PENTAGON

ALSO BY ALLEN DRURY

The Advise and Consent Series
ADVISE AND CONSENT
A SHADE OF DIFFERENCE
CAPABLE OF HONOR
PRESERVE AND PROTECT
COME NINEVEH, COME TYRE
THE PROMISE OF JOY

Other Washington Novels
ANNA HASTINGS
MARK COFFIN, U.S.S.
THE HILL OF SUMMER
DECISION
THE ROADS OF EARTH

Novels of Ancient Egypt
A GOD AGAINST THE GODS
RETURN TO THEBES

Other Novels
THAT SUMMMER, A California Novel
THE THRONE OF SATURN, A Novel of Space and Politics

Non-fiction
A SENATE JOURNAL
THREE KIDS IN A CART
"A VERY STRANGE SOCIETY"
COURAGE AND HESITATION (with Fred Maroon)
EGYPT: THE ETERNAL SMILE (with Alex Gotfryd)

PENTAGON

Allen Drury

Doubleday & Company, Inc.
Garden City, New York
1986

All characters and incidents in this novel are
fictitious. Any resemblance of any character to
any actual person living or dead is entirely
coincidental. Any resemblance of any incident to
any actual incident past, present or future is
unhappily due to the times we live in.

Library of Congress Cataloging-in-Publication Data

Drury, Allen.
  Pentagon.

  I. Title.
PS3554.R8P46 1986   813'.54   86–8852
ISBN 0-385-15141-1

To
William Howard Eichstadt
Loving heart, brave spirit, true friend

*He always wanted the world to be a happier place,
and wherever he touched it, it was*

The Building sits by the river.
The island sits in the sun.
They are very far from one another.
They will come together, soon enough.

Huge, squat, sprawling, seeming almost to breathe like some great an-
tidiluvean animal awesome in its power and impact as it sits beside the river,
The Building sends out its tentacles to the farthest reaches of the earth.

Its critics call it "Fort Fumble"—"The Puzzle Palace"—and other things less
complimentary.

Its supporters call it the bastion of democracy, the defender of freedom.

Its power is enormous.

Its influence is everywhere.

What it decides or does not decide, what it does or does not do, affects not
only the life of every American but the life of every living thing.

Its actions can change the fate of nations, destroy or establish governments,
turn whole peoples from one path of destiny to another, wither or preserve the
earth.

It can, and does, decide the fate of millions of its own and many, many
millions more.

Its reach extends to all the continents and all the seas and beyond them into
space.

The mightiest nation, the tiniest dot of land upon the sea, may feel the touch
of its hand. Before it the denizens of earth, as it suits them, may bow in awe,
tremble in fear or jeer in hatred. It does not matter. The Building goes on,
impervious, set upon a course at once so irresistible yet so glacial in pace that it
takes years to start it moving, bring it to a halt or change its direction. In less
than five decades it has become a force of nature, like the tides. Now in the
closing years of the Anxious Eighties its influence upon America and the world
has never been greater.

Yet it is an intensely human place. People make its decisions. People order its
actions. People, in their thousands, give it life and purpose.

Upon them The Building confers life and purpose in return.

All day long it takes them in and spews them out. From the highest—

"SecDef"—the Secretary of Defense—to the most modest—someone in the motor pool, perhaps, or perhaps one of the ample black ladies who swing and sway down the seemingly endless, drab, vinyl-tiled corridors, with their lackadaisical brooms, their loud comfortable laughter and their casually overflowing refuse carts—all owe allegiance to The Building.

If they are among the approximately twenty-five thousand who work there—the figure varies from day to day as people start jobs, move to others, come in from the field, get transferred out—they arrive from their homes or posts in Virginia, Maryland, the District of Columbia. If they are high enough, they are chauffeured. If they are not so high, they ride the sleek gleaming trains of the Metro, remarkably clean and free of graffiti, or the many busy buses that link The Building to the neighboring countryside.

Some of them, both high and low, come in carpools, or, if these can't be arranged, or they live too far from public transportation, drive their own cars. Those who do park in carefully ranked lots in which the humblest find haven nearly half a mile from The Building. The mightiest park right out in front of the Mall Entrance or the River Entrance. In his office above the latter, SecDef can see them when he leaves his enormous antique desk for a moment's introspection and stares down thoughtfully at the serried ranks of vehicles and the carefully manicured miniature parade-ground where famous (or infamous, but in all events, necessary) foreign visitors are greeted with massed colors, twenty-one gun salutes, troops of the Old Guard and suitable welcoming speeches.

There also he can see the brown, slow-moving current of the Potomac and the familiar monuments of Washington, gleaming "across the river," as they say in The Building when they divide the world, as they invariably do, into Them and Us.

The Building never really sleeps, for somewhere, probably in several places simultaneously around the troubled globe at any given moment of day or night, there are things happening to which The Building must give attention. But it does slumber somewhat in Washington's later hours, its busy corridors mostly stilled, its constant traffic in and out temporarily in abeyance, only secret staff in secret places behind locked and closely-guarded doors keeping track of what is going on around the world, under the seas or in the busy skies above. Then as night fades and dawn illuminates the Capitol, the Washington Monument and Mr. Lincoln in his temple, light speeds across the Potomac to throw The Building's drab brown pillars and 7,748 (by official count) windows into sharp definition, and things begin to stir again. Ponderously The Building begins to shake itself fully to life. Through the River and Mall Entrances its hundreds of daily visitors begin to stream.

Some are officials from other government departments and agencies, such as the Department of Energy, which handles production of The Building's mightiest and most terrible weapons. If these people rank high enough, they too are chauffeured; if they are only couriers carrying messages for The Building from its competitive and suspiciously regarded colleagues across the river, they come by humbler means. Among others who come are a steady stream of uniformed officers, male and female, from The Building's many outlying installations and enclaves in the District, Virginia and Maryland. These arrive in the drab green Army shuttle-buses that run constantly back and forth to tie the whole together. They chat about paperwork, office crises, wives, husbands, kids, housing. Most of them look preoccupied, worried, tense.

Members of Congress such as Sens. "Cube" Herron, Luzanne Johnson and Jerry Castain, Reps. Mario Escondido and Karl Aschenheim come too, arriving on the regular shuttle from Capitol Hill, carrying in minds, hearts and briefcases their demands that their states or districts be given preference when The Building's contracts are handed out. They joke self-consciously with one another, looking momentarily at a loss. As if from nowhere smoothly deferential young officers magically appear to meet them, greet them and make them feel warmly at home.

Contractors come too, men like Roger Venable of Strategic Industries or Walker Stayman of General Growth Group, sometimes accompanied by their Senators or Representatives, more often in pairs or trios on their own: jovially confident if they are already at work on weapons systems projects, a little more nervous and apprehensive if they have not yet been granted the highly lucrative privilege of suckling at the constantly pumping public-money teat which The Building controls.

Occasionally scientific types like Dr. Donald K. Brattlefield of THOUGHT Inc., arrive, looking secretive and self-important—creators of Doomsday whose business one had better not inquire about because it is much better for one's peace of mind not to know.

Now and then there are little groups of giggling school kids, come to take the regular tours of The Building that are led by earnest young enlisted men and women who don't look or sound much older than the kids are and who keep the corridors echoing with their loud, self-conscious explanations. And occasionally there are foot-weary tourists from all over America who, having wandered in from neighboring Arlington National Cemetery where they have paid their dutiful respects to the Kennedys and to the Unknown Servicemen of World Wars I and II, Korea and Vietnam, want to see where it all begins and try to visualize, if they can, the vast river of their tax-money as it rushes faster and ever faster away from them.

And almost daily, also—earnest, humorless and grimly determined—come supporters of Causes who are convinced (often wrongly) that The Building does not agree with them. Some wave placards and distribute leaflets outside the River and Mall Entrances. Others come up the long steep escalator from the Metro in the bowels of The Building to work their way into the middle of the busy shop-filled Concourse and there stage sit-downs or lie-downs upon which they hope the media will focus national attention. Sometimes they throw chicken blood on The Building, which is then scrubbed clean again by the patient, much-practiced employees of the General Services Administration, which manages The Building's physical plant and grounds.

All who come to The Building, whether they be regular workers there or temporary visitors, think they will find therein at least a portion of what they desire.

For The Building is vast, and full of many wonders.

It is a place where people work, long and hard; a maze of corridors and passageways where battery-powered carts with blinking lights and beeping horns scoot along delivering mail, documents, supplies, their carefree drivers obviously having a great time scattering military and civilians right and left with their noisy passage . . . where foot couriers of all ranks and grades, walking fast—always fast and earnestly—hurry from office to office . . . where thoughtful majors, captains, commanders, sometimes even generals and admirals, walking slowly, consume ice cream cones or cardboard cartons full of popcorn which they have purchased at "The Big Scoop" in the "Pik-Quik," The Building's main cafeteria on the second floor, just at the top of the ramp coming up from the Concourse.

The Concourse is always alive and bustling with people, particularly during lunch and the morning and evening rush. Its concessions are designed to meet nearly every need, its completeness justifying the "city in itself" label so often given The Building: the women's store . . . the men's store . . . the drugstore . . . the post office . . . the book store . . . the magazine and newspaper stand . . . the greeting card store . . . the flower shop . . . the housing referral office, always full of incoming officers seeking haven for their families . . . the travel agency . . . Western Union . . . the novelty store . . . the candy shop . . . the bakery shop . . . the bank . . . the hospital, Army-run, down at the far end in a dimly-lighted enclave . . . the benches where people sit to watch television or the constantly passing parade—or, frequently, just to rest their feet ("Podiatry of course is very important here," the lieutenant colonel in charge of the hospital says) . . .

And once past security and up the ramps to first, second, third, fourth floors, one sees the inner landscape of The Building, which varies from vinyl-tiled Federal Blah to more imaginative attempts at decoration: the various special corridors hailing military heroes and civilian secretaries—the special exhibits of World War I uniforms, World War II uniforms, Korea—the paintings of battles recent or long forgotten, on land, at sea, in the air—the replicas of the surrender documents of World War II—the models of ships, planes, rockets, missiles —the Hall of Heroes hallowing the names of Congressional Medal of Honor winners . . . and many other exhibits, constantly changing, all designed to emphasize for The Building's occupants the importance of the work they do . . .

And the offices: in A Ring, looking down upon the pleasant sward at the center of The Building, ironically called "Ground Zero," with its hamburger stand, lawn and many benches, always crowded in good weather . . . in B, C and D Rings, offices hemmed in by masonry, many never seeing the light of day, artificially illuminated, most little more than cubicles crowded with desks, typewriters, word processors, computers, too many people in too little space . . . in E Ring, grandest of the lot, where SecDef, the Joint Chiefs of Staff and the individual service commands can actually look out and see that there is a world out there . . .

Five floors, each with five sides crammed every available inch with offices: a few spacious, some rabbit-warrens . . . some accessible to anyone, others behind doors that either have guards sitting in front of them or can only be opened by pressing the right buttons to activate the right codes . . . offices big and expansive like those of William Loyola "Loy" Buck, Secretary of Defense, and Gen. Zoren Chace "Zeecy" McCune, chairman of the Joint Chiefs of Staff . . . offices tiny, musty and hidden like that of that earnest and deliberately ignored whistle-blower, Skip Framberg (Crazy Skip, they call him in E Ring, where they have often tried to do him in, administratively) . . . offices filled with uniforms, like those of the upper echelons of the military . . . offices filled with civilians, like those involved with procurement, contracts, research and development, Congressional liaison, community liaison, service wives' organizations, Red Cross, General Services Administration. . . .

According to Gen. Elbert James "Tick" Tock, commandant of the Marine Corps, "This place is like a womb. It houses us, it nourishes us, it takes care of every little need. We have everything we could possibly want, right here. Get sick, go the hospital. Fight with your wife, buy her candy. Stay late working, buy her flowers. Birthday, buy her a cake. Need socks, shoes, toothpaste—hell, we've got it all."

And so they do, in The Building.

People—endless. Projects—manifold. Responsibilities—infinite. Importance —incalculable.

The Building tells you in its brochure, and perhaps rightly so, that it is the principal guarantor of "the preservation of peace with freedom for ourselves and our descendants."

"There can be no more demanding mission nor important goal," its brochure says.

Most who work there, and most who visit, believe this and so conduct themselves.

Some do not.

The Building officially denies this fact of human nature, for it is not a comfortable thought. Nonetheless, it happens. The Building is as perfect—and imperfect—as humanity itself. Sometimes this makes the mission even more difficult than it might otherwise be. Sometimes "the preservation of peace with freedom" falters and fails. Other times it is triumphantly achieved. Like everything about The Building, success, when it comes, can be overwhelming. Failure, when it comes, can be monumental.

A few times in a generation, perhaps, behind a general's stars, an admiral's gold braid, a civilian Secretary's carefully tailored or carefully rumpled suit, genius resides. More often a level—a very high level—of competence can be found.

Inspiration—sometimes. Diligence—more often. Genuine mediocrity—very seldom. Gross incompetence—almost never.

The Building is full of brilliant people, both civilian and military. It also has a System. The two do not always jibe. Much tension exists in The Building because of this. Unlike the labyrinth of King Minos, this one has many exits. Many, defeated, go. Those who remain do not have an easy time.

The vision that keeps some of them is preferment of one kind or another—rank, politics, pension, the lure of lucrative employment elsewhere, after they leave.

The vision for others is the hope that somehow, by their oft-frustrated labors, they can indeed contribute to "the preservation of peace with freedom for ourselves and our descendants."

But there is a price for this.

The Building exacts it from all—not least, from the millions of men and women under arms whose destinies—whose lives—The Building controls.

It provides the planes in which they fly, the tanks in which they fight, the vehicles in which they ride, the submarines in which they go beneath the seas, the shuttles in which they venture into space, the missiles and nuclear weapons they employ. It provides their food, their housing, their posts throughout the world. At the behest of "across the river" it sends them over the earth, into the skies, under the oceans, to the nearer shores of space. The Building dispenses billions beyond comprehension for projects that frequently are wasted and frequently fail. The feeling in The Building is: "You'd better have enough on hand than cry for it when you really need it."

The Building's occupants are divided about equally between civilian and military, and very few of them know at any given time what the rest are doing. Only at the highest levels, up where SecDef and the JCS and all their many assistants live, do they know; and even there, The Building's operations are so vast, so worldwide, so infinitely complex in ramification, that not even Loy Buck or Zeecy McCune—not even Army Chief of Staff Gen. "Brash" Burford, who knows practically everything about everything (and everybody)—can possibly grasp it all at any one given moment.

Up there in SecDef's comfortable offices on third floor, E Ring, over the River Entrance, or in Zeecy McCune's equally (but not *more* equally) comfortable offices on second floor, E Ring, alongside the River Entrance, or in Tick Tock's spartan (and proudly so, by God) Marine headquarters in nearby Arlington Annex, they get a lot of the picture that isn't allowed to escape to the general public—except when some enterprising member of the media (known generally in The Building as "the God damned media") gets hold of something and blares it forth with a fierce satisfaction derived from openly defying "national security" (known generally in the media as "their God damned cover-up").

Except when members of the God damned media manage to crack The Building's God damned cover-up, these are the things which, The Building hopes, will decide the future in favor of the United States: *this* secret space or underwater project, *that* fantastic weapons system, the "black" programs that go ahead virtually outside regular channels, because often that's the only way to get them done and keep them out of public view—which always means, of course, the Soviet view as well.

The Soviets are what is known universally throughout The Building as "the threat" or "the enemy"—usually capitalized even in conversation—The Threat. The Enemy.

Without The Threat, The Building would hardly exist. Certainly its major mission would not be "the preservation of peace with freedom" nor would the mission carry the heavy emphasis it does. Were it not for The Enemy, across the river in the White House and Congress they would not ask of The Building the near-impossible tasks they do, nor give to Loy Buck, Zeecy McCune, Tick Tock, Brash Burford and all their fellow brass and all their constantly proliferating deputies, sub-deputies, assistants, sub-assistants, aides, action officers, public relations officers, clerks, secretaries and everybody right down to the motor pool, the swing-and-sway ladies of the cleaning squad and the lowliest private (or lieutenant, since there are very few privates indeed in The Building) the endless billions of dollars they receive.

Nor would there be need for twenty-five thousand more or less to come to work there every day, for the world would be a much calmer place without The Threat and The Building would have much less to do. Nor would the hundreds of visitors be flocking in and out each day, for the errands that bring them there, and the benefits they seek, would not be half so important, or mean half so much, or be half so profitable in terms of cash or preferment.

As it is, The Building in these closing years of a sick, sad century, sits at the center of American life.

Its needs are imperative.

Its mission is overriding.

Its power is enormous.

Its influence is everywhere.

It is central to the operations and health of major segments of American industry—perhaps to all of American industry.

It is central to the security and future well-being of the nation itself.

It is central to the lives of all who cherish freedom, for without The Building and what it does nothing would stand between them and those who would impose upon them the end of freedom and the final enslavement of the human mind.

Huge, squat, sprawling, seeming almost to breathe like some great an-tidiluvean animal, The Building is so monumental in its impact and power that critics and supporters alike can only marvel—and, sometimes, shiver.

For the business of The Building is said to be Defense, but its real business— which its occupants push off to the backs of their minds and seldom talk about —is Death.

Death, if necessary, to make defense succeed.

Death, in certainty, if defense does not succeed.

Thus The Building sits beside the river.

Far away in a placid sea the island sits in the sun.

No one has ever associated the island with Death.

But Death is on the way.

And with it, The Building must somehow cope.

NANUKUVU

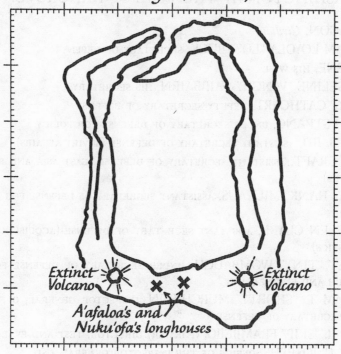

*(Defense Mapping Agency
Washington, D.C. 20305)*

Extinct Volcano

Extinct Volcano

A'afaloa's and
Nuku'ofa's longhouses

NANUKUVU, *island, South Pacific, genl. vicinity Gilberts and Marshalls; two
small extinct volcanoes; low ridges; sandy beach center, highest
elev. 923 ft.; moderate to heavy vegetation, mostly palm and scrub;
approx. 3 mi. wide, 6 long; pop. unknown, presumed uninhabited.*
—Gaines' Gazeteer, London, 1989

A'AFALOA, chief, fled from Gilberts in family dispute, 1979, with two wives,
four children, subsequently increased to twelve.
NUKU'OFA, younger brother, followed 1981 with two wives, one child, subsequently increased to ten.
Population at time of sighting of "great black whale" and "hot wind," twenty-
eight.

IN WASHINGTON AT THE TIME OF NANUKUVU:

PENTAGON, *Civilian:*

WILLIAM LOYOLA "LOY" BUCK, SECRETARY OF DEFENSE

IMOGENE, HIS WIFE

EVANGELINE "VANGIE" FAIRBAIRN, HIS SECRETARY

ROBERT CATHCART, DEPUTY SECRETARY OF DEFENSE

JOSEPH STRANG, UNDER SECRETARY OF DEFENSE FOR POLICY

JASON BARD, ASSISTANT SECRETARY OF DEFENSE (SOVIET AFFAIRS)

JAMES CRAFT, ASSISTANT SECRETARY OF DEFENSE (EAST ASIA AND PACIFIC AFFAIRS)

HENRY "HANK" MILHAUS, ASSISTANT SECRETARY OF DEFENSE FOR PUBLIC AFFAIRS

DR. HELEN CLARK, ASSISTANT SECRETARY OF DEFENSE (ACQUISITION AND LOGISTICS)

ERNEST "TINY" WOMBAUGH, UNDER SECRETARY OF DEFENSE FOR RESEARCH AND ENGINEERING

WILLIAM T. "SHORTY" MURCHISON, INSPECTOR GENERAL, OFFICE OF THE SECRETARY OF DEFENSE

JAMES H. "SKIP" FRAMBERG, (FORMER) DIRECTOR, TEST AND EVALUATION

HARRY C. JOSEPHS, OFFICE OF THE INSPECTOR GENERAL, OSD

RAYMOND C. CLARK, SECRETARY OF THE ARMY

HUGH MERRIMAN, SECRETARY OF THE NAVY

HILL B. RANSOME, SECRETARY OF THE AIR FORCE

PENTAGON, *Military:*

GEN. ZOREN CHACE "ZEECY" McCUNE, USAF, CHAIRMAN, JOINT CHIEFS OF STAFF

RENEE, HIS WIFE

GEN. WILBUR "BRASH" BURFORD, CHIEF OF STAFF, ARMY

VIOLET, HIS WIFE

ADM. JOHN ERIC "BUMPY" STAHLMAN, CHIEF OF NAVAL OPERATIONS

GEN. ELBERT JAMES "TICK" TOCK, COMMANDANT, MARINE CORPS

DOREEN, HIS WIFE

GEN. HARMON C. "HAM" STOKES, CHIEF OF STAFF, AIR FORCE

ZENIA, HIS WIFE

LT. GEN. ALBERT B. "AL" RIDER, USMC, COMMANDING, OPERATION FRIO

MAJ. GARY STUMP, USA, ACTION OFFICER, OPERATION FRIO

CAPT. ELIZABETH HOGAN, USN, SECRETARY TO GEN. RIDER, OPERATION FRIO

LT. BRODERICK TOLLIVER, USAF, ASSISTANT ACTION OFFICER, OPERATION FRIO

BRIG. GEN. HARRY AHMANSON, USA, CO-MANAGER, PROJECT FRIO

PENTAGON, *Media:*

WILLIAM "RED" ROBERTS, *Wall Street Journal*

DELIGHT JONES, PUBLISHER AND EDITOR, *Defense Eye*

HERBERT HOROWITZ, REPORTER, *Defense Eye*

"ACROSS THE RIVER," *Downtown:*

THE PRESIDENT

ALEKSANDR "AL" BRODOVSKY, NATIONAL SECURITY ADVISER

TERRAIL B. VENNER, SECRETARY OF STATE

ROGER T. VENABLE, VICE PRESIDENT FOR DEFENSE AFFAIRS, STRATEGIC INDUSTRIES

WALKER S. STAYMAN, VICE PRESIDENT FOR DEFENSE AFFAIRS, GENERAL GROWTH GROUP

"ACROSS THE RIVER," *Capitol Hill:*

SEN. HARLAN H. "CUBE" HERRON, CALIFORNIA, CHAIRMAN, SENATE ARMED SERVICES COMMITTEE

SEN. LUZANNE JOHNSON, LOUISIANA, SECOND-RANKING MEMBER, SENATE ARMED SERVICES COMMITTEE

BURTHOLD M. SANSTROM, STAFF DIRECTOR, SENATE ARMED SERVICES COMMITTEE

SEN. JERRY CASTAIN, INDIANA, CHAIRMAN, SENATE APPROPRIATIONS SUBCOMMITTEE ON DEFENSE

REP. MARIO ESCONDIDO, CONNECTICUT, CHAIRMAN, HOUSE ARMED SERVICES COMMITTEE

REP. KARL ASCHENHEIM, PENNSYLVANIA, CHAIRMAN, HOUSE APPROPRIATIONS SUBCOMMITTEE ON DEFENSE

One

1

It was March, and cold. Washington weather, frequently erratic, is never more so than when winter spills into spring. Sometimes this happens gracefully. More often it occurs with a violent reluctance that can turn the capital at a moment's notice from dazzling sun and sparkling days once more toward rain and chill and sometimes even snow.

Today appeared to be set toward the latter. When he looked back upon it, William Loyola Buck, who was Secretary of Defense and proud of it, would reflect that the day when what came to be known as "the problem of Nanukuvu" reached the Pentagon was a gloomy and forbidding one. Quite fitting, "Loy" Buck always thought, because its events were to pose one hell of a problem for the Department of Defense, whose head he had been for the past three years.

At the moment nobody knew anything about that. He himself, just arrived at 7:30 A.M. in the spacious office of the Secretary on third floor, E Ring, over the River Entrance, expected a day like any other for all who have held or will hold the job of "SecDef": a thousand minor details, a few big decisions, at least one or two crises around the uneasy globe to which the department must address itself. It was not a dull assignment, and like most of his predecessors he came to it each morning with a sense of anticipation and zest that he suspected few jobs in the federal government could match.

Riding the tiger wasn't always easy. For Loy Buck, as for many before him, it could be, and often was, nerve-wracking.

It was also, basically, fun.

This word he would never have dared use to anyone, not even to Imogene with her determined ways and her satisfaction at being known throughout Washington society—and throughout the building, where she was regarded with some fear by the wives of his subordinates both civilian and military—as "Mrs. B.," the woman who presumably could make Mr. B. toe the line. Not that she ever really did, of course, except when he amiably permitted it. Part of the reason was that he had always been the sort who could be expected to find running the Pentagon "fun." Not hilarious fun or lighthearted fun or irresponsible fun, but fun in a much more fundamental sense: challenging fun, the sort of challenge that had always kept him up to pitch and provided him with a fulfilling life from the first day he had gone to work at IBM aged twenty-two until the day when, aged fifty-four, he had left the corporation as president to join the Cabinet.

He had always enjoyed challenges, and God knew there was no lack of them here.

He turned for a moment from his huge document-covered desk—the nine-by-five-foot "Pershing desk" that had been built sometime in the 1870s, had been in the office of Gen. John J. Pershing after World War I, and had been used by every SecDef since the job was created in 1947—and stepped to the window facing north across the Potomac.

The river was dark and turgid, roiling angrily, covered with white-tops. Beyond it the stately city and its monuments gleamed fitfully as the sun whipped in and out of scudding clouds white at the edges, black at the center, heavy with the pledge of snow. The cherry trees along the Tidal Basin were whipping in the wind. There went the blossoms and this year's Festival, he suspected. Too bad: it was one of the capital's most innocent and endearing rituals. His own garden in Georgetown would suffer too. Imogene wouldn't have quite the lush backdrop of foliage she loved for the series of garden-parties she gave every summer. Life wasn't always so satisfying for Immy, who set stock on a lot of Washington's less innocent and endearing social rituals which to him seemed a waste of time, though he enjoyed them fairly well and used them for the purpose of advancing the Pentagon's interests. But he never really got any great charge out of them. If it weren't for the good of his department he would probably skip them all. If Immy would let him, which of course she wouldn't.

He had seen himself referred to many times over the years as a workaholic, and he supposed he was. Right now he heard the signal that it was time to get to it: Vangie's brisk footsteps coming down the dark, paneled corridor, the sharp click as the young Marine on the door came to attention with a salute and snap of heels. He knew she loved that, and he had encouraged it by issuing secret orders that she was to be accorded this honor every time she entered or left: a small flourish which pleased her and, he felt, a fitting tribute for one who was a veteran of the building's opening days in 1943 and had been confidential secretary to three SecDefs in succession, concluding with himself, whom she adored.

He gave her two minutes to straighten the desk she had left in immaculate order the night before, get out her notebook, adjust her glasses, give a final pat to the imagined disarrangement of the never-disarranged bun atop her small gray head. Then he pushed the buzzer. Bright and efficient as she had been for more than forty years, she opened the door and said, exactly as she had every working day in all that time, "You rang?"

"I buzzed, Vangie," he corrected with a mild chuckle. "The usual if you please. Cream and sugar this time, I think. I may even have two. It promises to be a busy day."

Coffee ran in endless gallons through the Pentagon. Somewhere in the building he supposed there was someone who had statistics on it: somewhere in the building there was someone who had stats on every possible thing you could think of under the sun. Coffee was the standard gift of greeting, the necessary complement of all meetings, conferences, social encounters, interviews, the one immutable constant in a constantly changing world. Coffee, coffee, coffee. He preferred tea himself but now and again he switched to the Pentagon's brew of choice. Evangeline Fairbairn had found that every employer she had ever had in the building had some distinguishing sign when he was really under pressure. With Loy Buck it was two cups of coffee. She turned and hurried out to get the first from the always perking pot in the corner of her office. When she returned he was seated at his desk, reading the *Early Bird,* that invaluable daily compendium of the news originated by Harry Zubkoff and now edited by W. B. "Clipper" Corbus.

"Vangie," he said, "the world is in its usual hell of a shape this morning. I trust you had a good evening."

"Oh, yes," she said in her curiously quaint, precise, old-maid's voice. "A couple of the girls and I went to Kennedy Center to see that new musical *Seasons."*

"We're going with the President Friday night," he said. "Is it any good?"

"Pretty good," she said. "It needs work."

"Alas, don't we all," he said, finally putting on the glasses that mild vanity always delayed until the moment his eyes began to protest and couldn't be denied. He slapped the *Early Bird* with an expression of disgust. "Now what the hell are they doing in Gabon?"

"What are they always doing?" she responded, knowing without further identification who "they" invariably refers to in the Pentagon. "Making trouble as usual."

He sighed.

"Yes, what else? Has Harry come in yet?"

"Any minute," she said. "I saw him going into the Pik-Quik to get a Danish. He said he overslept and didn't have time to eat anything at home."

"That isn't like Harry," he said, contemplating with some amusement for a moment a mental picture of his spick-and-span, spit-and-polish, always eager, always obedient, fiercely competent and fiercely competitive military aide, Brig. Gen. Harry Ahmanson, U.S. Army.

"Even perfection," she said gently, "has its moments."

"And the bachelor life its compensations," he agreed dryly. "But Harry late? Say not so!"

"Do you have anything for me at the moment?" she inquired. "If not, I'll get started on typing your schedule for next week. It looks pretty heavy."

"What else is new? Tell Harry to get his tail in here the minute he comes in. We're expecting the troops at eight-thirty."

"Not ten?" she asked in mild surprise: his daily meeting with his numerous deputies, under secretaries and assistant secretaries usually took place at that hour, to be followed immediately on this particular day of the week by their regular meeting with the chairman and members of the Joint Chiefs of Staff.

The times changed a little from SecDef to SecDef, but the basic routine remained the same. "You have the Secretary of State at nine, you know."

He had a quick mental picture of Terrail Venner, tall—slim—graying—distinguished—ice-cold—precise—and fiercely determined to keep the Defense Department from dominating foreign policy. This he was unable to do, since its influence was so all-pervasive and its foreign affairs experts were so shrewdly adept at the endless bitter in-fighting that went on between the two departments.

"Terry won't like having to rearrange his schedule," Loy said cheerfully, "but you tell him he's just got to. And notify everyone of the changed time, if you will. Zeecy McCune called me at home last night and asked that the conference be shifted because Brash Burford and Bumpy Stahlman have to go to the Hill to testify. So call Terry and make my apologies. Maybe we can do it this afternoon or tomorrow, if he'd like."

"He won't approve of that," she said with a little twinkle: nobody in the operative levels of the Pentagon liked Terry Venner very much. "You know how he is."

"I know how he is," he agreed with a grin. "And he knows how I am. So there we are. Get back to me with next week's schedule as soon as you can. I may want to try to work in a couple of days at the farm in Leesburg. Immy and I both need it, I think."

"*You* do," she agreed with the faintest partisan emphasis. "You're looking quite tired, actually."

"Oh, I hope not," he said. "I'm not feeling that way, though God knows I ought to be, the way this place operates all the time."

He watched her go with a fond expression. There went one of the real powers in the Pentagon. He supposed he was as responsible as any of his predecessors for making her so. But she had been there since God, as they said in E Ring; knew everything and everybody; in her prim, precise little way was a fiercely loyal supporter of each Secretary she had worked for; was a walking encyclopedia of the Pentagon; extremely competent; and a great friend if she liked you, an unrelenting enemy if she didn't. "Vangie can make you or break you with the Secretary," they said. It wasn't entirely true, but true enough so that everyone from the Secretary of State to the JCS took pains to stay on her good side. She was sixty-five and on the verge of retirement but already Loy was taking steps to have her rehired with the title "special consultant to the Secretary." The Pentagon wouldn't be the Pentagon without Vangie.

For a few minutes he read further in the reports: the usual unrelenting threnody of ups and downs. "They" were advancing here, subverting there, undermining somewhere else, never pausing in the incessant military build-up which had made their vast country so top-heavy with weaponry that he sometimes imagined it sinking into a huge hole in the ground. He told himself with a tired sigh as he read on that this would be a good thing if it could ever happen.

It wouldn't and that was why Secretaries of Defense, he reflected wryly, were nervous in the service.

Soon Harry Ahmanson strode in, terribly earnest and attentive as always, looking a little tired and unusually flustered but handsome and dynamic as he justifiably liked to think he was. They took up the agenda for the meeting.

Elsewhere in the building others were getting ready too.

Far from them all an infinitesimal dot on the map that none of them had ever heard of was about to move to the forefront of their many concerns.

At approximately the same moment that Loy Buck was preparing to meet his ever-growing troop of assistants in his office above River Entrance, Gen. Zoren Chace "Zeecy" McCune arrived at the Mall Entrance, emerged from his chauffeured staff car, bade a cordial farewell to his favorite master-sergeant driver, and started up the steps.

This was a departure from his usual practice of using the River Entrance adjacent to his own office. It came about because he was on his way to the fourth floor office of the chief of naval operations, directly above, to have (what else?) coffee with the Joint Chiefs before they went along to their meeting with Secretary Buck and the civilian side. It gave him a chance to turn back for a moment to contemplate one of his most favorite—and most sobering—views: a section of the neat white rows of crosses in neighboring Arlington Cemetery.

It was a good reminder, Gen. McCune felt, of one of the principal things he and his colleagues on both sides of the Pentagon were there for: not to kill infinitely brave young men and women, God knew, but to keep them from being killed, if at all possible.

In some sentimental and perhaps superstitious way that he recognized in himself, he thought it was good for the Pentagonian soul to be constantly in touch with Arlington Cemetery. It emphasized, with an emphasis no one could ignore, responsibilities as grave as those of any group of individuals on earth.

Contrary to some popular versions of the Pentagon, he knew that he and his military colleagues were not bemedaled monsters who slavered for the blood of the young, nor did they welcome with sinister glee the possibility of war now grown too awful to contemplate. They were as fearful of it and as opposed to it as the loudest protester in Lafayette Park across the river in front of the White House. It was just that they could not so irresponsibly escape the burden of dealing with its monstrous potential. They must devote themselves to the terribly difficult task of preventing it if they could.

It was a task made doubly difficult by the unending agitations and aggressions of the enemy, whose actions often forced them frighteningly close to precipitating the very disaster they were trying to avoid.

Gen. Zoren Chace McCune, United States Air Force, Chairman, Joint Chiefs of Staff—a name and titles which, Gen. Brash Burford said, should always be accompanied by drums and trumpets—was not, to the outward eye, so contemplative and philosophical a soul. At this moment, as at most in his public life, he was the epitome of the vigorous, dynamic and—yes, they called him this and it was true—glamorous military leader. He too was an impressive sight, awesome and legendary to the busy officers of all services who saluted him smartly as they hurried up the steps of the Mall Entrance past his motionless, brooding figure. His blond hair had turned full silver-gray at sixty-two but his six-foot-three-inch frame was as lean and erect as ever, his blue eyes as keenly perceptive, his ruggedly handsome face lined just enough by time and experience to make it fascinating to women and men alike, his air of command so ingrained and instinctive by now that he appeared a perfect fusion of man and mission.

"You always did know how to pose," Renee had once told him, not too kindly.

He had shrugged and replied mildly, "It comes natural. I don't work at it."

Which had annoyed her, as it was true.

Now he stood for another long moment looking at the crosses as he absent-mindedly but graciously returned the salutes. Then he turned on his heel and went in. A light snow was just beginning.

Upstairs in the CNO's office he was greeted with deep respect by the officers and ratings on duty. Their welcome held an extra warmth of admiration and approval that put them on a footing of camaraderie as relaxed as junior officers could ever be with the chairman of the JCS. He liked this, greeted several by name, which pleased them mightily; and was ushered into the inner office with great deference by Adm. Stahlman's principal aide, a rear admiral.

Bumpy and Gen. Wilbur "Brash" Burford, chief of staff of the Army, were already there. They assured him that Gen. Elbert "Tick" Tock, the Marine commandant, and Gen. Harmon C. "Ham" Stokes, chief of staff of the Air Force, were on the way.

"That's good," he said, while the rear admiral briskly brought him coffee, cream and sugar on a silver tray. "What do we have to worry about today?"

"Just the God damned Senate and House Armed Services Committees," Adm. Stahlman said with some gloom.

"*And* the God damned Senate and House Appropriations Committees," Gen. Burford added.

"And all their God damned little staffers who have nothing better to do than chew us out all the time," Gen. Tock remarked as he came in.

"It's how they make brownie-points," Gen. Stokes said, shrugging off his overcoat, tossing it on a chair and adding with a little mock-bow to Gen. McCune, "Sorry, Zeece, I dashed straight here from home. No time for ceremony."

"Typical Air Force," Brash Burford said. "You ought to get up earlier. You used to, or you wouldn't be a general now." Ham Stokes gave him a playful poke on the shoulder.

"Good old Brash," he said, sprawling into the big leather sofa that was already accommodating Adm. Stahlman's arrow-straight posterior. "Thank you," he said to the coffee-bearing rear admiral, who was dutifully going from elbow to elbow. "Just black, thanks. Any problems with the civs today?"

"Just the usual," Tick Tock said as the rear admiral, making sure that they were all well-coffeed and had a big silver pot at the ready on the table between the twin sofas, bowed deferentially and retired, shutting the door behind him. "I think the Secretary's getting a little pissed off with the way the media are ragging him about the overrun in the Army's fighter-plane contract with Three Gs. But that's par for the course. He'll huff and puff and then get over it. Loy doesn't fume for very long."

"Not as long as he knows it's going to be corrected," Gen. McCune observed. Gen. Burford smiled, a trifle stiffly.

"It's corrected already," he said. "It just takes those birds in the pressroom a while to find it out."

"And admit it," Ham Stokes said, a dour expression on his normally pleasant face. He pounded one black hand into the palm of the other. "Why in the *hell* are they never satisfied? Why can't they ever just *lay off?*"

"Oh, come," Gen. McCune said. "They aren't all that bad, Ham, and you know it. Lots of them are quite friendly. Red Roberts of the *Wall Street Journal,* for one. Sparky Morrison of the AP. And there are plenty of others."

"Not," Bumpy Stahlman said, his severe and saturnine face flushing a little as he remembered past encounters, "that little weasel Herb Horowitz of *Defense Eye."*

"Oh, *that* one," Ham said. "He's a born troublemaker, I grant you."

"What's his gripe?" Gen. McCune inquired. "It seems to me he's been on everybody's tail since the first day he walked into this place."

"Zeece," Brash Burford said seriously, "it's his boss, that other little weasel, Delight Jones. She's the real bitch in the ointment."

"Where'd she come from?" Gen. Tock wanted to know. "Anybody got any ideas?"

"She's a mystery," Gen. Stokes said. "She just appeared, apparently well-funded, announced the creation of the 'Defense Improvement Group'—or," he added wryly, "DIG—and started publishing the biweekly *Defense Eye.* Which has done nothing but give us hell since day one. I've often wondered—" he glanced quizzically at Gen. Burford.

"I understand both Defense Intelligence Agency and the F.B.I. have been working on it," Brash said. "So far, with no result. However, they're staying with it."

"Good," Ham Stokes said. "I'd be surprised if there wasn't *something."*

"Not always so easy to find," Tick Tock said. "Or, more importantly, prove. She and Herb *are* problems, though, no doubt about that."

"It'll all come out eventually if there's anything there," Brash said. "Meanwhile, they're having fun."

"And a lot of the rest of the media are having fun with *them*," Adm. Stahlman said gloomily. "Herb runs onto some rumor, no matter how far-fetched or how damaging, passes it on to her and then she passes it on to someone in the major media and next thing we know everybody's getting call-backs and they're all after us. That doesn't make me as tolerant as you seem to be, Zeece."

"Just one of the hair-shirts you wear if you're top brass in the military," Gen. McCune said cheerfully. "Don't brood about it, Bumpy. We'll all survive."

"Except when it gets to SecDef and the DepSec," Gen. Stokes said, pouring them all more coffee. "Then it gets a bit tetchy. Are Loy and Bob Cathcart speaking at the moment?"

"Barely," Gen. McCune said, and although they all liked Loy very much and definitely did not like Robert Cathcart, the Deputy Secretary foisted upon Loy by a President paying off political debts and known as "Bob Catheter," in the building, they couldn't help feeling a certain satisfaction. Anything that kept the Pentagon's civilian heads divided was fine with the Pentagon's military heads, though none of them would have dreamed of stating it thus candidly in public. When they were in private together they enjoyed gossiping about it like everyone else. Gossip was another of the many Pentagon by-products. It flowed through the building almost as torrentially as the coffee.

"Cathcart really isn't a very good man for us," Gen. Tock remarked. "I think we're his Cause. We're big bad evil people and he's out to get us."

"Why else do you think he rates so highly with the media?" Ham Stokes inquired dryly. "All those favorable editorials—the ass-kissing talk shows—the massive coverage of his weekly press conferences—"

"The only Deputy who's ever had the gall to hold his own press conference without the Secretary's approval," Bumpy Stahlman noted. "I don't blame Loy for being fed up with him."

"But what can he do?" Gen. Burford pointed out. "As long as Bob has the blessing of a man who's obviously going to seek re-election next year, Loy's stuck, I'd say."

"*Is* he going to seek re-election next year?" Tick Tock asked. "I hear rumors."

"So do I," Gen. McCune said. They all became attentive, for as chairman of the JCS, Zeecy had sources very close to the President—closer than most, in fact. They had been friends ever since they had been roommates at Annapolis, long before it became clear that the President would resign his commission at an early age to embark upon the political career that had eventually taken him to the White House; and before it became generally recognized that Zeecy, who had decided on graduation to transfer to the Air Force, was one of the golden ones who would carry his country's banner so successfully that he would rise with it to the highest position an officer of any service could hold.

"He's in perfectly good health, isn't he?" Tick demanded, going straight to the heart of what *he* had heard. Zeecy McCune looked him squarely in the eye.

"So far as I know," he said with a studied indifference that deliberately invited them to draw their own conclusions; which they did.

"Wow!" Ham Stokes said softly. "What is it, cancer?"

"I'm not saying anything more," Gen. McCune said bluntly. "In fact, I haven't said anything in the first place, except that I've heard rumors just as you have. Everybody hears rumors."

"Yeah, Zeece," Brash Burford said dryly.

"Anyway," Zeecy said, "what's with you guys? That's the important thing at the moment. What do we have to report to SecDef *this* week? That you're all stabbing each other in the back as usual?"

"Nonsense," Tick said, sternness belied by the twinkle in his eye. "We work together in perfect harmony. In fact it's so good that I sometimes think the building ought to put on an annual Pentagon Follies. Then we could have the JCS song. We could all come out dressed in the same uniform singing, 'Harmony—harmony—just a perfect har-mo-ny—' "

"Christ, Tick," Ham Stokes said, screwing up his face in an expression of exaggerated pain, "not at nine o'clock in the morning. Let's save that for some other time, o.k.? We all know it's true," he added wryly, "but we don't need to sing about it. It speaks for itself, right?"

"It does," Tick agreed, suddenly quite calm, his square, determined face and stocky, determined body all of a piece, bright eyes snapping shrewdly from beneath his close-cropped gray hair. "So don't any of you get any funny ideas about pushing the Marine Corps around."

"Nobody's getting ideas," Adm. Stahlman said.

"Oh, no?" Tick said sharply. "I hear rumors about *that,* too. Cube Herron was telling me yesterday when I was up there testifying—"

"Oh, *Cube,*" Bumpy Stahlman exclaimed. His tone found instant support. They respected—and feared—the constantly challenging chairman of the Senate Armed Services Committee. "What does he know about anything?"

"A hell of a lot," Tick Tock said, unmoved. "He knows a power-play when he sees one, and he told me he hears that Hugh Merriman is going to try to hold the Navy's cuts to not more than two billion this year if he can get away with it. Which means that the Navy will then try to take it out of the Marine Corps' hide if *you* can get away with it, Bumpy. But you won't, because Hugh has promised me he'll protect us."

"He's a Secretary of the Navy you can believe?" Ham Stokes inquired of no one in particular.

"He's a perfectly nice, decent guy," Gen. Tock said belligerently, "and I trust him. I'm surprised *you* don't."

"Just because we're both black?" Ham Stokes inquired lazily. "Now, come on, Tick, you know better than that. I don't trust him much. He's no friend of the Air Force."

"When was a Secretary of the Navy ever a friend of the Air Force?" Gen. Burford asked, his shrewd and amiable face extra friendly as he contemplated this inter-service friction to which he might be able to contribute something. "In fact, *I* hear on the House side that Hugh is trying to persuade Mario

Escondido to concentrate most of his economizing on the Air Force so that Hugh can get by with just that two billion cut you mention, Tick. Hugh's offering Mario two destroyers to be constructed in New London if he'll play ball with the Navy."

"And the slimy little grafter will probably go for it," Ham Stokes said with a distaste they all shared for Rep. Mario Escondido of Connecticut, chairman of the House Armed Services Committee. "If he makes one more noble speech about how we've got to cut defense spending and then turns around and tries to make one more secret deal for precious Connecticut, I'm going to throw up."

"He's not very lovable," Adm. Stahlman agreed. "Still," he added with some satisfaction, "he does seem to like the Navy."

Gen. Stokes snorted.

"Sure, as long as you buy him off. If you guys ever cut off the projects though, watch your asses because he'll be out to get 'em just as surely as he does ours. Or yours, Brash," he added, "sitting there so smug and above it all."

"Not at all," Gen. Burford retorted, amicability momentarily forgotten at Ham's acrid tone. "The Army gets by on its merits, thank you. We don't have to play that kind of game."

But at this they all hooted, and after a moment he relaxed and gave them a cheerful grin.

"Anyway," he said, "all it costs us is keeping a base or two open here and there."

" 'A base or two'!" Tick Tock exclaimed. " 'Here and there'! My God, Brash, you must have a hundred of them carefully spread over every state in the Union, maybe half of them really necessary, the rest just there to oblige our friends on the Hill. Try not to give us *too* much crap, please. There's a limit to what we can take."

"There's no limit to what *any* of us can take," Gen. Burford said cheerfully, "as long as it keeps those bastards on the Hill happy at appropriations time. We're all in this together, men, and it's war. War, I tell you! War!"

"Calm down, Brash," Gen. McCune said, amused, as Brash could always amuse them in spite of the fact that they all knew that he gave no quarter when the chips were down and his beloved Army was threatened. "There are bastards, true enough. But there are also plenty of people on the Hill who are really well-informed and highly competent, really devoted to both the welfare of the military and the good of the country. Those are the ones we really ought to cultivate. To hell with the others."

"Except at the moment it's the others who seem to hold most of the chairmanships and subcommittee chairmanships," Gen. Stokes pointed out gloomily. "And don't tell us you don't have to carry your hod of shit to the Hill, Zeecy, because we all know you do."

"Any of you fellows want the job?" Gen. McCune inquired.

"Avidly," Gen. Burford said with an engaging smile. "When are you going to vacate, Zeece?"

"You know when my term expires," Gen. McCune said, adding dryly, "Down to the last second. Get in line then. Until then, forget it . . . I take it, then, that there's really nothing we want to discuss with the civilian side this morning. No problems, no worries, no troubles, no gripes. Just a perfect har-mon-y, eh, Brash?"

"Suits me," Gen. Burford said.

"The less they know," Gen. Stokes remarked, "the better."

"And what they don't know," Adm. Stahlman added, "won't hurt them."

"Or us," Gen. Tock observed.

"That *is* harmony," Gen. McCune said with a chuckle.

They looked at one another, in a rarely united moment, with the mutually protective camaraderie of military subject to democratic control—or, as they saw it, democratic interference.

There were so many wars they had to fight.

With Congress.

With the civilians in the Pentagon.

With the White House.

With the Office of Management and Budget.

With the State Department.

With America's allies.

With each other.

It was a wonder they had any time left to even think about The Threat.

Gen. McCune glanced out the window and shivered. The crosses of Arlington were no longer visible. It was a white and swirling world.

"Look at that damned snow," he said. "It looks like we're going to have a real spring blizzard."

Thousands of miles from the nearest blizzard, all was still quiet on the island of Nanukuvu. But not for long.

Tapping one foot impatiently as he again stood restlessly at the window, the Secretary of Defense considered, with a wry expression few of them would have understood, the decidedly diverse group of individuals for whom he was waiting as the storm intensified outside.

Most were brilliant.

All were fiercely determined to protect their own turfs.

From them he faced the daily necessity of securing some sort of Consensus with which to run the Pentagon.

If the Pentagon could be "run," he thought gloomily.

All too often it seemed to him that it was set on some course that God had not devised and man could not fathom. Or control, no matter how great a kingpin of industry he might have been, or what resources of strength, will, vision, character and sheer persistence he might bring to it.

He had concluded quite early in his tenure that there were many times when the Pentagon eluded everybody and just careened along on its own sweet way, casually spewing out billions of dollars and rearranging millions of lives as it went along.

All around him he could feel, almost hear, the building at work. When he had first taken office Vangie had given him the official brochure that contained all its statistics, starting with the claim—probably valid unless some larger Soviet complex should eventually be found by curious explorers finally venturing in—that it is one of the world's largest office buildings, perhaps the largest: twice as large as the Chicago Merchandise Mart, three times the floor space of the Empire State Building, able to accommodate five United States Capitol Buildings in its five wedge-shaped sections.

It had been built early in World War II to consolidate the then War Department's scattered offices around Washington. Since 1947 it had been headquarters for the entire Department of Defense. It was constructed in a wartime hurry of seventeen months on the south bank of the Potomac just east of Arlington Cemetery. There had been no time since to do anything much aside from minimal necessary maintenance. As a result it had an air of shabby, tumbledown but reasonably comfortable dilapidation.

The cost of its five interlocking rings, decreasing in size down to lawn-covered, five-acre "Ground Zero," was $49,600,000. The addition of a refrigeration and heating plant, air conditioning (by now quite erratic), sewage plant, 30 miles of access highways, 21 overpasses and bridges, and 67 acres of parking to accommodate approximately 10,000 vehicles, brought the total cost to $83,000,000. It occupied 29 acres in the center of a 573-acre complex.

Inside, the statistics grew even more dazzling:

Gross floor area, 6,546,630 square feet. Usable space for offices, concessions and storage, 3,705,793 square feet. Length of each outside wall, 921 feet. Height of building, 77 feet, 3¼ inches. Number of floors, five, plus mezzanine and basement. Total length of corridors, 17½ miles. One hundred fifty staircases, 19 escalators, 13 elevators. Two hundred and eighty restrooms, containing 4,900 sanitary installations.

Six hundred and eighty-five drinking fountains, including Skip Framberg's famous "Purple Water Fountain" on which everyone guided when trying to find a way through the labyrinthine (and frequently RESTRICTED) passageways of the basement.

Outlets for electric clocks, 7,000. Eighty-five thousand lighting fixtures requiring 1,000 bulb changes daily.

Two restaurants and six cafeterias, including the Pik-Quik, the Executive Dining Room and the Big Scoop. Nine other snack bars. Six private dining rooms.

One hundred thirty-five thousand telephones, 75,000 main lines, upwards of 200,000 long distance calls per month through the main switchboards, plus all the innumerable direct communications with regional headquarters and forces in the U.S. and worldwide maintained by the services in their respective in-house communications centers.

Twelve million pieces of mail a year, and growing. Eight to ten truckloads of mail to be distributed each day, and growing.

And so on and on and on . . .

All of this the building had. And more. The "more" was people.

People made its decisions. People ordered its actions. People, in their thousands, gave it life and purpose.

Smart people, dumb people, bright people, dull people.

Great public servants like Zeecy McCune, humble public servants like the dedicated black who ran the motor pool, the earnest white who supervised the Pentagon's endless stream of publications.

People in uniform, people in civvies. Famous people and unknown people. Loyal people and, some few, disloyal.

Superb physical specimens like many he saw in the corridors every day; handicapped workers whom a decent government employs in jobs they can handle, receiving in return eager willingness, tireless devotion, the last, best measure of gratitude.

Shirkers and workers.

Savants and sloths.

Time-servers waiting only for retirement and pension.

Extraordinarily selfless and brilliant managers and scientists who drive themselves sometimes literally to collapse, in the never-ending battle to preserve freedom and thwart the incessant connivings of the enemy.

All kinds, all shapes, all sizes, all colors, all nationalities . . .

All of these The Building had.

People were its greatest strength.

As in any democratic society, people could also be its greatest liability.

It was his responsibility, insofar as any man could be held responsible for so huge an operation, to see to it that the strengths outweighed the weaknesses.

On that the balance shifted, day by day.

Right now his inner circle of assistants was converging on his office from all over the building: the deputies, sub-deputies, assistants, sub-assistants, aides, sub-aides who were responsible for the Defense Department's operations. ("Always room for one more," Mario Escondido had told him cheerfully when demanding, on threat of withholding funds, that he take on another "special consultant" from the great state of Connecticut.) There were thirty-one, at latest count. Some, as Cube Herron had pointed out at his most recent pitched battle with the Secretary behind the closed doors of the Senate Armed Services Committee, were more responsible than others.

"In fact," Cube had demanded, florid face flushed and calculating eyes filled with a hostility partly genuine, partly for effect, "why in the hell do you need thirty-one people to do maybe twelve different jobs, if they were organized right? Tell me that, Loy!"

"Because you and your colleagues on both sides of the Capitol keep insisting I find places for your friends," Loy had retorted, consistent with his invariable policy, on the Hill, that offense was the best defense. His sharp tone had taken Cube aback for a moment but as usual the Senator had managed to recover.

"Well," he had grumped—being one of the few Senators to whom the word "grumped" could accurately be applied—"you wouldn't have any if we didn't give you the money."

"That's right," Loy had said, unyielding. "And the end product often shows it."

After which Cube had turned abruptly to other things and they had dropped that topic. But it was true enough in some cases, though by no means all. The principal instance of political pressure, and the one that gave Loy the biggest headaches all the time, had not come from the Hill at all, as a matter of fact. Bob Cathcart, Deputy Secretary of Defense and as such No. 2 man in the department, had been imposed upon him directly by the President. And from that there was no appeal and no point in snapping back tart replies.

This President enjoyed being Commander-in-Chief a little more than some of his predecessors and there were times when he got his dander up and refused to take any back talk from the Pentagon. He was indebted to Bob Cathcart for heavy financial support in carrying California in the Presidential election. Bob was also former president of Three Gs—that vast corporate con-glomeration of contractors and sub-contractors that now held some $5 billion in Defense Department contracts. He had placed all his stock in blind trust when he accepted his appointment, but his influence in defense industry, and in California where most of Three Gs major components were located, gave him great clout in both Pentagon and White House. This posed a problem for Loy Buck, who was no mean slouch at corporate and political in-fighting, him-self. It prevented him from "having my hand on all the levers," as he liked to put it.

The Defense Department consequently was more deeply divided at the top than it had been for some time. It was not unheard of for Secretary and Deputy Secretary to be on frigid terms, but the present situation was aggra-vated further by notable differences in personality. Loy was the more open, candid and direct, Bob the more subtle, sly and devious—or so Loy saw him. Bob seemed big and somewhat lumpish, florid-faced and heavy-mannered. But he had his own agenda.

"I can't help it," Loy had told Imogene when she had chided him about it. "I just don't like the guy. He's always trying to undercut me with the White House, the media, the public and the services. That's a pretty complete list and I don't like it. He wants my job and I'm damned if he's going to get it. Or," he added dourly, "whatever other job he may be after."

Since this was an accurate description of the Deputy's tactics and a shrewd guess as to his ultimate ambition, and since Loy did not take many pains to hide his feelings by this time in his life, it had been some months since their relations had been more than minimally polite. This was always a topic of lively interest among the Joint Chiefs, as it had been already this morning. Whole strategies for winning some one of the endless internal Pentagon wars had been based upon whether Loy and Bob were speaking at the time. The only thing that gave Loy the edge was that Bob, whose ambitions quite likely did lie higher than Secretary of Defense, played to the media rather than the services when he had a choice. This made him a television hero, as Ham Stokes had acridly pointed out, but gave Loy a more solid base in the military from which to do the job he felt he was there to do.

This was exactly the job that Zeecy McCune conceived his to be: to keep kids—all kids, everywhere—alive, and to try, against whatever odds, to preserve both the safety of the nation and some semblance of stability in a highly unstable world made even more so by the other side's unceasing attempt to undermine it.

On these two subjects the Secretary of Defense and the chairman of the Joint Chiefs of Staff saw eye to eye, so that in the most important area of all— how the Defense Department might best achieve its mission to preserve liberty in the world, if such could be done—there did exist a unified point of view and a working relationship much closer than had sometimes existed between the civilian and military heads of the department. This was far more important, as both recognized, than whether Loy Buck got along with "Bob Catheter." Fortunately Zeecy was quite strong enough in public reputation and service support so that he did what he believed best without reference to whether or not it upset the Deputy Secretary of Defense. Which it quite often did, a fact which Zeecy enjoyed.

The Secretary's contemplation of this situation, which usually gave him the decisive edge in his many conflicts with the Deputy, was interrupted by four earnest young enlisted men and women, and Vangie. Under her direction they arranged chairs in a loose, informal circle around his desk, placed coffee pots and cups on strategic tables and then, with shy smiles which he returned cordially, withdrew. Vangie paused for a moment, checking everything; nodded once with a satisfied expression, started out and then paused.

"Mrs. B. wants to know if you'll be home in time for dinner tonight. She thinks it's time you had a quiet evening for a change. She declined an invitation from the Italian ambassador specifically so you could get a rest. I agree with her."

"You two women," he protested, humorously wry, "run my life. You both know perfectly well that it depends entirely on what happens here. As near as I can see now, yes. But who knows what may happen ten minutes from now?"

She sniffed.

"Ten minutes from now the herd will be here. Surely you don't expect any surprises from *them?*"

He chuckled.

"Vangie," he said, "my assistants all know your opinion of them and it terri-
fies them. Please greet them politely when they come in."

"I am always polite," she said in her precise little voice, "but I must say I've
seen better secretaries and under secretaries."

"I bow to your many years and vast experience in the Pentagon. As you
know, we take what we can get. Some of the best are making so much in
private business that they just can't afford to come here."

"You did. You thought it was worth it, to serve the country."

"Well, yes, I did. And so have many others. I'm satisfied with what we've got.
It's a good crew. Some I picked, some came up through the bureaucracy, some
were selected directly by the White House—"

"Those are the ones I like least," she observed with a slight smile. He smiled
too.

"Can't be helped. We just have to make do."

"I suppose the DepSec will skip the meeting," she said.

"Oh, no, he'll be here," he predicted. "Ready to make trouble, as always."

"You've got him on the defensive with that Army contract with Three Gs,"
she remarked. "One hundred and twenty million overrun, for goodness' sake!"

"I expect the matter will come up," he agreed.

"At the first sign he's getting rambunctious," she suggested, "don't let him
get away with a thing!"

He laughed.

"Vangie, sometimes I think you should have this job. You have a vindictive
streak that could come in handy."

"Not at all," she said primly. "I just want to be sure you do yourself justice."

"Very loyal of you, and I appreciate it. Tell Immy I'll try to make it."

"I hope you will," she said earnestly. "You really do need to slow down a little
once in a while."

But slowing down, he reflected as he returned to his desk and scanned the
Early Bird, was not a luxury permitted to Secretaries of Defense if they really
did their jobs—and most of them had, as he was satisfied he was doing in his
turn. The challenges were too many, the demands too incessant, the need for
decision too omnipresent and inescapable. It was one of the few jobs in Washington that could be said to approach the Presidency in its constant worldwide
burdens. As such, it did indeed require the best possible group of assistants. He
had spoken honestly: he was reasonably well satisfied.

From feisty Joe Strang through supremely self-possessed Helen Clark to
amiably tough Tiny Wombaugh, they were for the most part an intelligent,
dedicated and competent group. He ran quickly down the list of the most
important as he waited their arrival.

Joseph Strang, Under Secretary for Policy (which really meant "foreign"
policy and didn't fool a jealous State Department for one minute). Joe was one
more of those shrewd, sophisticated, cynical European imports tossed up on
America's shores out of the chaos of now-far-distant World War II, who have

greatly influenced American foreign policy, either in academe, White House, State Department or Pentagon, for the better part of the past four decades . . . now American citizens all, completely loyal to the country and grateful for what it has done for them . . . broad-gauged and philosophic in their overall view of world affairs, but possessed of a certain inbred, wearily sophisticated, centuries-old disillusionment concerning the hopes of man that no amount of adopted American idealism can ever quite take from them . . . consequently able to contemplate with sometimes chilling dispassion both a possible world victory for communism or a possible ending of the world itself . . . selected by university after university, Secretary after Secretary, President after President, simply because there is no getting around it, they are brilliant men who combine impressive mental capabilities with a decisive arrogance that frequently gives them an untouchable advantage over more hesitant native-born philosophers . . . Joe Strang was constantly at war with the State Department, as his own "little State Department" in the Pentagon sought with considerable success to preempt and control the policy-making process that Terrail Venner in Foggy Bottom knew by rights belonged to him . . .

Ernest "Tiny" Wombaugh, who with such a nickname, conferred years ago when Washington first knew him as a three-term Congressman from Michigan, inevitably had to be six-feet-seven and weigh 293 pounds in the morning, prior, as he often said with a jovial chuckle, to going to the bathroom (though he did not express it quite so delicately) . . . Under Secretary for Research and Engineering, following a highly successful post-Congressional career with Dow Chemical in Midland, Michigan, and then a ten-year hitch as president of the Massachusetts Institute of Technology . . . dry, pragmatic, blunt, no-nonsense, trying with varying degrees of success to ride herd on a scientific community determined to share as much technology as possible with the Soviets, and a military morbidly suspicious of even the most innocuous cooperation . . . given to the pointed joke, the casual guffaw, an outward appearance of casual camaraderie behind which one of the shrewdest brains in the country followed its own determined agenda . . . of two minds about the moral rightness of what he was doing, but justifying it, as did Loy Buck, Zeecy McCune and many another top official in the Pentagon, by telling himself constantly that it was all done for the safety of the nation and in the cause of peace . . .

Tom Garcia, Assistant Secretary for Command, Control, Communications and Intelligence, American-born child of wetbacks, as they had been known in those days before the age of carefully gentle euphemisms had been created to shield the American public as much as possible from all contact with reality . . . now they would have been called "undocumented aliens" from Mexico, but Tom, who was proud of his parents for having the guts to break away from their poverty-stricken, corruption-riddled society, preferred to use the old term without apology . . . particularly since his father had managed to stay in the United States, become a citizen, acquire with the aid of friendly Anglos his own small truck-farm, and send two sons and two daughters to the University of

New Mexico . . . Tom, the brightest, graduating magna cum laude, was offered a job with the Atomic Energy Commission at Los Alamos and very soon became known as one of the most brilliant young scientists in the field . . . now in his late thirties, instinctively inclined to be suspicious of the military but of such a basically amicable nature that they all got along together even when he was giving them hell, which was frequently . . .

The Doomsday Twins, as they were known in E Ring and Foggy Bottom—Jason Bard, Assistant Secretary (Soviet Affairs), and James Craft, Assistant Secretary (East Asia and Pacific Affairs) . . . two tall, thin, solemn-looking men who might have been cast from the same mold even though Jason Bard came from Washington state near the Canadian border and Jim Craft hailed from Baton Rouge, Louisiana . . . both early fifties, both academicians by vocation, Dr. Bard having been a twenty-year expert on Soviet affairs at the Hoover Institution at Stanford before being asked to come to Washington by Loy Buck, Dr. Craft having been equally noted as a Far Eastern scholar at the Georgetown Center for Strategic and International Studies before answering a similar call from Joe Strang . . . both grimly worried about The Threat, with whose ceaseless metastasizing they were in closer touch than most of the media critics who constantly assailed them; but both, contrary to outward appearances and the nature of their work, possessed of good senses of humor, a certain pragmatic approach to things, and the ability to relax with a game of handball, or a swim, at "POAC," the Pentagon Officers Athletic Club to which military and civilians of all ranks, grades and sexes repair for rest and recreation during lunch or other breaks in the building's heavy routine . . . both of them a little closer to Joe Strang than others in his "little State Department" . . . and thus comprising, with him, the operative trio who generated much of the strategy that eventually filtered up through Loy Buck to the National Security Council and the President . . . not very popular with either the military or the State Department, whom they often managed to outflank in their constant quest for the President's attention and agreement . . . but not really giving a damn, to quote Jim Craft, "as long as we take home the marbles . . ."

Rodney Stranahan, Deputy Under Secretary for Strategic and Nuclear Forces, short, dark, intense, humorless: a small man, as Tiny Wombaugh once put it not unkindly, driven by big devils; carrying on his shoulders the biggest devil of them all, the responsibility for nuclear procurement and the construction of the monstrous weapons that held humanity in pawn . . . very competent at this, and consequently an obvious and principal target for those many millions of his fellow citizens genuinely and frantically concerned about nuclear proliferation . . . not a retiring soul but feisty, articulate and combative, which meant that he was often sent out to act as point man in stating the Pentagon's case for continuing to increase the doomsday arsenal . . . which in turn meant that to date he had received a total of twelve rotten eggs, eight rotten tomatoes and two overripe cantaloupes in the face and had been burned in effigy a total of seven times on seven campuses . . . not concerned about that, as he assured Loy Buck after each episode, "but concerned as hell that the message isn't getting through that we have to keep building these Godawful things as long as they do" . . . assured by Loy and his other colleagues that he was doing a fine job, but knowing in his heart that as far as the public relations aspects of it were concerned he could not possibly succeed in convincing even the most friendly listeners that having to walk on the edge of the abyss was really preferable to being pushed over into it . . . absolutely convinced, himself, that there was no alternative to nuclear balance that could provide even the slightest guarantee that freedom would be permitted to continue in the world . . .

Dr. Helen Clark, Assistant Secretary for Acquisition and Logistics—tall, dark, striking, with beautiful dark eyes, sleek black hair drawn back severely into a tight bun at the nape of a long white neck, a lovely soft voice capable of swift implacable decision, a supremely self-confident manner fully warranted by her personal history and the disconcerting habit of staring thoughtfully at a collar-button, the lobe of an ear, an area of skin just above the neckline or some animate object known only to her but obviously moving through the hair of the unfortunate soul she happened to be talking to—a deliberate mechanism for throwing off balance anyone who wasn't as calm and self-possessed as she . . . which most of her male Pentagon colleagues were, being of considerable stature and ego themselves . . . so that she aroused rather more amusement among them than she was aware by using what was known as "Helen's neck-staring technique" . . . an extremely intelligent woman now in her early forties, who had married too young out of Stanford; been too critical of her struggling young scientist husband as they developed together a highly successful computer chip business in Silicon Valley; finally destroyed the marriage by being too right too often; and then persuaded her husband to let her buy him out at the time of the divorce, a move he always regretted bitterly because she went calmly on alone to build the business to the point where it now netted some $10 million a year . . . a very shrewd businesswoman and administrator, "lovely to look at, delightful to know and, I suspect, hell on earth to live with," as Gen. Burford had remarked to Loy Buck after the Army's first head-on clash with newly appointed Secretary Clark over a minor acquisition for the M-1 tank . . . on every Top Ten women's list in the country and, everyone was certain, planning ultimately to go back to California and run for the Senate . . . in the meantime, one of the most effective people in the Pentagon . . .

Henry Milhaus, Assistant Secretary for Public Affairs, tall, pleasant, self-possessed, quite capable, as a former Pentagon correspondent for *U.S. News and World Report,* of giving the media as good as he got . . . sharp, shrewd, "laid-back," unflappable . . . able to take the most subtly uninformative Pentagon press release and make it sound like a profound revelation—and able to withstand the scornful and persistent probings of his former colleagues as a consequence thereof . . . on constant call day and night . . . devoted to his job, one of the first to arrive and last to leave the building every day, which would have imposed some strain on his marriage were it not that Janet, who "used to be a newspaperman myself" for UPI, as she often liked to say, understood and supported him faithfully . . . personal choice of Loy Buck for his difficult and demanding position . . . assured of Loy's complete loyalty to him and completely loyal in return . . . imperturbable and sometimes acerbic front-man for every issue, every triumph . . . and every disaster . . .

Raymond C. Clark, Secretary of the Army, Helen's younger brother, who definitely was not considered one of the most effective people in the Pentagon, though the Army loved him because he was one of those service secretaries who become more Catholic than the Pope the minute they take office, so fiercely partisan and protective of their particular branch of the service that all other aspects of national defense sink to insignificance in their minds . . . this making him difficult for his fellow secretaries and officers of the other services to deal with, as he never wanted to compromise his constant demands for more money for the Army . . . also regarded with a mixture of admiration and amusement by many because he had taken office with a reputation as a great ladies' man and had proceeded to justify the reputation beyond all expectations both in the building and elsewhere in Washington . . . possessed of a quiet little wife, Karen, whom he had married when his career as a brash and highly successful young investment banker was just beginning to zoom . . . only a couple of months ago she had taken the unprecedented and embarrassing step of going directly to the Secretary of Defense and asking him to "make Ray stop misbehaving," the interview ending in floods of tears from Karen and an awkward promise from Loy Buck to "look into it and see what I can do" . . . now he was wondering how to go about it, because Ray certainly had to be warned; quite aside from his obligations to Karen, obvious womanizers being fair game for those who did not wish the United States well . . . and the prospect of snaring a Secretary of the Army in some sexual indiscretion being one the SecDef knew the Soviet embassy was no doubt considering with great interest . . . he might even have to request Ray's resignation if things didn't change . . . and of course they wouldn't . . .

The other service secretaries had their difficult aspects, he reflected as he heard the booming voice of the first arrival—Tiny Wombaugh, joking with Vangie—but none was as flamboyant as Ray Clark.

Hugh Merriman, Secretary of the Navy, was black, earnest, level-headed, steady; a former officer who had left the Navy as a captain to go into private law practice in Chicago, where he had done extremely well . . . a shrewd legal mind, a calm, unshakable personality . . . capable of being tough, as he sometimes was with Bumpy Stahlman, Tick Tock and the other Navy and Marine brass, but usually easy to work with even though he had on occasion allowed his partisanship for the Navy to lead him into open clashes with the other services . . . he and Ham Stokes did not get along at all, possibly because they were both black and either consciously or subconsciously jealous of each other's success . . . there had been an almost instinctive antagonism from the moment they had met two years ago when Ham received his fourth star and became chief of staff of the Air Force . . . the antagonism had only seemed to deepen, despite the best efforts of Loy Buck and Hill Ransome, Secretary of the Air Force . . . the two top blacks in the Pentagon simply didn't like one another . . . fortunately, as Hill Ransome remarked to the Secretary of Defense, they were not in the same service, which minimized the hostility to some extent . . .

Hill, the most amiable and tractable of the three service secretaries; mid-sixties, tall, distinguished, white-haired; decent, steady, not very inspired or very inspiring, the SecDef was afraid . . . Secretary Ransome was, in fact, somewhat dull; which, as Loy knew perfectly well, made him the ideal civilian in the eyes of the rambunctious Air Force over which he was supposed to exercise some control . . . no wonder Gen. Stokes clashed from time to time with the Secretary of the Navy: Ham was for all practical purposes the effective head of the Department of the Air Force . . . Hill Ransome just coasted along, cracking an amiable joke from time to time, enjoying Washington and his title but not really getting up much more steam about anything than he had during his many successful years as head of a major lumber company in Wisconsin . . . he had been in the Air Force himself in World War II, he liked to tell people; adding with a chuckle, "Course, I was a private first class and they had me helping to build buildings—right spot for a plain old lumberman, I guess." . . . No wonder they all love him in the Air Force, Ray Clark once remarked dryly to Hugh Merriman: let him hold a hammer, and he's happy . . .

This was a fair cross-section of the principal civilian aides of the Secretary of Defense as he and the public and their colleagues knew them. In addition there were many others upon whose counsel and cooperation he could call with confidence when the need arose. That they all had private lives, inner pressures, personal problems, gods they worshiped and devils they fought, he had time to be only superficially aware. The Pentagon, so big, so overwhelming, so powerful, often made basically impersonal relationships even more impersonal. It hindered him, as it did so many, in understanding those around him.

This particular job was too hectic and time-consuming to permit the careful study of impinging personalities that the slower pace of corporate life had made not only possible but advisable as a matter of simple self-preservation. In this building he had been the boss from the moment he arrived, subject to only one superior, the President. He called on people as he needed them: he didn't have to worry about their personal problems unless he wanted to. It was the same in the military. The top brass spoke and the rest jumped—or at least, he reflected wryly, they were *supposed* to jump. It didn't always happen that way, in the maze of competing interests and time-consuming delays that was the Pentagon.

It was only under the pressures of some major event that men and women here, as everywhere, were forced to reveal themselves in true pettiness or strength. Such an event, though he could not know it now, would be the problem of Nanukuvu.

The number of voices in his outer office increased, crescendoed. Harry Ahmanson peered through the discreetly tiny peephole that is a standard feature of all major Pentagon offices, ascertained that his boss was free, opened the door with the flourish he always liked to give to things and announced, "Mr. Secretary, the Deputy Secretary and the deputies and assistant secretaries"—and the meeting was on.

Far away on Nanukuvu something disturbed the calm of the lagoon. For just a second some agitation moved the limpid surface, some sound that was not quite normal broke the whispering silence of the night.

In his palm-thatched longhouse A'afaloa came awake with a start.

All around him the even breathing of his wives and children proclaimed that all was well.

Still, at sixty, he was a cautious and nature-wise man.

He got up stealthily, went to the door and stared out at the placid water.

It was flat and untroubled, shimmering faintly in the dying glow of an old moon about to give way to the first faint intimations of dawn.

Two hundred yards away his brother Nuku'ofa waved at him silently from the door of his house, listened for a moment, and went in.

A'afaloa returned to his pallet as stealthily as he had arisen. Next to him his senior wife Tuatama whispered, "Is it anything?"

"It is nothing," he whispered back.

But neither of them returned entirely to sleep. Something uneasy was in the night. They both wished day would hurry. Then unknown things were banished, their gentle kingdom basked in endless sunshine and warm trade winds, and the world belonged only to them and their happy families as it had for many years and as they prayed to the gods it always would.

"It seems we have two problems this morning," the Secretary said when everyone was seated, some with pads and pens at the ready, others sipping coffee. "One is the media and the other is the State Department."

"What else is new?" Tiny Wombaugh asked dryly, and there was general laughter.

"The morning papers are giving us hell about that Army contract overrun," Loy said. "I'm afraid I'll have to give somebody else hell. Ray, what's up?"

"I'll answer that," Bob Cathcart said before the Secretary of the Army could respond. "It was a simple overrun."

"Not so simple," Loy Buck said with the sharpness he could never keep entirely out of his voice when addressing the Deputy Secretary. "One hundred twenty million is no simple overrun, I would like to emphasize to all present. It's a serious matter and one we must all give attention to."

"Is the President giving attention to it?" Bob Cathcart inquired.

"You see him oftener than I do," Loy snapped. "You tell me. In any event," he added more calmly, "the committees on the Hill are sure as hell going to give attention to it, so I think it had better behoove us to have our answers ready." And deliberately turning his back on the Deputy Secretary, who was seated on a sofa to his right, he addressed himself again to the Secretary of the Army. "I repeat, Ray, what's up?"

"I'm looking into it," Ray Clark said, his handsome face, dark and striking like his sister's, taking on a defensive expression. "We've started an in-house investigation."

Somebody snorted and he swung around sharply toward Joseph Strang, who was seated—although at an obvious distance calculated to show that proximity did not imply approval—beside Bob Cathcart.

"And stop snorting, Joe! We *are* investigating."

"In-house investigations," Joe Strang said in his precise accent, "do not impress people on the Hill, in my observation. We are always having 'in-house investigations,' and nine times out of ten, as the media loves to point out, they come out as whitewashes. The media is entirely correct in this. Who is fooled," he concluded with a scornful expression, "by 'in-house investigations,' may I ask?"

"No one is trying to fool anyone!" Ray Clark retorted. "I've appointed a special board—"

"I believe it's called 'blue-ribbon panel,'" Tiny Wombaugh observed quietly to no one in particular and there was a snicker around the room. Ray Clark gave him an angry look.

"That's as good a name as any," he said shortly.

"Anyway," Loy Buck said, "we're issuing a statement out of my office to the effect that the matter is being investigated by the Army and that we will have a final report by one month from today—"

"Ouch!" Tom Garcia said with a sympathetic grin to Ray Clark. The Secretary of the Army did not look mollified.

"But—" he began. The Secretary of Defense raised a hand.

"One month from today. And I want some heads to roll. Somebody deserves at least a severe reprimand, maybe more. Don't hold back just because it happens to be a company associated with someone in the government."

"You'd love to get Three Gs, wouldn't you, Loy?" Bob Cathcart said. "How about IBM for a change?"

"IBM isn't guilty of anything at the moment," Loy said. "Three Gs is. Don't tell me you'd try to squelch an investigation to protect your old company, Bob. That *would* be a nice tidbit for the media!"

"It would be if you tattled," Secretary Cathcart said bluntly; and there was a little gasp.

The Secretary of Defense turned slowly and stared straight at the Deputy.

"Listen," he said, and his voice grated as it used to do in IBM board meetings. "Get this straight, Bob. I am not trying to 'get' Three Gs unless Three Gs deserves it. But when they do, by God I'm going to let them have it. So stop being defensive about it. If they've got a good explanation, they're home free. If they haven't, God help them."

"I'm not being defensive," Bob Cathcart responded with equal vigor. "My stock's in blind trust like everybody else's around here; it won't matter to me until I go home what happens to Three Gs. I grant you it will matter to me then, but if you are so much as hinting that in some way I'm trying to do something to shield that company from what it might deserve, by God I'll— I'll—"

He paused, looking slightly apoplectic. Helen Clark's smooth voice cut across the stunned silence.

"Gentlemen," she said calmly, "this really isn't advancing us very far this morning, now, is it. I'm sure we have a lot more important things to talk about, and I'm sure our responsibilities require it. I'd suggest we get on with serious matters. You said our problems today were really the media and the State Department, Mr. Secretary. What's the problem with the media?"

For a moment the Secretary hesitated. Then he turned to Bob Cathcart and spoke in a quieter tone.

"I'm sorry, Bob, I didn't mean to insinuate anything about you and Three Gs. I don't think Three Gs is going to come out of this looking very good, however, and I intend for all the facts to be put on the public record. It's the only way." He turned to Ray Clark, who had now decided to look defiant. "So wrap it up as fast as possible, Ray, and we'll get the hullaballoo over with as quickly as we can and get on to more important things." His tone turned brisk and businesslike. "The main problem with the media this morning apparently stems once again from our good friends Herb Horowitz and Delight Jones. Maybe you can tell us about that, Henry."

"Delight Jones and Herb Horowitz," Henry Milhaus said in his pleasant, clipped voice, "are the world's biggest pains in the sacroiliac, for us and everybody else in the government except their special pets. Of whom, unfortunately, there are some in the building. This place," he observed almost as an afterthought, "leaks like a sieve."

"I've done *my* damnedest to stop it," Loy Buck said. "But how many memos and investigations—in-house investigations, Joe," he interjected with a smile— "can we have? We could keep everybody in a soundproof cell and still somebody would leak. Especially since the military have learned in recent years that it's to their advantage to play the headlines. And," he added with a wry chuckle, "of course we've learned that, too."

"I don't mind *constructive* leakage," Joe Strang said with equal wryness. "It's the destructive that I find appalling. Particularly when it comes from State."

"Have they gotten under your skin again, Joe?" Rodney Stranahan inquired with amusement. "What is it this time?"

"They always get under Joe's skin," Hill Ransome remarked. "Terry Venner could tell you the time of day and it would irritate Joe."

"That's right," Joseph Strang agreed with a smile. "Particularly because he would always get it wrong."

There was general laughter at this. The Secretary brought them back to the problem.

"Go on, Hank," he said. "Tell us about the Deadly Duo's latest coup."

"A training accident last night," the Assistant Secretary for Public Affairs said. "At Camp Lejeune."

"Another Marine disaster," Bob Cathcart said and Hugh Merriman looked, for him, quite annoyed.

"These things happen," he said, "despite best precautions and best intentions by everybody. As Secretary of the Navy I accept full responsibility for it."

"That doesn't do much good," Bob Cathcart said. "It doesn't bring anybody back. How many were lost this time?"

"I believe there were seventeen," Hugh Merriman said evenly. The Deputy Secretary whistled.

"Jesus Christ," he said. "Your boys don't do anything in a small way, do they?"

"It was apparently unavoidable," Hugh Merriman said. "We're conducting a full investigation—"

There was a stir of amusement and Bob Cathcart whistled again.

"Not another in-house investigation! Do you think the Hill and the public are going to go for that?"

"They'll have to go for it," Hugh Merriman said in the same even tone, "as this is what's being done. If they want to conduct their own investigation, let them."

"They will," Secretary Cathcart predicted. "They're busy with appropriations right now, but after those are out of the way, they'll get around to it. You aren't home free, yet."

"We don't expect to be home free," Hugh Merriman said shortly. "Whatever went wrong, we'll find out and we'll correct it. We would like to do this with some privacy, but I gather our friends Horowitz and Jones won't let us."

"They and the rest of the media will only cry cover-up if you try to keep anything secret, Hugh," Loy Buck said. "You know that. Apparently Jones and Horowitz have already seized upon it, right, Hank?"

"The parents of one of the boys called them at six this morning and they called me," Henry Milhaus said. "They want an exclusive right to sit in on the hearing or they're going to tell 'the entire media,' as Delight put it. And—to quote further—'bring the full resources of DIG to bear in securing the widest possible publicity and public condemnation.'"

"'Public condemnation,' eh?" Tiny Wombaugh said. "That's prejudging the case, all right."

"Don't they always?" Jim Craft inquired dryly. "When did you ever know DIG to be anything but condemnatory?"

"'Defense Improvement Group,'" Joseph Strang said scornfully. "They improve defense, all right. They tear us down every chance they get."

"It's amazing to me," Helen Clark said, smoothing her sleek black hair with a white, long-fingered hand, "how they could have come from literally out of nowhere, apparently, and be as well-organized and well-financed as they are. It suggests other sources, to me."

"That's being investigated," Loy Buck said. "The only trouble is that they've become so well-established in six short months with friends in the media and support from the public that if we do find anything, we'll have the devil of a time convincing anybody. So what did you tell them, Henry?"

"I said that under no circumstances would they be permitted any exclusive right to attend the hearing, that the preliminary stages of the investigation would be secret, and that when it comes time to open them up, DIG will be accorded the same treatment as anyone else in the media."

"Good," the Secretary said.

"You're making enemies, Henry," Tiny Wombaugh said in an arch voice mimicking all the Pentagon's critics. Henry Milhaus snorted.

"Herb Horowitz and Delight Jones were enemies of this place the day they came out of the woodwork," he said. "I was their first contact and I was their first enemy. They don't scare me one little bit. But they will of course get all the biggies of the media involved in it, as they always do with their little scoops and snoops. It'll be on the news tonight and in all the dailies tomorrow morning."

"Another statement for me to issue," the Secretary said wryly. "I assume your staff is preparing it."

"It will be on your desk in half an hour," Henry said.

"Good," Loy said. "Now, as to State, I suppose you all saw their story in the *Post* this morning. The unnamed Assistant Secretary of State who says we don't really need to worry about Panama because 'the citizens of that country know full well that their best interests lie with the United States.'"

"*They* know it, maybe," Jason Bard said, "but the question is, does the enemy know it?"

"Always a good question," Tiny Wombaugh agreed. "What do you think, Jason?"

"I think we need to keep right on doing what we're doing," Dr. Bard said, "which is to keep our forces strong in the old Zone and around the embassy—stay on the alert—and keep calm."

"And try to stop any suspicious-looking trucks," Bob Cathcart said sardoni-cally. "Or is that too difficult?"

"That is not in my province," Jason Bard said calmly, "but I assume that those who are in charge of it are making sure."

"Yes, we are," Ray Clark said flatly. "The Army is fully prepared for any-thing."

"And so are the Marines," Hugh Merriman said with equal emphasis. "Nice of you to worry, though, Bob. It gives us heart."

The Deputy Secretary scowled.

"I don't want us to get into another damned disaster like some we've had. I'd like to keep a few boys alive, around here."

"Everybody wants to keep a few boys alive around here," Loy Buck retorted. "Does anyone else have anything to bring up this morning? If not, we'll adjourn next door and meet with the Joint Chiefs of Staff."

He stood up abruptly. The daily staff meeting ended on the same ill-tem-pered note on which it had begun. Outside the storm had settled in in earnest. The building was swathed in snow and gloom. From across the river only the dim glow of its thousands of windows through the swirling white indicated that its enormous bulk was there at all.

In the South Pacific dawn was just beginning to reach the waters around Nanukuvu. A faint touch of silver gray illumined an ocean placid as a mill-pond. A faint flush of rose tinged the underside of low clouds far away on the eastern horizon. Softly the gentle wind rustled idly through the palms. The world was good, and at peace.

In their longhouses the families of A'afaloa and Nuku'ofa began to stir. Twenty-eight souls, ranging in age from A'afaloa's sixty to Nuku'ofa's youngest baby of four days, inhabited the island. They had their chores, but there was time. Life had no problems on Nanukuvu save the catching of fish, the harvest-ing of taro, the collecting of the coconuts that fell conveniently of themselves, making human labor unnecessary. Placid day passed into placid night and so again into placid day, one upon another in a seamless web of time that had no arbitrary deliniations, not even the slow turning of the seasons, which in these latitudes barely troubled the surface of the earth or the mind of man. Life had its own internal rhythms on Nanukuvu, geared to the ancient Polynesian pace, unthinking, untroubled and serene.

Presently the first children and adults emerged from the houses, disappeared among the palms to take care of morning's needs, reappeared to gather drift-wood and light the communal cook-fire in the space between the grassy huts while others followed the same trails into the trees. Poi, coconut milk and dried fish comprised the morning meal. Afterwards certain children were detailed to sweep the area around the houses with palm-fronds. Others stacked the sleeping pallets in orderly piles along the walls. Still others swept the floors. The youngest began to play games in the sand. The wives and older daughters gathered under the trees to talk. The younger boys went off along the ridges to hunt for birds.

A'afaloa and Nuku'ofa, with six of their sturdiest sons, took the huge outrigger canoe that was their proudest possession and headed west along the lagoon to fish. Trolling as they went, they would reach the mouth of the lagoon in about one hour.

Today they planned to go beyond and spend most of the day in the open sea a few miles out. It would be a lesson day for the boys, who still had much to learn about the ocean, a happy day for A'afaloa and Nuku'ofa as they imparted the wisdom of a lifetime to sons with whom they were well satisfied and of whom they were very proud.

The vague mysterious menace they had felt in the night seemed utterly gone. Nothing now disturbed the tranquillity of their perfect little world.

Had they not remembered their sudden awakening, and waving to one another in the moonlight, they might have thought it all a dream.

Presently, as they watched the rhythmically rowing bodies of their sons propelling the outrigger with smooth efficiency over the warm limpid water, a pleasant torpor overcame them.

It would not be broken until they felt the surge of the tide at the entrance to the lagoon, and entered the open sea.

"General," the Secretary said to the Chairman of the Joint Chiefs of Staff when the meeting had moved, as was the custom, to the SecDef's private dining room next door, "do you have anything to report this morning?"

"Not much, sir," Gen. McCune said with the scrupulous deference he and his fellow officers always showed on formal occasions to the civilian side. "I'm sure we all know where the trouble spots are—"

"Everywhere," Loy Buck interjected. Zeecy smiled.

"Exactly: everywhere—and I know we're all in touch with them. They don't change much. Central America—the Philippines and Southeast Asia—the Middle East—the Gulf—southern Africa—South America—Mexico—you name it, we've got it."

"Nothing startling has happened, then, since you and I had our regular meeting last Friday," Loy said with a smile. Zeecy McCune shook his head.

"No, sir. Everything's in a hell of a shape. We wouldn't know how to react if it wasn't, would we?"

"We *hope* you know how to react," Bob Cathcart said with a disapproving expression that emphasized his refusal to be drawn into their basically serious banter.

"I hope we do, sir," Gen. McCune agreed calmly. "Have you noted any specific failures lately?"

"I'm not at all pleased with the way things are going in the Philippines," Secretary Cathcart said, not yielding an inch. "Nor in the Persian Gulf. Or in Central America, for that matter. I think you fellows ought to be a little more alert all around, if you ask me."

"We didn't, sir," Zeecy McCune said, just this side of insolence, "but since you offer, it is our impression that things are in reasonably good order in most places, considering what we're up against, worldwide."

"Of course you would think that," Bob Cathcart said. "I wouldn't expect you to admit shortcomings. Never."

"Mr. Secretary," Zeecy McCune said evenly, while his fellow members of the JCS tried with varying degrees of success to maintain polite, if frozen, smiles, "when shortcomings exist, I think we in the military are as concerned as you are about them. After all, we're on the line. It's our necks if things go wrong. We bleed, sometimes quite literally. We don't sit in the Pentagon—at least the great majority of us who are in the field don't sit in the Pentagon—and prejudge situations about which we don't, perhaps, know everything."

"Bravo," somebody murmured and Bob Cathcart swung around angrily, his big body tensing and his face looking even more flushed than usual. Bland expressions responded. After a moment he swung back.

"Well," he said, breathing a little heavily. "That's very smart but it doesn't answer the problem."

"What *is* the problem, Mr. Secretary?" Joe Strang inquired. "I don't know of any in particular at the moment."

"Military complacency," Bob Cathcart snapped. *"That's* the problem. It's always the problem."

"Now, Bob," Tiny Wombaugh said with the calm assurance of a man whose job does not depend upon the sufferance of another, "you're talking nonsense, in my estimation, so why don't you stop it? These guys are on the ball. They're about the best Joint Chiefs of Staff we've had in years, *I* think. We're lucky to have them. No complaints here, Zeecy. Carry on."

"Thank you, Tiny," Gen. McCune said with a little bow. "We try hard."

"We know you do," Loy Buck said in a tone that warned against any more argument on that point. For a moment the Deputy Secretary looked as though he were gathering himself for a retort but abruptly appeared to think better of it and subsided. The Joint Chiefs all made mental notes to *watch out for Catheter—he's on the rampage again about something.*

"Probably angling for an invitation to appear on '60 Minutes,' " Brash Burford murmured behind his hand to Ham Stokes.

"Sixty seconds would be more fitting," Gen. Stokes whispered back.

The Deputy saw the by-play and gave them a hostile look.

They smiled cordially in reply.

"How are we doing on the Hill at the moment?" Loy inquired. "I understand you and Bumpy are going up to testify this morning, Brash. Which committees?"

"I'm stuck with good old Cube Herron and the Senate Armed Services Committee," Gen. Burford said.

"And I have the great pleasure of meeting with Mario Escondido and his little gang of throat-slashers on the House Armed Services Committee," Adm. Stahlman said. "A prospect I do not entirely relish."

"Nor I," Brash Burford said, "though I will admit that Cube does know a good deal about our situation here, after twenty years on the committee."

"Even the most obtuse," Hugh Merriman observed, "are bound to learn something just by osmosis. I don't think he got that nickname from having three H's in his name. I think they took it from the shape of his head."

There was laughter. The Secretary of Defense professed to look shocked.

"That will do, Hugh," he said with mock sternness. "We can't have such talk about our great leaders on the Hill."

"The only thing that makes him bearable," the Secretary of the Navy observed, "is that Luzanne Johnson is No. 2 on the committee, so if Cube loses next year, we'll have her as chairwoman. Or person, as the case may be."

"Lu Johnson is a *woman,*" Gen. Tock said with such fervency that they all laughed.

"She's *my* kind of gal," Brash Burford sang, off-key.

"You're very musical this morning," Ham Stokes remarked and the Joint Chiefs looked amused.

"Someday you'll have to ask Tick about his idea for a Pentagon Follies show," Ham told the Secretary.

"Sounds like a good project," Loy said with a smile. "Count me in."

"Just what I meant," Bob Cathcart observed sourly. "Complacency. *And* frivolity. Doesn't anybody have a serious thought about our responsibilities, around here?"

"Oh, for Christ's sake," Loy Buck said, suddenly fed up. "If you don't like it, Bob, you can leave. Or resign. Everybody here is well aware of his or her responsibilities, but we have to laugh *sometimes,* otherwise we'd all go up the wall. Or I would, anyway. What's the status of our bills on the Hill?"

"The authorization bills are inching their way along in the Armed Services Committees," Bumpy Stahlman said. "That's why Brash and I are going into battle today. Same applies to the appropriations bills in the Appropriations committees. I know most of you folks have been up testifying on one or the other already this year, Mr. Secretary."

"And more appearances to come," Helen Clark remarked in her soft, decisive voice. She turned her beautiful eyes on Zeecy McCune and appeared, as usual, to be concentrating earnestly on some region near his adam's apple. "Tell me, general, how am I to answer when they ask me about the shortfalls in procurement? Shall I refer them to you?"

"You may, Madam Secretary," Zeecy said with a gallant bow and a broad smile. "I shall be glad to take all possible responsibility upon my shoulders for anything and everything you may wish to pass along to me."

"Oh, I wouldn't say it would be all *that* much," she said with an answering smile, lifting her gaze to look him squarely in the eyes with the quiet intensity that had felled many strong men on many occasions. "But I expect I'll be asked some pretty tough questions when I go before Cube and his pals."

"Ask Lu Johnson for help," he suggested, "she's a good ally to have."

"Yes," Helen Clark said softly. "So I understand."

There was a sudden suppressed amusement and for just a second Gen. McCune, the dynamic, the powerful, the perfect, came as close to looking flustered as any of them had ever expected to see. Brash Burford shot a quick glance across the table at Loy Buck and gave him the most fleeting of winks, which said: *It's true, then.* They had all heard the gossip in the last couple of weeks. But only Helen, as usual, had the cool self-confidence to bring it out.

"And of course, Helen," Loy said quickly as she looked away, a tiny smile touching her lips for a second, "we're all here to help too, you know. I dare say there isn't a man-jack of us here who wouldn't go to the Hill and die for you if necessary. So have no fear of Cube, or Mario Escondido, or anybody."

She laughed her pleasant laugh and gave a graceful little bow in turn.

"I'm overwhelmed," she said. "The Secretary of Defense, the chairman of the Joint Chiefs and *all* of you. What more could a poor defenseless girl ask?"

"To call you defenseless, Helen," Tiny Wombaugh remarked with a chuckle, "is to call King Kong a koala bear, to mix my vertebrates a bit. Gentlemen," he said with a sudden seriousness to the Joint Chiefs, "do you have anything for *me* this morning, aside from the memos, letters, phone calls and general brick-bats you all send me all the time? Is Research and Engineering doing all it can to Help Our Boys in Uniform?"

"You're doing pretty well, Mr. Secretary," Ham Stokes said. "In general, though, we in the Air Force have such a long shopping-list that I think I'd better continue to take it up with you via those aforesaid memos, letters and phone calls. Otherwise we'd be here all day."

"The Army likewise," Gen. Burford said.

"And the Navy," Adm. Stahlman said.

"And the Marines," Gen. Tock concluded with a smile.

Secretary Wombaugh smiled too.

"Now," he said. "Want to hear *my* shopping-list?"

"Please," Zeecy McCune said, holding up a hand in mock protest. "Not today, Tiny. We'll let you know. Personally, I think things are moving along pretty well on all fronts, from where I sit."

"It's a real love-feast," Bob Cathcart remarked to no one in particular. "Too bad it only takes an average of about twelve years to bring a weapons system on-line."

"That's the nature of the beast," Tiny Wombaugh said calmly. "We all try to hurry, but the system slows us down."

"Then why the hell don't you change the system?" Secretary Cathcart demanded. "The Soviets aren't sitting still, you know, while all you fellows piddle along with your endless reviews and changes and modifications and tests."

"Speaking of tests," Tiny Wombaugh said, ignoring him, "what's the latest with Skip Framberg?"

" 'Crazy Skip'?" Henry Milhaus said. "He's down in the basement cleaning sewers, last I heard."

There was general amusement at this description of the tall, raw-boned, idealistic but erratic and controversial redhead who had been demoted six months ago from his job as director of Test and Evaluation after feeding a story to Herb Horowitz about a carefully staged and highly suspect test of one of the Army's famous favorite mobile rocket-launchers. Now he was indeed in the basement, somewhere out beyond the "purple water fountain"—that famous landmark on which everyone guided when entering the labyrinths below—in a tiny little office without windows, churning out papers on study, research and analysis—still a potential time-bomb, and still apt to erupt in the media at any moment. But what else could be done with a difficult character like that? He couldn't be fired, he was civil service and, anyway, he was a Cause now, and sacrosanct. It would only cause a public stink to fire him; the only recourse was to demote him and hustle him out of sight. That also caused a stink, but only sporadically when somebody in the media remembered him and decided to interview him and "give the Framberg case another whirl." Meanwhile he bided his time and dreamed of vengeance. You don't resign in a fit of nobility when you have a wife and three young kids to support, but you do think about getting even. A certain uneasiness underlay the amusement with which his name was always mentioned in E Ring.

"I don't think," Bob Cathcart said loudly into the general chortles, "that there's anything funny about what happened to Skip Framberg. He's an honest man who had an honest complaint and he deserved a lot better of this building than to be swept under the rug."

"*That's* why the rug is so agitated these days," Ray Clark remarked. "I knew there must be something under there."

"Very funny," Secretary Cathcart retorted, "but he can still raise plenty of hell with you boys, and I for one hope he does."

"You wouldn't defend us, then, Mr. Secretary," Gen. Burford said, a dangerous little glint coming into his eyes at this disparagement of his beloved Army. Bob Cathcart snorted.

"Defend you! You're damned right I'll defend you, Brash, *when you're right*. I don't think anybody at this level was right about Skip Framberg."

"That test was honest also," Gen. Burford said in a level voice.

"Skip didn't think so, and he was the director," Bob Cathcart retorted.

"He is also a troublemaker," Loy Buck intervened flatly, "who tattles to the media and fancies himself in the headlines. We had to make an administrative decision about him and I made it. It isn't the first time you've disagreed with me, Bob, or the last, I suspect, but there it is. It doesn't help to have you encourage him. But the decision stands."

"You'll be sorry," Secretary Cathcart predicted.

"And you won't," Secretary Buck said crisply, "and there we are. Is there anything else, gentlemen?"

"How are we coming on the position papers for the NATO meeting in Brussels next month?" Zeecy McCune inquired. Loy gave him a quizzical look.

"You tell me how the secretariat of the Joint Chiefs of Staff is coming along with the JCS suggestions, Zeecy, and I'll tell you how the Pentagon is doing. We're ready in our shop."

"I wasn't aware they were dragging their feet," Gen. McCune said, "but I'll certainly get onto it the minute I leave this office."

"Please do," Loy Buck said. "I want to wrap it as soon as possible . . . So, then: no immediate crises this morning, everything proceeding reasonably on schedule, no more than the normal number of glitches. A relatively calm day in the Pentagon, I take it, so let's keep it that way if we can."

"A hell of a day outside, though," Hank Milhaus observed, nodding toward the swirling white slapping against the windows.

"Horrible," Helen Clark agreed as they rose to go to their respective offices. "It seems like a day when something *ought* to happen."

"Don't even say it," the Secretary protested with a smile as he saw them out. "I'm superstitious. We have enough to worry about, as it is."

This, he thought as the door closed upon the last of them and he returned to his desk and the accumulated calls from Hill, State, White House, home, media, friends, enemies, whatever, was typical of most of their meetings: some substantive business, some gossip, quite a bit of personal joshing—or animosity, as the case might be—nothing very earth-shaking, on the non-earth shaking days.

Earth shaking days were different.

He had presided over some meetings when the news from Lebanon, the word from the Gulf, the latest Soviet-Cuban demarche in the Americas, the latest terrorist bombing of embassy, airport or military base had brought them all grim-faced, tense and anxious to the table. Sometimes this had happened late at night. Then the building's lights suddenly flared, spotlights went on at the River Entrance, there was a burst of activity, cars and limousines arrived hastily from the District and nearby Maryland and Virginia. Then the cables hummed and the messages flew and the air was electric with crisis. Often this took civilians and military alike across the hall from his office into the highly restricted corridors and conference rooms of National Military Command Center, there to hover over the teletypes, radios and satellite communications linking the Pentagon with military commands all over the world and to receive direct reports, often by voice from the commanders in the field, describing the latest area of trouble in the always-troubled world.

These were the meetings that ran on sometimes for hours, sometimes around the clock, with little room for gossip or more than an occasional wise-crack to break the tension, until finally the crisis eased, the world settled down again—temporarily—the leak in the dike was plugged, the ruptured fabric of "civilization" was patched up, the fragile Humpty Dumpty of peace-that-was-no-peace was put back together to sit shakily upon his wall again, there to teeter in desperate uncertainty until the next time.

Then they all went home and slept for hours, returning finally to their accustomed routines in the knowledge that they had surmounted one more challenge—never knowing where the next might originate, or when they would again be called upon to meet and overcome it.

So far they almost always had. With luck, they would continue. But luck, he knew, with a sudden shiver as he looked out at the snowfilled world, was comparative and a frail reed on which to build survival. Much more than that was required. It was his hope, as it was that of all Secretaries of Defense, that the efforts of all in the building, each in his or her own way, would contribute to whatever might be needed.

All around him now he could sense the building humming along, its massive walls impervious to the storm, its hundreds of offices bright with lights against the gloom, its corridors as always alive with movement, the Concourse filled with bustle among the shops, military and civilian employees at their desks, working at their myriad tasks. Somewhere there was supposed to be a master plan to coordinate all this. He, if anyone, was supposed to know what it was. But he knew in his heart that this was largely illusion, no matter how intelligent, forceful and competent he might be. Half of any public job, he had concluded long ago when his duties for IBM first brought him into contact with Washington, was pretending that you knew what it was all about. The bigger the job, the truer this was. It was not a phony pretending and often it came near the fact, but it was a key to sustaining public faith and confidence, a national necessity to keep the whole machinery of government going. How much was pretense and how much reality varied from individual to individual. It was not until crisis struck that the basic truths of it really appeared and really mattered.

Thus in essence it was not important that meetings of civilian secretaries and Joint Chiefs of Staff, while sometimes grim, were more often casual and rambling as they had been today. When it was time to be grim, most had the capability. When it was not, it did no harm if they relaxed and were human. The machinery ground on.

He told himself, as he had so often before, not to worry.

With luck, it would all come right in the end.

The outrigger took the tide, slid swiftly out through the narrow channel, moved more slowly as it breasted the open sea. The palm-shrouded cleft through which it had come was scarcely two hundred feet in width; like almost the entire lagoon, its sides went straight down into the depths. A'afaloa and Nuku'ofa had never plumbed the true bottom but they knew it was very deep. The only place where there was any beach at all, and that did not extend out more than three or four hundred feet on either side before dropping off abruptly, was along the comparatively level area at the base of the U where their houses were built among the palms that came down to water's edge. For the rest, the lagoon was a great, elongated slot, approximately a mile across at fullest, perhaps six miles in length, with the narrow mouth and lateral ridges protecting it from all but the most violent typhoon-whipped tides.

Thus sheltered, it was an ideal place in which to live.

It was also, though they did not know it, an ideal place in which certain things might anchor.

The brothers had stumbled upon it inadvertently one day on a fishing trip when the smaller outrigger they shared and now used only within the lagoon had strayed from course during a long fishing trip out from the Gilberts. A'afaloa had already suspected that tensions within his tribe might make his departure advisable, and he had persuaded his younger brother to go with him on what he vaguely felt might be a search for a new home. When things subsequently developed as he had expected and he lost his battle to become chief, he had taken his wives and their then four children and set sail for the island to which foreigners had given the name Nanukuvu more than one hundred years ago.

A'afaloa knew nothing of this.

To him and his extended family it was known simply by the word for home.

Home it had become in short order, and when Nuku'ofa had followed with his wives and child two years later, it seemed that all was complete. Food and shelter were overwhelmingly abundant, there were fresh-water springs on the side of one of the two small extinct volcanoes, and with the amiable characteristics of their race and the close-knit affection of their familial background, they all got along very well. Both brothers had fine sons and daughters; soon, no doubt, some of the cousins would marry. Others might venture to explore as their fathers had and in time find other homes. For now, life on Nanukuvu was all they needed and all any of them wanted. They were in the blissful state of being unknown to the world; and nothing could have pleased them more.

The elders remembered dimly from their days in the Gilberts that there were other peoples, other tribes and—very distantly, usually only as a topic of occasional rumors that drifted by word of mouth through the endless islands that dotted the sun-washed sea—larger groups of tribes that sometimes warred with one another, for much the same reasons of greed or animosity—though on a much greater scale—as tribes did on some of the islands.

The brothers and their families knew virtually nothing of this. After they left the Gilberts and broke off contact with even their own people, their world became even more self-contained and self-centered. In time they were almost forgotten by those they had left behind. Nanukuvu, briefly a whaling station a century ago, had long since been forgotten too. Together they drifted in a pleasant lethargy that it seemed nothing could break. Once in a great while other outriggers might venture in after accidentally finding the tiny, tree-hidden entrance. Their occupants were always greeted cordially, given food and shelter for a night and politely requested to move on, which they invariably did with equal politeness, recognizing the brothers' serene hegemony.

Now and again, very high in the sky, a tiny bird of unknown nature might fly over, sending down a faint far-off drone and leaving a trail of white against the blue. But no one ever really noticed Nanukuvu. To those distant larger tribes it was, as the gazeteer so blandly reported, "pop. unknown, presumed uninhabited."

Now there were twenty-eight souls living there, huts hidden among the trees, leisurely activities unnoticed save by the casual passing visitors from the sea who, perhaps once in a year, invaded the quiet sanctuary of the lagoon and then moved on.

It was good, A'afaloa and Nuku'ofa felt. It was very good. They had found what they wanted, though they did not express it in the high-sounding words, vehement protestations and desperate exhortations of those larger tribes in faraway lands: they had found peace. The gods had decided, in their erratic, inexplicable way, that here and there, in a few small places on the face of the earth, they would permit such a condition to exist.

Now the outrigger was in the open sea, and after a few more minutes A'afaloa ordered, "Stop!" and the boys did stop, resting on their oars, dark bronzed bodies gleaming in the sun. Slowly and carefully A'afaloa began to explain to them certain things about the sea: certain signs that would tell you when it was gentle and kind, certain things to watch for when it was going to turn angry and unfriendly. He spoke of fish, too, and of all the ways to hunt and trap them, and how to dry and preserve them for a time if one wished to, and which to keep and which to throw away, and which were friends and which were enemies.

Much of this the boys had heard before, but it was pleasant for fathers to be drifting placidly on the gentle swell, imparting wisdom to sons in firm, dignified, all-wise voices to which the sons listened respectfully, just as A'afaloa and Nuku'ofa had listened to their father, many years ago.

It was while Nuku'ofa was confirming everything A'afaloa had said, repeating and embellishing in his deep, commanding voice, that one of his sons suddenly cried, "Look!" and pointed, eyes wide with wonder—though not with fear, for what could possibly disturb the paradise which was all he had ever known?

Quickly the brothers swung about and stared intently with their sons at the place where the sharp-eyed boy had pointed.

Something long and black and cylindrical had surfaced perhaps five hundred yards away.

Even as they watched it rose a little higher, so that they could see that it was only partially uncovered, and that there must be a much bigger body attached to it below the water.

Then as silently as it had appeared it sank beneath the gently rolling waves. Long hisses of surprise and astonishment escaped the brothers' lips.

It had appeared to be the back of a great black whale—a whale much larger, they told the boys excitedly, than any they had ever seen.

"Go back!" A'afaloa ordered quickly, and in thirty seconds the boys had the outrigger turned and were rowing desperately for the entrance to Nanukuvu.

A'afaloa and Nuku'ofa kept watch behind them with uneasy, troubled eyes. Presently they saw the whale surface again. This time it did not submerge. Before, there had been no indication that it had seen them. Now there was something about its posture, poised half in, half out of the water, that suggested that it was watching them intently.

Alarmed and deeply disturbed, the brothers each seized an oar and joined their sons in desperate hurry.

Behind them the great black whale watched with implacable silent concentration as they found the narrow opening and sped through it into the familiar quiet of the peaceful lagoon.

"With a name like 'Terrail Venner,'" Joseph Strang had once remarked, "where else could a man wind up but as Secretary of State?"

And in truth it did seem that Terry Venner's life had been predestined to bring him to his present high and uneasy eminence in the affairs of his country. Now, like all who would soon be directly involved with the problem of Nanukuvu, he looked out at the storm which was slashing with savage intensity at the windows of his seventh floor office in the State Department's chunkily unattractive quarters in Foggy Bottom. His thoughts were gloomy. He felt that he really would have been able to enjoy his job if it weren't for the constantly pushing crew in that damned building across the Potomac.

The friction that always exists between Pentagon and State Department had risen to new levels, it seemed to him, in the surge of the military build-up of the mid and later Eighties. Never averse to seeking influence in the field of foreign policy, the civilian and military heads of the Defense Department had gone all-out to grab even more in recent years. They had not only been re-armed to meet the Soviet advance, as the then President had intended: they had also been re-armed against their perennial antagonists in the State Department. In some ways he thought they considered this an even more important battle.

With great shrewdness, determination and tenacity they had managed to gather to themselves a weight in decision-making quite out of proportion to what he considered their true worth. He was willing to concede that they had some right to a voice in such matters, indeed a major right, but not to the extent of pushing around him and the Foreign Service and the entire bureaucracy of State. It annoyed and frustrated him and his colleagues all the time. In fact, he had often thought of resigning, though he had never voiced any such thought to the President. He wasn't quite that frustrated—yet.

At the moment—as of this hour on this particular hellish morning in the capital while winter was dying in one last grand convulsion—things were relatively quiet on the battlefront with the Pentagon. There had been the usual spate of foreign crises in recent weeks, the anticipated but never-quite-prepared-for attacks on embassies and consular offices, the diplomatic advances or rebuffs in sensitive areas, the unexpected minor conflicts that were always flaring out around the unhappy globe. But for some days there had been nothing really major. This had made it a good time, he had thought, in which to confer with Loy Buck and try to straighten out some of the lines of authority that seemed to have become all tangled up under the bland eye of the national security adviser, Al Brodovsky.

And now Loy's secretary, the invaluable and eternal Vangie, had called in her precise little voice to say Loy couldn't meet him at 9 as scheduled but would 11 A.M. do?

"No, it won't," Terry Venner said crossly. "I have one of the senior Saudi princes coming in for a conference and private lunch, and I'm sorry, but I just can't do it. You tell Loy I rearranged everything this morning so that *I* could see *him*—" he put a slight but noticeable emphasis on the order of the pronouns, because he considered it quite a concession for him to go to the Pentagon instead of the other way around—"and you tell him it's impossible to shift those plans now. I'll just have to call him back later in the week sometime and see what we can work out."

"He'll be sorry," Vangie said with just the right shade of regret. "He was so hoping to see you."

"I'll bet," Terry Venner said with a skepticism he made no attempt to hide. "I'll bet, Vangie."

"I'll tell him you'll be hearing from him, Mr. Secretary," she said politely. "Just call me whenever you're ready."

"My secretary will," he said sharply.

"Of course," she said calmly. "Thank you, Mr. Secretary."

And hung up on him, which he was not used to and which annoyed him even further. *He* was the one who hung up on other people—or had been, when he first took this job. Now Loy Buck and people who worked for Loy were hanging up on *him*. Terrail Venner was not amused. It was all so *indicative,* to use one of the favorite words of German-born Marisa, mother of their four children and fiercely staunch defender of himself. Marisa was always seeing slights, real or fancied, to his position and dignity, and certainly the way the Pentagon got away with treating him was enough to call out the word on many private occasions.

"It's just *indicative*," she would say in her still-heavy accent at each new apparent inroad upon his influence. "It's so *indicative*."

And yet he and Loy had been appointed to the Cabinet at the same time, he reflected as he stared moodily at the snow. They were the two who had been appointed first—he, in fact, ahead of Loy, since the President tended to be tradition-minded at times and wanted, he said, to recognize the State Department's seniority in the government. And he *was* supposed to be the senior Cabinet officer. Yet here was the Pentagon, into everything, throwing its weight around, pushing *him* around. So much for seniority!

For one who appeared to be tall, thin, reserved and glacial, Terry Venner at fifty-seven was a seething volcano, he told himself with the self-irony that saved him from many things, and was known only to Marisa and few others.

This was not at all the way he had planned that his career in the State Department would conclude—as a punching-bag for the Pentagon. In fact, after twenty-seven years as a career officer in the Foreign Service, after two ambassadorships, to South Africa and Japan, and after associating with a variety of Secretaries, he had always thought that he would direct foreign policy with a combination of the suave flair of a Dean Acheson and the ruthless skill of a Henry Kissinger. He had not intended to wind up as a wimp. And by God, he told himself angrily, he *wasn't* a wimp. But somehow he had to regain control of foreign policy. And how he was to do that, when the Secretary of Defense and his minions were aided and abetted by the President's national security adviser, he didn't at the moment know.

Aleksandr Brodovsky—known also as "Aleks" and "Al"—was another of those Europeans making American foreign policy whom Terry Venner, product of Beacon Hill, Choate and Harvard, didn't approve of very much, even if he did like him personally and even if Terry was married to a European himself. It had nothing to do with race or national origin, it was just that they had an instinctive cynical approach to things that he knew he did not have and could not acquire, no matter how Machiavellian he was sometimes accused of being by the more conservative elements of the media. He wasn't Machiavellian at all, he was at heart just as straightforward and undevious as most of his countrymen, no matter how his seemingly icy presence and generally unflappable calm might appear to others.

He wasn't very well equipped, in fact, to handle Al Brodovsky's type. He could meet Loy Buck one on one, and there his background, in contrast to Loy's typical poor-boy-up-through-the-ranks life story, gave Terry—or at least he thought it gave him—an advantage. But when it came to people like Joe Strang and Al Brodovsky, he seemed to find himself outmaneuvered more often than not. And he seemed to get little help from the President. It was all very annoying.

Time and again Terry Venner, who had come up the State Department ladder and arrived at the top thoroughly imbued with the department's easy-does-it—don't rock-the-boat—and-for-God's-sake-don't-be-*rude* attitude toward the Soviets and other obstreperous international elements, had found himself thwarted by the personal attitudes and convictions of his competitors. The Pentagon had always been far more hard line than State toward the Soviets, possibly because, as Zeecy McCune had remarked to him dryly one time when they had met at some function at the Soviet embassy, the Pentagon had to meet them on the ground.

"We can't meet them dancing in the air the way you diplomats do," the chairman of the Joint Chiefs had added with a disparaging—or what Terry Venner took to be disparaging—smile. "We have to consider the practical realities of it."

"And you think we don't?" Terry demanded, twenty-seven years in the State Department brimming with indignation. "We're just as practical as you are, believe me."

"Well," Gen. McCune had said, waving cheerfully across the room to the Soviet ambassador, oiling his way through Washington with practiced skill, "maybe you are, in your own minds, but it doesn't always seem so to us."

"That's because all you understand is waving bombs and ships and planes at people," the Secretary of State retorted. "Nuclear diplomacy, that's the only kind you understand."

"Don't think we enjoy it," Zeecy McCune responded with a sudden bitter vehemence that caused the wife of the Dutch ambassador, standing nearby, to turn around in unconcealed surprise. "I'd give you all of these—" he took his drink-free right hand and slapped it swiftly across the four stars on his left shoulder, "if we could just get a little honest-to-God peace."

"I guess we all want the same thing," Terry Venner agreed, somewhat mollified. "I didn't mean to imply you enjoyed the conflict with these people, Zeecy. I know it's a terrible burden for all of us."

"All of my professional life," Zeecy said, frowning unhappily. "And all of yours too, of course. And what do we have to show for it? Only tension and more tension. Nothing resolved, nothing settled. Only on and on, and God knows where it will ever stop."

"It's our job to see it doesn't stop with a bang," the Secretary of State said.

Zeecy shot him a sideways, gloomy look before he turned away to greet Luzanne Johnson and a couple of other Senate Armed Services Committee members.

"Ours too," he said. "May God attend our labors."

Unfortunately, Terry Venner reflected as the storm increased in intensity, buffeting the windows with a soft but clearly audible impact as the snow straggled down in great wet gobs, the Pentagon always managed to convince itself that God attended *its* labors rather more fully than He did anyone else's. When you put Joe Strang and the Doomsday Twins, Jason Bard and Jim Craft, together with Al Brodovsky, it took all the skill the State Department possessed to keep foreign policy from being swept entirely from its control. That was another battle that went "on and on, and God knows where it will ever stop."

He told himself again that he must get some clear definition of "parameters" —to use some of the Pentagon's own pet phraseology—so that the "interface" would be one they could both live with.

He had little hope of help from the President on this, at least at the present stage of negotiations. The Chief Executive didn't like to be bothered with Cabinet squabbles over territory until they were resolved by the disputants and could be brought up to him in settled form. Only after he and Loy had their talk and worked it out, Terry knew, would there be any point in taking it along to the White House.

At the same moment that he was indulging himself in these thoughts—he supposed it was an indulgence, to brood about it, because that really wasn't going to accomplish anything—Al Brodovsky was giving the President his daily national security briefing in the Oval Office. It was a task the national security adviser usually found pleasant enough, though the President did have a way sometimes of asking blunt and unsettling questions that required careful and diplomatic answers. Aleks prided himself on being able to handle these with a skill and swiftness that seemed to please "the Boss," as the President was known generally throughout the government. At least Al thought they pleased him. It was hard to tell sometimes, the Boss was such a shrewd and clever politician in the way he analyzed others' assumptions about him and skillfully adjusted his public utterances to conform.

At the moment he was sitting there doodling on a pad of paper, apparently listening intently, while Aleks brought him up to date on international events, particularly those involving the homeland Aleks had left with his parents when he was one year old. The Soviet Union could never seem to make up its mind whether it was going to release its Jewish citizens or keep them as hostages, but during one of the times when they were grudgingly being allowed to leave, Aleks and his parents had been lucky enough to get away. Distant relatives in New York had made them welcome. Aleks frequently blessed the day he came to America, for America had been very good to him—as, he often reflected with satisfaction, he had been good to America.

He had been a very bright boy who learned English with startling speed, got the highest possible grades in grammar school, high school and Harvard, and was generally conceded to be one of the most brilliant brains that ever emerged from the banks of the Charles. He had been two years and several social worlds behind Terry Venner, which, he would say to Terry's credit, Terry never indicated in any way whatsoever. He and Terry, in fact, were genuinely good friends. More so than Aleks was with what he thought of as "the Pentagon crowd," though it was with them and their generally hostile view of his native land that he sided more often than not in the constant debates that raged among the Administration's top foreign policy experts.

It was ironic, he thought as he almost lost the thread of his narration when the President suddenly exclaimed "Ah!" upon finishing an unusually elaborate doodle, that the national security adviser should catch hell from both sides of the fence. The far-right groups in the country went around muttering and publishing dark suspicions about his loyalty in view of his Russian origin, and the liberals were always after him because he was too outspokenly harsh in his attacks on the imperialistic intrigues of his homeland. As had happened to others before him, he had already been indirectly but firmly notified that he need not expect to return to the Harvard professorship he had left to accept his national security post: his critical attitude toward the Soviet Union was "no longer acceptable" along the Charles. Eventually he would either establish his own policy consultancy or go with something like THOUGHT Inc. or some other of the "Beltway Bandits," so-called because most of the major think-tanks were easily accessible from the interstate highway that looped around Washington. He often told himself with some amusement that in that capacity his views would continue to influence national policy far more than they ever could at Harvard.

For the moment, his job was to analyze as clearly as he could, and suggest as congently as he knew how, where overnight events fitted into the ongoing pattern of this miserable snowy day. He did so with his usual precise and encyclopedic skill, still not entirely sure, as he placed this piece of the puzzle securely alongside its mates and illuminated that murky corner of policy with shrewd, incisive insights, that the President was paying full attention. He knew there was one sure way to test this. He deliberately lowered his voice and slowed his pace. Instantly the President pushed his pad aside, gave him a shrewd look and inquired softly, "Am I tirin' you out, Al?"

"No, sir," Aleks said quickly. "Not at all."

"Good," the President said. "What you have to say is mighty interestin' to me, I want you to know, and I wouldn't want you to think I'm not payin' attention."

"Oh, no, sir," Aleks repeated earnestly. The President permitted a small gleam of amusement to come into the shrewd, dispassionate eyes that had accurately perceived the vulnerabilities of so many men during his days as Congressman, governor, U.S. Senator and Chief Executive.

"You're a good man, Al," he said. "Don't know what I'd do without you. You're very patient with me, I must say. Expect that isn't so easy, with all the pressures you're under tryin' to keep the foreign policy circus goin'. How are they treatin' you, over at State? And the Pentagon?"

Al Brodovsky smiled.

"I expect, Mr. President," he said, "that the complaints in those two places are about the way *I'm* treating them, not the other way around. I'm sure Terry Venner thinks I'm throwing everything the Pentagon's way, and vice versa. Loy Buck and his boys would like to run the whole thing, I'm sure."

"Loy Buck and his boys," the President echoed, "are one sharp bunch of cookies. Got a lot of clout, now, with all the build-up of the past few years. Expect they *would* like to run the whole thing. But you mustn't let 'em, Al. That would be dangerous. Not that there's any danger they'd try to do anything to hurt the democracy, of course, that's crap even if some of our big, pompous commentators do try to sound worried about it now and then. But it just isn't healthy to let things get out of balance. It's easy for Joe Strang and that crowd to think they've got all the answers to everything. We've got to keep the balance and keep it pretty firm, Al, and it isn't easy. Not that old Terry," he added dryly, "is all that strong a reed to lean on. I called him 'Mr. Icicle' to his face the other day." He chuckled. "He didn't like it, but he took it. Actually he isn't an icicle any more than you or I, he just looks and acts that way. He's a good sport, Terry, and he does know his foreign policy as well as any of 'em."

"Oh, yes," Aleks agreed. "I do try to keep a balance between them, as you know. But inevitably, I suppose, the military power has to predominate more often than not. After all, power is what it's all about."

"And nobody has power like the Pentagon," the President said thoughtfully. "Except me, and sometimes the way they run that shop over there, *I'm* not so sure." For a second he looked terribly tired, and Aleks thought of the rumors that were going around. He could neither confirm nor deny them. When you see a person every day, deterioration is sometimes hard to realize. Aside from occasional tiredness, the President seemed fine and as feisty as ever. He dismissed the thought.

"Do you have anything special you want me to do today?" he inquired.

The President looked up with the smile that could illuminate his face and send overwhelming millions to the polls to cast their ballots for him.

"Just keep things quiet, is all I ask, Aleks. Just keep 'em quiet. It's all I ask."

"Yes, sir," the national security adviser said with an answering smile. "I'll do my best."

On Nanukuvu, things were proceeding much as the occupants of the great black whale had anticipated.

In less than an hour A'afaloa and Nuku'ofa and their sons reached the beach. The women were off somewhere gathering material for weaving. All the children had now straggled off along the ridges to gather coconuts. The long-houses were deserted. The beach was empty. The sun was high and hot. All was quiet around the compound.

Prompted by some instinctive fear they could not have defined, they dragged the outrigger several hundred yards into the trees and covered it with fallen branches as though this could really hide it from a determined enemy. They all felt strongly now that the great black whale was hostile to them, though they did not know why or in what way. They also felt that whatever it intended might happen quickly.

When they hurried back to the houses A'afaloa ordered two of the sons to take up sentry posts, one at each end of the beach; dispatched two more to the other side of the level ground the two families inhabited in the curve of the island; and sent the final two running to lookouts high on the flanks of the two small volcanoes.

Then he took from the wall of his house the enormous conch-shell which he used on ceremonial occasions and gave it two long blasts—paused—two long blasts—paused—three long blasts—paused—one last blast—and stopped.

Far off he could hear the startled, dutifully answering cry of his senior wife Tuatama. Then all was silent save for the peaceful everyday sounds they were used to, the cries of gulls, the twittering of land birds in the trees, the rhythmic slap of tiny waves against the shore, the gentle rustle of the trade winds in the trees.

Within ten minutes all the inhabitants of Nanukuvu had come silently from the groves and gathered around him in a circle outside his house.

Gravely he told them of the great black whale, and of the fears he and Nuku'ofa and their sons had felt as they first watched it, then fled from it. It had not, he said, shown any signs of pursuing them; and yet he confessed that he and his brother and their sons were much afraid.

"We must hide," he told the silent women and children who watched him with huge, brown, apprehensive eyes.

Quickly he led the way along familiar trails to the secret cave in the side of the larger of the two volcanoes which he and Nuku'ofa had discovered many years ago and prepared for emergency.

They had never had to use it in all their years on the island.

But they knew they had to use it now.

They had just made sure that everyone was inside, with overhanging branches of palm-trees tied across the opening to conceal it, when A'afaloa's eldest son appeared, breathless and terrified, from his lookout on the other side of the volcano.

The great black whale had surfaced again.

Now it was just inside the lagoon.

Quickly A'afaloa blew two more short blasts on his conch to bring the other boys in.

Then he and Nuku'ofa, warning everyone to keep very quiet, went silently to the lookout and stared down, trembling, upon the gentle water that in all the years they had known it had always been so peaceful.

The great black whale was much closer now. It was moving with a relaxed, unhurried confidence straight toward the beach.

Now it was speaking to them. They could hear it growling as it came.

Two hundred feet offshore, where the beach ended and dropped away into the depths, it stopped.

After a moment little figures clad all in black bobbed up alongside it and began to swim toward land.

Now A'afaloa and Nuku'ofa knew that these were men; and knew with a bone-chilling fear that made their teeth literally chatter in the midst of the warm and gentle day, that their peaceful paradise, for reasons they would never understand, suddenly was peaceful no more.

For his part, Joe Strang felt as he walked slowly back along the busy corridors to his suite of offices on the other side of E Ring, he and his "little State Department" could have done very nicely without the incessant and usually quite obstructive opposition of the real State Department across the river. He was willing to concede—but only just—that the traditional home of diplomacy might have something to contribute to maintaining peace in the world. But it was minimal, he felt, compared to the combination of diplomacy and arms that this building could muster.

Joe Strang believed in the calculated application of power to the trouble spots of the world, and since that also seemed to be the favored policy of what the Pentagon customarily referred to as either "the threat" or "the enemy," he felt he was more than equipped to understand their policies and thwart their designs. He felt he knew the way they thought and how they operated. He felt he understood their plans. He took some pride in the way their various organs of official opinion often singled out himself and the Doomsday Twins, particularly Jason Bard, his Assistant Secretary for Soviet Affairs, for personal condemnation.

Joe Strang liked being damned up and down by *Pravda* and *Izvestia* and Radio Moscow. Whenever Moscow snarled out "the so-called Pentagon foreign policy expert J. Strang" or "the well-known anti-Soviet agitator J. Bard," he and Jason congratulated each other that they had gotten under the Soviets' skin again. They had found that this notoriously thin fabric was easily breached. When it was, Joe was confirmed in his conviction that he understood the men in Moscow and how to handle them. Through Al Brodovsky and Loy Buck he was often able to get his ideas placed before the President. As a result things happened in many parts of the world along lines Joe believed to be most effective in defeating the incessant outward-pushing imperialism of the Soviet Union.

Today he found on his desk one more of the continuing problems of Central America. He reviewed it carefully as he stepped out of the way of a hooting messenger cart and paused at one of the building's several ice cream shops to get himself a cone of chocolate chip—which would do nothing for his short, rotund figure, as Annalise was always telling him indignantly, but he *did* like it and often had three or four a day. He was not all that interested in the southern hemisphere except as a battleground, he acknowledged to himself as he resumed his steady, plodding walk. As a native of what just before World War II was still an independent Hungary, he was strongly and unshakably Europe-oriented, as most of America's top policy-makers of European extraction were. He dutifully took care of the rest of the world when it was necessary, which was most of the time, but his basic strategy was to defeat the enemy in Europe. Not with war, of course, that was too awful to contemplate, but by every other means of persuasion and threat at the command of the Pentagon.

This was where he ran squarely afoul of Terry Venner and his colleagues in Foggy Bottom. After all these years, Joe Strang thought with a contempt he could not suppress, they still were basically pink-tea-party in their approach to the threat. Events had forced them into taking, very reluctantly and with much foot-dragging, a relatively tough line toward Moscow, but on too many occasions still, he felt, they were halfhearted and wishy-washy about it. They would much rather have everything gentle and pleasant than take the harsh risks that Soviet policies made imperative, in his estimation. State's attitude wasn't quite peace at any price, he often told his colleagues, but it often came damned close to gentility at any price.

Terry Venner's tall, distinguished figure and glacially cool and precise manner seemed to contrast perfectly with Joe's own short, stocky, roly-poly form and his frequently quivering indignation. They symbolized in their persons, he felt, the sharp differences in their policies.

"Mr. Icicle," they called the Secretary of State in the Pentagon.

"Mr. Buzzfuzz" and "Mr. Pop-Off," they called Joe Strang at State. "Hatchet Man" they called Jason Bard for his hardline approach to the Soviets. Jim Craft was labeled "Fu Manchu" when he warned of Soviet designs on Asia or the South Pacific. For easy reference Foggy Bottom lumped the three of them together as "Dopey and the Doomsday Twins."

All of these terms had been passed along spitefully to the media years ago, and were used frequently in editorials and broadcasts that touched on policy arguments between State and Defense. It tended to give a somewhat juvenile aspect to what was in reality a deadly serious ongoing battle over the best course to pursue in dealing with the relentless, never-ceasing pressures of the enemy.

In this unending fight with State, Joe Strang was comfortably certain that when the chips were down he had the support of the national security adviser and, in many cases, the President himself. He and Al Brodovsky were not very far apart in their views of the Soviet Union. The President, while tending to veer a bit depending upon how the more vocal portions of the populace or the media seemed to feel on a given issue, also in general seemed to agree with him. He was definitely in the driver's seat vis-à-vis Terry Venner, he told himself with satisfaction as he approached his office. They had no outstanding clashes at the moment, but if one developed, he was ready for it. He congratulated himself complacently that he was exactly as he insisted his name be pronounced—not "STRANG"—not even "STRAHNG," in the European way —but *"STRONG."*

Both the Doomsday Twins—he often found himself slipping into State's derogatory terminology, it *was* catchy and convenient, if unjust—were waiting for him. He regarded them as extensions of himself and expected them to toe the line when he laid it down and echo his words when he uttered them. But he recognized, perhaps somewhat patronizingly, that both Jason Bard and Jim Craft were brilliant men in their own right, with ideas that frequently were helpful.

"Well, gentlemen," he said when they were seated in his office with the door closed and the various anti-bugging and anti-satellite devices turned on, "that wasn't much of a meeting today, was it?"

"Bob Catheter enjoys throwing his weight around, doesn't he?" Jason Bard responded with a smile. Joe Strang sniffed and dismissed the Deputy Secretary.

"Stupid. Uninformed and stupid. We have more serious things to do than worry about him. They should have been getting reports from *us*, not gripes from Bob and pleasantries from the Joint Chiefs. Which were all right, but immaterial."

Despite his tone he was not that critical of the military. He had his difference with them too but not much divided them when it came to the Soviets. Overall, they saw the enemy much the same.

"I was amused when Helen called Zeecy on Lu Johnson," Jim Craft said. "I'm beginning to think there's really something to it."

"There you go," Joe Strang said with some severity. "Gossip, gossip, gossip, just like the rest. But," he conceded with a smile that softened it, "they do make a handsome pair."

"Yes," Jason Bard agreed, and for a moment they were all silent, contemplating the gravely beautiful face, tall, graceful figure, soft southern voice and charming manner of the senior Senator from Louisiana. "But," Jason added finally with a small sigh for the chairman of the JCS, "there's always Renee."

"Yes," Joe Strang agreed, and again they were silent, contemplating the equally beautiful, equally graceful, equally charming—equally tough, under it all—figure of French-born Renee, Zeecy's wife of almost thirty years. "She's not one to give up easily."

"Oh, I doubt if it will come to that," Jim Craft said. "Renee's been through thick and thin with Zeecy all these years, and sometimes with considerable provocation, from what I hear—on both sides. They're a good combination. They remind me of a couple of gracefully aging racehorses going in tandem. They may kick each other once in a while, but they're going to keep on pulling together."

"Where does that leave Luzanne?" Jason Bard inquired; and it was symptomatic of the Senator's high standing with almost everyone that they really worried that she might get hurt.

"Luzanne can take care of herself, I expect," Joe Strang said. "Which makes life interesting in the Pentagon but does not advance us very far vis-à-vis the Soviets. What about *that*, gentlemen?"

"The usual in my area," Jason Bard said. "I think the U.S. made a little progress yesterday in Geneva. We got one word changed in one sentence. It was a great triumph."

At this reference to the perennial talks with the Soviets which had been poking along for years at their usual desultory pace, they again fell silent. What they contemplated now was what many of their fellow-citizens conceived to be the end of the world if it did not succeed. To them, as to all directly involved, it was a seemingly endless series of tactical problems that had to be solved one by one, inch by inch, day by day, sometimes minute by minute—always with the threat of world's end hanging over them, but so used to it by this time that they rarely stopped to think about it in those terms.

As the President had put it at his most recent news conference last week, "We just keep pluggin' along—just pluggin' along."

That was how they all thought of it, and that was the way it was. The doomsday scenario was in the backs of their minds but the immediate issue was how to work out a reasonably balanced agreement in the everyday world. Despite many years of trying and the efforts of many good men, this was still an objective unachieved. So things crawled on at Geneva, month after month, year after year, the situation unchanging and perhaps unchangeable, though the attempts continued to be made.

"And in your area, Jim?" Joe Strang inquired.

The Assistant Secretary for East Asian and Pacific Affairs shrugged.

"They're a worry in some places—New Caledonia, for instance, East Malaysia, the southern Philippines. Here and there in the islands, but not too much activity overall. Things are relatively quiet, for the moment. Of course the minute there's unrest of any kind they're ready to move in. You know what the Kremlin's game is and has been for more than seventy years: always make worse, never help to stabilize."

"Vicious bastards," Joe Strang said in a tired voice. "They really are the scum of the earth."

"Armed with history's greatest arsenal," Jason Bard observed. "Which puts them in a somewhat special category."

"Will you be seeing Loy this afternoon?" Jim Craft inquired.

"There's a small conference with Zeecy, I believe, at 3 P.M.," Joe said. "Something about Iran again. Crazy as ever, those birds. I suppose some of the JCS staff will be there. They always like to sit in and throw their weight around." His expression indicated it would do them no good.

"Were you there the other day when that Navy commander on the Joint Chiefs staff corrected Bumpy Stahlman?" Jim Craft inquired with amusement. "Spoke right up in meeting and told him, 'Admiral, I don't think you'd better say that without checking further with us.' Bumpy turned all colors, but the commander stood his ground, and I suspect he got away with it."

Joe Strang nodded.

"All of the chiefs have their own constituencies. And they're very powerful. That's why 'reform' of the Joint Chiefs of Staff set-up never really succeeds. Even Zeecy, hard as he tries, can't get entirely away from the Air Force: he has to take their feeling into account when he assesses things. Everything the Joint

Chiefs do has to be by consensus, the lowest common denominator. Nobody can come up with anything original, it has to go through so many hands and satisfy so many people. And Zeecy has no real power to make decisions or override anything, in spite of Congressional attempts at reform in recent years. It's frustrating for him and damaging to the country."

"That could be one hell of a handicap if it ever comes to a real showdown on something," Jim Craft observed.

Joe Strang frowned.

"Absolutely. That's why we just have to work around them whenever we can. It isn't often possible, but I try. Thereby earning my reputation as the biggest bastard in the Pentagon. But I dare say," he added complacently, "that I can survive *that.*"

"As long as Loy likes you," Jim Craft agreed.

"Right," Joe Strang conceded. He smiled. "He also likes Zeecy, very much. They get along better than any Secretary and chairman I've ever heard of. This complicates matters for me. And for all of you in this office."

"Of course Zeecy sees eye to eye with us on most things," Jason Bard remarked.

"Fortunately," Joe Strang said. He suddenly looked quite severe. "Otherwise I should have to bring him down a peg or two, I'm afraid."

His two principal assistants gave each other a quick look he did not see as he stared out at the furious snow. Their unspoken comment was: *Good luck if you can do it.*

"Gentlemen," Joe Strang said, standing up and making shooing motions with his hands as they both laughed. "Get along with you. We all have a lot of serious work to do, so let's get at it."

"Yes, sir!" said the Assistant Secretary for Soviet Affairs, snapping him a smart salute.

"On the double!" agreed the Assistant Secretary for East Asian and Pacific Affairs, duplicating the gesture.

"And don't come back," their boss told the Doomsday Twins as they went out on a wave of amusement that would have surprised their State Department opposites "until it's over, over there."

In their lookout high above the beach A'afaloa and Nuku'ofa dared do no more than draw in soft hissing breaths of astonishment and fear as perhaps twenty of the black figures emerged from the water, moved to the huts and disappeared inside. Some time later they emerged to rake methodically through the dead ashes of the breakfast fire.

The brothers could see that the strangers had brought out some of the sleeping mats, which they examined closely, then tossed aside. The bowls and cooking sticks the women had left neatly stacked near the fire were also pawed

over, discussed, thrown aside. Somewhere along one of the ridges a limb fell
with a sharp crack. Instantly the strangers leaped to form an outward-facing
circle, staring about them tensely, holding at the ready what the brothers recognized as weapons of some sort.

For several minutes no one moved.

Finally one of the group uttered a sharp command in an unknown tongue.
The circle dissolved. Its members fanned out through the trees. The brothers
grew even quieter, tense, motionless, utterly still. They could see that the
visitors seemed to be particularly interested in the large flat area, encompassing
their huts, that stretched across the base of the island from lagoon to sea.

In a few minutes some of the visitors emerged from the trees onto the beach
on the other side. A patient process of measuring began. Palm fronds were
stuck here and there in the sand, black figures carefully paced off the distance
from lagoon to sea and across the width of the level center. A handful stood
guard but now a general relaxation was apparent among them. It was as though
they had observed the island's inhabitants before and knew that they were
peaceful people from whom there was little to fear. It was as though, after their
initial instinctive caution, they knew they could easily handle whatever threat
the brothers and their families might pose.

All this time the great black whale sat patiently half-submerged, only a slight
hum indicating that it was alive.

Presently all of the visitors gathered again on the beach in front of the huts.
Their search was apparently completed. Their measurings were done. Whatever knowledge they had come to find, they had found. Again there was a
sharp command. The weapons were handed to one of their number who
placed them carefully in a small inflated rubber boat and began to row toward
the whale. The others plunged into the gentle water and began to swim swiftly
after him. In a few short minutes they had all reached the whale and disappeared inside.

The creature began to growl more loudly. It turned in a big half-circle and
headed toward the mouth of the lagoon. Now the brothers felt it was safe to
talk. They exchanged comments in low, excited voices.

For several minutes they watched the whale as it moved along the lagoon.
About halfway to the entrance it began to sink slowly beneath the water. Soon
it was out of sight, only a slight quick-dying ripple indicating its passage. The
brothers watched its trace as long as they could. Several hundred yards inside
the entrance the ripple disappeared altogether. For a long time they continued
watching, not sure whether it had actually gone or whether it was still lurking
inside the lagoon beneath the waters.

At last A'afaloa made the decision.

"It is gone," he said. Slowly Nuku'ofa nodded.

"Yes, brother, it is gone. May the gods grant that it never come back!"

"May the gods grant!" A'afaloa echoed with heartfelt fervor. And taking the great conch, which he had brought with him on their hurried climb up the slope, he blew three long blasts.

Soon all the inhabitants of Nanukuvu were gathered again in the space between the huts. Excitedly they chattered about the whale as the brothers related over and over again what they had seen.

At first they were all still nervous and many fearful glances were cast toward the mouth of the lagoon. But nothing now disturbed its calm. The gulls argued, the land-birds sang, the gentle breezes moved softly through the trees as always. Paradise seemed to have been re-established. Nothing appeared to have changed.

In a few minutes the novelty had worn off. They were beginning to become bored with it. It was time to resume the everyday patterns of life.

They would remember the visit of the great black whale as long as they lived but its mysterious passage was already losing its grip upon them.

The women and girls resumed their weaving and chattering. The youths ran about removing the palm fronds stuck in the sand, then stacked the sleeping mats and cooking utensils in their proper places.

A'afaloa and Nuku'ofa, tired from their rowing, their strenuous climb up the volcano and their tension while the visitors explored their home, lay down in their respective huts for a quick nap before the noontime meal.

Peace descended once again in its happy, familiar way upon Nanukuvu.

In a little while the gentle trade winds, which always increased a little when the sun passed zenith, began to blow across the center of the island from sea to lagoon.

In his office on E Ring near the River Entrance, the chairman of the Joint Chiefs, whose name had just a few minutes ago been taken in vain, or at least in gossip and jocularity, by Dopey and the Doomsday Twins, was reading the riot act to a young Air Force lieutenant who had been selected by two colonels on the joint staff to take the brunt of the chairman's ire concerning JCS slowness in preparing the NATO paper requested by the Secretary.

The young lieutenant, a newcomer to the Pentagon, told his wife ruefully that night that he seemed to have been selected to be the colonels' C.O.A.O.—Cover Our Ass Officer—a position he allowed he was not entirely comfortable with. At the moment he was standing at attention, a stance Zeecy did not often demand of anyone in the military, while the chairman let him have it.

It was not an unkindly bawling-out, for Zeecy was big enough and secure enough to be able to dispense with unkindness toward his subordinates.

It was a firm one, nonetheless.

"So, lieutenant," he concluded with a stern look and a secret amusement at the desperate earnestness of the anxious young face staring solemnly back at him, "I want you to go back and tell the sons of bitches who picked you out to take their licking for them that I want that damned paper on my desk by 1700 —*today*. Or it will be their asses, not yours. Which," he added, face breaking suddenly into his charming smile, "would be exactly what they deserve, right?"

"Well, sir—" the lieutenant began awkwardly. "Well, sir, I don't know—"

"Relax, lieutenant," Zeecy said. "You and I understand each other, don't we?"

"Yes, sir!" the young lieutenant said with a relief so strong that it almost brought tears to his eyes. "Yes, sir, I guess we do!"

"Good," Zeecy said. "Your name, again, is—?"

"Broderick Tolliver, sir," the young lieutenant said quickly. "Brod, they call me."

"All right, Brod," Gen. McCune said. "You run along now, and take my message. I'll see you around."

"I hope so, sir!" Brod Tolliver said fervently. "Oh, I hope so!"

And almost backed out in an obvious and touching glow—one more of those converts to the cause of Z. C. McCune, Zeecy told himself with a curious mixture of amusement and bittersweet wryness at his own practiced performance, with which the services were filled from one end of the earth to the other. All liked him. Most outright worshiped him. With the ranks of all services, Zeecy McCune could do no wrong.

With their superiors, it was sometimes another matter.

His face lost its pleasant expression, took on a frown as he returned to his desk and went through the reports that had accumulated during the meeting with the Secretary. Reports—endless reports. God, how he hated them, and God, how necessary they were if one wanted to keep any handle at all on what was going on in the military and more specifically in the Pentagon.

If you didn't stay ahead of them they could soon swamp you in a sea of paperwork so extensive that he had known it to stifle careers that once had been as promising as his. They were the bane of the services and the bane of getting anything done in the building. This, despite his valiant attempts to cut them back in his own domain by ordering one-page memoranda from the JCS staff—the famous "Zeecy Bullets" that were supposed to reduce everything to its simplest, most concise and most understandable form. They helped but inevitably were overtaken by the official need to have a record of everything— and the perceived need, he reflected ironically, to protect oneself against every possible attack from every possible quarter.

How to place responsibility where it belonged, and how to assure continuity of that responsibility, were among the most difficult tasks facing the managers of a building in which the politically-appointed civilian heads came and went on an average of two years and the longest a military officer could hope to stay in the same job rarely exceeded three years and more often fell below. Most of the top civilian officials found the Pentagon fascinating but it was also onerous and exhausting, and it was a rare civilian who loved it so much that he would sacrifice for very long the stability of his family life and the chance to make bigger money elsewhere. As for the military, while many also found the Pentagon fascinating and enjoyed their assignments there, it was basically regarded as simply a stepping-stone on the way up if they were still promotable or a way-station on the way out if they were no longer promotable. And always they worried about the record and did their best to make sure they couldn't be pinned for errors or mistakes. It was an obsession in the building which civilians and military suffered alike.

Some—Zeecy himself, for instance, or Loy Buck, or people like Tiny Wombaugh and Tick Tock and Joe Strang and quite a few others—were such independent individuals that they basically didn't give a damn, they were just there to serve the country as best they could and to hell with worrying too much about protecting themselves. Yet even they, he admitted honestly to himself as he peered out gloomily at the heavy gloom of the day, were concerned about reputation—and the record—and how well they would be remembered in the history of their times.

Even he, perhaps the most popular and charismatic military figure to reach national prominence in the past two decades, had to "carry his hod of shit to the Hill," as Ham Stokes had put it with typical bluntness and bull's-eye precision. Even he had to worry, even now in his final year as chairman of the Joint Chiefs, about reputation; the concern made sharper because, like many another on both sides of the river, there lived in the back of his mind the glimmer of an idea he could not help but feel was impossible but which nonetheless intrigued, as it had intrigued so many both civilian and military in the two hundred years since the first general had taken the oath of office as head of the great Republic.

Renee scoffed at this and told him that he was getting "too grand for his trousers." He agreed, telling her with deprecating wryness that, "There just aren't any wars to make anybody President any more." He had known Eisenhower after Ike had returned from Europe and become chief of staff of the Army. Zeecy had been a young Air Force officer on his first Pentagon assignment. What followed for Ike had been inevitable at that time. He had been a great commander, perhaps the last great military commander history would ever permit the democracies to have—because if another great military commander were raised up it could only mean that they were in another great war, and another great war was a self-defeating prophecy for everybody. It simply could not be: ergo, no more great commanders and no more leaps from battlefield glories into the White House.

There wouldn't be the opportunity—or the time—for any battlefield glories. Any major power that stumbled into a war this time was over and out.

So believed Gen. Zoren Chace McCune and so, he felt, believed every sane individual on the face of the planet.

Therefore he told himself sternly that the idea at the back of his mind was so much nonsense. Fortunately he didn't have much time to indulge it. He was usually much too busy and much too concerned about the day to day problems involved in containing the threat. And with containing his own ambitious service and the three others with which he had to work as chairman of the JCS.

Despite frequent stirrings in recent years—in fact, ever since Ike had been in the White House and proposed it, unsuccessfully, himself—there had not been any real reform in the Joint Chiefs of Staff system. Sporadic attempts had been made on the Hill. Various Presidents had argued for it with no more success than Eisenhower. Now and then a former JCS chairman such as Gen. David C. Jones had deserted his colleagues and lobbied extensively for a stronger chairman and a more responsive and less service-oriented staff. Former Army Chief of Staff Gen. Edward C. "Shy" Meyer (from whose nickname fellow West Pointer Brash Burford had indirectly derived his own) had proposed a strengthened chairman and a new "National Military Advisory Council" of senior officers divorced from their services to work exclusively on policy. The Packard Commission under President Reagan had made its recommendations. Senators Barry Goldwater and Sam Nunn had put in their reform bill.

None of the many proposals had succeeded in any really fundamental way. The dead weight of the system had always won. There were just too many empires involved.

The services opposed giving the chairman real authority because that would reduce their own . . . members of Congress opposed real unification because that would cancel their power to distribute appropriations to the individual services in the way best calculated to benefit their constituents, their districts, their states, and themselves . . . and many citizens were against reform because they had a vague feeling, encouraged by reform's opponents, that to have a stronger and more cohesive system would "Prussianize" the American military and pose a threat to democracy.

So the JCS stumbled along, top-heavy, overweight, cumbersome, cursed by the committee system, forced to reduce everything to the lowest common denominator of agreement, hampered by the Congressionally mandated fact that officers on its 400-member joint staff were restricted to three-year terms of duty and prohibited from serving on the staff again until a further three years had elapsed.

Lack of continuity, lack of clear-cut continuing responsibility, lack of decisiveness—slowness of reaction, slowness of response, inability on most occasions to move and move fast—these were what Zeecy McCune, like all who had been chairman before him, had to struggle with in the Joint Chiefs system. Sometimes it could be pushed ahead a little faster. Other times it moved at its own slow pace. In many ways it epitomized perfectly the Pentagon itself.

He sometimes thought ruefully that being chairman was the culmination of a military career, the highest honor and commendation a senior officer could receive from the White House and his peers—but it sure as hell had its problems. He could reign but not rule, cajole but not command. He had influence without authority, and if he tried to exercise the latter, somebody could always be counted on to run complaining to the Hill.

Theoretically, the "reforms" of recent years were supposed to have strengthened the chairman's position, given him real authority, placed him in a genuine command position vis-à-vis the services. In actual workaday practice, the first time the then chairman had tried to exercise these new powers there occurred what amounted to an in-house mutiny, carefully concealed from the public but fought out with ferocious intensity inside the building.

The then chairman was confronted, subtly and effectively, with a blandly polite slowdown in virtually all communications between himself and the services. Things that he was promised would be done simply weren't done. Papers and meetings that should have speeded action simply got sidetracked somewhere. Cooperations that were supposedly firmly pledged just somehow never quite came off.

The services, in effect, went on strike. In a smoothly obstructive way the whole ponderous machinery became even more ponderous. Within a month it was threatening to break down altogether.

Faced with this, the then chairman had done the only thing he could do, which was to cave in. What was he to do, spank his fellow generals? There was no point in complaining to the President—he wasn't really interested in internal squabbles and didn't really have the time. The then SecDef was powerless —he was told that it was "a military matter," and his exasperations were ignored as completely as those of the chairman. And certainly there was no point in complaining to the Congress. Once it had surprised itself by passing a "reform" bill, all of its parochial political self-interests came roaring back and the services found to their delight that their special constituencies on the Hill were still there to defend them, after all.

Theoretically, the chairman was much stronger. In practical fact he found he still had to walk on eggs and keep everybody happy, as chairmen had found themselves forced to do from the inception of the JCS. It was a cynical little inside game and he knew when he was licked. Despite deeply earnest public pledges of cooperation which, as Red Roberts remarked, "made the eagle sob right out loud," it was back-to-square-one, keep-everybody-happy, let's-find-the-lowest-common-denominator-we-can-all-agree-on.

There were more ways than one, the then chief of staff of the Army had confided gleefully to the then CNO, to skin a cat; and the services knew them all.

Thus while occupying what the public was led to believe was a strengthened position, Zeecy in reality was as helpless as his predecessors to exercise any real control over the JCS and the JCS staff.

If he tried too vehemently he got pushed back and sat upon.

Not that anybody, of course, ever sat upon Gen. Zoren Chace McCune for very long; but it *was* annoying to see so many things that needed doing and doing fast, and to be unable to exercise the qualities of leadership and decision that had brought him to his exalted post in the first place.

Particularly was this true in his relations with his own Air Force and with the

four proud and determined personalities who comprised the Joint Chiefs. Since
his thirty-year habit of command was not permitted here, it was fortunate that
he also had great innate talents of diplomacy and persuasion. He needed them
all in dealing with Adm. Stahlman, Gen. Burford, Gen. Stokes and Gen. Tock
and their jealous and highly vocal constituencies in the separate services.

He had been present at the same episode that had so intrigued Jim Craft,
when a young commander had spoken up and virtually reprimanded Bumpy
Stahlman by suggesting that he had better clear a position with the Navy
before committing himself to it. This had startled Jim, who had never experienced it before, but it was not uncommon in the JCS for the services to serve
notice on their commanders, usually through some junior officer, that they had
better toe the service line. Bumpy was a sternly proud and determined man,
but even he had deferred to the caution, withdrawn his statement and not
come back to it again until several weeks later after he had checked it out with
his fellow admirals. The same thing happened from time to time to the other
three chiefs; and it was not something they really objected to. They were
lifelong products of their respective services and fiercely devoted to them.
They would never admit it in public, but at heart they regarded themselves first
as spokesmen for their services and only secondarily as spokesmen for the
united point of view the JCS were supposedly there to formulate. This had
always been the case ever since the organization's rather haphazard beginning
by Franklin Roosevelt in World War II. And the personalities, while always as
disparate, had also nearly always seen things from their own narrow service
viewpoints.

He and his four colleagues, Zeecy reflected as he went over the problems on
his desk, had all come up approximately the same ladder. Three, himself,
Bumpy and Brash Burford, had attended the academies, graduated with high
honors and flaming ambition, and gone on from there. The other two, Ham
Stokes and Tick Tock, had come up through the ranks, Ham as an enlisted
airman, Tick as an enlisted (the only kind the Marines allowed) private in the
Marines. All five had shown exceptional merit from the beginning. As a rule
you didn't get to be chief of staff of one of the services if you were less than the
best, though now and then there had been glaring—and quickly glossed over—
exceptions.

Although the academies had given three of them a swift start out of the gate,
the abilities of Ham and Tick brought them along with an almost equal speed.
Both were proud of the fact that they were not academy products. Ham in
particular, as one of the handful of general-grade blacks in the services, felt he
had reason to be proud. He sometimes pointed out with some acerbity when
arguments got hot that, "I made it on my own"—the implication being that the
academy graduates had been given all the breaks and cosseted into their positions. Tick felt the same way. This was not true, because Bumpy, Brash and
Zeecy had all paid their dues, or "punched their tickets" as military slang had
it, moving up slowly rank by rank, going a little faster than most because of

their abilities and personalities, but following essentially the same recognizable patterns that all military careers have followed by the time they reach the top.

The shaky "peace" of the decades following World War II imposed its opportunities and limitations. All had served in Korea and Vietnam. Lebanon had taken them all to the Mediterranean at one time or another. Bumpy at one point had been naval attaché in Moscow, Zeecy and Ham had occupied in turn the parallel post for the Air Force. Brash had been involved in Asia and Central America. Tick had commanded Marines all over the world wherever his far-flung service had sent him. All had served at least two hitches in the Pentagon, all at one time or another had been assigned to the joint staff of the Joint Chiefs of Staff. All had suffered under poor commanders, been favored by good ones, managed to handle them all with sureness, skill and successful diplomacy. All had in time become excellent, and finally brilliant, commanders themselves. All had moved with what seemed now almost inevitable progression to the final position of chief of staff. Zeecy had gone beyond to become chairman. Both Ham and Brash might follow. Tick was too brusque and too much of a Marine, Bumpy was too stiff and formal: they would probably retire without having achieved the final brass ring on the merry-go-round. But all could be satisfied with jobs well done.

They were bright, they were brave, they were loyal, they were dedicated—they were military, at its best. They had done their duty, and in due course of time the highest rewards thereof had come to them.

They were also, Zeecy thought with an affectionate contemplation of their individual foibles, human beings.

Brash Burford, who was not nicknamed Brash for nothing: the bright boy who had graduated third in his class at West Point, always eager, always ambitious, tending at first, in the early days when he got his nickname, to be bumptious, but fortunately stopping early enough in his career so that it had not hurt him: now the nickname was only affectionate . . . intelligent, shrewd, possessed of probably the best and most sardonic sense of humor of them all . . . sixty years old, good-looking in a solid, no-nonsense sort of way, the good looks that instinctively inspire the trust and confidence of subordinates and superiors alike . . . often wry of manner but never disrespectful of country, flag, democracy, the tenets of the military faith that the Point inculcates in its best . . . curt and decisive in action, practical and pragmatic in approach, not given to much philosophizing about himself or his mission but always dedicated to it and defending it against all comers . . . passionately devoted to his own service, as they all were . . . a doughty battler in the internal Pentagon wars . . . friend of many, enemy of a few, able to handle himself successfully in almost any situation . . .

Ham Stokes, fifty-two, youngest of the chiefs, generally conceded to be the brightest and most competent of the small but increasing group of blacks who were rising in these years to the top levels of the services . . . born in Washington to parents of modest means, his father a Capitol policeman, his mother for many years a cashier at the local Peoples Drugstore . . . pushed by their dreams and his own ambition into using a quick and retentive mind to achieve top grades in grammar and high school . . . an Air Force volunteer at eighteen, soon selected for officer training because of his brains, ability, character . . . a top achiever and soon a highly resourceful and daring combat pilot— even reckless sometimes, his superiors felt uneasily, not wanting to lose him, but irrepressible and also lucky . . . not too much of a detail man but a driver, a pusher, a man who got things done because he could take a squadron, an office staff, a command group and *make it move,* as he often liked to say . . . like Brash, not given to much introspection—a doer, a force, a needed catalyst who had followed up the ladder behind Zeecy all of his service life, and in fact owed Zeecy a great deal because on several occasions Zeecy had been in a position to give his career the decisive push to get him where he wanted to go . . . tall and solid of frame, which he kept trim by daily trips to POAC to swim or play handball . . . possessed of an amiable face that did not always prepare people for his direct and occasionally acrid tongue . . . sometimes feared, not always liked, but always highly respected . . .

Bumpy Stahlman, sixty, who had received at Annapolis the nickname that now seemed slightly incongruous when applied to his ramrod-straight frame and the icily formal dignity that only relaxed when he was with these four equally-ranked military colleagues . . . an extremely bright boy from a modest family in Oregon who had graduated as captain of his class at the academy . . . but who, when he first arrived, had found the adjustment difficult for a while and had remarked with repetitive ruefulness to his classmates that, "It's kind of bumpy"—leading to the nickname that stuck permanently, even when he finally emerged as the pluperfect young lieutenant j.g. on graduation day . . . an extremely earnest, extremely hard-working young officer who had soon become the extremely earnest, extremely hard-working commander of men and ships, rising as fast through the naval hierarchy as he had through the academy . . . possessed of an endless eye for detail, rigid self-discipline and an instinctive need for perfection that did not always make him the most popular of leaders but won him the respect of all who knew or served under him because they could always count on the precision with which he did things and the success he almost always achieved . . . not the most dashing leader of men, as Brash sometimes remarked, but in a curious way one of the most inspiring because he was living proof that if you did it and did it right, you usually got the results you wanted to get no matter what the obstacles . . . of which he did not in truth have very many, it being recognized in the Navy very early in his career that here was one whose industry, intelligence and attention to detail would very likely take him wherever he wanted to go . . . not the most broad-gauged philosophic mind, either, but an earnest, honest, absolutely dependable and productive officer . . . now a chief of naval operations who really did operate the Navy: not a screw came loose or a bolt unthreaded, they said in the fleet, but what Bumpy Stahlman knew it and saw to it that it was put right . . . quiet, not flashy, perhaps a little somber, but invaluable . . .

Tick Tock, whose nickname of course had been inevitable from birth, particularly when he volunteered for the Marines at seventeen and began his own climb up the ladder . . . a bright, shrewd, ambitious, hard-working, hard-drinking, hard-fighting kid from a poor Alabama family who was "one tough son of a bitch" as his drillmaster at Lejeune had soon conceded admiringly . . . a tough son of a bitch but never a mean one, which was one of his great strengths . . . cut to the ideal Marine pattern, because in the Marines if you didn't fit the pattern, you soon found you couldn't hack it and either got invited out or left voluntarily . . . one who had never doubted he had found his vocation from the moment he took the oath . . . one who reveled in being a Marine, gloried in it, roistered in it, practically drowned in it: thought Marine, breathed Marine, drank Marine, lived Marine, was almost too much a Marine, in fact, except that in the Marines that was what they liked in a man, you couldn't be "too much" a Marine . . . they all liked Tick, from the lowliest private to the highest general, as his career moved steadily upward and his personal legend began to grow from Nam to Lebanon to Central America to wherever else the service sent him . . . not the greatest brain in the world, perhaps, but one of the most dedicated, loyal, tough and practical that had ever graced the Corps . . . a good man in a fight, a good man anywhere, kindly and considerate of his troops but a pugnacious and unyielding battler for his beloved service—always suspicious that the others, particularly the Navy, were trying to take advantage, and always in there slugging to prevent it . . . worshiped by the Corps, regarded with a sometimes amused tolerance by his fellow chiefs, all of whom bore bruises from past contentions with him and expended considerable thought before they engaged him head-on . . . fifty-nine, short, solid, square-bodied, square-faced, keen gray eyes, close-cropped gray hair, a face born to command for a spirit that always had . . . one tough (but generous) son of a bitch, who sometimes asked himself wryly what the hell he was doing in what he considered the patty-cake world of the JCS. . . .

And Zeecy himself, darling of the services and favorite of the gods, the very parfait, not so gentle knight who had come up through his chosen Air Force to his present eminence partly because of high intelligence, partly because of all-around character and partly just because he looked the part . . . the ambitious kid who had come from a wealthy family in California to the Naval Academy and whose first assignment had literally been to pose for a recruiting poster, his startling blond good looks and already distinguished bearing having caught the eye of the commandant in his first week of arrival . . . something it had taken him a while to live down with his classmates, but they very soon began to feel a certain awe around him, he was such a perfect match of man and role—and ambition, which burned so fiercely it almost seemed to give him a physical glow, and warned others, without his ever having to say anything, to walk wide and keep out of the way . . . the daredevil pilot who survived his deliberate change of service to become both the perfect field officer and the perfect administrator and had almost never set a foot really wrong since he graduated with top honors and began the long years of moving steadily and brilliantly toward his goal, which really was exactly what he had achieved, to become chairman of the Joint Chiefs . . . behind the golden public image, a man who had a philosophic turn of mind he revealed to no one but Renee and his closest friends, a thinker who was often deeply troubled by the fact that in his profession, leadership of men sometimes necessitated sending them to their deaths . . . who could reconcile this with an innate compassion for humanity and a desperate desire for peace only because he genuinely felt that the nature of the threat made any sacrifice acceptable . . . a born diplomat, among his many other talents, who knew when to order, when to persuade, when to yield, when to insist . . . the perfect charismatic leader who, inevitably, had always fascinated not only the men who accepted his leadership so willingly in the service, but the women who were always drawn to him irresistibly and now and then had been too attractive to pass up . . . which was a little hard to reconcile too . . . except that sometimes Renee's own realism made it easier . . . Gen. Zoren Chace McCune, sound of drums and trumpets. . . .

And along the way, of course, they had married. Almost everyone in the Pentagon military was married—aggressively so, one might almost say, wedding rings prominently displayed, domestic felicity constantly, almost defiantly, asserted—the form if not always the substance of happy union stressed with an insistence that was almost strident, as if to deny the slightest suspicion that being suitably married might have anything at all to do with the advancement of one's military career . . . until suddenly sometimes, in the most unexpected cases, the facade abruptly collapsed with startling and sometimes tragic consequences . . .

Not that this ever happened to the chiefs, of course—or only very rarely—because by the time you got to that eminence you had usually adjusted to your bargain and made the best of it. And in many cases the bargain had not been excessively difficult. Particularly not in the cases of Violet Burford, Doreen Tock, Clare Stahlman, Zenia Stokes and Renee McCune.

His affectionate contemplation of these five gallant ladies was interrupted by a call from the Hill passed along by the young female Air Force captain in his outer office. He noticed as he accepted the call with a lift of anticipation aroused by the caller's name, that the storm was as heavy as ever. It inevitably furnished the opening topic of a conversation that ostensibly concerned the annual bill to authorize Defense Department appropriations but in reality concerned a number of other things he was not at all sure yet that it should.

Nevertheless, when he spoke it was with the practiced smoothness that had always been the envy of his male acquaintances.

"Are we under the same blanket of snow, you and I?" he inquired without other introduction; and for just a second Luzanne Johnson hesitated, then laughed.

"It *is* snowing up here, yes," she agreed in a voice that sounded a little breathless for just a second—but only just. "It falls on Senators and chairmen of the JCS alike."

"I hope so," he said with the suavity of the old campaigner, for which he despised himself at the moment but could not seem to escape. "It makes it so much cozier."

"Yes," she agreed, a certain dryness entering her tone as she moved away from the invitation. "I want to know about this emergency request for more funds for Mexico, Zeecy. Tell me."

"Yes," he said with a humorous wryness, retreating obediently to fight again another day. "What's your difficulty with it, Senator?"

Now on Nanukuvu the day moved on in slow, pleasant rhythm just as always. The sun passed zenith. The gentle wind blew a little more strongly. The youths returned from the ridges with their bounty of coconuts. The women and girls prepared the noontime meal of fish and poi. The two youngest boys were sent to waken A'afaloa and Nuku'ofa. Sleepy-eyed, yawning and tousled they came from the longhouses and dropped down on the sand. Both were instantly covered with children, laughing, squealing, screaming with fun and excitement as their fathers roughhoused with them.

In a few minutes the meal was ready. Bowls were passed around. A comfortable, busy silence fell. Presently they were finished. The girls took the bowls to water's edge, scrubbed them clean with sand, rinsed them, stacked them in their customary place beside the fire. The boys went into the huts, brought out the sleeping mats, spread them about among the trees. Everyone went to sleep, including A'afaloa and Nuku'ofa, who had decided that there was no point in doing any more fishing, or indeed anything of any kind, today. The fish would keep. Life would keep. Everything would keep.

There was always tomorrow.

Always and always, there was tomorrow.

They had been asleep perhaps half an hour when they all came awake with a sudden frightened wrench.

From somewhere in the sea on the other side of the island they heard a long, muffled roar, not very loud but somehow so menacing that they froze, stricken with fright, unable to move.

"Look!" Nuku'ofa cried, pointing to the sky above the trees.

A pillar of smoke had appeared. It was not very tall and it was not very thick, for theirs was a tiny island and they were very few people, and not much was required to achieve the desired objective.

As they watched the pillar seemed to pause, float suspended for a moment and then begin to spread out on either side in a long, flat cap. And suddenly the winds that were blowing across the island seemed to grow in intensity and become very hot. But there was no after-shock to sway the trees, no after-blast to level the island, for this was something carefully designed to do exactly what it was intended for—"kill people, not structures," as they said in those larger tribes so far away.

Some of those tribes had abandoned this thing in response to clamors and pressures of which A'afaloa and Nuku'ofa and their families knew nothing.

Those who had inspired the pressures had gone right ahead with a grimly cynical humor to develop it and place it in their arsenal.

Now on Nanukuvu it was serving its purpose as efficiently as its users had known it would.

For several more minutes A'afaloa and Nuku'ofa and their families had time to scream and cry out to one another and run in circles among the trees frantically trying to escape what they knew instinctively now was their death. But it did them no good.

The island was too small.

They were too few.

Those who had planned this thing were too ruthless and efficient.

Dimly the brothers had time before they died to sense that this must come from the great black whale.

"What have we done to it, brother?" A'afaloa cried in despair as his lungs began to burn. "What did we ever do to it to make it hate us so?"

"Nothing," Nuku'ofa screamed, clutching at his throat as all around him their families began to fall writhing to the ground. *"Nothing!"*

But they had, of course, though they could never have understood it even if there had been time, which there was not.

It had been their misfortune to possess something the owners of the great black whale had decided they needed for their plans.

That was the crime of the inhabitants of Nanukuvu.

They were in the way.

Very soon the ripple again cut the placid surface of the lagoon and soon again the great whale surfaced.

From its belly the black-suited figures re-emerged. Now they were wearing gas masks and were swathed in even heavier outer garments. Again they swarmed up the beach. There were many more of them now. They moved with an efficient, determined haste to torch the huts, pull together a great heap of dry palm-fronds, gather the bodies and pile them upon it, set it alight.

Another column of smoke now rose into the sky to replace the first that had swiftly dissipated on the wind.

Distantly, a mere hint, at first very faint—then near—then louder—came a sound the black-suited figures recognized instantly.

The great black whale sank beneath the surface.

The black-suited figures swiftly hid among the trees.

The plume of smoke swayed and twisted in the wind.

The sound came nearer, a heavy, rapid, insistent rhythm.

Whupp, whupp, whupp, whupp, whupp, whupp, whupp.
No life was visible anywhere on Nanukuvu or in its lagoon.
But the plume of smoke continued to rise, and attract curiosity.
And the sound came nearer.
Whupp, whupp, whupp, whupp, whupp, whupp, whupp.

And that, Luzanne Johnson thought as she put down the phone after some ten minutes of determinedly impersonal conversation with the chairman of the JCS, was what you got for indulging, even for a moment, the idea of a flirtation, even the mildest, with one whose military abilities were not his only claim to renown.

Zeecy McCune, she addressed his distinguished image, you are *too* much. But it was all rather flattering, at that. And when it was the first time since your husband died that you really felt that someone really wanted you to become seriously involved, it was also a little hard to resist.

The senior Senator from Louisiana, who had now served ten years, eight of them as a member of the Armed Services Committee, admonished herself sternly that at forty-seven she was not a schoolgirl. Nor was she a flighty young military wife who might be overwhelmed by the glamor of a four-star general, as, according to the gossip she heard, had happened on a couple of occasions. She was one of the most highly respected and well regarded members of a body she valued greatly, and there were priorities.

They did not permit of anything—*anything*—involving General Zoren Chace McCune.

Nonetheless, she had to admit that she found him attractive.

She pulled herself up with a snort. Who *didn't* find Zeecy McCune attractive? Everybody, all ages, shapes, sizes, sexes, found Zeecy McCune attractive. Zeecy McCune was a mighty hard man to ignore. He could charm the rattles off a snake, according to her committee chairman, Cube Herron, and often did. Join the throng, girl, and get in line, she told herself sternly, if that's what you want. But first be darned sure it is.

As a member of Armed Services she had met Zeecy six years ago when he had been commander of the Pacific Air Forces, his last command before becoming chief of staff of the Air Force. There had been no particular interest then, she recalled—at least on her part. She had liked him, for it was also possible to like Zeecy very much as a human being quite aside from any physical appeal he might possess. He was very intelligent, extremely capable, calm, confident, decisive and authoritative. He had taken her and Cube and the committee staff director, Burt Sanstrom, up for an hour out of Guam in the Air Force's newest jet. He had put the plane through its paces. She remembered the occasion with a rueful amusement. She had come within an ace of getting sick and both Cube and Burt had gone all the way. She had the distinct impression that this was a result Zeecy had deliberately tried to achieve with all his zips and dips and wheels and whirls, and while she felt sorry for Cube, who was very likable in his somewhat heavy-handed way, she shared the general opinion of Burt Sanstrom, a cold-blooded little weasel who was disliked by most committee members and staff and was absolutely hated by all the top brass in the military.

She was sure Zeecy's principal aim had been to reduce Burt to a quivering, helpless, bedraggled lump of anguish, which he certainly was by the time Zeecy set the plane neatly down again on the runway at Guam. Cube managed to make it to the hangar under his own steam but Burt had to be held up on each side by two strapping young airmen. She was pale and shaking herself, inwardly, but managed to keep her chin up and walk at a steady pace even though Zeecy took her arm solicitously.

"I'm all right," she protested. "You don't have to help me."

"My pleasure," he said with a chuckle. "You're a better man than both of them put together."

"That wasn't very nice," she told him in half-serious reproof. "You might have given poor old Cube a heart attack. And as for Burt—" she chuckled suddenly. "As for Burt, I think that's exactly why you proposed that little jaunt."

"Senator," he said solemnly, "am I that transparent?" Then the famous "McCune rainbow," as Ham Stokes called it, broke through and he gave her the charming, quick-flashing smile that turned him momentarily into the little boy who had just robbed the candy-jar. "Oh, well," he said crisply. "It did him good to get some of that bile out of his system."

"Shush!" she said, pretending to be shocked but finally joining him in a burst of laughter that made Cube, up ahead, turn around and give them a startled and reproachful look.

"Now, see," she said in an amused whisper. "You've made the chairman think we're laughing at him. You'll never hear the end of it and neither will I."

"Good," he said with the sudden piercing look that had also been given a Ham Stokes label, "the McCune Bombshell." "That gives us something in common, for a start."

"Start of what?" she had asked, still deliberately sounding amused and determined to keep it that way.

"Who knows?" he had inquired blandly as they overtook Cube and went on to check on wretched, still-retching Burt. "That remains to be seen."

"Maybe," she had time to say in a firm half-whisper before they overtook Cube, "but not by me."

And since then she had heard hardly a word from him except for his annual appearances to testify before the committee, when they had greeted one another with a casual informality that they had kept, apparently by mutual agreement, on a friendly but businesslike basis. She had run into him and Renee at various Washington dinners and cocktail parties, had been invited along with the members of all pertinent Senate and House committees to his installation as chief of staff of the Air Force and, a little over a year ago, chairman of the Joint Chiefs. There had been various official JCS functions subsequently, and, as attritions of health and political defeat had removed some of her colleagues and cleared the way for her to rise to second-ranking member of Armed Services, she had been invited to several of the small intimate dinners that the McCunes gave from time to time in the chairman's official quarters at Fort Myer, adjacent to Arlington Cemetery.

But she had never indicated more than a normally friendly interest in the general, and in fact it was only recently that she had begun to feel any. Her marriage to Ken Johnson, whom she had been appointed to succeed in the Senate when he had been killed in the crash of an Army helicopter during a European inspection trip, had been a notably happy one, though not blessed with the children both had wanted. For a long time she remained faithful to his memory and entertained no thoughts of anyone else. Election in her own right six years ago, and her triumphant re-election last November, had seemed to stabilize and adjust a lot of things. Now she was so popular in Louisiana that it was as certain as anything in politics that she could remain in the Senate just about as long as she wanted, given good health, devotion to duty and no scandals.

She had been blessed with the first, trained in the second by her parents and had no intention whatsoever of ever having anything to do with the third. That was one of the principal reasons she had automatically rejected Zeecy's tentative little overture on Guam, although, being honest, she had to acknowledge to herself that she had often remembered it. But she certainly had no intention of becoming involved with a married man, and one of the most famous and conspicuous in Washington, at that.

And now, quite unexpectedly, he was trying again—with a gesture here, a little extra attentiveness there, a telephone call for no particular reason—and now this morning's quite blatant approach. She wondered why. It can't be my fatal charm, she told herself wryly, that hasn't changed any in the last few years. If anything, it's become less attractive as the demands of the Senate have worn me down. I'm getting to be a tired old politician, growing careworn and gray in my country's service . . . and quite unwittingly, for a moment, she began to hum, *The old gray mare, she ain't what she used to be*—until she realized what she was doing and shattered the comfortably cluttered calm of her office in the Russell Senate Office Building by erupting into her characteristic lighthearted peal of laughter that sounded the farthest thing from an old gray mare. More like a girl of sixteen, as her mother told her when she was able to get home to "Rive Tranquille," the old family home on the bayou deep in Cajun country.

Maybe it was time for her to go there right now, she thought, and get her mother's advice, which was wise and shrewd and unfailingly to the point. But she knew what Madame Labouchere would say: "Maybe you're inviting it and don't know it yet. Men are like dogs. They can smell it sometimes before you know yourself."

She laughed again in the silent office while outside the storm soughed against the high old windows. That was Mère, all right. And because Mère was so shrewd, and had passed it down to Luzanne, and because they shared with Renee a common heritage, she suspected that Renee already sensed the potential and appraised it in exactly the same realistic and unsentimental way. If so, she did not blame Luzanne, but rather her husband. And blame there, Luzanne suspected, was more a matter of form than substance, at this late date in their marriage.

Nonetheless, even if Luzanne was as hostile to the idea as she told herself she should be, Renee was not the type to let it pass without at least a show of resistance. Luzanne sighed. The last thing she wanted was a feud with Renee McCune, who was noted, in Washington's tightly knit, small-town social atmosphere in which everybody who was Anybody knew everybody else, for an acrid tongue and a ruthless attitude toward anyone who came near her glamorous property—even when the glamorous property himself was to blame.

The Senator made a mental note to find occasion at the earliest opportunity to have a little talk with Renee.

What she must also do, she told herself firmly, was make quite clear to Gen. Zoren Chace McCune that she wasn't having any, thank you very much. If it was necessary to become coldly formal with him, then she would become coldly —but, no. He would only laugh at her. The McCune technique would come to bear, she would be told to come off it, with a charming disrespect that would only shatter all her defenses, because of course she had a sense of humor too and it would take only a little prompting to make her dissolve in laughter that would absolutely destroy her entire position. The thought, in fact, made her chuckle again. And that showed her how vulnerable she was, right there.

And yet—and yet. He was not only glamorous and a major force in the affairs of the country, but he was an extremely appealing human being. And it was not something that happened to her every day, partly because she made very sure that it did not and also partly because her position was a quite formidable barrier for most men. She made it even more so by the cordially impersonal manner with which she treated them all. Even her closest friends in the Senate knew there was a point of joshing familiarity beyond which they must not go. When they tried, her manner became either excessively polite or, if she thought the recipient had as good a sense of humor as she did, excessively southern. Either way, they got the message. One of the most attractive widows in Washington went her way serenely unencumbered and serenely untouched—until now.

She buzzed for her administrative assistant, gave him quick directions on how to handle several pressing matters involving the state, discussed briefly what she intended to do when the Senate voted late this afternoon on one more of the endless requests for famine relief to appallingly overgrazed, appallingly mismanaged Africa, and said she would see him on the floor around 1 P.M. Then she stepped into her private bathroom and readied herself to go downstairs to the stately, old-fashioned hearing room of the Armed Services Committee and listen to Brash Burford defend the Army's request for an authorization bill that would boost its budget by some ten billion over last year. She liked Brash, as everybody did, but she couldn't go along with him this time. Zeecy had just answered some of her questions on Mexico but there were a lot of others she wanted to ask. She and Brash would have quite a discussion, she suspected, good friends though they were.

At the door she paused on a sudden impulse and turned back. She asked her secretary to ring Mrs. McCune at Fort Myer.

"Renee," she said when she heard the familiar, clipped voice, still heavily accented despite almost three decades of marriage to an American and being in and out of America on many tours of duty, "this is a wild shot in the dark, but are you doing anything tomorrow for lunch?"

"Eating," Renee said in what she always intended to be a jocular tone but which didn't always quite come out that way.

The Senator from Louisiana, who understood this, laughed comfortably.

"I, too. Why don't you come up and join me in the Senate dining room? We can gossip about all our friends."

"Oh?" Renee said, an instinctive caution coming into her voice that caused Luzanne to think: *Damn. She's suspicious already.* "Which ones?"

"Whichever ones you choose," Luzanne said a little more calmly than she felt. "How about it?"

"One o'clock?" Renee inquired.

"One o'clock," Luzanne replied.

"*À bientôt.*"

"*Au 'voir.*"

Also at Fort Myer, staring thoughtfully out at the storm that was now coming down with a steady, unwavering insistence that seemed to indicate that it would go on all afternoon and probably into the night, Violet Burford was busy in the dining room of Quarters No. 1, traditional home of the chief of staff of the Army, directing her maid in the annual washing of all the formal china—whether it needed it or not, as Brash usually joked; and it usually did. This morning Brash had left early for the meetings in the Pentagon and by now, she estimated, must be well into his testimony before the Senate Armed Services Committee. The authorization bill was going to have a fairly rough time of it in Armed Services this year, he had told her, and the appropriations bill that would follow in the Appropriations Committee would be equally under fire. The same thing would happen on the House side. The great bonanza that had come with the Reagan years was slowing down. The country was not so supportive now, as the still enormous deficit continued to plague the economy and the military build-up seemed to have reached and surpassed what many citizens regarded as a sufficient level.

Neither her husband nor any of his military colleagues, Vi Burford knew, would ever really regard *any* level as sufficient. It was not that they were insatiable warmongers, it was just that caution and worry about the future always prompted them to ask for far more than they needed and far more than they could possibly manage effectively and without waste. Monumental waste, in many areas. Insufferable waste—inexcusable waste—horrifying waste. Waste that was known to every man and woman who had ever served in the armed forces. Waste that created a permanent underlay of skepticism and cynicism toward every request for military funds.

But usually not, she firmly believed, criminal waste. She knew her husband was not a criminal, she knew he had never profited one red cent from any military contract and she knew the overwhelming majority of the military were the same. She was not a fool, however, nor an unthinking idealist after thirty-five years as a service wife. She knew there was some criminal waste, true enough—far more than there should be, for ideally there should be none. But people were human and, too many, avaricious. That funny little publication *Defense Eye* that was published by that odd little organization Defense Improvement Group—DIG—had something juicy to report almost every other day, it seemed, and so did many of the investigative reporters in Washington. And rightly so. They were correct. And they were needed. It was just that the fuss they raised and the emphasis they gave it seemed to her to be often out of proportion and out of balance. Their aim too often seemed to be, not reform, but revenge—on everyone and everything associated with the military establishment. And that, in some prominent cases, gave rise in the Pentagon to questions as to just what their basic motivation was and just where their basic loyalty lay.

None of this did Violet Burford, military wife, ever express to anyone except her husband and their military friends, even when, as often happened, she found herself seated beside some relentlessly hostile critic at a White House dinner or other social function. Her plain craggy face only became deceptively placid, her mind more alert, and with skillful, seemingly innocent questions and naïve expressions of surprise she would draw her dinner companion into some unintended alcoholic revelation of fact or attitude that she would dutifully report to Brash. Dutifully he in turn would pass it on where he thought it would do the most good. They all did that, all the military wives, particularly the JCS wives. They had the best little intelligence network in Washington, Brash sometimes said with a chuckle—"You gals could give the intelligence agencies a lesson or two, any day." It was a great help on many occasions, an invaluable aid in the constant battle to protect the military from the attacks that were made upon them—they felt, quite unjustly—all the time.

And Vi too felt the attacks were unjust, because she saw the picture from the wives' standpoint, and for the wives the military life was no picnic. Marriage to a military man was one of the greatest and most stringent challenges any woman could ever face, and a tragic number of them went under as a result of it. Some turned to alcohol, some to drugs, some to other men when their own were away, some gave way to mental depression, some lost few to physical violence that had even resulted, on a few suppressed but never forgotten occasions, in dead husbands, dead children, the ghastly debris of once happy marriages begun in high hopes and military glamor.

Even without more somber aspects, it was a rough, tough, unending struggle to hold together families constantly strained by constant transfers, lengthy absences of husbands and fathers long hours away from home, particularly on Pentagon duty, the constant exposure of the men to sexual and other temptations while the wives stayed home with the children and tried to find sufficient compensations within the narrow round of military social and philanthropic pursuits. They had their clubs, their Red Cross and other welfare activities, their bridge games, bowling leagues, garden clubs, handicraft classes and the like; but almost never did they have freedom to really express their own talents and personalities. Even more than their civilian sisters they were restricted to the narrow confines of the world in which their husbands lived; and within that world the rigid and exhausting classifications, categories and restrictions exactly paralleled those that controlled their husbands.

The sergeant's lady bowed to the colonel's lady and the colonel's to the general's; and always with the nagging fear that something the sergeant's lady might say or do would be taken amiss by the colonel's lady, and that would harm the sergeant; or something the colonel's lady might say or do would be taken amiss by the general's lady, and that would harm the colonel; and the general in turn might lose some ultimate preferment or coveted assignment because of something his lady might say or do.

It was a constant obstacle course, Vi Burford often thought, and while it was essentially the same for the men, at least they had the challenge of excitement and service and travel which all too often became simple drudgery for wives who must constantly pull up stakes, change homes, find new friends, worry about new schools and new companions for their kids.

Military service, despite the small, strained, awkward and sometimes quite absurd gestures made in response to the demands of the feminists in recent years, was now, always had been and would remain, a man's world. It could be no other way as long as the basic purpose was to keep the peace, and to keep it, if necessary, by killing. Women were not made to deal out death. Something in men enjoyed it—as long as the toss of the dice came right and they were among the lucky who survived.

When they did not, that was one more burden, the final and most awful, for the wives to bear.

No, it was no fun being a military wife; and those who came through it with marriages and sanity intact deserved enormous credit—so thought Violet Burford, who was one of them. Many times it had not been easy, many times the strains of separation and loneliness had pushed her and Brash to violent argument and even, on a couple of occasions, to the brink of separation. But they had survived, had kept the marriage and home intact, had raised Barbara and Jeff to be good, honorable, decent human beings with much to give the world. They had genuinely loved each other, and they had survived. Some she could think of had not been so lucky. One couple in particular on their own level still might not make it. There were others she knew personally or had heard about. Being in Washington and assigned to the Pentagon made already enormous pressures greater. It was a wonder any marriages survived in that atmosphere. That the majority did was the best tribute that could be rendered to the essential character and stability of the men—and even more, their wives.

Particularly, she thought as she carefully dried a Meissen bowl and set it back in its place on the sideboard, the wives of the Joint Chiefs of Staff, who had come up through the ranks and done it all. In one of his flights of kidding rhetoric that often amused and delighted them, Zeecy McCune had once toasted them as "the fairest group of damsels that ever soothed a weary warrior's brow." Everybody had laughed and applauded. They *were* pretty good— at least everyone seemed to think so. She gave the Meissen bowl a little extra buffing and regarded it with satisfaction.

There was Vi herself, regarded by many as the salt of the earth, one of those New Englanders with a face as craggily rockbound as the coast of Maine and a heart as broad as Texas, whom Brash had met when he was a cadet on his first leave in New York . . . a blind date who soon became his only date, and still was in spite of the fact that he, like Zeecy, had many opportunities over the years . . . the steady, indomitable, unwavering center of his life to whom he could always return when the pressures of the military became too much for him, as, not too often but often enough, they had . . . always there, always supportive, always steady, always encouraging him to go ahead toward the ambition he had confided to her on their honeymoon, the ambition he thought he might finally achieve now that Zeecy's term was running out . . . unfailingly gracious to everyone, intelligent, well-informed, providing the philosophic underpinning for his life that his own direct and pragmatic character could not provide . . . mother of Barbara, happily married to a lawyer in California and mother of two, and Jeff, presently an Army captain stationed in Panama, and on his way—on his way . . . plain as an old hedge fence and as honest, too— "so plain," as Renee McCune once remarked with some envy, "that she's beautiful"—a tribute to charm, character and genuine concern for everyone . . . "The best thing I ever did," Brash often tells people, and people always agree . . . getting a little forgetful of late, but, as she humorously tells Brash, "what can you expect when you start going downhill?" . . . a long way from downhill, in his loving estimation and that of her hundreds of friends . . .

And Doreen Tock, small, cute and cuddly at twenty-one, plump, jolly and comfortable at sixty, a real beauty when Tick "liberated her," as he put it, from her wealthy family in Philadelphia, a real beauty still despite her weight . . . rosy-cheeked, sparkly-eyed, full of laughs and giggles despite the family tragedy that still turns her eyes dark and brooding sometimes in the midst of laughter

. . . an unfailing support for Tick, both then and in all the tough and sometimes bitter challenges of his career . . . a devoted and supportive military
wife who has been, as he often says, the greatest contributor to his career—not
strictly true, as his own strong character, personal courage and inborn ability to
command have been perhaps even greater—but the one who defied her family
to marry her rough diamond from Alabama, smoothed his sharp edges, "taught
me how to eat with a fork" as he jokingly says, persuaded him to cut down the
drinking, cut out the roistering and get on with the career she could clearly see
would take him to the top of his service if his obvious ability, love for the Corps
and seemingly endless energy could only be channeled in the right direction
. . . never arguing, never pushing, but early adopting the practice of gently
offering him logical alternatives that usually won his acceptance . . . sometimes described cattily by the wives of other officers competing for the job
which he achieved as being "just as sweet as treacle," but regarded by most
junior officers and their wives as being one of the nicest and most likable
women they had ever met . . . tending to overindulge a bit in good food and
candy, which she confesses she just can't stay away from, but basically in good
health and vigor . . . concealing under her sweet sunny disposition a character just as firm and just as determined, in its gentle way, as Tick's; and equally
and always devoted to the welfare of Gen. Elbert James Tock, who for the past
thirty-four years has been her overriding family obligation . . .

And Zenia Stokes, fifty, strongly active supporter of ERA, women's lib and
the drive against sickle-cell anemia and other causes, who was well into her law
course when she married young Lt. Harmon Stokes and completed it at home
at night while juggling the demands of a new husband, a swift pregnancy and
twins born exactly nine months after marriage . . . "Ham's anchor," as Ham's
parents call her . . . a little tense on occasion but up to now basically steady
. . . neither reverse-racist nor chip-on-shoulder but very determined that
Ham should never suffer in the service because of race . . . largely because of
her influence in calming his sometimes belligerent tendency to overreact to
supposed slights, he almost never has . . . "a superb service wife," in the
admiring words of Zeecy McCune, who has known them both well ever since
Ham served as his top aide during Zeecy's tour of duty as head of the Air Force
Academy . . . very supportive of Ham's steady drive toward chief of staff,
which he achieved when Zeecy was appointed chairman of the JCS . . . very
supportive, though at times frayed a bit by Ham's late hours during his two
prior tours of duty in the Pentagon . . . frayed a bit by them now, if truth
were known, though she tries to tell herself, with not always convincing success, that he really *is* working, and she mustn't let her imagination run away
with her . . . having no real reason to suspect him of infidelity, but unable
sometimes to keep herself from snapping out at him when he comes home late,
which, given his own blunt tongue, seems to be leading increasingly to arguments that she knows she shouldn't get into but sometimes can't seem to resist
. . . an occasional poet, with a poet's sensibilities, who has written several

hundred, lately increasingly dour in tone, and is hopeful she can publish them one of these days . . . mother of two besides the twins, a lively and perfectly healthy girl and a boy who suffers from the sickle-cell anemia to which Zenia devotes a good deal of her time and energies . . . pretty, intelligent, capable: her own woman perhaps even more than Ham's . . .

And Clare, the tall, dark and laughing, who for thirty years cheered, kidded, comforted, deeply loved, and actually persuaded to loosen up once in a while, Bumpy Stahlman; who refused to give up her cigarettes and tragically paid the penalty six years ago; and who lives on in his heart—which closed in upon itself at her death, never to open again—and will never die there . . .

And finally Zeecy's Renee, the racehorse of Jim Craft's analogy, sleek and svelte and glitteringly attractive at fifty-nine, bride of his later youth when he was a military attaché in the embassy in Paris, highly intelligent, widely informed, swift-minded, precise, demanding, impatient of stupidity, intolerant of weakness, often difficult to live with but never dull . . . never able to provide him with the children they both had wanted . . . aging gracefully now that his roving days—they had thought—are over . . . cynical about some episodes in the past but determined to hang onto what she has no matter what the provocation . . . always a great assist to his career, as he often and publicly acknowledges . . . as sharp, capable and ambitious as he, the perfect ornament to adorn the rising leader and still determined to hold her own with the younger military wives around her, which she amply does . . . possessed of perfect taste in clothes and jewelry—the sheer, arrogant style of the upperclass Parisienne, which prevails so charmingly and so ruthlessly over all who get in the way . . . not always faithful herself, he suspects, when he has been overseas, but always there to stand beside him when he has needed her as his career moved upward . . . "a perfect wife for the chairman" as his fellow officers say admiringly, and as both of them congratulate themselves she is . . . a passionate relationship once, a practical one now, and one that neither of them thought they would ever sacrifice—until just lately, when all at once, quite unexpectedly, they suddenly aren't so sure . . .

Brought back sharply from thoughts of Renee, whose stylishness she had sometimes envied a little, Violet noted that her maid—wife of Brash's favorite driver, a master sergeant—was leaning against the sideboard, holding her stomach and sweating profusely. Vi had been through this before. The girl always insisted on working right up to the last minute because she said they needed the money, what with five kids already, and Jim's dependents' allowance barely enough to cover, these days.

"Well, Carleene," Violet said, not unkindly but with some impatience, "I really think you'd better stop for today. You'll have a tough enough time driving home as it is."

"You know we're right here on base, ma'am," Carleene said. "It's nothin'."

"Yes, well, I think you'd better scoot right now," Vi said. "We can finish this tomorrow." She smiled. "Or in a couple of weeks, if you have other things to worry about by tomorrow."

"May be," Carleene conceded. "He's gettin' mighty impatient to come out, this one. Bet he's gonna be a giant."

"Bet he is," Vi agreed. "Here, let me help you on with your coat and get you to the car. And then you skeedaddle, hear?"

"All right, ma'am," Carleene said, yielding gratefully. "I expect you're right, as usual."

"Not very usual," Violet Burford said with a chuckle, "but this time I am. Come along, now."

She helped Carleene bundle up, bundled up herself, saw Carleene out the door and down the slippery steps to her battered old Dodge station-wagon, and waved her off. Then she turned back toward the steps, placing her feet very carefully in the drifted snow.

She came to the steps, or thought she did, and started up. Suddenly and astoundingly, she was struck in the face by one of the two giant camellia bushes that flanked the steps. It was heavy with snow and she was drenched.

For a second or two it seemed to her that she must have blacked out, for when she looked around dazedly she saw from the quickly disappearing trail behind her that she had not gone straight toward the steps at all. Instead she had veered sharply to the right and run dead-on into the bush.

But she could have sworn she had been making straight for the steps.

She stood for several more seconds, carefully trying to reconstruct what could have happened. There was no explanation. It was very odd. Her heart began to race, her breath came short. She shook her head, very puzzled; and though it was really a very small incident, alarmed, in some obscure way she could not quite define or understand.

Very carefully she took aim at the steps again. This time she made it. Safely inside she took off her coat, cap and overshoes. Still damp with snow, she sat down on the big leather sofa in the living room and stayed there until her heart and breathing calmed down and the world seemed to be in order again.

Then she picked up the phone and called the number of the couple she and Brash liked best.

Doreen Tock responded, sounding, as she often did, as though she were just completing a mouthful.

"Dorry," Vi Burford said, "I've just had a funny experience."

The sound of the helicopter came nearer. The new owners of Nanukuvu continued to hide, motionless among the palms.

Lt. Hague Smith was a bright and able young man who had graduated from Annapolis in the top third of his class, decided to become a pilot and soon found his interest and enthusiasm channeled into helicopters, which fascinated him and were a major part of the Navy's anti-submarine force.

The enemy roved through all the seas and so did the Americans. Assiduously they built ever more sophisticated helicopters to track each other. Increasingly in these closing years of the century their forces went into unannounced but deadly combat. Unsuspected by their countrymen, unknown to all but those who had to know, American helicopter pilots from time to time would get a Soviet vessel somewhere off Europe, in the far Pacific, in the Indian Ocean, the South Atlantic or somewhere else where a target of opportunity inadvertently broke cover and revealed itself to constantly probing electronic eyes and ears. Highly sophisticated gear, capable of searching far below the surface, whose development and presence added many millions to the cost of each helicopter, made this possible. Equally sophisticated gear on the other side from time to time returned the compliment.

None of this silent warfare ever reached the public or the media. No challenges were issued, no gauntlets were flung down, no wars erupted as a result. It was war as real as any that ever occurred but it was secret war, in which each side took its losses, said nothing and retaliated when it could.

Lt. Hague Smith found this a constantly exciting and exhilarating challenge. He was very good at it, in fact. He had made no kills he was absolutely certain of yet, but he and his squadron had come close a couple of times, once off Santa Barbara, California, and the other time near Diego Garcia in the Indian Ocean.

He was hoping.

Now he was hoping in the South Pacific.

Safely at home in their Navy temporary housing near Pearl Harbor, his nice little wife Madeline and their two sweet little kids never dreamed how serious Daddy's business was. Madeline took care of the kids, went to bowling league, church group and the Navy wives' social services organization, and wished wistfully that Hague, whom she adored, had chosen some other career that might have permitted them to be together "like normal families." But she was "a good service wife" and didn't complain very much. She only had about thirty years to go and she might receive a reward at least partially commensurate with her sacrifices.

She was a potential Joint Chief's wife just as Hague was a potential Joint Chief.

There were a lot of them around, in all the services.

They managed.

For the last two months Hague had been assigned to the aircraft carrier *Dominant,* whose name was an affirmation of hope if not entirely, perhaps, an indication of reality. Still, she was a most impressive sight when she steamed slowly out of Pearl and headed south; and to the enemy subs, "fishing vessels" and aircraft of various kinds that tracked her along her way, she looked to be both an easy target and a potentially formidable foe. But this was of course the uneasy "peace" of the late twentieth century, and neither the men of the *Dominant* nor their putative foes had any real expectations of open combat.

For Hague Smith and his comrades in the helicopters flying off *Dominant's* deck, it was a different matter. Their sojourn in the South Pacific was a thrilling and potentially rewarding affair. In the area of their expertise, at least, it was possible to have a modest but satisfying little war. They didn't want a great big one, just enough to feel the thrill of it and maybe bag an enemy craft or two to give them the ultimate satisfaction they all hoped to get from their secret conflict.

Today Hague was out "just wandering," as he and the members of his select fraternity liked to put it: just roaming over the vast island-dotted expanses of the southern sea, looking for what they could find. No specific objectives, no particular targets, nothing special they expected to discover. "Just looking," in Mars' bargain basement.

He had been out about two hours and was preparing to turn back when he drifted idly toward Nanukuvu. The island was on the map, but only as one more of the myriad uninhabited dots that flecked the sea from Hawaii to the Antipodes. It was, in fact, officially uninhabited: so said both *Gaines' Gazeteer* and the Defense Mapping Agency in Washington. That did not necessarily mean, as Hague had discovered during other recent forays across these expanses, that it was always or consistently uninhabited. The Polynesians and Melanesians made a much-traveled highway of the South Pacific, foraying far themselves on their constant fishing trips. He had been told at Pearl that islands and atolls were often inhabited for a while, abandoned when their restless occupiers got the urge to move on, again inhabited when some new group or family wandered in.

Part of Hague's job, and that of those who had come before him and would come after, was to keep a casual but consistent eye on these tiny informal migrations; and also, of course, to keep a steady track on the enemy and what his subs, planes and "fishing vessels" were up to at any given moment.

Somehow, however, no one had ever paid much attention to Nanukuvu. Perhaps because the island's dense cover had concealed the habitations of A'afaloa and Nuku'ofa and their families, perhaps because planes of both sides had never happened to fly over at the precise moment the brothers and their sons were on the water, possibly just because of simple inattention induced by the belief that the island was uninhabited, their presence had never been discovered by observers from the two great tribes far away, until now.

Nanukuvu was supposed to be uninhabited and Hague had believed it to be; which was why his gaze, idly but alertly wandering over the endless gleaming reaches beneath him, had been attracted, with a sudden thrill that made the hair rise on the back of his neck, by first, the small mushroom-shaped cloud, and second, by the black pillar of smoke that soon followed as the mushroom cloud rapidly drifted across the island and disappeared.

He was a child of his century and he knew what mushroom clouds, whatever their size, were supposed to mean. The pillar of smoke was a puzzle but the mushroom cloud was a bone-chilling possibility. Both spelled human—or inhuman—beings.

In great excitement he instantly established voice contact with *Dominant,* now out of his sight on the eastern horizon; described what he had seen and requested permission to go in closer; was told reinforcements would be on their way immediately and was warned to be extremely careful and approach no more than five miles from the island; and with a surging excitement and a happy anticipation that at last he was going to see the action for which he hungered with all his young and exuberant heart, went headlong forward over Nanukuvu with all the dash and daring that might have been expected from his youth and nationality.

He made, in all, three passes over the island. On the first, flying as high and fast as he could go, he was able to discern only that the smoke seemed to be rising from a large mound of debris at the edge of the lagoon. On the second, coming in still fast but—since there had been no sign whatsoever of life or opposition—much lower, he could see what seemed to be bodies, or the remains of bodies, appearing, disappearing and reappearing in the swirls of smoke. And on the third pass, having described this in a tensely excited voice to distant *Dominant* as he went out to sea, made a wide swing and came back, he came in as low as he could and as slow as he could—and did not survive it.

On *Dominant* they heard what appeared to be an explosion . . . the abrupt end of his transmission . . . and silence.

Dispensing "hot wind" upon innocent and unsuspecting human beings was not the only capability of the great black whale. It had many other talents. Shooting down helicopters with deadly accuracy from beneath the seas was only one of them.

Beyond Nanukuvu the remains of Hague Smith and his craft fluttered into the sea.

Later that night—it must have been about 2 A.M., as a matter of fact, when Tick finally returned from the emergency meeting of the Joint Chiefs, Doreen told her husband about what she called "Vi's little episode," with a genuine alarm in her voice that got him seriously upset too. She could see that he already had a great deal on his mind, though he did not tell her about it then and she didn't expect him to, but with his usual generosity he was instantly concerned about their old friend. Doreen told him she had "just tried to calm her down and persuade her not to worry about it."

This she had accomplished with some success, having been her usual instantly sympathetic, kind and soothing self. Violet was much comforted, which was exactly what she had known she would be when she called Doreen. She felt much better after their talk.

Doreen pooh-poohed it, and after discussing it with her for a little while, Vi was reassured—or convinced herself she was—and pooh-poohed it too. They discussed Carleene, who also worked for Dorry, and were amused ("That girl can deliver at ten and be back to work at eleven," Dorry said); deplored the unseasonable weather; made a few amiable jokes about earnest Imogene Buck and her determined attempts to achieve a major place in Washington society; and concluded with happy predictions of how they would triumph Thursday afternoon when they had their regular weekly bridge game with Renee Mc-Cune and Zenia Stokes. By the time they hung up they were able to sound as though whatever had happened to Vi was a perfectly ordinary, if somewhat puzzling, event.

It was only after their talk concluded that Vi felt again a bleak and somber little chill; and Doreen, putting aside the box of chocolates into which she knew she dipped far too regularly, contemplated the frightening possibility that something really fundamental might be wrong with her friend. She thought she knew what it might be, and later Tick agreed. But it would be a while before they fully accepted the thought and dared mention it to Brash as a possibility that should be seriously explored by the Army doctors at Walter Reed Hospital.

For the moment, Dorry did not want to think about it; and so, after admitting it might be there, characteristically shut it out of her mind and returned to what she had been doing when Vi called, which was to supervise putting her own house in order for the small formal dinner she and Tick planned to give that night. (It would be canceled, as would several other similar events for the same reason, but she had no way of knowing that now.)

Tick's aide de camp had sent over to the Commandant's House at Marine Barracks two Marine corporals, female, and two Marine corporals, male, to prepare, cook, serve, and clean up after, the meal. They were an excellent crew, the same she always had, and their specialty was just such affairs as this. In fact, they worked together so well and so amicably, and were generally such pleasant and efficient young people, that Tick had seen to it that they would be kept together as a team in Washington for at least as long as he was commandant. Rank had its privileges, and this was one of them: to have your own personal catering crew, drawn from the service. Everyone of sufficient rank did, and none of the guests ever complained. Neither did the crew, since it assured them a soft and not very active berth in Washington and saved them for a while from the shores of Montezuma, Lebanon and other such uncomfortable duty posts.

Working for Doreen was great as her particular crew often told their friends: she was such a nice and considerate lady. The same approval was given Vi Burford. They weren't like Renee McCune, who was apt to be very picky in her direct and sharp-tongued way, or Zenia Stokes, who was usually rather absent-minded and preoccupied and was also inclined to be on the acerbic side when under pressure, which she seemed to be lately. Imogene Buck rotated her help among the services and was universally regarded with a combination of amused tolerance and frustrated dismay. She was always changing her mind, reversing her orders, trying this and trying that—sure sign, her helpers felt, that for all that she was Mrs. B., wife of the SecDef, she was basically a shy and insecure woman.

Which in truth she was, even after all Loy's years with IBM and all her years as a corporate wife doing all the necessary social things expected of her in that position. She was still, essentially, the same earnest, humorless, rather dowdy and unglamorous woman who had accompanied him somewhat awkwardly up the ladder of corporate success. Everybody automatically said "Loy's a brilliant man. As for Imogene . . ." and their voices would trail away and their expressions become wryly patient. Jane Cathcart, who reflected Bob's dislike of the Secretary anyway, often remarked, "I just *can't* see *why* he married her." Many agreed.

Being not totally devoid of sensitivity or perception, and always aware that more things came to her because of Loy than vice versa, she spent a good deal of her time feeling hurt and resentful. This required of him that he spend a good deal of his time being supportive; and this understandably placed a considerable strain on both of them. The Buck marriage, aside from its few first weeks, had not been one of the great passions of the century. Neither of their natures was conducive to it: he was one of those men, existing in their thousands in Washington, to whom power was a far greater obsession than anything sexual could ever be, and Imogene was just not particularly interested in that side of marriage. Reasonably interested, yes, because that was what was expected of well-brought-up young ladies of her wealthy Philadelphia background in the era when they got married; but "certainly not to the point where it matters all *that* much," as she had written her mother after the honeymoon.

She had done her duty and produced the twins, Loy, Jr., and Elizabeth; after that, interest had declined noticeably on both sides. Not that she ever felt she had real reason to worry about the stability or permanence of their marriage, of course: Loy was far too busy aiming to become president of IBM and far too aware that "a sound marriage" was as vital to that goal as the marriage of any would-be general or admiral. He didn't "chase around," as she put it, or if he did, it was short-lived and she didn't know about it. Nor did she want to know about it. She was quite content to go steadily along, raising the kids to be reliable and worthwhile young citizens and staunchly supporting Loy as he raced up the ladder, doing all she could in her somewhat uneasy and awkward way to help him with his goals and ambitions.

He respected her earnest assistance and her obviously deep and patient love for him, and would not have dreamed of leaving her or doing anything deliberately to hurt her.

The problem arose when they went to Washington and she suddenly realized that she was now the wife of someone extremely important indeed. Being wife of the president of the corporation was satisfying and rewarding, but being wife of the Secretary of Defense was to move onto a plane of far greater influence and importance. Washington was the city where the people you sat beside at dinner or met at cocktail parties *really* had power and *really* could make things happen: they really *were* the people who ran the country and moved the world. And none, save perhaps the President himself, had a more far-reaching mandate or a more globe-spanning ability to influence events and shape the course of history than the man who headed the Department of Defense.

Understandably, perhaps, this had worked some transformation in modest Imogene. In fact, her husband thought, it had gone slightly to Immy's head, though he never said this to anyone else and very rarely to her. When he did it was always in a gently chiding way, because anything more emphatic was apt to bring tears. She was obviously having such a good time, and obviously enjoying it so, that he did not have the heart to point out that she was making herself an easy target for individuals who wished to strike at him and the Defense Department through her.

Defense Eye, for instance, was typical. It was exactly this business of using service personnel to assist at Pentagon social functions that busy little Delight Jones and smug little Herb Horowitz had chosen to concentrate upon in their most recent blast against the military. Since Imogene by virtue of position was the major user, she was ideally suited to bear the brunt of attack.

Defense Eye always had its axe to grind, and there were some in the major media who were always willing to pick up its "exposés" and give them prominence. Delight Jones' little sheet, in fact never more than six poorly-printed pages, but bearing the pompously imposing and seemingly important imprimatur of *"The Defense Improvement Group,"* was perfect for this purpose.

It was typical of certain late twentieth century journalists and their late twentieth century readers that all one required to achieve instant national and world attention was a letterhead and a high-sounding name. The Committee for This, The Study Group for That—frequently consisting of no more than a tiny handful of people and an implacable desire to savage the government— were always being quoted in the papers and on the tube. All they had to do was issue a "report," a "position paper," a "study,"—or "charge," "announce," "denounce" or "conclude"—and instantly, with no check on who they were, where they came from, who was behind them, or whether there were any facts to support their claims, their words would be spread across the country and often the globe as though they were gospel truth. All it took was the letterhead, the vengeful spirit, the gall—and the name.

"The Defense Improvement Group" was most shrewdly chosen to achieve this aim.

So poor Immy was the frequent target, more often on this point of service help at social functions than on any other, although there was a general tendency to pick up every single little damaging thing that could possibly be found and throw it back at her. Her pearls had broken at a White House dinner soon after they arrived in town. Secondhand accounts from jealous wives speedily found their way into the local prints. "Cabinet members, Senators, Congress-men and at one point even the President himself were forced to scramble last night to recover the broken pearls of the wife of the new Secretary of Defense —" the clear implication being that she had somehow deliberately scattered them around the room so that all these distinguished gentlemen would have to go down on hands and knees and rummage under the tables. No one had, two of the waiters had taken care of it with quick efficiency, the pearls had not rolled far and all were back in her purse in five minutes. But, "Why do they try to make me look ridiculous?" she had complained to Loy.

"My dear," he had said crisply, "they just want to get at me, through you. I know it's unfair and I know it hurts, but that's just part of the game around here and you might as well take it philosophically."

"It's all very well for you *men* to be so calm about it," she said, "but I've never done anything to anybody in my life except try to be *nice* to everyone."

"I know," he agreed with an affectionate smile, "and people who are your real friends know that."

"I don't think I have any real friends in Washington," she said mournfully.

"Oh, come," he said. "Of course you do. I'm the one who doesn't, and that's why they hit you. Just remember it's me they're after. That ought to help a *little* bit."

"No, it doesn't," she said stoutly, "because that isn't fair, either. You're just trying to do the best you can for the country."

"There are some mighty disagreements as to what's 'best,'" he replied with a smile. "My 'best' is somebody else's awful, and if he or she has access to newsprint or camera, I'm going to get it. And so, unfortunately, are you. You really will just have to grin and bear it."

"I could answer back," she suggested in a halfhearted way, for she knew his response.

"Oh, no, you couldn't," he said. "You know perfectly well from company days that you can't argue with the press. It only gets you in deeper."

"Most people are more fair-minded than *they* are," she said stubbornly. "Most people *know*."

"Yes, I agree with you," he said. "But I really wish you wouldn't. It would only make matters worse."

So she hadn't. But she had noted, as Loy got deeper into the job and more settled and confident in it, that he didn't always take his own advice. When the media thought he was asking too much for defense, which was almost always, and began to pepper him with editorials, cartoons and unfavorable news sto-ries, he quite often replied with a cogent, and frequently acerbic, defense of his position. His first-year deference to members of the pertinent committees on the Hill had speedily given way to the same tart approach.

"No More Mr. Nice Guy," the *Post* had editorialized after his first such riposte. And when some intense young Congressman from New York, one of the type that always opposes every U.S. commitment abroad no matter how necessary or vital, brought it up in committee the next day, Loy had shrugged with an amicable grin.

"Are you really 'No More Mr. Nice Guy'?" the Congressman had asked with an exaggeratedly disapproving solemnity.

"You bet, Congressman," the Secretary had said with relish. "From now on I'm mean as hell. So watch it!"

And when the Congressman went into some long fandango about how this showed great disrespect for the Congress in general and himself in particular, Loy had simply observed calmly, "You'll get respect when you deserve it, Congressman. I don't believe you do this morning."

Which had provoked another long tirade filled with righteous indignation. At its conclusion Loy had asked calmly, "Can we move along to the next item, Mr. Chairman?" and not replied to the Congressman at all.

After that the Congressman and an ever-increasing number of his colleagues thought long and hard before tangling with the Secretary. And a not-so-amicable parody of Rudyard Kipling at the next Gridiron dinner began, "Walk wide o' the 'ead o' the Pentagon, for 'arf o' creation 'e owns!"

So, Immy felt resentfully sometimes, she *did* have a right to answer back; and was only mollified when Loy took occasion in a luncheon address to the National Press Club a year later to say, "I sometimes think I might have a little more success helping to defend the United States if I didn't have to spend so much time defending my wife against some of you gracious ladies and gallant gentlemen. I admire your bravery in attacking a defenseless woman who really wishes you no harm."

Which wasn't quite true, because by that time she *did* wish them harm, and plenty of it; but it had been greeted with a shocked gasp, and, for a while, a moratorium on Imogene. Now the snide attitude and the catty comments were beginning to creep back, but she found that she was finally becoming a little tougher. She still didn't like it but she didn't let it get her down quite so much as it had in the beginning. She found she really had accepted it, at last, as a necessary sacrifice on her part to assist Loy in his all-important work.

"I don't mind being the lightning-rod if it will help you," she had told him recently; and then, in a rare moment of self-humor had swung about to survey her short, plump figure in the mirror and chuckled, "Imagine! Me, a lightning-rod!"

Anyway, she thought with a thankful sigh now as she looked out at the garden already inches deep in snow, she didn't have to worry about any of that this night. She had telephoned the Italian embassy to cancel out on their dinner engagement there, and had been greeted with a swift interpretation of her reason before she had a chance to state it. "The snow, the snow! Yes, Signora, we are already receiving many calls." Actually that wasn't the reason at all and she had been prepared to tell a little white lie about an upset stomach. The real reason was that she felt, as she told Vangie, that it was high time Loy had a night at home with absolutely nothing to do except what he himself decided: perhaps the cabinet-making which was his principal hobby, or reading some book that had nothing at all to do with defense or international crisis, or maybe even watching something on television, if there was anything worth watching, which she doubted. Anyway, the principal thing was to get Loy away from the office and away from everything that had to do with defense.

They might begin it, she thought, by calling the children, Loy, Jr. and his wife in California, Elizabeth and her husband in Texas. Then they could have a couple of leisurely drinks and a simple meal—prepared by *her*—and then they could just relax. Maybe they could even get snowed in so Loy couldn't go to the Pentagon tomorrow—although in that case, as she knew from a previous occasion, the Army would just send a helicopter and airlift him across the frozen city and river and plunk him down at his job again. At his orders, of course. *He* wouldn't take advantage of the chance to get a rest.

There was almost no escaping the Pentagon, she soon realized after he had taken the job; and he really seemed to thrive on it. She had come to feel a real sympathy for all the wives, both civilian and military, who were involved with the defense effort. Such a monstrous undertaking, which only went on and on and never had a stop, consuming billions of dollars and millions of lives—even when it didn't physically consume them as in time of war, but just ate them up with the endless pressures that went into building and maintaining the military machine.

Imogene was not a militant pacifist such as Zenia Stokes had been on a couple of occasions, much to Ham's annoyance though luckily not to the detriment of his career. Imogene wasn't a militant anything. But there were times, and they came frequently as she watched Loy being chauffeured off to work promptly at 7:00 A.M. every day, often not to return until well into the evening, when she felt that she was thoroughly sick and tired of the whole business.

But—he wasn't. And therefore, like all the Pentagon's marital survivors, she made the best of it. Not without considerable complaining from time to time— she felt that she shouldn't be blamed for that perfectly human release—but with a dogged determination to stick it out as long as he wanted to. And she did make some effort to keep the complaining down to a reasonable minimum— "No more than ten times a week," he had remarked recently with wry but affectionate reproach. But damn it, she thought—with what for her was pretty strong language, even in the privacy of her own mind—damn it, Loy *ought* to slow down and take it easy. Otherwise, as she often warned him, he might have a heart attack, and then where would they be?

"In the first place," he replied, "you would be very well taken care of by both IBM and the government, and in the second place, it isn't going to happen. You know I get a regular checkup every two months—"

"There, you see?" she demanded, alarmed. "It used to be once a year. Then a couple of years ago it started to be every six months, and now—"

"Now," he said calmly, "it's just so I can keep an eye on what's going on. Nothing is. I'm in perfect health, so they tell me."

"But *you* must feel you aren't," she said, "otherwise you wouldn't be running to the doctors all the time—"

He shrugged, unconcerned.

"An ounce of prevention, and it's free at Walter Reed or Bethesda Naval Hospital, so why shouldn't I?"

"Don't tell *Defense Eye,*" she said dryly, "or the wicked witch of the west and her little elf Mr. Horowitz will get you."

He smiled and shook his head.

"How those two annoying little people can turn this town upside down with their rumors and gossip is something I marvel at. But I doubt if they'll take me on because they know I just don't give a damn. It *is* important that the Secretary of Defense be in good health, and it *is* important that he have checkups if he thinks he should have them, and it *is* probably the most sensible perk that goes with the office, so if they want to start a fuss, let them. Anyway, we waste enough time at the Pentagon discussing *Defense Eye* as it is. I'd rather not talk about them any more."

"Well," she said stubbornly, "you ought to at least get more rest than you do. You ought to just make time for it."

"You do it for me," he said with a grin.

"Will you cooperate if I do?"

He grinned again.

"We'll see."

"Yes," she echoed with a frustrated sound. " 'We'll see.' "

And tonight they would see, because she had checked with Vangie again just a little while ago and Vangie had said that she had relayed the message and Mr. Buck seemed to be agreeable to spending the evening at home. In fact, Vangie said, she thought a lot of people in the government would be spending the evening at home because of the storm, if nothing else. She thought that many of the nonessential military and civilians in the Pentagon would probably be dismissed by 2 P.M. so they could get on home before the roads became impassable, "and just the regulars will stay on."

"Loy's a regular," Imogene had said, sounding so forlorn that Vangie had chuckled, but sympathetically.

"Don't worry, Mrs. Buck," she had said, with the rare earthiness she revealed only to a few top-ranking people and their spouses, "I'll kick him out of here."

"Give him a good swift one, Vangie," Imogene had suggested and they had ended the conversation with fond, conspiratorial laughter toward the man they were dedicated to taking care of.

And now the phone rang, and before she even picked it up she knew that, sure as shooting, it would be Loy with some excuse about having to stay on at the Pentagon.

"Yes?" she said, sounding more defensive than she intended, but pushed by concern for him.

"Immy," he began apologetically, "I hate to do this to you, but something's come up that means I probably won't—"

"Oh, yes, you *will,*" she said fiercely. "You *can't* just stay at that old Pentagon all the time!"

"This time, Immy," he said gravely, "I think I'm going to have to, at least for a while. Don't wait up for me."

"Oh, *no!*" she wailed. "Not *again!*"

"Afraid so," he said. "I *am* sorry. But you'll understand when I'm able to tell you about it."

"What is it this time?" she demanded with a frustrated scorn. "A war?"

He sighed.

"Of a sort," he said in a tired voice. "The same one we're always in. Just a different place."

"Oh, damn," she said, again resorting to most unusual profanity, for her. "I love you and I do worry so about your health!"

"I love you, too," he said. "But now I've got to go. I'll see you later."

She heard the click of the receiver and replaced her own with tears in her eyes. Damn, damn, damn and *damn.* Damn the Pentagon, damn wars, damn the enemy and damn everything. She dashed a hand furiously across her eyes, took a deep breath and turned away from the phone. Shape up, Mrs. B., she told herself with a half-laugh, half-sob, you're in the Army, now.

Across the Pershing desk Loy thoughtfully studied the handsome troubled face that looked gravely back at him.

"Now, Zeecy," he said. "Start from the beginning and tell me all about it."

2 Within seconds after the abrupt termination of Hague Smith's transmission from Nanukuvu, orders had gone out from *Dominant* to the squadron already heading west that it should observe but not repeat NOT overfly the island. In the radio room the captain was already in contact with CINCPAC at Pearl and seconds after that CINCPAC was through to CJCS in Washington.

At that stage of the problem of Nanukuvu, things moved fast.

The call, relayed up through the ranks of the joint staff of the JCS, caught Zeecy in the midst of lunch in the JCS dining room. His guests were the military's principal problems on the Hill, Sens. Harlan H. Herron of California and Jerry Castain of Indiana—Reps. Mario Escondido of Connecticut and Karl Aschenheim of Pennsylvania—and the aide who gave the Pentagon the most trouble, Burt Sanstrom, staff director of the Senate Armed Services Committee.

There were other Senators and Congressmen, and other staff members, who were difficult; but these were the five who gave the Defense Department the most consistent hell. Zeecy had decided it was time to stroke them a bit at this midpoint in Congress' annual consideration of the defense authorization and appropriations bills.

He had tried to think of some excuse to include Luzanne but there just wasn't any. He was surprised at how upset and frustrated this made him feel. In addition to being pleasant for him, her attendance would have removed the luncheon a little from the cynical category in which he knew his guests were placing it. He felt rather cynical about it himself. As a consequence his tone was a little more sharply jocular than usual when the Congressional delegation arrived after debarking in the driving snow from one of the last Pentagon buses that would be able to make the Capitol Hill run before the weather shut them down.

"Cube!" he said when Sen. Herron led them into the room. "Jerry! Mario and Karl! Come in, come in. And you too, Burt. Always glad to see you all."

"You weren't yesterday," Mario Escondido remarked with his usual sledge-hammer subtlety. "We gave you quite a time in the committee, didn't we?"

"Oh, hell," Gen. McCune said expansively. "That's all part of the game, Mario. I didn't think you laid a finger on me. Until I tried to turn my head, that is. Suddenly I found it wasn't there any more."

Rep. Escondido's rotund little form shook with chuckles and the customary expression of self-satisfaction on his swarthy little face became even more pronounced.

"We took you apart a bit," he agreed happily. "It was good for you."

"No doubt," Zeecy said. "There are other ways I would rather have spent the day."

"You'll be coming over to us next week," Cube Herron said with considerable relish. "You'll think Mario and his boys were a flock of butterflies compared to what we'll do to you in the Senate."

"Oh, now," Jerry Castain said, tilting his handsome blond head to one side with a roguish air—"a real space cadet," the Senate press called him. "Don't be too rough on him, Cube. You've already had him before you once this year and he hasn't even started testifying before us in the Appropriations subcommittee yet. Leave a little for us, will you?"

"I think before you cut me up between you too much," Zeecy said, "that we'd better have a drink. Cube, what'll you have? Jerry? Mario? I'll get the troops in here—" He pressed a buzzer on his desk, the door opened instantly, a young Air Force sergeant, male, rolled in a liquor cart and a young airman second class, female, followed with a tray of hors d'oeuvres. Cube Herron and Mario Escondido took Bloody Marys, Jerry Castain his usual careful white wine, Karl Aschenheim a beer. Burt Sanstrom, small, thin, clean-shaven, middle-aged, grimly determined, stayed safely and ostentatiously with mineral water.

The sergeant made the drinks, the airman passed the hors d'oeuvres. The conversation turned innocuously to the weather while they were present. Zeecy nodded after one drink and two passes with the hors d'oeuvres tray— told them, "We'll eat in ten minutes"—and they were gone. He gestured his guests to the table.

"Find your own places, gentlemen. No protocol here. I thought you needed a private get-Zeecy session, so I've arranged for them to serve and leave us alone. Then you can *really* cut me up."

"We don't want to cut you up, Zeecy," Jerry Castain said with a protesting motion of his long-fingered hands. "We just want to have an amicable discussion of the problems you face on the Hill with this year's budget."

"Frankly," Cube Herron said with characteristic bluntness as they seated themselves, "you want too damned much. You birds always want too damned much. There's no end to it."

Zeecy, whose general strategy toward the Hill was very similar to the Secretary's—fast fire and no quarter—snorted.

"If we're going to start that game," he retorted, unimpressed, "let's talk about all the special requests we get from you guys. Every time *we* want to cut something, some base or other, or maybe something in Connecticut—"

"Don't you touch Connecticut!" Mario Escondido exploded, eyes bulging even more belligerently than usual. "We *need* Connecticut!"

"Of course," Gen. McCune said calmly. "Everybody needs everything. That's what I mean."

"What we *don't* need," Burt Sanstrom spoke up abruptly from down the table, "is one more snow-job from the Secretary and JCS, general. We need a few straight facts and figures and an honest budget that isn't padded with a lot of wasted money. We've *had* it with that."

"We've had it with the Hill, to some degree," Gen. McCune remarked. "But we all have to live together just the same."

"Not on your terms of an open-ended budget that doesn't give a damn about the economy—" Cube Herron began. Zeecy interrupted.

"Senator," he said sharply, "we're not fools, over here. We know the economy has to be in good shape. We also know that the Pentagon budget is the second biggest item in it and has the greatest effect on it of anything you people consider. That's why we're perfectly willing to trim the waste out of it— if you are. We'd like to do it together, though, not as enemies."

"Hmph!" Sen. Herron said. "The Hill and the Pentagon will always be enemies. We all know that. Who are we kidding?"

"Nobody's trying to kid—" Gen. McCune began and abruptly halted as the door opened and the sergeant and the airman first class came in with the food trolley and began serving "—anybody," he concluded and joined the general silence while the youngsters finished their task with swift efficiency.

"Thank you, troops," he said in the fatherly tone that had all the ranks eating out of his hand. "It looks very good, and we appreciate it."

"Thank you, sir," the sergeant said as they blushed and bowed and the Congressional delegation made appropriate sounds of thanks and approval. "Buzz when you want us to clear."

"We will, sergeant," Gen. McCune said. "Enjoy your lunches . . . Now," he said when they were alone again, "why don't you stop talking nonsense, Cube? You know perfectly well the Pentagon and the Hill aren't enemies. How could we defend the country together if we were? We aren't always friends, maybe, but we certainly aren't enemies. Particularly not someone like you, whose seniority and experience in military matters we all depend upon so much to assist us in our monumental task over here on this side of the river."

"Well," Sen. Herron said, looking flattered and mollified in spite of himself, though Burt Sanstrom, as he remarked to a staff member later, "wanted to vomit when McCune started laying it on with a trowel." (Not the first time, as he still resented and would never forget, when McCune had provoked that kind of reaction.)

"That's right, Zeecy," Sen. Castain said smoothly. "Of course we aren't enemies. And of course we have to work together. But to do that, it seems to me, requires a real spirit of understanding and cooperation on both sides. Right now, with a lot of people on both sides of the Hill under a lot of pressure from back home to keep the budget under some sort of reasonable control, we've got to look to you and the Secretary and the services to lead the way. That's why I'm glad we're having our frank little talk today."

And he beamed around the table, good-looking, vacuous and somewhat dumb—at least in Pentagon eyes—but, Zeecy knew, essentially well-meaning in his earnestly eager, far-out way. The casual cruelty of the media—"space cadet"—was not too far off the mark, Zeecy thought. Fortunately or unfortunately, depending upon his mood, Jerry was chairman of the Senate Appropriations subcommittee on defense and therefore vital to the Pentagon. The general found he still had a certain amount left on his trowel.

"Jerry," he said solemnly, "I don't think anyone could have stated it more clearly or with greater cogency. Understanding and cooperation, that's the ticket! Understanding and cooperation! We understand your problem with the budget—certainly no one understands better than *you* the vital necessity that Hill and Pentagon work together in unity to meet the terrible challenge to our freedoms, indeed to our very life as a nation. We *must* understand and cooperate with one another, Senator." His voice sank dramatically. *"We must."*

"So how do we cut the Pentagon as much as we're going to have to?" Karl Aschenheim inquired tartly, looking up from his luncheon steak for the first time and speaking in his faint but still lingering Pennsylvania Dutch accent. "With nice speeches from the chairman of the Joint Chiefs of Staff?"

"And from members of Congress, Karl," Gen. McCune responded calmly, not at all taken aback.

"Not from me," Karl Aschenheim retorted. *"I* want *results!"*

"So do we all want *'results'!"* Zeecy said with equal vigor, mimicking Karl's ponderous tone exactly. "Maybe Lancaster County is the place to start. Not many defense installations *there.*"

"Even if there were," Rep. Aschenheim said with equal calmness, "I wouldn't give a damn. Do you doubt it?"

Zeecy shook his head and laughed.

"No, Karl," he said, "I do not doubt it. I honestly do not. But you are, you must admit, in a special and ideal position to be objective. Maybe you are the perfect one to be Solomon, here."

"I don't mind," Karl Aschenheim said with a smile that conceded finally to Zeecy's amiable persuasions. "I can take it."

"And great for us that you can," Zeecy said. "Great for us . . . Cube," he said, "what do you think the chances are that—"

But they would never know what his question was, because just at that moment the door opened hastily. They swung around to face it, the others looking startled, Zeecy annoyed. The marine colonel who was aide to the general who headed the joint JCS staff stepped in, apologetic but determined.

"I'm sorry, sir," he said firmly, "but I'm afraid it's imperative that you take a message in your office. Immediately."

"Colonel—" Zeecy began; then he stopped and gave the colonel a searching glance that the colonel returned unflinching. Discipline took over. Zeecy nodded.

"Very well," he said, standing up and tossing his napkin on the table. "Gentlemen, I'm afraid we're going to have to continue this some other time, probably in front of your committees—" he smiled faintly—"when *everybody* can cut me up. Take your time, finish your desserts, enjoy yourselves. I'll be back in a few minutes if I can. If I can't—" he smiled again—"well, you'll know it soon enough."

"Zeecy," Cube Herron said in an alarmed tone. "You'll let us know—?"

"Absolutely," Gen. McCune said. "As soon as possible. Colonel, after you."

And they walked out, leaving the men from the Hill to worry and wonder. Zeecy did not return, and after another fifteen minutes or so Sen. Herron stood up heavily and said, "Well, boys, I guess that's it for today." He too smiled, wry and disturbed. "Watch the evening news."

But it was not on the evening news, nor would it be, Loy and Zeecy determined, if they could possibly prevent it. But of course they could not, though that was a while off, yet.

"So," Loy said, "what do you think we should do about it, Zeece?"

"My first instinct," Gen. McCune said, "is to go in and blast the hell out of them right now."

"Mine, too," Loy said. "Though there will be many voices, and many reasons, telling us why we should not."

"The longer we wait, the tougher it's going to be," Zeecy said. The Secretary sighed.

"It is ever and eternally thus," he said wryly. "Get on the other phone."

He pressed the proper button. The White House answered immediately.

"The President, please," he said.

"Yes, *sir*," the operator replied.

The mellow voice, calmly in command as always, came on the line.

Across the river, on F Street N.W. off 17th, Roger Venable of Strategic Industries and Walker Stayman of General Growth Group were lunching too, at Maison Blanche, still holding its own as the place to be seen between the hours of 12 noon and 2 P.M. There statesmen displayed their statesmanship, media people their fame, lobbyists their clout. Roger and Walker never acknowledged the term "lobbyist," which they felt was beneath their dignity as Washington representatives of two such mighty and prestigious corporations, but lobbyists they were, and rivals to boot. Friendly rivals, most of the time; although, as the S.I. and Three Gs shares of the Defense Department pie had zoomed upward into the billions in recent years and their influence in Washington had become correspondingly great, the friendliness of the corporations' representatives at times became more competitive.

It was so today, and the choice of luncheon partners showed it. Roger Venable was doing his bit for Strategic Industries by taking Helen Clark to lunch. Walker Stayman was doing his for General Growth Group by hosting William T. "Shorty" Murchison, inspector general in OSD, the Office of the Secretary of Defense. The maître d', whose job it was to know who in Washington was hating or loving whom at any given moment, and to seat them accordingly, had placed the two parties thoughtfully in clear line of vision.

Helen Clark had tossed a smile and wink at her fellow Pentagonian as she came into the crowded, buzzing, wood-paneled dining room with Roger Venable, who as always looked like a statesman himself, tall, gray, distinguished and reserved. Shorty Murchison, who lived up to his nickname by being short, fat, keen-eyed and so palpably honest that his mere glance could throw the fear of God into an erring contractor, responded with an equally ironic and obvious wink that made his host, Walker Stayman, smile nervously and look self-consciously about. Walker was forty-five to Roger Venable's sixty, new in Washington and still feeling a little conspicuous as the representative of one of the country's two biggest defense contractors.

"Nice girl, Helen," Shorty said to relieve Walker's apparent embarrassment. "And a damned good Assistant Secretary for Acquisition and Logistics."

"Oh, the best," Walker said hastily, returning Helen's cool smile and stately nod with a trifle too much obsequiousness. "But I suppose you make her jump through hoops just like you do all the rest of us."

"She knows I'm around," Shorty Murchison said with satisfaction as he went with unerring aim for the bread and butter. "I try to make them all know I'm around, in the Pentagon." He gave a beatific smile. "And you guys too."

"We know *that*," Walker Stayman said with a smile he made suitably rueful. One had to massage so many different egos in so many different ways, in this town. He was learning fast that it kept a guy hopping, to adjust to all the varying moods of all the people he must deal with in advancing the cause of General Growth Group. Three Gs was paying him a terrifically handsome sum to be its vice president in charge of defense affairs and he was determined to do everything he could to help Three Gs defend the country and make several hundred million bucks in the process. He and Three Gs were just as dedicated to the cause of America as anybody else, he often thought, somewhat defensively. What was good for the country was certainly good for Three Gs, and he was certainly anxious to keep it that way.

So here he was with Shorty Murchison, the annoyingly persistent little snoop, and over there was his strongest competition, Roger Venable, being his dignified best with Helen Clark, whose ego also was enormous and also required a sizable amount of stroking. Walker had been her partner at the White House dinner for the president of Pakistan scarcely a month ago, and had found her not at all hard to take. It was the first time he had met her. She was a damned attractive woman and he soon realized uneasily that she saw through most men without a moment's delay. But her company was enjoyable and he had not found it difficult to give her the impression that she had made one more conquest. She hadn't, of course, he was happily married and he trusted her with Three Gs' welfare about as much as he would a smiling cobra, but it didn't hurt to let her think so. He wondered now how he could gracefully go over and barge in on the conversation. He finally decided against it as it might offend a) Shorty, b) Roger and c) most importantly, Helen herself.

For his part, Roger Venable was equally intrigued by Walker's lunch with Shorty, although he was too smooth and experienced an operator to even consider involving himself in it. The inspector general had a fearsome reputation in the defense community, having been appointed to succeed an equally vigilant predecessor who had relished nothing so much as uncovering fraud in contracts and/or performance. The same applied to Shorty Murchison, if anything more so, and Roger Venable regarded him with a great deal of caution and respect. He was biding his time with the luncheon invitations: only someone new and gauche like Walker would rush right in and do anything so obvious. But Shorty was on Roger's list. Slowly, patiently and skillfully, Roger would throw out his net one of these days and haul him in. Not that this would in any way deflect the inspector general if he thought Strategic Industries was up to anything, but it would make him at least a reasonably friendly enemy. That was about all anyone could ask from the Pentagon, which seemed to have become permanently touchy a few years ago when a whole spate of cost overruns and absurdly overpriced items had surfaced in the media, which had screamed to high heaven even though the inspector general's office itself had uncovered the items and made them public. Once bitten, twice inspected, as he liked to say to his superiors at S.I.'s headquarters in Kansas City (Mo.), and the Pentagon certainly bore him out. They had really cracked down in recent years. Fraud and unnecessary overruns still occurred, but far less often than before. Shorty had a real band of vigilantes on his staff over there, Roger often remarked, and it took a lot of genteel lobbying to persuade some of them to be even civil.

Not so the Hill, he had found; and he knew Walker would find the same. Up there it was the same old story it had always been: the majority were decent, honest, desperately overworked and earnestly patriotic—but there were among them the weak, the venal and the vulnerable, as there were in any human endeavor, particularly a democracy where the expression of human characteristics had free rein.

There weren't an enormous number on the Hill, but there were enough so that corporate favors discreetly extended were sometimes ill-advisedly received. The free plane ride, the complimentary hotel room, the "inspection" junket overseas, the all-expenses-paid vacation at S.I.'s hideaways on Virgin Gorda or Maui, the bring-your-wife sojourn in the corporation's executive suites in London, Paris or Rome, the girl-provided weekend in Las Vegas—

these all had their takers on Capitol Hill. A great many, such as Luzanne Johnson or Karl Aschenheim, were incorruptible and not even worth approaching. But some others, such as Mario Escondido, loud in protestation and sly in practice, were easy targets.

Where that kind of thing worked, Roger Venable used it with a suppressed but virulent contempt for the recipients. Where it did not, as with Luzanne and Karl and many others, he was every inch the suave and dignified advocate, offering the occasional public meal in the very public place, relying on pleasantries, casual conversation, reasoned presentation and chastely impersonal argument to carry the day. On a surprising number of occasions, this worked. Rational argument was by far the most potent weapon of today's lobbyist, though there was enough of the other still left to give the profession a lingering shady reputation. He much preferred to be open, aboveboard, frankly partisan for his company but clear-cut and clean in his approach. He had long since found, as he knew Walker would, that he scored far more points being an honest lobbyist than he ever did by being underhanded.

This was particularly true with people in the Pentagon at the Helen Clark level. Her brother Ray might be another matter (the weekend in Las Vegas had already worked with Ray a couple of times), but with Helen and the majority of the deputies and assistants surrounding Loy Buck, morality, conscience and the Spirit of Old True-Blue formed the only pathway to persuasion. He knew that Helen, like Shorty Murchison, would order him out of the office if he ever dared suggest anything out of the ordinary. This was because Loy, of course, was so incorruptible himself and so annoyingly well-informed about corporate activities. He had been there, and he knew. Woe befall any around him who strayed from the mark for very long. Instinct told Roger that Ray Clark, for instance, was not long for the Pentagon world if he didn't shape up pretty damned fast; which did not, of course, prevent Roger from quite cynically offering Ray anything he felt he might fall for, in order to advance the corporate well-being and very great profits of Strategic Industries.

Thus musing as he looked about the busy room filled with the self-important movers and shakers of the capital of the free world, he was not prepared for the sudden amusement with which Helen Clark interrupted his reverie.

"Look at that!" she exclaimed, nodding to their left. "I think we're going to find ourselves immortalized in print, Bob. And undoubtedly Walker and Shorty too."

"Since half the media in D.C. seem to be here this noon," he responded with a smile, "I can't see that it's any secret that we're all having lunch."

"But—ah!" she exclaimed. "Ah—the twist!"

And turning full face to her left she smiled brilliantly and vigorously to the small, intense, dark-skinned young woman and her small, swarthy young male companion who were staring at them with a self-conscious defiance from across the room.

"Do you *know* those two?" Roger Venable demanded in amused disbelief. Secretary Clark uttered a carefree laugh.

"Only by reputation," she admitted. "Only by reputation. But isn't it fun to make everyone think I do!"

And waved again, as Shorty Murchison and Walker Stayman and several others looked with some surprise from her to her quarry and back again. Walker seemed a little bemused but she knew Shorty got it immediately. He gave her another ironic little bow and wink.

As for Delight Jones and Herbert Horowitz, they did not know for a moment how to take this effusive public greeting from the Assistant Secretary for Acquisition and Logistics, whom they had just attacked in today's edition of *Defense Eye* for "her complaisant attitude toward America's most voracious corporations and her blatant and adamant disregard for the public welfare in the letting of defense contracts."

They had conceded, quite far down in the story, that a lot of other people were also involved in letting defense contracts, but Helen Clark was the symbol they had chosen to attack. She obviously had to be guilty of various heinous crimes of commission and omission in the letting of contracts—wasn't everybody? And anyway, she was too damned glamorous to suit Delight, who did not exactly qualify as glamorous herself.

"What's with Helen and those two?" Walker inquired of Shorty, already falling into the "those two" locution with which a good deal of defense-oriented Washington referred to the publisher and (only) star reporter of *Defense Eye*.

"She's just having a little fun," Shorty said complacently. "You'll find that out about Helen. She has a pointed sense of humor."

"I'll remember that," Walker promised with a rather nervous little laugh.

"Best do," Shorty Murchison said. "She can be quite disconcerting if one isn't ready for it."

And disconcerted, at least for a few seconds, Delight Jones and Herb Horowitz seemed to be. Then righteous self-confidence and the fortifying knowledge of moral superiority came to the rescue. They had most of the corrupt bastards in this room exactly where they wanted them and the corrupt bastards knew it. So what was to worry if Helen Clark did give them the big hello? She was deliberately making fun of them, like all the rest. They'd get her, in due course: today's blast was only the beginning.

"Look at that!" Delight remarked to Herb after giving Helen a scornful look which did not seem to faze her at all. "If that worthless bitch isn't the damnedest!"

"Screw her," Herb Horowitz said succinctly, falling to again on the delicious trout he was consuming with great gusto. "She doesn't know what's good for her, that's all."

"She'll find out," Delight said dourly. "Why don't you do some more digging and see if you can't get some real dirt on her? She must be vulnerable: beautiful divorcée—world of men—Pentagon officers—big bucks. Think of all the millions she handles all the time. Some of it must stick to her fingers."

"If it does," Herb promised grimly, "I'll find out." He took another swig of the Napa Valley wine he always ordered here—damned good, if a little overpriced. The Defense Improvement Group had the money. DIG wouldn't let him down. The expense account covered it all. He enjoyed living it up with the rest of the in-crowd who frequented Maison Blanche. Especially when he and Delight knew how nervous it made all the government people when he and Delight came in here—and some of the media too, because *Defense Eye* was not averse to swiping at the more reactionary ones in passing. This nervous reaction occurred about three times a week, at least.

"How are you doing on that Marine death squad at Lejeune?" she asked, busy on her tournedos, which also were delicious. "Found out who's responsible for those training deaths yet?"

"Some poor bastard lieutenant seems to be in line to take the fall," he said. "God damned buck-passers. You might know some innocent son of a bitch with no rank to speak of would get stuck with it."

"Can't you carry it on up to Tick himself?" she inquired. "Surely the top brass can't remain sacrosanct forever."

"Boy!" he said. "You don't know the top brass! Of course they can."

"Not with *us* around," she said grimly. A mocking lilt came into her voice. "From the halls of Montezuma to the shores of Tripoli, if they get their asses in a sling they're sure to hear from *me*. Us." She gave a cheerful if somewhat rapacious grin. "How's that for the old hymnbo?"

"Perfect," he said admiringly. "You're quite a gal, Delight." And asked the question he had asked before. "Where'd you come from, anyway?"

"Oh," she said vaguely, as she always did. "Around. Usual D.C. stuff. You know. Ghetto kid makes good. Smartest little scruff in the block goes onward and upward to the Phi Beta Kappa key. Copy-girl on the *Post,* visions of Pulitzers dance in her head. Out on assignment, big deal. Greener pastures, bigger targets. Chance to work for DIG, jumped at it. Named editor of *Defense Eye* at once. Amazing responsibility placed in hands of immature child at advanced age. Watch out, Pentagon, here we come! And," she concluded with great satisfaction, "they *do* watch out, too, when *we* ring the bell."

"Who's 'we'?" he pursued, because he really didn't know, he had just answered a blind ad in *Editor and Publisher,* and here they were, two years after he had graduated from Columbia School of Journalism and served a brief apprenticeship on a chain of supermarket throwaways in Prince Georges County, Maryland.

"We's us," she said in the same fey way. "We's us, bruthuh, so why ask questions? You nail 'em, I'll print 'em, and together we clean up the God damned Pentagon and help this sick country fly right."

"Yes," he agreed with some doubtfulness he tried to suppress, because she always sensed it. "It sure needs it, all right."

"And don't sound dubious," she ordered. "Have some more wine and keep the faith. How's the trout?"

"Great," he said. "And the tournedos?"

"Greater. I hope Helen Clark chokes on her salmon. That would be a story for us: Assistant Secretary for Acquisition and Logistics acquires bite of salmon, logistics defeat her. Audit review shows tracheal termination. Whoops!"

"Delight," he said again admiringly, "you're some girl."

"And you're some God damned good reporter," she assured him. "Good day, when I picked you. Instinct told me: here's this hungry little Jew-boy—"

"Delight," he said, a warning anger coming into his voice. "You watch it, now. I don't like that kind of stuff, even from you."

"Who better?" she inquired. "Us bruthuhs and sistuhs, we *know*. Anyway, here he is, I told myself, and he's plenty smart, too; and then I talked to you and I added: and he hates the bastards. That's the key to it: *he hates*. So let's go get 'em and on with the show! That's what I said to me. And I was right, too, wasn't I? You do hate 'em, don't you? It sticks out all over."

"I strongly disapprove," he said stiffly, "of the militaristic element that has come to dominate our society and control our government, using the pretext of an insane arms race that continues unabated despite the Administration's phony pretenses that it is trying to end it."

"Don't write the editorials," she ordered. "I do that. You just hate 'em and get the stories, that's all I ask. O.K.?"

"I get some good ones, too," he remarked, deciding to drop it, though he still *would* like to know where Delight came from, and what DIG was all about.

"The best," she said. "And the biggies eat 'em up, too. All we have to do is plant something and before you know it, it's on the best front pages and featured on the evening news. We're class, honey. They eat us up. They really do. It doesn't matter much what we say: if we just say it strongly enough, they *listen*. And follow." She gave a satisfied nod. "We do a lot of good that way."

"We do manage to get some attention," he agreed with a smile.

"Keep at it!" she directed. "For instance, look at who Helen Clark is eating with: that damned shyster Roger Venable of S.I., ex-colonel from the Quarter-master Corps rewarded with a cushy lobbying job. And look at Shorty Murchison over there, no doubt bartering away his country's fortunes to that little wimp from Three Gs, Mr. Walker Stayman, who's so new in this town he still thinks everything is real. Can't you get something on those two?"

"It's been tried many times," he pointed out, "at least with Roger Venable. He's too smart to show his hand. Walker Stayman might be another matter."

"Get him in his infancy," she said with a grin, "or all will be lost. All but the dumbest learn fast in this town. He doesn't strike me as dumb. Just new. Incidentally, anything we can pin on Mrs. Lady Buck this week? She's usually doing some damned thing that makes good copy."

"I don't hear much over there about her these days," he said. "We've pretty well exhausted the servicemen-as-waiters bit for the time being, I think."

"She's such a dodo-bird she'll do *something* soon," Delight predicted. "Keep your antenna up."

"It always is," he said, truthfully.

"Yes, I know," she agreed. "Mine too. How about the Secretary? Chasing any young service women down the corridors yet? Any young service *men?* There must be something we can get on Loy Buck. He isn't *perfect.*"

"Just about," Herb said, a reluctant admiration coming into his voice in spite of his aversion to all such authoritarian figures. "Loy Buck is pretty near perfect as far as I can see. As people go around here."

"As people go around here," she said tartly, "nobody's perfect. Keep an eye on him. There's got to be something. How about Zeecy McCune? *He's* a chaser."

"He keeps it under control," Herb said. He grinned. "Or Mrs. McCune does. Anyway, he's too smart. And too high up. Everybody would cover for Zeecy."

"Again," Delight said, "not *everybody.* Keep at it."

"I *will* 'keep at it,' " Herb promised, a certain annoyance coming finally into his voice at this repeated admonition. "I'm not *dumb,* Delight. And no slouch, either."

"Of course you're not," she said, patting his hand comfortingly. She frowned. "Now what is Skip Framberg doing over there with Red Roberts? I thought they only let Skip out of his cage on alternate Wednesdays."

"I don't know," Herb admitted, glancing over his shoulder at the table by the window where the deposed former director of Test and Evaluation was lunching with the Pentagon correspondent of *The Wall Street Journal.* "Maybe giving him a story."

"A story we ought to have," Delight said sternly. "Keep after him."

Skip Framberg was tall, thin, rangy, red-haired, in his early forties. He appeared to be self-consciously defiant, as he always did since his demotion when he appeared in public with members of the media. Red Roberts at sixty-one was dean of the Pentagon press corps, having tramped the corridors with notable success for thirty years. His nickname did not come from the color of his hair but from the fact that as a young reporter he had been a most industrious womanizer who had come to work many mornings red-eyed from lack of sleep. This led, inevitably, first to "Red-Eye," and then, as marriage and advancing years curtailed the chase, to a permanent "Red," whose origins were now unknown to his younger colleagues. He always looked deceptively relaxed if not actually somnolent. He did not, however, miss a thing. He was generally regarded as the top Pentagon expert in the media. And—an increasingly rare trait in post-Watergate journalism—one of the fairest.

Now he noted the swift appraising glance from the *Defense Eye* table, just as he had noted similar glances earlier from Helen Clark and Shorty Murchison. To Delight he gave a skeptical nod, to Helen and Shorty a slight, satiric bow.

"Some of your best friends are here today," he observed dryly to Skip, who was toying halfheartedly with his scallops. "They're all wondering what the hell we're doing together and what kind of embarrassing story you're going to give me this time."

"Haven't got any," Skip said glumly. "Wish I had. I'd like to nail the bastards for you today. All bastards."

"Narrow your field of fire," Red suggested with a chuckle, hoping to head off one more of Skip's frequent and unfortunately boring recitals of how Loy Buck and the top brass had done him in for being honest and going public about that Army field test that had been so horribly botched and covered up. "Which particular bastard would you like to get if you really could?"

"Can't," Skip responded, still glumly. "They're all too well protected."

"Oh, you manage to embarrass 'em a bit now and then," Red said comfortably. "They all know you're down there in the basement beyond the purple water fountain."

"Might as well have the job of swabbing it out," Skip said. "Nothing much else to do these days."

"That's not the way I hear it," Red Roberts said, taking a shrewd shot in the dark. "What about that report?"

"What report?" Skip inquired with more animation.

"*You* know, for Christ's sake," Red said. "*That* report."

"Oh," Skip said. "So you heard about that? I wonder who—"

"Never mind 'who,' " Red said. "I want to know what, where, when, why. Which service is it this time? Air Force?"

"Army," Skip said tersely. "Getting too cozy with our friends from Strategic Industries, over there."

"Not Three Gs?"

"Not at the moment," Skip said. "No doubt they will, but at the moment it's S.I."

"What?"

"The usual," Skip said. "Entertainment. Free trips. Hotel bills. Overcharging."

"Sex?"

"With Ray Clark as Secretary of the Army?" Skip retorted with a gleam of humor. "Who needs more sex?"

Red snorted.

"Don't tell me S.I. has to provide *him* with any!"

"That's what I mean," Skip said. "But there are others who are not so fortunate as our distinguished Secretary."

"When do I get a copy of your report?" Red inquired. "In time for my next edition?"

"We'll see," Skip said. "I have to check out a few more things."

"All right," Red agreed. "But just don't give it to those two over there before I get it, o.k?" He nodded toward Delight and Herb, still glancing frequently in their direction.

"You have to admit," Skip said, "that *Defense Eye* does get a lot of exposure. I can release it to them without any documentation at all and they'll print it and raise enough hell so it gets picked up all over. Old-timers like you are so stuffy about *facts.*"

"You'd better be too, buster," Red said sternly, deciding it was time to bring this bruised but still hyperactive ego back to reality. "You still have a lot of clout with the media but you can sacrifice it very easily if you start swinging too wide. Some of my colleagues are quite willing to go with you as long as they think it will hurt the Pentagon, but there's still enough of us who have some principle so that you'll only hurt your own credibility in the long run. I like you, Skip, you got a raw deal, you're a good news source. But don't blow it."

"I won't," Skip said in an annoyed tone. "I'm not foolish, Red. But I think it's a good idea to keep a line out to everybody."

"Sure," Red said, "unless you put yourself in the position of being the eternal griper. Whistle-blowing is one thing, sour grapes is another. Too much of the latter and you lose the whole ball-game. Remember that."

"I will," Skip said in the same huffy tone. "And you remember I'm always keeping an eye out for things."

"Glad you are," Red said more lightly. "I know the way they feel about you in E Ring. They're afraid of you, Skip. Some of them think you really got shafted and even those who think you got what you deserved are damned worried about the trouble you can cause."

"But they were *wrong* on that test," Skip protested, so vehemently that the chief counselor of the embassy of Ghana, lunching at the next table with his counterpart from Algeria, looked over in open interest. "They were *wrong.*"

"Granted," Red said soothingly. "But keep it down, Skip, you don't want to make a scene. Granted, you blew that whistle and it needed to be blown. That was good."

"And they haven't changed a thing," Skip Framberg said bitterly. "Not one God damned thing. They're going right along just exactly the way they did before I released that report. They're so damned arrogant they make me furious. There are *lives* at stake in what they do. American boys are going to *die* because some of these tests are false and rigged so S.I. and Three Gs and the rest of them can keep their God damned errors and make their God damned profits. It's a crime. It's a *real crime.*"

"It is," Red Roberts agreed, reflecting how many times in thirty years he had written the stories of the whistle-blowers, all young, all earnest, all honest, all infuriated by the shortcomings of the Pentagon . . . and all making this seemingly inevitable transition from idealistic alarm-raisers—to media heroes—to perpetual complainers—to boring publicity hounds—to eventually innocuous characters silenced by their own notoriety and their inability to handle it on a moderate and measured basis that would enable them to continue to be effective and not just common scolds.

All the Pentagon had to do was hang tough and wait them out. They eventually took care of themselves, every time.

Skip Framberg, he estimated as Skip dug into his scallops with a sudden savagery and finally subsided, still grumbling, was about midway in his progression. He could still command enough media attention to raise some real hell and be of real embarrassment to the department. He still had many friends in the media, in the armed services and on the appropriations committees on the Hill. If something really big should happen and Skip should somehow get wind of it, he could still embarrass the Pentagon and perhaps have some effect on what it did. But it wouldn't last for long, Red reflected with the wisdom of three decades of experience. Another year and Old Skip would be old news indeed, virtually forgotten in his isolation out there beyond the purple water fountain.

"How about dessert?" he suggested. "And then let's catch the Metro back. Not much chance for a cab in this weather."

"Couldn't take one anyway," Skip said with a wry humor. "At least, I couldn't. They don't approve cabs for me on my expense account any longer. And they sure don't give me any official transportation."

"You mean Helen Clark and Shorty Murchison wouldn't give you a ride?" Red inquired with a grin. Skip snorted.

"They'd tie a rope around me and drag me behind their cars," he said. "But that would be about the extent of it."

They finished and gestured for the check, which Red paid. Helen Clark and Roger Venable, Shorty Murchison and Walter Stayman, Delight Jones and Herb Horowitz were doing the same. All around them luncheon was ending. The daily weekday show at Maison Blanche was almost over.

At the cloakroom Delight and Herb found themselves in line just behind Helen and Roger. No one spoke, but a wry and sardonic expression crossed Roger's face for a moment. Studied and open contempt was on Helen's. Delight exchanged glances with Herb; both for a moment looked furious, before they remembered where they were and smoothed out their faces into the standard bland expression official Washington uses when people do not like one another.

"Bitch," Delight said audibly as they followed the other two out the door.

"Bastard," Herb agreed with equal volume as they emerged into the driving snow.

"Let's take my publicly owned, taxpayer-supported, evilly-misused official Pentagon limousine, Roger," Helen said in a clear, distinct voice. "I'll drop you off at your office."

"With pleasure," Roger Venable said with a chuckle.

"Make it splatter, driver," he suggested as they climbed quickly in and slammed the door.

"God damn!" Delight exclaimed as she grabbed Herb's arm and jumped back. "They are *too much.*" She stood hands on hips watching the DoD sedan crunch away down the drifted street. *"Son of a bitch!"*

"Don't worry," Herb promised. "They'll pay for it."

"You bet they will," she said viciously. "You bet they will. Where are you off to now?"

"I thought I'd swing by the White House pressroom for a bit," he said, "as long as we're this close. I haven't been in for a week or so."

"I'll join you," she said. She uttered a contemptuous little laugh. "All the trained seals ought to be back from lunch by now. Maybe we can pick up an item or two that nobody else has the guts to run."

They trudged through the snow along F Street toward 17th in companionable silence. As they started to cross 17th, unexpected activity down the street attracted their attention. A DoD limousine flying the Secretary's flag came up 17th from the Mall, swung right toward the southwest gate of the White House. Something about the speed with which it did so made the staff of *Defense Eye* instantly alert.

"What's going on?" Delight demanded.

"Don't know," Herb responded with quick-growing excitement. "Let's get to the pressroom and spread the word. Maybe we can find out."

They began to slosh and slither through the snow as fast as they could. But when they reached the pressroom all was quiet. The press secretary's office had absolutely nothing to say in response to the sudden spate of questions that Delight and Herb were able to generate with their report of unusual activity at the southwest gate.

On Nanukuvu the fire by now was out. Only a pile of ashes and a few bones remained. With quick efficiency the ashes were raked into the lagoon where they began their slow inexorable progress toward the open sea. The bones were shoveled into body-bags and transported to the great black whale where they would presently be weighted and sunk.

At a safe distance out the five helicopters from *Dominant* passed and repassed. None of Hague Smith's colleagues were as daring as he, now that his daring had produced so disastrous a result. Presently two jets flew over at top speed, automatic cameras taking thousands of frames a minute. The new occupants of the island, hidden in the trees, did not stir. Once again Nanukuvu appeared uninhabited. But the men of *Dominant* and their superiors all the way up to the Commander-in-Chief, now confronting a worried SecDef and an equally worried chairman of the Joint Chiefs in the Oval Office, knew differently.

After a few more distant passes by the helicopters, a few more very high passes by the jets, *Dominant* ordered them home. Just over the horizon the radar of the fishing boat assigned to monitor the carrier discovered no further aerial sorties. The satellite passing regularly overhead photographed no more unusual onboard activities.

Both the island and the seas around it appeared to be completely calm again.

From the great black whale the word went out to half a dozen siblings in the neighborhood in a code the Americans intercepted but were unable at the moment to understand:

It is safe. They are running, as usual.

With an ironic little smile the whale's commander tore up his contingency orders. They were identical with those given and destroyed a dozen times since Hitler invaded the Rhineland in 1936:

If you meet opposition, withdraw.

No such opposition ever having been offered by the democracies, no enemy commander had ever had to follow the orders.

The commander of the great black whale was confident that he need not follow them now.

Perhaps he was jumping too fast to this conclusion.

But again, perhaps not.

Certainly he could not be faulted for thinking the historic odds were in his favor.

"Start from the beginning," the President suggested, chin resting on folded hands, shrewd eyes studying their somber faces, "and tell me all about it."

"Let me defer to Gen. McCune," the Secretary suggested. "He's talked directly to CINCPAC."

"And CINCPAC has talked to the aircraft carrier *Dominant*," Zeecy said. "And *Dominant* talked briefly to the boy who was lost. They don't know a great deal. He was a helicopter pilot on routine patrol near the Gilbert Islands. He reported an unusual cloud rising over an island which is called on our maps Nanukuvu—"

"Inhabited?" the President inquired.

"Nobody ever thought so," Zeecy said. "It was officially designated as uninhabited on our maps and also on those of Britain, Australia, New Zealand and Japan. Apparently, however, there were inhabitants, and the cloud this young fellow Hague Smith saw was apparently enemy action directed against them. The cloud was small but apparently could be construed as somewhat mushroom-shaped and he assumed that it must have been some kind of small atomic explosion, although by the time he got to the island it had dissipated. If his instruments did pick up any radiation, the record was lost when his helicopter was shot down. It may have been some combination of neutron bomb and gas bomb, of a nature not common but, as you know, possible. In any event, before he could reach the island this oddly-shaped cloud had been blown away by the trade winds. It was succeeded by another, more conventional pillar of smoke rising from a fire on the island. He was curious and went right on in, against orders, and unhappily for him, with fatal results. He was able to make two full passes over the island before being shot down, and reported that the smoke cloud was rising from what appeared to be a funeral pyre. He was able to perceive a sizable number of bodies, apparently those of the inhabitants, being consumed by the flames. At that point he was eliminated by the enemy and transmission ceased. Since then the island has been scouted by helicopters and jets from the carrier and it has been concluded that there is at least one enemy submarine, of the largest class, in the lagoon of the island. They are using intense stealth cover and massive jamming, but just enough signals have been picked up to indicate there might be others in the vicinity. Possibly as many as half a dozen, we think.

"It appears to be a well-planned action to take over the island of Nanukuvu and transform it into a major base servicing the entire Soviet submarine fleet in that area of the South Pacific. Which area, incidentally, is supposed to be under *our* informal but de facto control and protection."

"How strategic is Nanukuvu?" the President inquired.

A disgusted expression crossed the chairman's face for a moment.

"Well, *now,* of course," he said with some dryness, "it is *very* strategic indeed. And if all of our high-level thinkers in the Pentagon had been on their toes and giving some attention to strategic planning instead of how to protect their own turf, we would have recognized this a long time ago and gotten in there first. Our relations with most of those peoples down there are good, we could have worked out some sort of arrangement to use the island ourselves if it is that ideally suited for a base. Or at least we could have arranged and publicized a formal protective agreement that would have kept the enemy out. He doesn't like to come in where we're firmly established, or where we've given advance notice that we'll move if he does. But nobody," he concluded acidly, "thought of that."

"Why didn't you?" the President inquired with some dryness of his own.

"Because I depend on the people below me!" Gen. McCune retorted.

"So do I," the President remarked mildly, and for a minute or two nobody said anything because there wasn't much of anything to say. Then Loy Buck cleared his throat and leaned forward.

"If there's any responsibility for this," he said calmly, "it's mine and I take it. No doubt the services should be considering every possible strategic possibility in the world—"

"Yes, I think they should," the President interrupted. "That's their job, isn't it? You're not tryin' to tell me it's up to civilians like you and me, are you, Loy? Wait a minute. We can pass along our bright ideas when we are given sufficient facts to have them, but it's the military who're supposed to be thinkin' about these things mornin', noon and night. Somethin' missin' in that system over there, Zeecy, don't you think so?"

"Mr. President," Zeecy said, "with respect but some annoyance—justified, I think—I must point out that when you and I were young instructors together at the Air Force Academy in Colorado Springs, I wrote a paper and submitted it to the then JCS advocating a much larger role for long-range strategic thought and planning in the Pentagon. I've been a consistent advocate of that ever since and every time I've had the operative power to do so, I've ordered it done. I don't feel I've been derelict."

"Not sayin' you have, Zeecy," the President said mildly, "but when you ordered it done, *was* it done?"

Zeecy sighed.

"Not always, Mr. President," he admitted. "Not always. In fact, not anywhere near as often as it should have been. In spite of my orders and those of many others. Things sometimes don't proceed that neatly, in the military."

"But why not?" the President demanded with a sudden anger. "Why the hell not? What's the matter with all those lazy bastards over there?"

"Nobody's lazy, Chuck," Zeecy said sharply. The Secretary nodded vigorous agreement. "It's the system. I've given the orders, time and again. The Secretary has given the orders. A lot has been done—a hell of a lot. I don't want you to get the idea that *no* strategic planning and *no* overall thought is given to these things, in the Pentagon—that would be an absurd conclusion. But take me, for an example. I give the order—it goes down the line—other people give their orders—somewhere along the way maybe there *is* a weak link—somebody doesn't move as fast as he or she should—the chain of command slows down a bit. Meanwhile, I've moved on to some other assignment—or Joe Blow has, or Suzy Smith, or whoever—and sometimes it has to start all over again. Too often it just doesn't get done as fast as it should—if it gets done at all. Plus the fact that the way the system is set up now, we don't put the emphasis on planning that we ought to, and we don't give the rewards for it that we ought to. We still suffer from the command syndrome: if you want to get your bars or stars you've got to get out in the field and command the troops. We don't devote enough time and top manpower to just plain *thinking*. If we did, we'd be in a hell of a lot better shape vis-à-vis the enemy than we are. And things like Nanukuvu wouldn't take us by surprise."

"And whose job is it to correct that situation?" the President inquired.

"Everybody's," Gen. McCune said.

"And consequently nobody's," the President said wryly.

"We're working on it," Loy Buck said and the President smiled.

"Oh, sure. Just like I'm workin' on it in the Executive Branch. We're not perfect over here, either, you know. It has somethin' to do with everybody bein' human beings, I think. But—" his smile faded and he looked more grim—"we can't always afford that luxury. Particularly you in the military . . . And so—Nanukuvu. What do we do about it?"

"My instinct is to go in and blast them out of there," Gen. McCune said. "Right now."

"Half a dozen subs?" the President inquired. "That's quite an undertaking, Zeece."

"It will be more of a one six months from now," Zeecy McCune observed. "Or even six weeks."

"Even one week," the Secretary said. "I don't imagine they intend to be idle, now they're there."

"They're in a good position," the President agreed.

"And it can only get better," Loy Buck said. "Unless we act, as Zeecy says, and act now . . ." He paused and for a second studied this sometimes strong, sometimes equivocal figure before him. What a political chameleon he was! But, then, weren't all good Presidents?

Loy's expression became stern, his voice blunt. "Do you want us to go in, Mr. President?"

The famed caution—the look of careful, withdrawn, inner calculation Loy had come to know well in three years' association with this powerful, secretive man, and that Zeecy had known ever since they had been classmates—came into the President's eyes. As usual when pressed, he did not respond directly.

"They *are* in a good position, aren't they?" he repeated thoughtfully. "They often seem to get themselves in a good position, in these confrontations. Why is that?"

"Because they think aggressively and we think defensively," Gen. McCune said crisply. "It's as simple as that."

The President smiled.

"So we're back to thinkin' again . . . so what do *I* think we ought to do? I think if I had my way we'd do exactly what you two suggest. We'd go in and blast the hell out of 'em." He held up a hand at their instinctive movement. "Unfortunately it's not that simple, from where I sit. There are lots of things to consider, not least of 'em bein' whether we *could* go in and blast the hell out of 'em. And that brings us back to you fellows in the Pentagon. Can you? How ready are you? What do you have to put into it? How united would the services be? What kind of strategy could you work out? Those are the questions I have to have answered before *I* can decide anythin'. Have you had a JCS meeting about it yet?"

"Haven't had time," Loy pointed out in a tone just this side of exasperation. "We came here the minute we heard because we wanted to get some guidance from you, Mr. President."

"And here I am wantin' it from *you!*" the President said with a chuckle. "Chasin' each other around Robin Hood's barn, aren't we? Leastways, around the White House. Why don't you go back over there and huddle with your colleagues and *then* let me know what you think?"

"We can't take forever, Mr. President," Zeecy said tartly. The President looked mildly surprised.

"Nobody said you could, Zeecy. I'm contemplatin' a JCS meetin' just as soon as you can get everybody together after you get back in the buildin'. Let's see—" he glanced at the ornate watch with gold-nugget band that he had been given when he campaigned in Alaska, first Presidential candidate ever to do so —"it's gettin' on for 3 o'clock. Suppose you report back to me here by 6 P.M., how's that? In fact, I tell you what. For once in a blue moon there's not a damned thing on the social calendar in this busy house. Why don't you both come back for dinner and we'll have a National Security Council meetin'. Got to have one on this anyway, sooner or later. Might as well get right to it, don't you think, Loy?"

"I am pleased to see, Mr. President," the Secretary said with a smile, "that despite outward appearances of calmness and placidity, you do attach a certain amount of urgency to this matter just as we do."

"Hell," the President said with his charming by-God-you've-caught-me grin, "I'm upset as you are about it, Loy. I couldn't be more upset. I think we ought to kick those bastards so hard they wouldn't know what hit 'em. But—" his expression sobered, his tone became grave. "But I've got to be sure we can do it, first. So get on back over there and get busy and I'll see you here again at six. Tell everybody's wives I apologize for upsettin' their plans, but that's the way it goes."

"They're military," Zeecy McCune said with the unconscious complacency of the fighting male from time immemorial. "They'll understand."

The Secretary's limousine was waiting for them under the South Portico. The snow had finally stopped. Six inches lay on the District.

"Can we make it back over the river, driver?" Loy asked the young black staff sergeant who always drove him.

"It'll be a little slow, sir," the driver said with a grin, "but we'll make it." He chuckled with the familiarity of three years' friendship. "Even the Lord wouldn't dare stop the Secretary of Defense and the chairman of the JCS."

"You tell Him that, Parker," Gen. McCune suggested. "We want to be sure He understands."

Loy touched the button that raised the glass between front seat and back.

"What do you make of your friend?" he asked when it had guaranteed privacy.

Zeecy looked grim.

"Oh, he's worried. He's worried as hell. And so am I."

"Make that three," Loy Buck said. "About to become more."

As they drove slowly out the southwest gate six heavily overcoated figures stood huddled together awaiting their passage. They recognized Red Roberts, Delight Jones and Herb Horowitz, didn't know the others but knew they must be members of the White House press corps.

Red waved, with some irony. In the same spirit, they waved back.

"God damn!" Zeecy exclaimed. "They're like cockroaches. You find 'em everywhere."

"I hope they freeze their balls off," Loy Buck said with a chuckle. "Including Delight Jones."

But for all their amicable joking they knew that it was already a question as to whether the problem of Nanukuvu could be kept out of the media long enough for them to devise a viable solution.

On the island the new inhabitants, convinced, perhaps prematurely, that they would have a free hand, were wasting no time.

Summoned as soon as the squadron commander had decided that no opposition or further reaction would be forthcoming from *Dominant* or any other member of the armed forces of the United States, a sister submarine now lay alongside on the surface of the lagoon just a few yards from the place where A'afaloa, Nuku'ofa and their families had only that morning so innocently begun the day they had thought would be like all the others.

This was apparently the chief supply ship. From it a steady stream of small inflatable boats went to the beach, offloaded, returned to the mother ship, reloaded, returned to the beach.

Under the trees a contingent of perhaps a hundred men, also from this vessel, busily stacked building materials, stored caches of food and explosives, worked as impersonally and industriously as ants to prepare for the blasting, excavation and construction that would very soon, they intended, transform the island into a formidable fortress from which they could be dislodged only by the most extreme and difficult measures.

They all expected that there would now be nonmilitary challenges to be met, problems to be solved, diplomatic crises or at least tensions to be overcome, at the Moscow level.

These did not concern the commander. His initial mission had been accomplished. Its succeeding stages were already well underway. He and his men and their countrymen on the other submarines that lay around the island were in command of the situation. It was quite clear, as all remained quiet on *Dominant* and no signs of other activity were reported to them from around the South Pacific, that the United States had no intention of initiating a military response at this time. Later, they were confident, would be too late.

Presently the men under the trees began to sing while they went about their work. It was a pleasant sound, as the seagulls cried and the land-birds called and the soft caressing breezes blew through the rustling palms of peaceful Nanukuvu.

Loy Buck had already told Imogene, and in short order after the chairman of the Joint Chiefs returned to the Pentagon the other wives knew too. Doreen Tock was upset because she had to cancel her dinner party, but managed to be reasonably philosophical. Violet Burford felt a sudden pang of desolation because she had been counting on Brash's bluff presence to soothe her still uneasy concerns about what she referred to in her own mind as "my little episode." Zenia Stokes felt an impatient annoyance because this was to have been her night to attend a meeting of black wives on base to frame a resolution against South Africa, while Ham stayed home with the two younger children: now she would have to baby-sit, there was no time to get someone else. Renee McCune, adjusting smoothly as she always did after thirty years in the service, reflected calmly that now she could finish the book on Gen. De Gaulle that had intrigued her so much in recent days without having Zeecy underfoot to feed and entertain, or at least be reasonably cordial to—which she didn't mind, but they did find each other boring sometimes, there was no getting around it.

The thought brought an ironic smile. Half the women in the world wanted the chairman of the Joint Chiefs. She had him, and she was bored. Ah, well, *le mariage!* It was always so *incroyable.*

None of the chiefs voiced the thought and none of the wives had to have it spelled out, but they all knew that once the fatal words were uttered—"Hi. I'm afraid I'm going to be a little late tonight"—it meant that the whole evening was gone. Despite earnest protestations that they would be "not too late—keep something hot for me"—once the chiefs got involved in something it always seemed, from their wives' perspective, to go on and on, interminably.

None of the wives, of course, asked any questions, or protested very much, or allowed much disappointment to show: such stoicism went with being in the military, as Gen. McCune had somewhat complacently remarked to the President. Whatever feelings they had, they buried; whatever inconveniences they might suffer, they did not mention—or at least not very much. Nor did they feel any pangs of suspicion or jealousy, with the possible exception of Zenia Stokes, who sometimes, lately, found herself reflecting with some bewilderment that she seemed to be reaching a point with Ham where she could neither live with him nor without him. She *believed* that something unexpected had come up to keep him at the Pentagon; or did she? She *knew* that he was telling the truth when he indicated it was a serious matter that might keep him late; or did she? She was confident that he was faithful to her; or was he?

She gave her head an angry shake. Her long black hair swirled wildly for a moment around her small, pretty, clever face. She didn't know what kind of state she was getting herself into but she knew it wasn't good.

"You be careful, girl," she told herself as she caught her reflection in the mirror in the dining room, "or they're going to come get you in a big—black—bus."

Still and all, she *was* mad at Ham—at the Pentagon—at whatever it was that had upset her plans, meticulously organized as always, for the evening.

In "the tank"—the so-called "Gold Room" of the Pentagon, in the restricted labyrinth opposite SecDef's office on E Ring, where the Joint Chiefs hold their most confidential, no-holds-barred discussions—Gen. Zoren Chace McCune was waiting impatiently for his colleagues just before 4 P.M. Collectively they were known as "the pachyderms" to the junior officers who manned the area, and sometimes the speed at which they moved seemed to him to justify the term.

Across the hall the Secretary had returned to his office to confer with Joe Strang and such others as he might deem helpful on the subject of Nanukuvu. Ideally, he would find consensus on the best course to follow. Zeecy's task also was to find reasonable agreement among his colleagues. Later he and Loy could put it all together at the National Security Council meeting at the White House.

He knew the JCS discussion would probably be heated and lengthy. He had already called the President and suggested that it might make more sense to hold the NSC meeting at seven instead of six. The Chief Executive had agreed without a murmur.

"Y'all are goin' to be eatin' dinner here anyway, you know," he said amiably. "Might as well start it at a semi-civilized hour. Let me know if it appears to be gettin' even later."

"I will," Zeecy promised. "But I think we can wrap it up by then. I'll do my damnedest, anyway."

And he would, too, he thought, if he could keep Brash from being too ebullient, Tick too prickly, Ham too sarcastic and Bumpy too terse and humorless. What a crew! Never a dull moment, in the JCS. His eyes strayed to their formal picture on the wall, taken two years ago when he had become chairman. By *God,* they looked impressive!

And so they were, he acknowledged with a grin.

But human.

God, *yes.*

"What are you grinning about, you old Cheshire cat?" Ham Stokes inquired as he was shown in, very deferentially, by a young Air Force lieutenant—the same one, Zeecy remembered, to whom he had given a dressing-down this morning. What was his name? Brad—Brod. Broderick Tolliver, was it?

"Brod," he said, smiling cordially; and to Ham, "You've got a good man, there, Harmon."

"I have?" Ham said in mild surprise, turning to look at the lieutenant, who blushed. "I'm glad you told me, Zeece. I'll keep an eye on him."

"Do," Zeecy suggested, riding on the instinct that had rarely failed him in judging the caliber of his troops. "How's it going, Brod, all right?"

"Oh, yes, sir," Brod Tolliver said. *"Thank* you, sir!"

"You're welcome," Zeecy said. "Keep up the good work."

"Yes, sir!" Brod said fervently as he stepped nimbly aside to permit General Burford to enter. "I *will!"*

He saluted smartly and left.

"Seems to be a willing type," Ham remarked as he took a chair. "Friend of yours?"

"Not particularly," Gen. McCune said. "I gave him a chewing-out this morning, which he took very well—for somebody else. Seems to be a nice kid. I just thought I'd encourage him."

"Always glad to cooperate with good material," Ham Stokes said. "I *will* pay attention to him."

Zeecy felt the satisfaction he got from assisting the occasional young officer he met who reminded him, in some wistfully nebulous but heart-tugging way, of the son he and Renee had never had. Thus, he reflected, do military careers get assisted up the ladder. Sometimes on merit, sometimes on hunch, sometimes on liking, sometimes on a combination of all three. He thought he too would keep track of Brod Tolliver, particularly if the tentative plan he had in mind became reality and he needed, as he thought he might, a direct channel into what was happening.

"Brash," he said, "how did it go on the Hill this morning?"

The chief of staff of the Army snorted.

"The usual crap. Why don't we do this and why don't we do that, and don't forget my district or my state when you start passing out the goodies. Christ." He rubbed his eyes, obviously tired; also, Gen. McCune sensed, worried, though Brash thought he was concealing it.

"What's the matter? Did they really give you a hard time?"

Brash frowned as Bumpy Stahlman and Tick Tock came in together, nodded and took their seats.

"It's Vi," he said. "Something's bothering her. She wouldn't tell me what over the phone, and she denied it when I challenged her, of course. But you know how it is. After so many years, you get the signals."

"Dorry's worried, too," Gen. Tock said. "She told me about it."

Brash looked openly concerned for a moment. Then he took a deep breath and shook his head as if to clear it. His hands, which had ever so slightly trembled, became still. He was ready for action.

"Enough of that," he said firmly. "Whatever it is, it's my problem and I'll find out later. What's our problem here, Zeece?"

They listened in complete silence and absolute concentration as the chairman once again tersely recited the story of Hague Smith and the occupation of Nanukuvu.

"I asked the Defense Mapping Agency to send over their rendering of the island," he concluded, touching a button on a slide projector at his elbow. "This is it."

The lazy U of Nanukuvu, enlarged a dozen times, filled the screen that covered one wall. Still silently and with great concentration they studied it.

"Any photographs?" Bumpy Stahlman asked.

"None," Gen. McCune said. "Don't know why. Nobody ever considered it important enough, I suppose."

They continued to study it intently for several more minutes.

Tick Tock reached over and took the illuminated pointer that lay beside the projector. Its lighted arrow danced across the screen and came to rest on the outer edge of the base of the U.

"If you guys," he said to Ham Stokes, "or you guys," he said to Bumpy Stahlman, "or the two of you together, can bomb the vegetation off that flat area, the Marines can go in there with acceptable losses—or if we're lucky, with very few at all."

"If you're very damned lucky, I'd say," Brash Burford observed. "Give me that thing, Tick."

"Pleasure," Gen. Tock said, shoving it across the table.

"It seems that the Army's best bet," Gen. Burford said, "is to go in here—" the arrow rested for a moment to the right of the base of the small volcano on the right, then swung across to a comparable position to the left of the base of the volcano on the left—"and here. You're going to need some initial screening, no matter how much hell is bombed out of the place. Why not use the volcanoes as cover and then fan out there and meet in the middle? That's the way we're going to go about it."

"Oh, are you?" Gen. Tock inquired, beginning to look belligerent. "It hasn't been decided *whose* mission it's going to be, yet."

"I don't really see why the Air Force has to get into it at all, myself," Adm. Stahlman observed in an aloof tone. "We have another carrier, the *Vinson,* presently in the area, and together she and *Dominant* can certainly loft enough planes to take care of it. I don't think you people need to get involved at all, Ham."

Gen. Stokes leaned forward, big hands outthrust on the table like the paws of a lion.

"Well, don't you, now," he said, ever-present sarcasm beginning to surface. "That's very big of you, Bumpy. Always nice to know the Navy is concerned for the welfare of the Air Force. However, with the bombers we can bring in from Guam and Clark Field we can take care of it in one-tenth the time it would take you to do the job. And we could get there a lot quicker, too. I have a feeling the bastards aren't standing still: I'd guess they're in a hurry."

"They can't have very much in place," Gen. Burford pointed out. "It only happened this morning, after all."

"Which brings us," Gen. McCune said, "to the key point at the moment: should we make a response at all? What am I supposed to recommend to Loy and the President when the NSC meets? Strike? No strike? Hit 'em? Forget 'em? Bottle 'em up, blast 'em to hell, starve 'em out, ignore 'em? Let's get a few options on the table here. We can fight over who does the fighting, later."

"Good old Zeecy," Ham Stokes said with a laugh Bumpy Stahlman considered a trifle too hearty. "Always trying to keep us on the subject."

"You bet," Gen. McCune said crisply. "Somebody has to, and that's my job. Shall we take a vote?"

"How about a little discussion first?" Brash Burford demanded, not so amicably. "Don't try to railroad us, Zeece. It won't work here."

"Well I know," Zeecy acknowledged with a deliberately mournful air that made them all laugh and reduced the tension somewhat. "Would that it could. O.K., discuss. Just remember the Secretary and I have to go to the White House by about six-thirty."

"We have a while yet," Ham Stokes said, subjecting his watch to elaborate scrutiny. "My opinion is, we ought to go in and blast them, sooner the better."

"That was my initial reaction too," Gen. McCune said, "and that's fine, as long as it doesn't get into the media in advance. *Fait accompli,* well and good, but we can't have them breathing down our necks to begin with."

"Surely they don't know anything about it yet!" Bumpy Stahlman objected. "How could that happen?"

"No, they don't, yet," Zeecy agreed. "But they did see Loy and me at the White House earlier, and I'm sure they're sniffing like mad trying to find out why, right now."

"Thank God for the snowstorm," Ham Stokes said. "At least it reduces mobility a little. But not the telephone, of course. Anyway, who's talking?"

"Nobody, yet," Gen. Burford said, "but if it becomes a major problem, and our response has to become major, somebody will."

"We can meet that when it comes," Bumpy Stahlman said. "Right now, I gather it already *is* a major problem for us."

Without comment Zeecy advanced the projector and threw another slide on the screen. The entire South Pacific jumped out at them. Squarely astride most of its main routes of sea and air travel lay the big red circle that from now on in all their minds would surround the infinitesimal dot that was Nanukuvu.

"Bastards chose well, didn't they?" Tick Tock remarked. "Must have studied the map quite a while, to figure that one out. We should have been there first."

"Well," Gen. McCune said tartly. "We weren't."

"The story of our lives," Ham Stokes observed wryly. "So, come on!" he urged with sudden impatience. "Let's get 'em out of there!"

"You want a response, then," Zeecy said.

"Of course I want a response!" Gen. Stokes said sharply. "Hell, look at that map! You didn't mark it that way for us if *you* didn't want a response, did you, Zeece?"

"No," Zeecy said. "Of course not. Brash?"

"In one way, I don't see how we can avoid it," Gen. Burford said slowly. "In another, I wonder if we can't achieve the same end by some other means. I'm not sure we'll get public—or Congressional—support for a military action that far away, in such a remote area."

"Hell, they'll never know!" Ham Stokes said, pounding one huge hand on the table for emphasis. "They'll never know! We'll get in there, get out and get it over with. At least," he added pointedly, *"we* will. Of course if you want great big grandstand plays with amphibious landings, hand-to-hand combat, inch-by-inch heroics, all banners flying—"

"I resent that!" Gen. Tock snapped.

"And so do I!" Brash Burford agreed. "Nobody's grandstanding. We all want the quickest and most efficient operation—"

"Air, then," Gen. Stokes said flatly. "Air. It's the only way."

"And water," Adm. Stahlman said with frosty emphasis. "After all, it *is* an island."

"How true," Ham Stokes said sarcastically. "How true, Bumpy."

"And again we're off the track," Gen. McCune said with a sudden interruptive vigor that took them all by surprise, even though it was a rhetorical device he often used. "Will you guys for Christ's sake calm down and let's make the initial decision? Do we respond or don't we?"

"Of course," Bumpy Stahlman said calmly.

"Certainly," said Ham Stokes.

"In some way or other," Brash Burford agreed.

"Look at the map," Tick Tock said with a shrug. "You didn't use your red pencil for nothing, Zeecy."

"And I too," Gen. McCune agreed, "say yes. Now I'd suggest you all go back to your offices and get your top people to work on it and draw up your plan as though each of you was the dominant service. That way we'll have four options ready—"

"By when?" Ham Stokes inquired, and put up a playful arm as though to ward off the blow. "Don't say tonight."

"By the time Loy and I get back from the White House," Gen. McCune said briskly, "which should be around ten o'clock. You've already told the gals you won't be home for dinner, might as well put in some useful time around here."

"Slave-driver," Brash Burford said cheerfully.

"Masterful leader," Ham Stokes corrected with a grin.

"Damned dictator," Tick Tock growled, but amicably.

"Necessary," Bumpy Stahlman observed. "Necessary."

"Don't kid me, Bumpy," Ham said. "You've already got the Navy's plan all drawn up, in your head."

"Possibly," Adm. Stahlman said with what was, for him, a rare approach to jocularity. "The most brilliant things sometimes come the fastest."

"Oh, my," Zeecy said. "On that note, let's scatter."

"Let's," Gen. Stokes said, "before I throw up."

But as soon as they left the tank the light mood changed again to somber. The map imposed its own imperatives. The island deserved to be ringed in red. It would demand of them, they knew, much more than they had yet begun to contemplate, before the problem of Nanukuvu could be considered solved.

"What we've got to do over here," the Secretary said, "is pull together some kind of basic approach to the matter so that we can take it to the NSC meeting at seven. We know very well what the State Department's will be."

"Patty-cake, patty-cake, baker's man," Joe Strang suggested dryly. "Just *make* us be rude to them—*if you can!*"

Loy Buck smiled.

"Not quite that bad, Joe. You're a little rough on Terry and his friends. I think we can convince them of the strategic necessity for some kind of strong response. Particularly since the President seems to be disposed that way himself."

"The President," Joe Strang remarked, "is a weather-vane."

"And why shouldn't he be?" Bob Cathcart demanded sharply. "Isn't that his job, to reflect public opinion?"

"Some of us think, lead public opinion," Loy said calmly, before the Under Secretary of Defense for Policy could come back with a sharp retort to the Deputy Secretary of Defense.

Bob Cathcart flushed and gave the Secretary a hostile look across the expanse of the Pershing desk.

"I wonder if he knows there's disloyalty in the Pentagon toward him?" he inquired dourly. The Secretary shrugged.

"Why don't you tell him, Bob? I've just been over there seeing him and he didn't seem particularly disturbed by my presence or worried about my loyalty. But why don't you tell him about it?"

"Well—" Bob Cathcart said lamely. "Well— . . . How do we know," he demanded abruptly, "that the situation on this so-called 'strategic island' is as bad as the military say it is, anyway?"

The Secretary gave an exasperated sigh.

"For Christ's sake, Bob, Zeecy McCune doesn't lie! It's been reported to him accurately from the field, and he reported it accurately to me, and together we reported it accurately to the President. *You're* here because you're Deputy Secretary of Defense, which is something I can't do much about, and because as a matter of courtesy I feel you should be kept informed. What are you going to do now, call all your pals on the Hill and in the media and get them all excited about it before we've worked out an effective plan to cope? That would be an enormous help, all right. I'm sure the President would consider *that* loyal."

"You can tell the President," Bob Cathcart said angrily, "or I will—that there's a very deep division over here in the Pentagon as to what should be done about it."

Joe Strang nodded.

"A very deep division. You—and the rest of us. What do *you* think we should do, Mr. Secretary? Nothing?"

"I think we can afford to ignore it, yes," Secretary Cathcart said; and at their surprised and annoyed expressions, slammed the flat of his hand on the desk. "And why not?" he demanded. "What difference does it make if they have some piddling little base down there? They're in the area, they've been there for years, we've always known it. We're there too. So what? This isn't going to give them any great new advantage they haven't had already. After all, we have Guam—and we also have some other bases down there that we've always been damned secretive about, that the American public and our allies don't know about, but I'll bet the Soviets know about them, and have right along! I'll bet it's no secret to them!"

"It obviously won't be if you have your way, Mr. Secretary," Joe Strang snapped, round little face flushing angrily and round little body almost visibly quivering with indignation. "Haven't you told them?"

"By *God!*" Bob Cathcart roared, either in genuine anger or well-staged ferocity, they weren't sure which, "by *God,* I'm not going to take your aspersions on my patriotism and loyalty, you—you little *foreigner!*"

"You're too much!" Joe Strang cried, jumping to his feet. "You're too much, you—you—you silly *ass!*"

"Both of you!" Loy Buck said, rising to his feet and pointing sternly to their chairs. "Both of you, *sit down! SIT DOWN!*"

And presently, glaring at one another and breathing heavily, they did. Silence ensued. After it had gone on long enough the Secretary spoke in a cold and level tone.

"That is the last time that I ever want to see or hear that kind of exhibition by grown men in my office. You are obviously out of sympathy with the purpose of this discussion, Secretary Cathcart, so I would suggest you leave and not concern yourself with the matter any further. I will not go to the lengths of Secretary Strang, but I will express my hope that you will keep this matter confidential. American lives—many American lives—may well be at risk before this episode is over. It is imperative that it be entirely secret at this stage. Do I have your word on that?"

For several seconds Bob Cathcart stared at him, face red and working. Then he spoke in a husky, still furious voice.

"It is an insult to ask and it would be degrading to answer. I am not a schoolboy, Loy Buck. And I can make plenty of trouble. And I *will* leave!"

And he got up, stomped over to the door, flung it open and stomped out.

Vangie appeared briefly, a startled expression on her face. Loy shook his head, lifted his hands in a wry what-can-you-do? gesture and waved her away. She smiled briefly and closed the door. Joe Strang gave a lengthy sigh.

"I must apologize to you, Mr. Secretary," he said, voice trembling and accent becoming very precise as it did in moments of stress, "I expect if he had chosen to remain I would, after a few moments, have apologized to him. But he is such a—such a—*boor.* Fortunately he does not have many friends in the Department of Defense or you would have a real problem on your hands."

"He doesn't need friends here," Loy said ruefully, "as long as he has them elsewhere. I don't *think* he can do us much damage at the White House in view of the kind of crisis this is, but he can conceivably do us a lot in other places."

"I don't think he will, do you?" Joe inquired in a worried tone. "I mean, he wouldn't *really* do anything to hurt the country—"

Loy shook his head.

"Oh, no, not deliberately and not with any unpatriotic motivations, certainly. But ego does funny things, in this town. He might do a lot of damage just from sheer pique and wanting to be difficult. We'll have to hope it doesn't happen. Meanwhile, why don't you write me a quick position paper and get it to me by—" he glanced at his watch—"six-fifteen."

Joe Strang nodded, obviously relieved to be diverted back to familiar ground. "Jason Bard and Jim Craft are already working on it. I assume Zeecy won't have any trouble getting the JCS to go along, will he?"

"I'm sure they're agreed there's got to *be* a response," Loy Buck said with some wryness. "How—and when—and by whom—may be another matter. But that's not the main problem. The main problem is to get the President to agree. And that—" he remembered the Chief Executive's earlier equivocal response —"may not be so easy."

After Joe left he told Vangie to hold his calls and sat at his desk for a few minutes doing absolutely nothing—a practice he had adopted long ago in his first corporate days when it occurred to him that unless he deliberately made time for himself to think, he would probably not have any time at all. It was his habit to clear his mind of everything at the end of the day—not the end of *this* day, probably, because he had an idea this day had quite a few more hours to run—and then let things float back in of their own volition and in their own sequence.

There was no question what would predominate. The usual concerns—all revolving around either the progress of the various military authorization and appropriations bills on the Hill, or around the major areas of continuing enemy pressure around the world—were suddenly insignificant alongside a tiny red-circled island in the South Pacific.

There was no doubt where the focus of Washington—or of that little group of operative figures who really *are* "Washington"—lay now.

Nanukuvu was not a name any of them had heard before. It was now a name that none of them would ever forget. Before long, he was sure, its unfamiliar syllables would become public knowledge and spread far, far beyond the hitherto peaceful waters that were now the newest area of dispute.

Meanwhile there was what had been called, at various times and in various contexts, a "window of opportunity"—in this case the opportunity for the Pentagon, the State Department, the White House and those very few people on the Hill who really could contribute something helpful, to work out a strategy that would defuse what he had recognized immediately as a blatant and deliberate Soviet challenge—before it had sufficient time to freeze into a permanent part of Soviet strategy and Soviet power.

For the moment, this could, with luck, be done in secrecy—that secrecy which, in a sentimental sense, Americans always deplored but which, in a practical sense, they knew was sometimes necessary if anything at all was to be accomplished free from the withering blast of public scrutiny. There would be a time for that, justifiable and necessary. But right now, he hoped fervently that whatever might have to be done could be decided and set in motion before the whole wide world got into the act.

He was certain, even before Joe returned an hour later with a strongly-worded position paper and Zeecy called to say the Joint Chiefs were agreed on the necessity for some form of response, that the Pentagon would go into the meeting united. So would the State Department. The others, including Al Brodovsky, the national security adviser, and Eben Hartman, the director of Central Intelligence, would be the swing votes. The Vice President, a carefully neutral little political accident from New Jersey, was out of town attending a state funeral. Only one vote really mattered anyway: the man at the head of the table.

Convincing the President, as he had remarked to Joe earlier, might not be so easy.

He sighed, suddenly aware that the building was silent all around him. The sense of enormous bustle that accompanied all the days, even when it was muffled by office walls and endless corridors, had diminished almost to nothing. Most of the staffs, as Vangie had predicted earlier to Imogene, had been allowed to leave in mid-afternoon, about the time the snow had stopped. Presumably most of them were safely home, warm and snug against the weather which now had turned bitterly cold with a strong wind blowing. Only in major offices and in the secret rooms where radar, satellites and telecommunications of all kinds reported in with their nonstop eavesdropping on the world were lights on, machines humming, intent faces illuminated as they leaned forward to study endless reams of tape, paper, memoranda and reports, or to talk by scrambler phone directly to the many military observers who monitored, around the clock, the open wounds of a constantly hemorrhaging globe.

Relative silence, in the great machine he headed. Outside, a clear sky, a bitter wind, an almost full moon illuminating a world of blindingly dazzling white. And across the river, a President who apparently was not yet sure of his own response, a Chief Executive who was as always—as he had to—weighing the political angles . . . a man who must be convinced.

Not easy, he feared. Not easy at all.

Certainly it wouldn't be easy if Terrail *Venner* had anything to say about it, the Secretary of State told himself firmly as he shrugged impatiently into his cashmere overcoat, grabbed his umbrella, clapped on his famous black bowler hat ("Do something to make them remember you!" Marisa had directed on his first day in office. *"Wear* something!") and started for the door just before 7 P.M.

Although generally an abstemious man, he had ventured to mix himself one martini from the small liquor cabinet he kept on hand for visiting dignitaries. It had set him up considerably.

"I'm ready for them!" he said aloud in his silent office, thinking of those hordes of competing foreign policy "experts" who in his mind always seemed to be swarming across the Potomac from the Pentagon to try to preempt his turf. "I'm ready for them!"

With a zip and a dash that were quite unlike his normally sedate gait he swung briskly out of the office, said goodnight crisply to the several guards he passed as he made his way down the elevator and out the main entrance of the now deserted State Department and virtually sprang into the unmarked car for the five-minute ride to the White House.

He had let most of his people go around 3 P.M. when the other departments had closed down; now, as in the building he disliked so much across the river, only a few lights burned in the most top-secret offices. *Somebody* had to keep an eye on the world during the night, after all; you couldn't shut the Pentagon out of it, naturally, but at least you could try to go them one better. He prided himself that the State Department under his direction seemed to be quite as alert as the Defense Department to the unending trouble spots in the world. If he had not known of Nanukuvu before Al Brodovsky had called at 5 P.M. to summon him to an emergency meeting of the National Security Council, that was only because it was, in its opening stages, clearly a military matter. Its opening stages were over, now, and it was clearly in his domain.

He did not intend to let the Defense Department ride roughshod over State in determining what should be done about it. He knew what their prescription would be: bang, bang, you're dead! Well, he wasn't about to have any of *that*. At the moment the matter was completely secret. When it surfaced, as it surely would (though he didn't think he would be the first to tell the media), it would immediately have the most far-reaching diplomatic ramifications. His expertise and that of his department would be paramount then. There was no doubt of it. If he hadn't believed that, he would be a much more uncertain and much less determined man than he was right now. And God knew he *was* determined. Just let Loy Buck and Zeecy McCune try any of their tricks with the President now! He, Terry Venner, would be on the job.

Buoyed by this confidence, he found that he was ready for them when his car drew up behind that of the Secretary of Defense under the dimly lighted Southwest Portico. On the President's orders the press office in the West Wing had put the lid on at six. Shortly after that the last of the White House press corps regulars had gone home or back to their offices. In case any strays still lingered, the President had also ordered the subdued lighting at the Mansion, the deliberately cultivated air of nothing going on, on this rare evening when, as he had remarked earlier, the social calendar for once was blank.

Aleks Brodovsky had walked over from his office in the Executive Office Building, just next door across permanently closed West Executive Avenue. Eben Hartman had been chauffeured in, also in an unmarked car, from CIA headquarters in Langley, Va., and had entered the Mansion unnoticed through the East Gate on the other side. With the arrival of the two Secretaries in their unobtrusive vehicles, the National Security Council was complete. So far, they all thought, so good: not even *Defense Eye* was on the job tonight. It was an unusual, and quite pleasant, feeling to think that they could actually meet without being observed and reported. It added an edge of extra jauntiness to the Secretary of State's greeting when he, the Secretary of Defense and the chairman of the Joint Chiefs of Staff arrived together at the door.

"Loy!" he exclaimed. "And Zeecy! What a night, eh?"

"Cold," Loy Buck said and Zeecy echoed, "Damn cold!" as they shook hands and moved into the warmth of the basement reception area to surrender top-coats, scarves, hats to the smiling attendants. "I'm sorry, incidentally," Loy added, "about that appointment this morning, Terry. But things just got so hectic over in the building that I couldn't—"

"No problem!" Terry Venner said with an air so expansive that Zeecy shot him a quick, surreptitious glance and Loy Buck suppressed a startled little smile: this might be easier than they had contemplated if the Secretary of State was actually a little buzzed. Or was it just a feint to throw them off guard? Habitual suspicion of State caught them up short. Terry was never defeated, they had found, until the last argument was settled by the President himself.

"We'll have to try again next week," Loy suggested.

"It may well be necessary," Terry agreed amicably, "if this matter gets worse."

"Which it will," Gen. McCune predicted, "unless we can settle what to do about it pretty damned fast, tonight."

"I'm ready," the Secretary of State declared with a carefree laugh. "Onward and upward!"

Which was where they went, walking up the stairs to the Great Hall of the White House, and from there up the grand staircase to the family quarters. The President had directed the staff to serve dinner in the family dining room, with cocktails offered first in the comfortable seating area at the west end of the hall. The others were standing there talking when the two Secretaries and the chairman arrived. Without exception all were holding glasses of mineral water or, at the most—Aleks Brodovsky and the President himself—white wine. Loy requested wine, Terry asked quickly for soda with lime, Zeecy followed suit. They shook hands all around and after no more than ten minutes of social chitchat the chief steward announced dinner and they went in to the usual excellent White House meal. It was consumed with dispatch and desultory conversation, chiefly about the weather and whether it would, as predicted by the Pentagon's weather experts on whom many in the government relied when planning social engagements, break into spring again tomorrow.

Within half an hour the meal was over, the table cleared, liqueurs offered and refused, cigars likewise. The businesslike mood of the evening turned even more so. Terry Venner, his Pentagon opposites could see, was once more cold sober if he had ever been (even for a moment, which they were too suspicious of him to really believe) otherwise.

Two of Aleks Brodovsky's young NSC staffers entered, carrying the inevitable and necessary outsized map on a big pedestal; set it in place, plugged in the lights that illuminated it, vanished as quickly and quietly as they had come. An enlarged Nanukuvu filled one half of the map, a replica of Zeecy's South Pacific with its red-ringed dot the other. The members of the NSC studied them in silence until the President finally spoke.

"Gentlemen," he said, leaning back in a relaxed fashion but eyes shrewd and perceptive as always, "you know the situation. Does anybody have any specifics that would change the basic story?"

"We have no new information," Secretary Buck said. "Terry?"

"Nor we," the Secretary of State responded. "Eben?"

The director of the CIA, relatively young—forty-six—a tough, sharp mind carried over from the last Administration, shook his head.

"Nothing at all on the island itself," he said. "And nothing reported from any source in Europe or Asia that might indicate any undue activity that could be construed as having any connection with the incident."

"More than incident, I think," the President suggested. "Mass murder for one thing, though that's not much of an item these days for the fellows that did it. Plus the fact that those poor folks on that tiny little bit of land don't really have anybody to stand up for them, bein' as small and unknown to the world as they were. They didn't really belong to anybody, did they, Terry? Just sort of out there on the fringes in no-man's land, as it were."

"Officially, I think, under our protection, Mr. President," Terrail Venner said somewhat stiffly. "Which puts a whole different complexion on the matter."

"It does if we let it," the President observed. He shifted in his chair. "If we want to make an issue of it we have the excuse. Do you think we should? What about you, Loy?"

"I think we must respond," Loy Buck said, "at least to the extent of negating any potential advantage that might accrue to the aggressor."

" 'Negating any potential advantage that might accrue to the aggressor,' " the President repeated in an admiring tone that for a moment disconcerted the Secretary of Defense. "Now, *there's* Pentagonese for you. Better watch out, Loy, they're gettin' to you! You mean we shouldn't let the bastards get any stronger in the South Pacific than they already are, don't you?"

Loy fortunately had the grace and ability to smile at himself.

"Exactly right, Mr. President," he agreed crisply. "We can't afford to let the bastards get any stronger in the South Pacific than they already are. So, how do we prevent this? Do you want to make an issue of it? Or shall we just go about the business of cleaning them out as quietly and expeditiously as we can?"

"No fuss, no muss," Eben Hartman remarked quietly.

"Exactly," Loy Buck said. "I think Pentagon policy would be to keep both to the minimum."

"And fight an undeclared mini-war in the South Pacific?" Terry Venner demanded scornfully. "Do you think you could get away with that?"

"Zeecy?" Loy inquired.

Gen. McCune nodded.

"I think we could, yes. With a little cooperation all around in keeping it quiet, we could be in and out and nobody the wiser."

"If you could organize yourselves to move that fast," the Secretary of State remarked skeptically. "And if 'the enemy,' as you call them—" his expression reflected State Department distaste for such crudities—"let you keep it quiet. I think they'd be much more apt to take a righteous stand and complain to the U.N. and do the whole bit."

"So why don't *we* grandstand it first?" Aleks Brovodsky asked. "If, as you say, we have some juridical right to assert an interest there."

"Well," Terry Venner said. "At least as good as theirs, anyway."

"Oh, come," Eben Hartman said sharply. "Better. Confirmed by various treaties, our past presence in the area, and our de facto position as the strongest power there now. It seems to me we have a perfect right to give them an ultimatum to get the hell out, or else."

"Or else they stay there and say, 'Come get us,'" the President remarked dryly. "Which I agree with you, Terry, is the more likely. But suppose for the sake of argument that we should decide on a strike—"

"Oh, I *hope* not!" the Secretary of State exclaimed in open dismay. The Secretary of Defense gave him a disgusted look.

"And why not, Terry?" he demanded. "Are you really under any illusions that diplomatic persuasion would work, in light of all we've been through in recent years? They'd just stonewall it as they do everything else, in my judgment." He remembered Joe Strang's derisory jingle. "It's going to take more than patty-cake, patty-cake, baker's man."

"Well!" Terrail Venner said, flushing. "It's all very well to make fun of diplomacy, Loy, and I know you and Zeecy and the rest of you over there across the river really get a kick out of doing it, but nonetheless, that's the civilized way to go about things—"

"Even after those poor people on the island were apparently slaughtered in cold blood?" Gen. McCune demanded. "That's civilization? Well, maybe it is, as we know it in these later years of the great twentieth century. But it requires something a little stronger than discussions at the U.N., it seems to me, to furnish an adequate response. And I repeat, if it is to *be* adequate, it's got to be secret in at least its initial stages. Which I suppose upsets you too."

"I've already indicated," Secretary Venner said stiffly, "that I don't approve of covert actions."

"Is such a thing left?" Zeecy inquired. "If it's to be done, it has to be covert and by covert I meant *covert*. I don't mean blabbing it to all your friends in the media tomorrow morning if we decide to do something here tonight."

"My, my," the President murmured and the chairman of the Joint Chiefs, like his boss, had the grace to smile and rein himself in.

"I'm sorry, Terry," he said. "I didn't mean to get carried away. But damn it, if we decide on such a course of action, we can't have it undermined by leaks from *your* shop. You'll have to make certain that only those with a need to know *do* know, and it will have to be kept damned quiet, all around."

"*I* certainly would not violate such a ban," the Secretary of State said, not sounding much appeased. "But we haven't decided to do it that way, yet."

"Correct." Zeecy conceded, and again they turned to the President. But he was not ready to be smoked out.

He gave them a bland and impassive look.

"Al," he said, "why don't you give us your view of the overall strategic and diplomatic importance of this little speck of earth?"

"This little speck of earth and as many nuclear subs as they can cram into it if allowed to do so," the national security adviser amended with a smile. "Strategic, witness the map, very. Not overwhelming, but enough so that I can agree with the Pentagon that we want them out of there. Diplomatic, in some ways more important in the long run, because if they're allowed to stay they will soon have a major base from which to threaten a whole new area and once it's established, make no mistake, they'll let the whole world know and milk the diplomatic and psychological benefits as much as they can, which, as we know from much experience, are plenty. If we decide to move, and I think we must —" the Secretary of State tried not to look crestfallen but only partially succeeded—"then I also agree with the Pentagon, it must be without publicity"—he paused and gave Zeecy a thoughtful look, which the general returned with some challenge—*"and as efficiently as possible. I would not think it would be an easy exercise. It will have to be done right. And right away."*

"That is our responsibility," Loy said calmly. "I accept it. Zeecy accepts it. The Joint Chiefs accept it."

"Acceptance is all very well," the Secretary of State said with some spitefulness. "Doing is another matter."

"It will be done," Loy said sharply.

The President grunted.

"When?"

"When do you want it?" Zeecy asked with the bluntness of old friendship. The Chief Executive smiled.

"Tomorrow morning, 9 A.M. Enough time for you, Zeece?"

"Just about right," Gen. McCune said. Terry Venner snorted.

"And what about you?" the President inquired. "Tell us your solution, and how you'd go about it."

"Very well," the Secretary of State said, sitting straight in his chair, his patrician face outwardly as dispassionate and unemotional as usual, only a slight flush and a nervous little twitch at one corner of his mouth indicating emotions held tightly under control. "I realize I came into this meeting a minority of one, and nothing I've heard since has persuaded me to change my mind on that."

"Or anything else," Eben Hartman interjected wryly. Terry nodded.

"You're right, Eben. The best advice I have, and my own independent conclusion, is that the military route would be a most ill-considered and ill-advised one to take at the present time. The reasons are these: First of all, this incident is not known to the world at large. It is not as though it had occurred in Lebanon or Berlin. Therefore, as long as it remains secret—and diplomatically, also, it seems to me that it has to—then we're not in any imminent peril of the seizure of Nanukuvu being used as a means of pressure on anybody, or as a psychological weapon against us."

"What about later?" Loy Buck demanded. "What about when they're fully established and in a position to use it that way?"

"Ah," Terrail Venner said. "But you seem to contemplate that we'd do nothing, Loy. I wouldn't intend to sit still, if I were permitted to handle it my way. I'd break secrecy, all right, but I'd do it at my own time and on my own terms."

The President stirred.

"Specifics?"

"I would go to the U.N.," Terry said, a defiant note coming into his voice at the restless response from the Secretary of Defense, the chairman of the Joint Chiefs of Staff and the director of the C.I.A. "I would, as soon as tomorrow when they wouldn't expect it, call for an emergency session of the Security Council, lay charges against the Soviet Union and seek a resolution condemning what was done on Nanukuvu and what is apparently being contemplated there. Simultaneously I would approach Moscow directly, seek talks, make a very strong representation. I would, in effect, demand the removal of their submarines and any support structure they may intend to put in place. And I would, if I were you, Mr. President, go on television with maps, and explain the situation. And I'd propose that Nanukuvu be a jointly guaranteed area of peace in the South Pacific."

" 'A jointly guaranteed area of peace,' " the President repeated in a bemused tone. "That's a new one."

"And why not?" the Secretary of State demanded. "It could be a small but significant start on a policy that could grow little by little until it gradually became the basis for our relationships everywhere."

"When did you think of that?" the President asked. "It's the first I've heard of it."

Terry Venner, who hadn't even contemplated the idea until it had popped suddenly into his head two minutes ago, nonetheless now found it good and quite worthy of the mature and reasoned approach to things he felt to be characteristic of himself.

"Oh," he said in an offhand way, "we've been giving it some study. The occasion just hadn't arisen to present it to you yet. Now it has. Mr. President!" he said, leaning forward earnestly, his distinguished face and figure imbued with an almost quivering sincerity. "I beg of you, do not take the easy way out in this matter! Do not resort to force, of whatever kind, covert or overt! That way lies only disaster! Be patient, be calm, be cautious, be *diplomatic,* if you will. Surely that would be better than provoking some violent response that might well make it impossible to work out any kind of agreement—"

" 'Agreement'!" the Secretary of Defense exploded. "Hell's bells, Terry, *we're* supposed to work out an 'agreement,' which can only mean something that writes into language at least a portion of what *they* want and in effect rewards *them* for creating an utterly lawless, inhumane and illegal situation in the first place? That's your idea of diplomacy? I can tell you it isn't mine!"

"Well, now," the President said soothingly—a typical maneuver, Loy had time to reflect angrily, get them to fighting each other as he had on many occasions, and then step in as the peacemaker with something they'd both perforce accept. "Well, now, gentlemen, let's all calm down a bit. I think the Secretary of State has made a very good presentation, from his point of view. And I think the same can be said for the Department of Defense. What I'd like to do—" he paused and they all became very still—"if you agree with it—is to, in a sense, adopt both recommendations. Now, Zeecy," he interjected with a smile at his old friend's expression, "keep calm. I really want to take a two-pronged approach to this. Not publicly, at all, I'm with the Pentagon on that. Secrecy should be maintained as long as possible. The last thing I want to do is make a fuss in the U.N. right now, because it wouldn't do any good and it would only muddy the waters. It wouldn't matter that it was slaughter of innocent people who could in a sense be called 'third world,' it wouldn't matter that it was out-and-out ruthless imperialist aggression. All that would matter would be what *we* do in response to it. *We'd* be attemptin' to 'extend our power in the South Pacific,' no matter that *they're* the ones who are tryin' to do that. The truth wouldn't matter, it never does: *we'd* be blamed. It's a topsy-turvy world up there in the U.N., and everythin' gets stood on its head. Every time the U.S. gets in a pissin' match with a skunk, the skunk comes out ahead, in the U.N. That's the way they operate and nobody can deny the historical record of it. So, that's out. At least for now.

"What I do want to do is approach that rambunctious galoot in the Kremlin through direct channels and see how far I get warnin' him off. Not very far, I'll bet, but I'll go through the motions with you if you like, Terry—we'll keep up the forms. You call in Foxy Feodor from the embassy and we'll have a chat. After that I'll get on the horn to Moscow and *we'll* have a chat. And after I've been turned down cold by both of 'em, we'll 'keep the channels open,' as they say, but we'll begin to think about some other things. In fact—" he paused and took a sip of water—"we'll be thinkin' about them simultaneously. Terry and I will do the diplomacy bit, and you and Zeecy, Loy, and all your fine friends over there will get on the stick and get movin'."

"What—? how—? what—?" Terrail Venner protested, almost stuttering in his concern.

The President smiled.

"I mean while I'm dickerin' I want the Pentagon to get started buildin' up a mission to go after those babies in case we have to."

"But you can't *do* that!" the Secretary of State protested, too upset to be deferential. "If you order a mission it will develop a momentum of its own, these things always do, and it will be awfully hard to stop it—"

"If I say so," the President said calmly but with a firmness they knew it would be best not to question, "it will stop. I'm the Commander-in-Chief."

"It won't be easy, Mr. President," Terry insisted, voice shaking with emotion but determined. "It will be terribly difficult. Also," he added, concern growing, "you can't build up a mission at the same time you're talking peace! I mean it—it—it would be bad faith, Mr. President! It would—it would be two-faced! They'd—they'd charge us with all sorts of trickery and deceit! You just can't do it, Mr. President! It would be a betrayal of America's honor! It would be—it would be—*shameful!*"

"Now, Mr. Secretary," the President said, an edge in his voice, "that's goin' a bit far, isn't it? All I'm proposin' is what they do all the time, and have without a break for more than seventy years. I'm proposin' to keep smilin' but keep our powder dry. Don't worry about *them,*" he added sarcastically. "We won't fool 'em much. After all, they're already there, you know. We're the ones who have to take the risks to get 'em out. They'd think we're fools if we *don't* try to get 'em out. They're expectin' it, probably happily surprised it hasn't happened already. In any event," he concluded, tone suddenly adamant, "that's my decision and that's what's to be done. How do you vote?"

"I vote No," Terry Venner said loudly and the President smiled, more tolerantly, and said, "Well, I admire you for that. And the rest of you?"

"I'm with you," Eben Hartman said.

"A good approach, I think," said Aleks Brodovsky.

Loy Buck nodded.

"As you direct, Mr. President."

"We're on our way," Gen. McCune assured him.

"All right, then, gentlemen," he said, rising to his full height and holding out his hand to shake the Secretary of State's. "A good case, Terry, but not quite adequate for the problem this time, I think. Why don't you get in touch with the ambassador and ask him to come here tonight if he can."

"He's at dinner at the Swedish embassy," the Secretary of State said, looking glum.

"I assume you can get word to him. Suggest he not leave early and cause a sensation, but tell him I'd like to see him right after. Tell him to use the east gate and we'll try to keep it quiet." He turned to the Secretary of Defense. "Alert the boys on the hot-line that I'll be expectin' to put through a call about quarter to twelve our time."

"Then you don't think our talk with the ambassador will do any good—?"

Terry Venner's voice trailed away in disappointment at the President's expression.

"I said I'd go through the motions for you, Terry," he said, not unkindly, "but don't keep hopin' for a miracle. There won't be any."

"But maybe—" the Secretary of State said wistfully.

"There won't," the President said firmly.

And there wasn't; and at midnight the phone rang in the massive building across the river to which the Secretary of Defense and the chairman of the Joint Chiefs had returned shortly before ten, through the crystal-cold, diamond-bright, moonlit world of ice and drifted snow.

"Very tough response, just as I expected," the President said without preliminary. "I guess your boys had better get on it as soon as possible."

"They're standing by in the tank," Loy Buck said. "I'll pass the word."

And so the problem of Nanukuvu became official and the building went to work. The first step was to put it formally on the agenda, and this the Joint Chiefs did at approximately 12:17 A.M. when Gen. Zoren Chace McCune returned to the inner labyrinth of the National Military Command Center on E Ring from his quick trip to the SecDef's office across the hall.

He nodded tersely to his colleagues as they turned to face him, Gen. Burford leaning forward intently, Gen. Stokes outwardly relaxed but inwardly tensed for whatever contentions were to come, Adm. Stahlman sitting rigidly attentive in his chair, Gen. Tock already beginning to look pugnacious and combative.

"No dice," Zeecy said, taking his seat at the head of the table. "The President didn't expound, but Loy got the impression from his tone that it was hot and heavy and no good. Apparently as usual they're going to hang tough. So— away we go."

"Since this is obviously a naval mission—" Bumpy Stahlman began.

His colleagues cut him short.

"It can't be done without the Air Force," Ham Stokes said flatly, "and the Air Force can do it all."

"It can't be done without the Army!" Brash Burford objected sharply. "You can bomb hell out of 'em but somebody's still got to go in an dig 'em out!"

"And what's wrong with us?" Tick Tock demanded belligerently. "Amphibious landings have been our job forever, and we're not about to abandon 'em now, by God!"

"I repeat," Bumpy Stahlman said with the sudden iron vigor he could put into his voice when he considered it necessary, "this is above all and beyond doubt a naval mission. How do you get to Nanukuvu in the first place, if you don't have the Navy to get you there? Fly your troops in? And where will they fall back for replenishment and supplies, if it isn't on naval support? Don't try to con me, Brash, or you, either, Tick. You fellows can mount all the amphibious landings and all the parachute drops you like, but if you don't have the Navy to get you there you aren't going to get there, period. It's as simple as that."

"Not at all that simple," Ham Stokes said with equal vigor. "You've got blinders on, Bumpy. You and your damned Navy. Repeat, we've got plenty at Guam and the Philippines to get everybody down there that we need for mop-up. Because that's all it's going to be after we get through bombing."

"And what will they be doing all this time?" Brash Burford demanded. "Don't you think they have support ships somewhere in the vicinity—or maybe even enough on those big subs, if that's the size they are—to give us a hell of a run for our money? I'm sure they'll have support from somewhere, even if we don't know at the moment where it is. After all, we didn't know they were even in the area, did we?"

"What was wrong with naval intelligence?" Ham demanded.

"What was wrong with Defense Intelligence?" Adm. Stahlman retorted. "What was wrong with the CIA? With the National Security Agency? Where *was* everybody? At least *we* found them."

"At a price," Gen. Burford noted and Adm. Stahlman sighed.

"Yes, at a price, and a stupid one too, poor kid. He never should have gone in so close. But what can you do with American youngsters? It's their nature to be daring."

"And thank God for it," Brash Burford agreed. "It's what gives us the edge— that wonderful spirit. You can't beat it!"

And for a moment they were silent, comforted by this standard reassurance offered by nearly all the top brass in the Pentagon when required to rationalize growing enemy might: they may have us outgunned, outnumbered, out-equipped and outmaneuvered, but by God, our boys have the *spirit* and that's what counts!

There was still an outside chance—diminishing almost daily, but still glimmering elusively—that they might be right. It was enough, for a few seconds, to induce the euphoria that all too often enshrouds official thinking in the Pentagon, and in the country which it serves.

"However," Zeecy McCune said softly, bringing things back to reality, which he deemed to be one of his most important functions, "we still have a hell of a long road and a hard fight ahead of us. So how do we go about it?"

Thus returned to the widening gap that faced them—between the magnificent patriotism and fighting spirit of their countrymen and the steadily growing advantage, in arms of almost all kinds, in the hands of the enemy—they seemed for a moment nonplussed. Then they resumed where they had left off.

"I still say," Adm. Stahlman insisted doggedly, "that you cannot and must not diminish the role of the Navy in the retaking of Nanukuvu. Bombings are fine, amphibious landings are fine, parachute drops are fine, helicopter attacks are fine—but you have to have your floating base to back you up. The Navy's role," he concluded firmly, "is not only imperative, it is paramount!"

"Frankly," Gen. Stokes said bluntly, "my boys don't like to serve under an admiral, even if he's a flying admiral. It's the principle of the thing."

"And what principle is that?" Gen. McCune inquired from the independent eminence which his office theoretically, and quite often actually, guaranteed him. " 'My service *über alles?*' 'You guys get the hell off our turf or we won't play ball with you?' "

"You might say that," Tick Tock agreed, as bluntly as Ham Stokes. "Certainly *I'm* not here to let anybody crap on the Marine Corps. We get our fair share of this, or else."

"Or else what, Tick?" Gen. Burford inquired with a dangerous softness.

"Or else I'm going to the Hill and raise holy hell," Gen. Tock said. "And I can do it, too," he added with satisfaction. "Nobody has alumni in Congress like the Marine Corps. You better believe it."

"We are under express orders from the President," Zeecy said sharply, "to keep this operation secret as long as we can. I'd suggest you not go to the Hill, Tick. The damned place is even more a leaking sieve than this one."

"O.K.," Gen. Tock said. "Give us our fair share, then."

"That's blackmail," Ham Stokes said, and not in jest.

Gen. Tock rounded on him so abruptly that even though Ham was seven inches taller and at least forty pounds heavier, he instinctively flinched.

"God damn it!" Tick said, and it was an order. "Watch your language!"

"All right," Zeecy said loudly. "All *right,* Tick! Knock it off! Stop throwing your weight around. Your precious Marine Corps will be taken care of. Isn't it always?"

"Not unless I fight for it," Gen. Tock said, breathing hard. "It's always an uphill fight against you bastards."

"Oh, come now," Brash Burford said, trying to inject a little lightness that obviously did not mollify Tick very much, though they were very good personal friends: but not on this issue. "Poor old Marine Corps! You never get any glory at all! *Boy!*" he exclaimed with elaborate humor. "Talk about p.r. operations! There's never been the like of it!" His tone changed and became tougher. "And all *I* can say is, if you're going to get your oar in, then the Army will have to have an equal part. We're not taking any back seat to the Marines."

"What we'll do," Zeecy said sarcastically, "is use the great Grenada example when everybody fell over backward to keep both your services happy. The Army was placated by being allowed to go in at one end of the island and the Marines were placated by being allowed to go in at the other—and all the time the main concentration of hostiles and their equipment was right square in the middle, so you both had to fight your way in over awkward terrain, thereby prolonging the conflict unnecessarily for several days and costing us a lot more casualties than there should have been.

"So I tell you what we'll do with Nanukuvu—" his sarcasm grew as he took up the lighted pointer and flicked it across the wide, flat area at the base of the U which had so recently been the peaceful home of A'afaloa and Nuku'ofa.

"This of course is the key to it, and the only sensible place to attack, as I thought we all agreed the first time we saw this map. But to keep *you* happy, Tick, *you* can go in *here*—" he moved the pointer up to the outer edge of the left-hand tip of the U—"and to keep *you* happy, Brash, *you* can go in *here*—" and he moved it to the outer edge of the right-hand tip of the U—"and then you can both have the fun of fighting your way down along the ridges until you come to the center. This, considering that you'd no doubt be facing by that time a very well-entrenched, well-equipped and well-organized enemy, should guarantee you at least a healthy thousand or more casualties, lots and lots of medals and at least fifteen battlefield promotions. To say nothing of lots and lots of TV coverage and all the headlines your little hearts desire."

He paused and told himself that he too was getting a little overwrought and had better cut it out or he'd pop a gasket. But he had obviously made his point. Both Tick and Brash looked genuinely taken aback by the savagery of his sarcasm and the bluntness of his attack.

He might have known his flanks would be vulnerable.

"Which obviously makes both naval bombardment and naval supply absolute necessities," Bumpy Stahlman said with adamant quietness.

"It will be easy for you once we've completed our runs," Ham Stokes agreed pleasantly.

"Now, God *damn* it," Zeecy said. "Will everybody just lay off for a minute, please?" He took a deep breath and prepared to move in the direction he knew the chairman always had to move to get any kind of agreement out of the Joint Chiefs, the direction of compromise, placation, the least resistance and the lowest common denominator. "We'll do our best to accommodate everybody—"

"How?" his colleagues demanded as one man.

"By assigning certain tasks within the parameters of the mission," he snapped. "And by calling on each service for its appropriate contributions to each task. And finally by doing our damnedest to establish a joint command that will be agreeable to everybody—"

"Don't like joint commands," Gen. Tock said. "But," he added, and this time the others nodded agreement, "guess we've got to have one. It's the only practical way."

"Well, thank God!" Gen. McCune said, sarcasm returning. "At *last* somebody's talking practicality. Thank God for small favors."

"Who'd you have in mind, Zeece?" Brash Burford inquired, his tone not yielding much in the way of congeniality at this point.

"I have in mind to recommend to the Secretary," Zeecy said crisply, "Al Rider."

There was silence for several moments while they contemplated the thought of Al Rider—fifty, highly competent, highly intelligent, perceptive and intuitive; handsome veteran of many overseas assignments but basically a brilliant administrator, smooth, suave, pleasant, always amiable but with the necessary iron for decision underneath; popular with all ranks, a rising star headed for the JCS himself someday, everyone believed; next to Ham Stokes the most outstanding and highly thought of black in the services; and also a lieutenant general—and a Marine.

"Suits me just fine," Gen. Tock said with a satisfied look around the table.

"It would," Brash Burford retorted, but not as sharply as he would have had it been a Marine less obviously qualified.

"I think we can live with Al," Gen. Stokes said. He smiled. "Even if he is a grunt."

"After all, he's *your* grunt," Bumpy Stahlman observed, but amicably so it had no racial sting. Ham nodded matter-of-factly.

"That, too," he said. "I like Al, he deserves his reputation. Let's bring him on board."

"Don't tell me," Gen. McCune said, "that we've got unanimity *already.* Whatever in the hell happened?"

"I want the Army to be second in command, though," Gen. Burford said calmly.

"Just a minute!" Gen. Stokes said, instantly ready to do battle.

"The Navy expects—" Adm. Stahlman began.

"All right," Zeecy said, holding up his hands. "All right, just—just calm it, will you? In a mission of this kind, which is going to involve all elements, I don't see any reason why we can't have three subordinates, as far as that goes—providing it's understood that Al has complete and overriding authority and that everything channels through him. Do I have your words on that?"

He looked challengingly around the table until Brash nodded for them all.

"It's done," he said. He glanced at his watch. "Can't we wrap this up and get out of here? We'll have our individual recommendations for Al's approval tomorrow. Or today, rather."

Zeecy shook his head.

"It's only 1 A.M. Keep calm. We've got to finish at least the basics tonight. Loy's still over there in his office waiting to know what we've decided, and the President's across the river expecting Loy to call before he goes to sleep. So hang tight."

"They really want us to put speed on this thing, don't they?" Ham remarked as though he hadn't quite believed it before.

Zeecy nodded.

"Obviously they do. What about equipment?"

"I like the latest models of the LSD and the ALCAC," Tick said, pronouncing the latter 'alkack' in the Pentagon way. "They're fine for the amphibious operation this is basically going to be."

"I'll let that pass," Ham Stokes said, "but if you're going to use the ALCAC, I want to run a few experiments with it to test some things we think ought to be tested."

"What in the hell does the Air Force want with a 'Landing Ship Dock'?"

Brash Burford demanded. "Or an 'Advanced Landing Craft Air Cushion' for that matter?"

"For *that* matter, Brash," Gen. McCune remarked, "there might be some who would wonder why we need both those vessels anyway. Your ALCAC floats on a cushion of air and carries men and supplies to the beach—after it is disgorged from your Landing Ship Dock, which instead of carrying men and supplies directly to the beach itself, as landing ships used to do in World War II, now carries air cushions filled with men and supplies *near* to the beach— and then releases them so that *they* can go to the beach. Thus we have, thanks to past military officers and our friends on the civilian side, many of whom got kudos, promotions and cushy jobs out of it, plus all the contractors and subcontractors who made a bundle out of it, plus all the members of Congress who got votes out of it by forcing allocation of funds and contracts to their states and districts, *two* very expensive vehicles—to do the job that one did before. There *might* be people who wonder about that, Brash."

For a moment they stared at him, astounded by his tone and sentiments.

"By God, Zeecy," Tick Tock said finally in a hushed voice, "there are times when you sound like a God damned communist."

"Oh, I am," Zeecy said dryly. "I just think that once in a while it's good for us to see ourselves as others see us . . . *So*. We go for the LSD and the ALCAC, right?"

"With bells and whistles," Ham reminded calmly, using the Pentagon slang for anything that encumbers, overloads, or seriously handicaps a weapons system. "We've been thinking for quite a while that there ought to be some additions to the ALCAC."

"If you're going to do that," Brash said, "then we've some ideas that we want to get on there too."

"Well, if *that's* the case," Tick said firmly, "I expect on second thought that the Marines can come up with a few things also. We haven't been entirely satisfied with either piece of equipment in recent maneuvers, as a matter of fact."

"Actually," Bumpy Stahlman confessed, "even though these are Navy craft, we have a few reservations about them ourselves, particularly, as you say, the ALCAC. It might be a good idea to have a brief test program before we get too deeply into the mission—"

"*Christ!*" Zeecy grated out. "Do you realize those bastards are out there on that island building defenses *right now?* This very minute as we sit here? They aren't waiting around for our 'test program' to be completed and all the bells and whistles to be put in place! Let's go with what we've got, for Christ's sake, and stop all this wasting time that people charge us with so often. Aren't we *ever* going to prove them wrong?"

Again they looked at him, surprised and startled. Bumpy Stahlman gave their reply, quite calmly.

"Zeecy," he said patiently, "we know it's been a long night, and we know you're under a lot of pressure from Loy and the President. But after all, we can't rush into these things too fast. If there's a real need for modification we've got to do it. We can't send our boys out in inadequate equipment."

"Who said it's 'inadequate'?" Gen. McCune demanded. "It's been perfectly o.k. up to right now when we need it, and suddenly you guys are demanding all sorts of changes that don't make any sense to me!"

"They'll all have to go through channels and be approved by proper authority," Brash pointed out in the same soothing tone. "Anything that doesn't pass muster won't be signed off on. There are lots of safeguards built in. You don't need to worry that anybody's going to *waste* anything."

"Except time," Zeecy said with a bitterness he wasn't quite able to conceal. "Except time."

"No, no, no!" Tick Tock said vehemently. "Not at all, Zeecy, not—at—all! We're all committed to moving fast on this. We'll see to it!"

"Yes," Gen. McCune said, "I'm sure you'll intend to, in absolute good faith. But I've been around the merry-go-round in this building too often, Tick. You'll try, but the system will thwart us, every time . . . at least," he said, more calmly, "that's how I see it. I hope to hell I'm wrong, but if you all insist on modifications the mission is going to be under terrible handicap right from the start. And meanwhile out there— . . ."

He fell silent, gazing with a brooding intensity at the map of red-ringed Nanukuvu far away in the distant sea.

Ham Stokes cleared his throat cautiously and spoke with a respectful but firm emphasis.

"Nonetheless," he said, "speaking for the Air Force—*your* Air Force, Zeecy —I feel we must insist on certain tests. This is an opportunity to remove some glitches that we've noticed for quite a while. We wouldn't want to let it slip."

"I think we all feel the same way," Brash Burford said firmly and they all nodded.

The chairman sighed and spread his hands before him on the table for a moment before sitting back in his chair.

"All right. You're outvoting me, then. I'll carry your recommendation back to Loy and the President. We'll see what happens."

"What *can* happen?" Ham Stokes inquired blandly; and nobody replied.

"Well!" Zeecy said with a sudden briskness, cutting his losses as he had learned long ago one must do sometimes. "Now: what do we call this thing? And bear in mind somebody's going to leak it to the media sooner or later, and that we want to throw them off so we can retain at least a little bit of surprise. Which may be hopeless, but let's try."

"As a matter of fact," Brash said slowly, "I've been thinking about that since this afternoon. It's in a very hot place, so how about 'Operation Frio'—'cold,' in Spanish? Hopefully that will throw them off. They may think we're planning to mess around down near Argentina or some place in the Antarctic; or they may associate it with the North Pole. We can even run a short maneuver with our arctic units and invite the reporters to come along."

"Include the Marines in that, Brash," Tick said. "It's a good idea."

"And of course," Zeecy couldn't resist, "if you do that, there'll have to be some Air Force input as well."

"And the Navy," Bumpy Stahlman said as they all chuckled. "Don't forget the Navy."

"Never," Zeecy said. "Ne—*ver*. O.K., then, Operation Frio it is. And at least promise me this: let's aim for no more than one month on all these things and then let's get going, o.k.?"

"O.K.," Gen. Burford said solemnly.

"We can do it," Gen. Tock promised.

"On the double," Gen. Stokes agreed.

"Chop-chop," Adm. Stahlman said.

"Good," Zeecy said. "Where is Al Rider right now, Tick?"

"Hawaii."

"Good. Get on the horn to him before you leave the Command Center and tell him to get his ass back here."

"He'll be surprised," Gen. Tock said with a smile, "but, I think, delighted. Al likes to be at the heart of the action and he's good at it too."

"Very," Gen. McCune agreed. A sudden thought popped into his head—out of nowhere, really, except his instinctive, much-experienced assessment of men and his earlier feeling that he wanted an inside source in the mission as it developed.

"About his staff, I have a young fellow I want on it. You remember him, that young Brod Tolliver you met this afternoon?"

"Sure," Ham said. "I looked him up. He's good stuff. You want him to be Al's aide?"

"Well, I don't know about that," Zeecy said. "Al may have somebody else in mind. But I think young Brod ought to be in there someplace. I have a feeling he's a comer—let's help him along. Somewhere close in where he can contribute something. We'll work it out."

"No problem," Ham said.

"We'll have our staff recommendations for Al, too," Brash Burford said quickly, somewhat alarmed by what appeared to be the start of an Air Force attempt to take over. "By the time he gets back here tomorrow—today. Hell, it's almost 2 A.M., you know that? I've got to get home to a worried wife."

"Just quickly, before we break up," Bumpy Stahlman interjected hastily, "I want to make sure that the Navy's representation is settled too."

"Get it to Al as soon as he shows up," Tick advised. "That's the way to do it."

"O.K., fine," Zeecy said, rising and stretching and uttering an enormous yawn. "Oh, *man!* I'm *tired!* Thank you, gentlemen. See you in the morning."

"Can I give you a ride back to Fort Myer?" Brash inquired.

"No, I'll have to call on the motor pool, thanks," Zeecy said. "I still have to get back to Loy. And he still has to get back to the President."

Neither took very long. The Secretary was pleased that they had agreed on the mission, though disturbed, as the chairman intended him to be, by the chiefs' adamant insistence on "bells and whistles," which would inevitably slow things down somewhat. But, he said, perhaps the President could help with that.

When he called the White House he learned that the President, contrary to earlier assurances, had finally given up and gone to bed. But he had left word with Al Brodovsky, who was still in his office in the Executive Office Building hoping that he too might speedily go home to much-needed rest.

"He said to tell you," the national security adviser relayed, "that he's behind you a hundred per cent in everything you have to do to get this job done as fast as possible. He's going to call all the chiefs in the morning and tell them that in person. So I guess we're on our way."

"I hope so," Loy Buck said, looking thoughtfully at Zeecy, who was waiting patiently in the chair across the desk. "I'll get to the civilian side of it tomorrow."

"Is there going to be one?" Aleks inquired in some surprise.

"There may be," Loy said. "There seems to be some talk of equipment modification."

"God damn it," Aleks said with a tired annoyance. "Don't they realize there's a matter of haste involved here?"

"I realize it," the Secretary said. "Zeecy, who is sitting opposite me at this moment, realizes it. You and others realize it. Some don't. And that will include, I'm afraid, some in my shop, as soon as word of the mission gets around. But we'll do our best."

"He'll want to help you there, too, I think," Al Brodovsky said. "I'll make sure he emphasizes it to everybody on both sides in the morning."

"Zeecy and I will appreciate it," the Secretary said. . . . "He's worried about delay too," he said to Zeecy when he had hung up. "The Boss is going to go after it in the morning. Let's hope it works."

"It's got to work," the chairman said. "There isn't a great deal of margin for error."

"No," the Secretary agreed, sounding more glum than he intended.

They emerged from the River Entrance into the crystal night. The wind caught them sharply by the throat, leaving them momentarily breathless. Across the river the white city sparkled in the still strong moonlight, a thing of ivory and diamonds, set in a dream. Its lights were dimmed, its monuments dark, its streets virtually deserted. Only a handful of homegoing cars still passed near the water. It was a lonely world.

They shook hands quickly and said goodnight. Loy chuckled as he entered the limousine that would take him to Georgetown.

"Operation Frio is well named," he observed. "It's certainly beginning on a damned cold night."

"An omen of success," Zeecy suggested. His expression became wry. "We hope."

The Secretary chuckled again, waved, was driven away. The chairman was chauffeured off to Fort Myer.

Imogene had long since gone to bed.

Renee, as always, was still up and reading when her husband came in.

Squat and powerful, all the offices that were visible to the outside world entirely dark now, the building brooded beside the river.

Far away on Nanukuvu the new inhabitants labored busily on.

3 Next morning when Harry Ahmanson, brigadier general, U.S. Army, aide to the SecDef, came to work the weather was already beginning to revert to spring. The icy wind had dropped and then ended shortly before 4 A.M. By 6 the temperature was rising rapidly. Warm winds were blowing east out of the Shenandoah Valley and the Blue Ridge. The unexpected storm had gone to sea and died. On its heels came the more customary soft seasonal breezes that were already turning the snow-covered world to slush and would very soon send the last traces of stubborn winter gurgling finally into the ground.

In Virginia, in Maryland and everywhere along the tree-lined streets and omnipresent gardens of the District of Columbia, the lush green jungle growth of the upper South, having been momentarily distracted, was about to lunge forth again and overwhelm the land.

A pleasant excitement was in the air.

The season was back on course.

Harry Ahmanson left the packed underground Pentagon station of the Metro, nimbly blended himself into the throng of military and civilians hurrying to their jobs, surrendered the ticket that had carried him, with transfers, from his bachelor apartment in northwest Washington, and walked through the steadily-clanging turnstiles toward the long, heavily-laden escalator that rises steeply to the Concourse. He was looking forward with anticipation to a pleasant weekend that would permit him to join friends on the picnic outing to Harpers Ferry, West Virginia, which they had been planning when the weather had so surprisingly turned.

The friends included several of his military associates and their wives; Hank Milhaus, assistant secretary for public affairs, and his wife Janet; and, as usual, "a girl for Harry," who in this case was Helen Clark, assistant secretary for acquisition and logistics.

This had been his own idea, even though, like many men, he found Helen a little disconcerting at times. Perhaps that was what intrigued him—because he *was* intrigued. Also like many men, he considered Helen something of a challenge. If one captured that citadel, he imagined with a wry inward smile, as he pushed through the swinging glass doors at the top of the escalator and passed into the ever-busy Concourse now roaring with coming-to-work bustle, you would no doubt be instructed exactly how to go about it. Everything would be neat, concise, orderly: nothing would be left to chance. He was not really sure it was worth the effort: the mental strain of it all might well wipe out any emotional or physical rewards to be gained. Romantic notions might well be canceled and romantic illusions abandoned.

This did not particularly dismay him, as he was not a particularly illusion-prone individual. He was, in fact, as calm, efficient, unromantic, unflappable and self-assured as Helen herself—"cold," in fact, as Vangie had once described him, with a rare open disapproval, to Imogene Buck. This might make the two of them a good match if, as at forty-six he considered increasingly unlikely, he were ever to abandon bachelorhood and the freedoms which he seldom exercised but still liked to think he had.

The reasons he did not exercise them very often were of course strictly attributable to his military career. Harry Ahmanson was in the game to win, and everything he had done for twenty years was pointed to that end. He was a good-looking man, tall, trim, personable, always neatly dressed, almost always in uniform even though the services really required it of their Pentagon members only once a week, and that purely for the sake of form. He was a West Pointer graduated in the upper third of his class; a veteran of several well-handled field assignments and of two previous Pentagon tours of duty; a lifelong single who had successfully managed to avoid entanglements of all kinds, though all kinds had been offered him from time to time; one who, while not married, still managed to blend with smooth astuteness into the marriage-conscious atmosphere of the services and somehow give the impression that he was—or had been—or was about to be; noted from academy days as one who would go far, a perfect, circumspect, clean-nosed, regulation-following, ambitious candidate for continuing promotion; one of the few who had spent twenty years in the service without acquiring a nickname.

Which perhaps said something.

He was poised now, he believed, to win his second star within a few months' time. He had been selected by Gen. Burford, who had long had his eye on him, to be aide to the Secretary. Loy Buck had accepted the suggestion without a moment's hesitation. Harry was satisfied that the Secretary felt that his confidence in Brash's recommendation had not been misplaced. Only once, and that only yesterday morning, had Harry even been ten minutes late to work; and that was due to a brief stoppage on the Metro and was not really his fault, though he did not bother to explain this to Vangie. He knew she didn't like him and reciprocated.

For the better part of a year, now, he had faithfully and with complete efficiency handled the Secretary's schedule, performed various confidential errands for him around the building and on the Hill, moved instantly to perform whatever task, minor or major, Loy asked of him. He felt, with ample justification, that he had been an extremely reliable, exemplary and helpful aide. He knew the Joint Chiefs were behind him 100 per cent and that Brash had already urged Loy to recommend to the President that he be promoted to major general as soon as a suitable vacancy occurred. Loy had endorsed the recommendation "with pleasure" and sent it on to the White House, where it had been favorably received.

So it was with a considerable inner satisfaction that he showed his pass at the Concourse checkpoint for the second floor and walked, with many hurrying others, up the ramp.

A few steps behind him, a fat, neat, precise little man came plodding along, lost in his own thoughts and not even noticing the tall military figure striding on ahead: Harry C. Josephs, assistant inspector general, Office of the Secretary of Defense, valued aide and confidant of W. T. "Shorty" Murchison, the inspector general, with whose dour views of contractor honesty and military efficiency he thoroughly concurred.

Harry Josephs, too, used the Metro, though he came in from Crystal City at the other end, beyond the Pentagon adjacent to National Airport. There he and his fat, neat, precise little wife had a neat precise little apartment in which, childless, the only fractious elements they permitted were two cats, by now too elderly to do much except sleep and go along placidly with their owners' unvarying routine.

Both Harry and his wife had been civil servants all their lives. She was now retired after thirty years as a secretary in the Department of Labor. He was still going strong, at sixty-two, as Shorty Murchison's right-hand man, the culmination of four decades of earnest service, all of them in the Pentagon. He could be retired himself by now if he wanted to, they could be off to the neat little house in Winter Haven, Fla., in which they had cautiously and wisely invested fifteen years ago, but his wife realized without complaint that this was not to be, at least for a while, yet. The world of regulations, surveys, studies, probes, examinations, statistics and endless paperwork was made for her Harry, and her Harry was made for it. Wisely she said nothing, talked to the cats, and dreamed of the day when they might be off to their lakeside lanai and through with government once and for all.

Not so, of course, Harry. After serving in various offices in the Defense Department he had finally, six years ago, found his perfect niche in the office of the inspector general, OSD. The hunt for dishonest contractors and the pursuit of military waste became the crowning of his career and the passion of his life. To it he brought a fierce determination and a meticulous attention to detail that had landed many a contractor and subcontractor in court and caused many a harried officer to curse the day Harry Josephs began to poke into *his* operation.

Shortly after taking up his new duties, Harry had become close to the then inspector general: everyone in that office seemed to have the same kind of detailed, meticulous, patient, skeptical and suspicious mind. When Harry's friend left and Shorty Murchison was brought in by Loy Buck from his high-ranking job with IBM's certified accountants, Harry moved even closer to the center of things. He and Shorty had hit it off splendidly at once. Shorty had the greater flair and personality but he recognized immediately that in Harry he had "an invaluable ferret," as he had once put it privately to the Secretary. Stung by sporadic but persistent scandals that were always given full media treatment to the detriment of the department, Loy (like many a frustrated SecDef before him and no doubt many to come), had given orders to his inspector general to "turn your people loose and give 'em hell." Shorty needed little encouragement and Harry even less. The suspicious cost overrun, the bookkeeping sleight of hand, the bland insistence by some military officer that certain lavish and wasteful expenditures were an entirely inevitable necessity for "meeting the threat," were red flags to Harry. He was not always successful in hauling them down but far more often than not he did so. Contractors usually *meant* to be honest, military men usually *meant* to control waste, but when they didn't, as was too often the case, Harry was there to nail them.

Next to Shorty himself he was, in his quiet, mouselike way, probably the most feared and hated man in the Pentagon.

So he went happily about his work, satisfying his mind with the bulldog success with which he brought wrongdoers to book and warming his heart with the knowledge that what he did was utterly moral, worthwhile and of genuine benefit to the country. Not many men in Washington, or in the world for that matter, were as content and fulfilled as Harry Josephs. Given the absolute right to choose his own job, he could not have picked one more suited to his experience, temperament and abilities.

Thus, on this second day of the problem of Nanukuvu, walking up the ramp apart but soon to be together, went "the two Harrys"—"Military Harry" and "Civilian Harry" as they would swiftly be dubbed in E Ring—who would soon find themselves in tandem, in charge of Operation Frio's companion project.

Civilian Harry was the first to be told.

It did not take long for the news to get around the building to those most closely, and most secretly, involved.

"Zeecy," Brash Burford demanded with an exasperation that came clearly over the line, "what in the *hell* is going on?"

"I don't know," Gen. McCune said calmly. "What is?"

"Do you know that Loy intends to establish a 'Project Frio' to go along with 'Operation Frio' and have the civilian side handle all the modification work on the ALCAC?"

"No," Zeecy said thoughtfully, "I didn't know that."

"Well, it's true," Brash said with some bitterness. "And that isn't all. He wants to put that insufferable little snot Harry Josephs in charge of it."

"Hell!" Gen. McCune said, with considerably more animation. "That's a hell of a note! Who told you that?"

"I have my sources," Brash said. "You know who."

"Is he sure?"

"He overheard Loy talking about it to Vangie a few minutes ago," Gen. Burford said. "Those two are thick as thieves. I think Loy values her opinion more highly than he does ours."

"She's been here longer," Zeecy said with some attempt at wry humor that did not mollify Brash.

"Well, I don't like it!"

"Is it definite?"

"My source thinks so," Brash said, and Zeecy, aware that their man inside the SecDef's office, that very model of a model brigadier, Harry Ahmanson, was usually correct in the information he passed on to them, sucked in his breath with a sound of concern.

"This bears looking into," he said, more as a comment to gain time than as any profound analysis.

Gen. Burford snorted.

"It bears one hell of a fight! I'm not going to sit by and let that two-bit pencil-pushing jerk tell the Army what to do. And no more will the rest of us!"

"No," Zeecy agreed thoughtfully. "I won't either, as a matter of fact."

"I should hope *not,*" Brash said, more calmly. "It would be absolutely impossible. Every time we wanted to do something to modify that craft the way we want it, Josephs would be there with his little calculator telling us it's going to cost too much. We can't have *that* and get anything accomplished!"

"It *would* make it difficult," Gen. McCune agreed.

"Furthermore," Gen. Burford said, "this is a *military* project, it isn't some damned civilian picnic. We've got a job to do down there on that island and we can't be bothered with a lot of piddling little civilian bookkeeping if we're to get it done."

"I think you have a point," Zeecy conceded slowly, "but whether Loy will see it that way—"

"Loy has to be convinced," Brash interrupted. "Convince him!"

"Want to go with me?"

"I'll go," Brash said promptly. "Hell, we'll all go. All you have to do is tell the boys what's up and we'll be there beating his door down."

And fifteen minutes later, after Zeecy had called a startled Adm. Stahlman, an outraged Gen. Stokes and a sputtering Gen. Tock, they were beating it down—if not physically, at least with an onslaught of indignation that tended at first to amuse the Secretary.

"My God," he said when, in response to the chairman's urgent request, he faced them across the big desk, "what have I done to warrant this mass attack? You know I have to be up on the Hill to testify before House Appropriations in half an hour."

"It won't take us half an hour to tell you what's on our minds," Zeecy said crisply. "The name is Josephs."

"Yes?" Loy inquired blandly.

"In fact," Gen. McCune went on, "it's more fundamental than that. It starts with the whole concept of a civilian group to manage what is essentially a military matter."

"How do you know all this?" Loy inquired mildly; not surprised, for things in his office frequently reached the JCS like lightning.

"We have our sources," Zeecy said, echoing Brash's earlier comment to him.

"Yes, and I know who he is," the Secretary said. Their expressions remained grave and impassive. "I'm not surprised he keeps you informed. I don't fault him for that, his career lies more with you than with me. And I do like him and find him most competent . . . Anyway, it's no secret. I was going to call you all in later today and thrash it out with you." He punched a buzzer two times. Harry Ahmanson, brisk and polite as ever, peered around the door.

"Yes, sir?"

"The chiefs are upset because you told them about Harry Josephs and Project Frio," the Secretary said, "so I'm going to have to talk it over with them now rather than this afternoon as I'd planned. So will you please call House Appropriations and tell them I may be as much as an hour late due to an unavoidable situation. And, Harry—I don't mind your reporting on me, because you don't hear much top-secret stuff anyway, but at least keep it in the family, o.k.? Don't tell anybody else?"

"I don't, sir," Harry Ahmanson said coolly, apparently not at all abashed. "And of course if I *should* overhear anything top secret, I would first—"

"Clear it with me," Loy Buck concluded for him in a pleasant but very firm tone. "Then we'll all be happy."

"Yes, sir!" Gen. Ahmanson agreed smartly. "Of course."

"Good," Loy said. "That's all, thank you, Harry." He paused while Harry withdrew, still imperturbable. "Notable gallantry under fire," the Secretary murmured. "He will go far."

"I hope there won't be reprisals," Gen. McCune said. "He was only doing his duty."

"To whom?" the Secretary inquired. "That's one of the funny things about this place: loyalties *hop about so*. . . . Anyway," he said briskly, "to get back to business: yes, I think there should be a Project Frio parallel with Operation Frio—"

"Why?" Gen. Tock interrupted bluntly.

The Secretary gave him a look and replied with equal bluntness. "To keep you boys from running off with the Treasury, that's why. And to try to impose some limits of sensibility on what you do. You're proposing to modify what seems to me a perfectly sound item, known as the Advanced Landing Craft Air Cushion, or ALCAC—'Al-cack,' as you boys call it—and I'm damned if I know why. Do you?"

The ALCAC as it now stood was an improved or "advanced" form of the original Landing Craft Air Cushion that had been developed by the Navy in the early 1980s at an approximate cost of $400 million and some seven or eight years of interservice bickering and wrangling during the development period.

The official justification for it was that it would permit amphibious landings on any type of shoreline and would also permit an assault to proceed inland on its air cushion some distance before discharging troops and equipment. Subsequently it had been decided to improve it in various aspects, leading to the creation of the Advanced Landing Craft Air Cushion, at another cost of approximately $300 million and more interservice battling.

What was now proposed by the four earnest gentlemen before him, Loy reflected, would be go 'round No. 3 for the LCAC. Why, as he had said, he did not know.

In response to his challenge, no one said anything for a moment. They all looked at Zeecy. He returned the look squarely, took a deep breath and responded calmly.

"I must confess, Mr. Secretary, that I have some reservations on that myself. However, I have expressed them to the chiefs and they remain convinced that this mission provides a priceless opportunity to test certain additions to the ALCAC which they believe desirable. In effect, I got voted down. I still have my reservations. So I think it best that this time I not attempt to speak for them, since basically I don't agree. Ham, you started this whole thing in the tank last night. Suppose you argue the case."

"All right," Gen. Stokes said, "I will. The Air Force feels there are certain things, some of them of a secret nature, that we want to test out, having to do basically with communications between the ALCAC and air cover. There's no need to go into them here, but suffice it to say we do believe them necessary and that's why we want to test. Brash?"

"We've felt for quite some time that there needs to be a change in configuration," Gen. Burford said. "Our interest isn't anything particularly secret, it's more a matter of convenience and effectiveness in pre-combat operations and landing."

"We, too," Gen. Tock said. "That's our basic thrust. The thing has what we consider to be some glitches that we want to iron out."

"Good," the Secretary said crisply. "Then since your aim is the same, you can conduct a joint Army-Marine experiment, which will be quite a saving in both time and money—"

"Now, just a minute—" the commandant of the Marine Corps and the chief of staff of the Army began together, which might have been amusing but for their alarmed and dead-serious expressions.

"Go ahead, Tick," Brash said. "You tell him."

"Mr. Secretary," Gen. Tock said earnestly, "apparently we *still* haven't made it clear to you how fundamentally the Army and Marine missions differ—"

"No," Loy agreed blandly, "I'm afraid, despite many, many educational sessions you've had with me on the subject, that you haven't. Basically it has always seemed to me that your missions are the same: take ground, hold it and advance. Have I missed something?"

"You've missed the whole concept, with all respects, Mr. Secretary," Gen.

Burford said. "The whole thrust—the whole tradition—the historic develop-ment—the needs of battle—"

"Exactly," Gen. Tock said, beginning to look a little flushed. "It's an entirely different thing, Loy, and that ought to be obvious."

"Even to a dumb civilian like me," the Secretary suggested. "Well, Tick, I'm afraid it isn't. The island of Nanukuvu—on which, incidentally, we mustn't forget for a second, our friends are busily digging in like little ants right this minute—seems to me exactly in the pattern of the South Pacific campaigns in World War II. It's a take, hold and advance mission. Or should be."

"With the addition of adequate air cover," Ham Stokes said, shifting his big frame forward in a position to do verbal and psychological battle. "Don't forget that."

"*And* sufficient naval support," Bumpy Stahlman said firmly, sitting, if possi-ble, even more rigidly upright. "It would be a rather serious error to ignore the Navy, which after all transports the Marines. To say nothing of bombardment and logistic support."

"Jesus!" Loy exclaimed with the sudden deliberate anger he had long ago found to be effective in corporate boardrooms. "You guys are going to mess up the equipment, you're going to mess up the mission, you're going to let the whole thing go by default simply because each of you has to maintain his own petty little empire and defend his own petty little turf. What the hell are we planning here, anyway, a ladies' tea-party?"

"It isn't petty!" Tick Tock said angrily. "God damn it, it isn't petty! There are fundamental principles involved here, God damn it, and that's the truth of it!"

"Well," the Secretary said, apparently not yielding an inch, "I don't doubt your sincerity, and I know you have precedent on your side, but it's a damned poor way to mount a mission. You haven't justified your method to me, yet."

"We will," Tick promised loudly. "By God, we *will!*"

For several moments they were silent, breathing heavily and staring at the Secretary, who returned them look for look. It was the chairman who finally brought them back to that plane of agreed concession upon which people have to function in the Pentagon if, under its present system, they are to function at all.

"If I may suggest," Zeecy said in a calm and comfortable voice, "we aren't going to get anywhere shouting at each other. I think we can all concede, Loy, that there are times when the way we operate in the military does seem baffling to civilians—"

"I was in the Army once," Loy remarked, tone not conceding much. "Most wasteful, inefficient operation I ever saw in my life. Wasteful of lives, too, which is my main concern here."

"We aren't going to waste any lives," Zeecy said, still calmly, "but I think, to avoid it, we're going to have to be permitted some leeway in working it out among ourselves. That's why I for one want to keep this thing secret as long as possible. Otherwise Congress is going to get into the act and we're going to have half the committees on the Hill trying to micromanage everything. To say nothing of State, the White House and NSC."

"The President wants speed," the Secretary said. "He doesn't want waste and he doesn't want inefficiency, and above all, he doesn't want any more casualties than are absolutely unavoidable. You agreed last night on Al Rider to manage Operation Frio because you finally had to acknowledge that some one individual has to be in charge, even with substantial input from the rest of you. At least *he's* going to be in command." He gave a wry little smile. "We hope. By the same token, if you're going to get into this kick of modifying the ALCAC all to hell and gone, we're going to have to have somebody in charge of that who's in a neutral position and can see all sides. *You* take care of the military plans, *we'll* take care of the equipment."

"Just give us the kind we need," Tick Tock growled, and Brash Burford said explosively, *"Yes!"*

"We'll give you the kind you need," the Secretary said. "And just *you* keep the experimenting down, o.k., otherwise we won't be fielding this mission until long after you and I have left this building and galloped off into the sunset. *And we simply can't wait that long.* Right?"

"But Harry *Josephs?"* Gen. McCune murmured in a tone of quiet but adamant disbelief. "Harry *Josephs?"*

"Harry Josephs is a completely competent individual," Loy Buck said flatly.

"The ultimate civil servant," Bumpy Stahlman said with what for him came close to derisive disgust.

"The ultimate cipher," Brash Burford agreed.

"Maybe," Loy said. "But one who can, and will, see to it, with absolute single-mindedness, that Project Frio gets carried out as efficiently, economically and speedily as possible. And without a lot of unnecessary damned frills—or, as you fellows like to put it, 'bells and whistles.' "

"I don't really know," Ham Stokes said with a certain aloof thoughtfulness, "whether the Air Force can work with him."

"I'm not sure we in the Army can, either," Brash Burford said.

"We sure have *our* doubts," Tick Tock agreed, and Bumpy Stahlman nodded slowly.

"It will be a *most difficult* problem. In fact—"

"In fact, what?" the Secretary demanded, good-naturedly but with a growing sharpness. "What are you ornery bastards going to do, go on strike?"

"We aren't bastards, Loy," Zeecy McCune said in the mild tone he had decided would be best from him for this entire discussion. "We're just very concerned about whether we can accomplish our mission with somebody like Harry Josephs meddling in. After all, what has he ever managed, when you come right down to it? Anything except a computer?"

"He is an absolutely honest, dedicated, trustworthy public servant who has devoted his entire life to the welfare of this country," the Secretary said, and raised a hand to forestall protest. "And yes, I know that's exactly what all of you are, too. That isn't the point. The point is that he's outside the military, he's not interested in turf fights and service rivalries, he just wants to get the job done. That's why I've chosen him."

"Oh, then, he already *is* chosen," Zeecy said.

"He is," Loy said firmly. "Didn't Harry Ahmanson tell you that?"

"Harry Ahmanson," Zeecy said slowly, and his military colleagues, with a sudden pleased anticipation, could see the wheels going around as he spoke—and so, of course, could Loy—"Harry Ahmanson doesn't always know everything. *But,*" he concluded thoughtfully, "he *could* know everything, couldn't he, if he were to be appointed co-manager of Project Frio."

"Better make him manager," Brash said, picking up the ball with smooth efficiency.

"He can handle the military details," Ham Stokes suggested, coordinating as effortlessly as though they had rehearsed it.

"And Harry Josephs can be co-manager and handle the money side and make sure the contractors behave," Tick Tock said happily.

"Much the better solution," Bumpy Stahlman agreed with a gratified air, as though of course it was all settled. *"Much* the better."

And polite, respectful, interested and concerned—and, for the moment at least, completely united—they regarded the Secretary with pleased, expectant expressions.

In spite of himself, Loy Buck began to laugh.

"You guys!" he conceded at last. "You guys! What an operation! *What* an operation! . . . All right. That's the price, hm?"

"We don't want to put it on that basis," Gen. McCune said with a pleasant smile. "But on the other hand, Loy, we *would* feel a lot better."

"All right," Loy said again. "As long as I've got my civilian Harry in there, you can have your military Harry. Is that a deal?"

"It's a deal," Zeecy said, and reached out his hand to shake the Secretary's across the enormous desk.

"Civilian Harry and Military Harry," Tick said dreamily. "I *like* that."

"You got it wrong, Tick," Ham Stokes said. "As usual. Leave it to the Marines. *Military* Harry and *Civilian* Harry. *That's* the order."

"We won't establish any order," the Secretary said with some return of sharpness that momentarily quelled the celebration. "They're going to be co-managers and don't you forget it."

"Quite right, Loy," Zeecy McCune agreed solemnly. "Quite right. So—" He stood up, held out his hand again. "On with Project Frio!"

"And *you,*" Loy said as he shook hands with them all. *"You*—get on with *Operation* Frio and let's get those babies off that island!"

"Yes, *sir!*" they said in unison.

But after they were gone he sat for a long time staring moodily straight ahead.

"How to instill a sense of speed," he finally said aloud to the silent room. *"How to instill a sense of speed.* That's the problem."

And, he might have added, how to make the sense of speed effective throughout the system once you *had* instilled it.

Far from the building and the delicate necessities of Pentagonian compromise, the new inhabitants of Nanukuvu labored on. There may have been similar negotiations in the Kremlin, the world would never know, but once committed to their mission there was no doubt that it would be accomplished to the best of their ability, as fast as possible, without hesitation or further discussion. The purpose now was single-minded, its execution as near to inevitable as absolute dictatorship could make it. No qualms, no questions, no trying to satisfy competing interests. Once a decision was made, competition was not permitted.

Interservice rivalries there may very well have been—though robotized by their system, they were still human enough for that—but all had been subordinated to the single overriding purpose of defeating the United States. Their command structure, once decided, was not subject to challenge. Their equipment, once standardized, was not to be changed by bells and whistles. And their morale, contrary to a considerable amount of comfortable wishful thinking in the building by the river, was quite as high as that of their opponents, because they, too, loved their country—and had within them the extra goad of hatred which they had been taught from infancy and which was now an instinctive and automatic part of them, as it could never be of the easygoing Americans.

By the time the last snow had trickled away through the gutters and brought the Potomac to a record high tide for late spring, the prefabricated foundations for an extensive command center had been laid down among the palms of Nanukuvu. Small controlled atomic blasts were being used to begin the smoothing and hollowing out of concave berths along both sides of the lagoon from beach to narrow entrance. The entrance itself, though retained in its natural, concealed configuration, had already been scoured of underwater reefs and other obstructions to the passage of larger vessels. And on the shore, hidden among the trees, the mound of supplies grew steadily as the rubber boats plied back and forth between the beach and the three giant submarines that now lay side by side along the edge of the underwater shelf.

Now and again there were radar traces, and occasionally actual sightings, of the various patrols from *Dominant* that were apparently maintaining surveillance. But none came close and none gave signs of hostile action. Nor was there any undue American activity reported anywhere in the South Pacific.

Despite this seeming acquiescence, however, initial euphoria had given way to customary caution on the island.

There was no telling how long the condition of quietude might last.

The Americans might appear supine but they still had the capacity to be dangerously unpredictable.

The commander of Nanukuvu, aware that time as always was of the essence, drove his men, now divided into three eight-hour shifts, furiously ahead.

Two

1

Placed alongside all the other problems worldwide of the U.S.-Soviet relationship, the Secretary reflected on a hot, humid afternoon three months later, the problem of Nanukuvu had been at inception, and to some degree still was, a gnat on the hide of the elephant.

But in today's frantically explosive world it could become a tiger on the flank at any time.

He was a little surprised, in fact, that it had not already done so: the Soviet development of the island was so rapid and the Pentagon's pace in meeting it, despite constant proddings from himself, the President and the chairman of the JCS, so unnervingly slow.

The enemy's hold on Nanukuvu now appeared to be secure and, insofar as could be determined by radar, satellite and close-pass observation, nearly complete.

A large command center was now in place under the palms where A'afaloa and Nuku'ofa and their families had once lived their peaceful lives. It consisted of what was apparently a headquarters building, two barracks, several supply dumps and a small repair-shed on the beach from which a new channel now ran out to the deeper water beyond the shelf. A series of small atomic explosions had been detected immediately after the occupation, indicating excavations in the lagoon. Increasingly frequent passage of submarines in and out seemed proof that the excavations had been successful. They still used "black" techniques, jamming and "stealth" for cover, but moved so freely that it seemed clear the lagoon was now a completely viable base for them.

Now work appeared to be starting on missile emplacements and other defensive fortifications along the outer rim. At this rate Nanukuvu in a few months would be a major fortress in the South Pacific. There could no longer be doubt if there ever had been: its occupiers were there to stay.

"A nest of vipers," Bumpy Stahlman called them. The comment seemed to describe perfectly what Nanukuvu had become in the eyes of the Pentagon.

But the challenge still had not been met. The difficulties of doing so had increased a dozen-fold if not a hundred-fold. And still the building maintained its customary ponderous pace.

Those most concerned professed urgency, it seemed to the Secretary, but practiced the-system-as-usual.

So far there had been no attempt by the new owners to use the base either militarily or diplomatically to affect the situation in the area. If they did, Loy

Buck knew, there would be a renewed sense of crisis in the building. Until then, speed must depend on the desire of its leaders to make speed. He thought with a sudden angry impatience that this desire was not very obvious to him.

Aside from himself, the President and the chairman of the Joint Chiefs, everyone was pretty much business as usual.

Zeecy was after everybody all the time but it didn't seem to do much good. He himself made periodic calls, sometimes every day; they appeared to be equally unproductive. Three times since the frigid night when the problem of Nanukuvu had blown in on the storm, the President had talked individually to each of the Joint Chiefs, culminating a week ago with a burst of direct profanity to Brash Burford that Brash had dutifully passed along to his colleagues. Their reaction appeared to be startled but not unduly alarmed.

The Secretary seemed to detect slightly more urgency on the civilian side than on the military, but not much. Each time a new intelligence report came in detailing progress on the island, he had it circulated to the chiefs, to Al Rider, to the two Harrys, to Bob Cathcart, Helen Clark, Tiny Wombaugh, Joe Strang and the Doomsday Twins—all the top people on both sides of the building who were involved in either Operation or Project Frio.

The results always appeared to be the same. Each time the subject was raised there were stout assurances of compliance, diligence, application, duty. Then he would get busy, or they would get busy, with some other of the hundred demands that seemed to press in upon them each day as they sought to do their part in managing the Pentagon's global business. Nanukuvu would sink back to somewhere around tenth priority for most of them. And another day would go by without substantial progress.

The principal reason, Loy suspected, was that the Joint Chiefs and their staffs and most people in his own shop thought they *were* making progress. And in Pentagon terms, he supposed they were.

The two Harrys had agreed, after a long period of wrangling, on a staff and three civilians to manage Project Frio.

Gen. Rider had returned to the Pentagon and immediately created his own personal staff of an Air Force officer—young Brod Tolliver, who didn't quite know why he was there, but found it exciting—an Army officer and a Navy officer to do the preliminary work on organization of Operation Frio. But lacking agreement among the chiefs, not much more could be done.

Gens. Stokes, Tock, Burford and Adm. Stahlman had presented their separate requests for bells and whistles on the ALCAC to Harry Ahmanson. Harry Josephs had promptly said they would cost entirely too much, had dug in his heels and refused so far to give his approval. Since the informal structure of Project Frio—which was partly, the Secretary knew unhappily, his fault—required unanimity at the top, the project had virtually come to a dead halt in recent weeks.

Gens. Stokes, Tock, Burford and Adm. Stahlman had presented their individual plans for the re-taking of Nanukuvu to Zeecy and Zeecy had held five meetings so far, all unsuccessful, trying to get each to modify his request in a way that would permit Al Rider to form a genuinely effective joint force. It had now been three weeks since the last such meeting, and Operation Frio was temporarily also stalled.

Tiny Wombaugh, as Under Secretary for Research and Engineering, had also been presented with the ALCAC requests and had also dug in *his* heels on the same grounds as Harry Josephs: modifications were an unnecessary waste of time and money. This had further crippled Project Frio.

Helen Clark, as Assistant Secretary for Acquisition and Logistics had been similarly cool to the whole idea but had made some progress in sounding out both Strategic Industries and General Growth Group as to whether they would be interested in bidding on the ALCAC modifications if and when their final form was approved. Both said they would, which appeared to be one small plus.

Loy and the President had both "tested the waters," as the President put it, on the Hill with people like Cube Herron, Mario Escondido, Luzanne Johnson and Karl Aschenheim, to ascertain whether they would back funding for "a special project of great importance to national security." They had all said they would if they knew what it was. Neither the President nor Loy was ready to tell them, and in that area also, things seemed to have come to a standstill.

Terrail Venner at State and Joe Strang in the Pentagon had kept up a running tug-of-war for the support of Al Brodovsky in the White House. The national security adviser was committed to the Pentagon solution but found that the longer it dragged out, the more persuasive Terry's demands for conventional diplomacy became. Two more meetings of the National Security Council on the subject had ended inconclusively.

All in all, Loy concluded wryly, it could not be said that much progress had been made on the problem of Nanukuvu—except by the Soviets. This was a disturbing and frustrating thought; and he determined now, as he began his usual restless pacing in front of the window overlooking the river that something must and would be done without further delay. But he did not know exactly where to begin; and so, as always when in doubt on military issues, turned to the most obvious source.

"Zeecy," he said when the chairman appeared ten minutes later in response to his call, "what are we going to do about this damned Nanukuvu thing?"

Gen. McCune sighed heavily.

"I'm damned if I know, Loy," he said gloomily, "and that's the truth. I try to keep the pressure on in my side of the building, but there's a million and one things that demand attention, as you know, and without some overt threat out there, it tends to lose its urgency. I think it's rather remarkable we've done as much as we have, considering the track record around here."

"The only thing we've really done is set up a couple of frameworks," the

Secretary pointed out. "We've fleshed out Project Frio with the two Harrys and you've got Al Rider ready to go with Operation Frio. And that's about it."

"Al's getting damned frustrated, frankly," Gen. McCune said. "He's already asked me right out if he couldn't get back to the field because he says he isn't getting anything done here. And that's bad."

"You tell him from me," Loy said firmly, "that it's highly important that he remain exactly where he is because we need him, and we'll have plenty for him to do, very shortly."

"I've already told him that," Zeecy said, "but I'll be glad to add your endorsement. I don't think it'll convince him unless things really begin to move. He can see as well as anybody that they aren't, so far. I don't see the two Harrys setting any speed records, either. Civilian Harry is being exactly the kind of bastard we thought he would be."

"Harry Josephs," the Secretary said, "is a highly conscientious man who can't understand, any more than you and I, why it's necessary to modify the ALCAC when it's proven itself in a number of places and when it's going to be part of a mission involving a lot of other elements anyway. It isn't as though it were the *only* thing that's going to be used."

Gen. McCune spread his hands in a don't-look-at-me gesture.

"I've done my best. I opposed any attempt to meddle with it from the very beginning. But Ham and the boys are determined and they would have dragged their heels if we hadn't gone along. So, what can you do?"

"All right!" Loy said sharply. "What you can do is tell them that if they're going to do it they're to *get on with it.*"

"O.K.," Zeecy said with equal sharpness. "Then tell Harry Josephs and Tiny Wombaugh to get the hell out of the way and let them make their damned experiments and then maybe they *will* 'get on with it' . . . Look, Loy, I want this to move, just as much as you do. But part of this isn't a military responsibility, you know. It wasn't *our* idea to set up a civilian project alongside."

"No," the Secretary conceded, "it was mine. And the reasons were, one, as I told the boys, I wanted somebody around to make sure they didn't steal the Treasury, and two, I'm looking toward the day when this is going to hit the Hill and the media, as it certainly will and I'm astounded it hasn't already. When that time comes, I want to be able to point to the fact that we're maintaining civilian control over expenditures and potential waste. They'd never go along if we didn't have *some* restraints in place."

"They may not go along anyway," Zeecy said with a return of grimness, "unless the enemy does something to get them excited and make them see that yes, it really is a threat. It's so damned far away, and the Soviets are being so discreet about it so far, that it would be awfully hard to instill any sense of emergency. As things stand now."

"They can see it," Loy said in a disgusted tone. "They're not stupid, they know perfectly well what the situation is."

"Yes, but they have to convince the folks back home, you know, and a lot of them will be skeptical of it. The South Pacific doesn't play very well in Podunk all these years after World War II. Especially with the example of Vietnam to scare off people from everything within a radius of ten thousand miles. The Soviets knew what they were doing when they supported North Vietnam, all right. They were making a long-term investment in the psychological future. It sure as hell paid off." He sighed. "And not only among civilians, either. We've got a hell of a lot of people in the military who are still spooked by the Vietnam example. I wish everybody could shake it, but it isn't that easy. It still cripples the country and the building in a thousand ways."

"And the Hill," the Secretary agreed unhappily. *"And* the media . . . *But.* Those of us who have the responsibility can't let it cripple *us* forever. We've got to get on with it, because the enemy sure as hell is. So—what do you want me to do? Get the two Harrys in here and bawl the hell out of 'em? And you do the same with the chiefs?"

"We've tried that," Gen. McCune pointed out. "I've held five separate meetings with those stubborn prima donnas and last time I got Al Rider in and he practically went down on his knees with tears in his eyes trying to get them to yield half an inch all around so that we can go forward with planning the mission. It didn't do any good. Nobody's ready to yield yet. 'Things have got to mature a little,' Bumpy Stahlman said in his gently superior way." The chairman gave a snort of disgust. "Hell! 'Mature a little'! It'll be the year 2000 before this mission gets underway, at this rate."

"It damned well better not be," Loy Buck said grimly.

Zeecy shrugged.

"O.K., tell Josephs and Wombaugh to get out of the way and let the boys have their little games, if that's the only way to get them to cooperate."

"For how long?" the Secretary demanded. "Suppose I do, will they take a year to do it?"

"They damned well better not!" Gen. McCune said in an ominous tone.

"All right. There's got to be a unanimous urgency here, or it isn't going to work at all."

They were silent for a few moments, contemplating without much enthusiasm the difficulties inherent in the democratic system, exacerbated and increased by the Pentagon system, which permits human imperfections to run rampant—until the time comes when they simply must be curtailed for the common good.

"Maybe it's time for a full court press," Zeecy suggested finally. "A full-scale, no-holds-barred, highest-level thrash-out. How about that?"

"I've been thinking about suggesting it," Loy said. "You know him better than I do. Will he go for it?"

"Oh, he's ready," Gen. McCune said. "He called me yesterday demanding to know why there hasn't been more progress. And he's been calling the chiefs too."

"And me," the Secretary said. "And Tiny. I will say for him, he's one President who keeps his eye on detail."

"When it really concerns him," Zeecy said, "and this does . . . O.K., why don't you suggest it to him, then? Any time that's convenient to him, we'll be there."

"And so will we," the Secretary said. "I'll get to him some time today and let you know."

"Good," Gen. McCune said as they both stood up. "I feel relieved. I think maybe we'll finally get somewhere. I've been worried as hell, frankly."

"I, too," Loy said. "I, too. They aren't sitting still, down there on the island."

"No," Zeecy McCune said grimly. "They are not."

He had almost reached the door when the phone rang. Instinctively he looked back.

"Yes?" the Secretary said. "Who is it? *Who?*" He raised his hand for Zeecy to stay. "O.K., put him on . . . Yes, Skip," he said, tone carefully neutral. "What can I do for you? . . . Oh? . . . Oh, you have? Well, that's interesting . . . Yes, we can use any help we can get. Why don't you bring it by my office tomorrow morning at nine. I think I'm free, if not Vangie will call you. . . . O.K., Skip, thanks for calling. We appreciate it . . . *Well,"* he said in both wonderment and annoyance as he hung up. "What do you make of that?"

"What does *he* want?"

"He has a proposed design for the ALCAC modification that he wants to show me," Loy said.

"The *what?"* Gen. McCune demanded.

"The ALCAC modification," the Secretary said, not quite knowing whether to laugh or be furious.

"Now how in the *hell,"* Zeecy exclaimed, "did he hear about that?"

"This little building," the Secretary said dryly, "has great big ears. Somebody's spilled the beans."

"And if it's reached him," Gen. McCune said, "it's one swift hop, skip and a jump to somebody like Delight Jones—"

"Or Mario Escondido—"

"Or both," the chairman concluded. *"Hell!"*

"If you can't lick 'em," the SecDef remarked wryly, "join 'em. Or have them join us. Who knows? Brother Skip may be back on board in no time."

"And just when he was learning to love the purple water fountain," the chairman remarked. "Well: keep me advised, will you? And let me know about the President."

"Instantly," Loy Buck promised with a rueful chuckle. "In both cases."

And that, Skip Framberg thought with a great deal of satisfaction as he hung up on an obviously surprised and baffled SecDef, ought to show the bastards a thing or two. If they thought they could take one of the best men they had *ever* had and banish him to the basement and keep him there *forever,* they had another think coming. If they thought he didn't still have friends in the building, they were mightily in error. He had them all over the place. And they all realized what a rotten deal he had received, and how inevitable it was that he would sooner or later turn the tables on all the enemies who only wanted a free hand to waste the public money and rob the country blind while they indulged their greed and their endless ambitions for preferment.

Skip Framberg took a very dim view of the military establishment and of the civilian leaders of the department in which he had been an employee for the past ten years. He was not exactly disloyal to them but he certainly regarded them with a great and often bitter skepticism, made deeper by the way in which they had treated him after he had gone public with the results of that faulty Army test nine months ago. They had virtually implied that to be disloyal to them was to be disloyal to the country, whereas in his mind nothing proved his loyalty to the country more than what he had done in the Army case. If he hadn't been so loyal to the country he wouldn't have blown the whistle. If he hadn't been so concerned about the country, the way its money was used and its sons' lives were jeopardized by faulty equipment, he would never have gone to Red Roberts with his story. And Red, who was equally concerned, wouldn't have brought it up in Hank Milhaus' regular DoD news briefing and turned it into a national case.

That was loyalty to America, in Skip Framberg's estimation: not to sit quietly by and help to cover up what he sincerely believed to be gross and dangerous inefficiency, but to blow the whistle and get it out in the open and trust to exposure to right the wrongs.

And all exposure had done was strip him of his authority and relegate him to a musty little office in the basement out beyond the purple water fountain. That was justice for you, he often told his wife bitterly. But his day would come. And now, perhaps, it had.

One of his allies in the Army episode had been funny old Harry Josephs, that diligent beaver of the inspector general's office who had blown a lot of whistles himself but somehow, shielded by Shorty Murchison and the self-righteous mantle of the Office of the Secretary of Defense, had escaped unscathed. It just went to prove, in Skip's mind, that the Pentagon was divided into insiders and outsiders, and if you were on the inside like Harry Josephs you could do a lot of things you couldn't do if you were an outsider like Skip. Of course Skip's former position as director of Test and Evaluation had been a part of OSD also, but somehow that didn't seem to qualify him for the same protection. He didn't think it could be a matter of personality, because no one was more drab and quiet and unnoticeable in defending the public interest than Harry Josephs and no one was more contentious and combative and uncompromising than Skip. It was his nature and his instinct to believe that you had to fight the bastards and fight them hard. He reflected that this approach gave him ten times the friends in the media that Harry Josephs would ever have. He had that satisfaction, anyway.

He could only conclude that the reason Harry Josephs survived unscathed, while Skip was punished by being stripped of his authority, was because Brash Burford had a lot of friends on the Hill who joined in quashing anything that put the Army in a bad light. It was all politics, that was the whole thing. He had never seen a place like the Pentagon that was so riddled with politics, except maybe the Hill itself; and the Hill didn't have the direct control over people's lives that the Pentagon did. Which made Skip even more righteous and angry when he came across what he considered one of its many collective misdeeds.

However, despite their differences in personality and unequal success in surviving Pentagon politics, a curious friendship had grown up between himself and Harry Josephs during Skip's battle with Loy Buck and the top brass over the Army test. Harry was really the one who had discovered the way the test was being rigged—held in smooth terrain, when the system would have to be used mostly in rugged country; held in the warmth of summer, when mostly it would be used in colder climates; held without even simulated attack, when of course there would be constant opposing fire; and so on. Harry was the one who had initially passed this on to Skip. A suspicious claim for money—wouldn't you know—was what had tipped Harry off. He had wondered if it didn't indicate something deeper and had privately contacted Skip. Skip had taken it from there, queried a couple of disgruntled technicians whom he knew in the test crew, secured the facts, challenged the powers that be, tipped off the media—and wound up behind the purple water fountain.

But he and Harry still had lunch occasionally, and still exchanged notes now and then. It was on one such occasion a couple of months ago that Harry had told him about Project Frio. Not why it was being organized—or what its objectives were—or where, if anywhere, its mission was supposed to find fruition—because Civilian Harry had not been told those things, nor would he be. But Harry Josephs did know officially that it was to organize equipment and materiel for some unspecified mission, and that one of its principal tasks was apparently going to be to modify the ALCAC.

It was this that annoyed Civilian Harry, and it was this that annoyed Skip Framberg. Both of them were vaguely curious about the ultimate purposes of Project Frio, but that was really aside from their basic interest. People in their positions were seldom told the final military usages of what they did: they were not, after all, military. It was their job to see to it that support items were perfected and secured with as much efficiency and as little waste as possible; and to both Skip and Harry Josephs, modifying the perfectly serviceable AL-CAC was exactly the sort of thing that caused their whole beings to quiver with indignation. Nonsense like that was exactly what God had put them in the world and in the Pentagon to prevent.

It was an absolute waste of time and money! So thought Civilian Harry and so thought Skip Framberg.

"Keep me advised," he had told Harry Josephs grimly. "They've hog-tied me so I can't do much any more, but you know I've still got some pretty good leads to the media. I'll do what I can."

"You bet," Harry Josephs said, and good as his word, he arranged to meet Skip accidentally at the Pik-Quik one day a month or so later. While they were in the salad line he murmured to him the tale of how he, Civilian Harry, was holding up the whole of Project Frio because he refused to approve the unnecessary modifications of the ALCAC that the Joint Chiefs seemed so bound and determined to proceed with.

Skip had gone back to his basement cubbyhole and brooded for a good many days about how he might best help to torpedo this senseless enterprise. But it was not until, completely out of the blue, he had received a most unexpected visitor a week ago that he had hit upon what he perceived might be the best way to go about it. And had also begun to get some inkling of what Project Frio —and its companion, Operation Frio—were all about.

His visitor had arrived late one afternoon when the building was beginning to empty. The corridors and the Concourse were streaming with tired home-going military and civilians, the escalators to the Metro were packed from top to bottom, buses, heavily loaded, were grinding off at rapid intervals to Virginia and the District. Shadowy basement hallways were almost deserted. Nobody had rounded the purple water fountain for half an hour, when there came a sudden rather furtive knock on his door. He opened it to find one of the last people he would ever have expected to see down there.

"You'll forgive me for barging in, Skip," Bob Cathcart said gruffly. "Just thought I'd drop by for a chat."

"Glad you did," Skip Framberg said, feeling as though his tightly-curled red hair might literally be crackling with excitement at this most unexpected intrusion by the Deputy Secretary of Defense. "Glad you did, Mr. Secretary. Come in, come in, and do sit down"—sweeping a pile of reports and papers on his one extra chair off onto the floor in nervous haste. "My quarters are a little tight here, but you're certainly very welcome."

"Thanks," Secretary Cathcart said, settling his big frame uneasily in the rickety chair. "Quite a change from the old days, Skip."

"Yes," Skip said with the bitterness he could never quite keep out of his voice when discussing this. "It isn't D Ring."

"Do you have anybody?" Bob Cathcart inquired. "I mean, a secretary or anything?"

Skip looked bleak.

"Just me. A secretary would be the beginning of status, and you know me. I don't rate Status."

"It's a damned shame!" Bob Cathcart said indignantly. "A God damned shame and I'm going to tell Loy Buck about it!"

"He knows," Skip said. "I'm sure he ordered it."

"Damned shame," Bob Cathcart repeated. "God damned shame. It's typical of the high-handed way he runs this department. And gets away with it, by God. You got one of the dirtiest deals I've ever heard of, and hardly anybody pays any attention any more. It's criminal!"

"Oh, I still have my friends," Skip said, somewhat uncomfortably. What the hell was Bob Cathcart's interest, anyway? Skip had been around the Pentagon long enough to know there must be something: the pure and disinterested like himself did exist, but seldom, he felt, in the highest places.

The Deputy Secretary gave a grim little smile.

"I'll bet you *do* have your friends, and thank God for that. You can still light a fire when you want to. That's important."

"I like to think it's good for the country," Skip said, sounding rather prim though neither of them noticed.

"It is!" Bob Cathcart exclaimed. "By God, it is! Especially now," he added darkly, "when all sorts of damned nonsense is going on."

"No more than usual, I hope," Skip said with a smile. The Deputy Secretary nodded vigorously.

"Oh, yes, more than usual! Now we've got this damned Frio business—"

"What's that?" Skip asked, trying to sound casual though his pulse quickened and his heart beat faster as he thought of what Harry Josephs had told him.

"Project Frio," Bob Cathcart said. "Modifying the damned ALCAC and all that crap. I suppose my old outfit Three Gs will get a slice of it, but I still say it's a lot of damned nonsense." He gave him a keen look. "Haven't you heard of it? I'm sure you still have your spies around the building."

"Well," Skip said, uncomfortable again, "not so you'd notice. I did hear, though—" he deliberately looked thoughtful and as though he were trying to think where—"I did hear, though, something about the ALCAC, yes. The Joint Chiefs want to put some bells and whistles on it, isn't that it? I thought we got that thing perfected four or five years ago. What's the problem now?"

"That may *be* the problem," the Deputy Secretary said with a humorless little laugh. "Nobody's tampered with it in four or five years, so it must be ripe for a replay. Money and promotions for somebody! Let's tear it apart and put it back together again! *That's* the ticket!" He uttered a disgusted sound. "Lot of damned nonsense all around, in my judgment."

"Are there other things they want to do?" Skip asked cautiously, because it suddenly seemed important to him to find out as much as he could about this enterprise that had Harry Josephs so indignant and the Deputy Secretary so upset.

"Oh, the whole thing's crazy," Bob Cathcart said. "I told Loy when it first happened that we don't have any business down there in those islands, any-way—" He stopped abruptly and shot a sharp glance at Skip, who hoped he looked impassive. "Anyway, that's beside the point. The main reason I dropped in was to get your advice on the ALCAC, because I know you were involved in the testing when it first came on line. I'm trying to fight it and I need some support. Maybe you can help."

"Me?" Skip asked with a deprecating laugh. *"Me?* I'm a non-person, Mr. Secretary, you know that. I'm a purple water fountain warrior. Nothing I can do."

"But your friends maybe can," Secretary Cathcart said. "If you drop the word."

"Well—" Skip said more doubtfully then he felt, "I don't know . . ." He took a deep breath and gambled. "I'd need to know a little more about it—"

"Just that there's some damned project on," Bob Cathcart said shortly, "and they want to modify the ALCAC, entirely unnecessarily in my opinion. That's all."

"But they must be contemplating some mission that requires it, obviously," Skip said, taking a chance on bluntness.

"Oh, they are," Bob Cathcart said sarcastically. "Never fear, they are. But it isn't going to do them any good. By the time they get ready the bastards will have dug in like ticks, and there we'll be. Anyway," he concluded abruptly, "you think about it, o.k.? And see what you can do."

"Well," Skip said slowly, "of course if there's a legitimate mission that really requires modification, then I wouldn't want to be in the position of opposing it. I mean, I'm in bad enough, now. I can't afford to lose my job, I have a wife and kids—"

"You can always go to work for Three Gs," the Secretary said bluntly. "We'd fix you up."

"Working for a huge corporation," Skip Framberg said with a sudden stiffness, "is not my idea of how best to serve my country."

For a moment Bob Cathcart studied him with an intentness that made Skip realize why this seemingly rather empty and blustery man had risen to the position he had in the business world.

"Fair enough," the Deputy Secretary said with a sudden grin. "Fair enough, you have your principles and I've always admired you for them, Skip. That's why I've always supported you in your battle with the Office of the SecDef. And that's why I'm hopeful you'll help me in this fight to stop this unconscionable waste of taxpapers' money on the ALCAC. To say nothing of that other stupid—" He stopped with an angry scowl. "Well, stop one, maybe the fuss will stop the other."

"But you still haven't told me," Skip protested, more vigorously now, because he really did feel he wanted to know more about this.

"Can't," Bob Cathcart said. "Sworn to secrecy, and all that. Tell you someday, maybe, when it's all over."

"But surely if you want to stop something, you can always go to the President," Skip said. "You're a friend of his."

"I'm afraid Loy and the Joint Chiefs got to him first," Bob Cathcart said ruefully. "I've talked to him, but it doesn't do any good. They've convinced him it's a threat to our security and he's going along with it . . . at least," he said thoughtfully, "as long as there isn't any public howl. Maybe if there were—

. . . anyway," he concluded in an offhand tone, "we'll see. How are things going with you, generally?"

"Oh," Skip said, accepting that the confidences, such as they were, had apparently ended, "I manage. It isn't what I'd prefer to be doing, but as long as I'm here they can't ignore me. And—" he smiled—"I issue a report once in a while."

"Yes, I know," the Deputy Secretary said with an admiring glance. "That one you gave Red Roberts a couple of months ago on the ties between the Army and Strategic Industries got a very good play, I must say. Glad you didn't take after Three Gs! You still wield a mean pen, Skip."

Skip, flattered as he was meant to be, permitted himself a modest smile.

"I manage."

"Indeed you do," Bob Cathcart said emphatically, standing up to go. He stuck out his hand, shook Skip's vigorously. "Well, Skip: take care. It's been nice to talk to you. Keep in touch if you need anything."

"Just rehabilitation," Skip said wryly, and Bob Cathcart gave him a rueful smile.

"That I can't do much about," he said, "under present conditions. But if I ever get the chance—"

"I'd certainly appreciate it!" Skip said with a fervor half-mock, half-genuine, thinking as Bob Cathcart went out the door: having another corporate type as SecDef is exactly what we want I *don't* think.

They parted with mutual smiles and he watched the Deputy Secretary's departing back with a thoughtful expression until, with a last wave, he turned at the purple water fountain and disappeared.

Back at his desk Skip sat very still trying to put it all together. He had been around long enough so that his guesses were well-informed and shrewd. Project Frio was apparently a coordinate or coequal part of some mission "down there in those islands" where "the bastards" were "going to be dug in like ticks." Bob Cathcart thought attempts to dislodge them were "stupid" but the SecDef and the JCS had the President pretty much convinced that they should do so, barring some public flak against the decision which he, Skip, was supposed to generate by using as fulcrum the plan to modify the ALCAC. This modification indicated that a landing was contemplated on one of "those islands" which were "down there," and therefore "Frio" was obviously intended to mislead and the situation was probably somewhere in the Caribbean or the South Pacific.

A Soviet airstrip? A naval base? A sub base?

By the time he got through speculating Skip didn't know exactly where or when but he had a pretty good idea what and he had some good clues with which to start unraveling the rest.

So how to go about cracking it open, if he decided to accept Bob Cathcart's not-so-subtle prodding and do so?

Inspiration came.

An ironic smile crossed his face. Was *he* going to have fun with Loy Buck!

He picked up the phone and made his appointment with the startled Secretary. Then he gave his desk a superficial tidying, slung his jacket over one shoulder and walked out of his tiny office, locking the door behind him.

For the first time in months he found himself actually whistling as he walked down the poorly lit, deserted underground corridor toward the purple water fountain, the Metro, and home.

At about the same moment the chief of staff of the Army was going through the final pieces of paperwork that had accumulated on his desk when he had returned from the Hill shortly after one-thirty. He had testified that morning before Jerry Castain's Senate Appropriations subcommittee on defense and the experience had left him cursing as always—inwardly, because Jerry had insisted on taking him to lunch in the Senators' dining room and Gen. Burford did not feel that he could be so ungracious, or unwise, as to tell Jerry exactly what he thought of him and his staff.

Jerry had been at his most space-cadetish. Meetings of some twenty-three other Senate committees and subcommittees had prevented attendance by his usual colleagues. The staff had thus been free to have a field-day with Brash, who had not been in the mood for it to begin with and became increasingly less so as the persistent needling went on.

There were a couple in particular he didn't like, a sassily superior young miss from Radcliffe and a fiercely bushy-haired young man from Columbia who had landed, in their first jobs, squarely on top, as they conceived it, of the military-industrial complex they mistrusted and despised with a fervor equal to, if not greater than, Skip Framberg's. Even though Jerry from time to time uttered a mild, "Now, now," the Army and the Pentagon in general were obviously considered to be guilty until proven innocent. Brash was thoroughly sick of the girl's triumphant intensity and the young man's ferocious righteousness. By the time the hearing ended he was ignoring them and addressing his replies directly to Jerry, who followed the proceedings with his usual rather dreamlike air. Brash found himself thinking, as he often did when talking to younger members of the Senate: *This* is a United States Senator? Fortunately there were a number of others he respected a lot more. Jerry wasn't *bad,* but he *was* a space cadet.

At lunch he had looked at the general with his occasional wide-eyed concentration and demanded,

"Well, Brash, are you going to be appointed chairman when Zeecy retires?"

"I don't know," Brash said shortly.

"Would you *like* to be?"

"Hm," Brash said, taking his time, waving to Cube Herron across the pleasantly small and intimate room crowded with Senators and their impressed constituents. "That's an interesting question."

"Answer it!" Jerry said with the coy air that, as Tick Tock had remarked to Ham Stokes after a recent hearing, "makes one want to vomit."

"Naturally," Brash said, slowly and thoughtfully buttering a roll while Jerry appeared to hang eagerly on every word, "one could only be flattered by being chosen for the highest post a military man can aspire to—"

"Stop waffling, now!" Sen. Castain exhorted.

"—but," Brash concluded, unhurried, "all of that is up to the President and one has no way of knowing what his conclusions may be until he announces them. So, frankly, Jerry, I just don't know anything about it."

"That's a neat piece of sidestepping," Jerry said with a chuckle and Brash chuckled amicably back.

"Yes, it is," he agreed. "You fellows on the Hill aren't the only ones who learn double-talk."

"Hmph!" Jerry said, dissolving into genuine laughter as one of the dining room's jolly plump waitresses came to the table and requested their order. "I guess that tells *me!*"

"I hope so," Gen. Burford said with a comfortable laugh. They paused to order and when the waitress had gone he inquired, "Where do you get these young kooks who dominate the committee staffs these days, anyway?"

"Oh, those two!" Sen. Castain said with a chuckle. "They're from Indiana. Her father is a big steel man in Gary, he heads the top law firm in Indianapolis. What could I do?"

"Put them to straightening the files in the back room," Brash suggested. "Have them index all the subcommittee hearings between the years 1891 and 1903. Things like that."

Jerry chuckled again.

"I *know* they're pests," he admitted cheerily, "but once in a while they do dig up some interesting stuff."

"It wasn't necessary to dig up Skip Framberg," Brash said, not so cheerily. "I know all about Skip Framberg."

"Oh, well," Jerry said. "It's good to keep you fellows on your toes, over there. A lot of things can get out of hand in the testing process. What are you testing these days, incidentally?"

"Quite a few things," Gen. Burford said, thinking: Now what does that mean? Has he heard something up here about Frio?

But the Senator's question was apparently quite innocent because he just said casually, "But nothing unusual."

Brash shook his head and said, quite truthfully, "No, nothing special going on at the moment." Because of course now, three months after the occupation of Nanukuvu, nothing as yet really was.

"Well, let us know," Sen. Castain said. He uttered a burst of laughter whose exaggerated sound made old Sen. Dominick of Michigan turn around grumpily and give him a quizzical stare. "We'll sick the kids on you!"

"You'd better not," Brash responded with a smile. "I've got enough problems."

And in spite of himself a fleeting look of worry crossed his face. People said a lot of things about Jerry Castain but no one ever said he wasn't quick when he wanted to be.

"You're worried about something, Brash," he said with the sudden genuine concern that could make him quite likable at times. "What's wrong? Something in the Pentagon? Anything we can do up here to help?"

"No, thanks," Gen. Burford said; and because Jerry in his sincere moments could be quite appealing, and because Brash was really filled with worry that not even Tick and Doreen Tock's continuing sympathy and concern could assuage, he added in a lowered voice, "It's a personal matter."

"Oh, well," the Senator said quickly. "But still—if I can help. Is it a health matter?"

"How did you know that?" Brash demanded sharply and Jerry made a little soothing gesture.

"Just a guess. It couldn't be a command problem, you're on top of the heap. It couldn't be money, ditto. So I thought maybe—" He gave the general a sudden keen glance. "Are *you* feeling all right?"

"I'm fine," Brash said.

"Mrs. Burford, then," Jerry Castain said; and Brash, after a moment's hesitation, nodded. "A lovely lady. Tell me about it. If you want to."

So, with a sudden rush of relief he had never dreamed this seeming lightweight could evoke, Brash did, from the first episode in the snow to several other little things lately: increasing forgetfulness, including how to sign her name; a recurring inability to read her watch; a sudden uncertainty as to which door led to the kitchen and which to the den.

"Nothing very big," he concluded. "But cumulatively—" he looked grave— "worrisome."

"It is," Sen. Castain said with equal gravity. "In fact—" He paused and looked thoughtful. "It sounds like my mother."

"What's her problem?"

Jerry hesitated and then decided: he's a brave man, better let him have it straight.

"Alzheimer's," he said and the world came crashing down around the chief of staff of the Army, so violently that for several seconds the cheerful noises of half a hundred conversations were lost to him. Jerry's concerned young face and the Senate dining room disappeared and there was nothing in the universe but the word that seemed to go ringing endlessly down some hollow corridor in his brain.

"Brash," Jerry said. "Brash!"

"Yes?" Gen. Burford said dully, the world beginning to come back into focus.

"Brash, you mustn't let it get you down," Jerry said earnestly. "I may be utterly and entirely wrong, and pray to God I am. But it's something you should have them check out very thoroughly at Walter Reed. Has she been there yet?"

"No," Brash said with a deep sigh that seemed to come from the very interior of his being. "So far she's refused to go."

"You must get her there," Jerry Castain said firmly. "And don't wait any longer."

Gen. Burford gave him a bitter look that fortunately no one noticed.

"What's the hurry?" he inquired. "It doesn't really matter, does it?"

"Now, stop!" Jerry ordered, dropping his voice, but urgently. "Just stop it, Brash! It's a precaution and a necessary thing. If I'm wrong—that's great. If I'm not— . . . You must get her there. Have you told anyone else?"

"We're close to Tick and Doreen Tock. Vi called Doreen right after that first episode in—in the snow."

"And they haven't suggested this?"

"They've hinted," Brash admitted, realizing now that indeed they had but he had refused to accept it. "But sometimes it takes somebody—somebody—outside—to bring things into focus."

"I'm glad if I have," Jerry Castain said quietly and for a moment he didn't seem space-cadetish at all but rather a gravely concerned young man, "because you shouldn't waste any more time. Either of you. Get on it."

"I will," Brash promised humbly. "I will."

And now he was back at his desk in the rapidly emptying Pentagon, trying to concentrate on the endless routine matters he had to deal with all the time. Matters such as a colonels' promotion list, which of course wasn't routine at all for the men and women involved but a matter of deepest concern. And a formal opinion he must give on a new laser technology. And the constant review of policy concerning liquor on bases. And whether changes should be made in the auditing of officers' clubs. And whether wearing the uniform at certain overseas bases was advisable. And drugs, diminished but still a problem. And whether he or his deputy should attend the upcoming NATO conference in Brussels. And plans for a formal reception for the head of the army of Thailand. And—

And so on—and on—and on—in an establishment which, worldwide, comprised some 800,000 men and women as the Army's share of an estimated total U.S. uniformed force in all services of approximately 2,200,000 compared to Soviet strength estimates that now ranged as high as 5,000,000. Together with some 350,000 civilians who worked for the Department of the Army, total Army personnel stood around 1,150,000, stationed at the Pentagon, and at posts and bases, most known, some secret, in continental U.S. (CONUS), Europe, South America, Africa and Asia. Some 35 U.S. Army divisions faced a Soviet Army estimated now to be well over 200 divisions. The annual budget for the Department of the Army ran in the neighborhood of $80 billion, many thousands of times what the Continental Congress voted to field and maintain the ragged motley that followed George Washington and gave to their descendants the priceless gift of liberty.

And what a history the ragged motley began, Brash often thought with a welling-up of emotion that always seemed to hit him hardest at those ceremonies such as Memorial Day services at the Tombs of the Unknowns in Arlington, when he was required to be at his most solemn and dignified. There were times, seeing the earnest young faces at attention around him and thinking of the long and gallant history behind them and what they might face in the future, when, he told Vi, he wanted to bawl like a baby. But of course the chief of staff couldn't do that, even though he had come perilously close on occasion and always found himself unable to suppress a few tears that crept surreptitiously out of control. He had learned to ignore these and aides who noticed them always tactfully looked the other way, most of them being moved themselves. The delegates to the Second Revolutionary Convention had certainly started something when they met on March 23, 1775, at St. John's Church in Richmond, Va., listened to Patrick Henry cry, "Give me liberty or give me death!" and responded with their enabling resolution:

> *Resolved, That six compaines of expert rifflemen,*
> *be immediately raised in Pensylvania, two in Maryland, and*
> *two in Virginia; that each company consist of a captain, three*
> *lieutenants, four serjeants, four corporals, a drummer or*
> *trumpeter, and sixty-eight privates.*
>
> > *That each company shall as soon as compleated,*
> *march and join the army near Boston, to be there employed as*
> *light infantry, under the command of the chief Officer in that*
> *army.*
>
> > *That the pay of the Officers and privates be as*
> *follows, viz. a captain, @ 20 dollars per month; a lieutenant*
> *@ 13 ½ dollars; a serjeant @ 8 dollars; a corporal @ 7 ½*
> *dollars; drummer or (trumpeter) @ 7 ½ dollars; privates @*
> *6 ⅔ dollars; to find their own arms and cloaths.*
>
> > *That the form of the enlistment be in the following*
> *words;*
>
> > *I have, this day, voluntarily enlisted myself, as a*
> *soldier, in the American continental army, for one*
> *year, unless sooner discharged: And I do bind*
> *myself to conform, in all instances, to such rules and*
> *regulations, as are, or shall be, established for the*
> *government of the said Army.*
>
> > *Upon motion, Resolved, That Mr. (George)*
> *Washington, Mr. (Phillip) Schuyler, Mr. (Silas) Deane,*
> *Mr. (Thomas) Cushing, and Mr. (Joseph) Howes be a*

committee to bring in a draft of rules and regulations for the government of the army.

From that day forward the names of battles rang down through history: the long erratic start-and-stop of the Revolution, Lexington and Concord . . . Ticonderoga, Bunker Hill, Valley Forge, White Plains, Savannah, Charleston, Yorktown . . . the War of 1812 . . . the Mexican War of 1846–48 . . . the Civil War, its terrible tragedies and great gallantries living on in the legends of Union and Confederate descendants alike, Bull Run, Shiloh, Second Bull Run, Vicksburg, Chancellorsville, Gettysburg, The Wilderness, Cold Harbor, Atlanta and the rest . . . the Spanish-American War of 1898, basically "the Navy's war" except for Teddy Roosevelt, the "Rough Riders" and San Juan Hill . . . World War I, 1917–18, Belleau Wood, the Marne, the Somme, Meuse-Argonne, Château-Thierry . . . World War II, 1941–46, Bataan and Corregidor, New Guinea, Burma, the Philippines—Casablanca, Kasserine Pass, Salerno, Cassino, Overlord, D-Day, Battle of the Bulge, Remagen Bridge . . . the Korean Conflict, 1950–53, Inchon, Panmunjom, the 39th Parallel . . . the Vietnam War, 1962–73, Pleiku, Danang, Hue, Saigon, endless frustrating forays in the jungle, no great victories but heartbreaking gallantry, bravery and devotion to country by youngsters who often had no real idea why they were there . . .

And the names of major bases and installations, many well-known almost from the beginning, some brought to unforgettable prominence in the memories of hundreds of thousands of World War II inductees, others less familiar but all part of the worldwide organization for which he was responsible as chief of staff:

Fort Dix, New Jersey . . . Gila Bend, Arizona . . . Camp Roberts, Fort Ord, Presidio of Monterey, Presidio of San Francisco, California . . . Fort Benning, Georgia . . . Schofield Barracks, Hawaii . . . Fort Leavenworth, Kansas . . . Fort Polk, Louisiana . . . Fort Devens, Massachusetts . . . Fort Drum, New York . . . Fort Sill, Oklahoma . . . White Sands Missile Range, New Mexico . . . and so on, across every state and every U.S. territory, and the territories of friendly NATO members and other allies around the world . . .

And the times of feast and the times of famine, always alternating in the unfortunately traditional American way, until today the comparative U.S.-Soviet figures, on paper at least, were appalling . . . but, he constantly reminded the Hill and the critics, words in one army often did not mean the same in the other, the size of Soviet divisions did not necessarily equal the size of American divisions—and it was of course a main objective of Soviet propaganda to give the impression of overwhelming ground strength . . .

What the U.S. Army lacked in actual man-to-man strength, he always argued, it made up for in the spirit and morale of its soldiers and the sophistication of its weapons. Reflecting on those weapons now, as he did when the manpower figures became too oppressive to be thought about, he was satisfied that the Army was in good shape and getting steadily better:

In the Army's own categories published each year in a handsome volume of text and photos entitled *United States Army Weapon Systems,* the first rank went to what was known as the "close combat mission"—the M-1 and M-1A1 Abrams Tank . . . the M-60A3 Tank . . . the light-armored, full-track Bradley Fighting Vehicle Systems . . . the M-113A2 Armored Personnel Carrier . . . the AH-64 Apache airborne anti-tank weapon, the Hellfire airborne anti-armor missile . . . the Light Helicopter program . . . the Dragon medium-range, wire-guided anti-tank missile . . . the M-249 Squad Automatic Weapon, developed by the Army but designed for use by all four services, one of the rare weapons to have such all-service acceptance . . . the M-K19-3 Automatic Grenade Launcher . . . and so on . . .

And the "Air Defense" category; the Patriot all-altitude missile system . . . the Roland, a European-designed, highly mobile, all-weather, short-range, air defense missile system . . . the Hawk medium-range air defense guided missile system . . . the Chaparral short-range air defense surface-to-air missile system . . . the Stinger, a heat-seeking missile "to provide air defense coverage to even the smallest of combat units" . . . and so on . . .

And the "Fire Support" category; the Pershing II ballistic missile system . . . the Multiple Launch Rocket System . . . the Self-Propelled Howitzer . . . the Self-Propelled 8-Inch Howitzer . . . the Medium Towed Howitzer . . . the Copperhead cannon-launched guided projectile . . . the Battery Computer System for greater artillery effectiveness . . . the Firefinder artillery and mortar locating radars . . . the Armored Personnel Carrier . . . the Field Artillery Ammunition Support Vehicle . . . the Armored Combat Earthmover . . . and so on . . . and so on . . . and so on, through binary chemical warfare systems to the helicopters such as Black Hawk, successor to the "Huey" of the Vietnam War . . . and the tactical nuclear weapons . . . and the various combat service support vehicles such as the High Mobility Multipurpose Wheeled Vehicle, the Commercial Utility and Cargo Vehicle, the Heavy Expanded Mobility Tactical Truck . . . and all the various components and special items of Command, Control and Communications (C3) . . . and individual soldier equipment . . . and so on . . .

"By God," Cube Herron had told him one day during a particularly heated meeting of the Senate Armed Services Committee, "if you fellows don't have a tank, a gun, a missile, a truck, a plane or a system for every single possible thing that could happen on the face of the planet, I'll eat my hat!"

"Eat it, Senator," Brash had told him calmly, "but be thankful we do, because we never know when or where we're going to need them."

And since *United States Army Weapon Systems* also thoughtfully included at the bottom of each entry a detailed list of all the contractors who helped produce it, with their addresses in the various states neatly set forth, neither Cube Herron nor any other member of Senate and House protested too loudly at what in many instances appeared to be repetition, overlapping, duplication and redundancy of missions, weapons and systems.

From time to time these redundancies troubled Brash, as they did many in the military and many on the Hill; but once a given configuration or system had been established it was almost impossible to cancel or change it without running head-on into all the vested interests both military and civilian that were involved in its production. So sooner or later nearly everyone who came roaring to the fray crying for reform gave up; and the redundancies rolled on. And why shouldn't they? Brash demanded when pressed: the Soviets did exactly the same thing, piling weapon upon weapon, version after version, variation after variation of the same thing in warehouses, depots, bases. It was all part of the system, which seemed basically no different on either side.

At any rate, this was his domain, in the eminence to which he had risen in almost four decades of faithful service to his country. And now, just as he hoped to move on up to the final triumph, the Lord was attacking him without warning.

He was devastated by sudden overwhelming shame.

Attacking *him!*

It was nothing compared to the attack on his wife.

Good, gentle Vi, of all the decent people! He could not believe it. And yet, as he considered the symptoms and all he had read or heard about the disease as it had become a generally recognized diagnosis in recent years—and as he thought of the indirect hints the Tocks had offered out of their own tragedy— he was forced to admit that Jerry Castain was probably right.

That seeming lightweight—the "space cadet." How pointless it was to label people, how easy to misjudge. No one could have been more instantly sympathetic and concerned than this youthful Senator who was generally regarded in the Pentagon as "unpredictable . . . unreliable . . . kookie . . . off-base . . . serves the racquet instead of the ball . . . swallows the bottle instead of the pills . . . gets off the escalator halfway up . . ." and so on.

Brash had thought he had learned that lesson about people way back at the Point, but it was still an easy error to slip into: he supposed one never really outgrew it, in spite of one's best intentions. He promised Jerry in his mind that the Army, at least, would treat him with more respect from now on. Perhaps in return Jerry would not be so erratically picky about Army policies and occasional mistakes as he sometimes was. But whether that was the result or not, Gen. Burford determined that he personally would never criticize him again.

Of course he would continue to fight him when it came to appropriations and policy, because that was his job as head of the Army; but it wouldn't be contemptuous, the way it used to be. He promised himself and Jerry that.

After a few more moments he stopped going automatically through his papers and pushed them aside. He wasn't going to get anything more accomplished today, that was for sure. He reached for the phone.

"Tick? Good, I thought you might have gone home already. How about a drink at the officers' club at Fort Myer? I need a good stiff one."

"Sure thing," Tick said, as though he had been expecting such a call for quite a long time, as indeed he had. "Have you heard from Zeecy?"

"Not yet. Why, what's up?"

"You will," Tick said. "We're supposed to be at the White House tomorrow morning. Full-scale review of Nanukuvu, I gather. The Boss isn't pleased with progress, apparently."

"I'm not either," Gen. Burford said. "But it isn't the Army's fault."

"Ours either," Gen. Tock said firmly. "We'll have to talk about that too."

"O.K.," Gen. Burford said, tacitly accepting the implications of the "too." "Six o'clock?"

"Roger."

And so, finally, Brash was going to have to face up to it, Tick thought as he turned back from the phone to his own endless stream of papers in his office in Arlington Annex.

Face up to it and come to grips with it and somehow live through it, as he and Doreen and Lisa and the kids had been forced to do for the past ten years.

The commandant of the Marine Corps had his own responsibilities, on a smaller scale than those of his fellow chiefs but equally vital for his service and the country. He had faced, and successfully faced down, many crises and many challenges, both in the field and in the office. But none had ever been quite so tough as the challenge of his son.

He put his signature to a dozen pieces of paper and tossed them in the out basket for his secretary to send back down through channels. She was a civilian who had been with his two immediate predecessors and was invaluable and infallible. Everything would be done exactly right and according to regulations. She was one of that indispensable breed, like the SecDef's Vangie, who kept the Pentagon running. Without clerical staffs like them, both civilian and military, the building would disappear beneath a mountain of paperwork that threatened, unless disposed of every day, to bury the world.

For a little while pride in the Corps managed to push thoughts of his son temporarily into the background. He congratulated himself that everything was going well for the Marines at the moment—aside of course from Frio, which was becoming more of a headache than any of them had envisaged, thanks to the enemy's diligent progress. In general, the Marines were in good shape. He prided himself that they were ready for anything, but he was glad that at the moment they were not out there exposed to hostile fire, as they had been a few years ago in Lebanon, for instance. Everything was relatively quiet at their various stations around the world. And at home, aside from the unhappy accident at Camp Lejeune three months ago that *Defense Eye* and some others in the media were still hammering the Corps about, there were no outstanding problems.

It was a tidy service, and that was one of the things he loved about it, aside from all its great traditions and stirring history, which were quite capable, at the most unexpected moments, of bringing tears to his eyes. Unsuspected by few except his wife and his closest associates, Gen. Tock was a very sentimental man and nothing brought this out in him more deeply and inescapably than the Corps. He was quite helpless in the contemplation of its past magnificent record and the almost unbearable bravery of its current young men and women. He was not at all helpless in the face of its organizational and command problems, to which he brought a completely impersonal yet basically compassionate objectivity.

And why shouldn't he? he asked himself now as he opened the final sealed envelope on his desk and found it to be a confidential report from the commander of one of the Pacific bases about a sex ring out there involving three officers and three enlistees—all male, unhappily. His face grew red with anger, he cursed vehemently aloud—and then calmed down. CALL ME, he scrawled on it in big red letters, initialed it, stuck it in an envelope, addressed it by hand to the commander, and tucked it in his coat pocket to drop in the mail himself on his way out. People *would* be human, he had found out long ago. No need to crucify the bastards. Just get 'em out of there and send 'em home *and keep it out of the papers*. That was the important thing: protect the Corps. He had served no greater master in all his years in service.

Because after all, it was a great Corps to protect. He relaxed and all the many good things about it came flooding to mind.

Like the Army and the Navy, it had begun in the Revolution, which was one reason all three services tended to regard that late-comer the Air Force with a slightly patronizing air. The Continental Congress established the Corps on Nov. 10, 1775, as a distinct category but without a separate named command. Marines were enlisted for service on a particular ship in the embryonic Navy, their assignment being to serve as snipers and boarders during close combat at sea. It was not until fifty-nine years later, in 1834, that Marines were enlisted for service in the Corps itself rather than on an individual ship, their increasing use in land combat bringing about a situation in which they were under command of the Navy at sea, the Army on land. And it was not until sixty-six years later, when the Navy in 1900 began its conversion from sail to steam, that the Corps found itself recognized as a separate entity with its own command structure, used for separate and specific missions—first to guard the Navy's increasingly far-flung refueling bases around the globe, and then to become the spearhead for the amphibious assaults on land targets that became a major aspect of warfare in the middle years of the twentieth century. And now to form a vital component in joint forward-based strike forces, on alert for rapid deployment around the troubled globe.

In 1947 the Corps acquired by act of Congress the general worldwide guard duties which, in the later years of the sad, sick century, began to make the Corps not only "First to fight," as it proudly proclaimed, but also first to take the brunt of terrorist attacks on U.S. embassies and diplomats abroad. Too many Marines began to come home in flag-draped coffins from both the halls of Montezuma and the shores of Tripoli to be the focus of the Arlington Cemetery burials performed with such spit and polish. It was a development the Corps deplored but it was a duty only the best Marines were chosen for and it was one no Marine ever shirked. The Marines didn't shirk any duties, Tick thought proudly: they never had. For more than two centuries they had fought their country's battles on the land and on the sea, and nobody in any service had a better record or a more stirring list of heroes.

And look how they had grown: from the scared but valiant handful who rode the bucking seas in sailing ships in the Revolution to the approximately two hundred thousand men and women today who were stationed, like all the services, across the earth wherever America had a friend, a foe or an interest: and that was everywhere. The initial minuscule budget for the entire Corps that today might perhaps support one small company had grown to the approximately $5 billion that now was necessary to support the nation's most compact and battle-ready force.

Not for the Marine Corps, Tick knew, the waste and overlappings of material and equipment that made the other services such targets for criticism. The Marines did not have very many items that were specifically and only for the Marines: that was one of the advantages of being partner in the Navy-Marine team. The Marines, too, had their LTVP-7 amphibious assault vehicles; their Landing Vehicle Tracked; their M-939 series 5-ton tactical truck; their 5/4 ton High Mobility Multipurpose Wheeled Vehicle; their Dragon Medium Anti-Armor System; their M-60A1, the Corps' main battle tank; some separate and distinct artillery weapons; attack helicopters; the AV-8B aircraft built on the proven concepts of the VSTOL (Vertical and Short Take-Off and Landing); and so on. But for the most part they borrowed from the Navy and the Army, adapted what they took for their own purposes and came as close to real integration of the services as it was perhaps possible to come in the present uneasy association of forces within the Pentagon.

This did not mean that the Corps was any less jealous and protective of its individuality vis-à-vis the Army and the Navy. It just meant that it was run by practical men who, as leaders of the smallest service, had to use whatever they could get wherever they could get it and make the most of it.

It also relieved the Corps of a lot of headaches directly related to the design and procurement of equipment.

He was as aware as anyone that there were instances of needless duplication, of little changes to justify big budgets, in the Navy's arsenal of ships, planes and weaponry; but that was basically the Navy's problem. By dint of shrewd and incessant public relations work—aided by the undeniable bravery that gave the p.r. such a solid and defensible basis—the Corps managed to glide smoothly along in the Navy's shadow without having to take the brunt of the Navy's frequent battles with the Hill and other critics. But it was only there that it discreetly sought the Navy's shadow. In all other aspects of public visibility and public acclaim the Marines stood forth proudly and emphatically on their own, aided by what Tick had accurately described as one of the strongest lobbies on Capitol Hill—those members of Senate and House who look back with proud nostalgia upon the glamorous days when they too were members of the Corps.

A tidy service, discreetly inconspicuous when it came to budget battles, duplications, cost overruns, outrageously overpriced purchases, sex scandals, spy rings and other embarrassments that from time to time plagued the sister services. Marine dirty linen, of which there was not much, was washed as fast and secretively as Tick proposed to do with the minor but potentially embarrassing episode at the Pacific base. Marines did not malinger, misbehave, subvert or betray—or if they did, the matter was disposed of in rapid and ruthless silence. Marines were tough, brave, no-nonsense fighting men and dedicated, diligent, no-nonsense supportive women: such was the public image, rigorously maintained. And such, with very few exceptions, the actual fact.

He was right to be proud of his service, he told himself: and right to have the feeling that, generally, it was in excellent shape for the duties it was called upon to perform.

Of course there was, now, the problem of Nanukuvu—and the problem of Frio, which in both its phases seemed to be bogged down a bit. Not, in Pentagon terms, very much—after all, your average weapons system took twelve to fifteen years to bring on line, from idea to finished product, and your normal military mission sometimes as much as two or three years before everybody's requirements were met and everything was organized and ready to go. But in terms of what was apparently a rather impatient President and an evident desire on the part of the Soviets to get themselves a tidy little submarine base in the South Pacific as quickly as possible, perhaps things *were* moving a bit slowly. Perhaps they *could* be pushed along a little faster.

But not, he reminded himself sternly, to the jeopardy of the best interests of the Marine Corps. He had some good people working on the ALCAC, and they had assured him just this morning that they would have their recommendations ready in about another two weeks. After that, of course, there would have to be some thrashing out in the JCS, but that shouldn't take too long, even though he knew the others would have their own little shopping lists ready for Project Frio to work on.

As for Operation Frio, the Marines' timetable was far ahead of everybody else's. He and Al Rider had blocked it all out two months ago. The Marines knew what *they* wanted to do. It was the other services, as usual, that were holding things up.

He and Al had assumed that Al's selection to be commander had meant that the Marines would really be in charge. Not all this futzing around with the

Army's desire to get in the act, and Ham Stokes' monotonous insistence that the Air Force be given the paramount role, and Bumpy Stahlman's continual fidgeting about his precious damned Navy and how much it ought to be allowed to do.

He uttered an exasperated sigh at the thought of his fellow chiefs, all so—so *selfish* about their services. If they would just let the Marines handle it, it could all be so simple. Why were they such damned obstructionists?

He stood up, put on his jacket, checked to make sure the letter to the Pacific outpost commander was safely in the pocket, and started out. The phone rang before he reached the door and he turned back quickly as his secretary picked it up and then buzzed him.

"Adm. Stahlman," she said.

"Hell!" he said, and thought of Brash, and Brash's sad problem, and his own. He'd have plenty of time to battle with Bumpy at the White House tomorrow morning. "Tell him I've left."

"Right."

He took a deep breath and straightened his shoulders as he plowed along with his determined gait toward the car that would take him to the officers' club at Fort Myer. He didn't relish his talk with Brash. But Brash needed him—and it had to be done.

For his part, Adm. Stahlman was ending his usual neatly-packaged, busy day in the same way he always did, by carefully going over once again in his mind all decisions he had made since coming to work at 8 A.M. Like those of his fellow chiefs, these ranged all the way from such relative trivia as approving plans to coordinate the arrival of an aircraft carrier in San Francisco with the mayor's plans for a civic reception, to more serious matters such as a couple of incidents in the Mediterranean fleet similar to the one Tick's Pacific base commander was worried about, to really major matters such as what the Navy's official position should be on certain hitherto innocent categories of ships.

He had concentrated on each decision without haste, waste, emotional involvement or excessive mental perturbation. "Bumpy," Ham Stokes had once remarked, "works like a metronome." And so he did, unhurried, unflurried, cool, calm, completely competent. The concept of the Navy, its history and traditions, the bravery of its men and women, the enormous part it played in protecting the safety of the United States and her allies—all of these could, on occasion, bring tears as readily to the eyes of Adm. Stahlman as to anyone else. But they were carefully controlled tears, almost never visible to anyone watching: the neat, precise, well-ordered tears of a man whose only two truly consuming emotional commitments in a lifetime had been to his wife and his service. He had lost his wife and over the years his commitment to his service had settled into a well-delineated and well-guarded area of his heart, from which it was taken on suitable occasions and then carefully put away again after the occasions had passed.

This did not mean that he did not fight like a bulldog, every minute of every day, for the Navy and its proper place in the scheme of things. It just meant that he did not do so with the emotional excitability of Tick defending the Marines, but with a cool determination that reminded some older Navy hands of the late Adm. Ernest King, CNO in World War II. This made him a very effective battler for the Navy indeed—to the point where senior retirees told each other, "We're lucky to have him," and personnel on active duty said with affection, "Old Bumpy's got his eye on us," and thanked the Lord that he had, and on the Navy too.

Not even Brash Burford, he told himself now with satisfaction, not even Ham Stokes with all his far-flung fly-boys, could claim to preside over a greater portion of the earth's surface. The Navy was on every ocean, beneath the surface of every sea. It could be rationally argued, as he often had rationally argued on the Hill and elsewhere, that this would not have been necessary were not the Navy's global opponents doing exactly the same.

Their presence, in fact, was a constant irritant and a constant danger—not so much the danger of deliberate attack, though now and then, as with Hague Smith's colleagues in the Pacific, little deadly games were played that never got reported in the media. Rather it was the danger of some inadvertent clash that *would* become public, that *would* abruptly escalate into worldwide tension, that would put both navies and their countries on some collision course from which only a miracle could extricate them from the ultimate disaster.

Miracles, Bumpy thought grimly now as he prepared to put his desk in order and go home to a solitary meal and several hours of reading in the CNO's quarters at Tingey House in the Washington Navy Yard, were not easy to come by these days.

"The only miracle that counts," he had told the graduating class at Annapolis in May, "is absolute attention to duty. Given that, accidents don't happen and other kinds of miracles to correct them aren't necessary."

Or so he had believed all his life, and so he had conducted himself. It was a rigid standard and a tough one. But he felt it was the only way to prevent the final clash that would end the world. If by absolute attention to duty you could stop things before they happened, then the battle was mostly won. If you veered from that narrow path by so much as a figurative inch, in the world's present climate, you could be over the edge of the abyss and gone so fast there wouldn't be time to say John Paul Jones.

For instance, take Hague Smith, whose woeful little widow Madeline had written recently that she planned to be in Washington with their two young-sters sometime in the next few months and wanted to see him; a request he had considered carefully for several days and had finally decided to grant. He did not like to get too involved with widows and orphans—that did sometimes threaten to crack his almost implacable reserve. And he also did not feel that

Hague Smith himself deserved such a concession to those he had left behind, because Hague Smith had stepped over the edge of the abyss of his own foolish volition and had paid the penalty.

But Bumpy was not inhuman, and he had the impression, after studying the boy's record and talking via satellite to his commanding officer, that Hague Smith had been a nice young man whose main fault was overzealousness and a certain dashing willingness to take chances. *You don't take chances,* Bumpy had thought grimly when Hague's commanding officer had offered this almost as an excuse. It wasn't an excuse. But still, the boy had paid his price. And the spirit was hard to fault even if the action had been foolish. And the poor young wife and children weren't to blame. And so—

He dreaded it but felt it had to be done. The Hague Smith spirit had to be channeled, his death showed what happened when it ran wild; but to have it there in the Navy and in all the other services was a precious and invaluable thing. Like all the chiefs, he really did believe that the spirit of American youth was the single greatest weapon in the American arsenal. And he did believe that, all things being equal, it could decide the issue, every time.

Except, of course, he thought bleakly, that all things were *not* equal now, and that was the problem. They hadn't been equal for a good long while, despite valiant efforts in recent years to get them back on a footing of equality. The enemy still had the United States outmanned, outgunned and, in many volatile areas of the world, outflanked. The issue was still in very grave doubt. This Nanukuvu business was an example—perhaps *the* example, at the moment.

He too had heard from Zeecy, scarcely five minutes ago, about the White House meeting tomorrow morning. He was not prepared to offer excuses for what he thought would probably be criticized as the slowness of the services in meeting the situation out there. He had asked his people to prepare a study for him on what further modifications might be needed or desired on the ALCAC, and he had drawn up with his top aides what seemed to him a perfectly sound battle-plan, controlled by the Navy, for knocking out the Soviet emplacements. It was not his fault if both the ALCAC study and the battle-plan were not quite ready yet—it was just the system. It was almost impossible to explain to outsiders the tortuous channels through which things worked themselves up, down and sometimes sideways through the military and civilian bureaucracies in the Pentagon: they just did. It was just the way it was. He had given orders three months ago that speed was essential; but when a thing had to go through perhaps twenty or thirty different offices before it could be signed off on by himself, it just took time.

And a good part of it, he thought with some bitterness, was either the fear of what the Hill and the media would say or do if haste caused error, or it was directly attributable to some rule or requirement that Congress itself had mandated by law—some example of political micromanagement designed to keep *them* in the clear if something went wrong.

This constant buck-passing, within the services, between the services and particularly between the services and the Hill! It had not been like that—or at any rate, nowhere near as much like that—when he had been a young officer starting out. He could remember a time when lines of authority were reasonably direct—when a task could be clearly assigned and honestly accomplished —when everybody was motivated by the same general desire to get the job done—when people weren't afraid to take responsibility.

Not so now. Now it was a matter of who's-going-to-get-the-blame-if-things-go-wrong; and, if-they-could-go-wrong-then-let's-don't-get-too-involved; and, let's-pin-it-on-the-other-guy-before-it-happens-so-he-can't-pin-it-on-us; and, let's-require-so-many-things-to-be-done-that-almost-nothing-can-be-done-and-then-we'll-*really*-be-safe.

He had a sudden vivid, almost physical sensation of sea-spray in his face, a deck surging beneath his feet, a proud bow breaking and conquering the surging waves. *That* was the Navy, salt spray and bucking deck and racing sea— that was what *he* belonged to! Not this other stuff.

Bumpy was rather old-fashioned, when all was said and done.

But successfully negotiating the perilous shoals of Pentagon and Hill, White House and media was his assignment now, and he thought with satisfaction that he did it well. The problems he faced were often more subtle—and frequently ten times more petty, in this Washington world of politics—than his predecessors had faced but he liked to think that he was the worthy custodian of a service and a tradition that went back more than two centuries to the day in 1775 when the Second Continental Congress approved the acquisition and outfitting of two tiny naval vessels.

Two years later John Paul Jones sailed the ship *Ranger* into Quiberon Bay, France, and was given the first formal nine-gun salute accorded a naval ship carrying the flag of the new United States.

John Paul Jones, Bumpy reflected, was the first of that line of phrasemakers that the Navy seemed to have produced with fair regularity to inspire its later sons and daughters:

John Paul himself, in the *Bon Homme Richard,* fighting and ultimately defeating the superior British frigate *Serapis,* when asked if he was ready to give up: "I have not yet begun to fight!"

Capt. Oliver Hazard Perry, defeating a British squadron in Lake Erie in the War of 1812: "We have met the enemy and they are ours!"

Rear Adm. David Farragut at the Battle of Mobile Bay, 1864: "Damn the torpedoes, full speed ahead!"

Commodore George Dewey in the Battle of Manila Bay, 1898: "You may fire when ready, Gridley!"

And, from the beginning, the pride of service, still controlling today, that burgeoned when the tiny new navy engaged in rapid succession in the Revolution, a minor tiff with France, the war with the Barbary pirates, the War of 1812—a pinprick navy in those days, which did little more than harass Britain, then and for a century thereafter the world's greatest naval power—but a pinprick that grew in time into a major force that changed the balance and began the long journey through history that would eventually take the American flag into all the seas and all the oceans.

Triumphs exploratory, diplomatic, naval: the first successful Antarctic exploration, 1840; Commodore Matthew C. Perry signing the treaty with Japan that opened that closed society to trade with America and the world, 1854; decisive blockade of the South in the Civil War; capture of the Philippines, Cuba and Puerto Rico to decide the Spanish-American War, 1898; Commander Robert A. Peary reaching the North Pole, 1909; successful conveying of millions of American troops to Europe in 1917–18 without a single loss to German submarines . . . and then post-war doldrums and decline as America tried to turn its back on the world . . . uncertainty and unreadiness for what was obviously coming in 1939 . . . and the shame of Pearl Harbor, Dec. 7, 1941.

But from that, recoil, rebound, the irresistible drive back in the Pacific: the great victories of the Battle of the Coral Sea, May, 1942; the Battle of Midway, single most decisive naval battle of World War II, a month later; the Battle of the Philippine Sea, June, 1944; the Battle of Leyte Gulf, October, 1944 . . . and in the Atlantic, the successful convoying of men, munitions, supplies of all kinds, to Britain and the Allies; the greatest armada ever assembled, which on June 6, 1944, successfully supported the D-Day invasion of Normandy to begin the final collapse of Hitler Germany . . . followed within a decade by intensive naval bombardments and troop transport in the Korean War . . . then the Vietnam War . . . then the development of nuclear submarines . . . participation in the space program . . . decline in strength while the enemy was rapidly building his, particularly in the confused and confusing Carter years . . . resurgence in the Reagan years . . . and the present state of what Bumpy knew, with a deep and frequent sigh, to be somewhere between modest parity and potential disaster.

All of this, with its accumulations of history and tradition, *his* Navy. "You sound as though you really own that service, old man!" Clare used to josh him in the days when Clare was still around: he could hear her, with a wince of pain he supposed would never go away, joshing him still. And look at it now, the manpower, the fleet, the weapons:

Approximately 600,000 men and women, stationed, like those of all the services, in almost every friendly corner of the world; an annual budget of around $100 billion; weaponry whose inventory, part classified, part public, was growing in individual items at a rate which even he as CNO needed regular up-dates to keep abreast of, starting with the ponderous monarch of them all, the *Nimitz* class nuclear powered aircraft carrier and going on from there:

The refurbished *Iowa* class of out-of-mothballs battleships; the *Ohio* class Trident strategic missile submarine; the *Los Angeles* class nuclear powered attack submarine; the *Ticonderoga* class cruiser; the *Virginia* class nuclear powered guided missile cruiser; the *Arleigh Burke* class guided missile destroyer; the

Kidd class guided missile destroyer; the *Spruance* class destroyer; the *Oliver Hazard Perry* class guided missile frigate; the *Tarawa* class amphibious assault ship; the *Wasp* class multi-purpose amphibious assault ship; the *Whidbey Island* class landing ship dock; the *Austin* class amphibious transport dock service life extension program; the *Pegasus* class patrol combatant-missile (hydrofoil); the *Emory S. Land* class submarine tender; the *Cimarron* class fleet oiler; the *Yellowstone* class destroyer tender; the fleet oiler; the aviation logistics support ship; the fast logistic ship; the fleet ballistic missile resupply ship; the *Powhatan* class fleet tug . . . and so on, through the various support and repair vessels, to the ALCAC, the present focus of their concerns, and concluding with the lesser submarines, the nuclear powered research submarine; the *Mystic* class deep submergence rescue vehicle; *Turtle* class deep submergence vehicle; and the *Safeguard* class salvage ship.

And the airborne elements, of which the Navy of course demanded and received what it regarded as its fair share and only right, too, he thought: the fixed wing planes, the helicopters, the missiles . . . and the torpedoes, guns and fire control systems . . .

All of them, he told the Navy's critics stoutly in his own mind, fully justified even if they did duplicate a lot of functions of other items in the overall U.S. arsenal, and in some cases duplicated, in basic essentials, each other . . . such as the Seahawk helicopter (Mission: "Extend the sensors and weapon systems capabilities of surface combatants for anti-submarine warfare, anti-ship surveillance and targeting") and the Seasprite helicopter (Mission: "Extend and increase shipboard sensor and weapon capabilities against several types of enemy threats, notably submarines of all types, surface ships and patrol craft that may be armed with anti-ship missiles") . . . and the submarines which, aside from varying degrees of size and sophistication in weaponry and equipment, were essentially the same, with essentially just one mission: kill the enemy . . . and the surface ships, which in class after class, again aside from degrees of variation in size and sophistication, had, essentially, one or both of two purposes: attack and/or support . . .

He had never been one of the "questioning admirals" (of whom there were a few—in his opinion, too damned many). The Navy needed everything in its inventory, in his opinion; he was here to see that it got them; and with a method of quietly adamant rigidity that often proved more effective than the more blustery methods of Tick or Brash, he did very well.

He was a hard man to attack or thwart, Adm. John Eric Stahlman: he was so —so *Navy*, as Ham Stokes had remarked more than once in annoyed but grudging admiration. He never yielded unless he absolutely had to, and he never gave up even when all the odds seemed against him. Aided by the enormous personal dignity he had acquired over the years, he sailed on— outwardly, at least, as serene as one of his own aircraft carriers in summer weather; even though for the Navy, as for them all, the weather now was far from summery.

Yet in the broad perspective, he could not feel too gloomy. This was the history and the tradition and the power: he felt that in the last analysis it equipped the Navy, even now, to meet almost any challenge that could be flung at it. It was just a matter of getting everybody to pull together and work fast; and by normal Pentagon timetables he didn't really think three months was an unconscionable time for things to get geared up to handle the problem of Nanukuvu. It would, after all, be a major operation once they got into it. It was not something to be lightly undertaken. The JCS were not privy to all the infighting between State and Defense at the diplomatic level: he rather suspected that Terry Venner was gaining ground in his attempt to stop the military mission and confine the response to diplomatic protests. But from the military standpoint, *it took time.*

The President wanted to see them all tomorrow morning. Bumpy wondered exactly how forceful the President was going to be, now that the Soviets were becoming so solidly entrenched on the island that it would be virtually an act of war to root them out. If the Pentagon could have moved at once maybe it could have been done without great consequences. But the Pentagon just didn't work that way. The machine was too ponderous even when there was full cooperation. He expected, with a sudden ironic twist at the corner of his mouth, that the Boss, who had appeared to be somewhat equivocal about what to do when it first happened, might be even more so now.

He rolled down his sleeves, put on his jacket and cap, strode out to the outer office where he said a crisp and impersonal goodnight to the two female officers still typing correspondence, and went down to his waiting car.

As he entered the house he still expected, to this day, to hear a lighthearted, "He—ll—o—o!" But there was only silence. He changed stoically from uniform to tee shirt and jeans, took a TV dinner out of the freezer and prepared it for the microwave. He never wasted much time at the table: there was always plenty of reading to do, in other, less reminiscent rooms.

Gen. Stokes, on his way home from Andrews Air Force Base where he had participated in ceremonies marking the departure of the chief air minister of Turkey, wondered what Zenia would be up to tonight. It was one of her mysterious nights when she had "a committee meeting" to attend. He never thought it was anything else, but the frequency with which she engaged in this activity did annoy him from time to time.

"Can't you *ever* stay home and look after the kids?" he had inquired with some exasperation around 3 P.M. when she had called to say she'd be out.

Her response had been tart, which was increasingly the case:

"I could ask you the same, but I wouldn't want to jeopardize the defense of the free world."

"Don't be sarcastic," he said in a tired tone. "It's been a long day, and I'm not through yet."

"Well, *I'm* going out," she announced firmly. "I have a committee meeting. I've asked Sally if she'll baby-sit until you get home."

Sally was sixteen, white and lived next door. Her father was an Air Force brigadier general who was director of contracting and acquisition policy.

"Can't you find somebody besides Sally?" he inquired. "There'll probably be a dozen boyfriends underfoot by the time I get home."

"Then hurry up and get here," Zenia suggested. "It'll be all right if you aren't *too* late."

"I'm never later than I have to be," he said, more mildly than he felt. Why couldn't she get off this kick, anyway?

"That's as may be," she observed. There was a pause. He debated whether to fill it with conversation or just let it drop. She solved it for him.

"Well, goodbye. I really hope you won't be too late."

"Goodbye," he said. "I'll do my best."

"I'll bet," she said, and hung up before he could frame a rejoinder.

He sighed, big frame leaning forward over the desk, big hands holding the papers he had to initial or sign or send back down the chain of command for further work. He too had a good secretary, a female lieutenant colonel, white, who had accompanied him in his last three duty posts and had become as indispensable as all the good ones seemed to be. There was a politeness between them—to this day they scrupulously addressed each other by rank—but she was highly efficient and she understood his frequent frustrations and the way he sometimes wished he could chuck all the desk duty and get back to the sky.

He particularly wished it right now, after getting the call from Zeecy and learning about tomorrow's full-dress review of Nanukuvu at the White House. If the damned Navy and the damned Army and the damned Marines had only left the Air Force alone to do its job in the very beginning, Nanukuvu would already be a fast-fading memory in the history books. But, no: everybody had to get into the act. So the usual futzed-up mess had been created, and now nobody was moving very fast in a situation that obviously should have been terminated two days after it began. If it was subject to termination at all.

Ham Stokes had felt from the beginning that the new inhabitants intended to stay; and of course, as was obvious, the longer the response was delayed, the more difficult it would become to dislodge them.

There had been a sense of urgency in the beginning.

What had happened to it?

As far as the Air Force was concerned, he did not feel that his people could fairly be charged with dragging their feet. He had asked them for recommendations on the ALCAC and had ordered the preparation of a battle-plan geared to the needs and abilities of the only service that could do the job as quickly and efficiently as it must be done, namely his own. Both reports, he was assured, were almost ready. Three months' lapsed time did not seem too unreasonable. When he felt impatient, he knew from long experience that impatience did no good.

These things, here, moved at their own pace.

Unlike the field, they could not be accelerated by one commander's impatience.

They took time.

He prided himself that nobody could make things move faster or more effectively than Ham Stokes when he got on the rampage. But there was a point at which further desk-pounding did not produce results, in the Pentagon.

The sheer weight of people! Each with his or her task to perform, each with his or her concept of the overall mission, each with a certain area, however small, of responsibility or authority to which each clung, willing to do battle to the death to protect it against challenge or diminution.

He sometimes thought he should announce Ham's Law:

Speed is determined by the number of people it takes to make speed. Speed is decreased in direct ratio to the increase in the number of people.

In the Pentagon, Ham's Law ruled supreme.

And yet, leaving aside Nanukuvu—which the President had evidently decided he was not going to permit anyone to do—Ham felt that the Air Force was in good shape around the world. It faced tough competition but it was still a most formidable fighting force. It had begun formally with the creation of an Aeronautical Division of the Army Signal Corps on Aug. 1, 1907, three and a half years after Wilbur and Orville Wright made the first heavier than air flight at Kitty Hawk, N.C., in December, 1903. It now consisted of approximately six hundred thousand men and women, flying or supporting aircraft of all types whose exact number fluctuated constantly and in many categories was classified, but which totaled in the hundreds of thousands and literally covered the globe. Its cost also fluctuated and in many areas was classified. It was presently running over $100 billion a year.

Its history was one of significant dates, famous battles, famous men—and many of all three that were not famous, yet were greatly significant in the irresistible growth of the service from its first tentative, controversy-filled days to its present commanding position in the national defense.

In 1911 the Aeronautical Section had one plane and one pilot. In 1914 Congress created its successor, the Aviation Section, with 60 officers, 260 enlisted men and an appropriation of $250,000. Its first use as a military weapon came in 1916 when one of its pioneers, Capt. Benjamin Foulois, led the First Aero Squadron into Mexico as part of the Mexican Border Expedition ordered by President Woodrow Wilson. A year later American entry into World War I brought the first great burst of growth as America and all major nations recognized that Wilbur and Orville Wright's invention, which the brothers had naïvely thought could be used for peace, might well become a completely devastating weapon of war.

World War I: sudden growth, followed, in American fashion, by sudden lapse; and the subsequent struggles of Gen. Billy Mitchell, who was court-martialed for his pains, to prove that the airplane could be used to decide the fate of nations. Most particularly—and most fatally for his career, though he was honored many years later by Congress—he said and proved that it could be used to sink ships.

For a time alarmed and determined Navy opposition crippled the growth of the Air Force, but not for long, as pioneering exploits such as Charles Lindbergh's transatlantic flight and the obviously growing imperatives of the coming second world conflict established their own inexorable logic. Blunders, stupidity, crushing defeats at Pearl Harbor and Clark Field in the Philippines when the Japanese attacked; phenomenal recuperation and growth as America rallied and her air forces came back to play a major role in deciding the battles of Europe and the Pacific.

And so in due course to the golden glories of the space program—walks on the moon—probes into the deep infinitudes of space—the steady creation of ever-faster, ever more accurate planes—the somber addition of spy satellites, cruise missiles, the ICBM and the MX—and the ability, now, to destroy the great globe itself and all who live upon it . . . a little over eight decades away from Kitty Hawk, and the hopeful experiment of the Wright brothers already transformed by the mind, the greed, the fear and the fatal self-destructiveness of humankind into the carrier of death and the messenger of oblivion.

These philosophic concerns, though he acknowledged their existence and perhaps their validity, did not concern the chief of staff of the Air Force overmuch.

His service was now spread across the world wherever America had commitments, and that was everywhere. The major names marched through his mind in sonorous parade. He was responsible for every one of them:

In continental United States, major active Air Force installations in almost every state . . . names familiar such as Andrews in Maryland, Westover in Massachusetts, Langley in Virginia, Wright Patterson in Ohio, Eglin and Patrick in Florida, Barksdale in Louisiana, Maxwell in Alabama, Randolph and Sheppard in Texas, Grand Forks in North Dakota, Kirtland in New Mexico, Luke in Arizona, March, Edwards, Travis and Vandenberg in California, McChord in Washington, Elmendorf in Alaska, Wheeler and Hickam in Hawaii . . . names less familiar such as Chanute in Illinois, Francis E. Warren in Wyoming, Wurtsmith in Michigan, Dobbins in Georgia, Seymour Johnson in North Carolina, Griffis in New York, Pease in New Hampshire, Indian Springs in Nevada, Keesler in Mississippi, Malmstrom in Montana . . .

And in Europe, United States Air Forces in Europe, USAFE, bases in the Netherlands, Spain, Belgium, West Germany, West Berlin, Italy, Greece, Turkey . . .

And in the Atlantic, bases in Greenland, Iceland and the Azores . . .

And in Central America, a base in Panama . . .

And in the Pacific, bases in Japan, South Korea, Okinawa, the Philippines. . . .

And the various commands, including the Air Force Communications Command, the Air Force Logistics Command, the Air Force Systems Command, the Air Training Command, the Air University, the Air Force Academy, the Alaskan Air Command, the Military Airlift Command, the Pacific Air Forces, the Strategic Air Command, the Tactical Air Command, the Space Command, the Accounting and Finance Center, the Audit Agency, the Commissary Service, the Legal Services Center, the Office of Medical Support, the Security Police, the Operational Test and Evaluation Center, the Reserve and Air National Guard, the— . . . it was quite possible to go on for fifteen minutes.

And the constantly expanding arsenal of Air Force weapons, some unique, more duplicative of the other services but in existence because the Air Force, like the rest of them, cooperated only reluctantly in developing joint weaponry, joint purchasing, even, in many instances of which Nanukuvu threatened to become one, joint tactics:

The supersecret Advanced Technology Bomber, ATB; the B-1B bomber; the aging but still effective B-52 Superfortress . . . the strategic medium-range low-altitude bombers, F-111 and FB-111A; the fighters, the F-4 Phantom II, the F-5E/F Tiger II, the F-15 Eagle, the F-16 Fighting Falcon, the Advanced Tactical Fighter, ATF, the F-106 Delta Dart . . . the attack and observation aircraft, the A-10 Thunderbolt II, the AC-130 A/H, the O-2A, the OA-37B Dragonfly, the OC-10A Bronco . . . the reconnaissance and special-duty aircraft, the SR-71A/B Blackbird, the U-2 and TR-1, the RF-AC, the EC-130, the EC-135, the EF-111A Raven, the E-3 Sentry (AWACS), the E-4B, the EC-18B ARIA, the EC-130 E/H . . . the transports and tankers, the C-23 Sherpa, the CT-39 Sabreliner, the C-130 Hercules . . . the various types of helicopters . . . again, one could go on and on.

Like all who were directly involved and responsible, Ham Stokes knew perfectly well that all these fancy names and numbers and codes and designations concealed perhaps five or six fundamental and really necessary items—just as Bumpy knew this about *his* weaponry and Brash about *his* weaponry and Tick about *his* weaponry—all those innumerable named, numbered, coded and designated items that each service had in its arsenal.

But each fancy name and number and code and designation represented some powerful element in each service that must be satisfied—or some powerful Senator or Congressman whose district, state or constituency must be protected and given industry and jobs—or some major contractor whose equipment and employees must be kept busy so that in the event of a real national emergency they would be in operation and ready to start producing something really pertinent to the national defense. If, that is, there was time.

Waste, duplication, overlapping of projects, a multiplicity of slightly differing items of weaponry and equipment to do essentially the same job that one agreed-upon model could do. But, he thought wryly, who's to agree? When so much is at stake for so many, when such enormous profits and so much career enhancement await those who diligently order, and those who blandly produce, such enormous redundancies?

He knew these were thoughts that might startle some civilian critics of the military, who did not believe them capable of such self-criticism; but he knew few top-ranking officers who did not, in their innermost private contemplations, arrive at some such distaste and dismay for the system that produced so many enormously expensive and wasteful duplications and overlappings.

And yet—and yet.

The system ruled them all, and it was a most unusual man who tried to change it, or was even partially able to do so even if he thought he could.

And of course, to take the most immediate specific, there was no doubt in his mind that modifications of the ALCAC were desirable, because out of them could come some substantial and necessary improvements in communications that could be of value to the Air Force. There was no certainty of this, but to deny the experiments would be to foreclose results that might possibly be of benefit. In his opinion it was well worth the effort and expense.

Having thus swung full circle in an elapsed time of ten seconds—what Zenia called his "convenient double vision"—he was not even aware that he had done so. His responsibility was to the Air Force. In wishing to put bells and whistles on the ALCAC he was simply discharging that responsibility.

He was unable to view it any other way: the Air Force mission was unique, all-important and must not be tampered with. Ordinary rules of economy and budgetary restraint did not apply when it came to the specific project that might benefit the Air Force.

The Air Force was different.

How a highly intelligent, usually bluntly logical human being could move thus with perfect sincerity along two diametrically opposed lines of thought he did not stop to analyze because he was not conscious that it was happening. All dedicated servicemen were like that. On an intellectual plane he could recognize, as he just had, waste and duplication and overlapping in his own service. But when it came to challenges to what his own service wished to do, suggestions that it be held to the same standards of restraint he often and loudly advocated for the others, there was an instantaneous shifting of mental gears and the whole perspective changed 180 degrees.

When Zenia pointed this out with some irony his reaction was always strong: "I don't like it when you make fun of the Air Force!"

This in turn provoked her into the sort of argument, lately becoming all too frequent, which usually wound up in a discussion of mutual shortcomings, followed by recriminations which, alarmingly, seemed to be increasingly bitter.

He didn't want to fight with Zenia; he didn't want to have frictions and tensions; he didn't want to even think about the possibility of divorce, though it was coming more and more often to mind. He just wanted what he had always wanted, a family relationship that would support and sustain him while he achieved what he knew he was able and destined to achieve. Divorce at this point was simply unthinkable.

There was the fact that they still loved each other—he guessed; and the fact of deeply shared concern for the children; and the fact that divorce would be absolutely devastating to his career at this particular time when he was hoping to succeed Zeecy as chairman of the JCS.

It was out of the question.

Nonetheless tension was rising in his marriage for no specific reason he could determine with absolute certainty. Custom, habit, familiarity, boredom— the years—all the usual clichés probably applied to some degree. But it seemed to him there must be something more than that, to cause her to run the risk of disturbing his mental and emotional tranquillity at the very time when it was most important to him to have them.

Ham Stokes had never been a particularly introspective or analytical man when it came to human emotions and relationships. When he had first seen Zenia MacDonald he had wanted her and she had wanted him: it had been as simple as that. Later had come what he regarded as all the emotional frills that women seemed to find necessary, but as far as he was concerned it was a mating made in heaven, a comfort and refuge for what had been a restless and searching heart, and above all, a great and necessary assist and support for his career.

He had not worried too much about asking Zenia to give up *her* career, because essentially, she hadn't. They had moved around a lot in the service, of course, but she had always been able to find some kind of legal work, usually assisting servicemen and their families on whatever base they happened to be stationed, and always managing "to keep my hand in," as she often put it. She didn't sound dissatisfied when she said that, although he could see that she might well have preferred a husband with a more settled job that would have permitted her to join some prestigious law firm and stay there. But neither the frequent moves—nineteen in thirty years, which was not at all an unusual average for any of the services—nor the four children, had appeared to create any major disruption in her legal interests. It was true that the major career advancement had been his, but, after all, wasn't that the way it was supposed to be, in the military? There really would have been a divorce a long time ago if that hadn't been conceded.

No, it wasn't lack of settled career, or the arrival of the kids, or even what he referred to with sometimes scathing sarcasm as "your precious social con- science" that had seemed to sour things lately—although if he had to choose any single factor to blame, it probably would have been this last. He had suffered it with what seemed to him great patience for many years, even when it *had* been a potential threat to his career. He thought it was fair time now for her to knock it off and settle down.

She knew the reason, of course, and lately she had begun to refer to it in what he could only consider a jeering manner. Every time he came forth with "your precious social conscience," he got right back, "your precious JCS chairmanship." He didn't like this, one little bit.

"You know perfectly well," he had said only last night, trying to be calm, "that the chairmanship is something I've dreamed of and worked for, my entire military career. Are you going to make me blow it, now?"

"Nothing can make you blow it," she had replied firmly, "except yourself. Not my 'precious social conscience,' as you put it, and thank God one of us has one, but just you, yourself."

"And what can I, myself, do," he asked sarcastically, "when I've already reached the highest position any black has ever achieved in any of the services?"

"You can be too overbearing and you can take too much for granted," she said with the decisive manner she used when declaring some home truth to one of the kids. "You haven't got a hammerlock on that job, you know. Zeecy may be for you, and maybe the SecDef, but there are plenty of others in the running and it's up to the President, isn't it? He may have somebody entirely different in mind."

"Well," he said, retreating as he often did to what he considered safe ground, "you don't help it any with all your 'causes.'"

"My 'causes,'" she retorted, "haven't hurt your career so far, and they aren't going to hurt it now."

"That's only because—" he began, and stopped. As usual she wouldn't let it rest until he said it right out.

"Only because what?" she demanded. "What are you trying to tell me?"

"Only because we're black and there's a sort of reverse liberal snobbism at work, even in the military. It's all right for you to be for a nuclear freeze and join protests against the MX and the cruise missile, and all the rest of it, because you're black. You're the in-house protester, and it's all right. They wouldn't take it from Vi Burford or Doreen Tock or Renee McCune, but they'll take it from you because it's good for the image to have one like you around. After all—" and his tone unfortunately again became sarcastic—"you're the wife of Gen. Harmon Stokes, and it looks good in the media when we graciously permit Mrs. Gen. Stokes to demonstrate against the military. Particularly when it can all be dismissed with a patronizing pat on the head and the assurance—which is also quite patronizing, actually—that *of course* we wouldn't be so petty as to let it hurt General Stokes' career."

"Then what are you worrying about?" she demanded triumphantly. "If that's true, then what I do can't really hurt your career, and if you don't make chairman it won't be because of me. Now, will it?"

"Oh, for Christ's sake," he said in a disgusted tone. "You do love to make legal arguments, don't you?"

"I should," she said with satisfaction. "I'm a lawyer. Maybe I'll find myself a good firm in D.C. and settle down, now that you're either going to become chairman or retire. One way or the other we're probably going to be staying here, aren't we? Maybe it's time for me to get established at last."

"Go ahead," he said indifferently, "as long as it's a halfway decent firm."

"It will probably be one that thinks the way I do," she remarked.

He snorted.

"I don't really care how you think, as long as it doesn't hurt me."

And was unable to understand why she turned pale and looked as though he had actually struck her. There were even tears in her eyes. He couldn't understand this at all. He was only stating the truth, and he didn't have much patience with people who couldn't take it when Ham Stokes told the truth. It was one of the things he was noted for.

In Quarters No. 1 at Fort Myer, Vi Burford sat and waited with a sort of resigned patience for Brash to come home. Resigned patience, she reflected sadly, seemed to be something she was feeling a lot of, lately. It seemed to be becoming necessary.

Although she still professed to be as puzzled as Brash about the nature of her "little spells," she had finally concluded in her own mind what they indicated. For her, privately, it was no longer "my little spells." It was "my illness." A couple of days ago she had slipped up for a moment and referred to it thus to Brash. He had looked so stricken that she had hastily corrected herself and pretended it was just a silly exaggeration. But she had given it a great deal of thought in the depths of many nights and the long stretches of many days, and she had also, finally, come right out and asked Doreen Tock what she thought. And, finally, Dorry had told her.

So now there was nothing to do but just wait—and try to help Brash be strong. It was so important that he not be bothered or upset at this crucial time when the President and the SecDef, and all the other people who were consulted before a consensus was reached on a new chairman, were making up their minds. He must continue to be what she had always proudly considered him, one of the finest officers and most admirable chiefs of staff the Army had ever had. Major ingredients in this had always been his even temper, his sense of humor and his unflappable calm in the face of crisis or necessary decision.

They both knew, far more than the world ever did, that the strongest element in that calm had been the unwavering love, loyalty and support of his wife.

He had done his best to return this, but for Vi Burford up to now it had never seemed to be really necessary. She was always so steady, so even-tempered, so completely calm herself, that while she greatly appreciated all the innumerable loving things he had done for her over the years, she had never had quite the same need for reassurance. Neither of them had ever mentioned this—he couldn't quite bring himself to admit it, and she was so modest that she would never have dreamed of embarrassing him by articulating it. But they both knew that when all was said and done, the rock Gen. Burford's life rested upon was Violet Burford. That was one reason why the Tocks, whom they had never met until appointment to the JCS but had quickly become fond of, were so devastated by what they believed to be the true nature of Vi's illness.

"It will just kill Brash," Dorry had remarked and Tick had nodded grimly.

"And just when he needs to be at his best," he said.

"Is he going to make it?" she asked, their conversation a tacit admission that Tick, for all his bluff abilities and dedication to the Corps, was probably not.

"Ham's his competition," Tick acknowledged, matter-of-factly and without rancor: a Marine, after all, took what came and made the best of it. "At the moment I'd put my money on Brash, but if this really throws him, as it well may, then . . . I don't know."

"I hope he gets it," Dorry said flatly. "I like Ham and Zenia, and I know all the reasons why it would be a great thing if somebody like—like him—became chairman, but naturally I want it for Brash."

"We'll see," Tick said, still grimly. "He's going to need all the help we can give him."

"They both are," Doreen said sadly. "Poor people."

Yet as Vi Burford sat waiting in the gentle summer twilight for Brash to come home, she did not feel that she was "poor people." In her innermost heart she was often rebellious, often sad—but also resigned and patient and beginning to be filled with a strange serenity that came, she supposed, from her determination not to worry Brash—and, perhaps, from something even deeper. She had never been a particularly religious woman, but she had long ago concluded that when you really needed strength the Lord gave it to you if you regarded Him with sufficient respect and submission to His will. She was too realistic to think that the will was always for the best—sometimes it seemed to her, as it did now, that He was far more cruel and ironic than He was compassionate and loving—but that it was a will that could not be defeated and must in the long run be accepted, she had long believed. Out of that acceptance she found that she was indeed gaining strength, far more than she would ever have dreamed possible on the snowy day when she had first suspected that something was going fundamentally wrong with her hitherto well-ordered and productive life.

She reviewed briefly now the status of her obligations—the children grown and happily married, Brash on the threshold of the triumphant culmination of his career, her own life in a sense triumphant also, and complete—and felt that she could safely begin to withdraw mentally and emotionally from everything except the overriding necessity to support and strengthen her husband so that nothing at all could disturb the peace of mind he must have to achieve the chairmanship. It was a goal as political as everything else in a democratic society, and they knew, as everyone in the military knew, that many factors far removed from character and skill went into promotions and selections. Those two things were necessary, of course, no fool or incompetent ever made chief of staff or chairman of the JCS; but once that was said, a lot of other things entered in, in the tricky world of Washington. There was the SecDef to consider, what his feelings and commitments were—the President—powerful members of Congress—popular approval—the media—many, many things went into the making of a chairman of the JCS. It was necessary to move with a sure foot and a steady hand when you neared that eminence. It was also necessary to move as much as possible with a clear mind and an untroubled heart.

She made up her mind once and for all, as she sat there while the heat-pummeled earth turned slowly toward night's restoring coolness, that she would not trouble Brash with her illness any more than could possibly be helped, until the time, now less than a year ahead, when the chairmanship would be decided and the tensions of competition be over. She too felt that of the present chiefs, Brash and Ham Stokes were the two likeliest competitors, unless the President fooled them as he might and reached down into the ranks to select someone else. This had happened in the past and could happen now; but that was not the estimate on which they had to proceed. They had to proceed on the supposition that Brash was in the running; and that supposition decided, as his best interests always had, what she must do.

So she composed herself, waiting in the warm deepening dusk, and began thinking practically of how to manage the challenge fate had handed her. It would not be easy—the episodes of forgetfulness, of sudden physical quirks and oddities, of the unexpected stumble either mental or physical always lurking, lurking—but she must find the strength to do the best she could. And above all, she must not admit to Brash what she thought the matter was, nor submit to medical tests and evaluations that would make it impossible for him not to know.

She heard a car drive up, pause, and drive away; heard him enter the historic old house filled with the memories of so many famous Army leaders of the past; heard his customary, "Hey, troop!"—and sensed instantly that he probably knew. Something different, something she recognized without even defining it was in his voice: fear.

"I'll fix myself a drink," he called. "Have you got one? Like another?"

"No, thanks," she called back. "Did you have a busy day?"

"Oh, the usual," he said, still in the kitchen, ice clinking in glass, sound of pouring, bottle being returned to shelf, cupboard closed. She did not turn when he came out on the porch behind her, leaned down, kissed her cheek, took the hand she reached up to him over her shoulder and gave it a sudden squeeze that conveyed more desperation than he probably realized.

"How about you?" he asked. "Everything go all right?"

"Not bad," she said as he sat down in the deck chair beside her and stretched out his legs with elaborate casualness. She smiled. "Nothing dramatic."

"That's good," he said, reaching out to squeeze her hand again. He managed a quite respectable grin. "Me, either. Just the usual good old Army crap."

"I'm glad it didn't pose any challenges," she said, managing to sound humorous and wry.

"Nary a one," he said, "except that damned Nanukuvu again. But, we'll get over that."

"Good," she said. "I know it's been troubling you."

"A little," he admitted. "But it will pass."

He took several sips from his glass, hesitated an almost imperceptible second, and then spoke in an offhand manner.

"Vi," he said, "do you suppose you ought to go to Walter Reed and get a checkup on this funny little business of yours?"

"No, I don't," she said firmly. "What makes you think so?"

"Nothing," he said quickly. "Nothing at all. I just thought maybe—well, maybe you'd feel better about it, that's all."

"No, I'm fine," she said. "Unless, of course, you'd feel better if I—"

"Oh, no," he said hastily. "No, I just thought maybe you—"

"No," she said, quietly but with a finality he did not dare challenge.

"O.K.," he said after a moment. "If you feel comfortable about it."

"I'm fine," she repeated. "Just fine."

He reached out a hand again suddenly and again gave hers a hard squeeze.

"That's good," he said, congratulating himself that his voice was quite normal, not a quaver in it that he could detect. "That's *good.*"

So a silence fell and for a while they said nothing, sitting side by side in the fading light until presently it was time to go in to dinner and they went; accompanied by the quiet terror that would haunt them now through all the days that they might have left together.

Also at Fort Myer, in the quarters of the chairman, JCS, that shrewd and pragmatic lady, Mrs. Gen. McCune, was directing the invaluable and indispensable Carleene in putting the final touches on the elaborate chocolate mousse that Renee wanted to serve Zeecy. If he ever got home, that is, which as had often been the case in almost thirty years of married life, she was not at all certain of at the moment. Not that this still bothered her in an emotional way—that had ended, with her usual great realism, perhaps thirty days after their honeymoon—but simply because he was *hers,* and damn it, it was time for him to *be* there.

Carleene, who understood the moods of her ladies pretty well—she got passed around among the wives of the chiefs and the SecDef like some old bean bag, she often told her husband, but it was fun, never a dull moment—realized that Mrs. McCune was feelin' pretty restless tonight. Carleene didn't blame her, being married to a handsome devil like Gen. McCune, who had never, she suspected, managed to keep his pants zipped when opportunity came along. For men like Gen. McCune, she knew, opportunity was there practically every old minute of every old day. She was glad she was married to easygoin' old Jim, who had many fine qualities as father and husband, not the least of the latter being that, whatever he might *wish,* he was a plain, ordinary, down-home lookin' man with a face like an old bulldog that not many women gave a second glance to. Which was a good thing for him, as Carleene, for all that she was a wiry and seemingly frail little thing who had six kids including the newest little three-month-old slugger, would have reacted very violently if she had ever caught him strayin'.

But Mrs. Gen. McCune, who undoubtedly had caught the general strayin' on Lord knew how many occasions, seemed to take it all in stride. Carleene expected she had some mighty sharp words for him sometimes—she could cut anybody down in two seconds with that dry French accent of hers—but they stayed together. She suspected, in fact, that there never had been any serious question that they wouldn't.

"I bet she's gone her way sometimes, too," she told Jim when the subject came up, as it often did, "and I just *know* he's gone his way. But they's used to it. They're not goin' to change, I reckon. Ever."

And of course they wouldn't, although there were times, like these recent weeks, when Renee had allowed herself to reach a level of annoyance that was quite unusual, for her. She didn't know how far things had gone with Luzanne Johnson—not as far as Zeecy would have liked, she suspected with an ironic little smile—but mentally she had a sense that they were a lot closer than she liked. It was possible to hop in and out of bed mentally with a lot greater frequency—and sometimes a great deal more satisfaction—than circumstances and reality permitted. She could stand the physical competition, that was nice for anybody while it lasted but it never lasted long; but the mental competition, when it came from someone fully as attractive and intelligent as she was, she did not like. One little bit.

So there was an extra sharpness in her voice tonight as she told Carleene— for perhaps the thousandth time, she estimated with exasperation—how to top off the mousse in just the right way with Renee's own special recipe for whipped cream, macadamia nuts, cherries and assorted liqueurs. Carleene could manage this a dozen times perfectly, and then suddenly—*zut!* She seemed to forget all about it and Renee had to start all over again.

They were all alike, she told herself scornfully, thinking back to the days when her father, who himself had eventually risen to general, was a captain in then French-owned Cameroon. They were just different, that's all. They weren't quick, they weren't intelligent in the sense that she was intelligent, they weren't good at all the complicated things that made real civilization work. They were perceptive, intuitive, shrewd—very shrewd at stubbornly getting their own way—but they just weren't *civilized.*

So thought Mrs. Gen. McCune, who had learned long ago that to express such sentiments in racially conscious—and self-conscious—America was not the thing to do if one wanted to assist one's husband in his steadily rising career. And she could honestly say that she always had assisted it, and not Zeecy nor anyone else could fault her on that. But they couldn't prevent her thinking it.

"*Carleene!*" she said sharply. "*First* liqueurs, *then* the nuts, all right? It is a matter of timing, is it not? And proportion?"

"Yes, ma'am," Carleene said amicably. "Sometimes I just *forget.*"

"Eh, well," Renee said with a shrug, because after all, she had learned in Cameroon that there was no point in ranting on about it, "we're all human." *Your kind less than some of us, however,* she thought while her face arranged itself with some effort in a patient smile. "So let us proceed with more care, if you please. It is not, after all, grits."

"No, ma'am," Carleene said with a chuckle. "It sure ain't."

"Very well," Renee said firmly. "Forward!"

The second time, after the initial mistake had been dumped down the garbage disposal, was more successful. There was *some* hope, after all, Renee told herself dryly. One just had to keep a sense of proportion.

And, she thought more grimly, one had to keep a sense of proportion about Sen. Johnson, with whom she took pains to maintain a reasonably cordial, if mutually wary, friendship. Perhaps because the maiden name was Labouchere, the background Louisiana French, the racial relationship still creating a certain mutual perception, quickness and understanding, she did not find this too difficult to do. She only wished, with as near to wistful regret as Renee McCune ever permitted herself, that they could be real friends instead of uneasy ones sparring across the handsome head of Gen. Zoren Chace McCune. Not that Renee ever permitted herself any *real* friends, of course. That way, she had always believed, lay unpredictability, uncertainty, ultimately shattering betrayal of closeness and trust. But insofar as she was capable of it, she would have enjoyed having Luzanne Labouchere Johnson for a friend. It would have given her someone she could really talk to in this wasteland of petty military minds, always obsessed with the "three p's," pay, promotion and pension, and the tiresome problems of meeting the enemy, in which she had found herself all her life.

She suspected that genuine friendship was what Luzanne would like to have with her, because she had sensed in their conversation at that luncheon three months ago that the Senator, while flattered and perhaps even a little bit thrilled by Zeecy's interest, did not really want or intend for it to go any further. With her customary native directness, Renee had precipitated the subject. With the softening of three hundred years in America, Luzanne had attempted to couch it in subtler diplomacy. Renee, as she always did with everyone except Zeecy, prevailed—though once she had started the conversation it did not go quite so disconcertingly for Luzanne as she had hoped.

"Now," she had said as soon as they had been shown to their table in the

Senate dining room and had taken their seats along with the usual thrilled constituents, gracious Senators, assorted lobbyists, staff members and political power-brokers from across the continent, "I understand from my husband that you are one of the best friends the military has on Capitol Hill. One of the best friends, indeed, that *he* has."

"Suppose we order," Luzanne suggested with a pleasant smile, "and then we can discuss your husband. Whom, incidentally, I must say I admire tremendously. It must be a great satisfaction to be married to such a man."

Renee gave a wry little chuckle and touched one hand lightly to the perfectly coiffed silver-gray hair which she had spent two hours this morning at her favorite salon getting in shape to impress the Senator.

"It passes the time," she said, at which Luzanne broke into a peal of her charming laughter. Renee, after a puzzled second, joined her.

"Oh, Renee!" Luzanne said. "You are so—so—well, let's order, shall we? Then we can get back to Zeecy."

"It is why we are here, is it not?" Renee inquired. "I," she said, turning to the waitress who had come to the table in response to Luzanne's wave, "will have the shrimp salad, please. And coffee."

"Admirable choice," Luzanne agreed; and decided she would meet Renee on her own ground. "So what has Zeecy told you about me? Aside from my support for the military, that is? And for him personally?"

"His observation is the same as mine," Renee said. "That you are most intelligent, charming, able. And that he values you highly."

"Indeed," Luzanne remarked. "I must say it's mutual. He is a most competent officer. And an excellent chairman of the Joint Chiefs. He will be much missed when his term expires."

Renee shrugged.

"They come and go. He has served his time, and well, I think. It is time for him to retire. He is, after all, an old man."

"Ancient," Luzanne agreed solemnly. "But it is not apparent in either of you."

Renee gave her a sudden sharp glance but Luzanne was waving gayly across the room to Jerry Castain, who was holding forth to a worshipful group of awed Hoosiers. Her expression was as pleasant and innocent of guile as always.

"My!" she said. "What a good salad!"

"It suffices," Renee said dryly. "Then, if he is so ancient, and *I* am so ancient, why is it that you and he are—are—"

"What, Renee?" Luzanne inquired. "I don't think we are anything, except good friends. And in fact—" she looked thoughtful—"perhaps we could not even be called that. Good working acquaintances concerned with the military, might perhaps be a better way to put it."

"He is very conscious of you," Renee said, picking delicately at her salad. "He is aware that you exist."

"And am I aware that *he* exists!" Sen. Johnson said with a fervor whose true nature, real or mocking, Renee could not quite decide. "How could any woman not be, he is so—so handsome—and so dashing—and such a perfect model of what a great officer ought to be. He really is my ideal!"

"You are more than that to him, I think," Renee observed. Luzanne turned upon her a sudden candid gaze.

"Well, Renee," she said in a matter-of-fact voice, "that may be, and if it disturbs you I am sorry. But I want you to know, I think you have a right to know, that if there is anything like that, it exists on his part and not on mine—"

"Entirely?" Renee interrupted. Luzanne paused but her gaze remained open and candid.

"Perhaps not entirely," she admitted. "He is, as we agree, a very handsome and appealing man. And a delightful character—even if, as I suspect, he is, like all men, not all that easy to live with all the time. But as for anything—anything —serious—on my part, that's out of the question. I like him, I'm flattered that anyone should show any interest in me, even platonic, at *my* ancient age, but— no, Renee. Not guilty, here."

"I think he is guilty, in his thoughts."

"That may be," Sen. Johnson said. "I'm not responsible for that. All I'm responsible for is me. And on that score, Renee, you can rest easy."

"It will simply intrigue him more," Renee predicted as she took the final peck at her salad. "I know my husband. You have your own beauty and charm, which are great. And your fine intelligence, which I must admit. And your own high position of United States Senator, which I am sure intrigues many men. And now you have the extra appeal of the chase. You will not be easy, like—" her mouth twisted for just a second and Luzanne had a sudden unsettling glimpse of what it must be like to be Mrs. Zoren Chace McCune—"so many others. You are a challenge. He will not rest until he has you."

"Then he will be restless, Renee," Luzanne said quietly, "for a very long time, indeed."

And there it had remained. Renee abruptly dropped the subject and for a few more minutes they had chatted of inconsequential things. Then bells rang to indicate a vote on the Senate floor, Luzanne kissed her hastily, said, "My dear Renee, thank you for coming, I feel we've had a necessary talk, bless you, take your time, this all goes on my bill"—and hurried away to her duties.

Renee had picked up her purse and gone thoughtfully home, reassured about Luzanne's sincere intentions though from experience skeptical of them—grateful to her—liking her very much—but not reassured about Zeecy.

As she had said, she knew her husband.

And now, three months later, she began, hardly knowing it, to pace up and down the living room of the chairman's quarters at Fort Myer while Carleene continued to putter in the kitchen and grow increasingly anxious about when she might be allowed to go home and tend to faithful Jim and her lively brood.

Renee did not think he was seeing Luzanne, though she was highly sensitive to the fact that his interest had not diminished. It had, in fact, as she had known it would, increased. He was still extremely conscious of the Senator, mentioned her frequently, recounted her astute questionings at meetings of the Senate Armed Services Committee, commented every time her name appeared in the media, which was often for she was a favorite, and was just very—very—*aware.*

Renee knew he would never leave her physically but she was bleakly certain that mentally and emotionally, for the time being—and she could only hope it would be a short time—he was, as so often before, somewhere else.

Actually at that particular moment he was exactly where he was supposed to be physically, mentally and emotionally—seated at his desk in E Ring, hammering away at the progress, or lack thereof, of Operation and Project Frio.

It had been a long and frustrating day, much of it devoted, since Loy had told him of the President's insistence on a full-scale review, to trying to get the military side of both projects into reasonable shape to present at the White House tomorrow morning. He felt he had accomplished a little, in that he had been assured that formal reports were being prepared on all sides, apparently by everybody. But he was not sanguine about the prospects for Presidential approval when they were delivered.

Preparing progress reports was something many people in the Pentagon were very good at. The problem that often arose was that the reports were frequently far more concrete than the progress. Literally thousands of pages arrived at thousands of desks every day, solemnly recording the status of innumerable enterprises. More often than not, if it could have been measured on a ruler, the advance described as having occurred in the time between a given report on a given project on a given day, and the next report on the same project weeks, or even months, later, would show perhaps half an inch.

If that much.

But the amount of paper was overwhelming—the number of man- and woman-hours devoted to running the duplicating machines simply astounding —and the language carefully crafted by many skilled and experienced veterans of the Pentagon paper wars to give an impression of urgency, speed and diligent accomplishment.

This did not fool anybody, though a great many both military and civilian were willing participants in the agreed pretense that it really meant something. It certainly would not fool the President, who ever since Zeecy had first known him at the academy had been a sharp and impatient mind cleverly camouflaged by a slow and pleasant regional accent.

Thus when Brash, Ham, Bumpy and Tick had each in turn solemnly assured him that "I'm having them get up a good report over here—everything's going fine in *my* shop," Gen. McCune had given each the same reply.

"I certainly hope so, because I don't think the Boss is going to be satisfied with a lot of b.s. this time. He's apparently getting impatient for results. So look to it."

They had each promised him earnestly that they would, and now at the end of the day he was sure that the machines were humming, the pages were mounting, the staplers were busy and the briefing officers were staying late to prepare the short papers that each of the chiefs would deliver while a hand rested casually from time to time on the lengthy full report beside him.

All of these full reports, he suspected, had been in preparation for weeks against just such a day; and all, he suspected, would be about as useful as they always were on the Hill: they would be filed for the record and the interrogators would then plunge immediately into questions that would throw all the carefully prepared strategy into catch-as-catch-can disarray.

The President, he was sure, didn't want all that paperwork. He *would* regard it as b.s. And he would not be pleased. But there was no stopping the machinery once it got into motion.

During the day, the chairman in his direct calls and conferences had formed the impression of two largely formless enterprises moving without much consistent plan, purpose or leadership toward a goal that was never more clearly defined than "getting those bastards out of there." Three months after the occupation of Nanukuvu no real specifics had been developed. Yet it was beyond question that everyone involved was as able, as concerned, as determined, as patriotic, as well-intentioned—and as frustrated—as he and Loy Buck were.

Al Rider, for instance: Lt. Gen. Albert B. Rider, USMC, fifty, married, father of three, veteran of Lebanon and Grenada: another of the able blacks who were moving in increasing numbers into the higher ranks; a calm, steady, good-natured, competent, courageous officer who had something of Ham Stokes' desire to "get things done," but a less abrasive and consequently more popular way of going about it. Today he had dropped by to see the chairman without knowing that the chairman wanted to see him.

"Just instinct," he said with his comfortable smile as he seated himself with an at-home air in the chair across the desk. "Seemed like a good time to talk. I guess we're both getting a little anxious, general."

"Yes, general, I guess we are," Gen. McCune agreed. "I think it's time for you to call me Zeecy, incidentally. Everybody does."

"Well, not *every*body," Al Rider said, smiling again. "But I'm flattered—Al here, of course." He leaned forward, suddenly earnest. "I'd like to get on with this."

"You and me both, Al," Zeecy said. "How do we go about it? Give it all to the Marines, the way Tick wants? You're a good start."

"Oh, no," Al Rider said, smile broadening. "I know Tick would like that, and I'm sure I would too, but as I get it, this really is supposed to be a joint operation and that's fine with me, I'm ready to cooperate. But so far—" he looked frustrated—"they aren't giving me much to go on. Not even the Marines. As I told you the other day on the phone, I'm about ready to request field

duty again, I'm getting that disillusioned about it. Meantime out there in
Nanukuvu they're preparing a hell of a nice little greeting for us if we ever do
get to them. And it's getting worse every day. I don't like the prospects."

"I don't either, Al," Gen. McCune said, "but the last thing we can let you do
is go back to the field before this job is done. We need you here."

"I don't see why," Gen. Rider said mildly. "It's not as though I'm all that
great."

"Yes, you are," Zeecy said. "You're a doer and you're also a diplomat. And
that's not always a combination to be found in the military."

"Particularly in the Marines," Al Rider suggested with a sudden grin. "Well
—anyway, it's damned upsetting to feel I've accomplished so little in three
months' time. I need specifics—and I need plans—and I need definite manpower commitments—and I need to freeze weapons requirements—and I
need—" He broke off and asked with a quizzical look, "Just between you and
me, Zeecy, do you really think there's any need to fiddle with the ALCAC?"

"No," Gen. McCune said scornfully. "Not at all. As I said to the boys the
minute they proposed it. But—you know how things go. Ham Stokes wants to
do something with it—so Brash immediately had to get into the act—and then
Tick couldn't stand being left out—and finally Bumpy had to point out that of
course it *is* a Navy craft, and therefore the Navy, by rights, should have a hand
in it. And presto, bingo—*Project* Frio sprang full blown from the brow of Jove.
Or from the brows of the JCS, anyway. And *it's* not making any headway,
either."

"No, I gather," Gen. Rider said thoughtfully. "I've had a couple of talks with
Harry Ahmanson—"

"Like him?"

"He keeps his nose clean," Al Rider said noncommittally. Then he nodded.
"Oh, sure, we can get along. Except, as you say, he isn't getting much of
anywhere, either. But we've got to get *somewhere,* it seems to me, and pretty
damned fast."

"The President's going to have a full-scale review tomorrow," Zeecy said, "to
which, I'm sorry, you and Harry, and the other Harry, aren't invited, simply
because of numbers, I expect. But you can be sure nobody's going to blame *you.*
I'll be there to see to that."

"Thank you," Gen. Rider said, "but I'm not worried. The facts are there.
None of us at my level can move until some decisions are made up top." His
eyes got a musing look. "I wonder . . . Do you think the President *really*
wants this?"

Zeecy hesitated and then decided to level with this obviously broad-gauged
and reflective gentleman.

"To tell you the truth, Al, just between us: I don't really know. He's given us
that impression, but on the other hand—warts, as my dear mother used to say.
As long as it's secret, which by some miracle it still is, he has a lot of options
and I think he's determined to go ahead with it. If it became public, as it may at

any time, then . . . the ardor might cool. Or so, at least, is my impression of him based on a friendship going back thirty years. He was always a complex character and being President has made him even more so. All Presidents are complex, I suppose—or if they aren't, we make them so by our infinite perceptions of them. But some are more so than others. He, I would say, is more."

"Hm," Al Rider said. "That somewhat complicates things, doesn't it?"

"Not yet," Gen. McCune said. "But it could."

"Well," Gen. Rider remarked, "I guess all I can do is tend to my business and keep asking the chiefs to help me get things organized and hope for the best."

"It should move more smoothly after tomorrow."

"Hell, it's got to," Al Rider said, rising and holding out his hand for a farewell shake, "because they sure aren't sitting still on the island."

"No," Zeecy agreed as he walked him out. "They are not."

Later in the day he called in General Ahmanson. The tone was different but the underlying unease the same.

"Harry," he said, when it soon became obvious that Harry the cautious and ever careful, unlike Al Rider the open and assured, was not going to volunteer, "how are things going over in your shop?"

"I wouldn't want to say they were bogged down—" Gen. Ahmanson began slowly.

"Why not?" Zeecy demanded. "They are, aren't they?"

"Well," Harry Ahmanson said with a small smile, "they are not proceeding with dazzling speed, I will say that much."

"And the fault is that of—?"

Harry Ahmanson gave a small, noncommittal shrug.

"Myself, I suppose. I'm in charge."

"But is it that simple?" Gen. McCune inquired. "Surely some responsibility must lie with the chiefs?"

"It would seem a fair presumption," Harry Ahmanson agreed.

"O.K.," Zeecy said, "let's make it. How about Civilian Harry? Are you and he getting along?"

"As well as a civilian and an officer can get along when they're supposed to have equal authority," Harry Ahmanson said. He spoke with a sudden vigor, honestly disgusted. "It's a half-assed setup, frankly."

"I agree," Zeecy said, "but just remember you're in there because we wanted you to be. Otherwise it would have been all Civilian Harry, and what a mess that would have been."

"He's a pain in the ass," Gen. Ahmanson observed, not so cautious on the safe ground of what everybody, at least in the military, thought of Harry Josephs. "If he nit-picks as much once we really get rolling as he's done in the preliminary stages, God help us. We'll never get through with modifying the ALCAC."

"Do we really need to?" Gen. McCune inquired. Gen. Ahmanson frowned but his response was once again conditioned by caution.

"If it has been decided by the chiefs that it is necessary for the success of the mission . . . then, yes, I suppose we do."

"What's your opinion?"

"I don't have one," Harry Ahmanson said blandly. "I'm just in there to do the job, aren't I?"

"Oh, Harry, for Christ's sake, you can have an *opinion,*" Gen. McCune said. "It's a boondoggle, isn't it?"

"No," Gen. Ahmanson said. "Since you insist. I'm not entirely sure that it is. It may be that some good can come out of modifying it—I don't think we really know, at this stage. Perhaps it's worth trying, if that's what they want. We might be surprised."

"But what about time?" Zeecy demanded. "Isn't that what the basic mission is all about, *time?* It's holding us up, isn't it? It's a time-consumer and for the purpose in hand, it really isn't necessary. The job can be done with the ALCAC as it stands, can't it? Why waste the *time?*"

"If Operation Frio were that far ahead of Project Frio," Harry Ahmanson remarked calmly, "I should be more concerned about time. But I don't think *that* can be claimed . . . can it?"

"Hmph," Gen. McCune said, forced into a grudging smile. "You have me there."

"Exactly," Harry Ahmanson said. His expression became for a moment quite candidly serious.

"Frankly, general—"

"Zeecy," Zeecy said automatically.

"I'm not comfortable with that," Gen. Ahmanson said matter-of-factly. "With respect. Frankly, general, I *am* concerned about the slowness with which we're moving. But if the chiefs can't seem to hurry up their recommendations, what am I supposed to do about it? Not even Civilian Harry," he added dryly, "could perform that miracle, I suspect."

"No," Zeecy conceded, "I guess you're right. Well, all I can do is keep urging them to hurry it up. And you do the same, if you will, please. There's a White House meeting about it tomorrow, maybe you know—"

"No," Gen. Ahmanson said, "but I'm not entirely surprised. It should have been held two months ago."

"Well!" Zeecy remarked. "You *do* have opinions, after all."

"When they count," Harry Ahmanson said with a sudden smile that made him quite human. "I think they have some pertinence, here."

"Yes," Zeecy said. "Well. In any event, there will be a meeting, and after that, we hope, things will begin to speed up all along the line."

"I *hope* so," Gen. Ahmanson said, sounding for the moment exactly like Gen. Rider, "because things on Nanukuvu are not improving—for us."

So there you have it, Zeecy thought as he prepared to call it quits and go home to Renee, who no doubt would have her usual good meal ready for him. The chiefs were issuing reports and the operational heads were going crazy with virtually nothing to do. And he and Loy were trying to ride herd on the whole thing and get it into shape. And despite all pleas for haste and urgency, the system just wasn't allowing it.

He made up his mind that he would, if he could, steer the White House conversation tomorrow into a discussion of just what that system was. It might be a revelation to the President, who, like nearly all Presidents, was rather uncomfortable with his awesome powers as Commander-in-Chief, and with the military, and preferred to have his associations with both of them strained through several layers of indirect contact. Tomorrow, Gen. McCune promised himself with wry determination, he was going to rub the Boss' nose in it. After all, he *was* Commander-in-Chief.

He had dismissed his staff half an hour ago but he went to the door and glanced out to make sure they had obeyed him. Reassured, he picked up the phone and dialed the private Senate number he had become quite familiar with in recent weeks. Its owner answered at once.

"Still working," he observed.

"Just like you," she said. "I thought the chairman didn't have much to do. Don't you ever rest?"

"Not when I'm trying to get this juggernaut on the road. It's like trying to move a mountain of mud."

"What are you trying to do with it?" she inquired casually. "Anything in particular?"

"Just the usual," he said dryly. "Secure all borders, put out all fires, solve all problems, stop all wars, preserve the peace, keep the enemy at bay and usher in paradise on earth. It's a simple mission we have over here, but don't get me wrong—we love it."

"It sounds a great deal like ours," she said in a tone as wry as his own. "But I've had the impression lately that there's something more you're up to."

"Oh?" he said innocently. "How's that?"

"I don't know," she said. "Just a hunch—woman's intuition, if you like. Something in your voice, lately. Out of all the generalities, something specific has arisen to bug you. I don't know why I feel that way, but I do. I don't suppose you'll tell me what it is."

"Not yet," he said. "The day will come, but not yet."

"But it isn't going well," she suggested.

"No," he admitted, because she had a way of going to the heart of things that persuaded him to be candid. "It should be going much better, at this stage."

"Is it anything we could help you with, up here on the Hill?"

"Lord, *no!*" he said, in such a tone of genuine protest and alarm that she started to laugh, that silvery sound of which he had become so fond in their increasingly frequent after-hours conversations.

"Well, you needn't take my head off," she said. "We aren't *that* bad."

"Some of you, no," he agreed. "Some of you, yes. And all of you, sooner or later, both good *and* bad."

"And the military, of course," she remarked with some tartness, "the ultimate and infallible judges of which is which."

"Insofar as it affects the military, yes," he said, and they both laughed.

"A one-track point of view," she observed, "but I suppose inevitable . . . so you won't tell me."

"Sorry about that."

"Perhaps I should get the committee staff working on it," she said in a thoughtful tone. "Burt Sanstrom, for instance. Some of the younger and more suspicious interns—"

"You've got to be kidding!" he exclaimed; adding, "I hope?" in such an uncertain voice that once again the silvery laugh burst forth.

"Maybe," she said lightly, "maybe not. No, of course I'm kidding. But I'm friendly, remember. If somebody like Cube Herron gets suspicious, or Mario Escondido over on the House side— . . ."

"Yes, I know," he said, "then there could be hell to pay. This is not a matter," he added with sudden seriousness, "that will be assisted in the slightest by Cube and Mario playing for headlines and five-minute segments on the evening news."

"Really serious?"

"Really serious," he replied gravely.

"And not going well at the moment?"

"No."

"I wish I *could* help. Sooner or later it's going to have to come up to us anyway, you know."

"When it's all over, done and accomplished, I hope and pray. The Hill won't be involved a minute sooner if I can help it."

"In this town?" she inquired. "Really, now, Zeecy!"

"We can only hope," he said quietly. "The implications are already grave. That would make them even graver."

"Oh, dear," she said, sounding genuinely alarmed. "That does sound ominous."

"It could be."

"All right, I won't press any further. But do let me know if there's anything —*anything*—I can do to help."

"You could have a meal with me some night," he suggested promptly, and for the third time her charming laugh rang out.

"Oh, general!" she said. "You can be subtler than that!"

He chuckled.

"Indubitably. But why should I? It's hardly an astounding suggestion. Or unexpected, I imagine. Right?"

"Now, where," she demanded—telling herself, *This is crazy, why don't I just simply say No and stop the nonsense?*—"*where* do you think a United States Senator, and a female one at that, could have a private dinner with the chairman of the Joint Chiefs of Staff and go unnoticed?"

He chuckled again.

"I haven't given much thought to that, because I don't really think it's going to happen. However, if it were, then no doubt I'd think of something."

"No doubt," she said. "Well—banish the thought, Zeecy."

"You're not interested, then." He uttered an exaggerated sigh. "Ah, well, so much for the last flight of a tired old pilot. I had imagined—I did entertain such glowing hopes—it would have been such a marvelous—ah, well. I guess I'll go shoot myself instead."

"I guess you'll go straight home to Renee," she said firmly—but, he noted, with a continuing note of amusement, "and stop this silly talk. I'm sure she's waiting for you with a delicious dinner."

"We *are* eating home tonight," he agreed. "Only night this week, as a matter of fact. Have you been invited to Loy and Imogene's garden party Sunday afternoon?"

"Isn't everybody?"

"Good," he said. "Maybe we can meet under a rhododendron and plot."

"Plot nothing," she retorted, vigorously but still with that undercurrent of amusement that made him think: *yes, Luzanne, you're very firm about this.* "Particularly with Renee there."

"She's leaving for France on Saturday. She still has a sister and two brothers and their families in Paris that she goes to see every summer. I'm going to be a bachelor for a month."

"Oh?" she said, and in spite of her best intentions it was a little more than a routine query.

"Absolutely," he said. "So you see—"

"I don't see anything at all," she said, the laugh coming to the surface again. "No, general, I don't see anything at all. So goodnight. But if there *is* anything I can do on that other matter—"

"Not right now. Just hold good thoughts and wish us luck."

"Oh, I do."

"Fine. See you Sunday."

"Without rhododendrons," she said and yet again the laughter bubbled up.

"What's so funny?" he demanded as he prepared to hang up. "I'm eating my heart out over here."

"Oh, sure," she said. "Oh sure, I'll bet, poor thing."

"Well, it's true," he said, chuckling too. "Goodnight, Senator."

"Goodnight, Zeecy," she said, her voice suddenly sounding quite fond and embracing—but that might just be southern talk, he told himself wryly. "Thank you for calling."

"I wouldn't have missed it," he assured her with mock fervor, "for the world."

Luzanne, she told herself as his familiar, confident voice went off the line with a final chuckle, something doesn't quite coordinate, here. You *say* you're not interested—you *think* you're not interested—but you keep on acting as though you *were* interested. And all because he persists in calling from time to time and kidding you about it. Not too often. Maybe once a week. Maybe every other week. Just enough to keep you interested. Just enough to make you look forward to it a little, and wonder what's happened when he doesn't.

Ah, yes, a clever campaigner, Zeecy. Veteran of many such, she had no doubt, and, of course, a very shrewd politician as well. Likes to keep all his contacts in good shape, does Zeecy. Likes to stay in touch with Senators, especially if they have clout. Especially if one of them is a woman.

And yet for all her determination, she admitted to herself honestly, what was she herself up to? Here she was, talking to him about all sorts of odds and ends as though they had been comfortable old lovers for years. That must be part of the Zeecy technique too—to persuade one into just this sort of easygoing, casual, old-shoe relationship. And then—pow!

"Pow, nothing!" she told herself aloud in the silent office, laughter bubbling once more. "No pow, no pow-wow. Roger, over and *out!*"

But still she was intrigued, much more so now, she had to admit to herself, than she had been three months ago when she and Renee had had their talk and she had been so firm about her intentions. She was weaker now. She had, in fact, been waiting for him to call and would have been quite puzzled and chagrined if he hadn't.

She knew this was very foolish. But there it was.

She got up briskly from her desk; picked up her purse and the flowered umbrella brought in case of one of the sudden thunderstorms that often hit Washington around six in the summer evenings, said goodnight on her way out to the last secretary who was still typing. The girl, a young intern from Louisiana, said with a weary but gallant smile that she hoped to be through by seven. Luzanne walked along the now deserted corridors of the Russell Senate Office Building to the muggy, threatening dusk outside, and caught a cab to her spectacular apartment in "Washington Harbour," on the Potomac in Georgetown.

Like Bumpy Stahlman at the Washington Navy Yard further down-river, she was planning a quick snack and a lot of reading, particularly the House Appropriations defense subcommittee hearings that Karl Aschenheim had sent over by messenger earlier this afternoon. She liked Karl a lot and appreciated his kindness in giving her an early look. She also wondered now, Senator's instinct coming back, whether Karl had heard anything about this mysterious worry of Zeecy's. She decided to call him and ask, tomorrow.

She was in the midst of making herself a salad when the doorman rang and said some flowers had been delivered for her. He had put them through the security scanner, he said, and they were indeed flowers. She told him to send them up, feeling a little quickening, which she knew was foolish; and knowing as soon as she saw the name of the Pentagon florist in the Concourse what they were.

Arranged on the hall entrance table, in the beautiful Lalique vase she had received as an official gift when she had attended her first NATO conference eight years ago, the gleaming rhododendron leaves looked handsome indeed.

From his small apartment across Francis Scott Key Bridge in Rosslyn, Virginia, Lt. Broderick Tolliver, USAF, could just have seen Luzanne's lighted windows if he had known where to look in all the glitter that was riverine Georgetown at night.

This probably would not have meant very much to him, since United States Senators had not yet begun to impinge upon his world except as a vaguely menacing group up there on the Hill who from time to time seemed to possess the capacity to send his superiors into a high state of nervous tension and irritability. One of the things he liked about his newest commander, amiable Al Rider of Operation Frio, was that he seemed entirely calm when contemplating these often difficult individuals. Gen. Rider, in fact, had even spoken specifically of Sen. Johnson only a day or two ago and had described her as "a decent and sensible legislator who does her best to be fair and helpful to us."

Brod Tolliver would have been interested to know that he was virtually looking in her window, though, being a polite and almost too-well-brought-up young man, he would probably have blushed at the thoughts this aroused, and turned tactfully away.

As it was, he stood there staring moodily out across the gleaming dark waters of the Potomac as they reflected the lights of Washington Harbour, the Watergate, Kennedy Center and all the other developments that in recent years had gobbled up the once rundown riverbank and turned it into a paradise for real estate promoters and people who could afford to live there. Behind him his wife Kathleen, who, he was pleased to be able to say, worshiped the ground he walked on, was busily preparing dinner. She was not the greatest cook in the world, and knew it, which sometimes occasioned frustration, tears and the need for comfort. Being a healthy young animal as well as a polite one, Brod enjoyed conferring comfort, and poor dinners quite often resulted in delightful desserts. As a result of this and other frequent impulses, Kathleen was already four months' pregnant after six months of marriage and Brod was already thinking that he would have to begin looking for a modest little house somewhere near the Pentagon if he was to remain on duty there for any length of time.

Now that he had been assigned to Operation Frio it was beginning to look as though this might well be the case. Things just weren't moving on Operation Frio, and after he had been cleared for security and had been told what Operation Frio was all about, this alarmed him considerably. He had never been in the South Pacific but he possessed a sharp and analytical mind that would have loved to concentrate on really long-range strategic planning if such a thing had been encouraged in the Pentagon. As it was, it was obvious to him from even a cursory analysis that the occupation of Nanukuvu by the enemy and its rapid conversion into a strategic submarine nest boded little good for the United States and its vulnerable antipodean allies, to say nothing of the Philippines, Indonesia, Papua-New Guinea, Micronesia or anybody else in the area. He could not understand why this did not provoke greater urgency in the office, deep in the inner recesses of third floor, B Ring, where Operation Frio was taking shape under the innocuous title on the door of "Cumulative Assessment Group."

Brod's assessment was that it was time for Operation Frio to damned well get going. According to the accounts he had read, it was now three months since the enemy had slaughtered the island's innocent inhabitants and begun construction of the base. Most of the essential elements now seemed to be in place. Constant surveillance and monitoring indicated that several subs were virtually home-ported there already and it was estimated that as many as fifteen could be: enough to blow up the entire South Pacific if they ever set out to do it. And so far, only words, memos, "meetings" and "reports" in the Pentagon.

Brod Tolliver was not an academy graduate, he was only a lowly enlistee whose attractive personality, analytic brain and obvious common-sense had brought him rapidly along so far; but he was certainly not a dullard. It was quite obvious to him that if Operation Frio, and what he understood to be its civilian component, Project Frio, didn't get off the dime, it soon would take a major confrontation to root the enemy out of there. It had been ground into him, as it was into everyone these days, that *nobody* wanted a major confrontation in this day and age; but he wasn't so sure. If you were solidly entrenched, virtually impregnable except to all-out assault, and facing an opponent who appeared to be tiptoe-shy of using his own power, then you might not mind at all if a "major confrontation" took place.

It would hardly be major, in your mind.

You would know that if you just sat tight and bluffed it out, your opponent would presently move, disgruntled and disgraced, away.

Brod desperately did not want this to happen to *his* country, but he was very much afraid that it would if the two Frios and the whole damned mission didn't get off the ground pretty damned fast. He had observed that this was very clearly the attitude of Gen. Al Rider. It also was the attitude of the confidential secretary who had been assigned to Gen. Rider, a large, plain, awkward, often gloomy Navy spinster named Capt. Elizabeth Hogan, who lived with a mysterious "sick mother" and seemed to be carrying the weight of the world on her shoulders most of the time.

Because he had a lot of charm and was amicably disposed toward the world, Brod had achieved some success in getting Hogan to relax a little and forget her troubles now and then. Over lunches they shared with increasing frequency in the Pik-Quik they had found agreement that Nanukuvu was a problem fully as serious as Gen. Rider seemed to consider it; and with a freedom he was not

permitted and they weren't either, at least in public, they often cussed out the
Joint Chiefs and wondered to each other why the old fuddy-duddies didn't stop
dragging their tails and *get moving.*

Curiously, though, Brod and Hogan also shared the feeling that the Army
major, Gary Stump, who had been assigned to Gen. Rider as his action officer,
didn't share the same urgency. Gary Stump was one of those small, trim,
compact, sleek young officers, suavely handsome, smooth-spoken and sharp,
who are so obviously ambitious that everyone around them automatically as-
sumes that their only interest in life is their own advancement. Yet although
Gary Stump created this impression—deliberately created it, Brod and Hogan
finally agreed, puzzled—they somehow didn't quite believe it.

"Gary has his own agenda," Elizabeth Hogan had remarked recently and
Brod had nodded.

"He does," he said. "But what is it?"

"Maybe *he* doesn't know," she said with one of her rare chuckles.

"Maybe we should watch and find out," he suggested, and she had nodded
quickly. Something in Gary Stump touched some deep chord of suspicion in
them—they couldn't say why, or what it was. They had become much aware of
him lately, and wondered if Gen. Rider had also noticed anything. It wasn't the
sort of thing you could talk to the general about. It was all so amorphous and
vague, as Hogan pointed out—"just a feeling."

"You can't hang anybody on that," Brod had agreed.

But they were a little surprised that Gen. Rider, who appeared to be such an
astute, competent and perceptive officer, should not have shown in some way,
however small, that he too found something in Maj. Stump that did not ring
quite true.

However, he didn't seem to, and so things poked along in the office in B Ring
even though Brod Tolliver, as assistant action officer, worked very closely with
Gary and shared the laugh when Gary remarked, as he often did, "We're the
action officers, but there sure isn't much action!" There was just a gap somewhere when Brod expressed his own impatience with the slow progress they
were making. In some indefinable way, Gary didn't seem to care. Or maybe,
the thought crossed Brod's mind now as he stood at the window and stared
across at Georgetown, Gary *did* care, and was pleased.

He himself, as he often told Kathleen, had felt nothing but the greatest
excitement and pleasure when word had come down from the nearest thing to
heaven the military had, the office of the chairman of the JCS, that he was
going to be plucked up from his interesting but obscure job in the Air Force
information office to be given a "special assignment" with Gen. Al Rider. He
had been granted a brief interview, much more comfortable than his first one,
with that legendary figure Gen. Zoren Chace McCune, and had perceived that
for some reason unknown to him Gen. McCune was reposing an unusual
amount of trust and confidence in him. He didn't know that Zeecy had made
similar spontaneous judgment calls quite often during his career, and that

usually his judgment of men had proven correct. Zeecy mentioned to Brod in passing that he had rarely been disappointed in one of his selections, and one of the reasons, Brod realized, was that he made it casually but unmistakably clear that he didn't expect to be.

"Trust 'em and they'll trust you back and do their damnedest for you," was one of Zeecy's principles. It had rarely failed him, and he and Brod both knew that it wasn't going to fail him now.

"Your main job," Gen. McCune had said with a chuckle that didn't lead Brod into the error of assuming that he was kidding, "is to keep a sharp eye on everybody else and let me know about it from time to time. Without a word to Al Rider or anybody, that is. Understood?"

"Yes, sir!" Brod said smartly.

Gen. McCune had laughed.

"You'll do," he said. "I'll leave it to you to decide if everything isn't what it should be, and how to get the word to me without alerting whoever's to blame." He chuckled again. "I'll deny I ever spoke to you if you get caught."

"I would expect it, sir," Brod Tolliver said and Zeecy had stood up to see him to the door, taking his arm in the confidentially intimate manner that always melted the lower ranks to worshiping jelly.

"You're a good man, Lt. Tolliver," he said, "and I know you won't let me down. I suppose you have a cute little wife: handsome young officers like you *always* have cute little wives. Right?"

"She isn't bad, sir," Brod said with a sudden sunny smile.

"Well," Zeecy said, "you give her my best and tell her she's got a good man and she's to hang onto him—tight!"

"She does, sir," Brod said, and blushed a bright crimson as Zeecy laughed heartily, gave him a clap on the back and pushed him, gently and with a flattering familiarity, out the door.

Brod had not seen him since, but he had spoken to him on a phone from the Concourse yesterday afternoon when Zeecy had sent along a confidential note requesting that he do so. His report had been what Zeecy had expected: they were ready to organize the mission but so far there wasn't any mission to organize.

"It's the chiefs, isn't it?" Zeecy had asked. Brod had hesitated for a split second and then said exactly what Zeecy was hoping for, from him.

"It is, sir," he said firmly. "They aren't moving fast enough."

"Exactly," Zeecy said. "If you get any ideas how I can get 'em to move faster, let me know."

"Raise hell, sir," Brod suggested and then gulped, stricken by his own temerity.

"Easier said than done, young Brod," Gen. McCune remarked, "as you may find out someday. I think you just might, if you keep on the way you're going."

"Thank *you,* sir!" Brod said, deeply thrilled, and walked away from the Concourse phone in a happy daze, almost bumping into a messenger cart, a janitor

lady, three majors and a full colonel as he made his way back to the security
checkpoint for the ramp to the third floor.

Now as he waited for Kathleen to call him to the table he was a little bit
heartened by the news Gen. Rider had imparted to him, Hogan and Gary
Stump this evening just before they left the office.

He had talked to Gen. McCune, Gen. Rider said, and Gen. McCune had
told him there would be a full-scale White House review tomorrow morning,
headed by the President himself, of exactly where things stood on Nanukuvu
and the two Frios. Gen. McCune had indicated, Gen. Rider said, that the
President was going to really raise hell—at least, Gen. Rider said with the slow
grin that lit up his honest and amiable face so attractively, Gen. McCune *hoped*
he was going to raise hell. And so did he, Al Rider, hope so. And so, he
assumed, did they.

"You bet, sir!" Brod had said fervently.

"We could use it!" Hogan agreed with unusual heartiness, for her.

"There might be some," Gary Stump had said with a sleek little smile on his
sleek little face, "who might say: *it's about time!*"

But whether he was one of those who said so was not entirely clear, though
the moment passed without Gen. Rider, apparently, noticing.

And now here he was again, going around in circles about it, Brod thought.
With a loud, "Aw, the hell with it!" that quite startled Kathleen, he swung
around suddenly to the table where she was just serving up a rather dubious-
looking ham and cheese casserole, gave her a resounding kiss and an enormous
hug, gulped down his meal with constant exhortations that, "It's good, it's
good!" to ward off what appeared to be imminent tears, and within twenty
minutes was rolling around on the bed with her stark naked, painfully tumes-
cent and blissfully oblivious. For the moment Nanukuvu was really a *very* long
way away.

2

At the moment when Brod Tolliver was, as it were, re-endorsing Kathy's pregnancy with a wonderfully agonizing explosion that seemed to tear his body apart and put it back together again, the SecDef and his wife were getting ready to go to dinner at the Moroccan embassy.

Loy was silent and preoccupied as he thoughtfully put in his studs and tied his bow tie. If someone like Skip Framberg had heard about Nanukuvu—or, at least, Project Frio—how long would it be before *Defense Eye* and the rest heard about it too? Perhaps it was time for one of those strategy conferences that Hank Milhaus liked to hold with the top people in Defense when he anticipated some imminent flap in the media. The Assistant Secretary for Public Affairs was very good at organizing the various civilian and military spokesmen into a united front.

This sort of gathering-together to repulse attack was one of the most constant and characteristic of all Pentagon activities. Hank had once estimated that at least half the time of the top civilians and military was spent on managing the media: either to secure its dissemination of favorable information on the one hand, or to anticipate and if possible defuse damaging attacks, on the other. Half the time! It was an absurd figure, in Loy's estimation, but there it was: in a media-dominated world, there was virtually no choice. If you wanted favorable coverage for the Department of Defense, you had to work for it. If you wanted to fend off destructive attacks on the Department of Defense, you had to work for it.

"You have to keep ahead of 'em," Hank had warned when Loy first took office, "or sooner or later, they'll wear you down."

The concept of constant war with the media was a new one for Loy, who had sometimes had his problems as head of IBM but had not found them nearly as all-pervasive or time-consuming as they were in the Pentagon. And now with Skip Framberg apparently about to blow the whistle on Project Frio, it probably *was* time for one of Hank's little sessions, because Lord knew what form the flak might take or how destructive it might be to a satisfactory solution of the problem of Nanukuvu.

The Secretary had no idea how Skip had acquired his knowledge, but he had always known that Skip still had very active pipelines into the Office of the Secretary of Defense. Loy wondered briefly whether he had handled Skip correctly when he had in effect banished him to the purple water fountain when Skip had blown the whistle on the Army test. Brash Burford had demanded "the most stringent disciplining," as he put it, and the other chiefs and Zeecy had backed him up even though there was reasonable question if Skip's position, while flamboyant and deliberately publicity-seeking, had not been right.

Loy had expressed considerable misgivings about so stringently rebuking one whom he had from the first perceived as a born troublemaker, but he had been too new in office to withstand the massed insistence of the JCS. He would be much tougher and less responsive now, but he suspected he still would make the same decision, for the most fundamental of reasons: when Skip chose to put it on a basis of, in essence, "Choose me or choose the Pentagon," the Secretary really had no choice. So he had worked out a half-loaf that he hoped would be better than none. Now Skip was back, no doubt primed and eager for revenge.

He sighed and Imogene, surveying herself in the full-length mirror across the room, turned immediately and gave him an intent look.

"Are you all right?" she demanded. "Are you sure you want to go out?"

"Immy," he said, "you know perfectly well that's an absurd question. We're scheduled for this and we can't back out now short of a national emergency or a major coronary. Washington official parties just don't work that way. Of course I want to go. I'm just thinking about the Pentagon, that's all."

"I will be *so glad,*" she said, "when you're out of all this and we can both stop 'thinking about the Pentagon.' *The Pentagon!* I wish you'd never heard of it! It makes me sick!"

"Me, too," he said with a smile, "but it's an incurable illness for the time being."

"Why?" she inquired. "You aren't a slave to the President, you know."

"Slave to the country," he said, half-amused, half-serious. "Or at least I *feel* I am. No, I agreed to do this job and I will as long as he's in office and wants me. It just gets a little difficult at times, that's all. It will all smooth out—" he made a wry little face—"sometime."

She sniffed.

"Not soon enough for me . . . I still think," she said with a sudden reversion to her earlier worry, "that you ought to banish that stupid Delight Jones from the building. She's *such* a troublemaker, and she does seem to hate me so. I'd feel a lot better with her out of there."

"You and the rest of us. But she's far from stupid, and of course you know why I can't: the entire media would be up in arms, and it wouldn't stop the news hemorrhaging anyway. Plenty of people over there are ready to spill their gripes to any reporter who'll give them a hearing. And there are plenty of gripes and plenty of reporters."

"Of whom she's the worst," Imogene remarked with another sniff.

He smiled.

"At least one of the most representative—of a certain type. We're lucky there are some others who provide a balance."

"Hmph!" she said. "I haven't seen much of it."

"Admittedly a little hard to find, sometimes," he agreed, "but it's there."

And would be, he hoped as they finished dressing and went downstairs to await the arrival of his limousine, when Nanukuvu became public knowledge. Meanwhile he had a personal problem: how to manage Skip so that he would not go immediately to Delight or Red Roberts or some other pal and tell everything he knew. He knew Skip hadn't done so yet, because Skip obviously thought he had something with which to strike a bargain with the SecDef. But if he wasn't satisfied, Loy knew the media would have another story.

He would have to handle that one very carefully or the problem of Nanukuvu would become even more complicated than it was already. With the slowness in the Pentagon it was a wonder it was still secret at all.

How to remove that particular obstacle, he did not exactly know at the moment. He, Zeecy and the President had all worked hard on the chiefs, urging, exhorting, demanding: the machinery had ground on at its accustomed pace. The meeting tomorrow might speed it up, that was the point of the exercise: because the growing enemy strength on Nanukuvu was posing an increasing problem for the Pentagon position.

A couple of months ago he and Terry Venner had finally had their private luncheon. "SUMMIT" HELD TO EASE STATE-PENTAGON TENSIONS the headlines had promptly reported; though who in hell, unless it was the table crew and he knew it wasn't, had told them, Loy couldn't imagine. Fortunately it wasn't a factual story, just a lot of rumor, hint and gossip, and no reports had leaked out of what the participants had said. That wouldn't happen unless Terry went public and so far he hadn't. Certainly Loy wouldn't.

It had been a rather warm session, though. In a way he felt sorry for the media that they didn't have the details. It was the sort of scrap they loved to report.

It had been held, at Loy's suggestion, in the commander's private dining room at Fort Lesley J. McNair, the lovely old traditional Army post that juts out on a small peninsula where the Potomac and Anacostia rivers meet near the southern boundary of the District of Columbia. There amid immaculate lawns, the gentle lapping of the two rivers and such historic structures as the quarters where Mary Surratt, one of the convicted Lincoln assassination conspirators, was housed prior to her execution, things always seemed to turn back to an earlier, statelier, somehow gentler time. Loy hoped the atmosphere would be conducive to constructive discussion. There was also the advantage of the post's relative isolation from the Pentagon and the District, and the fact that nobody in the media would expect to find the two Secretaries meeting there.

"Now, Terry," he had said when they had finished an excellent luncheon accompanied by an excellent California wine, "what's your gripe?"

For a moment the Secretary of State seemed taken aback at this bluntness, which of course was exactly what Loy intended. Then a tentative and rather frosty smile had crossed his face.

"I wouldn't say they're 'gripes.' Just points between us that need clarification."

"That's diplomacy for you," Loy said in an admiring tone, whose sincerity Terry couldn't quite determine. "*We* have gripes, *you* have points that need clarification. Somehow we've got to learn to speak the same language in our two departments. Otherwise we never will get things straight."

"The solution seems simple enough to me," Terrail Venner said in his most aloof manner. "Just tell Joe Strang and your other ambitious policy-grabbers to *stay off our turf.* How's that," he inquired with a bland smile, "for diplomatic language?"

"Better," Loy conceded with a laugh in which Terry joined, looking wryly pleased with himself. "I don't see that the suggestion is valid, though. Foreign policy is your domain, not ours—"

"Now, Loy," Terry interrupted, sounding not at all diplomatic but downright annoyed, "stop being disingenuous. You know very well that the Pentagon meddles into every foreign policy matter on the face of this earth. Joe and the Doomsday Twins and the rest of his crew just can't keep their hands off. And neither can you, or anybody on the military side either, for that matter. You *know* that."

"I know we naturally have a very basic interest in what goes on," Loy said, "but I wouldn't call it 'meddling.' I would call it assuring that the proper perspective and balance are maintained in considering our many problems abroad."

The Secretary of State snorted.

"Talk about diplomatic language! If that doesn't take the cake! Meddling is what I said and meddling is what I mean. We want it stopped, Loy. Or at least put under some reasonable control."

"Well, I'm sorry," Loy said blandly, "but if there seem to be gaps in the advice which is given the President, or if there is some light we can cast upon a given situation that somebody else is unable to provide, then I'm afraid I regard that as part of our mission. After all, we're all creatures of the President. We have to give him whatever advice and guidance he asks us for. You can't expect us not to respond, Terry, just to keep State happy."

"It isn't a question of keeping us happy!" Terry snapped, flushing, not at all diplomatic now. "It's a question of overweighting everything on the military side so that normal diplomatic procedures can't have a chance to work. It's always wanting to go for the military solution without giving us time to see what we can do. It's this—this build-up over Nanukuvu, for instance, instead of letting us try to work something out quietly behind the scenes—"

"That was tried the first night of the occupation," the Secretary of Defense interrupted sharply. "The President called Moscow, he talked to that murderous empire-building guttersnipe, he tried to put it on a private basis, and he got the usual stonewalling. So he asked us to get busy."

"And have you?" Terry Venner inquired with a sarcasm that made Loy Buck think that he, too, must have his pipelines into the Pentagon; but, then, who didn't?

"We're moving, yes," he said. "We're getting things in shape."

"Not very fast," the Secretary of State remarked with an icy smile. It was Loy's turn to flush.

"An operation like that doesn't materialize overnight. It takes a lot of planning and a lot of preparation. My best people are working on it—"

"How long will they be at it?" Terry inquired. "It's been three months—"

"When the President is ready to act, we'll be ready!"

"Hmph," Terry said. "I thought everybody was ready that night. I was told I was out of line, so sit down and be quiet. So," he concluded with disapproving dignity, "I did. And here we are. Anyway," he said with the tenacity that made him, in Pentagon eyes, such an annoyingly determined adversary, "that isn't solving the major problem here, which is how to keep your people from preempting every crisis that comes along and trying to force a military solution."

" 'My people,' " Loy said angrily, *"don't do that.* We honestly try to work out a peaceable solution and most times we succeed. With or without," he couldn't resist adding, "the State Department's help."

"Why should *we* help *you?"* the Secretary of State demanded with an anger of his own. "Foreign policy is *our* affair. *You* help *us,* for a change! How about that?"

The Secretary of Defense shrugged.

"In a world dominated by armaments? How can that be?"

"There's still got to be room for *diplomacy,"* Terry Venner said desperately. "There's still got to be room for *peace."*

"I hope so," Loy said, "with all my heart. But in the meantime, until we can get the world stabilized sufficiently so that diplomacy has a chance—"

" 'Stabilized'!" the Secretary of State said bitterly. "You think this constant state of tension is stabilization?"

"It's apparently as near as we're going to get," Loy Buck said crisply, "so you might as well learn to live with it. We have to."

"You've given up, then," Terry said, still bitterly. "You've stopped hoping, you've—just—given—up." He folded his napkin precisely, as most well-brought-up little boys still do, and placed it neatly beside his plate. "Well," he said bleakly, "we haven't! But I guess there's no point in discussing it further. The Pentagon will continue to meddle, just as always."

"Given our responsibilities in defending this nation," the Secretary of Defense said calmly, "we will continue to be deeply involved in foreign policy, yes."

Later he regretted his tone, which had been too harsh—too harsh. But, damn it, why was State always trying to maintain that it occupied some morally superior high ground and why did it always try to claim that it was the only entity that really wanted peace? They all wanted peace—any sane man wanted peace, when the alternative was the destruction of the planet. But means and methods differed so widely, particularly within free governments. The Defense Department couldn't afford to yield too much control to State, otherwise it would all be slaps-on-the-wrist and "accommodation of opposing viewpoints." He was convinced that the enemy viewpoint in today's world was determined to destroy the U.S. viewpoint. This conviction was shared overwhelmingly throughout the Pentagon. What choice was there, then, but to build and build and arm and arm and hope that what the enemy called "the correlation of forces" would eventually come into sufficient balance to discourage the enemy's imperialistic adventurism?

He was sorry for Terry, because the Secretary of State was an honest, dedicated, troubled and sincerely idealistic man. But, my God, idealism! There was a limit to what idealism could do, confronted by such an antagonist as faced the United States.

So at any rate, believed the Secretary of Defense; and now as he and Imogene arrived at the Moroccan embassy, he tried for a little while to put the problem of Nanukuvu out of mind. It was not a successful attempt: the wife of the West German ambassador was on his right, the wife of the Indian ambassador on his left. He was caught between minds as worlds apart as ham hocks with sauerkraut and silverleaf on custard. The one was too heavy, the other too bland.

He sank presently into a silence that caused Imogene, seated down the table, to give him several alarmed looks which he saw but ignored. His partners turned to the gentlemen on the other side. He was left to review what he would be able to tell the President at tomorrow's meeting. It was not exactly earthshaking.

Presently he gave it up, regained an animation that pleased Imogene, as he could tell from her archly approving glances, and began to chat again with the ladies. The ambassador made his little speech thanking them all for coming. They left the tables and went into the drawing room for the obligatory postprandial chat. Promptly at eleven the party ended and they all went home.

By that time he was in quite good humor.

All he had to worry about now, he told himself wryly, were his civilian aides, the military, Skip Framberg, Delight Jones and the President of the United States.

The military were basically Zeecy's headache; all the rest were his. He was not sure which of them was the more formidable, but it didn't really matter. He would just have to hunker down and take them as they came.

At the moment when the SecDef's limousine was gliding away from the Moroccan embassy and heading for home, *Defense Eye*'s editor and its chief and only correspondent were sitting in one of the duskier discotheques, under the freeway on the Georgetown waterfront, trying to make each other hear over the surrounding cacophony. They had dined in leisurely fashion at the Jockey Club, where they had been with, though not together with, several Senators and their wives, a few ambassadors ditto, the Secretary of Commerce and his party, the King of Jordan and *his* party, and a spare Washington hostess or two. From there they had clambered into Herb's battered old Nissan and had drifted almost inadvertently to this temple of grace and culture which both from time to time frequented, Delight Jones usually by herself, Herb Horowitz usually accompanied by whatever young lady from Pentagon or Hill he had "been able to con into it," as his editor put it with characteristically ferocious humor.

Tonight they were there together, discussing the events of the day and plotting with a woozy amicability how to make them even more embarrassing for the powers that be than they were already.

"About time you found something big at the Pentagon," Delight shouted to him over the din—practically the seventeenth time tonight that she had said this, Herb reflected with an annoyance aggravated by his fourth brandy Alexander.

"I'm looking," he shouted back, "I'm *looking*. I can't help it if the bastards are so quiet lately."

"Always a bad sign," Delight observed, pulling him toward her and speaking in a more normal tone directly into his ear. "They must be up to *something*. We can't keep on running that same tired old story about Lady Buck's entertaining. You've milked that 'til the cows are cross-eyed. What else is new?"

"The usual crap," he said, managing to communicate at a relatively low volume himself. "I think there may be something breaking with both Strategic Industries and General Growth Group pretty soon. I've seen Roger Venable of S.I. and Walker Stayman of Three Gs over there this week. My sources tell me they've been huddling with Helen Clark and Tiny Wombaugh on some top-secret project or other."

"Aren't they all?" Delight demanded with a savage grin. "Every damned thing's top-secret over there, including how many times the Joint Chiefs go to the bathroom. I'm sick of it!" she declared with a sudden loud, dramatic emphasis. "Sick of it, sick of it, sick of it!" Then she burst into laughter and waved gaily to a tourist couple from Minnesota who were staring at her rather strangely.

"Look at those country dudes," she said, pulling Herb toward her again and pointing with one long, bony, glittery-nailed finger toward the couple, who continued to stare, mesmerized. "Real down-homers, been here three days, seen Mr. Lincoln in his temple, seen Mr. Jefferson in *his* temple, been to the top of the Washington Monument, seen the town, Smithsonian, Air and Space Museum, Unknown Soldiers, Vietnam Memorial, Library of Congress, Declaration of Independence, whole bit, Senator's had 'em to lunch, Congressman's wet his pants being obliging, isn't *anything* folks won't do for 'em, now they're slumming in Georgetown and *now*, by God—" her voice rose to a yell that penetrated clearly and caused the tourists, finally, to blush, look indignant and turn away—"NOW, BY GOD, IT'S TIME THEY WENT HOME! Right?"

"I don't know," Herb protested as mildly as possible when communicating at several decibels above normal. "I don't think they do anybody any harm. They have a right to be here, after all. It's their city."

"*Their* city!" Delight exclaimed. "*Their* city! If they only knew what goes on in *their* city, this pretty place with all the pretty monuments. *Their* city. If they only *knew!* Ha, *hoo!*"

"We try to tell them," Herb said stoutly, hoping by this to calm the tide, but Delight was on what he called "one of her rampages" and he knew it would have to run its course. She snorted so hard she had to stop and blow her nose. Then she resumed, full voice.

"We try, do we?" she cried. "We *try?* Oh, Herbie boy, I guess you *do* and so do I, but I know there's a hell of a lot we miss, I just know it. DO YOU MIND?" she shouted at a gyrating couple who almost landed in her lap, glaring at them as they romped obliviously away. "There's plenty we miss, Herbie boy, *plenty*. Like, who's Zeecy McCune sleeping with these days, ditto Helen Clark, ditto Loy Buck, ditto—"

"Delight," he said, emboldened by the fifth brandy Alexander, "are you sex-mad? You're always talking about who's sleeping with whom. People do a lot of other things in this town besides sleep with each other, you know. They run the country and the military and a whole hell of a lot of other things. And most of the time, I've observed, they think the things they do are a hell of a lot more important than who they sleep with. It doesn't really matter to them *who* they sleep with. It doesn't really *matter* to them whether they sleep with anybody or *not* as long as they can make their mark in this town. Why don't you think about something else?"

"Herbie boy," she said, clutching his arm in a viselike grip from which he tried unsuccessfully to pry himself loose. "Herbie boy, they may do a lot of other things but I just like to know who they're sleeping with—I just like to know. It comes in handy, sometimes, when you really need to get a story. Haven't you learned that yet?"

"That's not how *I* get *my* stories," Herb said stiffly. Delight hooted.

"You're still *pure!*" she exclaimed. "You still think it's all real, that crap about journalistic ethics. Well, let me tell you, Herbie boy—"

"Just 'Herb' will do!" he snapped with a sudden real annoyance. "I'm not your average school kid, you know!"

"Well!" she cried on a burst of laughter. "Wow*ee,* that's some temper there, Herbie—Herb. All right, then. All *right.* I still want to know who they're sleeping with. So make a note whenever you find out, because you never know when it'll come in handy. You can just hand it on to me, if it's too much for your pristine conscience to bear . . . So you saw Roger Venable and Walker Stayman in the building this week?"

"They weren't sleeping together," he said in a spiteful tone and she hooted again.

"Stranger things have happened, Herbie—Herb. And some of 'em in the Pentagon, too. I just want to know what they were up to, who they saw, where they went, what they want—"

"I told you," he said loudly as the music, temporarily in abeyance while the band took a break, roared up again. "They saw Helen Clark and Tiny Wombaugh. It could be some kind of new project, though I don't know what yet. I've put in a request for an interview with Helen or Tiny—"

"Won't get either one," Delight said promptly. "They're all scared as hell of us over there. Better try down the line somewhere."

"That, too," he said. "I have a few leads out. Meanwhile, Red Roberts told me he thinks there's some sort of secret military thing underway. He doesn't know what. Maybe it's related to what Venable and Stayman are after."

"Well, Red isn't going to share it with *us*, if he does find out, that's for sure," Delight said, looking suddenly sour. "The *WSJ* and the rest of them are all alike, they'll pick up something we've started and run with it but they're pretty damned chary about sharing anything *they* find. Red's in the Pentagon's hip pocket, anyway."

"Why do you say that?" he demanded. "I've never seen that to be the case. I think he's a decent guy with a lot of integrity who calls them as he sees them and doesn't play any favorites. Of course he has a lot of friends in the Pentagon, he's been there so much longer than most of 'em including the SecDef and the JCS and anybody else you want to name at the top level, but that doesn't mean he's their stooge. *I* don't think he is."

"Listen!" Delight said—"Mr. Innocence: When you run the kind of operation we're running you start by being suspicious and distrustful of everybody and go on from there. You don't trust anybody and you don't think anybody's a nice guy and you think the worst of everybody until you have damned good proof to the contrary. And I mean *damned* good proof. You don't get sentimental about somebody just because he's been around a long time. I say Red Roberts is a Pentagon stooge! He can't help but be!"

"I'm not going to argue it with you," he said, looking at his watch and beginning to yawn. "I've got to get home and get some sleep."

"Me, too," she agreed, whipping out her credit card. "We'll let the company pay for this one. Big conference in Georgetown. Have you talked to Skip Framberg lately?"

"No," he said, surprised. "Is it time to?"

"He might know something," she said. "He still has a lot of lines into what's going on even if they do keep him in the basement. I have a hunch it's about time for him to unload about something. Go see him. Or I will if you don't want to."

"*I* will!" he said sharply. "It's my beat."

"Produce, Herbie boy," she said airily. "Produce, produce, produce! Something's got to break pretty soon. Or we'll make it break. Go see Skip. Or I will."

"Get the check and let's get out of here," Herb Horowitz said, tight-lipped. "Maybe we can draw straws for it."

But they didn't have to, because of course next morning Skip came to them.

First, however, he went to see the SecDef. On this morning when the President appeared to be finally fed up about Nanukuvu—and when, on Nanukuvu, they were just beginning to work on the next stage of their deadly preparations —Skip found Loy Buck to be in a terse and preoccupied mood that tipped his visitor that all was probably not going well with the mysterious project, or projects, that seemed to be underway.

In fact, Loy was not feeling pleased at all. He was annoyed with Skip for being the bothersome soul he was, and he was even more annoyed with his own subordinates for not having moved things along much faster on Frio. He had already had conversations with Tiny Wombaugh and Helen Clark that didn't please him very much, and he *knew* his conversation with Skip Framberg would not please him very much.

The wry mood of acceptance with which he had gone to bed last night had given way again this morning to what he felt was quite justified irritation.

Tiny, of course, had been his usual jovial, unexcitable, unimpressed, immovable self. Helen had been blandly calm as always. Between them, they had made him feel both frustrated and faintly foolish. He was ready for Skip by the time he got there.

"Now, Loy," Tiny had said, and in mind's eye the Secretary could see him pacing up and down beside his desk as he liked to do when telephoning, great height and enormous bulk lightly swaying from side to side as though on a dance-floor, receiver tucked into and almost hidden by the heavy folds of flesh that ringed his neck, "now, Loy, temper won't do any good. I've told Helen and told her and *told* her to get things moving, and she in turn has told and told and *told* everybody in her office who's involved to do likewise, and we've both had innumerable conferences with the two Harrys, who are as frustrated as we are—and there it is. I mean, you can push the building just so fast, you know."

"Yes, I know," the Secretary said. "God *damn* it. Now I've got the President breathing down my neck, and what am I supposed to tell him?"

"Tell him we're all working away just as fast as we can," Tiny said in a soothing voice. He chuckled. "Tell him it will all be taken care of by election-time next year."

"If it isn't taken care of before that," Loy Buck said bluntly, "forget it. He won't want anything like this in an election year."

"Yes," Tiny remarked, "that aspect of it has occurred to me. However, there really is some aspect of national security and overall strategy involved here also—"

"Then get to it!" Loy Buck snapped. Tiny chuckled again.

"We're gittin'," he said, sounding not at all disturbed. "Slow, maybe but sure, we're gittin', Loy. Don't let it get to you. I repeat, you know how things are in the building. Lots of us would like to move a lot faster. I suspect nine-tenths of us would like to move a lot faster. And if we didn't have to put up with the other one-tenth—*and*, of course, with each other—we'd manage it. But since everybody who's involved has to make his or her own record, and has to be sure there are sufficient copies of everything to provide adequate protection in case of challenge or failure—and the contractors in turn have to get all *their* ducks in a row too and get all *their* records in shape too—and protect *them*selves too —well, you know, Loy, it just amounts to Pentagon speed. Not what your average man in the street would consider *real* speed, but *Pentagon* speed . . . If I sound bitter," he concluded dryly, "I am. But there, as I said, it is. Let me know if the President has any brilliant ideas about how to expedite things. We're always open to suggestions. What the hell's the point in modifying the ALCAC anyway? Whose bright idea was that?"

"The JCS," the Secretary said, "and I can't dissuade them now. You know what a phalanx they put up when a civilian has the nerve to challenge them. They may fight among themselves like cats and dogs sometimes, but when it comes to us, brother, it's another world."

"I thought Joe Strang was going to try to stir up the reform group on the Hill again. At least he told me he was. Whatever happened to that idea?"

"What always happens to it?" Loy Buck inquired. "Do you really need an answer?"

"Not this morning," Tiny said. "I've got a lot of papers to shuffle around today. Can't take the time for *that.*"

Five minutes after they had parted with Loy's promise to report on the White House meeting as soon as possible, the Secretary's phone rang. The cool tones of Helen Clark fell with melodic self-assurance on his ear.

"Mr. Secretary," she said softly like iron velvet, "Tiny says you're displeased —even more displeased than usual, I take it—with the progress on Project Frio. I just want you to know that I am too. What would you suggest?"

"That's your responsibility, Helen," Loy Buck said tartly.

"Which I am discharging," she responded calmly, "to the very best of my ability. I don't know what else I can do except beat people with the blacksnake whip a lot of them seem to think I have. I've got both Strategic Industries and General Growth Group lined up and ready to make bids on the ALCAC as soon as the chiefs get their recommendations in to Project Frio. I've had repeated conferences with General Ahmanson—"

"Yes," Loy agreed with a deliberate dryness that for just a second interrupted the velvet flow; but only for a second.

"—and with Harry Josephs, and while Harry Josephs is still balking at the potential expense of the ALCAC idea, I think he's beginning to come around."

"A conscientious public servant," Loy Buck observed.

"Indubitably," she agreed. "But at times obstructive. He has no particular incentive to be cooperative if he doesn't agree with something. He told me the other day, 'I'm over the hill. All I have left is honor. It's important to me to protect that.' Which struck me as a trifle pompous but perfectly sincere. And admirable."

"Unlike Harry Ahmanson," he said, still dryly, "who has that second star to protect and so is, I am sure, eating his heart out at the slowness with which things are moving."

"He also is an honorable man," she said with a stiffness that prompted Loy to think: Ah ha, fair maid, yon E Ring gossip must be true. He had never known Helen to show the slightest emotion about anything. There was some there now, all right: tightly controlled, but apparent to a perceptive ear.

"Yes," he agreed, "both Military Harry and Civilian Harry have their good points, I do believe. And if the problem is, as you indicate, Civilian Harry, then maybe I should have him in and discuss it with him."

"It might help," she said. "I don't mind his being conscientious, but he is holding things up just as much as the chiefs, I think. Both S.I. and Three Gs are complaining to me. They want to get started as soon as possible. As I assume Gen. Ahmanson and the chiefs do too—although," she added, "it sometimes seems as though the chiefs think *they* have forever."

"Zeecy and I are after them all the time," he said. "The President has been too. But—" he realized suddenly that his tone was becoming quite uncomfortable and defensive as he automatically repeated the cliché—"these things take time."

"They shouldn't take this much, Mr. Secretary," she said. "I don't know what all this is about, but I assume it is—or," she couldn't resist adding, "was— a matter of some urgency."

"Not 'was,' yet," he said firmly. "*Is*. I want you to transmit it to all down the line, to both Harrys, to S.I. and Three Gs and anybody else you have involved in this, that from this point forward things are to move fast and no nonsense. The President is making this a top priority—"

"He is?" she interrupted. "I haven't been sure."

"He is," Loy said firmly. "I'll let you know the results of the White House meeting, but I'm sure it will be positive, affirmative and not subject to any misinterpretations."

"I hope so," she said politely. "That would help. Meanwhile I shall continue to do *my* best."

"You know," he said, "that's a funny thing I've noticed about the Pentagon: with relatively few exceptions, everybody in this place *does* try to do his or her best. Why is it, then, that so many things are subject to delay, disruption, duplication, false starts, revisions, reconsiderations, wasted motion, wasted time, wasted money, lethargy, slowness, frustration and general failure to achieve the results people think they are setting out to do?"

"Too many people," she said crisply, "too much money and too many constituencies to satisfy, in the building, on the Hill, in the White House and in industry. Cut them all in half and you'd get three times as much accomplished."

"Easy said," he remarked. "Not so easy done. When you get the successful formula for *that,* Helen, you come tell me."

"When I get the formula for that, Mr. Secretary," she said with a laugh, "I'll have your job. But I don't think you have to worry. It ain't never gonna happen, no how."

He sighed, humorous but frustrated.

"You're right there," he agreed. "I'm afraid you're absolutely right . . . Thanks for calling, Helen."

"Always a pleasure," she said.

"Likewise," he said; and thought as they hung up that it was. She was a very bright, shrewd, competent woman, one of the best in the building; a little cold, maybe, but perhaps that went with the kind of success she had achieved in business. So what if she and Harry Ahmanson were having an affair? They might be a perfect match. Certainly if they weren't there wouldn't be any false sentiment on either side about terminating it. Nor would there be the slightest public indiscretion.

Vangie knocked and came in with accustomed familiarity almost before he had a chance to respond.

"Skip Framberg's out there," she said with obvious disapproval. "He says you're expecting him."

Loy smiled.

"I am. I didn't tell you about it because I was afraid you'd tell me I couldn't do it."

"Well," she said, smiling a little too but still disapproving, "I should have strongly advised against it, if you had asked."

"What am I supposed to do with someone like that, Vangie?" he inquired. "You must have seen a hundred such troublemakers pass through this building—"

"At least."

"Yes. What's the magic formula for defanging them?"

"About what you've done, I reckon. Reassign them. Correct what they were complaining about, if possible. And let them wear themselves out trying to keep themselves in the headlines." She paused thoughtfully, trim gray head at a thoughtful angle. "I don't like Skip personally," she said, "but I'm not so sure that he didn't have a point on that Army test. General Burford isn't perfect."

"It wasn't Gen. Burford, of course," he said, "it was his people down the line. He just felt he had to stonewall it in their defense."

"I've often wondered why," she said. "I've seen it happen repeatedly, in forty years. The military always does stonewall. Or tries to. I think Skip went about it the wrong way, he went to the media first and then made his formal complaint here, but he may have had a point. Maybe the Army should have listened. However, once he'd chosen to make it a public issue, I think you had to stonewall it too."

"*Is* there enough outlet for legitimate complaint in this building?" he mused. "I often think about that, Vangie."

"I've seen it get out of hand on a few occasions," she said, "which is one reason for stonewalling, I guess. But, no, I don't think there is. I've seen a lot of suggestion boxes over the years, and a lot of memoranda inviting the ranks or the staff to make constructive suggestions." She smiled a trifle wryly. "A lot of directives *commanding* them to, too. But somehow it never does much good. Somehow there are never very many suggestions and somehow they never seem to be quite 'constructive' enough."

"It's no wonder minds like Skip's get fed up, then."

"I agree," she said. She looked thoughtful. "But of course one does have to stay within channels, when all's said and done. Otherwise chaos."

He sighed: and decided he had best lay a little groundwork.

"Yes, I know that's the rationale. I sometimes wonder if it's good enough. Maybe Skip's paid the penalty long enough. Maybe I should rehabilitate him." Thinking: *maybe he's discovered sufficient leverage so I'll have to.*

Vangie sniffed and forty years of Pentagon came to the fore.

"Only if he's got something on you," she said. "It wouldn't be worth it otherwise."

He uttered a startled laugh.

"Vangie," he said, "you amaze me. What a cynic! Why would you ever think a thing like that?"

"Hmph," she said with a dry little smile that summed up the wisdom of those forty years. "He's here, isn't he?"

"Right you are," he said, giving her a mock bow, still much amused. "Show him in."

So it was that Skip, who like many scientists was so self-centered that he rarely wasted time bothering to notice other people's reactions to him, did feel in this instance that the SecDef was cordially disposed. He knew Vangie didn't like him but he had never felt any real personal animosity coming from Loy Buck even if Loy had been the administrative factor in banishing him to the purple water fountain. Now he felt that Loy might really like him after all. Wasn't his expression pleasant and his attitude one of friendly welcome?

"Skip," he said, holding out his hand. "It's good to see you again."

"It is?" Skip said, glow fading as he abruptly remembered why he was here. "I've just been right down there in the basement."

"I know," Loy said, "but you know how it is in the building. So many things are going on, everybody's in his own niche, we're all so busy—one just loses contact."

"I could have come up any time you wanted to see me, Mr. Secretary," Skip said stiffly, beginning to get mad all over again. Just another snow-job from Loy Buck, that's all he was to get, as usual. He could see that.

"Sit down, Skip," the Secretary said cordially, gesturing to a sofa along the wall, slouching himself comfortably into one end of it. "What *does* bring you up here, anyway? I hope it's nothing that will cause me *too* many headaches. God knows I've got enough of 'em!"

"I'm sorry," Skip said, seating himself rigidly at the other end, refusing to relax and be buddies. "I guess you asked for it, Mr. Secretary."

"Did I?" Loy Buck inquired, really seeming to look back over the years to the day of his appointment. "No, I don't believe I did, Skip. I had greatness thrust upon me. Sometimes I wonder if it's all been worth it. Do you ever have that feeling about your work here?"

"I like it here!" Skip said in an alarmed tone, forgetting entirely that he had asked for—demanded—the interview, wondering: *what's he getting ready to do, fire me?* But then remembering: *he can't do that, I'm civil service.*

"I know you like it here, Skip," Loy Buck said soothingly. "And we like having you here. I only regret that the past nine months have been a little—let's say a little awkward for you. I'm hoping we can rectify that very soon."

"Oh?" Skip said, taken quite off base by this smooth preemption of what he had intended to initiate himself. "Do you?"

"Certainly," the Secretary said firmly. "Made-work in the basement is hardly the way to make use of the talents of a man so highly intelligent and capable as yourself."

"Then why—?" Skip demanded in a suddenly exasperated tone.

"Skip," Loy Buck said, "you know the Pentagon. You know what I'm up against here. You know what the situation is with the services and how every civilian official, even myself, has to walk a narrow line between them all and try to keep them all happy. I virtually had an Army revolt on my hands when you blew the whistle on that test—"

"It was a fraud!" Skip said, face getting almost as red as his hair, "a complete and utter fraud!"

"I don't think it was that bad," Loy Buck began, and raised his hand to forestall Skip's threatened rejoinder. "But it was bad enough. The country owes you a great deal for discovering the inadvertent laxities which occurred—"

" 'Inadvertent laxities'!" Skip cried. "Inadvertent my ass! They were deliberate and you know it!—Mr. Secretary," he added, almost in afterthought.

"Well," Loy said comfortably, "whatever, you blew the whistle and rightly so. And the Army corrected it."

"Not publicly," Skip said bitterly. "And not completely, either. And *I* wound up beyond the purple water fountain. And *you* put me there, Mr. Secretary!"

"Only because I was under such pressure from the Army that I had to do *something*. And they *did* correct it, don't forget that."

"They owe me a public apology," Skip said flatly. "Sure they 'corrected it,' enough to get by with a cursory hearing here and a lick and a promise from Cube Herron on the Hill, but not enough to really make that machine safe for our kids. That's what's important, Mr. Secretary, *the kids,* who have to operate the damned thing and put their lives on the line in it. Isn't it bad enough to have the error at all, without some fuck-up general compounding it by trying to pull a cover-up because he thinks his stars might be in jeopardy if he tells the truth? *And where is he now?"* he exploded loudly. "Working for Three Gs, the half-assed dangerous moron!"

"Did you ring, Mr. Secretary?" Vangie inquired politely from the door, pen and pad ready, expression bland: innocent, wide-eyed and ready to provide whatever diversion her boss required.

"No, thanks, Vangie," Loy said with a pleasant smile. "Not at the moment, thanks. I'll let you know if I need you."

"Well— . . ." she said vaguely. "If you really *don't*—"

"I appreciate the thought," he said, with a wink at Skip that obviously didn't appease him one bit, "but, no."

"Very good," she said. "I'll be right here if you want me."

"That she will," Skip said bitterly as she turned her neat little self around, walked neatly out and neatly closed the door. "Listening right there, the eavesdropper!"

"Only when you shout, Skip," the Secretary said calmly. "Only when you shout. That's when we start to call in the white squad. Now," he said, tone suddenly much tougher, leaning forward and pinning Skip with his eyes, "what do you want with me, Skip? I'm a busy man as you damned well know and I'm due at the White House in forty-five minutes, so whatever it is, spill it and be on your way. And don't forget I'm getting ready to bring you back to E Ring, if that's what this is all about. It's going to be done." He paused and then added, "If all goes well."

" 'If all goes well,' " Skip echoed. "Well, isn't that nice, Mr. Secretary! I think that's lovely. In what capacity?"

"We'll discuss that," Loy said, reverting to his usual amicable tone. "It's open to negotiation."

"You bet it is," Skip Framberg said flatly. "After we discuss Project Frio."

But if he thought this would disconcert Loy Buck he was mistaken. The Secretary didn't even blink. He just looked politely curious.

"What aspect of it would you like to discuss, Skip?"

"Then there is one!" Skip said triumphantly. "There really is one!"

"Of course there is," Loy said calmly. "As you know, we're a little wacky around here, but we don't usually establish project names just for the hell of it. Of course there's a Project Frio. What did you want to say about it?"

"And it involves modification of the ALCAC," Skip said.

Loy nodded.

"Among other things. Is that the aspect you wanted to discuss with me?"

" 'Among other things,' " Skip echoed with a tight little smile. "But we'll start with that. Here's *my* idea!"

And he drew a folded paper from his pocket, unfolded it and tossed it along the sofa to the Secretary. It was a completely drafted and, as Loy could see, extremely well-engineered modification of the Advanced Landing Craft Air Cushion as a highly skilled and highly knowledgeable civilian might see it. Whether it would satisfy the military he had no idea, but he determined in that split second that if everything checked out, he would certainly present it to them as the compromise he himself would support.

The irony of it made him smile a little to himself and Skip of course was on it at once.

"What's so amusing, Mr. Secretary?" he demanded. "It's a perfectly sound design."

"So it is," Loy agreed pleasantly. "I'm no engineer but I've picked up a little curbstone knowledge over the years. I can see it's perfectly sound. *I* like it. I may even get behind it with my full recommendation, assuming everything's in order. How about that, Mr. Skip Framberg?"

"Well," Skip said, astounded at how easy it all seemed to be—made suspicious thereby—but inwardly too flattered to continue his belligerent approach —"well, I'm pleased, Mr. Secretary, of course." Then he remembered his basic purpose in coming here and tensed up again. "But I'm only releasing it to you if I'm satisfied the mission itself makes sense."

"Technically and legally, of course," Loy said mildly, "you really don't have any choice but to release it to the department. But I wouldn't want to force it from you." He refolded it and tossed it along the sofa. "You can have it back."

"Now, wait a minute!" Skip protested thinking: *he is so damned tricky. It's no wonder he is where he is.* "I understand the legal situation. Certainly I understand it."

"And you understand that a lot of people in this building are at work on things whose ultimate use and purpose they don't know and are never told. It all gets put together by higher authority. Theirs but to provide the pieces, ours to put them together. All right, Skip?"

Skip placed the paper this time squarely in the center between them and sat back with his arms folded and a stern expression on his face.

"That should be quite adequate," he said, "for any landings anybody wants to make in the Caribbean or Central America."

"Now why," the Secretary inquired blandly, "would anybody want to name a project Frio and then go land in the Caribbean or Central America?"

"Or the South Pacific," Skip shot out triumphantly; but again the Secretary only looked bland.

"Or the South Pacific? 'Frio' means 'cold,' you know."

Loy's expression became kindly, he even had the nerve, Skip thought disgustedly, to lean forward and pat Skip's knee with a gesture that was fatherly, patronizing and, Skip felt, deliberately and mockingly insulting. "I'm afraid you'll have to guess again, Skip. You'll have to do better than that. It's a good try, but you'll have to guess again."

He picked up the paper and this time tucked it in his coat pocket with a firmness designed to show that he accepted and intended to keep it.

"Thank you for this. It will be most helpful when I get down to the hair-pulling stage with the Joint Chiefs. I can assure you that you'll get full credit if it's finally approved."

"And when do I come back to E Ring?" Skip inquired, deciding with a sudden angry impatience that there was no point in sparring any longer with this master at it. "When do I get my apology from the Army? My *public* apology?"

"Several questions at once," Loy observed with a smile. His eyes narrowed thoughtfully. "It wasn't E Ring anyway, was it? It was D Ring. Though E Ring," he added with a sudden embracing smile, "is not at all out of the question, Skip. I'll have to give it a little more thought."

"And the apology?" Skip demanded. "The *public* apology?"

"That may be a bit more difficult," the Secretary said with a man-to-man candor. "Apology, yes, perhaps we can arrange something with Brash Burford—"

"I don't want it just from Brash Burford," Skip Framberg said bluntly. "I want it from you."

For a second Loy's eyes narrowed again, a little more dangerously this time. But his tone was as calm as ever. He shrugged.

"Maybe that too, Skip. We'll have to see. As for it being public—well—that gets into various areas of consideration and policy. Let me think about it. Meanwhile, we should have something for you in a week or two about coming back up here in some suitable position . . . providing, of course, that we can count on your complete discretion concerning Project Frio, its nature—whereabouts—mission—whatever." He smiled, again in a kindly way. "Stop guessing, Skip. You'll be informed when it's necessary—if it's necessary. Isn't that SOP?"

Skip took a deep breath and a long gamble.

"Well, at least," he said, "I'll be pleased to know that when they land in the South Pacific they'll be using my design."

The Secretary laughed, apparently in quite genuine amusement.

"Always trying, Skip," he said, standing up and proffering his hand. "Always trying. You never give up, do you?"

"No, Mr. Secretary," Skip said as he returned the pressure with very minimal warmth, "I do not."

And he didn't, either, he thought with a resurgence of anger as he stalked out, nodding curtly to Vangie on the way and more cordially to the young Marine standing duty at the corridor door.

He had just been given, he realized as he stalked off along E Ring to the escalator that would take him down toward the bowels of the building, a typical Loy Buck snow-job, just as he had feared. His design had been "accepted," his apology had been denied, his probing about Project Frio had been virtually laughed off and he had only received a half-promise, tenuous at best, that his exile in the basement would be ended. Nothing definite, nothing clear, *nothing worthy of Skip Framberg.*

He was, suddenly, furious.

And with another of his sudden inspirations, he knew what he was going to do about it.

He stopped abruptly, absentmindedly returning the greeting of some colonel he remembered vaguely from test evaluation days, and stood for several moments thinking in the hall. Then he resumed his return to his cubbyhole, almost running down the stairs and along the dusty corridors until he reached it.

He picked up the phone, put in a quick call to the office of the Deputy Secretary of Defense, who by luck happened to be in. His secretary, after a moment's hesitation, put Skip through.

"Mr. Secretary," he said after they had exchanged quick greetings, Bob Cathcart obviously quite surprised to be hearing from him again so soon, "I'm glad I caught you."

"Glad you did too," Bob Cathcart said, sounding as though he regretted yesterday's confidential chat. "What can I do for you today?"

Skip took a deep breath and made his voice matter-of-fact and businesslike.

"I thought you'd be interested to know I've just seen Loy Buck," he said, "and he's decided to use my design to modify the ALCAC for those Caribbean landings."

"South Pacific," Bob Cathcart corrected and then caught himself with a hasty muttered, "God *damn!*" that came clearly over the line. "Congratulations!" he said hastily. "That's great, Skip! The Caribbean can be a real tricky place, and it's good to know we'll have a really well engineered vehicle to help us out. Congratulations!"

"I thought you'd like to know," Skip said happily. "Enjoy the White House."

"I'm not going," Bob Cathcart said with genuine gloom and then uttered a hearty laugh designed to make Skip forget all about his indiscretion. "I'm too lowly. Anyway, I don't care. A great place to visit, but I wouldn't want to live there!"

Not much, Skip thought dryly as the Deputy Secretary hung up still blustering heartily: half the people in this town want to live there.

He dialed another number, said quickly, "This is Skip. Can you meet me at Clyde's in Georgetown at twelve? I may have something for you."

"Honey," Delight said, "ah'se on mah broom an' *takin' off!*"

3   In one of those rare moments of being left alone which he was able to achieve from time to time—not without difficulty, he reflected—the President of the United States was sitting in the Oval Office awaiting the arrival of what he thought of as "the Pentagon gang."

Not "gang" in an invidious sense, just "gang" in the sense of ganging-up—on him, because he was quite sure there would be some smooth, well-coordinated rationale for the delay in the twin projects that were supposed to furnish the answer to the problem of Nanukuvu. He decided he would blow any such smooth-talking defense out of the water immediately so that they could get down to the nub of it and start working on a solution. He didn't propose to waste an hour on phony palaver while they all shined their shoes and polished their stars. He wanted a little action, for a change.

The occupation of the island was now three months old, and according to every intelligence report that had reached his desk, was proceeding with great success from the enemy's point of view. Constant surveillance by satellite and aircraft had kept track of the various ongoing accretions of strength, the growing number of submarine facilities, the barracks, the supply depots—everything still relatively new and unfinished, but well underway. A right tidy little Gibraltar in the Pacific, that was the apparent aim. Meanwhile back at the ranch, he thought with annoyance, things were not going so well.

Why this was he could not exactly determine, and he knew perfectly well he was not going to determine it this morning. There would be "explanations," "reasons," "justifications," "defenses" and of course earnest assurances that all was now ready and that from now on all would proceed post-haste. But as to exactly *why* things were as they were, and exactly *who* was responsible for things being as they were, he would not be truly enlightened. Not because of any particularly sinister conspiracy of silence or obfuscation, but just because, in the Pentagon, there rarely was a villain who could be positively identified and fairly disciplined. Sometimes somebody was singled out—as far down the ranks as his superiors dared descend in assigning responsibility—and, luckless fellow, he took the fall. But whether he was really the one responsible, or whether it was one or more of those above him, was almost never really clear. Scapegoats were available when needed but rarely was it possible to find real culprits.

Nobody and everybody was responsible in the Pentagon. They were like a school of squid, he sometimes thought: at the slightest sign of danger, they all exuded ink and took cover in the cloud.

If there had not been endless examples of loyalty, patriotism, devotion to duty and often really brilliant achievement in the Pentagon record, both in the building and, in time of crisis, in the field, he would have despaired of the country's safety long since. But somehow the gigantic machine had always managed to function—so far. Never perfectly, because its components were only human, and while supposed to be held to a higher standard of behavior than most, did not always make it. But often enough so that the nation had survived as a free country and had managed to maintain most of its obligations overseas at a reasonable level.

So far.

How much longer this could happen in today's world, he did not know, and often, like all Presidents, found himself in the grip of very gloomy thoughts about it. Yet he knew that the overall caliber of most of those in the Department of Defense, both military and civilian, was fully equal, if not well above, that of any group of individuals of comparable size and endeavor in the general population. There was, in fact, no such comparable group and no such comparable endeavor. The Pentagon was unique, it reached around the world, its hand lay everywhere. The majority of those who occupied positions of trust within it were worthy of that trust in every respect, mental, ethical, administrative. Why was it, then, that men and women so often brilliant and outstanding when taken individually seemed too often to move en masse with a frustrating slowness and lack of vision that too often made national survival a miracle instead of the assured and inevitable thing it ought to be?

Too much self-protection and buck-passing, yes; too much adherence to past traditions and past battles, yes; too much stress by too many on the "three p's," pay, promotion and pension, yes; too much red-tape, yes. But he felt those didn't explain it all.

Maybe it was just the sheer ponderous size of it. Maybe it was just too big: too many people, with too much money, trying to do too many things. Yet every time you tried to cut back areas of obvious waste—as he, unlike some, had genuinely tried to do—in came the political side as exemplified by the Hill, and beyond the Hill all the folks back home whose livelihood depended upon defense-related industries. You *can't* do such-and-such to my state, or district! You *must* do so-and-so for my state, or district! You *can't* close that plant and take away our jobs! You *must* keep us working or we'll go under—and vote you out of office.

It all became a terrible, a really insoluble maze of competing, interlocking, inextricably entangled interests . . .

Well—anyway. Here was Nanukuvu, one small but vital element in all the vast range of problems he faced—and what was to be done about *that?*

At this moment, while he awaited their arrival and enjoyed the unusual quiet in the Oval Office, his own task seemed entirely clear to him:

Raise hell and get things moving.

The installation, according to the latest intelligence he had received, was estimated to be only about a third completed—still time for decisive action by the United States. And by some miracle secrecy still prevailed.

As long as it did, the opportunity for direct and unhindered action remained open to them all.

He was convinced and determined that they must make the most of it.

This was what he told himself, as the meeting began.

The first to arrive, using his privilege as national security adviser to come in ahead of the rest, who would be assembled in a group and brought in together promptly at eleven, was Aleks Brodovsky. He was, as always, neat, quiet, self-possessed, understated, unassuming. And firmly in charge.

"Got all the answers, I suppose," the President greeted him with a smile. Al Brodovsky smiled back.

"Not exactly. To a dozen other things, maybe, but not to Nanukuvu—yet."

"That's not like you, Al," the President said. "I thought you knew everythin' 'bout everythin'."

"Don't believe all you read, Mr. President," Aleks said. "I like to fool State and the Pentagon into thinking I do, but it isn't really true."

"Keep 'em convinced of that," the President suggested. "It's the only way to keep 'em under control." He looked suddenly grim. "Doesn't look too good on the island, does it."

"No, sir," Al Brodovsky agreed. "Time's getting short."

"Couldn't agree more," the President said. "But how to get that across—" He frowned. "I can exhort, insist, threaten, demand—and the bureaucracy goes right along doin' as it damned well pleases. It's damned frustratin', you know, Al? You come into this job all fired up about what you're goin' to do to save the world, and—whammo! You run into that stone wall—or maybe I should say that wave of molasses, because it's just about as slow and just about as sticky—and suddenly all those bright, clever, rarin'-to-go ideas get modified and slowed down and memoranda-ed to death, and before you know it you're settlin' for half a loaf and thankin' the Lord you're lucky enough to get that much—if you do . . . Sometimes I feel like chuckin' the whole thing. Why should I put up with it for another four years?"

Al Brodovsky smiled.

"I'm not one of the people who's interested in the answer to that," he said, "but a lot of other people certainly are."

"Well," the President said triumphantly, "I'm not goin' to tell 'em! I'm not goin' to tell 'em one little smidgin until next year. They can eat their hearts out. Frankly, I was feelin' a little poorly a while back, but I'm over it now and the doctors tell me I'm in great shape to go again if I want to. But don't you tell anybody that, Al. We'll just let 'em guess. And I still may not. I still may not."

His secretary buzzed three times and he stood up and came around the desk.

"Here comes the thunderin' herd," he said. "You lead the discussion, Al. I'll just come in from time to time when it seems necessary. O.K.?"

"I was going to suggest that, Mr. President," the national security adviser said. "Much more effective if you do it that way."

"Clever man, Al," the President said sotto voce as the door was opened. "Glad I picked you to do the job, you never fail me. And here," he said, raising his voice in apparent expansive good nature, "here comes old Terry, big as life! You're lookin' mighty warm today, Mr. Icicle, I'll say that!"

"Well, Mr. President," Terry Venner said, momentarily flustered and off balance at this jolly greeting, as the President had intended, "it *is* rather warm outside. Summer, you know, summer!"

"It's a bitch, in Washington," the Chief Executive agreed, shaking hands heartily as the Pentagon group came in just behind. "And here come all those powerful people from across the river, all decked out in their medals and ribbons. Kind of got you outnumbered, haven't they, Terry? I admire you for comin' in here alone, I must say. *You* don't need six battalions and an honor guard like Loy, here. How are you, Mr. Secretary?"

"Mr. President," Loy said, shaking hands, not quite so flustered as the Secretary of State but pushed a little off balance himself in spite of his best determination, "good to see you. You know why we're all here—so you can give us hell collectively instead of one by one."

"Pshaw!" the President exclaimed. "I wouldn't do that, now, would I, Zeecy?"

"Not much," Gen. McCune said with a laugh. "Not *much.*"

"Anyway," the President said, shaking hands in quick succession with Gen. Burford, Gen. Stokes, Gen. Tock and Adm. Stahlman, followed by Joe Strang, looking pugnacious, "you fellows just make yourselves comfortable. They're supposed to be bringin' in some coffee—yes, here it comes."

Two of the kitchen staff discreetly rolled in a cart containing a big silver pot, cups, saucers and sweet rolls, and as discreetly withdrew.

"Help yourselves," the President directed, "and have a seat."

When they were all seated on the chairs and sofas drawn together in an informal circle at one of the windows overlooking the rose garden, he positioned himself in a leather armchair with his back to the window and glanced from face to face. His visitors looked respectful, expectant—and, as far as he could tell, determined to defend their positions and, if necessary, go down fighting. He suppressed a smile and turned to the national security adviser.

"Al," he suggested, "why don't you lead off?"

"Thank you, Mr. President," Al Brodovsky said; cleared his throat; and leaned forward, hands on knees, cool, calm and, although he didn't emphasize it and didn't have to, just as determined as the chiefs were.

"Gentlemen," he said, "the President is not satisfied with the progress made so far on either Operation Frio or Project Frio. He made this abundantly clear to all of you in the Pentagon in direct phone calls in recent weeks. The results have been disappointing. He thought it might help to get together and thrash it out. Loy, perhaps you might kick it off?"

The Secretary of Defense nodded and turned to Gen. McCune.

"Gen. McCune," he said, "are you gentlemen ready to present your case?"

"I believe we are, Mr. Secretary," Zeecy said, and bowed slightly to the President. "And Mr. President." The President waved a hand and said, "Forget me. I'll just listen for a while."

"Very well," Zeecy said. "Gen. Burford, perhaps you would like to lead off?"

"Certainly," Brash said. He opened his briefcase and took out a thick white document, obviously a prepared statement. His hands trembled a little and he looked tense and a little peaked, the President thought, which was not like Brash. The President made a mental note to check and find out about this: if it meant anything serious, it might have some bearing on the JCS chairmanship appointment later on. Meanwhile, he moved fast to intercept what was obviously intended to be a lengthy formal presentation.

"Now," he said, holding up a hand. "I don't intend to interfere, gentlemen, but I do think it would be contributin' greatly to both the speed and value of our discussion if we dispensed with formal statements and just got right to the heart of it. O.K.?"

"But, Mr. President—" Brash protested and his colleagues also looked upset.

"I would appreciate that," the President said firmly, looking around the circle. A disturbed silence fell, broken finally by Zeecy with a shrug.

"You're the boss, Mr. President," he said. "I'm sure the chiefs thought it would be helpful to offer in-depth presentations, but if time won't permit more than a few cursory surface observations—"

"Now, Zeecy," the President said with the bluntness of position and the candor of old friendship, "come off it. I know these 'in-depth presentations.' With all respects to you and the chiefs, they're always self-servin', they can't help but be. Why don't we just let Al, here, ask some questions and get on with it."

He looked around the circle again with an expression that did not invite debate.

"All right?"

After a moment the Secretary of Defense, with a rather wry expression, agreed for all of them.

"All right."

The Secretary of State could not restrain a small, satisfied smile.

"Perhaps we should take up Operation Frio first," Al Brodovsky suggested calmly as though the interruption had not occurred. "What's the problem there, Loy?"

"No particular problem," Loy said, marveling inwardly at how defensive and partisan he felt about his people now that they were under attack, and at how smoothly he, probably one of their most stringent critics, could slip into the role of their defender. "Just the slowness inherent in a large organization when it is called upon to move fast, I think. It has been emphasized to the chiefs, and I know they have emphasized it down the line, that the problem of Nanukuvu is a top priority and its elimination a matter of vital concern to the United States."

"Both of those things are obvious," Al Brodovsky said, and Loy Buck flushed slightly. The national security adviser ignored it. "They don't explain why, three months after the occupation of the island, there still has not been any agreement on a feasible plan for recapturing it or at least neutralizing it and denying its use to the enemy. Why is this?"

"Zeecy," Loy Buck suggested, "why don't you respond to that? You've also had some discussions with the chiefs, I believe."

"I have," Gen. McCune said crisply. "Both the Secretary and myself, Mr. President, have made repeated representations to the chiefs. You yourself, I believe, have done the same."

"Then why has nothing happened?" Aleks Brodovsky inquired.

"I wouldn't say that 'nothing' has happened," Zeecy retorted, tone sharpening. "We have established the Operation Frio mission and have assigned highly competent people to it, including General Al Rider, a Marine, at its head, as you know; and the Secretary has established Project Frio to handle certain elements of equipment and materiel to support the mission, also with a highly competent staff headed jointly by Gen. Harry Ahmanson, USA, and Harry Josephs, a longtime civil service employee in the office of the inspector general, OSD. I think a good interface has been established between the two projects. I can't say this is 'nothing.'"

"Results aren't much," the President observed. "Maybe you need more competent people to run it."

"Al Rider is one of the most competent general officers I know," Zeecy said. "Harry Ahmanson is also highly competent, and I am sure the fame of Harry Josephs—" he smiled a trifle dryly—"has spread even to the White House. They're all beavers for work and they have good staffs working for them."

"The staffs just don't have anything to work *on,*" the President remarked. "Other than that, they're perfect."

"But to return for a moment to Operation Frio," Aleks Brodovsky said smoothly before either Zeecy or Loy, both of whom looked upset, could reply, "why is it, gentlemen—and I would address this directly to the chiefs—why is it that you have not yet come up with a joint plan of operations in the face of a steady enemy build-up that is rapidly turning Nanukuvu, if it has not already done so, into a really formidable base in the South Pacific? This is puzzling to the President, and to me."

The chiefs glanced at one another and by tacit and instantaneous consensus deferred to Bumpy Stahlman. The admiral was at his most stiff and starchy when he replied.

"Mr. President," he said, "it is not surprising when civilians, even civilians as well-informed as Mr. Brodovsky, are unaware of the process that goes into the creation of a joint operational plan of any kind. Let alone one which, let us face it, would be, ipso facto and without question, a plan for an act of war."

"Why?" the President inquired. "Why, admiral? They don't own that island. Nobody does, really, but if anybody can be said to, it's ours by virtue of a general protective presence in that part of the South Pacific. *They* have committed the act of war, gentlemen, not we. It's a hazy area, but I think it could be argued that we have every right to dislodge them if we can." He shifted in his chair. "Maybe we can't, I don't know. Maybe we've waited too long. Is that the problem?"

"I am not yet ready to admit, Mr. President," Bumpy Stahlman said with the same stiff dignity, "that an adequately trained and equipped force of the United States of America cannot dislodge a temporary gamble launched by the enemy."

"I'm not prepared to admit it, either," the President said softly. "But it may be true."

There was a shocked silence as he had intended. Bumpy finally responded.

"Well, Mr. President, if that is the way you truly feel, then perhaps we had better dismantle Frio altogether and concede a key position in the South Pacific without further ado. Especially since you yourself made a direct representation to the Soviet General Secretary and received a rebuff that was evidently too strong for you to pursue further."

Again there was silence. It was the President's turn to look, if not shocked, at least definitely annoyed. The general attitude of the top brass—that the civilian heads of government were a burden whose opinions had to be suffered but not given much weight when it came to really important military matters—rarely surfaced quite so frankly. The feeling was always there, more than a little contemptuous but usually kept out of sight. His colleagues were at once startled, pleased and apprehensive that Bumpy had allowed it to color his tone so candidly.

"I did, as you say, make a 'direct representation' to Mr. KGB in the Kremlin," the President said coldly. "He did, as you say, rebuff me. That does not mean that I don't intend to get after him again about this. I've been countin' on you fellows to give me a little added muscle before I do. I haven't seen it yet and that's why we're here. If you boys have any explanation for this that makes more than a modicum of sense," he added, sounding a mite contemptuous himself, "let's have it. How about you, Gen. Stokes? You fly fellows always have an explanation for most everythin', I've noticed. How come you're so tardy?"

"I can see I'd better not bother with this," Ham said wryly, tossing his prepared statement on a coffee table and leaning back to prop one leg over the other. "The Air Force doesn't have any 'explanation,' Mr. President, we don't feel we need any. We wanted to go in there the first day and bomb the hell out of them. Instead we got all sorts of flutterings from Mr. Venner, there—" he looked without fondness at the Secretary of State, who returned the compliment—"and also, I might say, some feeling that perhaps you yourself were not quite ready for so strong an approach at that time. So we didn't push it. We have our ideas for a coordinated plan and whenever the group's ready, we're ready too."

"You still want to bomb hell out of 'em and make it basically an Air Force operation," Gen. Tock growled.

"You could say that," Ham Stokes agreed blandly. "But the Marines'll get their licks in, Tick, don't worry. We'll leave a little something for you to do."

"Hmph," Tick said. "We've got our plan ready, Mr. President, it's been ready since about two days after the occupation. And we've got a damned good Marine in charge of the mission. So we're ready, any time the rest of these birds want to sit down with us and work it out."

"The Army's ready and has been since day one," Brash Burford said shortly.

"The Navy," Bumpy Stahlman said, "won't boast, but I think it is safe to say that we're equally prepared."

"Then why haven't you gotten together and agreed and had the staff draw it up and then presented it to us?" Al Brodovsky inquired with some exasperation. "If everything is so perfect why are we sitting here three months later wondering when things are going to get pulled together? Gen. McCune, you're supposed to be the one who has the overview of the JCS. Perhaps you can tell us."

"I suppose," Zeecy said slowly, "that it has to do basically with the JCS system. Frio has been 'going through the process.' Simply because my colleagues say—and truthfully—that each service has its own plan does *not* mean that all the services have been able to work out *one* plan. And that's where we started this discussion and that's where we are now." He gave his colleagues a disapproving look. "I'd like to know myself, Mr. President, when it's going to happen."

"It's been going through the staff just as things always do," Adm. Stahlman said defensively. *"You* know how that is, Zeecy."

"Yes, I know," Gen. McCune said, deciding that this probably was not the time to tell the President about that, after all. "But I'm sure the President wants to know why you haven't been able to move it along faster."

"Can't we at least set a time?" the President inquired in a weary voice. "How about tomorrow morning? And I mean, seriously, *tomorrow morning.* And get it back to me by day after tomorrow. How about that?"

The chiefs looked at one another in open dismay.

"I'm not really sure, Mr. President," Brash said slowly, "that my staff people can have their paperwork ready by then."

"It's a concern we all have," Bumpy agreed. "Possibly they'll be ready day after tomorrow—possibly. And then we can meet the following day—" he looked around—"all day, if necessary."

"I have to make a speech in Colorado Springs," Ham Stokes said. "It'll have to be day after that."

"And I have to address the Commonwealth Club in San Francisco—" Tick said.

"All right, then," the President said in exasperation, "the day after that! Is everybody agreed?"

Brash nodded.

"We can at least go over the ground pretty thoroughly by then."

"We can be back to you in a week," Tick said firmly.

"If that's the best you can do—" the President said. They all nodded vigorously. "Very well. One week from today, a coordinated plan of military action for Operation Frio. Now: what about Project Frio? How are we coming on that? Not any better, right?"

"We should have our recommendations for modification of the ALCAC in to Harry Ahmanson by the end of the week," Brash said.

"We too," Bumpy agreed.

"Ours aren't major," Tick said, "but it's taken a little time to get everybody in line. I think we'll be ready."

"We may run into next week," Ham said. "These communications things can be pretty tricky. My people are working on it . . . Of course, you have to dislodge Civilian Harry. He's an obstinate little bastard. He still doesn't think there's any need to change the ALCAC at all."

"Neither do I, really," Bumpy Stahlman said. "It's an efficient piece of equipment. But," he added quickly as his colleagues looked at him in some surprise, "since the opportunity has developed to make it even better adapted to our various missions, the Navy certainly feels we should participate."

"We're arriving then at roughly the same time-frame for both aspects of Frio," Al Brodovsky said. "That at least is something."

"No, you're not, really," Terry Venner spoke up for the first time, "because getting the plans completed is only the beginning. Gen. Rider still has to organize the mission. Gen. Ahmanson and Mr. Josephs still have to arrange letting the contracts and getting the work done on the ALCAC, plus whatever other materiel problems they're called upon to solve in cooperation with Gen. Rider. This is just the beginning for you people. What do you think will be the situation on Nanukuvu by the time you all get through? *When* will you all get through?" he concluded triumphantly. "Tell me *that,* if anybody knows!"

For several seconds they simply looked at him, in not too friendly a fashion. Then Tick snorted.

"Hmph!" he said. "Wouldn't want to commit myself to that, Mr. Secretary; but I don't think you'll have to wait very long. I think we can promise that."

"You'll be lucky to get moving in a year," Terry predicted. "Maybe it'll even be two—"

"Now, just a minute—" Ham Stokes began loudly, but the President held up a hand and Ham, grumbling, subsided.

"I think maybe you have a point, Terry," the President said softly. "Meanwhile, I see a suggestion comin' on, from *you.* What is it?"

"About what I said at the beginning," the Secretary of State said, looking tired, annoyed and frustrated himself. "We can still take it to the U.N. We can still make a record. I can sound out the ambassador again and see if the General Secretary is any more receptive to a call from you—"

"He won't be," Loy Buck interjected.

"He may be," the Secretary of State said. "It takes them a while to feel secure about something. Then they'll usually talk about it."

" 'Secure' about something!" the Secretary of Defense exploded. "My God, man, being *secure* about Nanukuvu means they'll have it completely and entirely under their control and we'll never get them out of there. That's what it always means when they say they're feeling *'secure'* about something. It means they've *got* it."

"Well, *you're* letting them have it, with all your delays and service games and futzing around!" Terry Venner snapped. *"I'm* not! I'm trying to suggest to the President an option he might follow with a lot more rapidity and a lot more success than the Pentagon's option would give him!"

"I don't agree with that," Joe Strang said loudly, swiveling around his chubby frame, heavier by several hundred more chocolate-chip cones since the first day of Nanukuvu three months ago. "I think it's absolute nonsense to follow the diplomatic option without a most vigorous assertion of the military option to keep it company. If you want the President to call him and hint what we're planning in the Pentagon and *then* invite him to talk, well, maybe, yes. But you can't just go hat in hand and beg him to back off from an operation they're obviously investing a great deal of effort in, unless you're in a position to back it up with force if necessary."

"Well, you aren't right now," Terry Venner said flatly. "So how about *that*, Joe?"

"Then we should keep our mouths shut!" Joe Strang snapped.

"And do nothing?" the Secretary of State demanded. "I thought everybody was all upset because we're doing *nothing*, right now. Isn't that what this is all about? I'm trying to offer something we *can* do, right away, not some Pentagon pie-in-the-sky that's going to take *years* to get off the drawing-board!"

"Oh, hell!" Loy Buck retorted. "Stop being dramatic."

"I'm not being dramatic!" the Secretary of State said. "I'm suggesting the civilized way to go about this. You're planning to commit an act of war in the South Pacific. I'm trying to keep the peace. That's the difference!"

"We're planning an act of war!" Ham Stokes exploded. "Who the hell seized that island in the first place? You people really manage to get things upside down over there in Foggy Bottom. It's no wonder we're always having to pull your chestnuts out of the fire."

"That's not fair, general!" Terry Venner exclaimed. *"That's not fair!"*

"Gentlemen," Aleks Brodovsky said firmly while the President looked impassively from face to face and kept his counsel, "I think probably that's enough. I think the Secretary of State has offered a reasonable option—a parallel option, not an alternative, because I think the preparations for Frio must go ahead and the sooner the better. I'm inclined to agree with the Pentagon that the bottom line is that we're probably literally going to have to go in and get them out of there. But I think a fair warning makes sense. Not specific details of what we plan to do—when you gentlemen decide what that is," he interjected dryly—"but that we *will* do *something* unless they dismantle the installations and get out of there. Fortunately so far we can conduct both these options with a reasonable assurance of secrecy—" He broke off abruptly and demanded, "What's the matter, Loy? You know something we don't know?"

"Does the name Skip Framberg mean anything to you?" Loy inquired wryly. "It does to us."

"We've heard of him," the national security adviser said. "Don't tell me he's onto this. How did that happen?"

"He is to some degree," Loy said, "and I don't know how. Certainly I don't think it came from any of us. He dropped in to see me a couple of hours ago. You'll be interested to know, gentlemen, that he has a modification of the ALCAC, which he presented to me with his compliments. It's a good one, too. I may even decide to give it my endorsement."

"Son of a bitch!" Brash Burford said softly. "How did that snotty little bastard—"

"He didn't say," Loy said. "But he did say he thought his design would be good for landing in, consecutively, the Caribbean—Central America—or the South Pacific. He mentioned the South Pacific twice."

"Son of a bitch," Brash said again. His face flushed with anger. "If I ever find out that any son of a bitch in *my* shop spilled the beans to that two-bit little troublemaker I'll crucify him. So help me, I'll crucify him!"

"That won't help any," Bumpy Stahlman said. "The problem now is to contain the damage. How much does he know, Loy?"

"He doesn't know much," the Secretary said. "Just enough to know the name of the project and that 'Frio' does not, in this case, mean 'cold.' Just enough to be able to start the media on the trail. That should be quite sufficient to give us all a lively time."

"Can't you buy him off some way?" Joe Strang inquired. Loy shrugged.

"I'd already told him I was thinking about bringing him back upstairs—which I was," he said firmly as Brash looked restive. "It's the best way to defang that type, in the long run. He's quite substantial, much more than just a headline hunter. He's a serious young man, Brash. Dedicated. Difficult. Determined." His tone was half mocking, half respectful. It was hard to tell what he really thought of Skip. "He upped his price immediately, of course."

"What does he want?" Brash inquired.

"A public apology." The Secretary chuckled. "From me. And you."

"I'll be God *damned*—" Gen. Burford began.

"The strong implication I got was that if he doesn't get them he'll go running to the media about Frio—or as much as he can guess about Frio. He may have done so already. Anyway, he will, I'm sure of that. So, Mr. President, new options to consider. We probably aren't going to be secret much longer. Or at least not *as* secret. Then what? Do we still proceed full-steam in the Pentagon?"

"And will you *now,*" Terry Venner inquired, in a tone as close to exasperation as he felt advisable in addressing the President, "exercise the diplomatic option, which seems to me even more valid if this becomes public?"

For several moments they were all silent. Outwardly amicable, inwardly secretive, sometimes devious—as all Presidents are sometimes devious—the man they watched dominated the room. Zeecy, who knew him best, thought *I know that look.* He had seen it in academy days when his then-classmate was contemplating how to finesse a difficult professor or emerge with praise, plaudits and not too much risk from a difficult situation. *He's going to be tricky,* Zeecy predicted to himself. *When it comes to tight corners, he's always tricky.* Which was perhaps a good thing for his country when *it* was in a tight corner, but not always for subordinates such as faced him now. Quite often he left them uncertain and hesitant in the wake of his sudden shifts of position.

"Well, now," he said finally, turning his chair around to face the rose garden. "I'll have to think about that."

They looked at one another blankly behind his back: Loy at Terry, Terry at Loy. Finally Terry cleared his throat.

"Is that all you're going to say, Mr. President?"

"It may be, at the moment," the President said, not turning around.

"But how are we to proceed on that?" Loy asked. "That doesn't give us much guidance, does it? Do you want us to keep up the pressure in the Pentagon? Shall we continue to organize the mission?"

"Do you want me to approach the ambassador?" Terry inquired. He and Loy exchanged a baffled look. "I mean—really, Mr. President. What *do* you want us to do?"

The President swung his chair around until he faced them again. A contrite expression crossed his face.

"I'm sorry," he said. "I'm *not* being much help, am I? Of course I want you fellows to keep on with what you're doing. You get that mission in shape, Loy. You keep the diplomatic channels open, Terry. And maybe I'll give our friend in the Kremlin a buzz one of these days. After all—" he smiled blandly—"it wouldn't do for us to drop our efforts now, would it? Nanukuvu's just as much a problem whether it's secret or not, isn't it? How could we *not* go forward?"

"*We* don't know, Mr. President," Zeecy said, taking a chance, but provoked by what he felt to be willful equivocation. "But you suddenly don't seem to be as enthusiastic as you were a couple of minutes ago. What are we supposed to conclude from that?"

"Not a thing," the Chief Executive said in the same bland way. "Not a thing. Of *course* we're going ahead. We just have to take into account that we may not have quite so much public support from now on, that's all."

"We haven't had *any*," Zeecy said more patiently than he felt, "because the public hasn't known about it. Or any opposition, either, for the same reason. Now we're probably going to get some of both . . . You know what would make us in the Pentagon feel a lot better about it, Mr. President?"

"Can't imagine," the President said with a comfortable smile.

"If this does become public to the point where an official stand has to be taken, we'd appreciate it if you'd go on television and make one of your A-B-C talks to the country explaining exactly what's happening on Nanukuvu, exactly why Nanukuvu is strategically important in the South Pacific, and exactly why it's important to the United States that we get the enemy out of there. That's exactly what we in the Pentagon would like you to do."

"It would be very helpful to all of us," Terry Venner agreed quickly and Zeecy nodded appreciation of his support. Again they all looked at the President, who now returned their collective gaze with an open and candid air.

"That's what I mean by having to think about it. If it becomes public, there are so many new factors that have to be taken into account . . . the media . . . the Hill . . . the peaceniks . . . the U.N. . . . the Soviets . . . so many new aspects. You've got all the pressures to consider . . ."

His voice trailed away and again it was Gen. McCune who took a chance on old friendship and spoke for all of them.

"But those are things you have to overcome, Mr. President," he said firmly. "If it's really important to the United States to get rid of that base out there, you're going to have to take the brunt and lead the way. That's what always has to happen if things are going to get done. America will defeat itself again unless you do."

The President, who had been following him very closely but with an expression whose purport they could not fathom, pursed his lips and leaned back in his chair.

"Well," he said, propping his chin on his fingers and staring thoughtfully at the floor, "that's giving it to me straight, Zeecy, I will say that." He smiled suddenly. "I expect that's what I need now and then, a little remindin' of my duty from an old friend who's known me since my salad days. Never known me to fail before though, have you, Zeece?" And when Zeecy hesitated just a fraction too long, his smile broadened and he looked him straight in the eye. "Well, have you?"

"No, sir," Zeecy said crisply. "Not when it really mattered. That's what you really have to decide, sir: whether it really matters."

"That's right," the President said, standing up suddenly so that they perforce had to follow his example. "That's exactly right, and that's where I've got to do some really serious thinkin'. Meanwhile, you boys keep right on pushin' full speed ahead with all your various projects, Frio this and Frio that, and you with your diplomatic maneuverin', Terry, to get things ready for me to talk to that smart number in Moscow one of these days, and we'll see what happens."

"But—" the Secretary of State said in an uncertain tone.

The President chuckled, took him by the arm and started walking them all to the door.

"Shucks, Terry," he said in a jovial voice, "don't *worry* about things so. It will all work out."

"We sincerely hope so, Mr. President," Loy Buck said bluntly.

But the President made no reply, only smiled upon them all and shook hands firmly with each as he saw them out the door.

Outside in the sweltering noontime air Terry's limousine was the first to draw up under the South Portico.

"Well, gentlemen," he said with an ironic smile as he prepared to get in, "I seem to hear a rather uncertain trumpet leading us to battle. I hope we can all keep our footing in this mad, headlong charge."

"Good luck," Loy responded with equal irony as Terry rolled away with a final wave. "Hang together or we'll all hang separately."

He turned to the chiefs and Joe Strang with a wry smile.

"One thing: he's running again, if anybody had any doubt."

"Like a jack-rabbit," Zeecy agreed in a disgusted tone. "Like a God damned jack-rabbit!"

"Where does that leave Nanukuvu?" Adm. Stahlman inquired.

Gen. Stokes snorted.

"Under a pile of bunny-bullets, I'd say."

An uneasy silence fell as they waited for the Secretary's limousine. As it arrived Al Brodovsky peered out and waved goodbye with an apologetic air. It didn't help much.

Next morning Hank Milhaus, as he had expected right along, became the first line of defense against the additional handicaps that from now on would join those already hindering a swift solution of the problem of Nanukuvu.

When the Assistant Secretary of Defense for Public Affairs had accepted his appointment after a dozen excellent years as Pentagon correspondent for *The Wall Street Journal* he had done so with considerable misgiving about "jumping the fence," as he had put it to his friends in the media. There had been many pointed comments, most friendly because he was highly liked and respected, but some snide, about how he was about to "move across the river and lie for his country."

He had argued this out with Loy Buck at considerable length and with some heat before agreeing to join the Pentagon. Loy had assured him that he would not be asked to do anything that would offend his conscience or violate his principles.

Yet, like so many when they move from the this-is-how-it-should-be-done side of Washington to the this-is-actually-how-we-have-to-do-it side, he had soon found that it was not so easy to pontificate or hold the line on that particular subject. There had been times, quite frequent, when he had found himself standing on the podium in the press conference room across from his office on the second floor of E Ring, defending the Department of Defense against a hail of questions that almost invariably started from the passionately-held premise that all the building's occupants were crooks, scoundrels, liars and thieves.

And that all their questioners, with equally adamant conviction, were pure as the driven snow, absolute paragons of morality and virtue, and exclusive hold-ers and infallible guardians of all truth on all subjects, particularly anything pertaining to the big bad military.

Somewhere in all this, he supposed, there was a healthy balance to be found —healthy for the building, for the media and for the country. Except, he soon concluded, very few on either side were really interested in balance. It was constant war, in the Pentagon, and having enlisted voluntarily on the side of the department he soon found himself using weapons as ruthless, if not always so blatant, as its critics.

Therefore he came forth prepared to do battle on this morning when he held one of his regular weekly press conferences—as distinct from the unex-pected ones that he was always being required to hold at all hours of day and night, either through media insistence for *their* purposes or mandated by his superiors for *their* purposes. It was, as he often told Janet, a hell of a job. But, he confessed when she kidded him about it, he loved it. He won some and he lost some but at least it was never dull. It kept him on his toes and despite the hours and pressures, he really thought it kept him young. He did indeed look perhaps a decade younger than his actual forty-seven years.

He had been informed of the occupation of Nanukuvu by the Secretary within two hours after Zeecy McCune had passed the word to Loy. He had been kept constantly apprised of the enemy's progress ever since, on a genuine need-to-know basis because there was no telling when something would leak to some alert reporter and he would suddenly be confronted with a disconcerting question in open meeting. The private background questions he often got could be handled with a candor sufficient to satisfy most of the reasonable reporters who asked them. It was the wild ones he had to worry about and try to anticipate—the ones who deliberately set out to put him on the spot and embarrass the department in the most public and damaging way they could think of.

The publisher of *Defense Eye* was one of these and he knew the moment he saw her sitting in the front row next to Herbie Horowitz, one long skinny leg dangling over the other, hair in its usual wild frazzle, highly intelligent eyes hooded and implacable, sharp-featured little face following his every motion with deliberately unnerving intensity, that she meant trouble this morning.

The television lights went on. The cameras started rolling. The twenty or so reporters who had shown up for what they obviously expected to be a routine wrangle over the department's most recently publicized achievements, blunders or plain outright screw-ups leaned forward with an expectant air. He stepped forward and took the microphone with an easy assurance.

"I haven't got anything special for you this morning," he began—and Delight came in right on cue.

"Hank," she interrupted, "what's this Project Frio we keep hearing so much about?"

Inwardly he skipped a beat but outwardly he was as calm as ever.

"I'm not sure I know what you're talking about," he said as everybody's ears obviously pricked up, "but if you hear so much about it, then obviously I should. Perhaps you could describe it to me."

"Project Frio," she repeated. *"Project Frio! You* know!"

"I'd still like you to tell me, Delight," he said patiently. "It sounds interesting. I could check on it for you and get back to you if I only knew what—"

"You know," she said flatly. "You're just being coy, now. It has something to do with something in the South Pacific."

"Oh?" he responded with exaggerated wonder. " *'South'* Pacific? 'Frio'? When I went to school, that meant 'cold.' At least the way Miss Barnes taught Spanish sophomore year in high school, it did. But maybe the language has changed since then."

"Maybe it has," she said, but he noted she sounded a little less certain. "It's a project! In the South Pacific! Or the Caribbean! Or somewhere, for God's sake. You *must* know what it is."

"Delight," he said solemnly, "you've got me, kid. I'll have to check on that and get back to you."

"Oh, come *on!*" she said, beginning to sound a little frustrated. "Why do you people always have to play games with the country? *Tell us what Project Frio is!* You're spending the taxpayers' money, aren't you?"

"That strikes me as something of a non sequitur," he remarked as Red Roberts and a few others looked amused and he thought maybe he could swing them against her as he had sometimes managed to do before, even though they often picked up on things she managed to uncover. "We always spend the taxpayers' money. Doesn't everybody?"

"Very funny," she said dourly. "Very damned funny, I don't think! What's such a big secret about Project Frio, anyway?"

He looked blank.

"Is there any?"

"Damn it," she said, looking really angry now, *"Defense Eye* wants to know what this cover-up is all about. Something's going on!"

"Something's always going on," he said blandly. "If *Defense Spy* wants to get excited about this mysterious Frio whatever-it-is you've dreamed up, then I suppose that's your privilege. It's your newspaper. Or is it?"

"What's that supposed to mean?" she demanded while Red and several others laughed outright.

"I don't know," he said innocently. "Sometimes I just wonder."

"Well, don't 'just wonder' on taxpayers' time!"

"There you go again," he said. "You take a very proprietary air toward the taxpayers, Delight. I wonder if they appreciate how much you do for them."

"More than you do, anyway!" she snapped. "It's *Defense Eye*, too, not *Defense Spy*, I'll thank you to remember!"

"To each his own," he said. His tone turned crisp. "Anyway, I think we've wasted enough time on that. I'll check out whatever it is you want to know if you can just give me some specifics. Meanwhile," he said, using the diversion he had kept in reserve for many weeks, "I thought you all might be interested to know that we're soon going to hold talks with—"

"Why is it necessary to modify the ALCAC for Frio?" she interrupted loudly. His tone became firmer.

"—going to start discussions with Argentina on mutual defense matters in the South *Atlantic,* Delight. And I've already said I'll be glad to check out anything specific you people want to bring me. So can we move on to something of more substance now, please?"

"Is the Argentine business Project Frio?" Red Roberts inquired.

"Oh, come on now, Red," he said comfortably. "We're not going off down that path *again,* are we?"

"It can get pretty cold in Argentina," Red observed with a chuckle that Hank hoped meant he wasn't buying Delight's bait. "In the southern end, anyway."

"It sure can," Hank agreed with an answering chuckle, hoping Red would keep on with it. Obligingly, he did.

"Why is it considered necessary to hold discussions with Argentina at this time?" he inquired. "Is there anything developing down that way at the moment that we're concerned about?"

"Nothing in particular," Hank said thankfully, "but it's been some time since their defense minister has been up here to talk to the SecDef and Mr. Buck thought it would be a good idea to invite him here for a general discussion of matters of mutual interest. The usual thing," he added in an offhand tone. "It happens often with a lot of countries, as you know. Pretty routine, on the whole."

"You'll let us know if it's anything more important," Red said. Hank nodded. "Immediately."

"What about that false billing charge against Three Gs in connection with parts for the new Navy helicopter?" the AP inquired; and they were off into a long, detailed discussion of the steps that Shorty Murchison, as inspector general, was going to take to investigate this latest possibly not-so-innocent blunder by some hitherto unknown employees of one of the nation's two largest defense contractors.

In the middle of it Delight, who had been ostentatiously sulking in her seat, got up abruptly and stalked out with a backward glare to which he replied cheerfully, "And you too, lady!"

Everybody laughed and he plunged back into Three Gs and breathed a sigh of relief—temporary relief, maybe, he thought as the conference broke up. But at least for the moment he seemed to have put the lid back on Frio.

He made a mental note to tell Loy to shoot that invitation to Buenos Aires within the hour. And to suggest that he give a little more thought before he got too kind to Skip Framberg.

He watched the news and read the papers carefully for the next twenty-four hours, but nowhere did he find mention of Frio, nor did he receive further queries from *Defense Eye* or anyone else. For the time being it seemed to have trailed away in the wake of their inconclusive discussion. He hoped devoutly that it would be considered "just another of Delight's red herrings." Her probings often were, though never often enough to satisfy the Defense Department.

On Nanukuvu the first missile-launcher of the twenty expected arrived right on schedule on a submarine from Cam Ranh Bay in communist Vietnam.

All was proceeding well, the commander thought.

Three

1

BLESSED ARE THE MERCIFUL, FOR THEY SHALL OB-TAIN MERCY.

So said the sign.

Its proprietor, on this cool October morning, was sitting on the concrete buttress alongside the steps of the River Entrance. He wore a blue woolen skull-cap, a tattered red woolen shirt, a tattered camouflage jacket and tattered camouflage pants. His feet were tucked into a tattered camouflage sleeping bag against the unseasonably chilly weather. He wore glasses, had long, sandy hair and a thin droopy moustache. He was perhaps twenty-five. He appeared to be a nice, earnest, well-meaning, harmless young man.

After a lengthy scrutiny to which he paid no attention, two security guards at the top of the steps had decided he was. They were right. Nobody even noticed him as hundreds of civilians and military hurried briskly in and out.

This, perhaps, accounted for his lonely, resigned, disconsolate air. He was the only picket this morning, in a place that sometimes attracted hundreds. Because of this, and because picketing at the River Entrance usually wasn't half so dramatic or colorful as the occasional sit-ins and lie-downs in the center of the Concourse, no reporters came by to find out what his protest was and no television crews hung upon his every word in preparation for the evening news.

He was obviously there out of genuine conviction, which made him relatively unique, rather colorless and not at all as newsworthy as his more flamboyant, camera-smart brothers and sisters.

Significantly, however, all were treated alike by the Pentagon, whose occupants did not consider it a normal day if someone wasn't picketing or protesting somewhere in the building or its environs. Diligent attempts were made to confine this to the entrances and the Concourse, but within those limits free speech, free assembly, free demonstration were guarded as zealously by the Defense Department as they were exercised zealously by its more publicity-conscious critics. The building was not often given credit for this, but it was a matter of satisfaction to its occupants. It was part of what they felt they were protecting and as such they suffered it with patience if not enthusiasm.

It was quite possible that if the names "Operation Frio" and "Project Frio" had been known to the world, the lone demonstrator might have been joined by dozens, even hundreds more.

They would have believed, mistakenly, that the United States was fully prepared to launch an all-out smashing drive against a tiny island many thousands of miles away in the South Pacific.

They would have been convinced, quite erroneously, that America was about to precipitate, with high hopes of successfully concluding, a major confrontation with the Soviet Union that would result in the Soviet Union's withdrawal from its newest strategically located bastion in the distant sea.

They would have assumed that the building was actually as all-powerful, all-knowing, supremely efficient and perfectly organized for mayhem as many of them honestly believed it to be.

This would have indicated how much *they* knew about it.

But it would also have helped to strengthen the comforting national assumption that action, stern and implacable, was the building's inevitable and unwavering response to every new encroachment by the enemy upon the steadily diminishing areas of freedom in the world.

The building would not have been averse to having this assumption strengthened, because today, seven months after the occupation of Nanukuvu, four months after the White House meeting that was to have put everything in order, things were still not moving very well with Frio. Partly this was due to a certain slackening of Presidential pressure, whether for the reason attributed by those attending the White House meeting, or some other. Far more important were the delays inherent in the building itself.

Things were happening, but they were happening, in customary Pentagon fashion, at their own traditional, balletic pace.

Fortunately for those involved, this was still by some miracle occurring in secrecy. But this protection had always been extremely chancy. Now in October it was finally going to end.

For the duration of his few earnest hours at the River Entrance, however, the building still seemed to its lone picketer to be an ominous, implacable and inevitable mass looming over the world.

BLESSED ARE THE MERCIFUL, he admonished it, shivering and hunching his shoulders deeper into his battered old camouflage coat, FOR THEY SHALL OBTAIN MERCY.

Whatever his exact intention in issuing a Biblical advisory whose meaning was somewhat obscure in this context, the building, as far as he could tell, did not respond. Ominous, implacable and inevitable, it ignored him against a sky of scudding gray clouds and answered nothing back.

Which did not mean, of course, that its leaders and its occupants were not merciful, or that they did not with conscious volition intend to be merciful in all their dealings, insofar as the magnitude of their tasks and the pressures of getting them done—to say nothing of the pressures of the enemy, which also had a lot to do with it—permitted them to be merciful.

It was just that there were so many of them, and that even the major titles, jobs and positions, so often repetitious as between civilian and military and so often redundant within both civilian and military, rarely permitted a clear vision of exactly who was supposed to be doing what, let alone time to concentrate on such nice but abstract concepts as being merciful.

For instance—in figures that often fluctuated upward, almost never down:

In OSD, the Office of the Secretary of Defense, currently 690 people considered of sufficient importance to list in the *Department of Defense Key Personnel Locator* prepared by the Directorate for Organizational and Management Planning, OSD, starting with the Secretary and senior staff of four, plus secretarial staff—the Deputy Secretary and three, plus secretarial—the Executive Secretary to the Secretary and seven, plus secretarial . . . running on through the Under Secretary of Defense for Policy, Joe Strang and ten, plus secretarial . . . Deputy Under Secretary for Trade Security Policy/Director Defense Technology Security Information and six, plus staff . . . Assistant Secretary of Defense, International Security *Affairs* and nineteen, plus staff . . . Assistant Secretary of Defense, International Security *Policy* and twenty-five, plus . . . Director of Net Assessment and nine, plus . . . Defense Investigative Service director and twelve, plus . . . Defense Security Assistance Agency, director and twelve, plus . . . Assistant Secretary of Defense, Comptroller and twenty-nine, plus . . . Contract Audit Agency, director and eighteen, plus . . . Strategic Defense Initiative Organization, commanding general and fourteen, plus . . . Assistant to the Secretary of Defense (Intelligence Oversight) and three, plus secretarial . . . Uniformed Services University of Health Sciences, chairman and thirty-five, plus . . . Office of Small and Disadvantaged Business Utilization, director and three, plus . . . National Security Agency/Central Security Service, director and four, plus staff . . . Assistant Secretary of Defense, Command, Control, Communications and Intelligence, Tom Garcia and fifteen, plus . . . and so on through the Defense Communications Agency, director and thirteen, plus staff . . . Defense Mapping Agency . . . Defense Intelligence Agency . . . Assistant Secretary of Defense, Health Affairs . . . Director, Operational Test and Evaluation . . . Director, Program Analysis and Evaluation . . . Inspector General, Shorty Murchison and ten, including Harry Josephs, and staff . . . Assistant Secretary of Defense, Legislative Affairs and twenty, plus staff . . . Reserve Affairs . . . Public Affairs . . . Acquisition and Logistics, Helen Clark and forty-four, plus staff . . . Under Secretary of Defense, Research and Engineering, Tiny Wombaugh and four and staff . . . and on and on to the number of 690 as of the time of Nanukuvu . . . more responsibilities, under various titles but dealing with the same subjects, occurring in OSD—the Army—the Navy—the Marines—the Air Force . . . offices of legislative affairs, under various titles but dealing with the same subjects, in OSD—the Army—the Navy—the Marines—the Air Force . . . offices of foreign policy, under various names but dealing with the same issues, nations and crises, in OSD—the Army—the Navy—the Marines—the Air Force . . . and these only a very few examples out of many.

OSD, Army, Navy, Marines, Air Force, all fiercely convinced that they had to have their own individual units to do almost identical things; all fiercely protective of their own staffs and budgets no matter how redundant; all fiercely determined that nobody, but nobody, should interfere with the sacred structure to which substructure after substructure had been added over the years since Congress after great and bitter laborings passed the "National Security act of 1947" that was to have brought about consolidation and economy, done away with duplication, repetition and redundancy, put an end to waste of time, waste of money, waste of effort . . .

The Defense Department wallowed like some great ship, while the enormous weight of barnacles on the hull grew and grew and grew and grew, year after year after year after year.

The lone picketer at the River Entrance today need not have felt so forlorn nor so hopeless; nor should he, or anyone else across the full range of the ship's many enemies, have really bothered to attack it in the hopes of running it aground. Barring some truly major overhaul and restructuring, some truly fundamental reorganization that would be more than just a stately game of musical chairs designed to make the public think something was really happening, the ship would founder all by itself, one of these days.

There were times and this was one of them, when Helen Clark felt that she would be much happier back home in Silicon Valley in California, tidily making millions on items whose successful manufacture depended in the last analysis on her own shrewd management and astute business judgment. Instead she was stuck here in the Pentagon, as she put it to herself, trying to push, shove, pull and haul a combined civilian and military bureaucracy that seemed incapable of the speed which she understood to be necessary to meet the problem she knew only as "Project Frio." She did not know its true nature or its ultimate conclusion, but she had been given the impression that it was a matter of pressing urgency. Seven months had passed and it presumably was still of urgency. But . . .

She had done all *she* could, she told herself now as she went over some of the major contracts that passed through her office every day. It was impossible to review them all—the department let some fifteen million a year on various items large and small, which averaged out at a little over forty-one thousand a day if you put it on that basis, and it was all her large and capable staff could do to keep the paper moving.

Many were minor and routine, duplications or extensions of previous contracts, only needing to be approved and passed along to the next stage in the process. But enough were new and major so that they had to be carefully and painfully studied by herself in the OSD, plus all the many people who did the same work, on the same items, in some one or more of the services. Sometimes it took many months or even years for the documents to work their way through these many duplicating reviews; but sometimes, she supposed, things were caught that wouldn't have been caught otherwise, and that justified at least some of it.

She was directly involved in only a small but major portion over the course of a year, but it was still an appalling task—one of the least attractive, though one of the most vital, aspects of her job.

Only a genuine sense of public duty and the need for a record of public achievement if she should ever decide to run for the Senate kept her at it; these and the fact that she really did enjoy what Harry Ahmanson referred to as "the wheeling and dealing side of your job." She recognized that one part of her nature was quite masculine—Harry lately was taking care of the other part—in that she really did enjoy the give-and-take of commercial enterprise, the striking of bargains, the making of deals, the business of meeting, and more often than not beating, men at their own game of business and industry. She liked to match wits with them, because she had learned some years ago, when divorce gave her the opportunity to assume full command of her own enterprise, that her wits were frequently as good as, and quite often better than, nine-tenths of the men she met.

She had not been entirely joking when she had told Loy Buck that if she could figure out a formula to cut the Pentagon's work force in half and thereby increase its productivity by two-thirds she would have his job. She never doubted that she was quite capable of handling it. And she never doubted that a formula was possible if one could only get it past the phalanx of vested interests that kept the system as it was.

But that, of course, was dreaming and she knew it. Even Military Harry, who saw eye to eye with her on most things, fell back on the complacent Pentagonian retort to those who complain about the way things are done in the building: "Oh, well, it's probably going to take another war and *then* the system will be reformed."

Helen felt, with far more urgency than some of the military minds she dealt with: have another war and there won't *be* any system.

Not any system at all.

Her secretary buzzed. She picked up the phone and said crisply, "Secretary Clark. May I help you?"

"Secretary Clark here, too," her brother said amicably. "How are things, Hel?"

"Did you just call to chat?" she inquired, but also amicably, "because if so, I've got about ten million contracts to get through this morning. But I'm glad you did, actually, because I want to ask you why the Army *still* hasn't put in its final recommendations on modifying the ALCAC for Project Frio. I don't mean the preliminary report we got a couple of months ago but the *final* report. What's the matter with your department, anyway?"

"It's almost ready," Ray Clark said in a defensive tone. "That's really what I called about. I was talking to Brash Burford only yesterday and he promised it'll be in by day after tomorrow. For sure."

"I'm glad to hear that," she said dryly, "since it's now seven months since I first heard about Frio."

"The rest of them are the same way," Ray protested. "The Navy isn't any better. Or the Marines. Or the Air Force. We're all moving along."

"Slowly. The SecDef told me after that White House meeting four months ago that everybody promised the President that all recommendations were to be in within a week. What happened?"

"It wasn't specified that *final* recommendations would be in," her brother said. "He just wanted something to indicate that everybody was actually working on it."

"I'm glad he understood the department's intentions," she said, again dryly. "I'm just surprised he hasn't had everyone on the carpet again by this time."

"Well, he has a lot of things on his mind," the Secretary of the Army said. "You know how it is. Things tend to get lost in the shuffle."

"So they do," she agreed, and decided to probe a little, "I'm glad Frio isn't very urgent any more."

"Oh, but it is," he said sharply. "Don't you think it isn't. We want to get that ALCAC thing straightened out just as fast as possible."

"Pentagon speed and my speed," she said, "are two different things. I'll never get used to it. Never. The Army will have everything completed by day after tomorrow, then? Maybe I can use that to bludgeon the rest of them."

"Be my guest," he said. "And give my best to Harry."

"I will," she said impassively, fingering the single strand of pearls around her long, white, lovely neck. "And do give my best to Karen. How is she these days?"

"We're probably going to get a divorce," he said in a sour tone. "She's really impossible. She went to Loy Buck again, complaining about me. You don't *do* that sort of thing."

"With sufficient provocation," she remarked, "some people might. Karen obviously does. Has Loy said anything to you?"

"Loy doesn't care as long as your private life doesn't get into the papers," he said smugly.

"I wouldn't be so sure," she said.

"Well," he retorted. "You're in no position to talk."

"I'm not married," she said sharply. "You are. My advice to you is to cool it if you want to stay around."

"But—" he began.

"I'm sorry," she interrupted, "I've got a couple of other calls coming in. Must run."

"Can't we have lunch someday?" he inquired in a plaintive tone that put them suddenly back thirty years, big sister and little brother.

"Oh, of course," she said, yielding to it as always. "Have your secretary call and set it up with mine. Next week sometime."

"Thanks, sis," he said. "The Army report on the ALCAC will be in right away. It really will."

"Better be," she said more sternly. *"Something's* got to move, around here." Without farewell she punched a lighted button, said, "Secretary Clark. May I help you?" The calm comfortable voice of Strategic Industries' vice president for defense affairs came over the line.

"Roger Venable, Helen. Got a minute?"

"Hi, Rodge," she said. "Sure. What's on your mind?"

"Well—" he said thoughtfully. "As a matter of fact, that ALCAC contract. When are we going to get a look at it? Is it still kicking around over there? Hasn't anybody whipped it into shape yet?"

"Haven't I, you mean?" she asked with a small, unamused laugh. "I tell you, Roger, I've been around the barn so many times with these gentlemen over here, trying to get them to settle down and let me have their final recommendations so I can get the papers out to you, that there have been times when I thought I'd scream the building down. Not that it would do any good, of course: they'd just tell me it was working its way up through channels. Everything is. It's the nearest thing to perpetual motion ever devised, the slow, turgid, inexorable and inevitable progression of paperwork through the Pentagon. It doesn't always get anywhere, but it keeps moving. Not as fast as I'd like, but then, who am I? Just one among what sometimes seems to be infinitely many."

He chuckled.

"You sound a little disillusioned, Helen. You shouldn't. It all works out eventually."

"I think I'm still in transition," she said. "I've been in this job a year and a half, now, and I still haven't made the change from business to government. I still want things to happen when I say the word."

"That's because you were boss. And of a relatively small outfit. Not everything in business—big business—moves as fast or as efficiently as you might have been able to do on a small scale. Business can be a pretty slow, turgid, sloppy proposition, too; just as incompetent, just as inefficient, just as full of buck-passers and four-flushers and phonies as anything you'll ever run into over there. And some extremely brilliant and efficient people too, of course. Anyway, that's the way life is and we've got to make the best of it. When does S.I. get to see the contract?"

"The day Three Gs does," she said promptly. He uttered a humorous groan.

"Don't tell me you're going to give our competition a crack at it too," he said in mock protest.

"You know the regulations," she said. "Equal advantage, equal competition, lowest bidder and the rest of it. Subject to some administrative leeway when the lowest bidder is obviously or dangerously inferior to the higher, but in the main, pretty cut and dried. You know the regs better than I do."

"I doubt that," he said with a comfortable chuckle. "I guess we'll have to find out what Three Gs intends to bid and undercut them a few bucks, if you're going to be a stickler for form."

"You bet," she said.

"We'd still like to know when."

"As would I. I'll try to get back to you in a day or two with some indication of time-frame. Would that be all right?"

"If that's it, that's it."

"But don't get your people excited, because first it has to go through DSARC." (Which, in Pentagonese, she pronounced "Dee-sarc.")

"Why DSARC?" he demanded, sounding upset and annoyed. "It's only going to be modifications of the ALCAC, as I understand it. Or am I wrong?"

"That's how I understand it too," she said, "but DSARC still has to get involved."

"But DSARC went over the whole thing when it was originally approved. And again when the 'advanced' model was created. How many years did that take? And why is it necessary to review modifications now?"

"I don't know how many," she said, "but quite a few. And they always review everything."

"I hope it isn't going to take ten years!" he said sourly.

"There are a lot of pressures for speed," she said, "so hopefully it could get through DSARC in short order."

"I hope so," he said, sounding gloomy, "because we're ready to go at S.I. We'd like to have that contract."

"So Walker Stayman tells me at Three Gs," she said.

"Has he been talking to you privately again too?" Roger Venable demanded with semi-humorous annoyance. "I forbid that."

"Three calls last week."

Roger Venable sounded surprised.

"It isn't going to be *that* big a contract, is it?"

"I really have no idea," she said. "The service recommendations are supposed to be in within the week and I'll know a little better then. I'll call you."

"I'd appreciate it," he said, "DSARC! Well, well."

Yet his wonderment, she suspected, could only be deliberately disingenuous, because of course he knew from much past experience that *everything* had to go through DSARC. DSARC was one of the two biggest checkpoints and/or bottlenecks in the whole weapons procurement and development process. The Defense Systems Acquisition Review Council was composed of the Under Secretary for Research and Engineering, presently her boss, Tiny Wombaugh, or his representative; a representative of the Joint Chiefs of Staff; and four or five others, ranks and numbers varying from time to time but the skills required being basically always engineering, cost analysis and test evaluation.

The other checkpoint and bottleneck, which did not enter into the problem here because modification of the ALCAC did not fall into its highly classified, esoteric and really major weapons categories, was the Defense Advanced Research Projects Agency.

Between them DSARC and DARPA accounted for most of the armaments of the United States of America and most of the delays in getting them on-line. Their systems of initial approval—review—testing—revision—final approval— were in many respects identical. So was the time, often seeming endless, which it took them. The major difference seemed to be that DARPA was, as its name stated, engaged in "advanced" research on highly sophisticated weapons, while DSARC basically concentrated on the more mundane. DSARC also handled the acquisition and production of both.

They were the formidable twins of Research and Development, and hardly anything joined the arsenal before it had first passed through their lengthy and ponderous processes.

Thank goodness Project Frio did not qualify for DARPA as well as DSARC, she thought with relief, or it never *would* be completed. DSARC alone was bad enough.

DSARC was the mechanism devised by OSD to establish and review—constantly—the procedures for securing and building weapons systems. It decided which programs were large enough and important enough to go through its processes, which meant almost anything of any significance at all. It devised and promulgated the regulations governing applications for contracts and compliance with them, which resulted in a volume as thick as two large telephone books and enough rules to decide the number of angels on the head of a pin. It tried to assure the maximum of competition in the letting of contracts or, when there was only one feasible supplier, to try to make sure that the best possible financial deal for the government was worked out with him. It ran periodic engineering, cost analysis and test evaluation checks at regular stages in the development of each system.

After initial approval of the project idea and its design, DSARC's various functions were delegated out through the building to appropriate military and civilian offices. Its internal battles, of which there were many, represented basically a tug and haul between research and development—between those who said let's test and test and test again until it's absolutely perfect and those who said let's test and test until it's reasonably efficient under any foreseeable circumstances and then let's go ahead and get it the hell done.

This was greatly complicated by the constant intrusions of Congress, whose members in recent years had insisted upon more and more testing in an effort to increase safety—and at the same time had insisted upon more and more speed and more and more economy, neither of which was compatible with the time and expense necessitated by more and more testing. Plus all the other reasons that prompted members of Congress to intervene, basically related, as always, to the needs and interests of various states and districts and the relative seniority and power of their Senators and Representatives.

Under all these handicaps and conflicting pressures, DSARC soldiered on. Sometimes (as its staff people were apt to boast, innocently and, it would seem to the observer, somewhat naïvely) it was possible with this system to complete a given weapon "as quickly as five to seven years," a goal "which can be reached if there is sufficient money and too much bickering doesn't get in the way." Some projects, on the other hand, could languish as long as twenty-five years between initial idea and final completion. The average ran somewhere between twelve and fifteen years for major weapons systems.

Meantime, the enemy was not sitting still.

Nonetheless, this was the mechanism, created out of all the needs and all the pressures of a democratic society faced, in defense of its freedoms, with the need to spend enormous sums to build enormous weapons systems. It was seldom perfect, often created terrible delays, sometimes wasted unnecessary billions in pursuit of its mission; but like many things in the building was a creation of the necessity posed by the threat. It was as slow, as imperfect and yet at times as brilliant and as capable of serving the country as the best among the citizenry. It was a peculiarly democratic institution, and as such its achievements were sometimes fantastic. Its bumbles, when they could not be cured, simply had to be endured.

And now into this next stage of progress through the Pentagon were about to come Project Frio and the modifications of the ALCAC. Helen Clark knew there was no way to avoid this, even in the interests of presidentially-mandated speed. Or was it mandated by the President? No one, now, seemed very sure, uncertainty about White House intentions being another inescapable democratic fact of life. In any event, in the building they had to proceed on their initial estimate of the situation and continue until the President said Stop, if he did say Stop. She was determined that as far as she was concerned, she was going to keep her record clear and continue to do her best to move things ahead.

In pursuit of this she picked up the telephone and directed her secretary to "get Josephs in here." Within five minutes the door opened and Civilian Harry, looking as always rather like a stooped, graying, humble little mole, was ushered in.

She stood to receive him, holding out her hand for a brisk but friendly handshake which he returned with his usual flaccid pressure. *Honestly,* she thought to herself, *you'd think the man was an utter wimp.* But she knew very well that he wasn't. He had too many scalps under his belt, too many victories over both civilian and military wrong-doers, to warrant anything but the most respectful handling. Particularly since she too had lately become dedicated to the cause of a second star for Military Harry, and they both knew very well that Harry Josephs was keeping an eye on *him,* too.

"Harry," she said, gesturing him to a comfortable armchair alongside her desk and returning to her seat, "how are the cats?"

"Oh," he said in his slow, cautious voice, with a slow, pleased smile, "I didn't know you knew we had any."

"Gen. Ahmanson tells me you carry their picture. May I see it?"

"Why, yes," he said. "Why, yes. Yes, you may."

"Thank you," she said and studied it carefully when he handed it across the desk with a shy pride. Two fat, complacent American tabbies who looked just like everybody else's fat, complacent American tabbies stared lazily at her out of the snapshot. But she and Ray had been raised with cats and dogs and she genuinely loved them both.

"They're *beautiful,*" she said with an enthusiasm that pleased Civilian Harry, as she had of course known it would. "They remind me of a pair Ray and I had when we were kids. They were inseparable."

"So are these," Harry Josephs said. She smiled.

"They must be great company for you and Mrs. Josephs . . . Harry, is there anything we can do to speed up Project Frio? I've just had a call from Roger Venable at S.I. and yesterday I had one from Walker Stayman at Three Gs. They're both very anxious to bid on the modifications of the ALCAC, and very puzzled as to why we can't show them the specifications yet. Do you know anything about that?"

"I suppose, Madame Secretary—" he began carefully.

"Helen," she said. "For heaven's sake, Harry, how many times do I have to tell you?"

"Well, all right," he agreed with an awkward little smile, "if you insist— Helen—I'm sure you know as well as I that it's the usual slowdown in the JCS staff. It takes them so long to *do* anything."

"Maybe they're afraid of *you,*" she suggested with a sudden shrewd glance from her beautiful dark eyes and the throaty laugh that went with it—both effective weapons in her arsenal when used on ordinary men. She told herself with a wry inward amusement that Harry Josephs wasn't an ordinary man, he was a walking computer. He looked at her with what appeared to be genuine astonishment.

"Me?" he said. "Why should they be afraid of me, Helen? They aren't doing anything wrong, are they?"

This time her laugh was quite genuine as she agreed, "No, Harry, I don't think they're doing anything wrong. But it's been pretty generally known around the building from the first that you are opposed to modifying the ALCAC, and so maybe it's inhibited them. They may have a feeling you're breathing over their shoulders, just waiting to jump on them when you see their recommendations."

He looked quite offended.

"I won't if they're honest," he said stiffly. "Although I must admit, I'm very skeptical about the ALCAC. It seems a perfectly sound craft to me."

"I'm sure it is," she said soothingly, concentrating her gaze in the general region of his Adam's apple. "But if they feel it's necessary to have some modification, don't you think perhaps we should all cooperate willingly and permit them to go ahead?" She raised her gaze until it met his and gave him a between-us smile. "You know they're going to anyway."

"Yes," he said glumly, "I suppose they are. But that isn't going to make it any less a waste of the taxpayers' money."

"Perhaps it won't be," she suggested. "General Ahmanson, while somewhat skeptical himself as I'm sure he's told you, is inclined to think that if they really believe some changes could be of value, then we probably ought to stop opposing and give them enthusiastic support. In the interests of moving ahead."

"General Ahmanson," he said, "has his own motivations. Of course he isn't going to oppose the JCS. He has a new star coming."

"Oh," she said comfortably, though tempted to make a sharp rejoinder in Military Harry's defense, "I think his motivations are a little nobler than that. I'm sure he's as interested as you are in saving the taxpayers' money."

"I've never known a military man above a certain level yet who really and truly gave a damn about that," he said in a tart tone that surprised her. "They want what they think they need and they don't care how much it's going to cost. Unless it upsets the Hill, that is, and threatens something else they want. At least, that's my observation after being here a long time."

"You're very severe," she said with a smile gracefully rueful for all the officers who had run afoul of this, "and I'm sure the taxpayers really owe you an awful lot for saving them money. But Harry, Frio seems to be something that's a major priority and I feel we really must move it along, now. After all, it's seven months since we first heard about it."

"Not long for the Pentagon," he observed with a small, dry smile.

"Nonetheless," she said, letting her tone become firm and businesslike, "I think we must give them the benefit of the doubt and get on with it. Otherwise it could be fairly said, I think, that part of what could be a very serious and crippling delay is due to the obstructionism of Harry Josephs. I don't think you would want that to go on your record."

For a moment he said nothing, simply staring without much expression and blinking slowly like some baffled old rodent. Finally he shook his head and pursed his lips in what appeared to be absolute puzzlement that anybody would address him like that. Maybe nobody in the building ever had, she thought: if not, about time.

"I don't think it's that bad, is it?" he asked finally.

"It could be."

"Is Frio that important, Helen?" he inquired in the same puzzled tone. "Do you really know that?"

"To tell you the truth, Harry," she said, knowing it wouldn't do any good to tell him anything else, "I don't really know, myself. But I do know, as of course you do too, that there has been constant pressure from Secretary Buck and from the White House to get it moving. Today it just seems time, that's all. It just seems that the delays have gone on long enough. We need to get something out to S.I. and Three Gs, who are the two contractors of interest. I would appreciate it if you would cease your opposition and begin to cooperate, now."

"Did Secretary Buck ask you to say that to me?" he asked in the same baffled way.

"He has remarked to me several times in the past few weeks," she said, "that he appreciates your patriotism and diligence but he does think perhaps you're overdoing it a little. He has indicated quite clearly that he would feel better about it if you could now begin to give the project your unqualified enthusiasm."

"He wanted me appointed, though," he said slowly. "At least, I think he did."

"I believe he asked Mr. Murchison to release you from your regular duties to concentrate on Frio, yes. But I don't think he wanted you to obstruct the project—just to make sure it doesn't waste any money or get into any excessive cost overruns."

"There, you see?" he said with owl-like triumph. "That's exactly why I've been hesitant. I don't see how it can *help* but waste money and create cost overruns. And incidentally, Helen," he added earnestly, "there shouldn't be any such thing as *'excessive'* cost overruns. They're *all* excessive. There shouldn't be *any.*"

"Harry," she said, finally permitting some impatience to surface, "you know it's impossible to get by without *any,* in most projects. About all we can do is keep them from being *excessive.*" Her tone toughened. "So, then, I have your pledge to cooperate and to get this thing moving?"

Again he gave her his slow, puzzled, blinking stare.

"Well," he said finally, "as long as we're agreed that we're going to keep a close watch on everything—"

"The closest," she said, giving him a friendly smile, rising gracefully to say goodbye. "And don't think your vigilance isn't appreciated by the Secretary and by me, Harry. It's exactly what's needed for this particular project."

"I only wish we knew what it is," he said as he went out, small, serious, humorless, colorless and a formidable force to be reckoned with. "It might help if we knew what it is."

But they both knew they were not going to be told, at least not now. Harry Ahmanson had a reasonably good idea—he had gradually put clues together to come as close as: "something to do with some enemy action in the South Pacific." But that was as much as he had been able to discover, even though, she suspected, there must be at least half a dozen officers on the JCS staff, plus the chiefs, and as many civilians in OSD, who knew.

All, she suspected, feeling as frustrated as she. And the DSARC process hadn't even started yet.

One of the officers who knew, and perhaps the only one who did not feel frustrated about what he knew, was at that moment enjoying his regular lunchtime swim at POAC ("Po-Ack")—the Pentagon Officers Athletic Club, which was in a separate structure, out beyond the small parade-ground at the River Entrance where welcoming ceremonies were held for foreign dignitaries and other notable visitors.

Maj. Gary Stump, USA, small, dark, sleek and compact, swam like the seal he somewhat resembled when he hit the water, having been a child of Southern California and aquatic all his life. At thirty-five he was, he felt, in perfect physical condition. This not only enabled him to pass the regular physical examinations required by the Army but gave him the feeling of confidence that comes with perfect health. It also equipped him more than adequately for whatever might come his way, either in line of duty or at such places as POAC.

POAC had originally begun as a health facility strictly for officers. That had lasted a few years and then membership had been thrown open to all Pentagon employees, military and civilian, of all ranks and both sexes, as well as all civil service employees in the Washington area of grade 11 and above. Complimentary membership had even been extended to Presidents, Vice Presidents and Secretaries of Defense, though as far as was known none had ever used it.

Its dark, rambling quarters, gradually sinking on a jerry-built wartime foundation, contained separate locker and shower rooms for men and women, but in all other aspects POAC was now completely coeducational. Its approximately eight thousand members paid nine dollars a month for the use of its facilities, which included pool, hot tubs, sauna, general gymnastic equipment and squash, handball and racquetball courts. It also furnished start-and-return for the Pentagon's many joggers, most of whom used their lunch hours to run beside the river as far west as Key Bridge and Rosslyn, Virginia, as far east as Hains Point.

Its operations were divided in true Pentagon fashion: it was under the overall direction of the Army's catch-all Military District of Washington and its manager was Army, its administrator Navy and its recreational service officer Air Force. It was the observation of its manager that most Army played racquetball, most Navy played squash and most Air Force handball. "When *they* play it," he had told Gary once, "we call it Hannibal-ball. Those Air Force guys are really out to prove something. Man, they're *grim.*"

Most of the two thousand who, on the average, used POAC every day, were not grim, but neither did they seem particularly relaxed as they went about their exercising. The pressures of working in the Pentagon were too heavy, even when things moved as slowly as they were with Frio: even moving slowly has its anxieties, in the Pentagon. There were also the three p's, the constant worry about job performance ratings, the constant worry about the effect of long hours on family relationships, the constant competition for place and preferment which gnawed at nearly all of them save those relative few, military and civilian, who were simply serving time to retirement. For most, working in the Pentagon, as they often remarked, was like working in a pressure-cooker. For many of them POAC was a welcome and necessary release.

Like the Pentagon itself, POAC was old, run-down, shabby but functional. Its atmosphere, like that of all athletic facilities, was hot, steamy and redolent of sex of all kinds. This, though very few were ever permitted to realize it about this thoroughly masculine, very model young officer, was what Gary Stump liked best.

Now, as he swam in leisurely fashion his daily thirty laps, carefully distributing his glances with mathematical impartiality between the unappealing females and brawny males who swam as diligently as he all around him, his thoughts were drifting idly from chest to thigh to Frio and back again. For once they were not concentrating quite so much on the scenery as they were on Frio. Gary Stump was quite pleased with the way Frio was going, and his anonymous associates were too.

His assignment to Operation Frio, discreetly tucked away on third floor, B Ring, behind the innocuous sign "Cumulative Assessment Group," had come as a considerable surprise to him. It had proved to be an exciting and satisfying one when he had found out what it was all about. Nothing could have better served the purposes to which he had early dedicated himself—or been dedicated, rather, when he found his destiny removed suavely but effectively from his hands after his first assignment in Germany some fifteen years ago.

On that occasion, five days after his arrival in Wiesbaden, he had not done nothing any different from what he had done on a thousand occasions since about age fifteen. But that time his partner had turned out to be a Russian who had been sent across the border from East Germany to accomplish exactly what he had accomplished. And Gary Stump, after an initial period of shock, outrage and fear, had shrugged and decided that the pay was good, the prospects interesting and the challenge something that would give life the extra spice he liked to have. He had come of a broken home and a father savagely wounded in Korea and desperately embittered against his country. Education in Gary's youth had not been designed to strengthen one's faith in America. This made it even easier for him to accept his new life as an agent of his country's enemies.

Nor had it been hard to remain with it, and to get away with it. The pay *had* been good: Gary was one of the amoralists, the group that can be bought because, in a society whose standards are all too often based on greed and self-interest, money talks more loudly than it does in many others. Because he had determined to make full use of his natural attributes and abilities, both of which were exemplary, he had managed an effective and apparently impregnable cover.

So he had left Germany, gone through officers' training with a brilliant record, served for a time at various posts in CONUS, spent three years at Schofield Barracks in Hawaii and a year and a half ago had been assigned to the Pentagon. He had carefully and brilliantly made himself an expert on cryptology and communications (although in these amazingly slack security days you hardly had to be an expert to gain access to those sensitive areas, you almost just had to walk in off the street and ask) and in consequence had been able to supply his mentors with a steady stream of top-secret material for the past eight years. His private life he had kept entirely secret, known only to a few absolutely reliable like-minded friends in the services and even fewer in the civilian world. Never once had the slightest suspicion of any kind touched Gary Stump, that brilliant, able, suave and smoothly accomplished young major of whom every one of his associates thought so highly.

At least, he mused as he moved gracefully but slowly out of the way of a handsome crew-cut with a wedding ring on one hand and a West Point ring on the other who bore down upon him, quite deliberately, a little too fast as he turned to begin another lap—at least up until *now,* every one had thought highly and without suspicion of him. Now there were a couple whose suspicion he could sense, and he didn't like it one little bit, though with them both he maintained an absolutely untroubled and friendly attitude.

Tolliver and Hogan, he thought scornfully, Hogan and Tolliver. He couldn't try to get them reassigned, that really *would* make them suspicious. But he knew they didn't like him and wondered about him; not in *this* way, he reflected with some amusement as the crew-cut overtook him and swam swiftly by, kicking a small wave in his face as he passed, but just with some general uneasiness that he had caught sometimes in Tolliver's quick glance or Hogan's dull, stodgy appraisal. There was a little reserve there, a holding back, a feeling of slight but inescapable hostility that made him angry because, God knew, he had done nothing whatsoever to justify it. He had given them no cause to be suspicious, for in fact, aside from telling his friends that nothing was happening at the moment, he hadn't done a thing: there hadn't been anything to do. But he knew that Hogan and Tolliver were bothered by something about him. His native intuition, which was great, and his sensitivity to others' reactions, which had been honed to a high pitch in his years of duplicity, told him so. It had posed no problem so far but it could when Operation Frio reached the point of actual challenge to the occupiers of Nanukuvu. Then he would become active again, and then his office-mates could become a problem.

He contemplated idly what he should do about it. The amusement came into his eyes again, as his new aquatic acquaintance thrashed past once more, at the thought of Brod Tolliver. Seduce Tolliver; what a thought! It would be a challenge, but he told himself wryly that while it might be worth the trouble, it wouldn't be worth the time. Brod might tumble eventually, it was possible with almost anybody given the right circumstances, but it would be an endless process. He was such an All-American boy, so devoted to his cute little wife and the child that was becoming more imminent every day: Operation Frio would be in the history books before *that* one fell. Hogan, he thought, and his eyes narrowed and he no longer paid attention to the disappointed West Pointer, might be another matter.

Hogan was forty, unhappy and desperate. Her sick mother kept her tied down to the point where Gary guessed that she had very little social life, and almost certainly no social life with a man. Probably she got invited to things with the girls, she seemed to pal around a bit with a couple of other female officers who had worked with her in Adm. Stahlman's office before her assignment to Frio; now and again she mentioned some play at Kennedy Center that she had seen in the company of an Air Force colonel and his wife whom she had met some years ago when she was stationed in Japan. But aside from that, there was no indication of any social life for Hogan.

He swam thoughtfully on, oblivious now to others around him, planning his campaigns. He would be extra nice to Brod, make a point of having a lot of lunches with him, invite him and his little wife to dinner or a play, turn on the charm, overwhelm his vague uneasiness with constant, generous friendship. With Elizabeth Hogan he would get more basic. She wouldn't know what hit her, he told himself with a cynical smile as he left the pool and headed for the men's locker room and the long line of naked noontime athletes waiting for the showers. It wasn't that he didn't know what to do: he just didn't like it very much. In a good cause he could perform quite brilliantly. And from his standpoint, if not the Pentagon's, his was a good cause.

He worked his way patiently up the line, got a shower, soaped and rinsed off with considerate dispatch, keeping his eyes carefully to himself, which was not always the case. His Army friend was down at the end, giving him cautious glances; he ignored him, for now. Closer by, though, he became aware that someone was looking him over, quite thoroughly, for just a moment: a thin, amiable, youthful face, a generous smile, an expensively-cut shock of graying hair. Well, I'll be damned, he thought with a sudden amazed recognition; *well, I'll be damned.*

The thought seared across his mind: there might be more than Hogan available to assist him in subverting Operation Frio. And, with luck, perhaps many more things as well.

He was already considering how to make contact as he flung his towel in the hamper and went back to his locker, humming.

On the Hill, the lunch hour was also in full swing. In his private office, hidden back on the Senate side in the ancient labyrinths of the Capitol off the rotunda, the chairman of the Senate Armed Services Committee was entertaining at his regular monthly luncheon for the other four people who, with himself, were the Pentagon's most powerful friends and/or enemies in Congress. Which they were at any given moment depended on a lot of things, Sen.

Harlan H. "Cube" Herron of California told himself as he looked around the table at their familiar faces, raised his glass of wine and said, "Here's to the God damned budget!" It was being its usual pain in the ass and everybody on the Hill was thoroughly fed up with it.

It was with a wry enthusiasm that their glasses were lifted by the ranking member of his committee, Sen. Luzanne Johnson of Louisiana; Sen. Jerry Castain of Indiana, chairman of the Senate Appropriations subcommittee on defense; Rep. Mario Escondido of Connecticut, chairman of the House Armed Services Committee; and Rep. Karl Aschenheim of Pennsylvania, chairman of the House Appropriations subcommittee on defense.

Cube Herron, who was in his fifth term, by now was probably the greatest overall expert on defense in the government, bar none. That included Loy Buck, with whom he maintained a mutually admiring if frequently prickly relationship; Zeecy McCune likewise; and the other chiefs. Seniority got kicked around by all the critics of Congress, Cube often told his constituents, but there was no substitute for staying a long time in one job and really learning what it was all about. You knew far more than transitory secretaries and transitory generals and admirals. And you also, at seventy-two, found your views pretty well set and your positions pretty well unbudgeable, particularly by here-they-come-there-they-goes whose two- or three-year tenures were no match for his twenty-seven.

He gave an audible sniff at the thought and Luzanne Johnson uttered her light and carefree laugh and inquired, *"Now* what's the matter, Cube? You've been looking like a thundercloud all morning."

"Am," he said, a sudden smile turning his often red and choleric face into that of a white-haired, aging but still mischievous little boy—an appealing aspect that accounted for the fondness with which most of his colleagues regarded him in the relatively rare moments when they were not being mad at him about something. He was an obdurate codger, possessed of exhaustive knowledge and formidable influence. This frequently made him anathema to the Pentagon. But everybody had to recognize that he was the expert, even though Mario Escondido, whom Cube privately regarded as a greedy, favor-seeking little jerk, liked to pretend that he knew something about it too.

Cube often remarked to Luzanne that Mario would know something about it if he'd only stop trying to grab everything for his district and try to understand what defense was really all about.

"It isn't supposed to be his private pork-barrel," Cube often said. "It's supposed to be for the benefit of the country."

Cube, whose native state of California had long ago been ticketed by the Pentagon, very wisely, to receive a large and steady flow of defense contracts, research projects, military installations and other goodies designed to keep him and his constituents happy, was pretty adept at getting what he wanted, too. But he wasn't crude about it. Rep. Escondido, he often grumbled to Luzanne and his other Senate cronies, was *crude.*

Now Mario piped up as they prepared to fall to on the steaks and salads sent up from the Senate dining room. He spoke in his usual quick, excited way, dark eyes snapping and chunky little frame leaning forward so aggressively that his upper belly jiggled the table.

"Cube!" he said as though it were a call to battle. "Cube!"

"What the hell is it?" Sen. Herron responded, though with a trace of a smile in spite of his general feelings about Connecticut's finest. "You sound all excited, Mario. What's the problem?"

"I am excited!" Mario proclaimed. "Do you know what I heard from my sources in the God damned Navy this morning?"

"Obviously not," Cube said. "What did you hear from your sources in the— hell, Mario, out with it."

"I've heard somebody over there is working on some battle plan for the South Pacific," Mario said. "Now, what the hell is that all about?"

"Don't know," Cube said, looking blank.

"Don't they always work on battle plans over there?" Jerry Castain suggested. "The media always makes a big deal of it when one of them surfaces, but hell, doesn't everybody do it? The Soviets do it, we do it, the Brits do it, the birds do it, the bees do it, even little fleas—I mean, what's the big deal, Mario? So there's a plan, so what? It's the Pentagon's job to be prepared for everything, isn't it? Don't discourage them!"

"Well," Congressman Escondido conceded, slowed down a bit, "yes, I suppose so. But *my* source says—that *he* thinks—that there's some specific target in mind this time." He looked around the table belligerently. "*I* want to know what it is!"

"There's always a target in mind," Karl Aschenheim said in the slow, deliberate manner that usually silenced all but the most obstreperous, which Mario of course was. "Otherwise, what's the point in planning? Don't get so excited, Mario. You'll rupture something."

"Rupture the Pentagon," Mario said darkly, "if they don't give me some more battleship rebuilding jobs for Connecticut. Anyway: I'd like to know if something suspicious is going on over there. Do any of you hear anything? Luzanne, how about you?"

For just a second the senior Senator from Louisiana looked a little flustered, leading her colleagues to think: Ah, *ha!* But her tone was perfectly calm.

"I haven't heard of anything," she said, "except what I mentioned to you two or three months ago, Cube, that I got some sense of something a little unsettling from some of my friends over there. They still seem a little concerned. But I don't have any idea as to what it might be. Anyway, when you think of the thousand and one things they have to worry about all the time, it's no wonder they sound concerned now and then. Don't *we?*"

"You didn't hear anything about the South Pacific," Mario Escondido pressed.

She shook her head.

"Nothing specific about anything. Just some minor worry, probably. Let it go, Mario. We'll hear soon enough if it's anything really important."

"Well," Rep. Escondido said, not sounding much appeased. "I *hope* so." He leaned back and characteristically changed the subject abruptly. "Who's going to be the next chairman of the JCS? Has anybody heard?"

"I get some talk from Loy," Cube said. "It seems to be narrowing down to Ham Stokes or Brash Burford as far as anybody knows. I don't think the President's given a hint."

"He wouldn't," Jerry Castain said disdainfully. "He likes to play everything close to the vest, that one. Who do you like, Cube?"

"I like Brash," Sen. Herron said. "I know all the reasons why Ham Stokes would be a good choice, excellent officer, right color, ideal political appointment if you're running for re-election as I think our man is. But Ham comes on a little strong, for me. We've tangled a good many times." He smiled slightly. "Not that I hold that against him, you understand."

"Certainly not," Karl Aschenheim said dryly. "We all understand that, Cube. *I* like him. Like Brash, too, as a matter of fact. He seems to be a little off speed lately, though. Preoccupied about something. Don't imagine it's anything important, though."

"As a matter of fact, it is," Sen. Castain said. "Vi Burford's not well. He's talked to me about it several times. It's driving him up the wall because she refuses to go to Walter Reed and get checked out. Says it would upset him too much and affect his chances to be chairman, if they found anything. Very loving of her, of course, but her refusal just makes him even more frantic."

"What is it?" Luzanne inquired with a troubled frown. "Cancer?"

"No, I don't think so," Jerry said. "We think it's Alzheimer's."

"Oh, *dear,*" Luzanne said. "How sad. Poor Vi. Poor Brash. Are you sure?"

"Pretty much," Jerry said. "My mother has it and the symptoms are the same."

"No wonder he's been off speed," Mario Escondido said, for once taken a little outside of himself by someone else's problems. "Maybe it *will* affect his chances to be chairman, then. Maybe Ham will be inevitable. I don't like him, either, Cube," he added, back to his own concerns. "He was going to put two Air Force research facilities in my district but when I forced them to keep the J-2 in production he got really mad at me and gave them to New Jersey instead." He looked grim. "I won't forgive him for that."

"The J-2," Karl Aschenheim said, referring to a famous case last session when Mario had indeed forced the Air Force to continue producing an outmoded version of a sub-searching helicopter simply because one of its major subcontractors was in his district, "is a waste of the taxpayers' money and you know it, Mario. It's not only behind times now in state of the art, but it's sufficiently old-fashioned in view of the latest Soviet advances so that it could be a really dangerous machine for our boys to fly. As," he added in a tone of some disgust, "we all told you at the time."

"Listen!" Mario said, words tumbling over one another in their usual fashion. "Five hundred people work in that plant! *Five hundred jobs! Five hundred families! Five hundred paychecks! Five hundred—*"

"One thousand votes," Sen. Herron interrupted dryly. "We all know how it is, Mario. Nonetheless, that's a no-good, dangerous aircraft. You got your fellows lined up in conference and you beat the Senate on it when we wanted to eliminate it, but you can't change the facts of it. It's a no-God-damned-good aircraft! Now stop trying to tell us it is!"

"I didn't tell you it was," Rep. Escondido pointed out. "I'm not talking about that at all."

"Well, somebody should, by God," Cube Herron said. "Somebody should!"

"You all did," Mario said, "and the House conferees beat the Senate and I won. So forget it."

"I suppose we will," Cube Herron said, "until somebody dies for it. Then we'll remember, Mario."

"Who will care then?" Rep. Escondido inquired blandly. But that was too crude even for his veteran colleagues, who looked at him with unanimous and unconcealed distaste.

"You're a bit much, Mario," Luzanne Johnson told him finally. "A bit much."

"They like me in the district," Mario pointed out smugly. "Can't quarrel with that . . . So what'll we do, Cube, let the President know we want Brash to be chairman, or let the Black Bomber have it by default?"

"I'll express my views when it comes right," Sen. Herron said. "You do likewise, if you want. We can't do much to influence it one way or the other."

"Oh, yes, we can," Mario Escondido said grimly, "and I intend to . . . What's Zeecy McCune going to do when he retires, Luzanne?" he inquired, switching course so abruptly it took her off balance, as he had intended.

"Why, I don't know," she said, looking flustered again for a moment. "How should I know, Mario?"

"I thought you two were pretty thick," Mario said. "Am I mistaken?"

"I like to think I'm a good friend of the McCunes, yes," Luzanne said. She gave him a long, cool look, aplomb recovered. "But in any event, Mario, I don't really know that it's any of your business, is it?"

"Just asking," Rep. Escondido said airily. "Just asking."

"Well, knock it off," Jerry Castain ordered flatly. "She's right, it's none of your damned business. Cube," he said before Mario could make the angry retort his flushed face promised, "I *am* a little intrigued by what we were talking about earlier. Do you suppose you could get Burt Sanstrom on it and see what he can find out? We don't want any Grenadas sprung on us in the South Pacific when we aren't looking."

"Nothing down there to do a Grenada on, that I know of," Sen. Herron said. "But I'll mention it to Burt. He likes to dig in the Pentagon dirt. Maybe he'll turn up something."

"If anybody can do it," Jerry Castain said, paying tribute to the well-deserved fearsome reputation of the Senate Armed Services' staff director, "Burt can."

"They hate him," Cube Herron said with satisfaction, "but when he talks, they listen." He chuckled without much humor. "They've got to."

"He's a lot better than my kids," Sen. Castain confessed. "They mean well but most of them are such crusaders. Burt doesn't waste time on that. He goes after 'em, sweet and simple."

"He usually gets results," Cube Herron agreed. "How about you, Luzanne?" he inquired in an impersonal tone far from Mario Escondido's and therefore acceptable. "Do you think it would do any good for us to ask Zeecy?"

"You can try," she said matter-of-factly. "If it's something really top-secret you won't get anywhere."

"I'll give it a whirl," Sen. Herron said. "Ol' Zeece and I, we hit it off pretty well. I suppose I could demand to know, but then he really wouldn't tell me."

She smiled.

"He can be stubborn."

"And of course," Karl Aschenheim pointed out, "secrecy *is* part of his job." He stood up and extended his hand. "Cube, thank you for the lunch, as always. Sorry to rush away, but I've got some constituents coming in at one-thirty. See you next week."

"Same time, same place," Cube Herron said.

"It's a wonder to me," Jerry Castain remarked, "that the media have never tumbled to this little gathering of ours. But thank goodness they haven't. It lets us talk about a lot of things. Including the J-2, Mario," he said as a not-too-jovial parting shot.

The swarthy little Congressman from Connecticut smiled complacently.

"You take care of your constituents, Jerry," he said, "and I'll take care of mine."

"You bet," Jerry said as he gave them all a quick wave and went out the door. "I've got some waiting right now."

He didn't really, as far as he knew, but it made a good farewell; and if there weren't any when he got back to the office, there would be before the afternoon was over.

Sure enough, as soon as he came in through his private entrance, seated himself at his desk and hit the buzzer to let the staff know he was back, his receptionist called.

A young woman and her two children were there, she said. The young woman was from Fort Wayne and her late husband had been from South Bend. She said her name was Mrs. Hague Smith and she seemed to be quite upset.

2

In the Pentagon press-room on the second floor, E Ring, along the corridor lined with photographs of famous correspondents and battles of World War II, Red Roberts was sitting at his terminal wondering idly what he should use as his lead item in the account of the day's activities that he would file with his office later in the afternoon.

There had been the usual spate of releases. This general had been assigned here, that admiral transferred there. An assistant secretary of defense had resigned, her successor had been announced. The regular "Activities Report: Program Division" had been released, listing all the speeches that would be given during the week by the SecDef, his major assistants, the chairman of the JCS and the chiefs and their major assistants. From the office of the inspector general, OSD, Shorty Murchison had issued a report on fines assessed against five major subcontractors in the latest cost overrun case. Secretary of the Army Ray Clark had issued a statement in connection with awarding of a posthumous commendation to a lieutenant-colonel in Army intelligence, killed by government forces while on a mission in Central America. And the Pentagon wives' club was planning a raffle in Alexandria, Va., to raise funds for families of servicemen missing in action.

Also, Hank Milhaus had held his regular press briefing in the morning and Red had spent a couple of hours after lunch checking out something in it that had interested him. But he hadn't been able to run it down and he was wondering now if he should abandon it altogether or relegate it to a minor mention in some other story.

It had been provoked, Red recalled with an ironic smile, as many of Hank's more uncomfortable moments were, by that scourge of the venal—that angel of vengeance—that defender of the taxpayer—that upholder of all things pure and wonderful (and embarrassing to the Pentagon)—Ms. Delight Jones of *Defense Spy*—or *Eye,* as she insisted on calling it, although Red and all her other colleagues jocularly used the Pentagon's scornful designation in their private conversations.

Delight was something else, they all thought; and even though they quite often picked up her stories and thereby had already made a national name of a publication that had seemed to come from nowhere and seemed to exist on a wing and a prayer and some mysterious and unknown backing, they regarded her as more of an oddball on the Pentagon scene than as a really responsible journalist.

Nonetheless, she got attention and quite often she helped to shape the news. Which, they sometimes speculated, was probably what she was there for.

This morning she had been on her high horse again about something she had raised with Hank months ago without result—a "Project Frio" that Hank had not seemed to know about then, and professed not to know about now. Red and the Pentagon press regulars had been mildly interested, as before, but not enough to follow it up right then. There were, as Hank had truly said, hundreds of "projects," "operations," "groups," "committees" and "councils" going on in the building all the time, some public, some secret, most routine. Occasionally one of them would surface and he and his colleagues would get intrigued and check it out as much as they could depending upon its security nature. If it was really secret they never got far. If it was public it was usually innocuous and worth no more than a line or two. Ultimately, on most things of that kind, they were allowed to find out just about what the Pentagon wanted them to find out. It was a lucky hit when they were able, usually through some disgruntled source like Skip Framberg, to get more.

Maybe Skip, Red thought now, was behind this one. He had not seen Skip lately. Since Loy Buck had brought him back upstairs to be a vaguely defined "special assistant to the Secretary for progress evaluation," Skip had been rather elusive with his old friends. His new title was meaningless and nobody seemed to know exactly what he was doing. Maybe he was as essentially unemployed as he had been down in the basement beyond the purple water fountain. Maybe he was still disgruntled. He might be worth a visit—or rather, a rendezvous somewhere outside the building where they wouldn't be under the eyes of the OSD staff.

Red, the conscientious veteran, had decided after Hank's conference that he would check out Project Frio a little further. In the couple of hours he had devoted to it he hadn't been able to find out very much. He had tried a number of sources around the building that were usually pretty good but they all looked blank when he mentioned Project Frio. Whatever it was, if it was anything— and Delight, angry and frustrated, had kept insisting that it was even though she apparently hadn't been able to find out anything specific, either, in several months of trying—it wasn't going to surface through regular sources. The Pentagon frequently leaked like a sieve but on this one everything seemed to be clamped down tight. Maybe it didn't even exist at all except in Delight's imagination—a rather highly-colored thing, they had all discovered.

So after a while he abandoned it again, for today. But Delight's persistence had achieved one thing, anyway: it had finally made him curious, too. He thought he would keep after Project Frio, now, keep it up top in his mind, mention it around the building, test it out on everybody he talked to, see if somewhere, in some inadvertent slip of tongue, some lift of eyebrow, some slight, almost imperceptible shift of expression that would deliver its message to the trained reporter, he might come across its traces.

The first step, of course, would be Skip. He couldn't call him in his office, his phone was probably monitored, and he couldn't buttonhole him in the corridors to make a date for a talk, somebody would almost certainly see them and carry it back. He would have to call him tonight at his home in Old Town Alexandria, maybe drop over later and have a drink. Skip probably didn't know it all but he could probably point him in the right directions. It would be worth a try.

Meanwhile he had a story to file. He decided to build it around the fines for the cost overruns. They liked that sort of stuff, in the office: they thought things like that were really what was wrong with the Pentagon.

In Quarters One at Fort Myer, house of the chief of staff of the Army, Doreen Tock and Violet Burford had enjoyed a quiet lunch cooked and served by a Carleene who kept giving Dorry significant nods toward Vi every time their glances met. Finally when Vi excused herself to go to the bathroom Dorry decided to put a stop to it.

"Carleene," she hissed, "for *heaven's* sake, stop acting like a spy in a grade-B movie! You don't have to give me all those signals about Mrs. Burford. I *know* she isn't well."

"Sure isn't," Carleene said, not at all abashed. "Got me worried sick myself. What we goin' do about her, Mrs. Tock?"

"I don't know," Dorry said, forgetting her annoyance in their mutual concern for Vi; Carleene, after all, was practically a member of all their families. "You see her oftener than I do. Does she seem to you to be getting worse? She seems pretty good today."

"That's it," Carleene said, frowning. "One day up, next day down. Sometimes it'll be almost a week, seems like, and then, bang! She's gone again, bumping into things, gettin' her words mixed up, forgettin' things. It's so sad."

"Yes," Doreen said, eyes filling with sympathetic tears. "It *is* sad. I *wish* she'd go to Walter Reed and get the truth."

"She's scared, Mrs. Tock," Carleene said, dashing away a tear herself. "Wouldn't you be? She doesn't *want* to know the truth. But she suspects, though, I'm sure of that. And the general, he knows. He told me all about it, couple of months ago. What could they do for her at Walter Reed?"

"Not much," Dorry said honestly. "Give her some drugs, maybe—arrest it a bit. Make things a little easier for her and the general."

"But not cure it," Carleene said.

"No," Doreen said bleakly. "No cure."

"I think she thinks she isn't botherin' the general," Carleene said. "She's worried about him wantin' to be chairman of the chiefs and she doesn't want to upset him while he's goin' after that. But he knows, anyway. So why not tell him?"

"Would you?" Doreen asked. Carleene gave her a long, troubled look.

"No, ma'am," she said at last. "I probably wouldn't. We've got to do what we can to help men, don't we? Most of 'em couldn't take what they have to take, without that. Least, not in the military."

"That's right," Dorry Tock agreed, mind racing back over the years to a young Tick, a mature Tick, a middle-aged and now gradually and inevitably slowing-toward-retirement Tick. "That's right, Carleene. Not in the military."

"I keep sayin' to her," Carleene said, " 'Go to Walter Reed, ma'am! Let 'em help you! Let 'em tell you what's wrong! That's what they're there for.' But she just won't. Mrs. Burford's a mighty fine woman but she's stubborn. And she thinks she's helpin' him. So," she said, turning away as they heard Vi coming back, "I guess we just have to go with it, ma'am. We just have to ride it out."

"Yes," Dorry agreed, picking up her coffee cup and pretending to take a sip as Carleene disappeared into the kitchen, "I guess you're right on that, Carleene."

"What's that?" Vi asked with a pleasant interest so like her old self that for a second it made Dorry want to cry again. But she mastered it and said calmly, "We're just agreeing that if it weren't for us women, our husbands would have had a pretty hard time making it in the military. Don't you agree?"

"They're such children," Vi said fondly, sitting down with just the faintest uncertainty, refilling her own cup with a hand that just barely trembled. "More?"

"No, thanks," Doreen said. "I'm drowning. Three cups is about two too many, so my doctor at Bethesda Naval Hospital tells me. Has yours at Walter Reed ever talked to you about coffee?"

"I don't really have one over there," Vi Burford said. "Anyway, heart and blood pressure aren't my problem."

"What is?" Doreen inquired with the directness of close friendship; and held her breath. Vi looked at her with equal directness for a moment, and shrugged.

"I don't know," she said casually; and then with a little gathering of breath that encouraged Doreen to feel that, finally, candor might be acceptable, "Why? Am I worse than I was, Dorry?"

"Can't you tell?" Doreen asked.

"I'm not today," Vi said stoutly; and then, quite suddenly, began to cry.

"Oh, Vi!" Doreen said, getting up as fast as her plump little body would allow and taking Vi, now shaking with sobs, into her arms. "There, there, Vi. There, there, dear. Hush. Hush"—adding automatically the meaningless words that always come on such occasions—"It will be all right. It will be all right. You've always been so strong. It will be all right."

Vi looked up with tear-red eyes and spoke through sobs. "No, it won't. No, it won't. It's never going to be all right again."

"Anything I can do to help, ma'am?" Carleene inquired in a troubled voice, opening the kitchen door behind which she had obviously been listening.

"No, thank you, Carleene," Dorry said sharply and then regretted her tone and softened it. "Or, yes, you can. Bring Mrs. Burford a hot towel, if you will please."

"Yes, ma'am," Carleene said, advancing. "I've got it here already."

At this Vi began to laugh a little through her sobs and they knew the corner was being turned.

"Thank you, Carleene," she said, taking the towel and burying her face in it gratefully. "I'm sorry to get everybody so upset."

"You're not," Doreen said firmly, taking her arms away gently and returning to her chair; and, "Oh, no, ma'am!" said Carleene, retreating discreetly behind the kitchen door again.

"Vi," Doreen said gently, after the sobs had subsided almost entirely and Vi's plain and honest face had restored itself to a tenuous but reasonable calm, "could we—?" It was her turn to give a significant nod, toward the kitchen door.

"Surely," Vi said, standing up and swaying a little just for a second before she steadied herself with what was obviously an act of will. "Come on into the den . . . Now," she said, speaking with some of her old brisk vigor, "what shall we talk about?"

"I'll tell you a story," Doreen said, her own voice growing shaky as she went on, but also by a determined effort of will, not failing her until almost the end, "about a bright young bride and a gung-ho young Marine and their little boy, Junior."

"Is this a once-upon-a-time story?" Vi asked, gently now herself in the face of Doreen's obvious tight control.

"It's a for-real story," Dorry said. Her voice trembled for a second. "It's a once-upon-a-time, here-and-now, still-going-on story. We've never told you be-cause—well, because we haven't really known you both that long, and we—we don't like to—to talk about it." She took out a handkerchief but being a strong woman under her lovable pink, plump, sugar-candy exterior, didn't use it for a while yet.

"The young bride and the gung-ho Marine got married, and for a long time they lived happily ever after. The young bride—" she smiled a little at herself —"got older and too fat, but before that happened she had two kids, a beautiful little boy and a beautiful little girl. And *they* grew up and got older. And the gung-ho Marine, who was young once too and nervous in the service, *also* grew older and became less nervous and began to acquire a lot of status and, eventu-ally, a lot of rank. And the world was in order, and everybody was happy."

"Sounds like us," Vi said and though she smiled her voice suddenly trembled too, for a second.

"Yes," Doreen said. She paused to dab her forehead and then went on.

"And the little boy and the little girl got married and *they* began to live happily ever after with their spouses and their kids, of whom the little boy had three. He was very bright and very handsome and very good—he and his sister," she interjected loyally, "both were—and he too was a Marine, and he too began to go up the ladder, and the future seemed very bright for him as it was for his daddy. And then one day—" her voice began to tremble again, but she went on—"we all began to notice some little funny things that didn't seem quite—quite right. His depth perception began to fail—and he didn't walk right—and he began to bump into things—and his memory began to go—and slowly but surely—" she began to cry softly into her handkerchief—"he wasn't so bright any more. He was still very handsome—and very good—but after a while—a couple of years, in his case—he just wasn't—wasn't *there* any more. And he hasn't been there," she said in a sudden bleak and desolate voice, "for quite a while, now. And he doesn't know us and he doesn't know his wife and kids . . . and he doesn't *go.* He just *stays.* And the government helps take care of him, but oh, Vi, *we want him back!* Or if we can't have that, then for—for his sake—we—we want him to go. But the doctors say he just isn't going to go for a while, yet—and he isn't coming back, either . . . and we just have to live with that . . .

"*But,*" she said more firmly, "and I guess this is the point of why I'm telling you this, Vi—we who are—are *here,* you might say, have to be very, very brave about it. But we've discovered that there *are* inner strengths we can call on, we *can* handle it when we have to, we can survive and keep going as long as we know that he isn't in pain, and is being—being taken care of . . . He worried dreadfully about us when he still—still knew about it, but he really needn't have. We're doing all right. It isn't easy for any of us, but we—we manage. And so will—will anybody who has to—to face something like that. So you—you shouldn't worry, Vi. You should have faith. And," she finished quietly, "you should go to Walter Reed and let them help. It would be best for you both, and for the family."

For several minutes there was a silence in which she cried again, a little, and then became calm. The only sound from Vi was one sudden loud sob, quickly stifled. Doreen did not dare look at her but had she done so she would have seen that Vi was staring far away into some distance, hidden by the shrubbery that framed the window, that only she could see.

Finally she spoke and when she did Doreen concluded instantly from her tone that her own well-meant effort, which had cost her much, had been in vain.

"I do thank you, Dorry," Vi said in the clear, calm, gentle voice that had been hers all her life. "I appreciate your sharing your sorrow with me, and if there is anything Brash and I can ever do to help, you must let us know. And I do appreciate your concern for us, too. You surely know how much one depends upon friends, and Brash and I consider our friendship with you and Tick to be one of the best we have ever had. We hope it will continue for a long, *long* time. For the rest—" her voice hesitated the slightest fraction then went calmly on—"of our lives, in fact. We're counting on it! And now," she said, rising gracefully and almost without visible tremor, "I'm sure Carleene wants to wash up and go, and I know *I've* got to take a nap. I find as I get older that I really appreciate a break in the afternoon and I know you must too. Give me a call next week and we'll do something. And give my love to Tick."

"All right, dear," Dorry said, equally calm though much disappointed. "You come to me next time. Maybe I'll invite Renee and Zenia too." Her tone deliberately lightened. "If you can stand the competition, that is!"

"Zenia?" Vi Burford said with a perfectly natural, humorous little smile. "She's quite a person, that girl. Quite remarkable. And they can't beat Ham when it comes to giving orders. I hope she has the time to fit us in."

"She will," Doreen predicted. "If she thinks it will help Ham in any way, she will."

"I admire her for that," Vi said as she opened the door and let in a breath of chill October air. "We all like to help our husbands all we can."

But you're not, Doreen thought as she gave Vi a quick kiss on the cheek, got in her car and waved goodbye to the tall, dignified figure bracing herself quite casually with one hand against the door. *You're not, dearest Vi, you're only being New England–stubborn, lovingly mistaken as your motives may be.*

"God *damn* it!" she exclaimed to herself most uncharacteristically as she backed carefully out the drive. "Damn it, damn it, *damn it!*"

In the doorway Vi stood for another minute or so, waving a final time and watching her go. With a long shuddering sigh she turned and went in, managing to hold herself together just long enough to pay Carleene and see her off too. Then she half-walked, half-staggered into the bedroom, disrobed, climbed under the blankets and lay for a long, long time staring up at the ceiling before she finally dropped off into restless and troubled sleep.

While Vi Burford fitfully slept away the afternoon and in the Commandant's House, Marine Barracks, Doreen Tock aimlessly ate a few more chocolates and tried without much success to concentrate on the latest historical novel she had picked up yesterday in the Pentagon bookstore on the Concourse, their husbands were in the tank in E Ring coming to terms at last with Operation Frio and the proposed joint service plan to solve the problem of Nanukuvu.

"The pachyderms," the lieutenant-general who was director of the JCS secretariat had told his office staff shortly after lunch, "are bellowing today."

And so they were, though in the privacy of that room their trumpetings were confined to one another. Which was just as well, Gen. McCune thought, because sometimes friendship, courtesy and decorum really came unstuck, on these occasions when the chiefs of staff sought to face one another down over their services' contending claims for power and preferment.

The plan had come finally up to them through what was known as "the JCS process," and, Zeecy reflected wryly, some process it was. He had first become familiar with it in his original Pentagon assignment twenty years ago. It had scarcely changed a copying machine or paper-clip since. It was a stately, frustrating, at times interminable ritual; and it was something of a miracle that this time it had produced a proposal in the relatively short time of seven months. This might seem slow to the White House, it might seem slow to him, it might seem slow to the public had they known about it, it might even—though they wouldn't admit it—seem slow to the chiefs themselves. But compared with the time that was normally consumed by a proposal working its way through the duplicating layers of the JCS labyrinth, the plan for Operation Frio had moved like greased lightning.

The only drawback was that the occupiers of Nanukuvu had, according to all intelligence reports reaching Washington, moved somewhat faster.

Nonetheless, "the process" had taken place in its customary stately way. Nothing could change the process. The processes of the process were sacrosanct.

First came The Idea. This could start, as members of the JCS staff put it, "from a thousand places." One of the chiefs might have some issue he thought needed attention; he wrote a letter to the chairman stating his reasons. The chiefs were then required to consider it.

Or one of the area commanders, CINCPAC, CINCLANT or some other CINC could get an idea and write the chairman. Again, the JCS were required to consider it.

Or the White House or the National Security Council or the SecDef could ask for a formal JCS position paper on some issue of military or foreign policy. The chiefs would acknowledge and the process would start to roll.

Or almost anyone down the line in the services, providing he or she went through channels and was approved at all the intervening levels (which almost never happened but was theoretically possible) could place a proposal before the chiefs. If considered and approved, it too would go through the process.

Once a decision was reached to start action, the matter was then passed to the office of the director of the joint staff, or "secretariat," who assigned it to the JCS action officer, who then selected the proper division of the secretariat (each division, inevitably, closely paralleled by a similar division in each of the four services) and sent it along to the action officer (often a major) of that division. His request for response was printed on white paper and was known as a *flimsy.*

The action officer of the appropriate division then *turned it blue* by sending out a *blue bullet,* printed, of course, on blue paper.

The *blue bullet* informed the appropriate matching division in each of the services that a working paper was being prepared, and requested each service to prepare a paper setting forth its particular views on the matter. Each service assigned its own action officer to this task and all the action officers then met with the JCS action officer in one or more sessions to discuss their respective positions. When consensus (which by custom if not by law had to be unanimous) was finally reached, it was put in the form of a working paper which then came back to the JCS staff and went through what was known as the *delete or put in* stage. A written rationale had to be submitted to justify each change. This meant that the basic working paper at this stage quite often went through two, three or sometimes many more revisions, which could stretch over many weeks.

(At about this time on Nanukuvu the channel had been dredged, the sub pens had been hollowed out, the barracks had been built and the supplies had been stored.)

After the *delete or put in* stage was successfully cleared, after the views of the JCS staff and the services had been finally melded together, it was time to *turn the paper buff,* and, sure enough, buff it became. Then back it went to the services, where it had to be approved, when he had time to get around to it in the midst of all his other concerns, by a flag or brigadier rank officer in each service. It then went to the *planners,* colonels or comparable rank, in each service.

At that point the JCS action officer prepared a *brief sheet* which again gave the background of the request and the arguments presented so far for or against it and sent that back through channels to the services. If all the services agreed that it was so important that it must be acted upon by the chiefs, it was sent to the chiefs' deputies and operations officers, all of two- or three-star rank. If these gentlemen and the planners were all in agreement, the paper was then *turned green,* and on green paper it came at last formally before the chiefs.

Either by telephone or in the tank, the chiefs then discussed it and decided whether or not to place it on their agenda.

(On Nanukuvu by now the first one thousand of a permanent contingent of two thousand had arrived.)

If they did so decide, the paper was *red-striped*—the front page was re-printed with a red-striped border—and it then became an *MOP*—Memorandum of Procedure—and was given a number.

(Nanukuvu was no. 27 of the current agenda.)

At that point the chiefs could either formally vote down the proposal, vote for it or take no action. Approval had to be unanimous. If they did nothing it was automatically approved at the end of five days.

(Today, when they were finally in the tank on item 27, the second thousand had just been delivered by submarines from Cam Ranh Bay and were busy settling in.)

In case of great emergency a matter could be taken directly to the chiefs. If they could not speedily reach unanimous agreement, it would be turned to *instant green* and sent immediately to the Secretary for decision.

For all the various reasons that had prevented it in the past seven months, Nanukuvu had never quite achieved emergency status. And so, having followed the regular process, the chiefs were now in the tank at last, hopefully to reach agreement on the plan for Operation Frio. They had invited Gen. Al Rider and his brilliant young action officer, Maj. Gary Stump, to sit in with them to assist in their discussion. That Maj. Stump had been invited into these sacrosanct quarters was indication enough of how highly he was regarded.

"Well," Zeecy said as they finished discussing item 26, a request from Pakistan for fifty more fighter jets, "here's Nanukuvu. At last."

"Don't look at me, Zeece," Ham Stokes responded. "*We* were ready seven months ago."

"The Navy," Bumpy Stahlman said stiffly, "is not here to go through all *that* again. Let's get on with the plan, shall we?"

"Good idea," Tick Tock agreed. "The Marines are ready."

"There you go, Tick," Brash Burford said, a trace of his old humor returning —all but Tick, who knew, had wondered with some concern why it seemed to be missing lately.

"Why not?" Tick inquired with a grin. "It's true, isn't it?" He nodded at the twenty or so pages of red-stripe. "You've got it there, Zeecy, we're all familiar with it, why don't we vote?"

"Just for the record," Adm. Stahlman said, "I think we'd better go over it once more. Zeecy—?"

"Let's let Al do it," Gen. McCune said, passing the document over to Gen. Rider, who grinned and passed it along to Maj. Stump.

"Gary," he said, "why don't you do the honors? You and I are going to have to live with it from now on."

"Certainly, sir," Maj. Stump said and began to read in the deep, clipped, precise and authoritative voice that was one of the things that made him such good officer material.

Operation Frio passed in review before them as their subordinates, over so many months, had finally worked out its details through successive stages of white, blue, buff and green. Exact details of how much equipment, what kinds, and how many men would be contributed by each service were carefully spelled out. The command structure was established. The order of battle was ordained.

The Air Force would get the bombing runs Gen. Stokes wanted.

The Navy would get the combined attack/support role Adm. Stahlman wanted.

The Army and the Marines would have the amphibious assaults and ground advances Gen. Burford and Gen. Tock wanted.

And everybody, presumably, would be happy.

The Air Force, it was true, would go in first, which would give it the opening publicity break. It would have a major outer-perimeter defensive role once the island had been thoroughly bombed.

Naval aviation would have to accept somewhat less than parity with the Air Force, but this would be compensated for by the Navy's continuing presence in bombardment, logistics and support.

The Army and Marines would be in the third time-stage but this would be compensated for by the fact that their ground roles would probably last longer, require more sacrifice and consequently give them more chance for favorable media coverage in the long run.

Also—and the necessity to reach unanimous agreement on this had been one of the principal causes of delay, since both Navy and Air Force were at first acridly opposed—it was stated that, "in order to make full use of the magnificent capabilities of both services, the Army will advance from the northern tip of the island along the northern ridge to the center, simultaneously as the Marine Corps advances from the southern tip of the island along the southern ridge to the center."

Ham Stokes snorted.

"And don't let either one," he said, "get there one step ahead of the other."

"I should hope *not,*" Gen. McCune agreed as both Brash and Tick looked as though they were about to do battle with the Air Force. Zeecy added quickly, "Thank you, major. Is that it, then?"

"That's it, sir!" Gary Stump said in his crisp, efficient way.

"I think we've all been over it enough," Bumpy Stahlman remarked. "The Navy isn't entirely happy with—"

"Bumpy," Ham Stokes interrupted, "nobody is ever *entirely* happy. This is a pretty good plan, considering everything."

"It seems to be the best we can devise," Tick said.

"It's the best we can agree on," Brash corrected.

"We *are* agreed, then?" Zeecy asked, and there were unanimous nods.

"Good," he said. "The question is, can it work. Al, what do you think?"

"Well," Gen. Rider said slowly, a twinkle in his eyes and the start of a smile on his pleasant face, "as long as a Marine is going to be in command, I think it will. You all tell your boys to behave, now."

"Don't worry," Zeecy said. "They will. You're satisfied, then."

Gen. Rider nodded.

"I think you've thought of about everything. The question now is: when?"

"And that," Zeecy said with a troubled sigh, "is a good question. Where do we stand on the ALCAC?"

"Our recommendations will go in to Helen Clark and Harry Ahmanson tomorrow morning," Ham Stokes said.

"Ours too," Brash and Tick said together.

"Ours should be reaching both of them," Bumpy Stahlman said with a small smile of satisfaction, "right about now."

"Damn!" Ham exclaimed. "Foiled by the Navy *again.* Anyway, they're done, thank God. Now it's up to Project Frio to match our progress with Operation Frio, and we'll be on our way, right?"

"Right," Gen. McCune agreed. "How soon would it take you fellows to be ready with your requirements as set forth in the plan?"

"Two weeks," Ham said.

"No more," Bumpy agreed. Brash and Tick nodded confirmation.

"Well, *good,*" the chairman said, at last sounding relieved and pleased about Frio. "Now we just have to keep after Helen and the two Harrys."

"That's right," Ham said. "We have to wait on the ALCAC."

"I'm sure it won't take very long, now," Zeecy said with more confidence than he felt.

"DSARC?" Gen. Tock inquired. "Manufacture of parts? Testing? I don't know, Zeece." He shook his head in honest frustration. "The damned civilians are always so *slow.*"

"They are that," Gen. Burford agreed. "But I guess all we can do is keep pushing. They move at their own pace but we'll just have to keep after 'em."

"I'll let them know what you think," Zeecy said in a tone he tried to keep from sounding too wry. "So, then," he said, standing up. "We're on our way, and thank God for it."

"I feel very good about it," Bumpy Stahlman said. "I think we've made real progress."

"Very gratifying," Ham Stokes said. Brash and Tick nodded vigorous agreement.

"Major," Zeecy said as they moved toward the door, "how are you liking your assignment to Frio?"

Gary Stump gave him a bright look.

"I think it's a great privilege, sir. And now it's going to be really challenging." He permitted himself a smile of just the proper degree of intimacy with one so far above him in rank. "Finally."

"Yes," Zeecy said with a chuckle. "You're right there, major. Keep the general in line, now," he added, giving Al Rider a friendly slap on the shoulder. "Don't let him make the mistake of thinking the Marines can do it all."

"I think he knows that, sir," Gary said, broadening his smile to include them both. His tone became frankly admiring. "He's a real team player."

"That's because I've got a good team," Gen. Rider said. "And Gary's about the best one on it."

"I wouldn't say that, sir," Gary protested with a modest smile.

"Well, *I* would," Al Rider said with a laugh, "and that's what counts, right, Zeecy?"

"You bet," Zeecy said with an answering laugh as they peeled off in the corridor to head for their respective offices, each carrying his copy of the plan. He stood for a moment watching them go, Al Rider and the major walking a little behind the others, engaged in animated and evidently friendly conversation.

Gen. McCune frowned. That wasn't quite the way he heard it from Brod Tolliver. Something was seriously bothering his young friend, and Brod couldn't tell him exactly what. "Just a hunch, sir," he had said only yesterday when he had called Zeecy from a phone in the Concourse. "Can't say why. It's just there."

"Keep your eyes and ears open," Zeecy had said. "If there is anything, it'll turn up sooner or later."

"Yes, sir," Brod had said gratefully. "I appreciate your letting me ramble on about it, when it's only a suspicion."

"That's what I put you there for," Gen. McCune had told him crisply. "Don't hesitate."

"I appreciate your confidence, sir," Brod said earnestly. "I won't overdo it."

Zeecy didn't think he was. There was something just a little too perfect, a little too smooth, about young Maj. Stump. Al Rider seemed to be a convert, however, and maybe everything was entirely in order. But Zeecy thought he'd keep it in mind. He trusted Brod's instincts and he trusted his own.

On B Ring, third floor, Gen. Rider and Maj. Stump approached the inconspicuous door with the chaste little sign CUMULATIVE ASSESSMENT GROUP. Al Rider waited while Gary stepped forward, punched out the proper code on the small bank of buttons alongside the lock and then stepped back to give the general precedence.

Inside they found Hogan's and Tolliver's desks deserted and a note indicating that they had decided to take advantage of the general's permission, granted when he and Gary had left for the tank.

"We've gone to the Big Scoop for an ice-cream fix," it said, referring to the highly popular ice-cream-and-popcorn counter in the Pik-Quik.

It was signed "Hogan," and Gen. Rider smiled.

"Do I detect a slight gleam of humor there?" he inquired. "A sly bit of raciness? 'Ice-cream fix'? That doesn't sound like Hogan."

"She *is* very serious, sir," Gary Stump said, going to his own desk and riffling through the telephone messages she had left for him. "But I suppose that's what makes her a good officer."

"She is good," Gen. Rider agreed. "Solemn, but good. Young Tolliver seems to be doing all right, too."

"He's a likable kid," Gary agreed with a casual but friendly indifference. "We get along quite well."

"I hope we all do," Al Rider said as he started into his office, "since from now on Frio is going to get pretty busy, at last." He paused and turned back to hand Gary his copy of the plan. "Run off an extra copy of this, will you, and then put one in my safe and keep one in the safe out here. You can go over it with Elizabeth and Brod when they get back."

"Surely, sir," Gary Stump said as the general went in and closed his door. He glanced at his watch. With a little luck Hogan and Tolliver wouldn't be back for another twenty-five minutes. Anyway, you had to take chances. He'd been taking them, in one way or another, almost all his life.

He stepped quickly to his desk, put on the pair of gloves he kept stashed away at the back of the bottom drawer, turned to the copier and went to work.

Down on second floor, E Ring, Gen. McCune sat for some moments staring thoughtfully into space. Then with a sudden decisive movement he picked up his private line and called the general commanding the Army's Criminal Investigation Command.

Also on the second floor, A Ring, on the windowed corridor that looked out upon Ground Zero, the central courtyard with its hamburger stand now shuttered and its benches empty against the early chill, Gen. Harry Ahmanson was feeling more pleased and relieved than he had in some time. Seated at his desk behind the door which, like Op Frio, bore only a small discreet sign—AGGREGATE ANALYSIS UNIT—he was studying the Navy's suggestions for modification of the ALCAC. The document had arrived from Adm. Stahlman's office an hour ago. Immediately he had made quick calls to the other services. He had been assured that their recommendations would all be in without fail tomorrow morning. Not since the creation of Project Frio had he felt such satisfaction. Maybe, now, they were going to get somewhere.

He fervently hoped so, because just a few moments ago Zeecy had called to tell him the chiefs had finally approved the plan for Op Frio. Zeecy had been in no way critical of his own progress, but Harry Ahmanson, being a conscientious officer who still hadn't received the second star he had been promised seven months ago, was very anxious to get moving and complete his part of the mission. He and Zeecy both knew the slowness was the chiefs' own fault and Harry had no worries about Zeecy's support. But having spent most of his adult life in the military, he was well aware that if there were ever any blame attached to the slowness of Project Frio, the JCS would turn on him in a minute. The blame for failure would land, suavely and implacably, squarely on his doorstep.

That was life in the services, Military Harry had early found out, and like most, he did not deem it prudent to challenge it. But it could be averted with sufficient foresight and skill, and now that the logjam over Frio seemed to be finally breaking he intended to do everything in his power to guarantee that it moved right along just as rapidly and efficiently as could possibly be. He and Helen Clark were in complete agreement on that.

His relationship with the assistant secretary for acquisition and logistics had developed rapidly after their plans for a picnic at Harpers Ferry had been interrupted by the unexpected snowstorm on the first day of Nanukuvu. The weather had rapidly returned to normal, spring had engulfed the land, and two weeks later the same group of friends had been reconstituted with the same "girl for Harry," and off they had gone to the Outer Banks of North Carolina, instead. This had been a two-day junket, and during the course of it things had progressed much more rapidly than either he or Helen, he suspected, had intended. There had been campfires and sing-alongs and plenty of good food and drinks in the big old house they had all rented at Ocracoke for the weekend, and by Saturday night he and Helen had found themselves taking long walks on the beach together. Their talk had ranged across the whole spectrum of Washington and world politics, with particular emphasis on the Pentagon and all its quirks and foibles. They had found themselves in agreement on almost everything. They were two sharp, shrewd, cool and competent minds and it was a genuine pleasure to communicate. She was particularly interested in his new assignment as co-manager of Proj Frio, he was particularly interested in how well they would be able to work together on it. They concluded that there would be very few problems; and soon sensed that their harmony on that might extend to more personal concerns as well.

He had driven her home, there had been more compatible exchanges, she had invited him in for a nightcap at her apartment at Washington Harbour, with its stunning view downriver to Lincoln Memorial, Jefferson Memorial, Washington Monument and Capitol; and after another twenty minutes of idle chitchat she had suddenly stood up, turned to him with a brilliant smile and said, "Why don't we?" He had smiled and stood up too. "I'll go for that," he said, and they were in each other's arms. They were more relaxed with one another than either had been with anyone in a long time. They recognized with a privately shared amusement that they were two of a kind; and it all went very well.

And was still going well, he congratulated himself, because after the first few weeks they had both rather expected it to gradually trail off. It had not. Instead it had grown deeper to the point where he was now quite seriously contemplating an end to the bachelorhood he had so carefully preserved free of blemish for so many years. He was not sure yet whether Helen was in agreement, but there were various indications that led him to believe she might be. She was not rejecting the idea outright, at any rate: it did not seem repugnant to her. He knew he was being weighed carefully in the balances of a calm and careful mind that took few uncalculated chances any more, and certainly not on the marriage relationship she felt had already let her down so badly once. He had already asked her and been assured that she was thinking about it, and certainly not unfavorably.

Once Frio was completed and he had his second star he intended to try to push the matter to a successful conclusion; or, rather, persuade Helen to push it to a successful conclusion, since she was the sort who had to be satisfied in her own mind that the successful conclusion of anything she tackled was her own doing. He had realized very early that this belief was very necessary to her, and being a skillful judge of human nature and an adept campaigner, he had subordinated his own ideas to hers and decided that he would pursue her until she caught him. Then they would both be happy.

He thought of her fondly now as he prepared to go over the Navy's paper on the ALCAC, which he knew she also had received this afternoon. They were going to have dinner tonight, as they did now at least three or four times a week, and no doubt would have some preliminary discussion of the craft before they turned to more relaxing pursuits. They were both very much aware of Loy

Buck's instructions: "Don't let the boys steal the Treasury on this one." He and Helen did not intend to, even though he knew Civilian Harry regarded him, as he did all military, with a dour and suspicious eye.

The vivid image of his co-manager flashed across his mind: slow, deliberate, meticulous, adamant in his diligence and virtually unshakable in his prejudices. He could not suppress a smile. Harry Josephs, civil servant par excellence, was not a bad sort when you got to know him, and over the past seven months Military Harry had made it a point to do so. He had even gone so far as to invite the Josephs to come to dinner with him and Helen at the officers' club at Fort McNair. It had been a surprisingly relaxed evening. Civilian Harry had consumed two martinis and three glasses of wine ("Who's counting?" he had demanded of Helen a little tipsily and she had put a cool hand on his and said calmly, "I am.") His mousy but pleasant little wife had kept him company on the wine. They had talked about Harry's lengthy (it seemed almost endless) career in the Pentagon; their childless life; their yearned-for retirement home in Winter Haven, Florida; their two cats, Lively and Livelier, who were now seventeen and no longer lively at all; and what they were going to do with Proj Frio if the chiefs ever "get off their fat behinds" as Civilian Harry put it with a surprising vigor that clearly startled his wife. Since part of the delay had been Harry's own opposition to the ALCAC modifications, this struck Military Harry and Helen with some irony, but they let it pass.

"We must all cooperate to see that it gets done just as soon as possible once the chiefs have put in their reports," Helen said and Civilian Harry had exclaimed stoutly, "Thash right!"

And now, Harry Ahmanson thought, he hoped to hell everybody would cooperate, because from what he heard from his friends on the JCS staff, things were moving right along on Nanukuvu.

He had not told Helen about this, or Harry Josephs, because officially they were not supposed to know anything about the ultimate purpose of their project. But it worried him as a military man and as a citizen, quite aside from the question of his own advancement. He wanted Frio to succeed for a lot of reasons, not least of them being the welfare of his country.

In this mood he read through the Navy's recommendations for the ALCAC: not too lengthy, not too difficult, not too unreasonable: why on earth had it taken them so long? Now, if the others were as reasonable—and if Helen could impress upon the DSARC people the need to reach speedy agreement—then just maybe—

He was lost in a momentary wild dream of getting the whole thing wrapped up in another two months when the phone rang and he picked it up to hear a voice he had not heard in some time, cold, biting and as always on the offensive: Burt Sanstrom, staff director of the Senate Armed Services Committee and no friend of the Pentagon, whose top officials regarded him with contempt and treated him with the utmost discretion.

"Harry?" Burt said peremptorily. "You're not with the SecDef's office any-more. What happened?"

"Burt," he said carefully, "nothing 'happened.' Higher authority decided I'd be more useful somewhere else, I guess. You know how it is in the military."

"Hmph," Burt Sanstrom said. "You and Buck have a fight?"

"No," Gen. Ahmanson said patiently, "Mr. Buck and I didn't have a fight, we get along just fine, always have and I hope always will. I'm just on another assignment for a while, that's all."

"Doing what?" Burt Sanstrom demanded.

"Aggregate analysis," Harry Ahmanson said smoothly. "That's the name of it, Aggregate Analysis Unit."

"I know those Pentagon names," Burt said tartly. "Nine-tenths of them de-signed to deliberately baffle the Hill and keep us in the dark at appropriations time. What do you *do*, I asked. Is it a secret?"

"If it were to involve anything that would be of value to the enemy," Gen. Ahmanson said calmly, "then I suppose it would be secret. As it is, nothing that has been analyzed so far is any secret."

"*Has* anything been analyzed so far?" Burt Sanstrom asked, and Harry Ahmanson cursed his suspicious instinct, which had often given the Pentagon trouble. But his voice was imperturbable as he replied.

"The name speaks for itself, I think. Analysis will have to be done—lots of analysis—*aggregate* analysis—before we can come up with anything at all. Why don't you call me back in a couple of months and I'll be able to give you a better fix on it?"

"I don't think you're telling me the truth, Harry," Burt Sanstrom said. "I think this phony name is a cover-up for something else. What *are* you analyz-ing, anyway?" He snorted. "Aggregates?"

"Various things which in the opinion of the SecDef are necessary to be analyzed," Gen. Ahmanson said blandly. "I'm afraid that's as far as I can go right now."

"Oh, then you *are* still working for Buck," Burt said triumphantly. "What's it about, an action in the South Pacific?"

For just a second Harry Ahmanson hesitated; just long enough for Burt to snort again and demand, *"Well?"*

"You remind me of someone, Burt," Harry Ahmanson said. "Do you know Delight Jones and *Defense Eye?"*

"Yes, I know her," Burt said coldly, "and I don't relish the comparison if that's what you're driving at. She or her stooge Herbie Horowitz bother me a dozen times a week about something."

"If she's that much of a bother," Gen. Ahmanson suggested with a chuckle that was designed deliberately to draw wrath, "why do you tell her anything?"

"I don't tell her anything!" Burt Sanstrom growled and Harry Ahmanson was on it at once.

"Oh, come now, Burt!" he said in a skeptical tone. "You *don't?* It's obvious to people over here where most of her so-called 'scoops' come from. Why kid me?"

"Now, listen," Burt Sanstrom said sharply. "That's all right, where Delight Jones gets her scoops. I may talk to her once in a while but we're not in cahoots, if that's what you mean. And furthermore, Harry, stop trying to lead me down the garden-path. Stop trying to throw me off the trail. I didn't call up to talk about Delight Jones and you know it. I want to know about that operation you're running to mount a strike in the South Pacific. What's it all about, Harry? You know I'll find out sooner or later. Might as well tell me."

"Burt," Harry Ahmanson said with perfect truth. "I swear by Cube Herron's sainted aunt that I am not running an operation to mount a strike in the South Pacific."

"Well," Burt Sanstrom said darkly. "Somebody is."

"How do you know that?" Gen. Ahmanson inquired scornfully. "Crystal ball? Or palm-reading?"

"No!" Burt said angrily. "Mario Escondido—"

"That little—" Harry Ahmanson began and then cut himself deliberately short with a dry little laugh.

"He's a vicious little jerk," Burt Sanstrom agreed, "but he has his sources in the building and they're usually pretty good. He's heard somewhere that somebody over there is planning some sort of emergency mission in the South Pacific and he wants to know what it is. So does Cube. So do Luzanne Johnson and Jerry Castain and Karl Aschenheim. So do I. I'm supposed to find out, and by God, I will. So you might as well tell me, Harry. I'll remember it if you do and remember it if you don't. So you might as well."

"Burt," Harry Ahmanson said solemnly and again truthfully, "I swear to you, I haven't been told a thing officially about any mission in the South Pacific. I just haven't been told."

"That doesn't mean you don't know about it," Burt said sourly. Harry Ahmanson said nothing. "Well," Burt said finally, "if you won't, you won't. But just don't expect an easy time of it when your promotion comes up to the committee."

"I don't expect anything from you, Burt," Gen. Ahmanson said, deciding suddenly that he had had enough guff from this one, "except threats and bad vibes. So what else is new?"

"All right," Burt Sanstrom said. *"All right!* But just don't look to *me* when you need help!"

"Is it o.k. if I hang up now, Burt?" Gen. Ahmanson inquired. "Have to run along. My aggregates and their analysis need attention."

"Very funny," Burt said. "I'll find out somewhere," he added in a remote tone, as though he were talking to himself. "I'll find out somewhere."

"Call me back if you do," Harry Ahmanson urged. "I like to be clued in on these things."

Burt hung up with a muffled and indecipherable sound of anger and disgust;

and the general, turning back to the Navy's ideas for the ALCAC, told himself that he had probably guaranteed a rough time for his promotion. But he would just have to rely on the fairness of Cube and Luzanne and the rest of the committee if Burt tried to make trouble. Even Cube didn't like Burt a great deal more than the Pentagon did: but he was a bulldog, you had to hand him that. He was remorseless and ruthless and he didn't give up. He'd find out sooner or later. He wouldn't stop digging until he did, unless it came out somewhere else.

Which, as a matter of fact, it was beginning to do in the office of the chairman of the Senate Appropriations subcommittee on defense. Jerry Castain was a little flighty at times but he too was a bulldog when he got really intrigued. And now, in this small, thin, worn-looking young woman—who, given a good rest and the additional twenty or so pounds he strongly suspected she could lay claim to before her world got shot to pieces in the South Pacific, could be a real little beauty—he felt he was definitely on the scent of something that might be pretty big.

Theirs had been a disconnected sort of interview and it was still going on, sandwiched between several votes for which he had been required to hurry all the way over to the floor and back again from his spectacular glass-walled office on the fifth floor of the Hart Senate Office Building. Several other constituents had also dropped in. They included the CEOs and board chairmen of three of Indiana's largest companies, who were in town fighting an administrative law case with the Department of Energy. There had also been a couple of families of soldiers killed in the latest bombing in Central America, and the widows of five of the Marines lost in the attack on Karg Island. And a women's delegation from Elkhart. And two lawyers from the Justice Department with information on the latest unauthorized transfer of technical information to the enemy. And so on . . .

A typical Senate afternoon, he thought with a sigh as he returned from the fourth roll-call. Thank goodness the debate didn't involve anything that required his participation. His time was, relatively, his own for a little while. In the midst of many interruptions he had managed to extract an interesting tale from little Mrs. Madeline Smith, widow of the late Hague, Hoosiers both.

She had come to him, she said in the first segment of it before he had to ask her to wait while he dashed to the floor, because she had not been able to get any satisfaction from the chief of naval operations.

"Bumpy Stahlman?" he had asked in surprise. "Adm. Stahlman? But he's a very nice guy."

"That may be," she said in a thin but defiant little voice, "and I don't doubt he *is* very kind. In fact, he was very kind to me. But he—he put me off, Senator. He didn't admit to *anything*."

"'Admit' to anything?" Jerry asked, suddenly alert. "What is there for him to 'admit' to?"

"That they killed Hague," she said. "That they made him fly over that island and he got shot down."

"Now, just—just a minute, Mrs. Smith," Jerry said carefully. "First of all, I'm completely in the dark on this, you know. You'll have to start from the beginning. Where is this island?"

"Oh," she said, gesturing vaguely, "out *there,* somewhere. I'm not sure. We were living just outside Pearl at the time. It was somewhere down south of there, quite a distance, I think. Hague was usually gone a month or so at a time." She shivered. "He never really told me much about what he did."

"What was he?" Jerry Castain asked. "I mean, what was his specialty? Was he a seaman or an officer—"

"He was an officer!" she said stoutly.

"Of course," he said hastily. "And a good one, I'm sure."

"The very best," she said, starting to cry a little but fortunately distracted by the children, who were quietly trying to murder each other under her chair.

"And was he—"

"He was assigned to the carrier *Dominant,*" she said, restoring harmony or at least armed truce with a couple of well-directed slaps. "He could tell me that much. And he flew a helicopter."

"How long had he been on helicopter duty?"

"A little over a year, I guess."

"Did he like it?"

"He loved it," she said, sounding almost scornful for a moment. "You know *men,* always shooting and killing each other—"

"Now, wait a minute," he said, a sudden excitement beginning to creep up. "We aren't at war out there. How come he was shooting or killing anybody?"

"I don't know," she said, looking at him with sad and thoughtful eyes. "He talked about it in his sleep."

"In his sleep?" he said, startled; and just then the vote signal buzzed and he had to excuse himself and jump up. "But don't run away," he ordered hastily as he hurried out the door. "I'll be right back . . . Keep those kids happy and keep her *here!*" he directed his secretary as he passed her desk; and when he hurried back, feeling some apprehension, she was still there.

"Now," he said, settling down again. "You were telling me about your husband's—Hague's—being on the *Dominant* and flying a helicopter and shooting and killing somebody."

"Yes," she said. "That's what he said in his sleep."

"But how *could* he?" Jerry demanded; and uttered again the sensible words that are held up so often as barrier against things international that make no sense. "We aren't at war!"

"I can't quote you everything he said," she remarked doggedly, "but he was fighting somebody, at least twice. And he said, 'Think I got him!' Each time. So," she said bleakly, "I guess maybe he did."

"What is the island's name?"

She frowned.

"Nankoo—Nanvoo—I don't know exactly. Something like that."

"And you don't know where it is—"

"Well, only generally. Somewhere down near the Marianas and the Gilbert islands, I think. At least, that's what Vernon said."

"Oh?" he said. "Then you do know a little bit about it, after all. Who's Vernon?"

"Vernon was his buddy," she said. "Vernon Muller. He and Millie lived right next door. They got married within a month after we did, and they had—have —two kids too. We were real pals, all of us. Vernon was a helicopter pilot too."

"I see," he said as the classic pattern began to emerge. "And they flew together and then something happened to Hague—and you got the official Navy version that he had been killed in a training exercise—" she nodded— "and you talked about it to Vernon and Millie—and at first Vernon wasn't going to tell you, because he didn't really know very much, it was mostly just gossip on the ship—" she nodded again—"and he wasn't supposed to tell you the little bit he did know—but you were all good friends and he felt very sorry for you— and so he did tell you."

"That's about it," she said in her little voice.

"And so what happened?"

And just then the voting signal buzzed again and he said, "God *damn* it!" excused himself again and dashed out, again apprehensive. But she was waiting when he got back.

"So Vernon told you," he said, out of breath but fascinated. "And what did he tell you?"

"That there was this island, Nankoo or Nanvoo or something, and Hague was supposed to go out and scout it because there was some kind of—" she looked doubtful—"some kind of *activity* on it that they wanted checked out."

"*Who* wanted checked out?" he demanded. "And what kind of activity? And by whom?"

"*They* wanted checked out," she said impatiently. "On the ship. Vernon didn't know what kind of activity but he heard later that night from another buddy of theirs on the ship that it might have been—submarines."

"Ah," he said in a voice soft but excited. "Soviet, I presume."

"That's what they thought."

"And Vernon and you think Hague was shot down by the Soviets?" he asked, scarcely daring to breathe lest he distract her. But she was in the grip of her narrative and her conviction and went right ahead.

"Yes," she said firmly. "Vernon thinks so and *I* think so. *Stop it!*" she snapped at the kids, who stopped.

"And do you and Vernon have any theory as to why the Soviets were there?" he asked, still softly. She shook her head.

"We don't know that," she said simply. "How could we?"

"That's right," he agreed. "How could you? But you think Adm. Stahlman knows."

"I think he does," she said. "Otherwise why would the Navy lie to me?"

"A good question," he said. "Did you ask Adm. Stahlman about all this?"

"Yes, I did," she said. "At first he wasn't going to see me at all, but after about three months of me pestering his office, he did." A faint smile touched her lips. "I guess he decided it was the only way to get rid of me. Well," she said and her expression hardened, "it didn't!"

"Good girl," he said. "I'm glad you came to me. I think you should believe, however, that Adm. Stahlman sincerely feels that it's best for all concerned, Hague, you and your country, that the exact circumstances of his death not be made public. I'm sure Adm. Stahlman thinks he's doing what's best."

"Oh, I'm sure," she agreed. "I liked him. He's a nice man. But he should have told *me* the truth."

"Yes," Sen. Castain said with a wry little smile, "I think perhaps he should . . . Now: where do I find Vernon?"

"Why?" she asked. "Don't you believe me?"

"Of course I do," he said quickly, "but surely you can see—"

"Oh, sure," she agreed immediately. "I'm not dumb. Of course you can't say anything just on my unsupported word. But, Senator—if he bears me out—you *will* say something?"

"If you can give me Vernon's full name and give me some idea where I can find him, and he bears you out as I've no doubt he will," he said quietly, "I promise you, I will say something."

"And make Hague's—Hague's—death—worthwhile?"

"And make Hague's death worthwhile. Now, Vernon's name again—?"

"Muller," she said. "Vernon B. Muller. He's a captain and I think he's still at Pearl. Anyway, the Navy will know."

"I'll find him," he said. He stood up, patted the now silent kids on the head, took her hands between his own. "Madeline," he said gravely, "are you all right? Do you have enough money? Is the Navy looking after you?"

"Oh, yes," she said. Her mouth twisted suddenly. "They take pretty good care of you, if you're a widow."

After she had gone, suddenly seeming frailer and tinier and more woebegone, he sat for a moment chewing on one of the distinctive hand-fitting "U.S. Senate" ballpoint pens. Then he picked up the phone, called the Navy; was promptly given Capt. Vernon B. Muller's address, home telephone number and duty telephone number at Pearl; put in a call and was told that he was "away from base on a routine training mission but will be back tomorrow"; called his wife and left word that he would call tomorrow; and went back to the floor looking so thoughtful that Luzanne Johnson kidded that he must have seen a ghost.

"Maybe I have," he told her, tone lightening. "But maybe I can bring it out of the everywhere into the here." He smiled. "Before Mario Escondido and Burt Sanstrom do."

"Oh?" she said, interested. "Sit down and tell me about it." She put a hand on his arm and pulled him down into the seat beside her. Across the floor old Sen. Dominick was having a verbal tussle with Dick Swenson of Minnesota. "Nobody's listening," she murmured with a chuckle. "I'd much rather hear about your ghost."

When he told her she too looked very thoughtful.

"That's probably why I've gotten that sense from the Pentagon of something not quite right over there lately. I haven't been able to find out what's going on but it sounds as though that might be it. If that boy wandered in somewhere where he wasn't supposed to be—"

"And of course," Jerry Castain said, "if *they* were somewhere where *they're* not supposed to be—"

"And if it's been decided to take some action—"

Jerry nodded quickly.

"And it hasn't moved along very fast—"

She frowned.

"That would tie in with Mario's query. When was this supposed to have taken place?"

"They notified his wife a little over six months ago. So assuming they didn't wait too long after the event—"

She nodded.

"And began planning to respond right away—yes, that would about fit. It would account for—" she hesitated: but she and Jerry Castain, Senate gossips said, were thick as thieves. She trusted him, for reasons the gossips assumed, perhaps unfairly, to be obvious. "It would account for Zeecy's mood in the last three months or so. He's been upset about something but he's refused to tell me what it is."

"Well," Jerry said, being a bit of a Senate gossip himself sometimes, "if he won't tell *you*—" But he smiled to take the offense out of it and she smiled back.

"You might be right," she said lightly. *"Might."* And then, just to throw him off a bit, and for the pleasure of it, "if he won't tell me and Renee, that is."

"Oh, is she still around?" Jerry inquired with exaggerated surprise. She hit his arm.

"Naughty boy," she remarked, and then smiled cheerfully up at friends in the press gallery who she could see were watching them with the attention to small details that occurred when somebody like boring Jim Dominick had the floor. "Something's been bugging the general, and maybe this is the way to get at it. Do you mind if I ask him about it?"

Sen. Castain hesitated.

"I'm thinking of making a speech on it tomorrow," he said slowly, "if I can get it all together by then. But if you want to do it yourself—"

"Oh, no," she said hastily. "Not at all. It's your baby, they're your constituents, you go right ahead. I'll give you whatever I get—if anything—and you make the speech." She smiled her charming smile. "I'll be a behind-the-scenes contributor. How's that?"

"Thanks, Lu," he said gratefully. "I do appreciate it, and who knows, maybe we can light a little fire under the building and get things moving. If that's what they want, and there's a real necessity for it."

She shook her head with a rueful little smile.

"That's always the question over there, isn't it. Do they want it—and is it necessary. The answer to the first is usually always yes but the answer to the second is often a little less clear-cut. Let me talk to Zeecy. I'll see what I can find out."

"Thanks, Lu," he said again as a quorum call began and he decided to go to his own desk. "This could be interesting."

"I'm sure it's going to be," she said. "We may be onto something quite serious. I'm just as concerned as you are."

But when she reached the chairman from a phone in the cloakroom she found him at first evasive, then annoyed and determined to stonewall.

"Look," he said finally. "There'll be a time for this and the time will be when everything's ready or when some definitive action has been taken. The time isn't now when things are still in a formative stage."

"There *is* something to it, then," she said. "Something's got to be 'ready' and some 'definitive action' has to be 'taken.' And Hague Smith *did* discover something he wasn't supposed to discover and he *did* get killed for his pains. Are you folks getting ready to start your own little war in the South Pacific?"

"Luzanne," he said patiently, "don't. Just—don't, all right? I'm not going to confirm or deny anything to you or Jerry Castain or Cube or anybody else on the Hill. Harry Ahmanson tells me Burt Sanstrom is already gum shoeing around. Harry didn't tell him anything and neither will I if he calls me. This is a situation of great delicacy and premature speeches in the Senate aren't going to help it any. I'm sorry that sounds blunt but that's the way it is."

"But we have a right to know!" she protested indignantly.

"Well, you *will* know, when the time comes."

She sounded genuinely annoyed with him for the first time since their relationship had become of more importance to both of them.

"You're just building up a lot of trouble for yourselves, you know that? It's going to be twice as bad when it does break."

"Oh, no, it's not," he said flatly.

"Well," she said, "Jerry's going to make a speech as soon as he's got enough to go on, probably tomorrow. And then—"

"Now, see here!" he said, sounding alarmed as he had the first time she had raised the possibility of public scrutiny, four months ago. "You tell Jerry—"

"*You* tell Jerry," she suggested, sounding, as she could, more the no-nonsense Senator than the delightful southern belle.

"*Damn!*" Gen. McCune said. "Damn and double damn . . . All right, I *will* tell Jerry. All we need right now is a lot of hue and cry just as things are falling into place. God, that irresponsible—"

"If he's irresponsible *I'm* irresponsible," she said. "I'm encouraging him to do it, because if he doesn't, Mario Escondido will, or somebody equally lovable. At least Jerry isn't a double-dealing, pork-barreling crook like Mario. Be thankful for that."

"Jerry's all right," he conceded grudgingly. "Better than most, though he does get in our hair too often to suit me. Maybe I can buy a little time if I explain the whole situation to him."

"Worth a try," she said in a remote tone. "You haven't explained it to *me.*"

"Are we seeing each other Friday night?" he inquired blandly.

She uttered an annoyed little sound.

"This is hardly the occasion *or* the place to bring that up. Your phone and this one are probably both bugged and even if they aren't this is no time to get into *that.*"

"It's always a good time to get into *that,*" he said with a chuckle. "Come on, Luzanne, relax. You know I can't say anything at this point. You'll be told as soon as anyone and probably sooner. Meanwhile, I just can't contribute to a public uproar that might very well abort the mission."

"There you go! 'Abort the mission.' Has it gone that far—it's a formal *'mission'?*"

"Yes," he said crisply, "and that is absolutely all I'm saying on the subject. You and Jerry can go ahead and blow the whistle if you like, but I warn you, you may very well be jeopardizing a great many American lives and a project of great importance to national security. Now, what about Friday?"

"I'll think about it," she said, not yielding much.

"Good!" he exclaimed with exaggerated relief. "I'll be able to live through the week, then, knowing—"

"Knowing nothing," she said, permitting herself to sound slightly amused. "Too bad Renee decided to go to New York this weekend."

"Well, she did," he said lightly. "It wasn't my idea but I didn't discourage it."

"You're incorrigible."

"But you like me."

"Not at the moment, no."

"But maybe by Friday."

"Maybe," she said. "We'll just have to see."

He answered that with a chuckle and hung up. She went back to the floor where Jim Dominick and Dick Swenson were still going at it. She told herself that their growing relationship was just as foolish as she had known it would be. But despite her best intentions it seemed to be happening. She was beginning to give in, just as Renee and Zeecy had both known she would. For the first time in a long time she felt a little out of control of her own life. She resented it but she was enjoying it too. It was an annoying, bothersome and pleasant sensation . . . while it lasted, which she promised herself would not be long.

She saw that Jerry had gone over to Cube's desk and was talking earnestly to him in the hushed voice Senators use for such conversations on the floor. She caught his eye and was beckoned over.

"What did you find out?" Cube inquired as she took the empty seat on his other side.

"He wouldn't talk, which I suppose I understand, but doesn't seem very wise to me under the circumstances."

"It doesn't to me either," Sen. Herron said.

"He did say, however, that we mustn't say anything or we might 'abort the mission.' So there *is* a mission, and I expect, Jerry, that it's to try to get them out of there, exactly as you and I have been guessing."

"God *damn* it!" Sen. Herron said with sotto voce vehemence, cherubic face flushing beneath its halo of fluffy white hair. "I've told them and told them and *told* them that they weren't to start anything without letting us know, no matter what the provocation. And now here they go again! God *damn* it!"

"Then you think I ought to make my speech," Jerry Castain said.

"Hell, yes," Cube Herron said. "You go right ahead. It's the only way to bring those bastards into line."

"That's what I think too," Sen. Castain said, "but I feel better, having your approval."

"You've got it," Sen. Herron said, looking defiantly around the room as though Pentagonian hordes were swarming toward them to assault some citadel of democracy they were sworn to protect—which was the way, unhappily, that the building's occupants were all too often regarded on the Hill.

At approximately the same moment in his office in the West Wing of the White House, Aleks Brodovsky was studying the message he had just received by special courier from the National Security Agency.

Its details were clear, its implications enormous. It was something he must show the President at once.

He picked up his direct line to the Oval Office, dialed and waited. After a couple of minutes the President responded; listened to the national security adviser's request; said he was talking to Terrail Venner, but why didn't Al come over. With some misgivings about whether he wanted Terry to know about this just yet, Al did. As he had anticipated, the Secretary of State was greatly alarmed and triumphantly insistent that the diplomatic approach to the problem of Nanukuvu which he had advocated so long and so unsuccessfully must now take immediate and top priority.

The President, as Al had also anticipated, did not seem so positive, though he agreed the matter was serious enough.

"Better get Loy over here right now," he said, "and let's kick it around a bit."

"Yes," Terry Venner agreed emphatically. "I should think so!"

3 When Al Brodovsky's call came, Loy Buck was feeling pretty good about the day, because late this morning Zeecy had delivered the plan for Operation Frio, and now he had just been informed by Helen Clark, who had been informed by Harry Ahmanson, that all of the service recommendations for the modification of the ALCAC had finally been received.

"They were originally going to get them in tomorrow sometime," Helen said with some amusement, "but I guess when they heard the Navy's was already completed they suddenly got busy."

"Nothing like a little service rivalry," Loy said with a chuckle. "Sometimes it *is* a good thing."

"I guess so," Helen said, sounding pleased. "Anyway, we're on our way."

"Now if you can just get DSARC to show a little speed—" the Secretary suggested.

"I've talked to them already," she said. "I told them you wanted action within forty-eight hours."

"At which," he said, "they fainted dead away."

She laughed.

"Not quite. It was a shock but I think they're really going to try."

"I hope so," Loy Buck said. "It's necessary."

How necessary, however, he did not realize until he reached the Oval Office and read the NSA message:

"Wish to advise satellite recon discloses significant activity on island of Nanukuvu which appears to consist of installation of twenty missile-launchers plus start of tree removal and leveling of earth along tops of both ridges of island. Purpose of latter unknown at this time but it would seem reasonable to assume enemy intends to build airstrips on both ridges. Extent of activity indicates plan is to accommodate all sizes aircraft up to and including largest bombers. Suggest urgent consideration."

It was signed by the director of the National Security Agency and when he had finished reading it the Secretary of Defense handed it back to Al Brodovsky with a worried frown.

"So!" the Secretary of State said, sounding triumphant. "What do you do now, Loy?"

For a moment the Secretary of Defense looked appraisingly at the Secretary of State. Then his glance swung directly to the man behind the desk and he inquired quietly,

"What do you want us to do, Mr. President?"

"What *can* you do, Mr. Secretary?" the President responded. There was silence for a moment.

"We can keep on doing what we're doing," Loy said finally, "only faster." At this Terry Venner looked scornful but Loy went quietly on. "The final battle-plan for Operation Frio was delivered to me this morning. The recommendations for modifications of the ALCAC for Project Frio reached my desk scarcely half an hour ago. There is the DSARC, or review process, to go through on those. I'm promised it will be completed by the end of the week. Then it's only a matter of manufacture and testing and we'll be on our way."

"Another seven months!" the Secretary of State predicted. "That's meeting an emergency, all right! Just about as fast as the Pentagon has met it so far!"

"I'm not defending that—" the Secretary of Defense began. The Secretary of State snorted.

"You shouldn't."

"—but I will say," Loy continued quietly, "that every effort has been made by the civilian side, and by the chairman of the Joint Chiefs, and I think, according to their lights, by the chiefs themselves, to move things along. Anyway," he said, cutting off the tart comment Terry was obviously getting ready to make, "if the National Security Agency is correct and this does indicate the start of major airstrips on Nanukuvu, then I would think the best estimate of when they will be completed is probably about six to eight months or maybe even a year. That's rugged terrain and you don't just chop off tops of mountains, even little ones, without considerable time and work. Particularly lava."

"Does that mean the Pentagon thinks it will have another six or eight months, or maybe even a year, to get ready?" the President inquired in a tone not exactly unfriendly, but pointed.

Loy shook his head.

"No, sir," he said, still quietly. "If you want us to launch an attack on Nanukuvu tomorrow, we could probably do it." His voice grew stronger suddenly, and bluntly challenging: "Do you?"

The President looked at him for a moment and then chuckled, one of his characteristic quick changes that were designed to, and usually did, throw his questioners off balance.

"Well, now, Loy," he said comfortably, "you're makin' me out to be pretty bloodthirsty, aren't you? Who said anythin' about attackin' tomorrow?"

"I seemed to detect some criticism of the Pentagon," Loy said with a not very humorous laugh—because he was apparently being confronted by the beginning of equivocation. "I thought it might be well to put it in perspective. I assume, however"—his tone grew challenging again—"that you *do* contemplate an attack *sometime*, Mr. President. You aren't planning to let them get away with it altogether, are you?"

"I'm contemplatin' pullin' their claws in some fashion," the President said promptly. "Haven't exactly decided how, yet."

"But you agree it must be done?" Loy pressed. The Chief Executive gave him a long, contemplative look.

"Somethin's got to be done, yes. What's your idea, Terry?"

"My idea," the Secretary of State said, "is to go to the U.N.—"

"We've heard all that a dozen times!" Loy snapped in a tone so impatient it stopped Terry in his tracks. An angry flush began to suffuse his lean, distinguished face. "Some small diplomatic representations have been made, haven't they? You talked to the General Secretary, Mr. President. You didn't get anywhere before. What makes you think he's going to get anywhere now, Terry?"

"Because now," Terrail Venner said stiffly, "he's beginning—at *last*—to get some of that military muscle you told him he had to have before."

"*I* told him before?" Loy Buck exclaimed. "That was his idea. He wanted it and we're getting it for him!"

"A little late in the game," Terry observed sourly.

"Now, you fellows!" the President exclaimed, chuckling again. "Just don't take each other's hair off, please, least not in my office. It *was* my idea that I needed some military clout behind me, Loy, and I want to congratulate you and your people over there, both civilian and military, on gettin' it together for me . . . finally," he added, as Loy started to relax a bit and then of course immediately tensed up again. "However, this new development down there *does* put a twist on it, doesn't it? It does make it an even tougher military problem, doesn't it? It's one," he added in a wistful tone, "that might have been easier to meet, I suppose, if the Pentagon had been just a *little* bit faster, Loy. Just a *little* bit more speedy. Just a little more efficient and a little less devoted to system. Then we could have gone after 'em on all fronts, maybe three months ago, maybe even four or five. Now things have stretched out so that we're just beginnin' to get ready as they're movin' on to the final phase—or maybe *not* the final phase. I expect the final phase they contemplate is bringin' in the nukes and then startin' to take action—all over the South Pacific. Pressure—threats —demands—nuclear blackmail. That's their agenda, or I miss my guess. And we're just now gettin' in a position where I can do somethin' about it." He looked sad. "Pity."

"Mr. President," Loy said, suddenly fed up with this characteristic combination of shrewd analysis and deliberate emotional charade, "whatever the shortcomings of the Pentagon, and I certainly make no brief for them and fight them in every way a Secretary can, the fact is we are, here and now, facing a dangerous situation that is suddenly being escalated drastically by the enemy—a quantum leap. As I said, it will be at least six months, probably a year, before the airstrips can be finished. We will be ready in the Pentagon in perhaps three months, if all goes well, to support whatever action you wish to take." He paused and looked squarely at the man behind the desk. *"Are you prepared to accept all the consequences of that action should you decide to take it?"*

The President gave him a look that for just a second was frankly angry. Then instantly he relaxed and smiled.

"Well, now, Loy," he said mildly, "I don't know that I need to be put on the spot like that. I took my oath of office just as we all did. I'm here to protect, preserve and defend the Constitution and the country just as much as anybody. If I decide to do it, then I decide to do it and take the consequences. Don't know as I need to be cross-examined about it."

"I'm sorry, Mr. President," Loy said, not sorry at all. "I apologize if that was how it sounded. But we really must know if you want us to go ahead. If not, we can save what is going to be an increasing amount of time and manpower and devote them to all the other pressing things that face us around the globe."

"And I don't like to be lectured on how to do my job, either," the President remarked, more sharply but again not revealing what Loy knew must be a deep annoyance. But damn it, somebody had to pin him down and Terry Venner sure as hell didn't have the nerve, or the desire. "You're not back at IBM, you know." He chuckled again. *I'm* the boss, here."

"Yes, Mr. President," Loy said, not giving an inch. "We still need to know what your marching orders are."

Again the President gave him a long look, shook his head and chuckled.

"Stubborn cuss!" he exclaimed. "I swear you're a stubborn cuss! Just keep on doin' what you're doin', Loy, and that will be fine with me. Just keep on doin' what you're doin'."

"But—" Loy began doggedly.

"Can't you see," the Secretary of State demanded, "that he can't do anything, really, until he's sure of what the Pentagon can accomplish? You say you'll be ready in another three months. Well, you haven't been in seven. How can he depend on you? The diplomatic solution," he said, his thin, aristocratic face looking at its most puritanically disapproving, "was, and remains, the only really viable one."

"In combination," the President said. "In combination, let's give Loy that. But if it's to be done in combination, Loy, you fellows over there are goin' to have to move right along, now. No more stumblin' and stallin'. Chop, chop!"

It was Loy's turn to give him a long look. Finally he nodded slowly.

"Yes, sir," he said levelly. "With your vigorous support, which I now see we have, we will be able to maintain and increase the momentum we have begun to achieve."

The President uttered a startled little laugh, obviously thought for a second of picking up the gauntlet, decided to let it pass.

"Good man!" he exclaimed approvingly. "Good man! Let that be an example to you, Terry. Let's get everything on line for the diplomatic approach too and then we'll let 'em have it!"

"State has been ready from the first moment," Terrail Venner said with a sniff.

"Vangie," Loy said when he got back across the river, "did you ever deal with a sleight-of-hand artist?"

"Not like you have to," Vangie said, knowing where he had been.

"Thank your stars for that," he said. "I'll bet—" his eyes narrowed—"I'll bet if this thing gets to the public—"

"It's a miracle it hasn't," she murmured.

"Yes. I'll bet if it does, he'll turn tail and run so fast we'll hardly see him."

"But how can he?" Vangie inquired, alarmed. "He just can't!"

"If there's a way," Loy said grimly, "he'll find it. Particularly with an election coming along next year."

"I hope not," she said. "Oh, I hope not."

I hope not too, he thought grimly as she went out, but I'm damned if I can see him doing anything else.

And so where did that leave the Pentagon?

The Department of Defense had its faults and many of them, and he was the first to admit it; but it also suffered on too many occasions from mixed signals from the White House. What was it supposed to do now? What *could* it do now, except proceed along the lines it was going, prepare the mission and hope that by the time it was organized and ready, a firm decision would have been reached in the White House to go ahead? He couldn't stop everything now. The internal momentum, though sluggish, had still reached a point where it would be almost more difficult to stop than to continue. And there remained the basic fact of what was happening on Nanukuvu. Nothing had diminished the seriousness and danger of that. It was now much greater.

He was too honest not to admit to himself that the Pentagon's slowness had a great deal to do with this. There were all the ifs: *if* they had organized a quickie mission, as Gen. Stokes and Gen. Tock in particular had wanted to do —*if* he had ruthlessly ruled out unnecessary modifications of the ALCAC and told them to go with what they had—*if* he had presented the President with an assurance of military backup in the first forty-eight hours and thus in a sense forced his hand—*if* the system had been scrapped for once and things had moved with the urgency warranted by the threat of the whole South Pacific basin implicit in the enemy's obvious determination to create a South Seas Gibraltar on the once-peaceful island of A'afaloa and Nuku'ofa—then perhaps the enemy could have been forced to abandon his plans and the whole episode, unknown to the world, could have been quietly disposed of without the added, and perhaps now insurmountable, hazards brought about by delay.

"Unknown to the world." That was the key. Terry Venner had wanted to go public from the first, take it to the U.N., try traditional methods, invite the usual uproarious condemnation of United States actions which somehow, by some miracle of tortuous rationale in the strange, erratic body, was almost never applied to the often vicious actions of the enemy. The end result would have been, if past patterns prevailed, de facto U.N. recognition of the occupation of Nanukuvu. It might still be, if it came to that. But as long as the episode was "unknown to the world," there was still a chance to work it out—*if* the President would support the efforts, however slow and imperfect, of the Pentagon and, when the Pentagon was ready, move with the decisiveness that the Pentagon, in the final analysis, desired.

The President had remarked that he, like all of them, had taken his oath to protect the country. So, the Secretary reflected with some bitterness, had the leaders, civilian and military, of the Department of Defense. But the President had the final say. His was the final leadership, his the necessary impetus for which there was no substitute.

God damn him, let *him* exercise it, then!

The Secretary's foul mood was not improved by a call from Gen. McCune, who passed along word that the Hill at last was on the trail of Frio, and that they might expect, sometime within the next twenty-four hours, a speech by Jerry Castain that would probably, in Zeecy's words, "blow the whole thing sky-high."

Loy matched him gloom for gloom by relating the contents of the NSA message and asking him to pass it on immediately to the chiefs. That would make six of them down in the dumps.

As a dismayed and disgruntled Secretary, bearing the added burden of all this difficult news, was being chauffeured home to Imogene and the small dinner she was giving for twelve including the Venners, a disgusted Burt San-strom was abandoning, for today at least, his fruitless attempts to track down the mysterious "South Pacific mission" first mentioned by Mario Escondido.

Burt's sources, of whom he did not have very many in a Pentagon generally hostile to his adversarial approaches, had been no more informative than Gen. Ahmanson. He had tried all the chiefs directly, and finally the chairman him-self, and all had been blandly unhelpful. Not even Skip Framberg, whom Burt considered to be as much of a friend as he ever expected to have in the building, had been forthcoming. Skip's attitude was funny, Burt often thought: supposedly they both had the same objective, to puncture the pretenses and disclose the shortcomings of the military. But when it came to the pinch Skip rarely gave him anything of value. It was as though Skip had his own priorities and was jealous of his own territory—as though he felt the Pentagon was his special area and he would use his own means and his own contacts to expose what he believed to be its errors. This was especially annoying to Burt this time, because Skip had hinted that he did know something.

"But," he had said, before ringing off rather summarily, Burt thought, "I'm not ready to go into that just yet."

Burt would have been even more upset if he could have seen Skip right now, sitting in an obscure little bar in Alexandria, not too far from Old Town where he lived, talking to Red Roberts.

He hadn't wanted to meet at his house, he told Red, because his wife and kids would be underfoot. But he did think it was about time to tell whatever he knew about this mysterious Frio thing that was kicking around.

"In fact, I may be part of it," he said, with a certain pride that struck Red as somewhat ironic given Skip's ostentatious hostility toward the powers that be. "I've put in a proposal to modify the ALCAC and the Secretary says they may use it."

"Modify the ALCAC?" Red echoed, surprised. "That means an amphibious landing, right?"

"I presume so," Skip said. "I don't know exactly, but that's my guess."

"Why do they want to modify it?" Red inquired. "I thought it was a perfectly good piece of equipment, given the fact it's a bit redundant. Why modify?"

Skip shrugged.

"I haven't been able to find out. Anyway, they do, and Buck said he might back my version of it." He frowned. "That was over three months ago, though, and nothing's happened yet."

"I guess you and the top brass are getting along better these days," Red Roberts said with the flattery he knew could always loosen up these whistle-blowers. "Isn't everybody who can kick 'em in the balls and wind up in E Ring. 'Special assistant,' too. How about that!"

Skip struggled not to look smug, as Red had known he would.

"Well," he said modestly, "I guess Loy felt he couldn't keep me in purgatory *forever.*"

"I should hope *not,*" Red said scornfully. "A valuable man like you? So what about this Frio business, anyway? Have you discovered what it's all about?"

"No," Skip said slowly, "except I've been told by a very high source—not the SecDef—that it's some sort of mission that's going to be undertaken on some island somewhere south. It could be the Caribbean or the South Atlantic—or it could be the South Pacific. I'm very much inclined to think it's the South Pacific, myself. I mean, everything's pretty quiet at the moment in the Caribbean and the South Atlantic. It's almost got to be the South Pacific, just by logical elimination."

"Quiet down there, too, isn't it?" Red Roberts suggested. Skip looked skeptical.

"They're stirring around," he said. "I get hints of it, now that I'm back upstairs. And I was told that this Frio mission is supposed to get them out of . . . 'that island down there.' It fits."

" 'Frio,' " Red said ironically. " 'Cold.' South Pacific. Well, that figures. That's the way they think. Have you told Delight Jones all this? She's been muttering about 'Frio' off and on for months." He smiled, not without satisfaction. "Hank Milhaus won't give her the time of day and nobody else official in the Pentagon will talk to her."

"Yes, I know," Skip said. "She often doesn't get anywhere. She's too raucous. They clam up. That's why I agreed to talk to you. I suspected what you had in mind. You're respectable. You'll be able to do something with it."

"I hope so," Red said, "if I can get a little corroboration elsewhere. No reflection, but you know I just need one more good source and I can write it. Who would you suggest?"

Skip gave him an intent look.

"Can I trust you?"

"Hell, yes," Red Roberts said. "Everybody in the Pentagon trusts me—" which was true—"that's why I'm the damned good reporter I am. I don't let 'em down."

Skip took a deep breath.

"Well," he said, "you could try *very close* to Loy. Not quite all the way up there—but *close.*"

"Not Bob Cathcart!" Red said softly. "It's common knowledge they barely speak, but I didn't know he'd go around spilling any secrets."

"He didn't mean to," Skip said with a disparaging little smile. "He's not really a very smart man even if he is—" his voice became scornful—"one of the stars of the military-industrial complex. Give him a try. You may catch him off balance. You know how to do it."

"Yes," Red agreed, "I think I do."

Half an hour later, back in his own apartment in Rosslyn, locked in his study away from his wife of thirty years and her liking for some of television's more lurid family sagas, he was on the phone to the Deputy Secretary of Defense in his big house in Georgetown, not far from Loy Buck's.

Fortunately he was in, not of course having been invited to the Bucks', and not having any other engagement this evening.

"Just a mo'," he said. "Got to take this on another line, can't hear a thing with this machine squawking away . . . Red, how the hell are you? Sure you don't want the Secretary? Nobody ever calls *me.* I'm flattered."

I hope you are, Red thought, that always makes things easier.

"Mr. Secretary," he said, "I want to talk to you about a serious matter."

"What's that?" Bob Cathcart said, and Red could see in mind's eye his big, florid face becoming grave with the weight of the world. "You know I'm always glad to help."

Red spoke calmly but rapidly, mentally keeping his fingers crossed.

"I want to know what the timetable is for the attack on that South Pacific island where the Soviet subs are holed in. Got any idea?"

For a moment there was stunned silence on the other end of the line. Then Bob Cathcart said explosively, "I don't know what the hell you're talking about!"

"Frio," Red Roberts said matter-of-factly. "I want to know about Frio. Somebody told me you know all about it."

"I don't know a thing," Bob Cathcart protested stoutly.

"I have enough to go on, you know," Red said quietly, "I just need to get a few details clarified. Is it true they're building a permanent base down there and we've decided to take it out?"

Again there was a pause and then Secretary Cathcart let out an angry sigh.

"I've been against the damned thing from the first," he said. His voice dropped, took on the confidential tone of official Washington going off the record. "Now, listen," he said softly, "I can't answer all your questions directly but maybe I can steer you so you won't go too far off base. Why don't you ask me a few?"

So Red did, and with a series of grunts, pauses, silences and significant sounds of one kind and another from the Deputy Secretary, was able to put together what he recognized as an incomplete but pretty good story. It would be enough to flush them out of the woodwork, he told himself with satisfaction as he filed it to New York around 9 P.M. Out of the flurry of Pentagon denials, leaks and general confusion, the full truth would begin to emerge.

He had written a fair story, because he always did, and he carefully balanced it with all the reasons why U.S. action might be justified. His lifelong dedication had been to get a good, honest, objective story, as much as objectivity could be achieved. He was not concerned with the ideology of it, as he knew Delight and many of their younger colleagues were.

It did not occur to him that from his relatively pure motives might come something as damaging to his country's purposes as anything she might write from what he regarded to be her less noble ones.

In his bachelor apartment on Capitol Hill three blocks from the Capitol, the junior Senator from Indiana was equally busy as the evening drew on.

He had decided that if Capt. Vernon B. Muller, buddy of the late Hague Smith, were returning from a "training mission" of any substantial duration south of Hawaii, he would probably have the rest of the day off.

The first time he called the captain's home he was told by a very youthful voice that Daddy would be back in about an hour.

The second time he called Mrs. Muller told him she expected the captain about an hour after that.

He cooked himself a small meal, ate it hurriedly, watched television for a little while and called for the third time. The captain was puzzled to be hearing from a United States Senator but rapidly warmed up as Jerry explained his purpose.

Cautiously and carefully but obviously wanting to be as candid and helpful as he could, Capt. Muller confirmed what Madeline Smith had said and added a few details of his own that he had not told her.

At the end of his recital, which was short, compact and efficient, as Jerry imagined he must be from the level, decisive sound of his voice, he said with his first show of nervousness, "Of course you won't tell anybody I told you this, Senator? My tail will be in everybody's gunsights if you do."

"Certainly not," Jerry said. He chuckled. "Senators don't have to reveal all their sources. They just *know* things."

"That's good," the captain said, sounding amused and quite at home with him by now. "I do think," he added seriously, "that this is a very important thing. I think we've got to get those bastards out of there, but I don't think we can do it with a handful of helicopters from *Dominant.* We've got to go all-out."

"We've got to make *some* decision fast," Jerry said. "That's for sure."

They parted with grateful thanks from him and an invitation to drop in and see him if they ever got to Washington.

"As a matter of fact," the captain said, "I'm due for Pentagon duty just about six months from now."

"Great!" Jerry exclaimed, always aware of the value of good sources in the building. "We'll get together then."

"We will," Capt. Muller agreed. "Maybe by then the bastards will be gone and everything will be peaceful again on the island."

"Let's hope," Jerry Castain said. "You be careful yourself, now."

"I don't take chances," the captain assured him, having just done so in what he considered a good cause. "See you in D.C."

Jerry went to his desk and pecked out his speech on his battered but beloved old typewriter. He did not intend to deliver it until he had checked it out with Adm. Stahlman. He fully intended, if Bumpy leveled with him, to withhold it if Bumpy requested that he do so on the ground of national security. Jerry was alert but not, he fairly told himself, irresponsible.

Reached at Tingey House shortly before midnight just as he got back from a dinner at the Naval Academy in Annapolis, Bumpy regretfully but firmly decided to stonewall it.

"I'm sorry you won't tell me, Bumpy," Jerry said, "because I think you're making a mistake. Have you discussed this with your colleagues on the JCS?"

"We've had some discussion," Bumpy said cautiously.

"Recently?"

"Fairly recently," Bumpy said, sounding uncomfortable as he recalled Zeecy's warning phone call that had reached him in the midst of dinner at the academy.

"And you all agreed to be uncooperative," Sen. Castain said.

"Jerry," Bumpy said, "that isn't fair. We agreed that it would be best at this time not to say anything at all about it. And," he added firmly, "I don't think you should either."

"Sooner or later," Jerry said, "somebody's going to. Better a friend of the Pentagon than an enemy. Right?"

"I still don't like it," Adm. Stahlman said.

"Neither do I, Bumpy," Sen. Castain said. "That's why I think it's time to speak out."

By 1 A.M. he had his notes in shape and ready to be typed by his secretary first thing in the morning. He was sorry to have to do it, but he didn't think the

JCS attitude as reflected by the Navy gave him any option. He felt there was really nothing for it now but to use the forum the voters of Indiana had twice kindly given him, and shoot the works.

Bumpy Stahlman, worried and upset, set up a conference call as soon as Jerry hung up. Everybody was home by then and both Ham and Tick sounded as though they had already been sleeping. Brash Burford sounded a little muffled, which Bumpy took to mean that he had also been asleep. In any event, they were all alert and listening intently when he told them stonewalling hadn't worked and that Jerry was definitely going ahead with his speech.

"So," he said, "what do we do now?"

"Continue to stonewall," Ham Stokes said. "What can they do about it?"

"It depends on how much resultant pressure there is from the Hill and the media," Zeecy said. "They can do a lot of things."

"Investigate," Tick said.

"Exactly," Zeecy said. "Make headlines. Shout. Bang on drums. Heap big scandal, another damned Pentagon cover-up. Oh, they can have fun."

"They will," Brash predicted bleakly. "Give 'em half an inch and they'll take a mile."

"So we tell them *all*, is that it?" Ham Stokes inquired sarcastically. "How can we do that without destroying the entire mission?"

"I get the sense," Bumpy said unhappily, "that Jerry thinks it may have failed already and it may be a good thing to destroy it."

"It sure as hell can't succeed with the sort of rumpus he may touch off."

"It's *got* to succeed," Ham said. "We can't have that kind of a base down there, subs, missile-launchers and *two* airstrips, for God's sake! We've *got* to get rid of it! As I said," he couldn't resist adding, "on day one. If the Pentagon had moved as fast as *I* wanted it to move, we wouldn't be in this bind right now."

"All right!" Brash said with a sudden anger that startled them. "Knock it off! We've all been guilty of delay. It doesn't do any damned good to point fingers now."

"Particularly," Bumpy came to his aid stoutly, "when most of the delay was simply due to the system. The Navy's part of it moved along in good time, it seemed to me. Certainly I haven't been conscious of deliberate delays on anyone's part."

"That's putting your finger on it, Bumpy," Ham Stokes said dourly. "It wasn't *deliberate* on anybody's part. That's the whole point."

"Well," Zeecy said, "I think we can leave all that to some other time, Ham, if you don't mind. Brash is right: no use pointing the finger now. What we've got to do is present a united front when the shouting starts."

"And do what with the mission?" Gen. Tock inquired. "Abort it?"

"Keep right on with it," Gen. McCune said grimly, "until we get orders from higher authority to stop it. I predict we'll known pretty soon after Jerry speaks what the situation will be on that."

"If we abort it and let that island go by default," Gen. Stokes said, "we deserve whatever we get in the South Pacific."

"I agree with you," Gen. McCune said. "But that isn't in our hands, is it?"

Tired, dismayed and apprehensive, they bade one another goodnight. Bumpy went back to his lonely bed to read briefly in a mystery story before hitting the light. Tick rolled in beside sleeping Doreen and was already beginning to snore again as his head hit the pillow. Ham listened patiently but without comment as Zenia completed her lengthy tale of what her women's action committee had talked about tonight. And Brash, tiptoeing as quietly as possible, got himself a glass of water, turned out the lights and slid quietly in beside Vi, who was breathing with an even, deep rhythm that seemed to indicate sleep. It did not, however.

He stifled a sigh and started to roll over on his side away from her but she stopped him with a hand on his shoulder.

"Are we at war?" she asked quietly and he promptly turned back to place a protective arm across her breast.

"Heavens, no," he said with a startled half-laugh. "What gave you that idea?"

"Oh, the late call," she said. "Every time you get one I have this fantasy that you'll have heard that the world is blowing up, but in order not to wake me you'll come tiptoeing back and go to sleep again as though nothing had happened. That isn't what occurred this time, is it?"

"You have the damnedest—" he began, amused. "Are you serious?"

"Quite," she said, and he knew she was. "I often think that, it's just the way I'm sure it's going to happen—if it ever does. Did the call bring it any closer?"

"Possibly," he said quietly. "It's always coming closer, isn't it, really? Day by day."

"But I thought you were stopping it," she said, staring up into the darkness. "You and Tick and Ham and Bumpy and Zeecy . . . and Loy . . . and the President . . . and all the brave men and women in the services . . . and the Congress . . . and—well, just about everybody. We all *want* to stop it, don't we?"

"You know that," he said. *"You know that."*

"Yes, I know," she agreed. "It's just the way I think, lately. Gloomy. Not like me . . . maybe," she said, startling him and making him hold his breath for what might come next, "it's because I'm sick."

"Oh?" he said cautiously, heart beginning to pound. "Are you?"

"You know I am," she said.

He nodded in the dark and then realized she couldn't see or hear that. "Yes," he said quietly, "I know. But I didn't know—"

She sighed.

"That I know? Yes, I've known ever since that day in the snow, and that was seven months ago. I've known ever since then and I haven't wanted to—to bother you . . ."

"Oh, Vi," he said, almost crying, holding her close. *"Bother me?* How in the world could I be *bothered* by you needing me? That's what I'm here for, isn't it? That's what I've always been here for . . . I hope," he said.

"You have been," she said, voice trembling but not quite giving in to tears herself. "Always and always, my dearest dear. Always and always . . ."

She drew in a deep, trembling breath and when she spoke again, sounded a little stronger.

"Dorry was here for lunch today. We had a long talk. She told me about their son—he has Alzheimer's. Isn't that awful, Brash, to have Alzheimer's at his age?" Brash made some sort of muffled assent, unable to articulate. She spoke very clearly then. "It sort of puts things in perspective, you know? At—sixty." She stopped for a moment but he didn't dare say anything, only waited, heart thudding painfully. "Brash," she said, "I think you'd better take me to Walter Reed tomorrow. I think I'd better go. Will you do that?"

"Of course," he said, beginning to cry openly now. "Of course I will, darling."

Then she cried too, and they lay very close together for a very long time, and he thought no more about the problem of Nanukuvu or the chairmanship of the JCS or anything else but the fact that the central light of his life was growing gradually dimmer until presently it would go out altogether.

4

Next day Red Roberts' story appeared in *The Wall Street Journal* and Jerry Castain made his speech in the Senate. Taken together they were the end of secrecy about Nanukuvu and the beginning of a rearguard action by the Pentagon which was not to end until Frio had reached the only logical conclusion possible under the circumstances.

Red's story was headlined U.S. SECRET MISSION TO ATTACK SOVIET SUB BASE IN PACIFIC?

"Washington—The United States is planning a secret attack on a Soviet submarine base in the South Pacific, Pentagon sources confirmed today. The attack could come within the next few months.

"The base, located on an unidentified island somewhere in the general vicinity of the Gilbert and Mariana islands, is believed to have been under occupation by Soviet air and naval forces since last March. The full extent of Soviet fortifications cannot be determined at the moment. But official sources who wished to remain anonymous indicated that they are 'extensive.'

"The base apparently is being planned as a major strategic bastion of Soviet power in the entire South Pacific basin which could threaten not only the U.S. position there but Micronesia, Australia, New Zealand, Indonesia and Malaysia as well. It will presumably house an unknown but strategically significant number of nuclear submarines.

" 'If successfully completed,' one official said, 'it will give them a virtual hammerlock on the South Pacific.'

"U.S. plans to meet this potential threat in an area which heretofore has been regarded as something of an 'American lake,' in the words of this source, are said to center around a mission known in the Pentagon as 'Frio.' The name, which in Spanish means 'cold,' was obviously selected to deflect Soviet suspicions concerning a possible U.S. response to the new base.

"According to international law experts in Washington [and Red had conscientiously called a couple he knew at the Georgetown Center for Strategic and International Studies before putting his story and himself to bed last night] sovereignty in the area is 'not very clearly defined.'

"The United States has treaty obligations there, these experts said, and the general assumption ever since World War II has been that American power provided a definite, if benign and rather vague, protective shield against Soviet encroachment. However, 'there are myriads of islands out there and lines in many cases have not been clearly drawn.'

"Under these circumstances, the experts said, it would be 'entirely possible to justify Soviet expansionism in the eyes of the world.' It is obvious, however, that Pentagon planners do not regard it in such a legalistically justifiable light. Reportedly they see it as a direct threat not only to the entire region but also as a direct challenge to American influence over a vast portion of the earth's surface.

"On that basis, the mission called 'Frio' has reportedly enlisted top concern and top personnel in the Pentagon over the past several months in an organized drive to mount a response that will ultimately be able to bring about Soviet abandonment of a base which it is believed has already advanced very far toward completion.

"The timing for such a possible response is not known at present. However, it is believed by anonymous Pentagon officials that it could be 'relatively soon.' "

Which did not seem to Red to be swinging too widely, though of course when Loy Buck, Zeecy McCune and the rest arrived at their desks to read the article as clipped and reprinted on the front page of the *Early Bird* they almost literally went through the roof.

"Well!" Hank Milhaus snapped when he met Red coming to work in the corridor outside the pressroom shortly after 9 A.M., "I hope to hell you're satisfied, you traitorous bastard!"

To this Red, who had begun his professional life as a responsible journalist about the time Hank was entering grammar school, at first contemplated an equally sharp retort, then thought better of it.

"I'm not a traitor, Hank," he said mildly, "and I think you'll come to regret that and apologize to me, when you stop to think about it. I'm just a reporter doing his job. I'm sorry if it's got you guys upset."

"Upset!" Hank exclaimed, beginning to calm down a little. "Loy's up the wall and Zeecy's chewing the rug. What did you expect them to do, sing hallelujah?"

"I gather my sources were pretty accurate, then," Red said.

"We're going to get them," Hank promised grimly, "if it's the last thing we do."

"Good luck," Red said. "But the people have a right to know."

"Right to know, shit!" Hank said bitterly. "You people think you have the right to kill American boys just to get a headline!"

"We're not the ones who can order the killing, Hank," Red Roberts said quietly. "That's generally done on E Ring."

To which the assistant secretary for public affairs made a loud sound of incoherent annoyance and disappeared into his office.

For the rest of the morning phones were busy all over the building as the media attempted to track down and match Red's exclusive story. He received the fitting accolade around eleven-thirty when he went to the Pik-Quik for an early lunch.

"Well!" a familiar voice said loudly in his ear. "If you aren't the great big journalist, man. I suppose you think you scooped me blind!"

"I seem to have, Delight," he said calmly. "Shall I put an extra cup of coffee on my tray for you? Come and sit down and let's have a talk. Maybe we can help each other develop my story."

"*Your* story!" she exclaimed loudly, so that all the colonels, majors, lieutenants, enlisted men and women in line turned around and told each interestedly who he was, all having also perused that universal first-thing-in-the-morning Pentagon reading, the *Early Bird*. "*Your* story! I've been after that story for months!"

"Well, you didn't get it, did you?" he asked tartly, putting her cup on his tray and adding another for Herb Horowitz, who had just appeared in a distant doorway to be greeted by a wildly frantic wave from his editor.

"You did a lot of steaming around but you weren't able to crack it. You got a hint somewhere but you weren't able to get any farther. Doesn't seem to me you have any call to be angry." He smiled wryly. "I'm getting enough flak from E Ring without you helping them pile it on."

"That's the *last* thing I want to do," she said as he paid and they made their way to the table Herb had staked out for them, "help E Ring! God, *no!* The day I help E Ring—" she gave a sudden cackle that made a couple of solemn majors eating together at the next table almost literally jump—"well, Red, that's the day you can tell 'em little old Delight has gone *off her rocker*—'round the *bend* —and bottoms *up!*"

"Thanks for the coffee, Red," Herb said, paying no attention. "I thought it was a damned good story, myself. Sorry we weren't able to beat you to it—"

"*Should* have," his boss said sourly but he ignored it.

"—but I'm glad you got it, anyway. It's opened the door. Now maybe we can stop the damned nonsense before it goes any further. Do you have any leads to follow up for tomorrow's paper?"

"Not yet," Red said, "but I have a feeling something may develop during the day."

At approximately twelve-fifteen in the Senate, it did.

"Mr. President," Sen. Castain said as soon as he could get the floor after the regular quorum call that always followed immediately upon their convening, "I rise to place in the *Congressional Record* an article from this morning's *Wall Street Journal* which I strongly advise all Senators to read if they haven't already."

"Without objection," said Sen. Dominick in the chair, "it is so ordered."

"And, Mr. President," Jerry said, "I would like to make a few remarks of my own in connection with it . . . First of all, Mr. President, I wish to highly commend the enterprise of one of America's most experienced and best-known journalists, William 'Red' Roberts, *The Wall Street Journal*'s longtime Pentagon correspondent, in breaking this story of what is apparently a clandestine Pentagon move that could embroil the United States most dangerously and gravely in a confrontation with the Soviet Union, very far from our shores.

"In an important sense, his account ties in with, illuminates and supports the remarks I had already prepared last night for delivery to the Senate today. You will see that I begin from a more personal and human episode, but we both arrive at the same point: the mysterious mission called 'Frio.' "

Thirty-four Senators had been on the floor when the quorum call had been dispensed with halfway down the list, but as word spread to the cloakroom and offices, many more began to drift in. By the time he finished ninety-five of the one hundred were there, listening intently.

"My story," he said, "begins approximately seven months ago and concerns a constituent of mine, a young Navy helicopter pilot, Lt. Hague Smith, who was assigned to duty on the aircraft carrier *Dominant* in the South Pacific. According to the Navy, Lt. Smith was a fine young man and had an exemplary record. I speak in the past tense, Mr. President, because Hague Smith died as a result of that duty. Out of his death, apparently, came the beginnings of 'Frio.'

"I am informed that Hague Smith was a brave and courageous young officer. He was also, it appears, an exemplar of that extra edge of daring and enterprise that can sometimes lead young Americans in service into areas dangerously beyond the rigid confines of duty. This is a marvelous quality in our young men —and women—in uniform, but it sometimes, tragically, leads to consequences they do not foresee. Hague Smith, in short, was a very brave young man but in some degree, perhaps, something of a reckless one. But for this quality of his, however, the United States would not have been apprised so soon of what is apparently underway in the far South Pacific—and would not have begun so soon to undertake the actions to meet it which are now apparently going forward in the Pentagon."

He paused to take a sip of water and added gravely, "I leave it to Senators to judge, on the basis of Red Roberts' revelations and mine, whether these actions in the Pentagon are a good or a bad thing . . . ."

The chamber was silent now, his audience enrapt.

"Hague Smith was on general scouting duty, employed on regular patrols out from his carrier to track, both visually and with all the sophisticated sounding gear with which a certain class of Navy helicopter is now equipped, the presence of Soviet submarines in the area. We do not know—at least we don't know in this body, the Navy may know but the Navy at the moment isn't saying— whether Hague Smith actually noted the presence of such submarines. He did, however, notice something out of the ordinary on a small island which is apparently named Nankoo or Nanvoo or something similar. This island, as Mr. Roberts has accurately reported, is in the general vicinity of the Marianas and the Gilberts, lying somewhere between them.

"As such it is indeed, as the Pentagon has evidently decided, of major strategic importance in commanding sea and airways to many important areas in the South Pacific basin.

"Although warned against it by his superiors on the carrier *Dominant,* Hague Smith went in over the island—not wisely, perhaps, but courageously. He was undoubtedly deeply concerned by what appeared to be unusual signs of enemy activity and he wanted to find out exactly what was going on, for the sake of his country. For this show of enterprise and daring, against orders but giving evidence of that courage we like to think of as characteristically American, he paid with his life. He was, in short, shot down, not in time of war but in time of what is known nowadays, perhaps euphemistically, as 'peace.'

"Following his death, the first steps of 'Frio' were taken. I am informed that *Dominant* has been kept in the area; that regular patrols now survey the island; that visually by satellite and by other sophisticated means of detection, constant watch is maintained on Nankoo, or Nanvoo.

"I am also informed that Soviet progress toward making this a virtually impregnable bastion in the South Pacific has proceeded at a very rapid pace.

"I refer you for the rest of the story to Mr. Roberts' account, which I have been able to confirm independently this morning, as perhaps some of you have too, from sources in the Pentagon.

"There *is* a mission, or project, or operation, perhaps several, known by the generic name 'Frio.' There *is* a plan, or purpose, or intention, to respond to the Soviet occupation of the island of Nankoo or Nanvoo in order to prevent its being transformed into an impregnable Soviet base in the South Pacific. There is, possibly, even a time-schedule, either on paper or generally in the minds of the Secretary of Defense, the Joint Chiefs of Staff and probably the President, as to when such an attempt to thwart Soviet intentions might be made.

"But, Senators," he said quietly, "the questions now arise:

"*Is it too late?*

"*Has the Pentagon waited too long?*

"*Can any counter-operation, however well-prepared and well-staged, successfully dislodge the Soviets from their bastion seven months after they started building it?*

"*Is it worth the time, the money and most importantly the brave young men who would have to be sacrificed, to remove what may after all be a relatively minor threat to national security—since the island is so far away and the effort to recapture it—now, having waited so long—would inevitably be so great?*

"*And, finally, do we, really, have the legal and moral right to conduct an operation, even if it did succeed, in an area where we have neither actual sovereignty nor a clearly-defined right to be there?*

"These, Senators," he said, picking up his notes and placing them neatly together as he concluded, "are questions to think about, as we contemplate the mission known as 'Frio.' "

There followed an angry debate, duplicated almost word for word on the other side of the Capitol when the news reached the House.

The Administration did receive some strong and vigorous support from those who pledged to back it in whatever it might deem necessary to meet the new situation in the South Pacific.

From those, more numerous, who for reasons or convictions of their own shared Sen. Castain's misgivings, it received strong and vigorous condemnation for even daring to *think* about meeting the new situation in the South Pacific.

Out of Jerry's nimble mind and facile pen had come the famous "Five Questions" that from now on would determine the national and international controversy that immediately erupted, and ultimately determine its outcome; and also determine, in one degree or another, the destinies of those in the building most closely involved with Frio.

There were now no more months in which the building might, at its own sweet pace and in its own sweet way, gather itself ponderously together to meet the problem of Nanukuvu.

The system had been true to itself and in so doing had lost its control of time.

Time now was on the side of its opponents foreign and domestic.

The hurricane that followed, as both the building and the White House had accurately feared, was tremendous and blew down many things, though it could not, of course, blow down the building.

The building stood, as it always has and probably always will until the ultimate catastrophe lays it low. But it suffered much—and more importantly, the United States of America, as so often before, suffered much—from the building's redundancies, its delays, its institutional opposition to reform and its adamant devotion to the system.

Red Roberts and Jerry Castain were only the first heralds of a mighty blast to come.

On the island work proceeded, right on schedule.

Four

1

Next morning the SecDef, as had been his practice at IBM, sought distraction from his major headache in other worries. Sometimes, he had found, they could be made to counterbalance one another. Sometimes one would even obliterate the other, temporarily. He hoped for a little while that this would be the case today.

But how could it, with the whole world clamoring?

Joe Strang had called him after the debate that followed Jerry's speech, very upset. So had Al Brodovsky, calmer but deeply concerned. So had the Secretary of State, worried and basically too decent to gloat. So, finally, had the President, his true mood, as always, impossible to determine. And so had Gen. Zoren Chace McCune, angry and frustrated.

The reports of the congressional debate that had come to Loy and Zeecy were thorough, as they should have been. The Office of the Secretary of Defense had its representatives on the Hill: at the time of Nanukuvu two on the Senate side, two on the House side. The Army had its representatives: two on each side. The Navy had its representatives: three on each side. The Air Force had its representatives: three on each side. The Marines had theirs: two on each side. Not to be outdone, the joint staff of the Joint Chiefs had theirs: two on each side.

From time to time in the past, and no doubt in the future, this small army of Defense Department observers of the actions of the Congress of the United States fluctuated in size a bit, but always each entity within the department had its own individual representation on the Hill. The excuse was that liaison officers were needed to answer members' requests for help with constituents' problems. Presumably the requests could not be handled by telephone directly to the building.

There also was the matter referred to euphemistically (America lived in the Age of Euphemism these days) as "making sure our point of view is adequately presented to the Congress"—in other words, lobbying. It cost the taxpayers quite a packet to keep the Congress informed of all the Pentagon's diverse views and the Pentagon of the 535 views of Congress. But everybody *was* informed, there was no doubt of that.

Such was the case with the uproar that followed Jerry Castain's speech and Red Roberts' article. The sum total of all the information reaching members of Congress was that the Defense Department had undertaken something behind their backs and by God they were going to find out what it was and why. The sum total of all the information reaching the Defense Department was that Jerry and Red between them had stirred up one hell of a row that was going to cause the department and the Administration big trouble.

Nanukuvu, which the Secretary of Defense had once thought of as a gnat on the elephant's hide, had now finally become the tiger on its back. Suddenly it was at the forefront of his concerns.

Not that there were not others, of course. The life and work of the Pentagon went on.

There was the Strategic Defense Initiative inherited from previous days, tagged by the media instantly and invidiously at its birth as "Star Wars" because the building had not been smart enough to preempt attack with some such friendlier term as "Space Shield." It was now in its advanced testing stage, a hoped-for vast net of missiles, lasers, satellites and other far-out items that were supposed to work together with absolute millisecond precision to intercept incoming Soviet missiles and explode them in space. Nobody knew whether it would work or not, but it was a great toy, costing billions upon billions, trailing behind it a huge supporting army of military, scientists, contractors, members of congress and their constituents, all working hard, and profitably, upon it.

There was the vast, and vastly complicated, communications system that was supposed to keep the President and the Pentagon—assuming they still existed after a Soviet attack, a rather chancy supposition—in command of whatever United States forces still remained around the globe. The chances of its working after a nuclear attack were also chancy, but it too was a great toy, costing billions upon billions and trailing behind it the same kind of camp-followers, all working hard, and profitably, upon it.

Then there were the more "conventional" weapons systems, the "strategic" or nuclear systems, the missiles and nuclear warheads that could destroy the world a hundredfold and by now were so ordinary in the minds of Pentagon planners that they were virtually "conventional" themselves. The ritual there was automatic and had become almost boring over the decades: just keep adding, building, piling up and piling up, horror upon horror, it's all a meaningless numbers game anyway once you get past the first hundred or so, so just keep going.

And the officially "conventional" systems, the planes, the guns, the tanks, the ships, the subs, the land weapons, the sea weapons, the hand-held weapons, the weapons fired from ships, tanks, subs, planes, and the men and women who had to be paid, fed, housed, sheltered, trained, encouraged and rewarded for doing their duty, which in its final stage—planned-against, trained-against, hoped-against but for some of them, perhaps all, inevitable—was Death.

All of these things the Secretary of Defense supported, because that was his job and because they were done in a cause he always and forever believed in, the safety and preservation of the United States of America.

For all of them the basic rationale was the same: *if we have them the cost of attacking us will be so instant and so great that the enemy will not dare attack us.*

Yet sometimes in the dead of night he would wake suddenly and think *how insane!* Grown men, playing with terrible things, making their terrible plans and creating their terrible weapons in some never-never land in which they were children still—monstrous children, playing with monstrous toys, in a playground so completely removed from reality that it was literally insane. Not in the first dictionary sense of "mentally ill," because those who did these things were very far from being mentally ill, they were for the most part brilliantly clever and capable men—but insane in the final dictionary rendering of "senseless"—*sense-less.*

Having no sense.

Having no *common* sense.

Having no sense of any kind.

Sense-*less.*

It did not help, in those cold and lonely hours, to know that the leaders of the Soviet Union were insane in exactly the same way.

This fact, which was a fact, did not remove the potential that the denizens of earth were now completely capable of destroying not only each other but the essence of Earth itself, the living, breathing, beautiful planet.

Nor did it change the fact that somehow—somehow—America must be protected against the Soviets; as they sincerely and with equally blind conviction believed that they must somehow—somehow—be protected against America.

Those were the nights when Imogene often awoke in response to his restless stirring and whispered over from the other bed—whispered, though the children were grown and gone years ago and thousands of miles away—"Loy, what is it, dear? Don't you feel well?"

"Yes," he always said in a normal tone, pulled back from staring into the abyss, "I'm feeling all right."

"Well," she always responded, a little tartly, "you don't sound like it to me. You're so *jumpy.* Maybe you don't know it, but you've been tossing and turning in your sleep—"

"I'm not asleep," he would say, coming back gradually to everyday living with his wife of thirty years, "otherwise I wouldn't *be* tossing and turning. Go back to sleep, Immy."

"Well, I don't know—" she always said doubtfully; and then usually for a few minutes talked to him about her plans for the week, or the lunch she had attended that day at some embassy or other, or perhaps the latest attack on her by *Defense Spy,* whose raucous lady never gave up.

And now he was staring into another part of the abyss, this one labeled "Nanukuvu."

He had watched the television evening news last night knowing exactly what he would see: the stern voice, the opaque, slightly protuberant eyes, the challenging expression and the air of invincible righteousness as it was made unarguably clear that the United States was up to some dastardly deed just because the Soviets had seen fit to seize an island "which exists in a virtual no-man's land—or sea—in the South Pacific." (A map showed the no-man's land, then disappeared as the crisp accusatory voice went on.) "That island's name, it has been learned, is not 'Nankoo' or 'Nanvoo' as mistakenly believed by Sen. Castain. It is 'Nan-u-ku-vu,' a name which Americans would do well to remember, since it promises to be a focus of great national concern in the days, weeks and possibly months, ahead.

"It is over this island, which apparently really belongs to no one, that the United States seems to be planning some sort of major confrontation with the Soviet Union. It is not clear at this moment by what right this government is doing this, a question which Americans might also want to consider . . ."

The most important and influential of this morning's editorials, faithfully clipped and reproduced in the very early hours by the diligent staff of the *Early Bird,* had the same tone. The one headed "Five Questions" was typical:

"It is hard to understand the rationale with which the United States is approaching the problem posed by Soviet occupation of a small uninhabited island in the South Pacific which apparently legally belongs to no one. In fact, it seems that there *is* no rationale save the old shibboleth that 'if we don't do it, the Soviets will.'

"Apparently the Soviets have, and there's the rub. Now the United States is trying to play catch-up in a most risky game that could conceivably escalate into a real confrontation in the South Pacific. Nothing could be more stupid, illadvised and inexcusable.

"It is obvious the Pentagon is largely to blame for the creation of this extremely dangerous situation. Its apparent desire to mix it up with the Soviets is as obscene as its preparations to do so have been sluggish.

"We think Sen. Castain hit the nail on the head in his short but brilliant speech yesterday bringing this sorry matter to the attention of the Senate and the country. His 'Five Questions' summed it up exactly."

And the five questions were quoted there and also in a special box on the front page, a layout replicated in many other papers across the country.

There were some voices upholding the Administration but they were far outweighed in number and national influence by those opposed. Given all that, Loy had been amazed by the calm tone with which the President had spoken when he called shortly after 9 A.M.

"Loy," he said comfortably, "how y'all doin' over there today? Hurricane howlin' 'round your ears?"

"Blowing a bit, Mr. President," the Secretary said with a rueful laugh. "We're trying to batten down the hatches."

"May be a little late for that," the President said. "May be just a little late, Loy. Perhaps if the Pentagon had moved a little faster in the beginnin'—"

"I don't think anyone over here has deliberately dragged his feet, Mr. President," Loy said with some sharpness.

"Oh, no," the President agreed, "I'm not sayin' anyone has *deliberately* done that. It's just been done. It's just the way it's happened. Which is too bad, because now we've got a real mess, just as we thought we might right along."

"What do you think we should do about it?" Loy inquired, expecting some equivocation. But the President surprised him.

"I think we should go right on doin' what we're doin'," he said promptly. "You keep buildin' up over there and I'll turn Terry Venner loose over here. Maybe this speech by Castain isn't such a bad thing, Loy. Bringin' it out in the open that we intend to do somethin' may be just what's necessary to get Smilin' Jack the Ripper over there in the Kremlin to listen to me. At least he knows now we're workin' on it."

"We're going to have trouble at home," the Secretary said. "The debate yesterday in both houses was against us, basically. The evening news was against us. The morning shows were against us. The majority of the major editorials we've seen over here so far are against us. It's going to be uphill."

"Well," the President said, sounding calmly sure of himself, "I may go on TV myself one of these days and make a little talk about it. They'll usually listen to me. I can usually calm 'em down when they get riled up."

"It may have to come to that," Loy Buck said. "It may well be necessary."

"We'll just have to see how it goes," the President said, "See how it develops. A little too early to tell yet, I think. You can always expect the news commentators and the major editorials to be critical, they always are. They wouldn't be happy bein' positive about anythin'. But we'll ride 'em out a bit, and then we'll see. Meantime you keep at it, over there. Good luck. We'll be talkin'."

"Thanks, Mr. President," Loy Buck said, "that's encouraging."

And so it was, as far as it went. He decided to take it a little further and had a worried Vangie put in a call to Hank Milhaus. Ten minutes later Hank sent his military aide to the pressroom to announce an emergency press conference, and also put it on the wire. A stream of reporters promptly made for the Pentagon from all over town. Half an hour later Hank faced them in the conference room, the largest attendance—about a hundred, he estimated—he had seen in a long time.

While they were arriving he had held his regular discussion with his opposite numbers at State, the National Security Council, the National Security Agency and the White House. They talked by conference phone every weekday morning, anticipating the major challenges for the day, deciding upon a united front to present to the media, arriving at an official Administration position to which they would all adhere.

Acting on the Secretary's instructions, he told them this morning that they must all stick with him on the official DoD position on Nanukuvu: the bare facts—as little contention as possible—no elaboration.

In short, stonewall.

Their agreement had been given willingly except for a shade of reservation in the voice of the State Department spokesman, which he sensed and immediately reacted to, figuring that with Foggy Bottom the best DoD defense was always offense.

"If you people don't like it, Bill," he said sharply, "you just do us a favor and keep your mouth shut, all right? That's an order from the President."

Which it wasn't, exactly, but he felt safe enough in extrapolating it from Loy Buck's firm order to him. Loy had told him he had just talked to the President.

The State Department press officer grumbled but subsided, and Hank thought that with a little luck State would cooperate. He told himself grimly as they hung up that by God, it better.

In any event, he himself would have the first word and that would give DoD some advantage. His air was brisk and no-nonsense when he strode to the podium, stepped up to the microphones and looked out into the glare of the television lights. A hundred or so skeptical faces, many of their owners eager to challenge and if possible harass him into some juicy quote, stared expectantly up. He felt tight inside but happy: he liked this kind of battle with former colleagues. They all spoke the same language: *Get the bastards if you can* on the media side, and *Don't give the bastards an inch* on the DoD side.

"First," he said, having had twenty-four hours in which to calm down and being, after all, a good friend of Red's, "I would like to congratulate my old friend Red Roberts on his enterprise in breaking the story he published yesterday morning.

"Some people here," he said with a dry smile and a glance down at Delight and Herb sitting in the front row, "are content to let loose a lot of gas about the Pentagon. Others really dig out stories as responsible journalists should. We all know which is which. And, Red," he said, ignoring Delight's angry stirring right under his nose and hardly ten feet from it, "I also want to apologize to you here and now for what I said to you yesterday morning. I was a little crowded by events, I'm afraid. I'm sorry. I hope you'll forgive me."

"Sure," Red said with the personal amicability they could always count on, whatever his dedication to his profession might lead him to write. "We all get a little hot, sometimes. Forget it. I have."

"Thank you," Hank said, honestly relieved. "I wouldn't want to permanently antagonize the best reporter in the Pentagon."

"Cut the love feast," Delight ordered loudly, and there were a few obliging chuckles. The remark did not sit well with the majority, however, and Hank let it lie there for a pointed moment before proceeding.

"Seven months ago almost to the day," he resumed calmly, "the Soviet Union occupied, without provocation and without excuse, an island in the South Pacific named Nanukuvu. This island is in a strategic location that could conceivably threaten the entire South Pacific basin.

"According to reports sent back by the only observer to fly over Nanukuvu at the time of the occupation, namely the late Navy helicopter pilot Lieutenant, senior grade, Hague Smith, of South Bend, Indiana, the island at the time was inhabited by a small number of native Polynesians. Their exact number is not known and probably never will be. However, Lt. Smith estimated that he saw at least a dozen bodies being burned on the beach, evidently killed by the invaders during the occupation."

He paused to let the furiously scribbling pens and pencils catch up. In the silence several people hastily reversed their tape recorders, checked to see if they were working correctly, and started them on *record* again.

"It is estimated by sources on the aircraft carrier *Dominant,* to which Lt. Smith was attached and which was and still is in the vicinity, that the lieutenant made three close passes over the island. As Sen. Castain accurately informed the Senate yesterday, Lt. Smith did this against orders but with conspicuous enterprise and bravery because he was obviously greatly concerned by this hostile Soviet action. As a result he was cold-bloodedly shot down by the Soviet invaders in time of peace.

"The Department of Defense has recommended to the President that Lt. Smith be honored posthumously for his enterprise and bravery. It is DoD's feeling that he received the ultimate punishment for disobedience and that what should be remembered now is his great courage and his dedication to the best interests of his country." (And that should make *you* happy, Jerry, he thought, so quick and obliging a response to your call to Loy last night.)

"Hank—" somebody began but he held up his hand firmly.

"You'll have your chance at questions. Let me finish.

"Since the day of occupation Soviet forces have been very actively reinforcing the island. A sizable number of personnel have been installed, together with various types of military equipment including nuclear submarines. The obvious purpose is to transform the island into a major military base.

"This action is regarded most gravely by the United States.

"Accordingly the United States is taking measures to effectively neutralize the Soviet presence on the island. For that purpose various activities have been underway for some time in this building and in the area of Nanukuvu. The nature of the activities cannot be disclosed at this time. Suffice it to say that they do exist, as Red Roberts and Sen. Castain have accurately reported. They will, we hope, effectively persuade the Soviets to abandon a dangerous gamble which potentially could create a most serious situation threatening the peace of the entire South Pacific basin."

He stopped and a number in his audience looked at him rather blankly.

"Is that all?" somebody asked.

"That's it," he said crisply. The customary tussle began.

"Hank," his first questioner said in a severe tone, "who owns the island of Nanukuvu?"

"Nobody 'owns' it," he said, "least of all the Soviets."

"Or the Americans," his questioner retorted.

"Or the Americans," he agreed, restraining a temptation to be sharp. "It lies in something of a no-man's land, actually, although we have for many years exercised what you might call a benevolent presence in the area."

"A colonial protectorate," someone suggested in a sarcastic tone.

"Not 'colonial' and not a 'protectorate,'" he said. "Just an island toward which we were friendly. And toward its inhabitants."

"Whom we did not know."

"That's right," he said blandly. "Whom we did not know."

"What right do we have to get so exercised about it, then?"

"Because it falls generally within a region of interest to us," he said. "And because if it were to be transformed from a peaceful island threatening no one into a major military base threatening everyone, the United States would be forced to take a most direct and concerned interest in it."

"How do we know what Soviet intentions are?" Delight demanded. "DoD got some crystal ball or something?"

"Not even a crystal ball, Delight," he said. "I guess you've got us coming and going, haven't you? Or," he added with a pleasant smile he knew would annoy her, "haven't you?"

"You can't prove they want to threaten anybody!" she snapped. He nodded.

"No, you can't *prove* a rattlesnake is going to strike you, either. But you get a little concerned when you see him coming along."

"Very funny," she said. "I'm talking about the Soviet Union, not a rattlesnake."

"There are some who might say—" he began and then abandoned it deliberately with a smile. "Any other questions, or shall we—"

"Just a minute!" a dozen voices cried in alarm. He waited patiently for them to sort themselves out. Red leaned forward and even the most aggressive youngsters yielded to his seniority.

"Hank," he said, "do we actually know the Soviets killed the people on the island?"

"We do know they killed Hague Smith," he said. "And we do know he saw bodies burning. And presumably the Soviets weren't burning their own people. Again, it's like the rattlesnake. You have to use a little ordinary logic, Red."

"Yes," Red said, "I'll accept that." There were murmurs: some wouldn't. "What, actually, have the Soviets put on that island?"

"I can't say any more than I have said," Hank replied. "Men, installations, weapons, subs."

"How do we know they're nuclear subs?" someone else inquired. "Is that 'ordinary logic,' too, or is it something we actually know?"

"Do you really expect them to send obsolete subs five thousand miles down there to enjoy the South Sea breezes?" he asked, releasing his own sarcasm a little. "We know when they have nuclear subs and they know when we have nuclear subs. Suppose we get back to sensible questions."

"I'm trying to *be* sensible," his questioner snapped. "It seems to me you're trying to justify a pretty flimsy case—"

"If that's your opinion, Bob," he said bluntly, "you go right ahead and broadcast it. You'll look pretty silly, but that's your problem."

"It seems to me," his questioner said acridly, "that the Pentagon is looking pretty damned silly trying to blow this up into some sort of emergency in the South Pacific."

"Well, that's your opinion," Hank said. "I'm afraid our opinion is controlling here."

"It may not be," his questioner snapped in a final sally, "when we get through informing the American people about it."

"No doubt you'll try," he agreed.

"Hank, if we can get back to the island itself," a reasonable and veteran voice inquired, "is it really in such a strategic position that it could threaten, say, Australia and New Zealand?"

"And also, as Red quoted his sources," Hank said, "Micronesia, the Philippines, Indonesia, Papua-New Guinea and Malaysia as well. Oh, yes, it's in a very strategic location. Why do you suppose they selected it in the first place? It was inhabited by innocent Third World natives—" somebody made a disgusted sound but he enjoyed giving them a little of their own back and went right on—"who could easily be disposed of, which means they could be easily killed and cremated and their ashes cast into the sea to disappear and take all evidence of the crime with them. It also sits in very dangerous relationship to major air and sea-lanes across that reach of ocean and its neighboring land areas. In a sense, Nanukuvu and its poor unfortunate innocent inhabitants—" again the scornful sound and again he ignored it—"were asking for it. They were helpless—they were trusting—and they were in the way. Remove them, and nature has given you an ideal jumping-off place for whatever evil plans you may have in that part of the world."

"And what are those 'evil plans,' Hank?" another voice inquired dryly. "They tell you?"

"I can only refer you to my reply to Delight Jones," he said. "There is such a thing as common sense, after all."

"It's hard to see it in this hysterical reaction to what seems a perfectly logical Soviet step," another voice remarked. "The island was there, not under anybody's specific sovereignty, virtually uninhabited—"

" 'Virtually'?" he snapped. "Is it all right to be murdered if you're only 'virtually' an inhabitant? Come on, for Lord's sake!"

"Hank," Red interrupted smoothly before the heat could escalate further, "leaving aside the rights or wrongs of their action and our response for the moment, what about the point Jerry Castain made yesterday that the Pentagon has been too slow to respond to the situation? Given our concern, whether rightly or wrongly, *has* the building moved fast enough? *Are* we adequately prepared to meet whatever might eventuate out there? *Is* the Pentagon making good time on this?"

"Thanks, Red," he said. "I appreciate your bringing this back to a sensible basis. The answer to that is, yes, the Pentagon is in good shape. I believe all aspects of the program—"

"Is that 'Mission Frio'?" somebody interrupted.

He hesitated and then decided to ignore it.

"—all aspects of the program," he repeated, "are well in hand and moving forward."

"Seven months after the occupation?" Red inquired before another argument could develop. "That seems a little slow to me for a real emergency. If that's what it is."

"You know the Pentagon, Red," Hank said with a comfortable smile, "better than all of us put together. For the problems posed and the work necessary to meet them in any adequate way, I'd say, yes, the Pentagon has moved reasonably fast and is doing a reasonably good job of preparation for whatever action may be required."

"Is 'reasonably' good enough, in the face of the crisis you indicate this government believes it to be?" Red pressed. "I don't mean to belabor the point but—"

"Why not?" somebody inquired sarcastically from the back of the room, and there was quite a lot of laughter.

"—but," Red said calmly, not bothering to look around, "it does seem slow to me. Is there really such a sense of urgency?"

"There is," Hank said quietly. "Believe you me, there is."

"Well . . ." Red said, and allowed his voice to trail deliberately away. "But," he added after a moment, "I dare say if anybody is derelict, the Hill will get to it, soon enough."

That one, Hank thought he had best not respond to. Instead he stood looking out upon them expectantly for a moment and then started to say, "If that's all, then—" But he was not to get away so easily.

"Wait a minute!" Delight said sharply. "I want to know what kind of action this government *is* planning to take when things *are* ready in the Pentagon, whenever that may be. How does it propose to handle the situation, if that's the aim? What are we planning to do? We need to know that before you hustle us out of here."

"I'm not hustling anybody out of here, Delight," he said with some asperity now that the conference was apparently beginning to wind down. "I'll stay here all morning, if you like. And of course you know I can't tell you what is being planned. First of all, I don't know, and secondly, I couldn't tell you if I did, and thirdly, I *wouldn't* tell you if I did. So there we are."

"I don't think anybody over here *does* know what they want to do," she said dryly. "I think the Pentagon is as confused about this as it is about everything else."

"Well," he said, still tartly, "just remember it's your necks, among others, that are involved in what's decided in this building, so maybe you shouldn't be so cavalier about it."

"Our necks and more importantly those of maybe thousands and thousands of innocent American boys whose blood will be shed for nothing on Nanukuvu!" she snapped and he uttered a muffled, disgusted, "Oh, *Christ!*" before taking the microphone firmly in hand and leaning forward for a parting shot.

"Listen!" he said. "Some of you can be as skeptical and nasty about what we're trying to do in this situation as you please. Thank God it isn't all of you, there are plenty here with the integrity and understanding to give us a fair shot. The facts are what I have related to you, and that's the situation. Nobody in this building is going to shed the blood of innocent American boys on Nanukuvu unless it absolutely can't be avoided, and we're doing our damnedest to prevent that. And nobody here is going to let the enemy build himself a major base in the South Pacific by default, either. Maybe," he concluded sarcastically, "maybe, Delight, *you* can tell us the perfect solution. What would it be?"

"Get the hell out," she said flatly, and this time there was vigorous applause from quite a few.

He looked at her for a long moment and suggested coldly,

"Make sense."

"*You* make sense!" she cried, voice rising. "You, God damned Pentagon, make sense! All this stupid 'preparing for action' and 'meeting situations' and 'facing dangers' and all that crap! All it ever means is killing and killing and more killing! Get out, God damned Pentagon! Get out, get out, *get out!*"

For a moment they were all struck silent in the face of her exaggerated but seemingly sincere frenzy. Finally Red spoke up with a wryly humorous air.

"On that note, Hank," he suggested, "maybe we'd better all call it quits and go home."

"Thanks, Red," he agreed, keeping his voice calm with considerable effort. "Maybe you're right."

He stepped down from the podium and walked out, not looking back. Behind him Delight was the center of a small but admiring circle; Red and older veteran colleagues trailed out shaking their heads. Judged objectively, Hank Milhaus thought it might come out somewhere in the vicinity of Righteousness 8, Pentagon 12. Weighed in the scales many of them would use in presenting it to the country, he knew it would be more like Righteousness 20, Pentagon also-ran. But that was a day in the life of E Ring, public affairs division.

Pravda said:

"U.S. imperialist circles, obviously preparing for war, have made false accusations that the Soviet Union is attempting to 'invade' an unknown island in the Pacific. These are typical attempts to hide America's own plans to launch nuclear war in the area."

Tass said:

"Imperialist liars in Washington are claiming that forces of the Motherland have occupied a mysterious 'island' in the South Pacific. It is strongly suspected that this means that the United States itself is contemplating such an imperialist move and is accusing the Soviet Union to hide its own plans for nuclear conquest."

Soviet television and radio said:

"The latest lie from Washington has even America's most obedient allies scratching their heads in wonderment. Washington claims that the Soviet Union has 'invaded' a mysterious unknown island in the South Pacific. It is well-known that America has such plans to extend its nuclear hegemony over the area. It is a typical trick of imperialist circles in the U.S. to accuse the Soviet Union of such tactics."

Nobody in that part of the world free from Soviet influence bought this story entirely, though of course, as usual, millions in Africa, Asia, Eastern Europe and Russia did. On the other hand, nobody in the non-communist world was quite willing to accept the Washington version completely, either.

The island *was* unknown, it *was* very far away, there *was* no proof except the word of the United States, which decades of incessant twenty-four-hour enemy propaganda had made suspect to many millions even in nations officially friendly. How was anyone to be entirely sure?

And even if they were, to quote *Paris Soir,* which summed up the western attitude quite well, what did America intend to do about it? Obviously, if it was actually a situation of an age of seven months, it might already be too late for America to take the effective action. Perhaps it would be best for Washington to put the face that was best upon it, or, if it felt the situation was really serious, to adopt the method diplomatic. France, with interests in French Polynesia, New Caledonia and elsewhere in the South Pacific, would be willing to help with this approach, but of course it could not contemplate, condone or support any kind of action military. That could only threaten the peace of the entire region and perhaps of all the world also.

In similar essence spoke the official and media voices of such allies as Britain, West Germany, Canada, NATO and Japan. The Philippines, Australia and New Zealand sounded more nervous, but they too insisted, perhaps a trifle desperately, that if the situation described by the United States did actually exist, then its solution must be sought through diplomatic means. Anything else, they all agreed, would carry the potential of utter disaster not only for the South Pacific basin but very possibly, as *Paris Soir* said, *pour tout le monde aussi.*

Contemplating all these reports as they came in, not only from the officials and media of allies both near to and far from Nanukuvu, but in confidential dispatches from American ambassadors in many other capitals as well, the Secretary of State prepared a final assault upon the White House. He was very optimistic that this time it would be successful.

The Secretary of Defense and the chairman and members of the JCS, receiving no further direct advice at the moment from the President, decided to follow his admonition to Loy to "keep on doin' what you're doin'." That, as the Secretary remarked, was still their job. There would be no change until they heard differently from the White House.

This did not, however, do very much to encourage morale; and as he parked his car far out in the lot, Lt. Broderick Tolliver found his spirits sagging. A vaguely defined but ominous feeling of depression, most uncharacteristic, seemed to be settling upon him. Brod was normally the most upbeat and ebullient of young men. Today, after two days of national and international uproar over Nanukuvu, he was definitely down in the dumps.

Brod, as Gary Stump had remarked yesterday afternoon to Hogan with the intimate amusement that he hoped would soon establish a bond between them, "really *believes* in Operation Frio."

He had been afraid for a moment that he had overplayed his hand when Hogan inquired with a startled air, "Don't you?"

"Oh, sure," he said easily, "but I don't worship the idea the way he does. He really eats and sleeps it. He really thinks there's a lot involved out there."

"So do I," she said firmly, "and so—" nodding at Al Rider's closed door— "does Big G. I thought we all did."

"We *do,*" he said, his glance still amused and intimate. "Hell, Liz, I want it to succeed as much as anyone. But I don't let it keep me awake nights, as I'll bet Brod does. We're getting there. Now that we finally have our marching orders from the JCS it shouldn't take too long to get things organized. So why worry?"

"He's just conscientious, I guess," she said in a tone that he took to be disapproving of himself: his campaign wasn't off the ground yet, obviously. "Perhaps we should all be that dedicated."

"Maybe," he said. He frowned. "Seriously, do you really think the mission is going to go through, now that there's all this fuss in Congress and everywhere else about it? It seems to me it's going to be a little tough for the Administration to carry it out. Don't you think so?"

Again she looked surprised and again he thought he had gone too far. But she only pursed her lips and said thoughtfully, "It's more difficult now. But I still believe with Brod and the general that it has to be attempted."

"I resent your excluding *me* from that, Liz," he said with his same easy air. "I don't want to be left out!"

"I didn't mean to imply anything," she protested quickly, flushing a bit and looking, he thought, even more ungainly and unattractive. The things he did to earn his money!

"Well, you definitely did," he said, sounding archly injured. Hogan's sense of humor, he thought, was on his side: she didn't have any.

"I'm sorry," she said with perfect seriousness. "It was thoughtless of me. I know you're as dedicated to the mission as we are, Gary. I didn't mean to imply otherwise."

"Well," he said with a sudden sunny smile, "I'll accept that. How about grabbing a quick cone at the Big Scoop? If Big G doesn't mind, that is?"

"Why, sure," she said, looking pleased and quite animated; and when Gen. Rider smiled and nodded and they went off chatting amicably to get their ice cream, Gary thought that he was back on track again.

Brod, just returning from carrying some papers to Proj Frio's "Aggregate Analysis Unit" on second floor, A Ring, had been in time to watch them go, with a speculative light in his eyes.

The speculation was still there now as he threaded his way through the thousands of parked cars and walked quickly toward the massive building looming ahead. The weather was still unseasonably chilly, which gave him a good feeling when he saw how uncomfortable it was making the large group of protesters who now milled with an uneasy aimlessness near River Entrance. The bastards deserve it, he thought. Their placards were the usual stuff, but this morning, given his feelings about the necessity for Frio and his general depressed mood, they struck him as more annoying than usual:

STOP U.S. AGGRESSION IN PACIFIC, they said. And, HANDS OFF MICRONESIA. And, NUTS TO NANUKUVU. And, NO NUKES IN PARADISE. And, TODAY NANUKUVU, TOMORROW THE WORLD. And off at the side, looking a little bewildered by his sudden newfound raucous associates but still gamely hanging in there, BLESSED ARE THE MERCIFUL, FOR THEY SHALL OBTAIN MERCY.

All of this, Brod thought, was so much obstructive crap, the same usual mix of mindless protest and machiavellian manipulation that greeted every attempt by the United States to show any kind of firmness anywhere in the world. Somebody punched the button and out they popped, complete with hand-lettered placards, scruffy clothes and self-righteous slogans. That was the thing about these professional nay-sayers that infuriated him most, he thought: they were so *self-righteous*. As a true-blue, flag-waving, earnest young patriot who might not be typical of his whole generation but was certainly typical of the majority who found their way into the services, Brod took this as a personal insult. *They* didn't have any monopoly on righteousness, or on the truth, either. There were two sides to everything, and if he was never quite able to see anything other than the military, well, that just showed what a good and loyal young officer he was.

Anyway, he felt this morning that he had just about had it with this ubiquitous crew, whose antics were being faithfully filmed by the networks and whose shouted slogans were being faithfully scribbled down by eight or ten reporters. He straightened his shoulders and walked right through the middle of the crowd, not being too careful whose toes he stepped on or whose ribs he dug in passing. Being of the same stocky build as Gary Stump, and almost as good physical condition, he went through them like a small determined tank, leaving jeers and curses in his wake to which he didn't even bother to respond by looking around until somebody screamed "damned military murderer!" as he started up the steps. At that he did whirl around and, concealing it from the guards who looked impassively down, gave them the finger. Then he turned smartly on his heel and disappeared inside the building, giving the guards a snappy salute and a wry grin as he passed.

In the office he found that Hogan, as usual, was already at her desk, and as he took his seat Gary Stump came in, professing to be a little breathless.

"Damn, you move fast, Brod," he said. "I've been chasing you all the way from the ramp."

"Why?" Brod inquired, but amicably; he was making it a point to stay on good terms, as Gen. McCune had suggested.

"No reason," Gary said with a smile. "Just companionship. I value yours. I see Liz has put us both to shame, as always. Do you live in this office, Liz?"

"No," she said with her usual awkward abruptness but looking pleased just the same, "I believe in getting here on time, that's all."

"A very model officer," Gary said in a tone nicely balanced between joshing and admiration. "Isn't she, Brod?"

"The best man in the outfit," Brod said.

Hogan said, "Oh, pooh!" but looked shyly pleased. Gary laughed heartily.

"Better than me . . . Say, you two," he said casually as they all started reading the *Early Bird*, "you haven't seen *the* document yet, have you? The secret scoop—the big deal—the battle-plan for dislodging the enemy from Nanukuvu?"

"You know we haven't," Brod said, looking at him a little curiously. "You were closeted with Big G about it all day yesterday. At least that's what you said."

"It was true, it was true," Gary said lightly. "Yes, he wanted to go over a lot of the details with me, because from now on we're going to be working our little asses off—excuse me, Liz, tails off—as the mission takes shape. And," he added firmly, "despite all the rumpus that seems to be going on on the Hill and elsewhere, it *is* going to take shape. Did you see those bastards at River Entrance?"

"Couldn't miss them, could we?" Brod said.

"They gripe my gut," Gary said frankly. "They have a damned nerve, criticizing what America is trying to do. Damned worthless subversives, in my book."

"Mine, too," Brod said and Hogan looked up indignantly also.

"They called *me*," she said, between annoyance and amusement, "a 'battle-scarred old hen.' 'Hey, you battle-scarred old hen, go lay an egg on Nanukuvu!' If I'd been able to lay an egg," she said with a rare show of spirit, "I'd have thrown it right at them!"

"Good for you, Elizabeth!" Gary said with amused admiration and Brod applauded vigorously.

"That's our girl, Liz!" he said. "Give 'em hell!"

"I'd like to," she said, half-laughing but still obviously annoyed. "They upset *me,* too."

"Our best answer to them," Gary said, "is to go right ahead as fast as we can with the mission. In pursuit of which, lieutenant—" he handed a folder to Brod —"and captain—" he handed the other to Hogan— "drop everything and read. Then you'll know where we're going from now on."

"All this damned hullaballo isn't going to stop it, then," Brod said, sounding relieved. Gary Stump looked scornful.

"Hell, no. They can scream their damned heads off, all over the damned world if they damned please. It isn't going to stop the building. The general says his orders are p.f., proceed forthwith, and that's what we're going to do. Liz, you'll ignore a few of my notes on that copy, it's my personal one." She looked pleased and Brod thought, boy, she must be falling to get a thrill out of something as trivial as that. "Brod, you get the virgin copy as befits our virgin member."

"Virgin!" Brod exclaimed. "A father in another month? Virgin?"

"Now, don't be sex-mad," Gary said lightly, with a very slight trace of coyness that struck Brod, like much about Gary, as being just slightly off true pitch, somehow. "Even though it becomes you. Of course I don't mean *that.* I mean virgin in the sense of being our youngest, newest, least battle-christened fighter in the Pentagon wars. You'll find some revelations in there about the relations between our noble services. Don't let 'em shock you."

"They won't," Brod promised, opening the neat green folder.

"O.K.," Gary said. "Have at it, then. I'm going to see if Big G needs me for anything." He stepped over to Gen. Rider's door and rapped politely. Al Rider told him to come in and he did so, closing the door behind him. With earnest concentration Brod and Hogan began to read.

Twenty minutes later Brod placed his copy neatly back in its folder and sat back. Hogan did the same. They looked at one another.

"I still don't think they've got the lines of authority clear enough in this thing," he said. She nodded.

"I don't, either. But if the general's satisfied, then I guess it's all right. He's the one who has to do it."

"I never really realized," Brod said thoughtfully, "how much compromise there has to be among the services at this level." He suddenly looked very serious. "That sort of thing could cost lives!"

"Oh, yes," Hogan said. "I haven't seen much of it in action, but what I have seen—oh, yes, it could. It has."

"But it shouldn't be that way!" he protested.

"No," she agreed rather bleakly. "But it is."

"I don't like it," he said slowly. "I—don't—like it."

"Well, keep your disagreement in the office," she advised, "or it won't take long to get yourself tagged as a malcontent. I'm sure you can talk it over with the general, he's a reasonable man—in fact," she said, blushing a bit but meaning sincerely the slangy term that came surprisingly from her lips—"he's a living doll—but I wouldn't express any doubts to anybody else."

He glanced at the closed door.

"Particularly not to Gary," he said, voice lowered, curious to see how she would react. She shot him a startled glance and lowered hers too.

"Why not? Do you suspect him of something?"

"Do you?"

"I don't *think* so," she said carefully. "I did at first, maybe, just something I couldn't really put my finger on. But the more we all work together the more I think he's all right. He's *very* efficient."

"He is that," he agreed. "And very decisive, and very intelligent. Good officer material all around. There's no doubt he'll go far in the service if . . ." His voice trailed away a bit, deliberately, and she reacted at once.

"If what?"

"If he doesn't trip himself up," he said. She looked earnest and puzzled.

"But how, Brod?" she asked. "I don't see anything that—that would bring that about."

"Maybe something we *don't* see," he said, and then decided that was enough of stating suspicions he couldn't support, to someone who appeared to be on her way to becoming a Gary partisan and might report back if he pressed too hard. "Oh, well," he said hastily as the door opened and Gary turned back to exchange some laughing comment with the general, "forget it. It's all my imagination. I'm sure everything's all right."

"I *think* so," she murmured, though a little more doubtfully. "He really is *very* efficient."

"Are you two through with your reading?" Gary asked pleasantly. "Good. Thanks, Liz." He took the folder from her and held it out casually in both hands toward Brod so that Brod automatically placed his own on top of it. Again for just a second something struck him as a little odd. It was not until some days later that he realized that this was an exact duplicate of the way in which Gary had handed them out, not touching Brod's folder either time.

"If you two have a minute," Al Rider said pleasantly from the door, "why don't you come in and we'll chat a bit?"

"Certainly, sir," they said with alacrity, feeling excited. He had always been pleasant but a little impersonal.

"Now," he said when they were seated, "Gary tells me you've read the document. What do you think of it?"

Brod deferred to Hogan, who hesitated a moment, then spoke out.

"I'm a little doubtful, sir," she said. She looked to Brod for support and he nodded quickly.

"So am I, sir," he said. "We think—" he glanced at Hogan, who gestured him to go ahead, "that the lines of authority among the services are still not clear-cut enough. We don't think you will really have a unified command. It will still be basically consultative. Will you be able to make decisions as fast as might be necessary?"

Al Rider sighed, his plain good-natured face dimmed for a moment by a troubled frown.

"Well, you know," he said, "frankly, that's my worry, too. With all respects to the JCS—and," he smiled, taking them flatteringly into his confidence, "one *must* show respect to the JCS whether one feels that way or not, right?"

They both hesitated, but encouraged by his candor finally nodded and smiled.

"With all respects to *them,*" Al Rider said, "I don't think it's such a hot number, myself. I made my position clear at every stage of the process but, as you can see, without too much success. I've been in the tank with them a dozen times arguing that somebody had to have a clearly defined line of command and each time I've run into such things as this proviso about the Marines coming down one ridge and the Army down the other. That's all very well, I suppose us Marines *can* use a little Army help once in a while—" he smiled again—"but we can't be very effective if each of us is going to command his own area. It's too much like Grenada, which came through as a great triumph in public but came very close to being botched up on the inside because the basic aim was not to take the island as fast and efficiently as possible, but to keep everybody happy while we were doing it. Well," he said with a sudden sternness, "I don't want that kind of thing duplicated on Nanukuvu!"

"Have you told them that, sir?" Brod inquired respectfully.

"Hell," Gen. Rider said, "I told you I went into the tank a dozen times and raised the roof. They were polite and said they wanted to be helpful, and I think they do, but the end result isn't what *I* would have liked to see . . ." He stared thoughtfully at the map of the South Pacific that faced him on the wall, Nanukuvu outlined in a big red circle. An adjoining map of the island alone, greatly enlarged by the Defense Mapping Agency, showed every topographical feature. Surrounding them both was a frieze of photographs, the latest dated just yesterday, showing the island right down to the last nook, cranny, tree, cover, barracks and installation.

"See those little brown things on the ridges?" he resumed presently. "Those are bulldozers."

"They're building an airfield!" Brod exclaimed and Hogan said excitedly, "No, Brod—two!"

"That's right," Gen. Rider said, "*two*. And we're still sitting here planning, only now I've got to plan with half a horse under me instead of a whole one as I begged the JCS to give me . . . but," he said, more upbeat, "we'll manage. I just wanted you two to know the whole situation we face because it's going to be very busy around here from now on and very important that we all pull together. They're adding to our space with the suite of offices next door on our right and giving us twenty more personnel as of next week. Gary will be coordinating all that, and it will be even more important that you two help him, and me, in every way you can. I know I can count on you to keep an eye on all the records, Elizabeth—"

"Oh, *yes,* sir," she said fervently, more animated than any of them had seen her before.

"—and Brod, you keep right on being Gary's right-hand man, and mine too, just as you've been, only more so. Stand by for anything and everything. All right?"

"Yes, *sir!*" Brod said, looking so young and earnest and determined that Al Rider, like Zeecy McCune, could not resist a surge of amused affection for him.

"Good," he said. "Gary and I went over all the details yesterday, exactly what we can expect from each service, amounts of materiel, types of equipment, specific personnel to be contributed by each—the numbers game that we'll be sharing with Project Frio. Some of it you'll be told, some of it won't directly concern you, but you can rest assured you'll be told everything you need to know, and more, because that's the way I like to run an outfit, always have and always will. It's my nature more than my training, I think. Some generals like to play everything close to the chest and keep even their own immediate subordinates guessing. I don't. I like everybody under me to know just as much as possible and I do my damnedest to make sure they do. It creates a hell of a lot better morale for you folks and it gives me the assurance that I have a team I can depend upon absolutely." He paused and gave them the kindly, all-embracing smile that had always aroused and instilled instant confidence in everyone he had ever dealt with.

"Oh, *yes,* sir!" they said together, overwhelmed by his candor and his trust. Had he asked Hogan to strip to her panties and walk down the hall on her hands, and Brod to jump out the window into Ground Zero without a parachute, both would have done it for him gladly at that moment.

"Wonderful!" he said. "Let's move out!"

"Yes, sir!" they said and he said, "Good!" They walked out glowing on the surge of his comfortable laughter.

"Well," Gary said with a chuckle as Brod closed the door behind them, "I can see he's given you the full treatment this time. Quite a guy, isn't he?"

"Quite a guy," Brod agreed.

"A living *doll!*" Hogan repeated solemnly.

"We have a lot to do," Gary said briskly. "Let's get to work!"

Their euphoria lasted at least an hour before the problems of Frio came crowding back and they realized that there was still a long, hard way to go, in a nation and world suddenly aware of, and in many places loudly opposed to, their mission.

No such euphoria prevailed, even briefly, behind the door marked "Aggregate Analysis Unit" on second floor, A Ring. Its principal occupants did not possess Al Rider's ability to inspire and lead, nor did they have the temperament to regard life with anything other than a calm, pragmatic, unchanging realism. This did not make for highs of emotion and idealism but neither did it make for lows of distress and dismay. It guaranteed that life went on at a steady, level, undeflected pace toward whatever goal might be set.

It could not be denied on this particular day, however, that the program managers of the "Aggregate Analysis Unit" were at least moderately shaken by the sudden startling burst of controversy that now threatened their enterprise. The two Harrys had missed being included in the direct fire for the time being but they were well aware that several dozen enterprising reporters were fanning out through the building and on the Hill in search of any still undiscovered aspects of Frio. It would probably not be long before Burt Sanstrom tipped off Delight or one of his other fellow players in the never-ending game of Get The Pentagon. Someone would come knocking soon on the door of the "Aggregate Analysis Unit."

"When that happens," Military Harry told Civilian Harry firmly as they paused in their joint perusal of the services' recommendations for the ALCAC, "the word is *mum.*"

"Yes, I know," Harry Josephs said with a harried air. "I won't say anything, even though . . ." His voice trailed away and Gen. Ahmanson gave him a severe look.

"Harry," he said, "you keep your reservations about the ALCAC to yourself, if you don't mind. There'll be enough curbstone experts jumping on that one without the co-manager adding fuel to the fire."

"Well, it's stupid," Harry Josephs said stubbornly, "and I still think—"

"Harry," Gen. Ahmanson said sternly, "shut up. Either that or go back to the inspector general's office and get involved in something you know something about."

"I know everything there is to know about the ALCAC!" Harry Josephs said indignantly. "And about everything else that goes on in this building, too. I was here when you were a greenhorn. Don't lecture me, Harry!"

"I'm sorry," Harry Ahmanson said, "but we *must* maintain a solid front. Otherwise the media will just have a field day with us."

"They are anyway," Harry Josephs pointed out. "And so is everybody else. You'd think we were the biggest criminals in the country." He sniffed. "We're only trying to do our job."

"That's *right,*" Gen Ahmanson said, detecting a note of fellow feeling that might be built upon in what he recognized to be a potentially major crisis for Frio. "And none of us, I expect, is going to escape criticism, at least from those people who make a profession out of criticizing the Pentagon. That's why we need to stand together and defend each other in this."

"I suppose we must," Harry Josephs agreed, appearing, at the moment, to be coming around to Harry Ahmanson's point of view. "Anyway," he said, sounding quite friendly, "I wouldn't want *you* to suffer from it, Harry. You've got another star ahead and undoubtedly more after that, and we certainly don't want you tagged with any failure of Project Frio."

"Project Frio isn't going to fail," Gen. Ahmanson said firmly. "We can't afford to let it fail, and not because of anything to do with me. That's a real problem out there in the Pacific and the U.S. has to solve it or just get pushed farther back in still another area of the world. It's all real, in this world we live in. That's what these quick-to-criticize bastards don't realize when they discover something like Frio. They think it's all a kid's game and nobody gets hurt." He frowned. "The U.S. gets hurt, plenty, if we don't succeed."

"That doesn't mean, though," Harry Josephs said, sounding combative again, "that there aren't plenty of solid grounds on which to criticize the Pentagon. *You* know that."

"God, yes," Harry Ahmanson agreed, "but not this particular mission, which has been forced upon us by the actions of the enemy and is no choice of ours. That's what we have to make people like that Jones woman understand—if she wants to understand. I don't think she does. She just wants to make trouble."

"Sometimes," Harry Josephs said, "she has a point."

"Oh, many times, no doubt," Harry Ahmanson agreed. "It's the way she goes about it. The adversarial approach. Of course," he added, tone joshing but pointed, "that's what you use on contractors yourself, isn't it. I'm amazed Three Gs and Strategic Industries are even interested in bidding on the AL-CAC, with you around."

"Helen tells me they're very anxious to go ahead with it," Harry Josephs said. "As I am sure she has told *you,*" he added with a primness that tempted Harry Ahmanson to utter a sharp retort. But he had no desire to really antagonize Civilian Harry.

"That she has," he said matter-of-factly. "She tells me they've been getting increasingly impatient for the past four or five months. Understandably so, I'd say. I can't blame them. The chiefs have been awfully slow."

"By our standards," Harry Josephs remarked with a sniff. "Not by theirs."

"Well, anyway," Harry Ahmanson said, "be that as it may, we have their recommendations now. They can't go on to DSARC without our approval, and they can't go anywhere after that without DSARC's approval, if anything's to be done with them at all, so—shall we approve them?"

"Didn't somebody say something," Harry Josephs asked vaguely, "about Skip Framberg having put in a specific set of recommendations also? Maybe we should take a look at those before we—"

"I believe he took them direct to the SecDef," Gen. Ahmanson said, "and I understand Loy's already sent them direct to Helen with orders to give them direct to DSARC. So I guess they're out of our jurisdiction. I think we'd better stick to what we have in front of us and let DSARC worry about Skip." He laughed suddenly without much amusement. "Sooner or later he's been every-body else's problem in the building, why not DSARC?"

"He means well," Harry Josephs said defensively and Harry Ahmanson im-mediately moderated his tone.

"I don't mean to criticize him if he's a pal of yours, Harry, but you must admit he has been a pain in the ass at times."

"Not for the righteous," Harry Josephs said serenely and Harry Ahmanson was so taken aback by this Biblical comment that for a moment he was at a loss for words. Then he laughed.

"Not a large group in the building, to hear Skip tell it."

Harry Josephs was not amused.

"Skip can be judged by his enemies," he remarked. "I would be proud if I had as many as he does, and of the same caliber."

"You do, Harry," Gen. Ahmanson assured him. "Oh, you do! Now," he said, briskly, "shall we o.k. these service papers and get them back to Helen so she can send them to DSARC? I think, considering the uproar, that we'd better move right along, now."

"Oh, very well," Harry Josephs said, sounding suddenly browbeaten and disheartened, "if you say so, Harry. I *would* like time to give them more study, but if you *insist*—"

"Well, now," Gen. Ahmanson said, vividly aware of his colleague's reputation as a troublemaker for uncooperative officers, "I don't mean to push you along at a speed you don't think prudent, Harry, but I also think we're under some obligation in this office to cooperate with the SecDef's obvious desire for speed. What advantage do you feel you would have if we took more time?"

"Oh, nothing," Harry Josephs said, seeming almost to have lost interest. "One never knows. Maybe something would turn up if I had more time to just —*study* them . . . but—" he sighed. "Oh, well. I don't want to be an *obstruc-tionist.* Helen told me I shouldn't be. *She* wants speed too. I guess I'd better sign. Here, give them to me."

"Now, just a minute," Harry Ahmanson said, holding the sheaf of papers out of reach. "We don't want you to feel, *or to say later,* Harry, that anybody put pressure on you or didn't give you time to do the thorough job your conscience dictates. *Are* you satisfied to send these on to DSARC, or are you not?"

"Give them to me," Harry Josephs said, sighing again—it was impossible to discern exactly what his mood really was—"I'll sign."

"Very well," Gen. Ahmanson said, placing them before him with a firm air. "Do so and then we'll discuss what we need in the way of additional staff for the rest of the project. I assume we'll be getting a lot of specific details down from Al Rider and Op Frio very soon about a lot of things besides the ALCAC, and at that point I imagine we'll need more than your secretary and mine and a filing clerk."

"I have a couple of bright kids in the inspector general's office I'd like to bring in," Harry Josephs said, almost absentmindedly scrawling his initials on the service recommendations, one after the other in rapid succession. "Shorty Murchison says he'll release them to me for as long as we need them."

"Good," Harry Ahmanson said. "Shorty's kids are always good. I don't have anybody in particular in mind. I think I'll leave my staffing to the JCS staff. They may have somebody they want included."

"That's the thing!" Harry Josephs exclaimed. "That's it, you see. You're all so damned *incestuous,* in the military. You can't bear the thought of a couple of honest kids from the I.G.'s office coming in here to help me keep an eye on things. You have to have somebody from the JCS staff to protect you from them!"

"Oh, come *on,* Harry," Gen. Ahmanson said. "That's not the point at all and you know it."

"What is, then?" Harry Josephs inquired stubbornly. "Every time I suggest something around here that will speed things up and in the process perhaps save the taxpapers some money, I'm told that—"

"Now, listen!" Harry Ahmanson exclaimed, beginning to get alarmed by this flood of injured righteousness. "You know damned well, Harry, that we in the military *appreciate* having you on this job—"

"It's the first time," Harry Joseph interrupted dourly, looking more than ever like a small, beleaguered rodent.

"But it's true!" Harry Ahmanson exclaimed. "You're an ideal colleague to work with because you're *aware,* Harry. You see things. You catch details. Why, my goodness, I'm sure I'd miss a dozen important angles if you weren't around to keep me on my toes!"

"I don't think you miss very much," Harry Josephs observed with a smile that was not unfriendly. "You're pretty sharp yourself, Harry. You and Helen both. You're quite a team. Why don't you marry her and retire and go back to California and help her run that plant of hers? You'd both be millionaires."

"She is already," Gen. Ahmanson said. "She's done very well without me so far."

"She'd do better," Harry Josephs said. "But I suppose you want your stars."

"Yes," Gen. Ahmanson said, "having devoted a couple of decades to them already, I *would* rather like to go the whole route if I can, Harry. But of course there is such a thing as absentee ownership for her and military transport for me." He smiled. "I dare say we'd manage to see each other quite a bit." He smiled again. "I'm thinking about it. And so is she, I hope."

"Oh, I'm sure," Harry Josephs said. "I'm sure . . . Which company do you think will make the best bid on the ALCAC, Three Gs or Strategic Industries?"

"I have no way of knowing," Gen. Ahmanson said, suddenly cautious at this abrupt change of subject: what was Civilian Harry's suspicious little mind up to now?

"Which one would you like to see get it?" Harry Josephs asked.

"I really have no preference at all," Harry Ahmanson said matter-of-factly. "Either one could do the job perfectly well. It really comes down in my mind to a question of speed—although of course that isn't the way the OSD judges things. It has to be on a monetary basis, I'm afraid."

"As so it should," Harry Josephs said firmly.

"Well," Harry Ahmanson said, "there we part company, but I suppose that's the difference between the military mind and the civilian."

"Might as well save a little money," Civilian Harry observed with a sniff. "I haven't seen much indication anybody thought speed was important, so far."

"Touché," Gen. Ahmanson said. "Can't argue with you too much there. But some of us have *felt* it was important, anyway. *We've* tried. From now on, things should speed up substantially."

"Unless there's such a fuss higher authority decides to cancel it altogether," Harry Josephs remarked. Harry Ahmanson shook his head, suddenly somber.

"I should greatly deplore that, myself. It would be terribly crippling. Anyway, it isn't going to happen. There's too much at stake. Which means," he said, deciding to terminate this unusually relaxed and intimate chat with his opposite number, "that the sooner we get these papers back to Helen and DSARC, the better. Perhaps you can have one of the girls run them over right away."

"Shouldn't we tell Three Gs and S.I. that they're on the way?" Harry Josephs inquired. Gen. Ahmanson looked a little blank.

"Why? They'll call in in the normal course of events and Helen can tell them."

"I thought maybe you'd like them to know," Harry Josephs said.

"You can call if you like," Harry Ahmanson suggested, deciding to look openly puzzled. "But I don't see the need to make a special deal out of it."

"No, no," Harry Josephs said. "Not at all. I just thought perhaps you would like your friends to know, that's all."

"They aren't my *friends,*" Harry Ahmanson said, aware that his voice was rising slightly, "at least not in the invidious sense you are apparently trying to imply, Harry. I know Rodge Venable, yes, and I know Walker Stayman. So what?"

"Nothing," Harry Josephs said, "nothing at all, nothing. I just thought maybe—"

"What?" Harry Ahmanson demanded; but his civilian counterpart didn't answer, studying his hands with a prim and proper air. "Look, Harry," Gen. Ahmanson said, "I am *not* taking bribes from Three Gs and S.I. and I have *not* been offered a cushy job when I leave the service if I'll give them a break on their contracts. So stop sounding like *Defense Spy* on a rampage. I'm not in a position to give them any preference anyway, even if I would. And I hope I'm not *that* stupid."

"Some are," Harry Josephs remarked in a superior tone. Harry Ahmanson snorted.

"Yes," he agreed. "I'm not. That's part of the Pentagon system that *I* don't belong to, though I'll grant you plenty have. Not me. So come off it."

"It always pays to be alert," Harry Josephs observed. Harry Ahmanson uttered a startled laugh: the conversation had been so typical of Civilian Harry's reputation in the building.

"Thanks a *lot,*" he said. "I appreciate your confidence in me, Harry. Now: shall we get one of the girls to take these papers to Helen—or do you want to— or shall I? Maybe I'll meet Rodge or Walker in the corridor and collect a bribe for giving them an early peek. How *about* that?"

"You can laugh," Harry Josephs said, "but *I* take *my* responsibility to the taxpayers *seriously.*"

"I'm not even going to dignify that with a comment," Gen. Ahmanson said. He picked up the service recommendations and started out the door. "Better get those two youngsters from Shorty's office in here first thing in the morning. Things ought to begin humming now."

"Do you really think so?" Harry Josephs inquired.

"Yes," he said, "I really think so."

2

They were beginning to hum on the Hill, too, where the senior Senators from California and Louisiana were meeting with the staff director of the Senate Armed Services Committee in the committee's ornate old quarters in the Russell Office Building. They were discussing whether—and if so, how soon—the committee should, as Cube Herron put it, "Yank Loy and Zeecy and their boys up here by the scruffs of their necks and make them tell us exactly what is going on with this Frio Business."

It was a typical day on the Hill for the Defense Department. A daily schedule of all Congressional hearings involving the department was issued by the office of the assistant secretary of defense for legislative affairs, for distribution to all the offices within the Office of the Secretary of Defense (each of the services issued its own similar schedule). On this day all with a need to know (and many who didn't, really, but it pleased the Hill) were informed that hearings would be held by:

. . . The House Armed Services Committee, chaired by Mr. Escondido, on a bill to create a "Joint Operational Planning Office" within the OSD, said office presumably to supersede (or, more likely, be added to) the JCS and all the other groups in the building that were supposedly already doing joint operational planning. The bill had been introduced by Mr. Escondido in the House and Mr. Castain in the Senate at the behest of Dr. Donald K. Brattlefield, president of THOUGHT Inc., one of the most active and ubiquitous of the "Beltway Bandit" think-tanks that clustered in Virginia near the Pentagon and contributed (for a handsome price) expertise, analysis and advice. Dr. Brattlefield, tall, thin, ancient, possessed of popping eyes, a frenetic manner and white hair streaming in a wind he seemed always to carry with him for the purpose, was one of the most powerful of all the Beltway Bandits, good every month for at least four letters to the editor and two op-ed pieces in the eastern seaboard's most prevalent newspapers. When "Bratty" Brattlefield spoke, both the building and the Hill jumped, or at least stirred uneasily. Bratty kept his clout in good shape and was treated with the outward respect due his ability to make trouble and the inward contempt warranted by his ceaseless and usually successful attempt to keep THOUGHT Inc., and particularly himself, prominent in the outside eye. Loy Buck, two generals, an admiral and three colonels would appear on that one. And, of course, Bratty.

. . . The House Administration Committee Task Force on Libraries and Memorials, on a resolution authorizing a small memorial on the monument grounds west of the Vietnam Memorial, for Marines lost in the Persian Gulf Encounter. The "encounter" had not been a particularly successful or popular episode in the history of American military actions, but it was generally agreed that *something* had to be done to appease widows and survivors. Gen. Tock and the commander (now ret. without reprimand) of the unfortunate mission were scheduled to testify. Also Lt. Gen. Walter B. "Holy" Waters, Chief of Chaplains.

. . . The Senate Appropriations subcommittee on defense, Mr. Castain chairing, on the latest proposed bill to update, modernize or otherwise modify the eternal MX missile. Old missiles, like old soldiers, never died. This one had as many lives as a cat and Jerry and his phalanx of bright young things were getting ready once again to cry, "View, haloo!" and "Once more unto the breach, dear friends!" in a probably vain attempt to scrub it once and for all. They wouldn't succeed, Jerry conceded dryly: after all these years there were far too many military contractors, subcontractors, constituents and jobs involved in the damned thing. But it was worth a few headlines and perhaps a minute or two on the evening news. So, what the hell. Deputy Secretary Cathcart, Under Secretary for Research and Engineering Tiny Wombaugh and the commanding general of NORAD would be on deck for that.

. . . The House Science and Technology Committee, on a bill to establish special science scholarships under DoD auspices in ten selected universities across the country. The chairman of the House Education and Labor Committee, at her request, would co-chair. Tiny Wombaugh, spreading himself rather thin for a big man, was also supposed to appear at that one as soon as he finished his statement before Jerry Castain on the Senate side. Also present would be a few scientific types from all four services and at least twenty members of the Senate and House, wanting to know why universities in their states and districts had not been mentioned in the original bill. It was pretty certain that they would be, in the revised version.

. . . The Senate Labor and Human Resources Committee, a hearing on the scope and impact of drugs in the military, less than it used to be, not as rare as it ought to be. Secretary of the Army Ray Clark, Secretary of the Navy Hugh Merriman and Secretary of the Air Force Hill B. Ransome would appear, each flanked by an exactly equal number of generals or admirals, as the case might be.

. . . The House Energy and Commerce Committee, on the latest developments in the Strategic Defense Initiative, or Star Wars. The fourth general to head the program was scheduled to testify on progress, which was still uncertain. He would be accompanied by two colonels and a major to run errands. No one from OSD would be supporting him today, because after a year and a half on the job he was due to move on to another duty next week; and anyway, the program, even now, was still considered "pretty iffy" in the building.

. . . The Senate Governmental Affairs Committee, to launch an investigation of military pay schedules compared with non-government civilians. A very large contingent was expected from OSD and all the services. A number of civilian groups had also signified their desire to testify. This was regarded as dull by the media but "a hot one" by the building. Its innumerable repetitions down the years always drew a large official attendance.

Seven committees, some requiring testimony by the same officials on the same morning on both sides of the Capitol: a typical Hill day for the Pentagon. Sitting like little kings, confident in the power conferred upon them by the voters—many of them determined to make damned sure that they overlooked no goodies that could persuade the voters to keep them in that power—the members of Congress demanded, and often got, the cooperation of the Department of Defense. That they did not always get it was a perennial and insoluble problem for those members, and they were many, who honestly worried about the building's enormous waste and its tendency to be alarmingly bull-headed when left unchecked by restraining civilian control.

Both Congress and the Pentagon had their little ways. Some in the Pentagon, like Loy Buck and Zeecy McCune, spoke up and spoke back and gave as good as they got. Others gave polite answers and retreated into the labyrinth to continue doing exactly what they wanted to do irrespective of Congressional prodding or displeasure. Congress in return insisted, demanded, cajoled or attempted to browbeat. It was an endless seasaw between the potential excesses of each. There were often great and justified aggravations and annoyances on both sides of the river. It was at best an uneasy relationship, made more so in recent years by Congress' increasing tendency to insist on stricter and stricter controls over both spending and operations—"their endless meddling," as it was often described by those in the building who had to deal with it, ignoring the fact that their predecessors had provoked it by their profligacy and arrogance. There were ample justifications for suspicion as seen from the Hill, ample reasons for impatience as seen from the Pentagon. It created an endless balancing act: which, after all, was perhaps exactly what the Founding Fathers would have approved of, had they been here.

And now Cube and Luzanne and Burt Sanstrom and very shortly, no doubt, Mario and Jerry and Karl Aschenheim, were about to plunge into the troubled waters of Frio. The justification, as Cube put it succinctly, was the general feeling that, "We're running blind," and that until what he called "the full light of public attention" was focused upon it, who knew what might be going on in the building that could endanger the present policy and future security of the United States?

"It's not that I don't trust Loy and Zeecy and the chiefs," Cube said, "but damn it, I *don't* trust them when I find out that something's been going for seven months without so much as a peep to us. Damn it, we have a right to *know* these things! We put up the money!"

"And," Luzanne agreed, "have to pick up the pieces if something goes wrong."

"What does Zeecy tell you about it?" Cube inquired. She shook her head.

"He still isn't telling me anything," she said in an annoyed tone. "They're still stonewalling over there. But Jerry is obviously right on the basics and so is Red Roberts. If there weren't such an uproar going on both here and abroad, which of course plays right into the Soviets' hands, I'd say let's have our hearing and make our own fuss. As it is— . . ."

"As it is," Burt Sanstrom said tartly, "Mario Escondido will if we don't. Or Jerry. Or Karl."

"They may anyway," Cube retorted. "We can't worry about that, we have our own row to hoe . . . What we *could* do," he said thoughtfully, shrewd old mind racing as it could still do when confronted with a challenge, "is hold a joint inquiry of both houses and invite Jerry and the House fellows to sit in with us. How would that be?"

"Mario would likely try to run away with it," Luzanne suggested. Sen. Herron snorted.

"Let him try. I can take the measure of that little squirt any day. Karl Aschenheim would be responsible, and so would Jerry, I think particularly since he's got his glory, now, being the one to break the story up here. What do you think?"

"It might be a good idea," she said slowly. "But maybe there's a first step that could be taken—a couple of them. First of all, line up Jerry and Mario and make sure they'll agree to it. And then call Loy and Zeecy and invite them to come up for a closed session to tell us all about it. If they won't, then— . . . Of course," she added wryly, "no guaranteed headlines in a closed hearing, so maybe Mario wouldn't go for it. But of course he could always leak it to the media."

"Loy and Zeecy won't go for it," Burt predicted with a sour smile. "Everybody is stonewalling over there. I wasn't able to get anything out of anybody when I tried. And I have some pretty good sources."

"Apparently not good enough," Cube observed and his staff director flushed but perforce said nothing. "All right, Lu, those are good ideas, we'll do it your way. Get me Mario, Burt."

"But—" Burt Sanstrom started to protest. "My secretary—"

"God damn it," Sen. Herron said in a tired tone, *"get him."*

"Yes, sir," Burt said grumpily, picked up the phone and dialed. In a moment he was through to the other side; requested the Congressman; said, "Mario? Hang on for Cube," and handed the phone to the Senator.

"Mario?" Cube Herron said with a wink at Luzanne, "great to hear your voice, you no-good conniving little scalawag." There was a sputter on the other end and he laughed comfortably. "Every word is true, Mario, and you know it. Say, listen. I've got a great idea here, thanks to our beautiful Luzanne, and I want your cooperation. Why don't we—" and he set it forth succinctly. There was further spluttering on the other end, a couple of "God damns!" from Cube and finally: "All right, you can be co-chairman if you want to. In fact, Jerry can be too—oh, Jerry can't be? He can if I say he can, Mario, it's my turf . . .

Come on, now, you can have some dinky little House hearing but if the Senate is rolling you're not going to have a chance at those headlines. Strictly second-string for you, boy. All the media biggies will be over here, so if you want exposure . . . Oh, all *right,* then. You *do* want exposure. Then it's a deal. Now don't you say a God damned word about it to *anybody,* understand me, until we've given Fort Fumble a chance to respond. If Loy and Zeecy say no, then you and I and Jerry will issue a joint statement—a *joint* statement, I said, Mario, I don't want you jumping the gun on us—and we'll get to it . . . When? Why, I'd say—" he looked over at Luzanne—"if it's no from them, as soon as next Monday, maybe?"—she nodded—"that all right with you, Mario? . . . God damn it, we've *all* got schedules we have to shift around, when did you ever know anything to be convenient on this half-assed crazy Hill? . . . No, I *won't* accept Tuesday, we're going to start Monday and if you aren't over here we'll go without you, so get your fat bottom over to the Senate Caucus Room at 10 A.M. Monday *sharp."* He grinned at Luzanne. "Or make it 9:30 if you want to beat us all to the cameras. O.K., Mario? . . . O.K., we'll see you. Until then, *be quiet!"*

And he put down the phone without ceremony and without much mercy for Mario's eardrums.

"Little snot," he remarked, shaking his head. "He can't wait to get his mug on those cameras. He doesn't know that *you're* going to be the beauty queen, dear. How about calling Zeecy for us?"

She laughed, her customary light and silvery sound.

"Certainly not," she said. "You're the chairman, you do it. And I'd suggest you start with Loy. Channels, you know. Channels!"

"All right," he said, "I will. Burt—"

"Yes!" Burt Sanstrom snapped, and dialed the SecDef's number. "Vangie? This is Burt Sanstrom. Where is he? . . . O.K., we'll wait. Sen. Herron wants to talk to him . . . Mr. Secretary? Hang on for the Senator."

"Loy?" Cube Herron said, looking more than ever like an old little boy, cherubic features twinkling beneath the halo of frizzly white, "what devilment are you folks cooking up over there today? Isn't Frio enough for you, for a while? . . . Yes, that's exactly what I want to talk to you about. How about you and Zeecy getting on your horses tomorrow morning and coming up here and telling us all about it? . . . Oh, Senate Armed Services and Mario Escondido, who wants in on the act and you're going to have to appease him somehow anyway if you want any peace of mind, so why not? Oh, and Jerry Castain, your nemesis who spilled the beans. Just to keep us all abreast of what's going on, and so you can swear us all to secrecy and prevent us from messing things up any more than some of us have already. How about that?" . . . His expression changed. He scowled at Luzanne. She made an unhappy face. "What's that?" His voice rose. "You'll talk to Luzanne and Jerry and me and the ranking minority member but you'll be damned if you'll talk to Mario? Now, look, Loy, he can make a lot of trouble for you . . . What? And you figure somebody's bound to talk if you meet with the whole committee? You're playing mighty hard to get, for a man who's dependent on us for appropriations *and* support *and* goodwill, which you're going to need plenty of as this thing builds. Is it still no? . . . Well, then I tell you what's going to happen, Loy. You fellows are going to get your asses dragged across the witness table in the Senate Caucus Room in public hearing starting next Monday sure as my name's Cube Herron, and there's nothing I can do to stop it or to help you much once it's begun. Think about that, Loy! Think about it! Have you heard from the President? Is he going to back you up on it? . . ." He gave Luzanne a grimly ironic smile. "Oh, you've heard from him but you don't really know whether he's going to leave you out there dangling if he thinks there's a chance he'll get hurt by this? He will, Loy, he will. You can count on *that* but don't count on *him*. Now, why don't you come up and have a confidential chat with us and then we can all stonewall it together? . . . I *know* we can't afford to reveal too much to the God damned Soviets, that's the point! Come on, now, Loy, be sensible! We want to be your friends, up here—at least I do, and Lu does, and Jerry does, and so do the majority. But you've got to level with us . . ." His tone changed, became impersonal. "All right, Loy. I've tried to help and you don't want help. So we'll see you Monday . . . That's right, 10 A.M. *sharp*. Sorry it has to come to that, but that's the way you want it, that's the way it's going to be. Have a good day." He gave a grim little chuckle. "Monday isn't going to be one. 'By, now . . .

"God *damn* it," he said, turning back to Luzanne. "Why do these bastards all get so arrogant when they get over there in the Pentagon? We're only trying to help him."

"I think he really is afraid of too much getting out," she said, "but of course it's going to anyway, now. I can see his problem. I also see ours." She smiled. "It's an insoluble conflict."

"Which we each have to decide according to our responsibilities," Sen. Herron agreed. "So there we are . . . O.K., then, Monday in the Caucus Room, 10 A.M."

"Sharp," she said. He grinned.

"I'll be sharp, dear Lu," he said with a grandfatherly pat on her arm, "and you'll be sharp and Jerry'll be sharp—and the Pentagon crowd will be sharp—but oh, Lord, what will we do with Mario?"

She laughed.

"Let him splutter. He can only make noise."

"He can also do damage," Cube said seriously. "I want this to be a responsible hearing, not a circus for a two-bit Congressman . . . Oh, well. I guess we'll just have to see how it goes. I can shut him up if I have to."

"Don't worry about it," she said. "After all, this is only Wednesday. A lot can happen between now and Monday. Maybe Loy will have a change of heart. He must be doing some pretty serious thinking, right about now."

And so he was, though he was certain his final conclusion would be just what he had told Cube. He would rather take his chances in public, where he could assert some degree of secrecy as a matter of national security, rather than in a private session where he would be subjected to a grilling that would allow few necessary evasions. And where, as he had remarked to Cube, more than one member would undoubtedly run right off to tell the media everything that had been discussed.

This propensity for leakage was endemic both on the Hill and in the building. It was one of the major problems hampering the defense program. It was especially frustrating because there was no effective or lasting solution for it. Warnings were issued to the civilian side, commands were handed down by the military, discussions were held from time to time between himself and pertinent committees on the Hill, and still the leaks reached the media. Thinking back over the past seven months he could see that it had been a miracle that Nanukuvu had remained a secret as long as it had. He regretted deeply now that the precious time had not been used to the fullest as it should have been. Instead the building had moved at its own customary pace. A few had felt the urgency. Most, including the JCS, had let things proceed in the set, traditional way. The System and the Process—and the services—had won again. Possibly, though it could not yet be said with certainty, the United States had lost.

He had to face the possibility that the delay might already have been fatal— that it was already too late to mount a successful mission—that there was no way, now, to deny the enemy his complete and triumphant conquest of a new and most dangerous bastion in the South Pacific.

The chance that this could still be accomplished diplomatically he felt had to be regarded, realistically, as virtually non-existent. The enemy had chosen his objective very cleverly, in an area very far from continental United States, a piece of real estate so tiny that many Americans, he was sure, were already concluding that it really was neither strategically significant nor of any real interest to them. Editorials, broadcasts, commentaries, much-publicized statements by the leading neo-isolationists of media, academe and Hollywood who had become so prominent in recent years—all indicated as much. There was a general putting-down of Nanukuvu, a general scoffing at its importance, the beginnings of a loudly vocal consensus that it was so hard to get at, in such a vaguely defined region, that what the hell, let the Soviets have it, it didn't make any difference: this last a very necessary conviction for an attitude unsupported by the facts.

All of this despite the irrefutable evidence of Soviet intentions and the unanswerable argument of the map.

The enemy had struck stealthily and except for the unhappy but fortunate intervention of Hague Smith his aggression might not have been discovered for many months. Realistically, Loy thought, it had probably been touch-and-go from the first. Nanukuvu was indeed so remote and so hard to get at that its difficulties for the United States might have been almost insurmountable under any circumstances.

Almost—but still, perhaps, not quite. He was not prepared to concede that to the critics yet. The building was finally awake and beginning to move. He felt that now there was a good chance that it could go forward under his leadership along the path that seemed best for the national security.

There *were* people in the Pentagon and in the White House, he thought grimly, who really *did* know more about what was going on in the world than columnists, editorialists, actors, rock singers and anchormen. They not only knew more, but they had responsibilities for doing something about it that such as those could lightly dismiss because they did not have the imagination to conceive what it was like to have them.

In this mood he skimmed quickly through the late-morning edition of Clipper Corbus' daily contribution to the mental health of the Pentagon, noting that it contained even more condemnatory editorials and columns than had appeared in the *Early Bird* that had greeted him when he entered his office at seven-thirty. The pack was in full cry, there was no doubt of that. He wondered, as he looked out upon the gray Potomac and the chilly little parade-ground where he would soon have to go to formally welcome the visiting prime minister of Singapore, how all this was playing in the White House. He had not heard from the President since their last phone conversation. He did not want to be the first to break the silence. Neither, evidently, did the Boss. They were playing, Loy recognized, a waiting game, and he was determined that he would not make the first move. The President was apparently making up his mind. An intervention that was not exactly timed and perfectly framed might very well bring about a result the SecDef did not want to see. He knew a President as sensitive to public outcry as this one was a skittish horse that might bolt, at the slightest wrong word, in a direction the SecDef did not want him to go.

This left the Pentagon, he thought ironically, rather high and dry at the moment; and the only solution for that was to continue to adhere to the last word from the Chief Executive and "keep on doin' what you're doin'." Loy did not know how things were moving on the diplomatic front—he'd have to call Terry Venner pretty soon and, with suitable banter and baiting, find out—but he knew that in this building some urgency was at last being shown. Helen Clark had called just a few minutes ago: the ALCAC recommendations had come over from the two Harrys, duly initialed by both. She had already sent them on to DSARC along with Skip Framberg's contribution, and had requested the executive secretary of DSARC to convene the pertinent members at 2 P.M. today. He had thanked her for this and she had promised cheerfully that she would "hold their noses to the grindstone until we get a decision."

"How soon will that be?" he wondered. She laughed.

"By 9 A.M. tomorrow morning, or a reasonable facsimile thereof. I would say by Friday."

"Good," he said. "Keep after them."

"Oh, I will," she promised, and knowing her to be as good as her word he had thanked her again and hung up gratified. She was a strong lady and he felt he was lucky to have her on his team; a gratification which unfortunately did not always extend to that bright, charming, able but often otherwise-occupied soul, her brother.

Ray Clark, he thought with a sigh, was one of those personnel problems that a busy executive should not have to be bothered with. If he rutted like a rabbit, that by rights was his problem, not the SecDef's; and having sad little Karen come in and complain about it at more or less regular intervals was ridiculous and something the civilian head of one of the world's two largest military establishments simply should not have to endure. But endure it he did, being a kindly and compassionate man, even though he really did not see much solution for Karen. The only real solution, as he had tried to suggest gently a couple of times, was to cut her losses and get out; but the storm of tears this idea produced was such as to make him regret that he had even thought it. On the three occasions when she had come to him he had always concluded by saying lamely that well, maybe, if she could just hang on—if she could just manage to be brave—things might straighten out—Ray might reform. But Ray wouldn't reform, he knew that as well as she did. They always ended on the uneasy note of hopeful hypocrisy on which such conversations always do end, and she went away appearing to be at least a little reassured. He hoped she wouldn't come back again but had little doubt she would.

As for Ray, he *was* a problem and promising to become more so, not only for Karen but for DoD. His reputation was spreading in the building as female secretaries, young female officers, even one or two female reporters, fell before his ruthless and incessant onslaught. His depredations upon the Pentagon's feminine population seemed to go on unabated even though he must have known that sooner or later his conquests would begin comparing notes. It was, after all, quite flattering to be pursued by the Secretary of the Army. It was the sort of thing that got talked about in the Pik-Quik, the Big Scoop and the Executive Dining Room. By now it was also probably being talked about in POAC, where Ray made it a practice to work out three times a week, although where he found the energy considering everything, Loy didn't know.

Anyway, before long now it was going to reach something like *Defense Eye,* and from there it would spread to the town's most notorious and determined investigative columnist, and from there to the wires and the rest of the media. More seriously, it had probably already been picked up by the enemy's agents, of whom Loy Buck was sure the building had a few—not many, he was also sure, but that they were in there working he did not have the slightest doubt. It would be sheer stupidity on the enemy's part if they weren't, and he had realized long ago that the enemy was far from stupid. OSD and the services were constantly alert for any indications, but some very strange lapses occurred in the security field, things so appallingly beyond common sense that one didn't see how grown men could let them slip by.

He just accepted it as a given that yes, there were a few enemy agents in the building despite all efforts to keep them out. For them, a swinging service secretary would be a prize, vulnerable target.

Loy had about reached the point where he had decided that Ray would have to go before he made some blunder that would put him really at risk. He was becoming too much of a worry. Only yesterday Zeecy McCune, who, Loy thought wryly, was expert on such matters, had made an indirect but pointed comment which indicated that Ray's reputation was spreading to the wives of the JCS. From there it was only a short step.

Ray might be one of the best secretaries of the Army to come down the pike in quite a while—he and Brash Burford seemed to have a real working rapport and Ray could always be counted on to fight the Army's battles intelligently, vigorously and well—but that didn't excuse the casual way he put himself in jeopardy. It had to stop. Since he and Helen had been direct appointees of the President it couldn't be done immediately. Loy didn't want to clutter the problem of Nanukuvu with an extraneous complaint of that nature to the White House. Let them get the island and its problems safely behind them and then he'd go after Ray. In the meantime, he could only hope the Secretary's luck at avoiding consequences would continue to protect him.

Brought back thus to the contemplation of Nanukuvu, the SecDef looked again out the window and sighed. The crack ceremonial troops of the Military District of Washington were already taking up positions on the parade-ground in front of River Entrance. On the fringes the protesters were waving their signs and shouting obscenities. He supposed he would have to ask the MDW commander to have them herded off to one side during the ceremony for the visitor from Singapore. This would mean camera shots on the evening news and photographs in tomorrow's newspapers but it couldn't be helped. The protesters would be delighted, of course: the media was the message, and the message didn't really matter. For those behind the protest it could be anything as long as it received sufficient publicity and was sufficiently damaging to the United States.

He was about to leave the office, hastily shrugging into a lightweight topcoat and quickly scanning the brief greetings suggested by the protocol office, when Vangie buzzed and he picked up the phone to accept a rare call from his putative second in command. Normally he did not talk to him more than a couple of times a week, usually at the morning conferences, which Bob attended sporadically, or when Bob called now and then to complain about something. Otherwise, the Deputy Secretary of Defense might have been on another planet. Fortunately OSD was set up in such a way as to accommodate the situation. The Deputy Secretary had very few duties that were not given him by the Secretary. Some Secretaries were close to their Deputies and gave them a lot. Loy had made sure some time ago that Bob Cathcart would have very little to do, most of it ceremonial and innocuous.

This meant, of course, that Bob was free to do mischief if he wanted to, and from time to time he had attempted to set up close personal ties to the military. But Zeecy and the chiefs were far too politically shrewd to get involved in anything like that. Their relations remained polite and distant.

On the whole, aside from giving a few disgruntled off-the-record interviews —which always surfaced somewhere in due course and made it quite clear to the public that there was friction at the top level of the Pentagon—Bob had been relatively quiet. Much quieter than Loy had anticipated, in fact, given Bob's longtime political and monetary support of the President in California, and his presumed closeness to the White House.

"Good morning, Bob," he said, deciding to be pleasant rather than hostile: that would probably come soon enough. "I'm in a little bit of a rush—the prime minister of Singapore is due in about ten minutes, as you know. What can I do for you?"

"You might have invited me to attend the ceremony," Bob Cathcart remarked, "but, oh, hell, forget it. Who wants to stand around in the cold wind watching the drill anyway? What does he want this time?"

"More planes," Loy said with some irony. "More missiles. A sub or two, if we can spare one. Not much, as our official visitors go."

"He's getting as hipped on defending that place as the British were," Bob Cathcart said. "Let's hope he doesn't aim all his defenses out to sea."

"He's smarter than that," the Secretary said. "What's on your mind?"

"I just got a call from Mario Escondido," Bob said and Loy said, "Oh?"

"Yes," the Deputy Secretary said. "He invited me to come up Monday and testify on Frio. I told him I would."

"That's good," Loy said, thinking: hell and damnation. "What am I supposed to do about it?"

"I thought you ought to know," Bob said. "I thought you ought to have some idea of the line I'm going to take. You won't like it, but I thought you should be prepared."

"I know you've always been opposed," Loy said, tone growing colder, "but I was hopeful you might be able to restrain yourself in public. It would be most helpful if DoD could present a united front."

"I wish I could," Bob Cathcart said, "but I've never been able to see it, from the first. It's so damned far away, and with the bases we have out there we've got them bracketed anyway, so why bother? It just doesn't seem worth it, to me."

"In that you know, of course, that you fly in the face of the best military advice we can get," the Secretary said. The Deputy Secretary snorted.

"Oh, yes, I know McCune and the rest fell into line. Isn't that what you wanted them to do?"

"They didn't have to," Loy said, restraining his temper but with some difficulty, now. "They had ample opportunity to make their opposition known, if they had any. Both to me and, I might add, to the White House."

"You don't think they'd really defy you, do you?" Bob inquired.

"Certainly," Loy said. "They have on many occasions. There was no question of defiance. We all agreed what should be done the minute we heard about it. It was an almost instinctive reaction."

"Shouldn't have been," Bob Cathcart observed sourly. "Should have been a lot of thought given to that one."

"There was. What's this leading up to, Bob? Are you getting ready to paint a picture for the country of a big bad Secretary going hell-bent for military action in spite of his advisers? 'Buck the War-Monger?' It's been done, you know. I'm sure you can find some in that scruffy gang out front that say exactly that. Why don't you go join them?"

"You're getting hot under the collar, Loy," the Deputy Secretary observed with some satisfaction, "and I wouldn't advise that. It will just throw you off base with the committee."

"I can assure you, Bob," Loy said in an acid tone, "that you are the last person on earth who can 'throw me off base with the committee.' Zeecy and the chiefs and I have been in complete agreement on this from day one, and they'll testify to that. So will everyone else the committee might decide to call. Except, of course, the DepSec. *He's* in a class by himself."

"Not necessarily, Loy," Bob Cathcart said. "Not necessarily. There's a lot of support for my position in the country—in fact, all over the world. This little adventure of yours is not very popular with a lot of people. Most of 'em seem to feel as I do, that it's an ill-advised attempt to find a military solution for something so remote that it can't possibly be handled that way. You'll find the sentiment in the country and on the Hill is pretty isolationist, Loy, when it comes to these far-flung enterprises of yours. We're over the gun-slinger days, now. We're settling back into common sense."

"If that's your opinion, that's your opinion," the Secretary said. "The record will show that all of us over here with the exception of you have been in complete agreement on Nanukuvu from the start. We'll make the case for it since it's now become public, which hampers us terribly in trying to mount an effective response, but there it is. Look, Bob: I've got to run, o.k.? Can't keep the prime minister waiting. Talk to you later."

"I just wanted you to know," the Deputy Secretary said loudly.

"Thank you, Bob," Loy said. "We all appreciate it. We aren't surprised and we won't be deflected. But thanks for passing the word."

"I've tried my best," Bob Cathcart said.

"So have we all, Bob," Loy said. "Thanks for all your help."

"Wait a minute before you slam down the phone on me," Bob said sharply. "Have you talked to the President? Is he on your side?"

"He's told me to 'keep on doing what you're doing,'" Loy said, "which is good enough for me."

"Has he told you that lately?" Bob inquired in a dry tone of voice.

"Lately enough," Loy retorted. "Why, has he told you something different?"

"I talked to him just a few minutes ago after I heard from Mario. It was an interesting discussion."

"I'm sure," the Secretary said. "Are you supposed to transmit some message to me about it?"

"Nope," Bob said smugly. "He just didn't seem very alarmed when I told him what I was going to say, that's all."

"That's good," Loy said. "That's very good, Bob. Now I really have to go. Thanks for calling."

"Thank *you*," the Deputy Secretary said. "Sorry to trouble you."

"Not at all," Loy said. "Any time."

Undercutting son of a bitch, he thought angrily as he opened the door to admit his new military aide, an Air Force brigadier general. Together they took the Secretary's small private elevator down to the motor pool on basement level where his armored limousine and driver were waiting. He could have taken the escalator down one floor and walked out River Entrance to the parade-ground, perhaps three hundred yards all told, instead of taking the limousine half a mile around the building, but he never traveled anywhere officially on foot. He wasn't allowed: too many opportunities. It was just part of the job.

Five minutes later he and the smiling little prime minister were standing side by side on the reviewing stand facing the massed troops and colors in the chill wind off the river. He was beginning smoothly, "Mr. Prime Minister, it is with a great deal of pleasure that I welcome such a good and valued friend of the United States to the Pentagon—"

Inwardly he was still thinking: that jealous, unpleasant, uncooperative son of a bitch. He's going to make all the trouble he can.

But at least, Loy thought with satisfaction, he would be able to fire the first shot when he delivered the department's opening statement to the committee. The speechwriters on the executive staff of the OSD were already at work on a first draft, with orders to have it on his desk by three this afternoon.

3

The doctor in charge at Walter Reed was a colonel in the Army Medical Corps and his approach was both businesslike and kind. How many tense faces, frightened eyes and brave expressions had he seen, he wondered wearily now as he sat behind his desk and began his low-keyed discussion with the tightly-controlled couple before him. From Korea through Vietnam and all the way-stations before, between and after, from terrified, hurting private to terrified, hurting general, all were proud, desperately calm, determined not to break down and give in—hoping against hope that if they could somehow just manage to hang on, God would recognize their character and their bravery and reward them by saying it wasn't so.

But doctors weren't God, though some of them thought so and some were considered so by grateful patients brought back from the edge of eternity; and when the facts were all in one direction there wasn't much to do but say it *was* so, as gently as one could. This he now proceeded to do.

He had never served with Gen. Burford but he had always heard good things about him and had admired his record as he had risen steadily to the post of chief of staff. He had heard from friends who knew them that Mrs. Burford was equally fine and equally admirable, that she was in fact "the general behind the general." Looking candidly into her sad but unwavering gray eyes and observing the way in which her husband never took his own from her face, he decided that they were quite a pair—a real team, a genuine marriage of hearts, minds, sensitivities, perceptions and mutual understanding. He could not help but wonder how her illness would affect the career that most in the Army thought would soon culminate in the chairmanship of the JCS. Not too drastically, he sincerely hoped; and sensed that, given the reserves they both seemed to have, it perhaps would not, though one could never be sure when fatal fears were finally transformed into reality.

"Mrs. Burford," he said gently, "I suspect that you already know what I am about to tell you. I know the general does."

"I expect I do," she said, hand holding tight to her husband's. "It *is*—Alzheimer's, isn't it."

"I'm afraid so," he said. "But," he added quickly, "it may be a long process. You may have several more good years ahead. There's no reason to expect any sudden degeneration."

She smiled wryly.

"Or any improvement, either."

"No," he conceded. "The best we can hope for is for you to hold your own. This could go on for quite a long time. We really don't know. It's unpredictable."

"But the chances are—" she said.

"The chances are," he said gravely, "that it will be difficult for you and the general and your family, no matter what. But with sufficient will and courage, which I think you both have, it can be managed. And, as I say, there may be a number of good years still ahead. We must hold to that. The main thing is to keep up your spirits, and to hope."

"It's the physical degeneration I mind almost more than the mental," she said with a little shudder. "It—it disgusts me."

"I know," he said softly. "I know . . ."

General Burford cleared his throat, a harsh and nervous sound.

"What should we do, colonel?" he asked. "I mean, is there anything special we should know as a—as a family? Aside from giving the medication, that is? Anything else?"

"Not much," the doctor said. "Follow the schedule on that—do whatever is necessary to provide physical comfort—*take care of her*. That's about it."

"I always have," Gen. Burford said simply and Mrs. Burford looked at him with an expression the doctor wished he could receive sometime from his own wife. He smiled.

"I can see that," he said, and stood up.

"I don't suppose," Gen. Burford said as they stood up too, "that there's any chance—I mean, you couldn't *possibly* be mistaken, colonel?"

"No, general," the doctor said gravely. "I'm sorry, but—there's no doubt."

"We'll just have to manage," Mrs. Burford said. A sudden fierce determination came into her voice. *"And we will."*

"Good," the doctor said, taking both her hands in his. "That's the spirit. You will."

"We *will*," she repeated, giving his hands an answering squeeze. "Give me your arm, Brash. I'm feeling a little wobbly right now, as a matter of fact. But," she added firmly, "it will pass."

"Yes," Gen. Burford said. "Yes, Vi, I'm sure it will . . ." He cleared his throat again, shook the doctor's hand with a quick, hard grip. "Thank you, colonel. You're very kind. We'll be in touch."

"Of course, general," the doctor said. "Call me any time."

He stepped out of his door for a moment after they left and watched them as they walked down the corridor, the general's figure stiff and unyielding, Mrs. Burford holding his arm, moving slowly but still with an erect and dignified carriage that spoke character in every line.

Well, general, he thought, I hope you make it. And Mrs. Burford, may you go in grace.

Back in his office an hour later, Brash sat for some time staring unseeing at the map of Nanukuvu that now held prominent place on his wall. His thoughts were much farther away than the island, lost in some reminiscent other world in which mental picture after mental picture of Vi flashed past: the girl he had met, the girl he had married, the wife and mother who had always been the solid rock of their family and of his own career. *"Everybody* loves Vi Burford!" the wife of his first commanding general had said, far back down the years in Manila; and so they had, and so they did still. She walked in an aura of love. How to draw from it now, and what should he himself do in the face of this implacable decision, by a God he could no longer respect or honor, to destroy her?

He had already consulted with the children, several months ago after one particularly bad day when she had worked very hard on a charity bazaar at Fort Myer, become overly tired and been driven home by Dorry Tock in a state of almost complete disorientation. It had fortunately not begun until they had almost reached Quarters 1, and only he, Dorry and Carleene had been present. The women had been the soul of kindness to Vi and to himself and somehow they had all managed to get through the frightening two hours before she began to come back to them. He had decided that it was time to begin calling up his reserves, as he put it to Barbara and Jeff when he talked to them that night.

They of course had been instantly responsive and instantly helpful. Barb had volunteered to leave her family and fly home for a couple of weeks to be with her mother. Jeff's wife Elise had suggested the same. He had thanked them all as calmly as he could under the emotional impact of the moment, but had declined with grateful thanks "until such time as it may be really necessary. Then I'll need you here."

He wondered if now was the time; and he wondered whether it might not be time for him to consider making the greatest and most fitting sacrifice for his wife that an officer in his position could make: to inform the Secretary that he was resigning immediately as chief of staff and retiring from the Army. This would terminate once and for all his lifelong ambition to be chairman of the JCS, but he would then be able to devote all of his time to caring for her.

He knew what Vi's reaction would be if he mentioned this idea to her: she would be utterly dismayed, sadly but strongly opposed. She would blame herself for it, which was not the point; she would, as always, take upon herself the responsibility and the burden of others' actions. Therefore he could not, for the first time since their marriage, seek her advice and support for a decision. Nor could he consult the kids, who would also be vehemently opposed. He would have to fight it out for himself, at least as far as the family was concerned.

Casting about in his mind now for someone he might talk to about it, he rejected the idea of Tick and Dorry. Tick, his most supportive friend at his own level, and the only one who knew the full situation, would tell him he was absolutely crazy. He could hear him now: "God damn it, Brash, that's ridiculous! She'll have all the help and care she needs, there isn't a thing you could

possibly do for her that others more competent can't, and you'd just be throwing away your chance for nothing. It's the last thing she'd want you to do. Don't
be a sentimental damned fool."

Asked if he would do the same for Dorry, Tick would hesitate but in the end
his pragmatic common-sense would control and he'd stick to what he wanted
to do. And that would be perfectly reasonable, and what any sensible and
ambitious man would do.

The Secretary himself he could not approach, because that would be to
disclose what Loy could probably only regard as the arrogant presumption that
Brash was even in the running for the chairmanship. Loy had never indicated
by so much as a lifted eyebrow that he was even considering the question of
Zeecy's successor, although of course it was inevitable that he should be. He
wouldn't be much of a Secretary if he weren't and one thing they were all
agreed upon was that few SecDefs had been as able as Loy Buck.

Everyone of any stature in the building, military or civilian, sooner or later
had occasion to find some fault with him on some point, it wouldn't be human
nature if they didn't, but taken overall, Loy came through with flying colors. He
had earned their respect and admiration and he had it in full measure. Brash
valued Loy's confidence in him and did not want to diminish it by seeming to
be greedy for preferment, even though he suspected that Loy in truth would
regard his situation with compassion and not think less of him at all.

Nonetheless, he couldn't do it.

Ham Stokes of course was out of the question, being the man Brash regarded
as his principal competition. He knew the building generally thought so too.

That left two possibilities, one of them Zeecy himself, who had always been
a sponsor of Ham's career, although a clear-eyed and at times skeptical observer of it; and the other being a man who was never very popular in the
Pentagon and was even less so now that he had blown the whistle on Frio, the
junior Senator from Indiana, Mr. Castain.

Brash could never forget the kindness Jerry had shown him that day at lunch
in the Senate when he had first guessed what Vi's problem was. Brash had not
gone out of his way to discuss it with him, but every two or three weeks since
he had received a call from Jerry. At first, in his helpless anger against fate, he
had tended to resent this interest, even though he told himself it was genuine
and coming from the kindest of motives. But presently, as things progressed
and her condition began noticeably to deteriorate, he had come to value Jerry's
disinterested and perfectly genuine support. He didn't know, however, where
Jerry stood as a Senator closely involved with the Pentagon and therefore
probably one of those whose opinion, if asked, would contribute something to
the final decision on the chairmanship. He too might be a Stokes partisan.
Brash rather doubted it, but Jerry *was* a little unpredictable—Brash had to
concede the Senator's Pentagon critics that.

And, of course, there was another question involved. Could Brash continue
to function at top capacity with his wife sinking steadily and inevitably toward

deterioration and death? Just how efficient an officer could he continue to be? Wouldn't it be best for the Army's sake and for his own, as well as Vi's, if he quit right now? Would he not be betraying the huge and admiring constituency he had built up over the years in his own service if he continued at psychological and emotional half-speed?

He did not think his state of mind had been reflected so far in his daily activities, although Zeecy had looked at him rather curiously only a couple of days ago and inquired abruptly, "Are you all right, Brash? You seem awfully preoccupied lately. Is something the matter?"

Brash had hastened to assure him that no, everything was fine. Zeecy had continued to look a little quizzical and uncertain, but his only comment had been, "I hope so. If there's anything wrong, I'm here to help. Remember that."

Brash had been properly and genuinely grateful but had protested again that everything was all right.

He told himself firmly now that this was true. He had watched his actions carefully right along, and aside from an occasional episode when he did indeed become preoccupied and momentarily lost his train of thought, he had not observed too much out of the ordinary in himself. He had, it was true, lost continuity a couple of times in recent speeches, one while addressing the Army War College at Carlisle Barracks, Pennsylvania, the other at the Century Club in New York. But he had quickly recouped, passed off his confusion with a joke that had covered nicely, and concluded successfully. And his judgment on such things as Nanukuvu and all the myriad other problems that came to his desk as chief of staff had not seemed to him to be noticeably impaired in any way.

Nanukuvu! That was a ticklish one for all of them, now that Jerry and Red Roberts between them had called in the whole world. He did not think it would have any real bearing on the selection of the next chairman providing there were no conspicuous errors on anyone's part, and he didn't think there were. It was true that Ham had advocated strong action from the very first, and that Brash and Bumpy and even Tick had been a little more cautious in their approach: that might possibly weigh against him in some minds when it all came out on the Hill. On the other hand, there was a big group whose members were opposed to any precipitate or even mild action by the United States anywhere in the world, no matter what. Bright young Congressmen, usually from New York, Massachusetts or California, media-stroking young Senators anxious for publicity, were always loud to criticize and quick to oppose. He disagreed sharply with their basic foreign policy, or lack of it; but being an old hand at the Washington game, he was not going to tell them so, or object if they saw his early brief hesitations on Nanukuvu as an endorsement of their beliefs and in return endorsed him too.

Cube Herron had called him a little while ago, as he was apparently calling everyone he could think of who might have something to do with it, with his invitation to appear at the hearing next Monday. Like all such Hill "invitations," it amounted to a command of the kind that very few in the executive branch of the government ever deliberately ignored. Brash frowned. Whatever points might or might not be made by the building's spokesmen, the hearing could only damage the mission. The Soviets once again would be given gratuitous and invaluable aid by America's open society and the almost compulsive desire of many of her citizens to expose her weaknesses, thwart her plans and generally rip her reputation and influence to shreds in the eyes of the world.

A very strange syndrome, Brash had always thought, but one that had dominated the nation's history for almost half a century, now. He supposed the hearing would be one more bath in abject abnegation for all those Americans who loved to savage their own country. Out of it both Frio and Pentagon could only emerge hurt, the enemy could only emerge strengthened and supported in his dangerous plans for the island. The Pentagon and Frio might be in trouble: the Soviet Union, as usual, would be home scot-free.

It was insane, in his estimation—absolutely insane. But that was the way it went, in America in the closing years of the weird century in which everything was upside down, bad was good, good was bad, right was wrong, wrong was right and golly, Molly, what a funny tea-party everybody went to.

What did it really matter, what one small four-star general did about his future, in such a topsy-turvy world?

But of course it did, and brooding about the insoluble nature of the times would not advance the solution of his own problems. He decided he *would* talk to Jerry about it. Maybe he *was* being too quixotic, maybe as Tick would say, too sentimental. On the other hand, there was Vi, the wonderful personality, the wonderful years . . . and the very few that were probably left.

He sighed heavily and turned again to all the worldwide problems of the Army that needed his attention. Whatever he might decide later, at the moment he was still chief of staff and these were his responsibilities. With an enormous but successful effort of the will he pushed aside his worries and returned to the duties he had been appointed to perform.

On fourth floor, E Ring, above River Entrance, his principal competition—or so they both sincerely believed—also had problems. Ham Stokes had always prided himself on his ability to concentrate on the needs of the Air Force to the exclusion of all else. But here he was, deep in unhappy thought about his domestic affairs.

It was not his nature to brood, and it was not his nature to be unhappy, because normally everything, both on duty and at home, went as he wanted it to. It was only in recent months that this ideal state of affairs had begun to disintegrate. Not in the Air Force, where his word was still law and his mandate still both respected and feared, but at home where Zenia was increasingly independent and increasingly hard to deal with.

The thing that was really getting to him, Ham thought now as he sat at his desk putting final polish on the speech he would deliver to a civic banquet in New Orleans next week, was that she was not so much hostile to him personally as she was to his concept of himself. That was what stung and that was where she knew how to get through his defenses and really give him hell. He found this alarmingly disturbing and something he did not quite know how to handle. No one had ever challenged him in quite this way before. It was probably something only a wife could do with just that combination of ridicule and exact aim at his most cherished beliefs about himself.

He had decided, with a heavy frown on his big, commanding face and an unconscious clenching of his big, emphatic fists, that it had to stop. One way or another, *it had to stop.* He could take a lot of things but he couldn't take much more erosion of his faith in himself and still continue to conduct himself with the force and competence that, in his estimation, made his appointment as chairman of the JCS a virtual certainty.

Nothing, he told himself grimly, *nothing* was going to get in the way of that long-cherished ambition, at least nothing that he himself could control or influence. And since his marriage had apparently entered upon a time in which he could neither control nor influence his wife, it might be that something fundamental would have to happen there.

Of all the delicate interlocking interests and considerations that went into the selection of a CJCS, a solid marriage was among the most important.

A candidate for chairman might possibly get a divorce after his appointment but a divorce beforehand would run squarely into the military marriage syndrome. It would shake everybody up, the whole web would quiver, a message would run down the network that it was possible for things *not* to be perfect; and that would never do. Things *had* to be perfect, that was part of the creed —at least, they had to be in public. Out of public view a lot of things went on, but in public, role-models had to be role-models had to be role-models, or suffer the career consequences. Even Gen. Zoren Chace McCune, who probably, Ham suspected, was not half the dashing devil gossip gave him credit for, observed most of the forms in public. A stable marriage—at least on the surface—was proof that you were Really All Right, a necessary endorsement in one's fitness file. Very few had the temerity to challenge this basic requirement of public appearance. Sooner or later "a good, solid marriage" was requisite if one had serious ambitions in the military. To sacrifice that image now, when he was just on the point of achieving his lifetime goal, was something Gen. Stokes could not seriously contemplate.

But something had to give. Zenia's various groups, boards, committees, conferences, were getting more numerous all the time; anything, it seemed, was sufficient excuse to get out of the house even though that meant increasingly heavy expenses for maids and baby-sitters for the younger children. She didn't seem to care. When he complained she usually had some pointed and/or flippant remark that told him she was not impressed with his opinion and no longer respected his objections to what she did.

It was true, as he had told her four months ago, that she was the beneficiary of a sort of reverse racial snobism in the Air Force. Its upper echelons rather prided themselves on her occasional defiance of military decorum, expressed in attendance at gatherings protesting military policies. She was, as he had told her again just the other day, the in-house protester, a distinction made even more acceptable to the service because she was black. She was the darling of *Defense Eye* and indeed of all the major organs of public opinion, which featured her prominently, interviewed her, quoted her, wrote about her with conspicuous frequency.

"You're really Mrs. Spotlight, aren't you?" he had inquired on one recent occasion.

She had given him an ironic smile.

"Sorry if I'm getting too prominent for you," she said, "but I imagine every mention boosts my value in the D.C. job market. When I join that law firm I'll be able to write my own ticket."

"I didn't know you were that devious about achieving your ambitions," he had remarked, thinking he sounded amused but, to her ears, sarcastic.

"I have a good example," she had shot back, which had provoked him instantly into an indignant sputter that by God, they could say a lot of things about Ham Stokes, but they couldn't say he was devious: everything was *right there*.

She had not commented on this with words, which might have been possible to counter, but with the knowing and superior smile she was using more and more as rejoinder to his increasingly self-defensive remarks. And how could they help but be self-defensive, in the face of that kind of treatment? It was getting to be a vicious circle he didn't know how to break out of—except by the method Gen. Harmon C. Stokes had always used to break out of tight situations, namely to go straight ahead and bull his way through by main strength and character.

So: divorce one of these days, if things didn't change—after his appointment as CJCS. For the time being, a separate room, scrupulous courtesy, a silent avoidance. Maybe that would still bring her around. If she were still willing to come down to earth, as he put it to himself, and resume being what she was supposed to be, a good—and *quiet*—wife and mother, he was willing to meet her halfway. But he wasn't going any further. She'd have to change substantially if she wanted to save the marriage.

And even that might not be enough unless it were accompanied by the respect she should give him both as an individual and as a member of their race who *had* achieved such a brilliant career and risen so unusually high. She was not respectful enough, he told himself now, frowning thunderously again: disrespect and a scarcely suppressed mockery and amusement lurked behind her words and glinted in her eyes. He had been a good husband, damn it, *and* a good father *and* a good provider. If she had been required to subordinate her career to his, well, that's just the way it was. If she didn't like it, why had she married him in the first place? He regarded it as a bargain she hadn't kept, not as what she once told him she regarded it to be, an obstacle to her own self-expression and career fulfillment.

One career being fulfilled was enough for one military family, he had told her bluntly, thereby provoking the last tears he had seen from her in months. After that she had seemed to close up somehow, though he couldn't understand why: it was the truth.

Everybody else respected Ham Stokes' dedication to the truth. Everybody else subordinated their needs to his and had through nearly all of his military career. Why couldn't she?

It wasn't fair, he thought angrily, particularly now when he was nearing the achievement of his life's ambition, now when the problem of Nanukuvu had moved into the public arena and he needed all his concentration for that. He too had received his "invitation" from Cube Herron, with whom he had met head-on in the past and with whom he would probably clash again here, although his own record, he was glad to say, was in the clear.

He was the original advocate of prompt and effective force to stop the occupation of the island and nobody could deny him that. The rest of them, particularly on the JCS staff, had piddled along and piddled along, all the smooth little colonels and majors and lieutenants who were so God damned busy all the time pushing paper, had taken their own sweet time about getting Op Frio through the process. But there had never been any doubt that Ham Stokes had made up *his* mind months before and had been ready to go long before the proposal had been turned white, buff, pink, blue, green, yellow, purple, magenta, cerise, puce, puke or whatever other damned color they might think of next. Even when he had been a member of the JCS staff years ago Ham had not thought much of the process. He thought even less of it now.

He and the Air Force didn't fuck around, he told himself dourly. They perceived a need, established an objective, went after it and *got it done.*

At least he liked to think they did, even if, in truth, there were probably just as many foul-ups, on an average, as there were in any other service. The Air Force just seemed more efficient and no-nonsense; and to some degree, because it thought of itself that way, possibly was.

So he was prepared to go to the Hill with no hesitations and state exactly what he had advocated right along. He knew the President still seemed to be wavering a bit and he could imagine what all this national and international uproar was doing to him; but that was all the more reason to take a firm position. Maybe it would help to light a fire in his gut. Ham, who did not think very highly of most politicians, felt that this one needed it maybe more than most. Right now, anyway.

It was no time, in his estimation, to turn tail and run. If that opinion affected his chances to be chairman, he thought grimly, so be it.

Again he was doing what Zenia often accused him of, taking two positions at once. A potential divorce might have to be deferred for a while for the sake of the chairmanship but the honesty of Ham Stokes' military beliefs wasn't going to be compromised even if it did affect the chairmanship.

There was no doubt now that the Pentagon would present a united front next Monday—with the possible exception of Bob Catheter, he thought scornfully; and who cared what the DepSec thought, anyway? Everyone else was ready to move. Their massed agreement could only come through on the Hill and in the media as an impressive display of unity and determination. There would be challenge and criticism, of course, but that could be ignored. The important thing was to show the President he had the support he needed in the Pentagon for strong, decisive action. Then they could move at last to neutralize Nanukuvu. He agreed with the SecDef's estimate that they had at least six months, maybe a year, before the most strategically important development of all, the two airstrips, would be operational.

If the Administration had the will, it had the time.

So it seemed to Ham Stokes as his thoughts moved on and became consumed by the idea of one more triumph for his beloved Air Force. Maybe he could rock along with Zenia for a while longer without doing anything too drastic: maybe he could even relax a bit on the Draconian measures he had been contemplating a few minutes ago to bring her to her senses. He was an odd combination of impatience and tolerance: most saw the first and didn't realize the second was there underneath. Zenia did, and probably didn't take his grumblings too seriously. Maybe he shouldn't either. Now that the plan for Operation Frio had finally been agreed upon, Nanukuvu was really what he should be concerned with, not the more difficult aspects of his marriage or their possible effects on his chances for the chairmanship. Let the Air Force do what he knew it could do with Nanukuvu, and the chairmanship would take care of itself. Quite unconsciously he found himself humming in a fashion that was corny, he realized with amusement, but inevitable given his position and background.

Nothing can stop the U.S. Air Force! he told himself with satisfaction.

Or Gen. Harmon C. Stokes, when he really got rolling.

A floor below and a few feet over, the chairman of the JCS was wishing he could feel as confident of the outcome as the chiefs and the members of the joint staff seemed to be. There was suddenly a new atmosphere in his offices in spite of the clamor in the media and on the Hill. He had passed the word to the head of the secretariat as soon as he had left the tank with agreement on Op Frio: it was as though he had injected a shot of adrenalin. The bureaucracy whose ponderous slowness and devotion to process had been largely responsible for the delays up to now was suddenly gung-ho to get moving. It was as though its members bore no responsibility whatsoever for the slowness that might very well have lost the United States its best and possibly only chance to neutralize Nanukuvu without a truly disastrous confrontation. The chiefs seemed to have the same curious ability to close their minds to their own responsibility. Once again, nobody was really responsible for anything: the system cushioned them all. The decision to move had apparently wiped out all memory of what had gone before. It was as though they were all starting from the beginning once more, and that the latest day was once again the first.

Except, as Zeecy knew with an unvarnished realism his position gave him the right to indulge, this was very far from the case. The first day was long gone, now, and on Nanukuvu they confronted an enemy installation already two-thirds of the way toward what was apparently intended to be its completed state: not only a major atomic submarine base in the South Pacific but two major airstrips as well. Like the SecDef he too bitterly regretted the time that had been lost.

He also knew that none of this must be allowed to surface on the Hill next Monday. It was vitally important that the Pentagon present a united front, otherwise not only would the building once again be vulnerable to attack from all its many critics, but Frio itself might very well suffer irremediable damage. He and Loy would have to refrain from answers that might give a public picture of discontent and divided counsel within the building at any stage of the mission. Any other impression could be fatal to Frio and thereby guarantee the enemy virtually unchallenged control of the island.

As the two men principally answerable, they would simply have to shoulder whatever blame might come because the mission had been delayed. He suspected with a grim irony that in today's climate the blame was much more likely to come because the Pentagon had had the nerve to even contemplate any mission at all. In either case, he and Loy would have to take the flak. And everyone else involved would have to support them.

With the exception of Bob Cathcart, he was confident that was the way it would be. Loy had already informed him that Bob, ever the wild card, had signified his intention to break ranks. Well, so be it, Zeecy thought: there was no way to stop him, his testimony could only be "put in proper perspective," as Loy had wryly described it—in other words derided, derogated and made to appear foolish and irresponsible. Both he and the Secretary were pretty good at that, Gen. McCune thought with some wryness of his own: Bob Catheter would know he had been in a tussle when they got through with him. As for Frio itself, he was reasonably confident that it would survive—providing it continued to receive the support of the one man who had to support it if it was to have any further life at all.

The President for the moment remained an enigma. He had apparently retreated into one of those evasive silences Zeecy remembered vividly from their academy days. Perhaps he honestly didn't know what he was going to do. The clamor, both at home and overseas, was still going on and would continue rising right up to the hearing. Inevitably this must be causing a lot of thought in the Oval Office. Against that lay his responsibilities as Commander-in-Chief, his constitutional duty to protect and preserve the United States which no President had to be reminded of, it was instinctive in all of them as it was in the great majority of Americans. It would come down, Zeecy suspected, to two things: whether the Boss really felt that a fortified, militarized base posed a genuine danger to the United States and to its allies in the South Pacific basin; and whether he felt that the continuing uproar over the effort to neutralize it would have a really serious detrimental effect upon his plans for re-election.

Gen. McCune knew his man well enough to know that he would have a very difficult time reconciling these two if he decided both were valid. Zeecy thought the President would come down on the side of removing the threat if it could be done; but he knew that if the decision was to abandon Nanukuvu without further protest it would be presented to the country and the world with great political skill and rationalization. He was certain that if the mission were abandoned the Pentagon would be left to twist in the wind, and that from it would fall a few sacrificial heads, not least of them his own.

He could stand this, he thought, and so could Loy if it came to that. They were nearing the end of their careers in any event. The effects on some others and above all the effect on the morale of the Pentagon in general would be for a time devastating . . . even though the Pentagon's own delays and the defects of its own system would have been in large part responsible for creating the time-lapse in which public controversy could develop. Few military in the building would stop to reason all that out, or would admit it to themselves or anyone else if they did. Civilian politics would be blamed for the debacle. Service politics, rivalries and jealousies would hardly be mentioned. Excuses and scapegoats would be desperately searched for and swiftly found. The main defense would be civilian shortcomings. The military's would not be acknowledged.

Therefore for a great many reasons it would behoove the Pentagon to stand firm now, and for the mission to be moved ahead just as fast as it could possibly be. He had tried to impress upon Cube Herron when he called that the hearing "should not repeat NOT" be dragged out a minute more than absolutely necessary.

"I'm with you, Zeecy," Cube said, "but that doesn't mean we aren't going to want to know everything we possibly can, short of absolute security, about what's going on over there. Also, we have Connecticut's finest with us, you know. I'll try to keep Mario under control but I can't guarantee anything."

"Yes, I know," Zeecy said, reflecting that this would be a very good excuse for letting Mario do whatever savaging of the Pentagon Cube didn't want to do himself. "I'm sure you'll try, Cube. We'd appreciate it."

"Funny thing," Cube remarked. "Loy said almost exactly the same thing. You boys been getting your act together already?"

"We haven't discussed it yet," Zeecy said, "there hasn't been time. However, of course we'll plan a little strategy. You wouldn't expect us not to, would you? —Or respect us if we didn't."

"That's right," Cube said with a chuckle. "But I expect there'll be somebody who won't stay in line. Somebody'll spill the beans, Zeecy. Somebody always does."

"No beans to spill," Gen. McCune said tartly. "Anyway, if you're counting on Bob Cathcart, I wouldn't. He'll sputter and fuss the way he always does but he'll be the only one. We're all pretty well agreed on Frio, over here."

"We sure aren't up here," Sen. Herron observed with equal tartness. "Doesn't stack up too well as we see it from the Hill, Zeecy. Lot of feeling against it, you know. It's not going to be a love-feast on Monday."

"What about you, Cube? Are you going to run out on us too?"

"Not saying yet," Cube replied promptly. "Going to wait and see."

"We regard Nanukuvu as an extremely serious situation not only for the United States but for many allies in the South Pacific," Gen. McCune said. "We'd be sorry to see you helping the enemy, Cube, inadvertently and innocently as it might be."

"Now, there you *go!*" Cube said indignantly. "That old 'helping the enemy' bit! God damn it, Zeecy, *some* of us up here are sincerely concerned about what's best for the United States, just as much as you are! We aren't *interested* in 'helping the enemy.' We're interested in what *might* be done, whether it *ought* to be done, whether it *can* be done, and if so, how can it be done most efficiently and expeditiously. It's on those points that you'll find me and every other responsible member bearing down on the Pentagon. As you damned well know, so cut the crap and let's don't have any of that damned 'helping the enemy'!"

"All right, Cube," Zeecy said, unmoved, "calm down. There *are* times when the Hill goes too far with us and you know it as well as I do. It's a rare member who deliberately wants to harm the United States—although," he added dryly, "I sometimes think there might be one or two—but inadvertently and innocently damage *can* be done. So you should be careful not to press too hard on certain points, and you should cooperate, it seems to me, in trying to keep the hearing on-track and as short as possible."

"I'm going to do my best," Cube said, more calmly, "but I'd just suggest you level with us, because if we get the sense that you're not, there'll be hell to pay. We don't like military adventures undertaken behind our backs, you know. *I* don't like it. In fact, Loy promised me when he first took office, and you did too, that it wouldn't happen while you were in there if you could possibly help it. Now here comes Nanukuvu, big surprise, and it turns out you've been working on it for seven months. How about a little good faith from the Pentagon, general? When are we going to see some?"

"Nanukuvu was a special case—" Gen. McCune began stiffly.

"They're *all* special cases," Sen. Herron interrupted. "Never knew one yet that wasn't a 'special case.' That isn't good faith, Zeecy."

"There were special circumstances surrounding this one," Zeecy said, not conceding. Cube Herron snorted.

"Well, if there were," he said, "you're going to have your chance on Monday to tell us all about them. So be prepared."

"We'll tell you everything we can consistent with security," Zeecy said firmly. Again Cube snorted.

"I know that one, too," he said as he hung up. "Better be good, Zeecy. I'm afraid the Pentagon doesn't have too many friends this time."

Which, the chairman knew, was entirely correct. There had been more hostile speeches in both houses, more condemnatory editorials and commentaries, more critical segments of the evening news; and overseas, more uneasy questionings from America's allies, more hostile attacks from America's enemies.

Only the major enemy had not spoken: the clever operator in the Kremlin was biding his time. No doubt, Zeecy thought with a tired annoyance, he would be reporting in soon, with his usual shrewd sense of timing and his usual flair for capturing the attention of an international community two thirds of whose members were conditioned by years of incessant anti-American propaganda to give him more than a fair hearing, anyway.

The general's tone was gruff when his secretary buzzed again and he lifted the phone to demand sharply, "Yes?"

"My, my," Luzanne said, sounding amused. "Things must be getting rough over there."

"They aren't exactly smooth," he replied, still sounding grumpy. Her tone changed to suit.

"I'm sorry. Maybe I should call back some other time—"

He relaxed.

"No, no. There won't be any better time for a while now, I suspect. I just talked to your distinguished chairman and he promises that you'll all give us hell on Monday. It's made my day."

"There *will* be some questions asked," she conceded. "A lot of people up here are really concerned about it. They're against secrecy instinctively and when it involves getting us into a military situation so far away—"

"I suppose that reflects your thinking too," he said. "There is no 'far away' any more. Everything's next door."

"Not psychologically," she said. "And not really in fact, in spite of planes and missiles and speed of communication. It's still going to take a major effort to neutralize Nanukuvu and don't think it isn't."

"I don't think it isn't," he said. His tone became musing. "You know, it's a funny thing—and perhaps significant. When this all began, the phrase over here was 'get those bastards out of there.' Now the phrase we've all begun to use is the one you just used—'*neutralize* Nanukuvu.' There's a great difference. It's interesting."

"It came natural to me to say that," she said, "because in general I'd say that's the way we look at it, up here. But I can see where it does represent a big shift in thinking in the Pentagon." She paused and he could sense a shrewd political intelligence working. "Maybe it will be possible to wind up not so far apart after all. I think the concept of 'neutralizing' would be much more popular up here than 'going in and getting the bastards out of there.' Maybe we should plot a little strategy along those lines."

"Not yet," he said. "Let's get the mission organized and really underway before we begin to think about trimming it back to fit its critics."

"Not just the critics," she said. "I'm disposed to be friendly. So are some powerful others. Jerry, for one. I don't think he's against you."

"I don't know about Jerry. I haven't quite figured him out, yet. But, then," he added wryly, "who ever does? Mario Escondido will perform the usual, aided no doubt by Burt Sanstrom. It'll be a lively time. I urged Cube to keep it short if possible. He said he'd try but might be helpless in the face of Mario. This struck me as a bit disingenuous but maybe you can help."

"I'll try."

"Good. Am I still seeing you Friday night?"

"If you still want to."

He laughed.

"Are you kidding? But no, of course you're not. The senior Senator from Louisiana never kids, she has no sense of humor. We all know that."

"Better watch out," she said, but lightly. "I may not have."

"That *would* be a strategic miscalculation on my part."

"Could be," she said cheerfully. "See you at seven."

"On the dot," he said with a comfortable chuckle that he hoped would invite reassuring laughter in return. When it did not he hung up both a little puzzled and a little alarmed. He couldn't believe he was being outfoxed at his own game. But maybe he was.

He was about to leave for lunch, which he and the chiefs were having with Loy in his office, when his secretary buzzed again. This time it was the head of the Army's Criminal Investigation Command, a major general.

"With reference to your inquiry about Maj. Gary Stump, sir," he said, "files show absolutely nothing of a suspicious nature. Apparently an admirable officer in every respect. Do you want us to pursue it further?"

Zeecy paused and then thought of his own uneasiness, and Brod's.

"I think perhaps you might, general. For a little while, anyway. I don't want to feel I'm persecuting the major, he may be exactly what you think he is. But a couple of us are a little bit concerned—for no particular reason, I grant you. Just—uneasy. How about having somebody keep an eye on him for a few days, just to see what happens?"

"Well, sir," the general said, obviously not approving very much, "if you really think—"

"Just to please me, general," Zeecy said with pleasant firmness. "Put it down to an old man's senility as he fades into the sunset, but humor me, all right? I'd appreciate it."

"Well . . ." the general said reluctantly. "All right, sir, if you *really* think so."

"I do," the chairman said crisply. "Thank you, general."

And replaced the phone before there could be further rejoinder. He was stretching his own quite nominal authority a bit to make such a request of one of the services, but on the other hand he was the chairman and rank had its privileges. Especially when he matched his own impressions with those of young Brod, who struck him as a very worthwhile and astute young man. He was stretching his authority a bit to push Brod along so fast, too, but that was an indulgence he permitted himself from time to time. He could remember his own career being given a boost at crucial moments by perceptive older officers. He felt that whenever he became a de facto sponsor of one of what were known generally as "Zeecy's kids," he was simply returning the investment made in him years ago by re-investing it in someone younger.

The corridors were bustling with lunchtime activity as he stepped along briskly to the SecDef's office, receiving and returning salutes by the dozens. The Pik-Quik would be jammed, the Big Scoop would be serving a long line of customers, the Executive Dining Room would be humming. Those officers and civilians of sufficient rank to have the time to eat out of the building would be on their way across the river. Many others would be getting their food-to-go in the major dining areas or in the snack-bars on the various rings and levels, taking their orders back to desks too loaded with paperwork and action memos to permit leisurely lunching. And at POAC, as always, those determined to keep fit and those determined to find a little relaxation were hard at the serious work of escaping, at least for a little while, the incessant pressures of the building.

This noontime, as so many before, the action officer of Operation Frio was prominent among them, executing the powerful dives and displaying the perfect technique that had always made swimming his favorite and most becoming sport. He had won a number of medals over the years in inter-service competitions, and when POAC held its annual field day Maj. Stump had twice taken first in diving and a first and second in the races.

Today, having completed a perfect swan-dive, he was floating idly on his back surveying the scenery with his usual impartial and precisely measured gaze. There were several beautiful women in the pool—where did they come from, he asked himself in ruefully amused dismay, when all he had was Hogan? —and a sizable number of equally attractive males, most of them in his general age group and several, as always, obviously aware of him. He had seen his West Pointer friend again a couple of days ago, and things had progressed to the point where they had exchanged hellos and mentioned casually what offices they were going back to. Names would be exchanged the next time, and after that a casual phone call from one or the other, and after that . . . he drifted lazily on, mind and body stirring with pleasant thoughts.

His other friend, the older, graying but youthfully smiling and very appealing one, he had not seen again until this moment, when he bumped gently against the side of the pool and paused to hang on with one hand while he rubbed his eyes and shook his head to clear the water from his ears.

Someone said pleasantly, "Wet, isn't it?" and he became aware that the one he had hoped to see was squatting at pool's edge just above his head. He took a deep breath and a long chance, though instinct and experience told him it was quite safe.

"I've been trying to figure out some excuse to come to your office," he said, "but I haven't been able to think of anything."

His new friend laughed with genuine amusement and said, "Well, now you don't need to, because here I am."

"Yes, sir," Gary said, turning to put both hands on the rim and hoist himself up and around in one swift, powerful motion so that he was seated beside him. "Here you are."

"You come here often," his new friend observed as he settled himself more comfortably and dangled his legs in the water.

"Yes," Gary said. "And you?"

"As often as I can," the other said. "It sometimes provides a welcome break from—" he smiled, taking Gary into a circle that suddenly seemed bright with light—"other things."

And quite casually he stretched his left hand against the concrete so that the heavy gold wedding-band gleamed and glistened.

"Yes, sir," Gary said, telling himself sternly that he must remember why he was here: not to get swept away but always to keep his mind on the work his silent associates demanded of him. "I don't suppose it's always so easy to find that kind of break, in your job."

"It does keep me busy," his new friend said. He grinned suddenly. "And restricted. That it does. And you, I believe, work for Gen. Rider."

"Yes, sir," Gary said, instantly cautious, bright light drained from the world. But his new friend only laughed softly, while across the pool there were shouts and laughter and nearby a handsome blonde swam past and gave him the eye.

"Tell her not to bother," his new friend suggested. *"We're* talking, right?"

"Yes, sir," Gary said, light flooding back, an answering smile playing about his lips. "How did you know I work for the general?"

"I have my spies," his new friend said, and instantly Gary froze again inside. But it was only a way of putting it, he decided the next moment, the other was so relaxed and so friendly as if he did this every day. Knowing his reputation Gary doubted very much that he did. In spite of another stern admonition to himself, he could not help feeling flattered.

"Tell me, sir," he said earnestly, "since you know Gen. Rider, and since you know who I am and I know—" the other was not offended or taken aback, only smiled attentively—"who you are—what do you think is going to happen with

Frio, anyway? Are we going to be able to do it? Are we really going ahead with it?"

His new friend looked thoughtful.

"I'll tell you," he said with a candor that was flattering, too, "I really don't know. I *think* we are, at least that's what I hear from my sources around the building, but then again—" he frowned. "There are a lot of problems still, particularly now that it's all come out in the open."

"That was very unfortunate, sir," Gary observed. "It's a shame to tip off the enemy in that fashion."

"Yes, it is," his new friend said somberly. "Too many things are made easy for them, as it is. We didn't need that, if we're really going to take action against them."

"But are we, sir?" Gary asked. "That's what we can't figure out, in our office. It *seems* as though we are, but then again—we just don't know. It really doesn't seem absolutely certain. It's confusing to us, you know? At least it is to me and my fellow staffers. I shouldn't speak for Gen. Rider. Maybe he knows for sure but we sure don't. It would be good if we could get some real fix on it."

"I tell you what," his new friend said. "What time do you get off duty?"

"Right around five, usually," Gary said, "although I expect hours are going to get longer very quickly now as Frio goes ahead—or at least our office goes ahead. I don't know about the mission." He gave the small, wistful smile that he knew from experience would be quite devastating in the right circumstances. "I wish we did."

"Do you have a car?" his new friend asked.

"Yes, sir."

"I tell you what. Why don't you meet me at The Courier bar in Georgetown—it's off M Street, maybe you know it? Perfectly legitimate place but relatively obscure. We're not likely to be noticed there. We can talk about it better over a drink. Maybe I can find out a little more before I see you."

"I hope so, sir," Gary said earnestly. "That would be great. Until then—" He held out his hand, the other gave it a quick grasp and a firm extra pressure.

"Until then." He looked across the pool and smiled with a pleasant vagueness that could indicate nothing but the most innocuous of conversations to anyone who might be watching. "By the way," he added casually, voice dropping, not looking at Gary, "are you tied up for the evening?"

"No, sir," he said. "Not a thing."

His new friend laughed.

"I probably should get home after we talk but I expect I won't be missed if I take my time."

"Good, sir," Gary said, heart suddenly pounding with an excitement that hardly became the seasoned campaigner he was. "I'd be glad of that."

"You can count on it," his new friend said, swinging his feet out of the water and standing up in one lithe sequence. "Until we meet."

"Until we meet," Gary echoed, rising to his feet, turning and diving into the turbulent pool in a movement as swift and graceful as his; and the world again was bright with light.

On the seventh floor in Foggy Bottom the Secretary of State at that moment was confronting one of his most frequent and most familiar opponents, aware that no matter how often they met in these sparring matches, there would be no change in the bland face and adamant attitude that confronted him across the table. The table in this case was set up for luncheon for two at one end of his spectacular office overlooking the Potomac. Across the river he could see the enormous squat brown mass that housed his principal adversaries in the government. Across the table was the squat, chunky, dark-visaged figure who represented his principal adversaries in the world.

He gave an inward, exasperated sigh.

He didn't really know which gave him the most headaches. He would like to put the two of them in a bag and dump them in the river.

But that wasn't the way it could be done, unfortunately. With each he was obliged to show at least the rudiments of diplomatic form. He was sure that the fact that this irked him as much as it did the Pentagon would have been a great revelation over there in the building. He wouldn't give them the small satisfaction of knowing, he told himself with a wry determination. They could keep right on considering him a cookie-pusher if they liked. It helped him surprise them sometimes.

His possibilities for surprising the owner of the shrewd Slavic face before him were, he knew, few and far between at best. Although he had not told his guest exactly why he was being invited to lunch this time, he suspected that Feodor knew, with the shrewd instinct for American reactions that they always seemed to have. It did not, after all, take a great deal of perspicacity to guess that an invitation to lunch with the Secretary of State, coming immediately after public disclosure of Frio, must inevitably concern the mission. Nor did it take a great deal of intuition to foresee that the substance of the meeting would probably be one more attempt by the American government to persuade the Soviet government to withdraw peaceably from its newest acquisition in the South Pacific.

Terry Venner was sure that the Kremlin position was prepared and that it did not vary in the slightest from the position stated already to the President by the Soviet leader when the crisis had first broken seven months ago. Then, it had been absolute, unyielding, slightly amused and more than a little contemptuous. He and the President had found, as leaders of all American administrations in recent decades had found, that basic Soviet positions did not change. There were cosmetic changes now and then, occasional bold public relations sallies to capture world attention and sometimes quite successfully muster world support. But almost never was there any perceptible real movement underneath to justify any hope that genuine peace could be worked out.

If they would only *leave people alone,* he thought in frustrated exasperation. If they would only cease this endless inexorable outward-pushing that always tried to gobble up everything and everyone that stood in its path. If they would only stop being the major active element in forcing the world to a point where ultimate catastrophe was becoming more and more likely. If they would only act like civilized beings and genuinely seek peace. If they would only stop being endlessly devious and treacherous. If they would only—

But they wouldn't. That was the reality each succeeding administration had to deal with. The difficulty had no relation to cries of "hysteria" and "anti-Soviet paranoia" that certain prominent Americans always automatically leveled against those who pointed out these unpleasant and unfortunate Soviet characteristics. It had to do with the facts of trying to deal with an international maverick government that wanted everything in the world its own way and would destroy, if it could, everything and everyone that dared say No.

In essence and actuality, the Secretary of State thought, he and the Pentagon did not disagree on the nature of the threat. Their basic disagreements came over what methods should be used to meet it. He knew there were some in State who, either from conviction born of fear or for genuinely traitorous reasons, wanted the United States to forego any firm action of any kind and rely solely upon the goodwill and restraint of the most implacable enemy it had ever faced. But the great majority in State, he felt, were genuinely loyal and patriotic people who were as greatly concerned as most intelligent Americans about the steady, ruthless, ongoing imperialist advance of the Soviet Union. They simply wanted more muted, more "civilized" approaches in dealing with it.

In considerable degree, having been so trained and conditioned by his years in the foreign service, the Secretary agreed. He did not see much point in raised voices, harsh rhetoric, public denunciations that only roused ill feelings in the Kremlin without deflecting Kremlin purposes. He would much rather approach them in what he thought was a "civilized manner" than engage in invective. If they were going to ignore you anyway, it might as well be in a reasonably pleasant climate—even if the Kremlin never made the slightest move to curtail its own raised voices, harsh rhetoric, public denunciations and invective against the United States.

"We're only responsible for this country," he often said when inner-circle Administration arguments grew hot upon this point. "We can't control what *they* do."

This belief, perfectly genuine and sincere, permitted one to remain civilized with considerable comfort and no great strain, even though it did very little if anything to change the ways of the enemy or deflect him in the slightest from what he intended to do.

"You are very somber today, Terry," the ambassador observed after one cautious sip of the white wine he then pushed aside in favor of mineral water. "Is it all those headaches caused by what my big, bad country is doing?"

"We do not like what you are up to on Nanukuvu, Feodor," Terrail Venner said, "and we would prefer for it to stop."

" 'Prefer' or 'insist'?" the ambassador inquired with the sly little smile he permitted himself from time to time. "It will make a great difference in how we think about it."

"Yes," the Secretary said dryly. "I am sure. I would prefer to say only that we 'prefer' not 'insist.' The Pentagon attitude may differ."

"The Pentagon attitude always differs," the ambassador said scornfully. "They would blow us up tomorrow if they thought we would not do the same to them."

"I am not authorized to speak for them," Terry said. "Suffice it to say that we prefer to prefer, not insist. But," he added as they began to eat the crab salads they had both ordered, "that is not to say that the time may not come, and soon, when we shall also insist."

"It is past time for insisting," the ambassador said with the sudden shift to coldness which was one of their standard gambits. "What good would it do you to insist? It is an impossible military objective, what your colleagues across the river are apparently contemplating. If it ever had the remotest chance of succeeding, it would have been right then, at that moment. Now it is too late, very much too late. It is, in fact, absurd." He frowned like a portentous thundercloud, as they often did when they sought to impress. "It would be suicide. And it might lead," he said, a dour note entering his voice, "to disasters far, far beyond Nanukuvu with consequences far, far more universal than the Administration thinks."

"*I* think," the Secretary said with a coldness of his own, "that we are quite aware in this government of all the horrendous possibilities you raise, Feodor. We are capable of raising them too. It does nothing but cloud the issue to have you resort to them every time there is an argument over something. You can blow us up—we can blow you up—so what? It's about that sensible an argument, when you come right down to it."

"Ah," the ambassador said, "but you have many more people who are afraid of it than we do."

"Maybe your ruling circles don't care," Terry Venner retorted, "but Shamizov told us the other day—"

"*Shamizov!*" the ambassador exclaimed with indignant scorn at the name of the latest defector, third-ranking member of the KGB. "What does Shamizov know about it! He is a coward anyway or he would not have run over to you with his tail between his legs. He knows nothing! Nothing!"

"Enough to get you excited," the Secretary observed. The ambassador gave him a horrible scowl.

"I am not excited! I—am—not—*excited!*"

"Pardon me," Terry Venner said. "I forget this kind of shouting is your normal mode of conversation."

"You will not entrap me!" the ambassador said in the same loudly indignant voice. "Oh, no, you will not, clever Terry! I know your tricks and they do not impress me! They do not impress me!" His tone reverted abruptly to normal and he dug into his salad as though he had never interrupted the steady flow of food to mouth. "What can you do about it anyway?"

"The President wishes to speak to the General Secretary about it again," Terry Venner said. The ambassador made a tired, disgusted face.

"Was it not enough for him to talk to the General Secretary when it first happened? Was he not satisfied with one refusal to discuss? What good is it going to do him to receive another? Such a conversation can only result as before. The General Secretary is even less willing to talk to him now that we are permanently settled on the island. He has much more in his hands now. Why should he discuss it with the President again?"

"Because the President also has much more in his hands now—" Terry began.

The ambassador shot him a triumphant look.

"But will he use it?" he inquired softly. "That is the question, Mr. Secretary. *Will he use it?*"

"I would suggest that you not test him too far on that," the Secretary said with more conviction than he felt: but it was necessary.

"Hmph!" the ambassador said. "We have been testing him from the first day and he has not responded. So much for the President!"

"He has responded," the Secretary said calmly. "He has ordered preparation of a military mission—"

"Your precious Frio!" the ambassador interrupted scornfully. "Congress will take care of *that!*"

"We shall see what Congress does!" Terry said sharply, again with more conviction than he felt. "In any event the final decisions do not lie with Congress—"

"Oh, no?"

"Oh, *no!*" Terry retorted in the same tone and with about the same conviction. "They lie with the Commander-in-Chief, who has ordered preparation of this mission and will order it carried forward unless there is a visible willingness on the part of the Soviet Union to withdraw its military forces from the island and participate in a general agreement to establish a jointly guaranteed area of peace in the South Pacific."

"A jointly guaranteed area of peace," the ambassador echoed, in much the same bemused, and amused, tone the President had used when first hearing the concept. "You mean the United States would actually, willingly, let us participate in such a joint arrangement?"

"We would," the Secretary said stoutly, thinking for the fourth time how positive one sometimes had to sound in his job, and how little real certainty often underlay it.

"I find that hard to believe," the ambassador remarked. "And anyway, why should we participate in a joint agreement? We have our bases there—including," he noted dryly, "Nanukuvu—and so why should we need any 'joint agreement' to protect an 'area of peace' that we have already established by our own actions? It is a good try, Terry, but I think I can assure you that it will not be greeted with wild ecstasy in the Kremlin. Who needs it?"

"*We* need *you* to remove your military threat and stop disturbing the peace of the South Pacific," the Secretary said with a real exasperation in his voice. The ambassador responded with a patronizing smile.

"We are not disturbing it, we are creating it. You must use your words with more precision, Terry."

"Nonetheless," the Secretary said with an angry firmness that finally appeared to give his opponent pause, "it is the desire of the President to speak with the General Secretary about this matter. Shall I inform the President that the General Secretary is willfully and deliberately going to ignore him without even giving him the courtesy of a hearing? Do you really think things have gone that far, that you can treat the United States like one of your satellites, Mr. Ambassador? If so, I'd suggest you knock it off."

For several seconds the ambassador, apparently genuinely taken aback by his tone, studied him carefully. Then he smiled in a more conciliatory way and shrugged.

"Very well, if he wishes to speak, let him do so. I am sure the General Secretary is always glad to hear his voice. I am a little puzzled, however," he said, growing more sarcastic as his composure returned, "why the President has not simply ordered the hot line activated and spoken directly to him, as he has done sometimes before. Why is it necessary to go through you and me? If he is really so firm on this, one would think—"

"He has his own methods," the Secretary said coldly, "and I am not privy as to how he selects them from among the many his advisers present to him. This time he has selected me. That is all you or I need to know. The President wishes to speak to the General Secretary tomorrow."

"So soon?" the ambassador said with genuine surprise. "That will not do at all. The General Secretary is a busy man. It takes time to arrange his schedule. It is quite likely that—"

"Tomorrow," Terrail Venner said firmly. The ambassador looked annoyed.

"Impossible! Absolutely impossible! He will speak to the President next Wednesday."

"Tomorrow," the Secretary repeated, though he knew he was not going to succeed. The ambassador smiled, a sudden broad grin.

"Oh, no," he said gently. "Not tomorrow, *before* the Congressional hearing. Next Wednesday, *after* the hearing. *After* there has been time for the President to hear from the Congress and the country. That is when they will speak."

"It will make no difference," the Secretary said.

The ambassador grinned again.

"Then it should make no difference that they speak on Wednesday instead of tomorrow. So it will be."

"The President will not be pleased."

"So? I am sure the General Secretary will be very much troubled to hear that."

The remainder of the luncheon passed in almost complete silence. They finished as rapidly as possible and bade one another a quick, formal goodbye. The sly little smile still played happily around the ambassador's lips.

The Secretary sat in silence while the luncheon things were cleared away. He felt disgruntled and depressed. He was not entirely sure that he had done the right thing—the President had not given him specific orders to arrange a conversation with the General Secretary, just a vague indication that he might be interested. He might repudiate the whole idea when Terry told him about it. And yet if he didn't talk to the General Secretary there would be no hope for a diplomatic solution. Either the military effort would finally be attempted, which in Terry's opinion could only lead to a major confrontation sure to terrify the world and end in failure, or there would be a tacit and humiliating acquiescence in the conquest of Nanukuvu and the permanent establishment of a major Soviet base in the South Pacific, with all its consequences for America and for America's helpless friends in the region.

All the wealth of the Indies, he thought in a memory of reading long ago, would lie open before them; and there would be no longer a guardian at the gate.

With a sudden irrational bitterness that disturbed him further, because it wasn't like him to be irrational no matter what the pressures, he felt that it was probably all the Pentagon's fault that things had reached this point. If their intelligence-gathering had been better in the first place—if their planning had been more astute and comprehensive—if they had been able to foresee that some such Soviet gamble in the South Pacific was almost inevitable, and had warned against it and prepared for it long since—if they had speeded up their cumbersome process when the crisis did come, and had been prepared to meet it as swiftly as it had to be met if it were to be successfully contained—if they had not been so strongly opposed to his desire to try the diplomatic approach when it still might have done some good—if they hadn't been so dog-in-the-manger about insisting on their own way of handling it and if their own way hadn't been so cumbersome, so protracted, so hampered by inter-service turf-protecting and so *typically military*—

But what was the good of that kind of thinking now? The Pentagon had simply goofed again, he told himself with the virtually automatic condemnation of Defense by State. Now let them wriggle themselves out of it. Cube Herron had invited him to testify too. He told himself with angry confidence that he was ready. He'd see how it went. If there was the slightest attempt by the

Pentagon crowd to pass the buck to *him,* he'd respond in no uncertain terms. Cube, he knew, would be delighted by this: he loved to pit the two departments against each other and see what came out of the scrimmage.

Terry Venner was deeply concerned about the good of the United States, both as Cabinet member and as citizen. But he wouldn't have been human, or a Secretary of State, if he didn't contemplate with some relish the prospect of the Defense Department falling on its face.

"What worries me," Red Roberts said to Jerry Castain as they lingered over late-afternoon pie and coffee in the almost deserted Senate dining room while the ever-recurring debate on tax reform droned along upstairs, "is that the damned Pentagon is going to fall flat on its face over Nanukuvu." He grinned his wry and knowing grin. "I've been around there long enough so that I really take a protective interest. I don't want them to do that."

"Neither do I," Sen. Castain said, "but you and I both know that they don't look very good at the moment. Why the hell can't they ever get their ducks in a row and *move faster* on things? And why didn't they take some of us into their confidence in the first place and say, 'Look, fellows, here's the situation, we need your cooperation, let's keep it quiet for a while to help us out, o.k.?' After all—" he looked as annoyed as his usual level good nature ever permitted him to become—"we're a pretty patriotic group up here, as a whole. We have our half-asses like Mario, but all in all we're not so bad. They don't have any monopoly on patriotism down there in the building, or on good sense, either. In fact they could use some, now and then."

"It's just ingrained in them," Red said thoughtfully. "And it's a two-way street. Some of you up here do an awful lot of prying and pressuring and pushing around, you know. They get an awful lot of flak from the Mario type, an awful lot of demands for special favors and special privileges and this for my district and that for my state, and how about giving some business to this contractor and making that sub-contractor happy? And then you have your military experts, too—the guys who used to be captains in the Army or privates in the Marines, or whatever, and they think that qualifies them to decide tactics and strategy for the Pentagon for the rest of their lives. There are a few little would-be generals and admirals running around up here in the guise of members of Congress who get real upset when the brass won't listen to their advice. So it works both ways."

Jerry nodded and took a thoughtful bite from his piece of apple pie.

"Well, anyway," he said after a moment, "you and I pretty well blew the whistle, didn't we?"

"That we did," Red agreed, "and that's really why I came up to see you today. I'm wondering what line your questioning's going to take."

"First I'm going to establish for the record that your account and mine are both correct. After that, we'll see. A lot of people up here are dead set against Nanukuvu."

"But can't they see—" Red demanded with some exasperation.

"The answer to that is," Jerry said, "that, no, some of them can't. And among those that do there are some who are either afraid of standing up to the Soviets just as a general principle, or are genuinely fearful that to do so would create a confrontation that could escalate into world catastrophe."

"We've let things slide that far," Red remarked with some bitterness.

Jerry nodded.

"We've let things slide that far. There was a time when an ounce of prevention could have made it unnecessary to even think about a pound of cure. A lot of loud voices in this country didn't want an ounce of prevention—they were too frightened. Now they're frightened, and rightly so, of the pound of cure. The fact is that this is *their* doing. They didn't have the foresight or the guts then, and it's for damned sure they don't have either now. So we have uproar in the country, uproar in the world, and a pretty good chance that we're going to have to turn tail and run from Nanukuvu if the Soviets stand firm and say *Boo!* You don't think they're going to say anything else, do you?"

"*I* don't, no," Red said, slowly stirring his second cup of coffee. "*I* don't think so for one minute. I think they're there to stay unless we can think of some way to knock them out of there. Without starting World War III, that is. But, hell, we've got to do it. Somehow."

"I know," Jerry said grimly. "That's why I thought very hard before I decided to go public with this."

"So did I," Red said promptly. "I don't believe in shooting from the hip like some of my distinguished colleagues of the media. Some of them tried to, and the Pentagon's been so slow it's a miracle they didn't succeed. Now, of course, they're having a field day."

"I'm glad you're not that kind of journalist," Jerry said with the sudden warm smile that could make him so likable. "I'm glad we have a *few* with integrity."

"I'm too old for anything else," Red said with a grin. "You have to be young and carefree and itching for a Pulitzer to be as irresponsible as some of 'em are. But there's still a few of us left who believe in trying to keep a balance."

"Quite a few," Jerry agreed. "And you do. It's the only thing that saves the media. From themselves."

"Thank you," Red said with a mock bow. "We try."

"Unlike some we could name. I'm expecting a couple of them later on. Your friends from *Defense Spy.*"

"Not *my* friends," Red said with a chuckle, "but we get along. It takes all kinds. And they do uncover some interesting things about Pentagon waste and Pentagon shortcomings. Delight was my first tip-off to Frio, as a matter of fact. I suppose they perform a necessary function."

Jerry smiled.

"In an unpleasant way."

Red smiled too.

"Yes, you could say that, I guess. They're pretty well feared and hated in the building. But they probably serve a useful purpose."

"You serve the same purpose," Jerry pointed out, "and with fairness and integrity, too. One doesn't have to be as biased as they are to be effective. It can be done."

"Well, thanks . . . What do you hear about the President's attitude toward Nanukuvu? Anything?"

Jerry gave him the knowing, skeptical, not-surprised-by-anything look of the experienced politician.

"I think he's hiding out with an ear to the ground and a finger to the wind. An ungainly posture but one that does not surprise me, coming from him."

Red laughed.

"You don't think much of him, do you?"

"He's not one of my buddies," Sen. Castain admitted dryly, "but as long as he can get 59 per cent approval in the polls and has the potential for a landslide next year, I keep my head down and don't say much. I may on this issue, though, if he equivocates too long."

"He has a great sense of timing. Whatever he does, he'll ride the tide."

"And get away with it," Jerry agreed. He smiled. "That's the annoying part."

"One more thing," Red said, "and then I'll let you go and return to my retreat across the river. What do you hear about the next chairman of the JCS? Is Brash Burford going to make it, or will it be Sledgehammer Ham?"

"Or, possibly, neither. I don't know, to tell you the truth, and I really haven't heard very much, except that they're the two obvious candidates. Brash—" he hesitated and then decided to trust this veteran newsman who did carry the standard of integrity high in everything he did—"Brash is going through a hard time right now. This is strictly off the record, but Mrs. Burford is ill and not going to get better, and it's beginning to throw Brash off stride quite a bit."

"Yes," Red said. "I noticed that at his last press conference a week ago when he talked to us about the next NATO exercises. He seemed quite distracted and not at all himself. That's a damned shame. Is it cancer?"

"Everybody's first choice," Jerry observed wryly. "No, Alzheimer's. Which in the long run can be just as devastating to all concerned."

"I'm sure," Red said, frowning in sympathy. "That *is* a shame. I still hope he makes it. Ham Stokes is a good general and a topnotch administrator but he leaves a trail of eaten bones behind."

"Maybe that's what the JCS secretariat needs," Sen. Castain said. "Maybe if we'd had more of that in the past seven months Nanukuvu wouldn't have got out of hand."

"Who knows?" Red said. "That's what you'll have to decide in the hearing. Which brings us back to where we started and I really must let you go. I've got to write a story and you've got to get back to the debate."

"The budget?" Jerry inquired wryly as they left the table. "They were debating the budget on the day I arrived here and they'll be debating the budget on the day I'm carried out on a stretcher."

"Which we hope will not be for a long, long time," Red said with a chuckle.

"I don't know," Sen. Castain said. "Sometimes I wonder if it's all worth it."

But, he reflected as he shook hands cordially and watched Red depart down the time-worn corridor and out the ancient revolving door of the Senate wing, there were a great many compensations. Not all of them were as obvious as public prominence and the privilege of being one of those who help to decide the destinies of the nation and the world. A lot of it lay in the people you met, like this decent, fair-minded veteran reporter who, with his colleagues, also helped decide the destinies of the nation and the world—and in the exciting and significant events of which you were privileged to be a part—and in problems like Nanukuvu, which were a worry and a headache and a danger but were great challenges and great opportunities as well.

He wondered how they would all measure up to Nanukuvu, here on the Hill; and how they would come through it across the river; and how it would leave the man who had his ear to the ground and a finger to the wind, once its tensions and troubles, which were now beginning to reach hurricane proportions, had passed.

Back on the floor, he saw that the attendance, which had been sparse when Red had sent in for him an hour ago, had dwindled further. Even Cube, who usually listened faithfully to his fellow chairmen, had abandoned old Sen. Dominick of Michigan, chairman of the Senate Finance Committee, who was droning on about the budget in his usual unrelieved monotone. Only a handful of Senators remained, some attempting to listen, some openly reading the *Congressional Record* or writing personal correspondence at their desks. He saw that Luzanne was still being polite, staying in her seat and appearing to listen. He walked over, intending to sit down and visit with her for a few moments before going back to his office. As he did so he looked up at the press gallery and saw the entire staff of *Defense Eye* staring down upon them with sudden interest. As he watched they glanced at one another, stood up and hurried up the stairs through the swinging glass doors to disappear into the pressroom.

He sat down beside Luzanne and whispered, "Oh, oh!" in the half-whisper Senators use for private conversations on the floor. "I think we're going to have company."

"They've been up there for the past half-hour," she said with a chuckle, "waiting for the moment to strike. Let's hope you're the only one they're after."

"I won't see them alone," he said in mock alarm. "Never!"

"Sen. Johnson," a staff aide whispered politely, "Sen. Castain—Delight Jones and Herb Horowitz of *Defense Eye* would like to see you both in the President's Room."

"And we," Luzanne whispered back solemnly, "would *love* to see them."

"After you," Jerry murmured.

"To the guillotine!" she said, and led the way out to the ornate old chamber just off the floor where Chief Executives up to Woodrow Wilson used to come on the closing nights of sessions to sign last-minute bills, and where now in later days reporters corner Senators to extract their earth-shaking thoughts on the latest earth-shaking events of an always quivering globe.

Delight and Herb, they could see, were definitely in a cornering mood.

"Sen. Johnson," Delight said abruptly when they were seated, the Senators on one of the worn leather sofas, herself and Herb in two of the big leather chairs, drawn up so closely that they were all virtually knee-to-knee with no escape, "Sen. Johnson, what do you think of the way the Pentagon has deliberately concealed its plans to launch an unprovoked aggression against a Soviet base in the South Pacific?"

"Now, just a minute, Miss Jones," Luzanne said sharply as Jerry also looked annoyed, "would you mind restating that question to make it less biased and a little less concerned with your own point of view?"

"That's what it is," Delight said, unabashed, "and *Defense Eye* is saying so. What do you think of it?"

"Not a thing," Luzanne said calmly, "as long as you continue to phrase it that way." And she made as if to rise, Jerry rising to help her.

"Now, just a minute yourselves!" Delight said angrily. *"Senators! I'm asking you a question!"*

"Senators," Herb said in a tired tone, "please sit down again. We're wondering if you have any thoughts about the Pentagon's plans for the Frio mission and whether you approve of their attempts to keep it secret up to now. Sen. Castain, maybe you'd like to address that, as the one who broke the story up here."

"All right," Jerry said in a tone as reasonable as his, and he and Luzanne sat down again. "I'm not very happy, and I don't think many in the Congress are very happy, about secrecy where something so important as the security of the United States is involved. I can, however, see the Pentagon point of view in wanting to handle it without crippling publicity and the general uproar that seems to have developed in the last couple of days. I'm really only sorry that they didn't make better use of the time they bought for themselves. If they had, the United States might be in better shape than it is right now."

"Do you think," Delight asked, making an obvious attempt to be reasonably polite, "that America is justified in complaining about a Soviet base in the South Pacific? When we have so many?"

"I'll take that," Luzanne said, "now that we're going to be staying with the facts." Delight's eyes snapped but Luzanne gazed at her steadily and she finally refrained from retort. "I think the United States is perfectly justified in being alarmed by such a major enemy advance into a region where the enemy has not, in the sense of a permanent base, been before. I think we have a perfect right to protest it and to do everything we can to secure enemy withdrawal."

"Why do you say 'enemy'?" Delight inquired, prominent eyes staring even wider. "Is that too much association with the Pentagon? They always use the word 'enemy' over there."

For a second Luzanne's eyes also snapped, but long experience told her the best way to handle hostile personal questions was always to be perfectly matter-of-fact.

"It's the term I prefer," she said calmly. "I think it sums up the situation pretty accurately."

"And we should 'do everything we can—' " Delight quoted.

"Using all peaceful means at our command," Luzanne said smoothly.

"What if we can't accomplish anything by 'peaceful means'?" Delight demanded. "Would you favor military action then?"

"Let's exhaust all peaceful means first and see," Luzanne suggested. "If they aren't enough, then we can decide where we go from there."

"Do you think they *will* be enough?" Herb asked.

She shrugged and gave him one of her charming smiles.

"Mr. Horowitz, your guess is as good as mine. We can only try."

"Sen. Castain," Delight said, "do *you* think we have a right to protest a Soviet appearance in that region? You said yourself in your speech—and Red Roberts," she added, obviously not pleased but giving the competition his due— "did too—that it's a very vaguely defined area of interest down there and that we probably don't have any real legal right ourselves. So how can we complain about the Soviets?"

"The Soviets are apparently introducing—or hoping to introduce—extremely heavy and dangerous armaments. This would upset the whole balance of peace in the region. This in turn would threaten not only American interests but America's allies. That being so, I just don't see how we can stand idly by and let this go ahead without the most strenuous efforts to bring it to a halt."

"Including military action?" Herb inquired.

"As Sen. Johnson says, that is something that would have to be decided after all other means have been exhausted. As far as we know in Congress, other means haven't been exhausted yet."

"What if you find out they have been," Delight said, "and it hasn't done any good? Then war?"

"I would want to know all the details first," Jerry said blandly. "Have you got any?"

For a second he could see that Delight was tempted. But she decided to stick with the truth.

"No, I don't," she said in a tart tone. "Aren't any of you Senators going to ask questions about that and find out?"

"Probably we are," Jerry said, and Luzanne said, "Give us time. The hearing isn't until Monday."

"We'll be there," Delight promised. "We'll be *right* there."

"I don't doubt it," Luzanne said. "We hope you'll be enlightened. We hope we'll all be enlightened."

"I thought you of all people would have been enlightened about it a long time ago," Delight remarked with a smooth insolence. "Didn't your friends in the Joint Chiefs tell you? I thought you had some."

For just a second Luzanne hesitated. Jerry tried not to look as alarmed as he felt. Then Luzanne laughed in a perfectly natural way and leaned forward to tap Delight gently on the arm.

"Oh, Miss Jones!" she said. "Miss Jones the demon reporter! Of course I know the Joint Chiefs, we all know the Joint Chiefs. But that doesn't mean they tell us anything, any more than they tell you anything. In fact, we're apt to hear about it a lot later than you do, actually. That's the way it's been with Nanukuvu." She looked, bland and innocent, straight into Delight's eyes. "Why? Did you think I have some special friend in the Joint Chiefs? Is there someone over there you particularly think might tell me secrets?" Her light-hearted laugh exploded. "My goodness, I'd love to have such a source! Do tell me, Miss Jones! Who is it?"

For a tense second Jerry thought Delight was going to call her bluff; but even Delight didn't quite dare. She tried to keep staring but she couldn't keep it up. Her eyes finally looked away, an angry flush mounted her cheeks. Beside her Herb Horowitz sat as frozen-still as Jerry. Finally she spoke in a harsh, antagonistic voice.

"I don't know *all* about your sources over there, Senator, *but I aim to find out.*"

"Good for you!" Luzanne said heartily. "Let me know when you do. I'm as anxious to know as you are. Jerry, don't you think we ought to get back to the floor?"

"Right," he said promptly, rising to his feet, taking her hand to assist. "Miss Jones—Mr. Horowitz—I'm sure we'll see you Monday. If anything comes up in the meantime, give us a call. We're both glad to help."

"Absolutely," Luzanne agreed. "Any time."

With a sudden movement that took Delight completely by surprise she reached out, seized her hand and gave it a warmly cordial squeeze, then turned immediately to Herb and did the same. Then she gave them both a cheerfully ironic little bow and swept out followed by Jerry, who burst into laughter Delight and Herb could clearly hear as he disappeared into the Senate.

"Bitch!" Delight growled. "I'm going to fix her! Bitch!"

"Oh, Delight," Herb said. "For Christ's sake, lay off. So she's probably sleeping with McCune, so what? Who gives a damn?"

"I do!" Delight said. "And I'm going to make sure everybody else does too!"

"You're sex-mad," Herb said, shaking his head.

"Yes, well," Delight said in the same ominous tone, "I can make her plenty sorry and I'm going to do it! Any bitch with her views shouldn't be in the United States Senate anyway. Damned warmonger!"

"Oh, come on," Herb said. "Come *on.*"

Sen. Dominick was still droning on when Luzanne and Jerry returned to the floor. Luzanne went to her desk, Jerry followed and sat down beside her. For several moments they said nothing as she silently, but to him obviously, struggled for self-control. He did not dare to interrupt. At last he ventured,

"Not a very nice lady."

"A bitch," she said in a tone he had never heard her use about anyone. "A real nasty bitch. But," she said, giving him a sidelong look and a slightly tremulous smile, "I suppose I deserved it. Except of course, you know, Jerry, the ironic thing is that I don't."

"Oh?" he said noncommittally, for though they had been close friends from the day she came to the Senate, he really wasn't sure he wanted to hear all this.

"No," she said. "Nothing really serious has ever happened between Zeecy and me, in spite of what people like that little tramp think."

"Are you sure you want to tell me about it?" he inquired. "I really don't need to know, you know."

"Somebody does," she said almost desperately. "I need to have someone I can talk to. I've tried to talk to my mother but she's bayou Louisiana and she just doesn't realize the goldfish bowl we live in up here. I mean, she knows it intellectually, of course, but she doesn't really *know* it. It pushes a lot of things out of proportion."

"Yes," he agreed, sympathetic but still noncommittal.

"I feel you'll understand because you're—you're—"

"Yes?" he said with an easy smile that said a lot for battles won long ago. "What?"

"You're my friend," she said simply, and something that had tensed inside relaxed again and became as steady and unshakable as always.

"Of course I am. So Zeecy's nothing, hm?"

She smiled and seemed suddenly much more relaxed.

"I wouldn't say exactly 'nothing.' But he's not *everything*."

"But something," he suggested and she smiled again.

"Oh, yes, I'm fond of him." She looked for a second like an earnest and stubbornly honest little girl. "More than fond. In fact, I've been thinking about seeing him Friday night. Renee's in New York and—"

"Really," he protested, "you don't need to tell me—"

"Well, I am," she said abruptly, "so be quiet!" Then she relaxed again with a soft little laugh and nudged his elbow with her own. "I'm sorry, I don't mean to be harsh but *be quiet,* because what I'm going to say is important."

"Yes, ma'am."

"I'm going to see him Friday night and I—I've been thinking that—that possibly . . . But now," she said, face abruptly somber, "after that—that *individual*—I just don't know. What do you think?"

"Golly, Lu," he said, "I wish you wouldn't put me on the spot. I don't know what to tell you. You're a grown woman. You decide."

"Tell me," she demanded. He took a deep breath.

"I think . . . I think . . . I'd give it a pass."

She looked very thoughtful but unflinching. Finally:

"Reasons?"

"All the obvious. I don't have to expound. You know them."

She was silent for a long time, so long that he finally glanced over. She was sitting very quietly, eyes straight ahead, beautiful face outwardly as serene to the watching eye, if a little preoccupied, as always.

"Thank you," she said finally.

"You're welcome," he said; and after a moment ventured, "And the decision is—?"

"I don't know," she said with a sudden bubbling little laugh. "Isn't that ridiculous? I honestly don't know."

"I think you do," he said. "And frankly, I'm relieved."

"Don't be too sure," she said with a teasing lightness that sounded quite herself again. "Talk to me Saturday morning."

Now he too laughed, as Sen. Dominick concluded and Vernon Atwood of Nebraska took the floor.

"I'm damned if I'll call you," he said as he squeezed her arm and stood up to leave. "You call me."

And on their quiet laughter, which was obvious enough to prompt a disapproving look from Vernon, who didn't like inattention when he spoke, Jerry went back to his office feeling much better about a situation that had worried him because it involved someone he genuinely cared about, and because it had for some time been a subject of not unfriendly but busy speculation on both sides of the river.

4 Across town in the pleasant book-lined study of their house in Georgetown, the wife of the Secretary of Defense was sitting with a notepad on her ample lap, drawing up the list of guests she intended to invite to a small formal dinner two weeks from now.

The room was warm and snug against the chill wind that was whipping away the last flowers of summer, the last of the camellias, the last of the rhododendrons, the last of everything she loved about a garden. Another summer dying —another year going—Imogene Buck shivered and for no reason she could quite put her finger on, other than the general melancholy of the season, tears came into her eyes and she sat there quietly crying for several minutes: a rather fat, dumpy, good-hearted and compassionate woman worried, as always, about her husband.

Loy had not told her much about Nanukuvu—she and Violet Burford were the only two wives who had been told anything at all—but she knew enough to realize that it had been a constant worry and headache for him. It was obvious as the weeks and months stretched out that things were not moving as fast as he would have liked.

He had not told her exactly why, but knowing his lifelong drive to get things done as fast and efficiently as possible, she suspected that the problem did not lie with him. It was something in what she thought of constantly as "the damned old Pentagon." She deeply resented its long-term effects upon her husband, which were finally beginning to surface here and there in ways that raised red flags for her. Loy was getting too tense and too snappish, which had never been like him even under the greatest pressures of private industry. He was working too long and too hard and worrying too much. His sleep was beginning to suffer. Once recently she had heard him muttering the island's name in the middle of the night. And he wasn't eating as well as she would have liked.

Now with Nanukuvu at last become public, and with all the resultant uproar that was swirling around his head, she was even more worried than usual that strain and tension might result in the heart attack she had feared ever since he started work for IBM so many years ago. He often pointed out that it had never happened but that couldn't prevent her worrying that it might. Now, with the heavy tide of opinion that seemed to be running against him and the Pentagon and the whole Nanukuvu business, she was terribly apprehensive that it might.

He had chided her for this at breakfast today but with the stubbornness of all the years of love and devotion she had refused to be diverted.

"I don't care," she said. "You're taking this whole thing too seriously *and it isn't good for you.* I wish you could just drop it all and get away for a vacation. We haven't been to Palm Springs in a long time. Why don't we go to Palm Springs? That would be nice."

"Still too hot."

"All right, Europe, then. It's beautiful now, the tourists are gone—"

"Immy," he said, with the sort of impatience he had shown lately, which troubled her so, "don't be foolish! I'm not going anywhere until we get Nanukuvu straightened out, and I probably won't be able to get away even then. It's big in the public eye at the moment but it's only one of my worries, you know. There are a dozen other things equal if not bigger. The SecDef doesn't just hightail it off on a vacation whenever he wants to. It isn't that kind of job."

"It is if you don't let it dominate your life," she said stubbornly. He uttered a disgusted snort.

" 'Dominate my life'! There's no way to avoid it . . . Now, look," he said, more patiently, "I've promised you that when I can find time for a logical break from the building and all its problems, I'll take it."

"You've said that since you started work there," she said, "and you haven't done it yet except for that week at your sister's in Florida two years ago. You've worked and worked and worked and *worked,* and what thanks have you got? Just obstruction from the military and kicks from the media and gripes and complaints from everybody."

"Immy!" he said sharply. "Cut it out! If I'd been the sort to turn tail and run I never would have taken this job in the first place. Certainly I'm not the sort to quit once I've taken it, as you know better than anyone. I've enlisted for the duration, or at least as long as the President wants me, and that's all there is to it. So you might as well stop cry-babying and be the great support you've always been."

"I'm not 'cry-babying'!" she exclaimed, though his scornful use of the term almost did provoke her to tears. "I'm just worried about you, and I have a right to be!"

"I know," he said, reaching out to squeeze her hand, his voice much softer as he realized finally how really upset she was. "I know you do, and I appreciate it more than I can say, you know that. I don't know what I'd do without you, really. But you mustn't let the Pentagon worry you so. I'm managing." He smiled and brushed her cheek with his hand. " 'T'ain't easy, but I'm doing it. So don't *you* let it get *you* down, either. All right?"

"Well," she said, not conceding much, "I still think it's time for you to get away. You've talked about it, I know, but that's all it's ever been, just talk. Meanwhile you're getting jumpy and nervous and irritable and *I just don't like it.*"

"You're letting your imagination run away with you," he said with a laugh
that wasn't quite as comfortable as he had intended. "You're the only one who's
complained about my being irritable. Vangie hasn't said anything, and you know
Vangie: she wouldn't hesitate to let me know. She's always fussed at me a little
just as you have, but she understands the problems over there. You can't just
walk away from them, and I won't unless the President wants me to. I've no
indication that he does."

He had left her looking forlorn and had been driven away through the chilly
morning in his armored limousine. He had realized once again as he approached the massive building hunkered down beside the river that what he
said was entirely true: there was no escaping it. It did dominate the lives of
everyone in it, especially those at the top: and now with Nanukuvu the focus of
worldwide attention, the building's pressures were heavier than ever. But to the
point where it was really affecting his personality and his ability to do his job?
He told himself with a sudden sharp annoyance that this was so much twaddle.
He appreciated Immy's concern, and Vangie's too, but there were really no
grounds. The department was going through a rough passage on Nanukuvu at
the moment, but they would all come through in good shape.

The day had appeared to confirm his confidence, even though the continued
silence from the White House created an underlying uneasiness that neither he
nor Zeecy could quite escape, no matter how much they encouraged one another to do so. It was obvious the President was thinking it over very carefully,
but occasions when a President kept his own counsel and left the Pentagon
dangling in the dark for a while were not unknown in the annals of the republic.

He would come around, they told one another with perhaps more assurance
than they felt: he simply had to. Anything else would be too dangerous to long-
range American interests to even think about.

Meanwhile those segments of the department directly involved in Nanukuvu
appeared to be moving smoothly along at last. Helen Clark had reported to him
that DSARC had held its first meeting on the ALCAC and appeared to be
making progress. Al Rider had stopped by to bring him up to date on the
detailed preliminary study he and Gary Stump had made of the men and
materiel that would be needed from each service for Op Frio. There had been
a long conversation with Cube Herron in which the Senator had promised to
do his best to keep the hearing on the track and not let it get off into diversion-
ary side issues of the kind they feared people like Mario Escondido and Bob
Cathcart might try to bring up. He had checked individually with all the chiefs
about the testimony they planned to give and had ascertained that all were
determined to maintain the solid front he felt the Pentagon should present in
the face of national and world outcry. He had conferred at some length with
Joe Strang and the Doomsday Twins about what they might say to offset Terry
Venner's expected criticisms of the Pentagon. And he had enjoyed a pointed
but essentially good-natured talk with Terry in which the Secretary of State

had filled him in on his luncheon with the ambassador and had promised not to be "any more critical of the Pentagon than I have to be." Loy had expressed wry thanks for this—even Terry had agreed that at this point any hot-line conversation between the President and the General Secretary would probably be futile. Loy had conceded in his turn that "no avenue should be left unexplored, at least it's worth a try"; and Terry appreciated that. And finally, at Hank Milhaus' urging, Loy had agreed to respond to the clamorous demands of the media that he hold a press conference on Nanukuvu, but only on condition that it would be next week after the hearing was concluded.

Between, around and among these various items concerning Frio he had conferred with the prime minister of Singapore; given him as much encouragement as possible on his request for more arms; accepted his invitation to visit next spring; approved the text of the latest Pentagon report on the massive Soviet program to steal America's technological secrets, a subject always greeted with great sarcasm by some segments of the media even though based entirely on fact; approved for release three more inspector general reports from Shorty Murchison's ongoing investigations of contract fraud; met for an hour with the commanding general of NATO, a West German, who had flown over secretly to report on the stealthy re-introduction of medium-range missiles along the East German border, which the Soviets stoutly maintained had been removed, and which had been—for almost two months; approved plans to expand his visit to Singapore to include Indonesia, Thailand, the Philippines, Japan and South Korea; received a delegation of families of hostages held in Lebanon and once again promised to do all he could; discussed other Middle Eastern problems in separate talks with the ambassadors of Egypt and Jordan; edited the preliminary draft of a speech he was to give to the Commonwealth Club in San Francisco next month; officiated at a ceremony dedicating a plaque in the MacArthur Corridor to one of the last of the general's aides to remain in beleaguered Bataan after Pearl Harbor; and asked Vangie to order a large bouquet of roses and a two-pound box of chocolates from the shops in the Concourse for him to take home to Immy, which Vangie did with a dry little smile and the comment that if she knew what was worrying Mrs. Buck, and she thought she did, that wasn't going to do much good.

All in all, aside from this last domestic note, a typical day in the life of a SecDef, he thought as he prepared to leave his office and ride the armored limousine back to Georgetown. Much of it the high-level routine that he went through every day—a few major items that required immediate action—usually some major crisis, in this case Nanukuvu, that demanded complete and diligent attention to get everything in shape all down the line for whatever challenges the department might face. And a schedule that usually brought him home somewhere between eight and nine o'clock, except on those evenings when he had to break away early to attend some diplomatic dinner or White House function.

He found Immy in a much better mood, improved further by his gifts of flowers and candy. She told him she wasn't a schoolgirl but she was obviously pleased and flattered, and for once they had the quiet evening at home that she was always hoping for. She was not entirely consistent in this, for she enjoyed entertaining herself and was already deep in plans for the black-tie dinner two weeks from now to which the First Lady had already agreed that she and the President would come. Another chance for *Defense Spy* to call her names, she told Loy dryly, but even on that sore point she sounded quite philosophical. They had a pleasant time seated in front of the first fire of the season, she doing needlepoint and the Secretary reading a novel instead of the official papers he usually brought home. By mutual agreement they had decided to skip television for the evening. "The world," Loy said, "will just have to go to hell without us."

He felt relaxed tonight as Nanukuvu appeared to be finally underway. There was still a considerable distance to go, and the bothersome hurdle of the Congressional hearing to get past, but on the whole he could feel for the first time in months, despite Presidential hesitations he believed would soon evaporate, that the building was on the right track and beginning to move.

Sharing this same conviction, which his earnest young heart welcomed with a genuine surge of relief, Brod Tolliver turned out the lights and secured the doors to Cumulative Assessment Group on third floor, B Ring at just about the time the Secretary was descending to the carpool in his private elevator to meet his armored car and driver.

It had been a long, busy day in Operation Frio. The days were suddenly beginning to get that way, just as the staff had expected would be the case as soon as the Joint Chiefs, as Gary Stump had expressed it repeatedly, got off their fat duffs and agreed on the plan for the mission. Workmen from the Pentagon office of the General Services Administration had already started rearranging and repainting the suite of offices next door. Ten of the new personnel had already reported for duty and Brod, Gary and Hogan were finding their hands full familiarizing them with the general details of the mission. All were cleared for some reasonable degree of security, but on Gen. Rider's orders really major security clearance was reserved for Brod and Hogan with the general and Gary, as his executive and action officer, holding the topmost security of all. The newcomers would be able to handle a lot of routine detail: what Brod with innocently pleased ego thought of as "the Big Four" would really run the mission. He secretly thanked Gen. McCune practically every hour on the hour for having arranged so important and exciting an assignment for him.

Gary, he knew, had been suggested to Gen. Rider by Gen. Burford, who in turn had received a recommendation from Gary's then superior officer pointing out what a fine and highly competent young officer he was. Hogan, the Navy's representative, had been recommended to Gen. Rider by Adm. Stahlman, in whose office she had been working. He had described her as "a plodder but a thoroughly nice person and most reliable, with a great eye for detail." Only Brod had the distinction of being "one of Zeecy's kids," which carried a special cachet and the almost guaranteed certainty that his career would receive a strong and compelling upward boost and be invested hereafter with a special presumption of predestined success.

He thought this was wonderful, because he had been convinced from his very first day at the Air Force Academy that his destiny lay with this glamorous service whose wings figuratively and literally spanned the farthest reaches of the globe. He had graduated fifth in his class, had qualified as a pilot, toyed for a while with the thought of going into the space program, finally decided that he would stay with the service. He came from a reasonably wealthy oil family in Wyoming, "not one of the big boys" as his father was wont to say, but of a financial stature quite adequate to relieve him of some of the pressures that afflicted young officers trying to raise families and make ends meet on service pay. He had been free to concentrate on his career and to it had brought notable qualities of intelligence, application and a certain philosophic overview which was rather rare in a service where the margin of error in the air was often very thin and where the bluntly pragmatic attitude of its present chief of staff epitomized the basic attitude of most of its members. Brod would have loved to concentrate on strategic planning, long-range concepts, "the Big Picture" as Ham Stokes sometimes described it with some sarcasm to his immediate subordinates. The chief of staff gave the concept lip-service and the Air Force participated—with due regard for its own interests, as did they all—in all attempts at joint planning that went on in the building. Privately, Ham and the great majority of his fellow officers were not really convinced that it was all that valuable.

Brod told himself that in fairness it should be recognized that this was possibly because the entire American military machine was basically geared to the idea of defense, not offense. If defense was your basic purpose it was a little difficult to establish too many long-range goals. You were inevitably forced, by an opposing military machine geared overwhelmingly to the concept of offense, to react rather than act. If you had no aggressive plans to extend your rule over other nations and areas of the world, you were inclined to feel that you did not really need much long-range planning. What were you planning for? Just to keep your country and its allies and your joint freedoms alive in the world. It was a simple objective and it inevitably forced American planning into a narrow and essentially negative mold.

Which left your opponent free to roam at will, creating worldwide mischief whenever it suited his aggressive purposes, while you sought constantly, and with only erratic degrees of success, to contain his imperialistic long-range planning all over the globe.

Nonetheless, Brod would have liked to do more along those lines, and he hoped the day might come when the concept of *thinking* was given as much stature, respect and career promotion as the concept of *doing* now received in all the American services. The pattern now was that you perhaps went to a staff school, or you served in the Pentagon for a while, or you were involved in some temporary strategic planning of some temporary mission, and then you were hurried back to the field where you ran up your brownie-points on really active duty. That was what you desired and schemed for and welcomed because under the present system you knew that this was the only way to really move up the ranks. Thinking wasn't "active"—its results weren't always immediately visible—it wasn't what real he-men considered worthy of their image of themselves—and it rarely created the image that superior officers liked to see when considering promotion lists. You could "think" all you liked: it was field command that really counted when it came time to award stars, bars, eagles and oak-leaf clusters.

So Brod knew perfectly well that his dream of being involved in long-range strategic planning was a very long-range concept itself. He knew that in time, no doubt, he would abandon this idea, which was essentially profitless in today's services in terms of power and promotion, and fit himself neatly and circumspectly into the standard pattern of a little bit of thinking and a lot of field command.

This pattern, which dominated all the services, would be all right if the enemy didn't think either; but it was clear enough in many places, and now most pressingly in the South Pacific, that he was thinking all the time.

Brod had been worried all through the earlier days of Frio, and though much relieved by the evident surge in activity, was still concerned about the obstacles that faced the mission as a result of the publicity that now surrounded it. He was not so naïve as to think that some hint of it might not sooner or later have reached the enemy, and he had always been skeptical that it could be accomplished with the degree of surprise that might be necessary for complete success; but this kind of worldwide hullabaloo was something new and disturbing to him. Perhaps because it was the first time he himself had been intimately involved, he had not previously realized the scope or nature of the national and worldwide orchestration of protest that could be mustered against any American project that opposed in the slightest degree the Soviet Union. He was sure that a lot of it, particularly the domestic variety, was entirely sincere and honestly motivated, but he was not stupid enough to think that all of it was. That crowd that had hung around River Entrance all day, for instance: he bet a lot of them had marching orders and would be there every day rain or shine until the issue was finally decided one way or the other. And the overseas uproar—which Clipper Corbus had covered for the Pentagon with surprising completeness in a special *Early Bird — Abroad* edition that had been on all their desks this morning—that too, he felt, was maybe 60 per cent managed and 40 per cent real.

He was realizing for the first time the basic nature and the very great extent of the massive danger that faced his country; and he found it a very shocking and frightening thing. He was determined, with all the fervor of his young, loyal and still very idealistic heart, to thwart its destructive purposes if he could.

Not, he told himself, that he as one individual could do very much to stop it from where he sat on his side of the issue. And yet it had only taken a handful of individuals on the other side, from Klaus Fuchs to Kim Philby and so on down the brief and shoddy list, to change fundamentally and beyond recall the course of history in favor of the Soviet Union. So maybe one individual *did* count. He was determined that *he* would, in whatever capacity might be given him.

He considered again, certainly not for the first time and certainly not for the last, the case of his co-worker, that model young officer, Maj. Gary Stump. He still was uneasy about Gary, even though he still could not put his finger on the reason why. Their relations in the office had always been pleasant, and recently Gary seemed to be going out of his way to be friendly. One obvious reason had occurred to Brod and he had dismissed it as something that didn't worry him because he was sure he could handle it without offending Gary if Gary ever tried to press the issue. More worrisome was the fact that Gary seemed to be launching a campaign to pry Hogan away from the quite close office friendship she and Brod had developed over the past few months. Maybe this was for Brod's sake, maybe for hers: Brod didn't know but he wasn't going to let that worry him, either—except as it seemed to contribute to his own vague suspicions that Gary's interest in them both was somehow a little beyond the personal. He only hoped Hogan knew what she was doing. From her increasingly kittenish responses when Gary was around, he wasn't so sure. He didn't know quite how to go about warning her further without causing a real problem; and Frio had too many problems, and he himself too much interest in continuing to be a part of it, to permit that to happen.

As far as he was concerned, Gary's purpose might be what it could be considered, but if so it was moving at the moment along conventional lines: an unexpected invitation to him and Kathy to be Gary's guests for dinner and the current play at Kennedy Center. If it went any further on a one-on-one basis, Brod would pass it off with the easy sureness that went with being a healthy young animal who had attracted a lot of attention over the years and had learned early how to distinguish between what he wanted and what he didn't. Meanwhile he had told Gary this afternoon with polite and quite sincere regret that he and Kathy couldn't accept because "Kathy's going to pop any minute now and we wouldn't want it to ruin your party in the middle of Kennedy Center." Gary had laughed and said he understood, he hadn't realized it was quite so imminent. It wasn't, quite, but it made a simple and acceptable excuse, and Brod hoped that would be the last of it. He still remained uneasy about Gary in relation to Frio, and for no reason whatsoever that he could define.

In fact, he told himself as he made his way out of the building through one of the few after-hours checkpoints that remained open to handle late workers, it would be a lot healthier for him if he just forgot it and took Gary at face value from now on. The mission was finally beginning to move, there was an awful lot to do, they all needed to work together in harmony and efficiency, and it would probably be a lot wiser if he stopped indulging in dark suspicions and pitched in with Gary and Hogan and Big G and the newcomers to make everything succeed. He told himself that from now on, barring something too flagrant or obvious to ignore, he would try to regard Gary as highly as everybody else regarded him, and stop harboring suspicions that were probably unworthy of him.

As he passed River Entrance he noted with satisfaction that a handful of protesters still remained, shivering in the wind that now had turned quite cold. It was supposed to be warmer again tomorrow but for now he hoped it would freeze their balls off. He did not feel any more sympathetic than he had this morning, even though this time he made no attempt to let them know it. He passed well to one side and walked briskly on out to his car in the distant parking-lot. Only a few other hurrying figures were doing the same. Behind them the building loomed massive and overpowering in the night, its porticoes illuminated, quite a few offices in E Ring still brightly lit. It never slept, he told himself—never slept. It was a comforting thought, perhaps more comforting than all the building's often confused and conflicting purposes might warrant. The sight of it couldn't help but give one some reassurance. It was so big—and so certain—and so *strong*.

Or so it appeared, sitting by the river in the chill October night.

He drove carefully home—he was a generally careful young man—west a mile or so along the Potomac to Rosslyn, his waiting apartment and his waiting wife. He was surprised and upset to find her in tears.

"Oh, *Brod!*" she cried, throwing herself into his arms with as much abandon as her present bulk would permit. "How *could* you!"

"How could I what?" he demanded in puzzled alarm, holding her as close as possible and kissing her hair. "I haven't done anything."

"Oh, yes, you did!" she cried, pulling back to thrust a late-edition front page in his face. *"Look!* And you've been on television too!"

"My God," he said stupidly. "Is that me?"

Indubitably, it was:

PENTAGON'S ANSWER TO PROTEST, the caption said: Is This the Finger That's on the Trigger?

And a chuckly little follow, good-natured and devastating, which related how "One Pentagon officer, apparently frustrated by protests against the Administration's newest adventure in the South Pacific, let demonstrators know what he thought of them this morning. We all suspected the Pentagon was getting a little fed up. But this much?"

"Oh, *Jesus,*" he said in a half-whisper, turning white. "What will Gen. McCune and Gen. Rider say? Oh, Christ. And this was on television too?"

"On the evening news," Kathy wailed. "They featured it. *In the first ten minutes!* You looked so—so *handsome*—but oh, Brod, *what you did!*"

"Could you tell it was me?" he asked, hoping against hope though with the newspaper picture clear as day it didn't really matter.

"Of *course* anybody could tell it was you," she said. "It *was* you! Oh, Brod!"

"But they didn't name me," he said, grasping at straws.

"They didn't *have* to," she said, indignation breaking through tears. "You're *you,* Brod. Anybody could tell!"

"Oh, my," he said, sitting down slowly, paper still in hand. "Oh, my goodness. Oh, hell. Oh, Christ. Thank *God* Gen. Rider had to go out of town today. But Gen. McCune—"

"Gen. Rider's going to hear," she said, drying her tears, "how can he help it?" Her tone became practical. "I think you'd better try to call Gen. McCune. I'm surprised he hasn't called you. Call him now."

"I don't want to interrupt him at dinner—" he began lamely but she wouldn't permit it.

"Brod Tolliver," she said sternly, "you call him. If he's as nice as you say he is, he'll forgive you. And if he's as smart as you say he is, he'll be expecting you to call—and he won't forgive you if you don't. So do it! And don't take a drink!" she added sharply as he started toward the wet-bar. "That isn't going to help!"

"No," he said humbly. "Of course you're right."

It took him ten minutes, arguing his way through the Pentagon switchboard and other outer defenses, to reach Quarters Six at Fort Myer. Mrs. McCune answered, her voice cool and distant as always. It took him another minute or so to convince her of his identity, but finally it was accepted.

"You want the general," she said. "Hold one moment."

In the background he could hear her say, "Zoren! It is a Brad—Brod—Toll—Toll—"

"Tolliver?" he could hear the general's awful voice reply. "Is it Brod Tolliver?"

"That's right, Tole-ee-vaire," she said; and to Brod, "He is coming."

He gulped and started to say thank you but before he could an astounding chuckle seemed to fill the room.

"Brod?" Gen. McCune said. "How *could* you!"

"I—" Brod stammered. "Sir, I'm—I'm *dreadfully* sorry—"

"Sorry?" Zeecy inquired on another burst of hilarity. "I wish I'd thought of it myself. Why didn't you come in and get me? We could have gone back and done it together!"

"Well, sir," Brod said, voice dropping to its normal level and beginning tentatively to sound relaxed, "I didn't think you'd be interested. I really didn't."

"Hell," Zeecy said, "I would have *loved* it . . . Seriously, now, young Brod, that really isn't exactly the way for an officer and a gentleman to behave, you know. Somebody is probably going to get very upset—probably the SecDef's protocol officer, he's a proper soul as befits his station. What kind of penance do you think you ought to do?"

"I don't know, sir," Brod said, voice husky again. "It really was stupid of me, I admit."

"Don't admit a thing!" Zeecy advised with another chuckle. "Haven't you learned *that* in the service? Anyway, aside from a disapproving editorial or two you'll probably get tomorrow, I doubt if anyone will really be seriously concerned, not even the protocol officer. I'm sure he'll agree with your sentiments and so will most in the building. They even smiled a little on the evening news, amazingly enough. You're on your way to becoming a legend, lieutenant. For the rest of your life in the service aging colonels and generals are going to remember you as 'Oh, yes, isn't he that kid who gave them the finger at the Pentagon?' But don't worry about it: more will approve than disapprove. Just please don't do it again. All right?"

"No, sir," Brod said fervently. "Oh, no, *sir!*"

"Good," Gen. McCune said. "How are things going now in the office?"

"Very well," Brod said, hardly daring to believe he was getting off so lightly but thankfully accepting it. "We're getting some extra space and additional personnel, ten already. Things are beginning to move right along, finally."

"Al Rider tells me he's pleased too," Zeecy said. "He also has kind words for you."

"Do you think he will," Brod asked, suddenly down again, "after—after—"

"If I know Al," Gen. McCune said, "he'll get a blowup of that picture from the newspaper and have it framed and displayed above the receptionist's desk where everybody can see it. Probably write 'Endorsed, Albert B. Rider, LTG, USMC' at the bottom."

"I hope so, sir," Brod said. "I *hope* so!"

"Don't worry about it," Zeecy said. "And our boy Gary? How's he doing?"

"Fine as far as I know, sir," Brod said. "He's very efficient. He and Big G— sorry, sir, Gen. Rider—seem to have everything pretty well lined up as to what's needed for the mission."

"Are you still suspicious?"

Brod hesitated.

"So am I," Zeecy said, "but we'll just rock along for a bit, o.k.? Keep your eyes and ears open."

"Yes, sir," Brod agreed. "I think we should."

"Yes," Zeecy said. "I'm glad you called me; I would have been disappointed if you hadn't. How's your pretty little wife?"

"Still pretty, sir," Brod said. He chuckled, quite relaxed now. "Not so little, at the moment."

"Great!" Gen. McCune said. "When's it going to happen?"

"In a couple of weeks, we expect."

"That's great," Zeecy repeated. "I never had a son myself, as you probably know. Always regretted that."

"Yes, sir," Brod said; and ventured to add, "Maybe that's why some of us have been fortunate enough to have your friendship, sir."

He was instantly stricken with trepidation at his own presumption; but, remarkably, Zeecy as always was Zeecy.

"That's right, young Brod," he said. "You're not a bad surrogate son—so far. But keep your damned fingers in your damned pocket, all right?"

"Yes, sir!" Brod said, laughing with relief. "I certainly will!"

And spent the next hour or so telling Kathy what a great and wonderful man the chairman of the JCS was.

At his end of the line, alone again with the one person in the world who knew him better than anyone else and to whom he was not, perhaps, quite so great or quite so wonderful after all the uneasy but unbreakable years, the chairman found that his brief moment of sentiment had not been appreciated. Instead, as usually happened when the sensitive subject came up, he was advised against a repetition.

"At least," Renee said, "in my presence. If you don't mind, Zoren."

The general sighed but managed a reasonably amicable retort.

"The only person in the world who calls me that," he remarked. "The *only* person."

"And the only one with the right," she said crisply. "So don't forget that, either."

"No, dear," he said, starting to take up the reading young Brod had interrupted, "I won't."

"Put down the book," she advised. "I want to talk."

"About what?" he said, obliging with the usual innocent air that now aroused only a minuscule portion of the annoyance it once could do.

"First of all," she said, "I *don't* think you should get too familiar with junior officers. You always have done that and I have never approved of it. It only leads to contempt."

" 'Contempt?' " he demanded, honestly astounded. "They worship me!"

"Well," she said. "That isn't healthy, either."

"Oh, Renee," he said in a tired tone. "Don't go Freudian on me at this late date. I know how to handle the troops. I've helped many and many a fine young officer get to where he wanted to go in the Air Force and scarcely a one of them has disappointed me or given me cause to feel it wasn't worthwhile." He smiled a little. "It's my private charity. Since," he couldn't quite resist, "I don't have a—"

"Son of your own," she finished for him. "I said, don't say that to me! It isn't my fault! *It isn't my fault!*"

But of course they both knew it was, and so he remained silent as she quietly started to cry, the only occasion and the only subject on which the perfect cool composure of perfect cool Mrs. Gen. McCune ever broke down.

"Darling," he said contritely, getting up and coming over to sit beside her on the sofa, taking her hand, helping her dry her tears, "I *am* sorry. I *know* I have no right to say that—"

"Oh, yes, you do," she said miserably, "that's what makes it so dreadful for me. You *must* not."

"I won't," he promised knowing suddenly that this time, at last, he meant it and that he never would again. "But," he added gently, "don't worry about people like young Brod Tolliver, either. He's a fine boy. It just pleases me to help them when I can." He smiled and spoke more lightly as she dried her eyes firmly and put her handkerchief away and the little squall seemed to have passed. "I'm a pretty good investor in human nature, Renee. I'm not such a bad judge, after all these years. And it helps the service. I help to keep up the quality. It's a worthwhile project. It's needed."

"Who is this Gary you mentioned?" she asked. "Him you do not like so much, and Lt. Tole—ee—vaire, he does not like him either. Is it just office rivalry or is there some reason?"

"We don't know," he said frankly. "I wish you could meet him, Renee. You're a great judge of people too. I'd like to know what you think of him."

"I would like to," she said. "Invite him here."

"No, I can't do that. There'd be no reason. He's a very bright, efficient, able young officer, who works with Brod Tolliver on the Frio mission there's such a rumpus about. They get along well, there's no personal friction: apparently he's perfect. But—there's something. So we're watching him."

"Poor Gary," she said dryly. "Being spied upon."

"Observed," he corrected, releasing her hand. "Observed . . . Is everything in order for New York this weekend? Anything more you need for the trip? Did the Pentagon travel office fix you up all right?"

"Unnecessary," she said. "Lucien and Annette—" the French ambassador and his wife, old friends with whom she was going to see a couple of major art exhibits and the latest Broadway musical hit—"have taken care of everything. Lucien has even chartered a private plane for us."

"Good," he said. "I'd fly you up myself, except I have to stay here and get things ready for that damned Congressional hearing on Monday."

"Not necessary," she said; and added, again dryly, "I am sure it is important that you be *very* well prepared for that particular Congressional hearing."

"Oh, yes," he said earnestly, ignoring her tone. "I expect a lot of lights are going to be burning in the building all weekend long."

"And yours, I am sure," she agreed, "the brightest of all. Well, we shall think of you, laboring so hard, poor Zoren, head on which so many burdens fall. We will be touched."

"Oh, come now," he said, joining her in old, accustomed laughter that often, as now, concealed an edge. "I'm not *that* badly abused. I'll manage."

She nodded.

"Yes, no doubt. And no doubt you will not be alone in your struggle through the weekend."

"Now, Renee," he said, tone becoming patient, "you know very well I shall be right at my desk, working away."

"Around the clock," she agreed, "twenty-four hours. I repeat, it will be touching to think of, that. And you will not even telephone anyone to help you through your torment."

Again he laughed and again she joined him, not amused.

"I make and receive probably a hundred phone calls a day," he said. "It won't be that heavy over the weekend but I *will* get some, I can't deny you that, Renee, I *will* get some."

"From your Senator, no doubt."

"We talk," he said calmly. "Quite often. She is hardly 'my' Senator, however."

"Not yet?" she said, eyes wide with exaggerated surprise. "You are slipping, Zoren!"

"Well," he said, turning to his book, "I won't even dignify that with a comment."

"What would you comment?" she inquired blandly. "There is nothing."

"That's right," he agreed with a smile, "there is nothing."

"Still nothing!" she said with a sigh of mock sympathy. "Poor Zoren!"

"Renee—" he began—shook his head with a wry frustration—and joined her in mutual, brittle, yet in a curious way not unfriendly, laughter. It was such an old, old game and they had been playing it so long.

"And now," she said, "I think that I, too, will read a book."

"Good," he said, opening his own. "I trust you've got a good one."

"A mystery," she said, showing him the cover. "It will do, though it is not half so interesting as life."

"Now *there,*" he said with a comfortable chuckle, "is a *profound* thought."

And she chuckled too, and in a comfortable silence they sat and read for a while, peaceably, side by side.

About the time they went to bed shortly before midnight the young Army sergeant sitting in his car across from a small, very discreet hotel on a side street near Capitol Hill saw one of the two men he had been following since six o'clock come out and pause for a second in the dimly-lighted doorway. He hesitated just long enough for the sergeant to take a picture with an extremely sensitive high-speed camera that required no flash. Then he obviously remembered where he had left his car, turned and walked quickly to it, got in and drove quickly away.

A few moments later the sergeant's primary quarry came out, was similarly recorded and drove with equal speed away.

The sergeant did not know the first man, though he looked vaguely familiar, but he did know the one he had been assigned to tail.

And he did know about that hotel. It was known to every intelligence agency in Washington, including the diplomatic, though those who used it, some of them amazingly high in the government and media, were not aware of this.

The sergeant uttered a long, low whistle. Then he started his own car and drove slowly and thoughtfully back to his quarters at Fort McNair.

5 Next day Al Rider returned to the Cumulative Assessment Group from a speech in Texas and as Gen. McCune had predicted, was at first more amused than upset by Brod's little gesture. But the east coast's most ubiquitous morning newspapers and its most egregious morning television shows had decided that today they would not be so amused.

The humorous note of last night's commentaries had given way to stern denunciations of "the young officer who apparently epitomizes, and perhaps was ordered to express, the Pentagon's attitude toward protests, however just and necessary, against the ill-advised Nanukuvu adventure." (So it had already become in the lexicon of the right-thinking.)

Brod's picture was again on front pages and small screens. His national notoriety received a new and deliberate boost. He and his impulsive gesture were now being used for the exact opposite purpose from that he believed in.

It upset him terribly and it made a highly pregnant and highly hypersensitive Kathy cry so hard that he really feared for a little while that she might go into labor prematurely.

It was only with a great deal of difficulty that he finally got her calmed down sufficiently so that he felt he could safely leave for the Pentagon. This time he went in the basement entrance and along the dark and dingy corridors, deliberately avoiding the now substantial crowd of perhaps two hundred who straggled in more or less orderly fashion along the edges of the parade-ground at River Entrance, holding high their banners and shouting their slogans at anyone in uniform who had to pass near them.

Because of Kathy's nerves he arrived twenty minutes late to find Hogan seated at her desk busy with her endless paperwork, Gary nowhere to be seen and the door to Gen. Rider's office closed. Presumably he and Gary were behind it, a fact Hogan confirmed after giving him a rather reserved greeting which alarmed him further.

"I must say *you've* made a splash," she commented, moving her papers about briskly. "I didn't know I was working with such a famous man."

"I didn't know I was going to *be* a famous man," he said forlornly. "I just had a sudden impulse to tell those crummy bastards off."

"Not very wise to give in to it," she observed and he nodded glumly.

"I know. My fault. It was stupid and childish. Has the general made any comment?"

"He didn't seem very bothered," she said. "In fact, he laughed. Gary seemed more upset than he was."

He looked surprised.

"Why is Gary upset? I thought he'd agree."

"He told me he thought it tended to lower the dignity of the mission and make it more vulnerable to attack. That was before," she added with a significant nod toward the closed door, "Big G called him in for a private conference."

"About me?"

She shrugged.

"I don't know, Brod. But if I were you, I'd keep my head down for a while."

"Yes, Liz," he agreed fervently. "I'll be so quiet you won't know I'm here."

"You'd better," she told him with a disapproving little sniff, "or you won't be."

Two minutes later Gary stuck his head out the door and asked, "Liz, has our media hero—oh, there you are, Brod," he remarked with rather elaborate surprise, Brod thought. "The general and I were wondering where you were. We thought maybe you were hiding out."

"No, I wasn't hiding out," he said, starting out annoyed but quickly moderating his tone at a warning glance from Hogan. "My wife is very upset by all this and being about to have a baby doesn't make her any calmer. I had to spend a little while quieting her down. I'm sorry."

"No problem," Gary said, not really sounding very cordial about it. "Too bad it happened in the first place. Want to come in? The general would like to talk to you."

"Surely," Brod said; adding as an awkward afterthought, "sir."

"What's that for?" Gary inquired with a smile that seemed a trifle scornful to Brod. "Are we playing soldiers in the office suddenly?"

"All right, Gary," he said shortly, getting up and heading for the general's door, "I'm coming."

"Here he is, sir," Gary said, stepping aside and gesturing him in with an ironic little bow. "The most famous lieutenant in the whole world. At the moment."

"Come in, Brod," Al Rider said and added pleasantly but firmly, "Sit down."

"Yes, sir," Brod said, thinking: now I'm really going to get it. He was very conscious of Gary standing behind his back and a sudden annoyance swept through him. Why didn't the little brown-nose come around where he could see him?

Fortified by Zeecy's support, however, which he had no cause to think had been withdrawn, he weathered his brief discussion with Gen. Rider in what he thought was pretty fair shape.

"You know of course, Brod," Al Rider said, a frown shadowing his normally open and untroubled face, "that what you did is not exactly what we expect of you as a representative of your service, the Pentagon and this office. Unfortunately you *are* being taken as representative of all three, particularly of the Pentagon. This is unfortunate."

"I'm very sorry, sir," he said. "It was stupid childish impulse. I had no idea I was being photographed—"

"You have to be alert all the time," Al Rider said, rubbing his eyes in a tired fashion with a big brown hand. "The media infest this place like fleas, you know, when there's any kind of demonstration. You offered yourself as a perfect target for them." He smiled a little, softening his admonitory tone, "I can't say I blame you. On the other hand I can't say I blame *them* either for taking advantage of you. I would if I'd been in their place."

"Yes, sir," Brod said. "I am very sorry, sir."

"Well," Al Rider said, smile broadening, "I dare say it isn't going to ruin Operation Frio."

"It isn't doing it much good, though, sir," Gary observed from behind Brod's shoulder. Brod restrained himself with some difficulty from turning around and responding.

"No," Gen. Rider agreed, serious again. "I think if you're to continue in this office, Brod—" Brod froze inside but relaxed as the general went on—"you're going to have to be absolutely circumspect from now on."

"Oh, yes, *sir!*" Brod said with the absolute earnestness that to his superiors was one of his most appealing traits.

"No more gestures," Al Rider said. "No snappy comebacks. Don't even look at 'em, just go right on by. That way you can't possibly get into any more trouble."

"Yes, sir," Brod promised fervently. "I *will* ignore them and I *won't* get into any more trouble."

"I hope not, Brod," Gen. Rider said, "because if you do I'm afraid I shall have to take real disciplinary action and neither one of us would enjoy that. It would spoil a very good record for you and it would rob me of a very fine assistant. So I don't want that to happen, o.k.?"

"O.K., sir," Brod said. "It won't! I *promise!*"

"Good," Al Rider said, smiling and relaxed again in his customary open fashion. "I'll count on that. You can get back to work now, if you like."

"Yes, sir," Brod said, standing and saluting before turning quickly to the door. "Thank you, sir."

"Well, sir," Gary said after he had closed the door firmly with a decisive little click, "what do you make of him?"

For a second Gen. Rider looked a little puzzled. Then he smiled.

"Not much. A likable kid and a very able and loyal one. Provoked and carried away a little bit, but nothing serious. It's a ten-minute wonder in the media; it'll pass. Why, Gary? Does he bother you in some way?"

"No, sir," Gary said, frowning thoughtfully. "I don't . . . think so. He's always *seemed* to be a very reliable guy. I suppose he still is. I just wonder, though . . ."

"What?" Al Rider inquired, interested.

"Well, I mean, sir," Gary said, "is anyone who's apt to fly off the handle like that really to be trusted with the secrets of this mission? It seems to me great discretion is necessary. I wonder if anyone with a temper like that really *can* be trusted. Wouldn't it be easy to provoke him into some indiscretion? Wouldn't he be—vulnerable, you might say?"

"That's interesting," Al Rider said, studying him thoughtfully. "I didn't realize you had these suspicions about Tolliver, Gary."

"Not suspicions, sir," Gary said earnestly. "Misgivings, let's say. Nothing I could ever quite put my finger on, you understand—nothing overt. Just a—just a hint once in a while. And now this, which certainly shows very poor self-control. I don't know, sir . . . I just wonder."

"Well," Al Rider said, "maybe you have a point, maybe you don't. I guess all we can do is keep an eye on him, don't you think? He's promised to behave and I believe he will. Maybe you're worried needlessly."

"It's not a worry, sir," Gary said with great reasonableness. "Just a—a concern."

"We'll keep an eye on it," Gen. Rider promised, opening the folder that rested before him on the desk, and thinking: I don't quite understand this sudden zeal about Tolliver. But Gary's no fool, and maybe . . . "Now," he said, dismissing it for the moment, "let's go over these estimates again and get them in final shape before we buck them back to the chiefs, shall we?"

"Yes, sir," Gary said, seating himself across the desk and opening his own copy of their highly secret papers. He smiled. "Shall we begin with the Marines?"

"Always begin with the Marines," Al Rider agreed with a grin. "That's the way to get ahead in *this* duty."

They spent the morning going over the facts and figures vital to the readiness of Frio. In the outer office Hogan and Brod continued acquainting the new staff members with the mission.

At noon Gary took his usual swim at POAC. He scanned the pool quickly as he approached it and realized that his new friend was not there, which of course served to bring back even more vividly his very vivid memories of last night—which, he suspected, was what his new friend might have intended by his absence. Or was he really not interested any more, and was that why he wasn't here? Or was it just that his responsibilities today prevented it? Or was it that—

He told himself disgustedly as he plunged in and began his regular thirty laps, looking neither to right nor left, that he was acting like a damned schoolboy with his first crush. He realized with a sudden alarm as he swam purposefully on that this was all too true. For the first time in many, many years he found himself powerfully and genuinely attracted. And that made *him* vulnerable, and that wasn't good.

Considerably shaken inside by this realization, although outwardly as smooth, sleek, self-contained and self-sufficient as ever, he completed his swim and went without further delay to the shower and then to his locker. When he dressed and left it he carried a paper bag containing an officer's cap that had belonged to Brod.

It had disappeared from the office several months ago when Brod had left it there overnight after changing into civilian clothes to go directly to a reception at the Riders. It had never been found. Gary suspected that it was time to take it home. Experience told him that it would be needed quite soon.

When he got back to the office Hogan told him there had been a call for him from someone who identified himself as representing something called "The Well-Favor'd Male." Maj. Stump's suit was ready, he said, and he could get it at the usual time and place.

Gary thanked her and said he was glad it was finally ready, it had taken long enough. He said he would like to take her to dinner and a show and let her see it sometime soon, and she blushed and looked flustered with anticipation.

Poor Hogan, he thought.

Some things were so easy.

And others were not.

On Friday afternoon the general commanding the Army's Criminal Investigation Command came in person to see the chairman of the JCS, not wanting to entrust his information to any other hand. He brought with him the sergeant, who was awed, respectful and obviously competent. They found Zeecy nearing the end of a busy day but he put everything aside to listen with absolute concentration.

When the sergeant had finished his report Zeecy, too, uttered a long, thoughtful whistle as he studied the two pictures.

"You're sure this is your man?" he asked. The sergeant nodded solemnly.

"Yes, sir, I can make positive identification."

"But you don't know the other one?"

"No, sir."

"Well, I do," the chairman said grimly.

"And I," the general agreed.

"Of course this is circumstantial," Zeecy remarked.

"Yes, sir," the sergeant said. "But pretty obvious circumstances, I'd say. I mean, they didn't go there to go to the movies."

"Oh, I don't know," Zeecy said dryly. "They probably have movies there too. Anyway, thank you, sergeant. You're very efficient. I appreciate it. May I keep these?"

"Yes, sir," the sergeant said. "Those copies are for you."

"Thank you," Zeecy said, "I'll make sure they don't go wandering around."

"What do you suggest now, sir?" the general inquired.

"This is interesting," Zeecy said, "but hardly conclusive. And I'm afraid, while this may account for some of the uneasiness felt by me and others, it may not account for all of it. Why don't your people stay with him a little longer? Would you mind?"

"Not if you say so, sir," the general said.

"I wouldn't think I'd have to make a point of it, general," Zeecy said with some tartness. "Even with this alone you're obligated to pursue it further and make a report if you get any real evidence, it seems to me."

"Of course, sir," the general said hurriedly. "I don't mean to imply that we could ignore this."

"I know," Zeecy said. He smiled. "It's been a long day and I'm probably getting a little snappish. I apologize. Good, then you will keep at it?"

"Yes, sir," they said in unison and his smile became personal and confidential.

"Thanks very much. I think it's important to our Frio mission or I wouldn't bother you further."

"No bother at all, sir," the general assured him. "Glad to help in any way we can."

"Good," Zeecy said. He looked at him with a quizzical smile. "Are you as surprised as I am?"

The general shook his head.

"Unbelievable. Considering the reputation—unbelievable. And—a real security risk there, too."

"The gravest," Zeecy agreed. "So: a couple of reasons for staying with it."

"We'll get back to you a week from today," the general promised. "Sooner, if warranted."

"Thank you, general," Zeecy said, rising and shaking hands with them both. "Thank you, sergeant. Your efforts won't go unrewarded."

"Sufficient reward if we can stop the enemy from jeopardizing the mission by exploiting personal vulnerabilities," the general said.

"Or anything else he might want to jeopardize," the sergeant remarked. "Sir."

Zeecy smiled.

"That's right, sergeant. You've got the idea."

After they had gone he sat for some minutes studying the two photographs.

Around him the building was beginning to empty for the weekend, save for those vital offices, such as his own, which were staffed and to some degree active every day of the year. The corridors bustled with the clatter of home-going feet and the sound of voices relaxing at the prospect of two days away from the never-ending problems of the Pentagon. He thought with a surprising touch of wistfulness how pleasant it would be to chuck it all, starting tonight, and relax in the luxury of two days away from this pressure-cooker. Then he told himself impatiently to knock it off. There was a lot to be done between now and the hearing on Monday, and not the least of what faced him was his rendezvous in another couple of hours with the senior Senator from Louisiana.

He considered very briefly the idea of sharing with her the information brought to him by the C.I.C., then dismissed it. It was all inchoate at the moment, interesting for her to know and as shocking to her as it had been to him, but not really her concern. And there was the traditional suspicion between Pentagon and Hill.

He knew he could trust her to keep it confidential, and yet . . . and yet. Things had a way of leaking, on the Hill, even with the best of intentions and the most solemn pledges of secrecy. Deliberately often; accidentally, sometimes. Burt Sanstrom or someone equally hostile might get hold of it. By some tortuous path never imagined at the beginning it might somehow reach the media, and wouldn't they love it. Big sex scandal in the Pentagon, hot damn! National defense secrets potentially endangered by sexual appetites of top-security personnel, goody-goody! Black eye for the God damned military, hallelujah! Oh, yes, they'd have a field-day. And from there it would go back to the Hill for another three-ring investigative circus and the circle would be complete. And heavy damage would be done to the Pentagon and with it, they believed in the Pentagon, to the country.

Fond as he was of Luzanne, and certain as he was that she wouldn't knowingly divulge anything, suspicion of the Hill was too strong. He put the idea firmly aside and also, presently, the photographs, which he secured in the small personal safe to which he alone had the combination. He told himself that if the C.I.C. did not come up with irrefutable evidence within a reasonable time he would destroy them and forget about it.

He was quite sure the C.I.C. would.

In several offices, including those of the JCS, the joint staff, the service secretaries and others directly involved in Frio, he felt sure the copying-machines were whirring again today and probably would be through the weekend. The prepared statements, the defensive documentation, the standard exercise of clearing one's own record as much as possible and putting the onus on someone else—the machinery almost always went automatically into gear whenever a Congressional hearing loomed. As always, most of this would be accepted without reading for the record; but for himself and Loy, at least, there would be respectful attention and gracious permission to deliver their statements. They had consulted about it several times already and had agreed upon strategy. Loy would present the over-all national security aspects of Nanukuvu, Zeecy would concentrate on the military aspects of the mission. No doubt the Secretary of State would also be allowed his full say. At the press tables the young KGB officers who manned the Washington bureau of Tass under the guise of correspondents would be taking it all down as busily as the members of the free press.

That was why, he told himself grimly, there were far more pressing imperatives than face-saving and buck-passing to justify a united and, if possible, extremely guarded presentation by the Pentagon and State. He knew Loy and Terry Venner had discussed the matter several times already—the SecDef had filled him in at considerable length on their conversations. He himself had checked with the chiefs twice in the past week. Now he was scheduled to meet them in the tank in five minutes for a final review of their proposed testimony.

They surprised him with their decision.

"Well," he said, after they were seated around the big table, with the big map of Nanukuvu and its crisscross of sea and air lanes twinkling on the wall, "is everybody in good shape for Monday?"

"I'm not getting in shape," Ham Stokes said calmly. "I'm not planning any statement. I'm not going to give Cube Herron or Mario Escondido anything to get a handle on. Let them come and get me if they want to. I'll tell it like it is. I'm ready for 'em."

"I think that's the best policy," Tick Tock agreed. "After all, the more you say the more you can trap yourself. Don't give the bastards any help, is my motto."

"When did you guys agree on this?" Gen. McCune inquired. "I thought, as of a couple of days ago, everybody was going to give them the full show-and-tell complete with maps and pointers. What happened?"

"We talked it over," Brash Burford said, "and we thought we'd leave that to you and the SecDef. We'll just be backup."

"If called upon," Bumpy Stahlman said. "We're ready if needed, but you two can carry the ball. Which," he added with a small smile, "I expect you were preparing to do anyway."

"No, not really," Zeecy said. "You're welcome to plunge in if you want to— the only proviso being that we don't really want to say very much, of course. We have to remember who's listening."

"The whole wide world," Ham Stokes remarked. "How the hell they think we can prepare a mission and have any kind of success now that they've blown our cover, I'm damned if I know."

"Perhaps they figure," Gen. McCune said with some tartness, "that since we've taken so much time we really must not think it's so important to *have* cover. That could be it."

"Damn it, Zeecy," Tick said, "will you stop riding us? You know why it's taken so long."

"Well, no," Zeecy said. "Not really. Why *has* it taken so long?"

"Well—" Tick said; and hesitated. "Hell!" he growled. "It just *has.*"

"That's right," Zeecy agreed, "it just *has.* Which is our greatest vulnerability, of course. However," he said, moderating his tone somewhat, "it can still be effective if we don't give the slightest sign of hesitation now. We've got to give everybody the feeling that we're going straight ahead just as planned, regardless, and that nothing's going to deflect us in the slightest."

"The juggernaut syndrome," Brash said with a flash of his old humor—it hadn't been present much, lately, Zeecy had noticed, and he had been worried about that and wondered why.

"Don't knock it," Ham said. "It can do an awful lot for you when you're facing an enemy."

"One who believes in it too?" Bumpy Stahlman inquired with some dryness. "Doesn't always work so well in that circumstance, Ham."

"Better than acting weak," Gen. Stokes said.

"I'm not suggesting that we act weak," Adm. Stahlman said with some asperity, "as you know very well. I think it's vitally important to act strong. And," he added pointedly, *'be* strong: it's easy to spot a bluff these days. The Navy's quite satisfied that *we* are."

"The Navy's quite satisfied," Ham said dryly. "O.K., Bumpy, I won't fight with you. We're satisfied too. We're still ready to move on out, any time."

"But you were the first one," Brash reminded, "who wanted to fiddle with the ALCAC and that's been part of the slowdown, right there. If it weren't for that—"

"You all joined in," Zeecy said firmly. "No point in going over that again."

"How's that doing, incidentally?" Tick inquired. "I was going to call Helen Clark today and get a progress report but got tied up and didn't. Where does it stand?"

"It's gone to DSARC," Zeecy said, "and she tells me she's putting on the pressure to get them to *move it.* Remains to be seen whether they'll do it or not."

"Damned civilians," Tock observed, "are as slow as—as—"

He started to grin and Zeecy finished crisply, "As we are."

"I was going to say molasses," Tick said with a chuckle, "but you took the words right out of my mouth, Zeece. Anyway, thank the Lord for that. As far as Al Rider and Op Frio are concerned, he tells me all's well there. Got their specs and recs in line and will have their final requests for us on Tuesday. As soon as DSARC comes through we'll be on our way."

"Then all we have to do," Gen. McCune said, "is come back here and decide on how we're going to neutralize Nanukuvu."

" 'Neutralize'?" Brash inquired and they all became very attentive. "I thought we were going to take it out. The battle-plan for *that* is still secret, isn't it? Jerry Castain hasn't got hold of that too, has he?"

"Jerry Castain," Ham Stokes said sourly, "is a pain in the ass."

"Jerry Castain," Brash said with a sudden anger, "is a fine person and a real friend of mine. Watch what you say about Jerry Castain!"

There was a moment's startled silence.

"Well," Ham said elaborately, "pardon me, I *am* sorry. I didn't realize he was a pal of yours, Brash. When did that happen?"

"He's very thoughtful and very kind," Gen. Burford said more quietly, "and he's been very good to—to us. I wouldn't want you to be too scornful of him,

Ham. We all wish he hadn't blown the whistle on Frio, but he has his responsibilities too, I suppose, and it could have been worse."

"Not much," Adm. Stahlman remarked. "We wouldn't be where we are right now if it weren't for Jerry Castain."

"And Red Roberts," Zeecy said, "don't forget him. They're both responsible men but I could wish there hadn't been time for Frio to attract their attention. However, no point in discussing that again. It did, and we go from there. We can still try the all-out assault, counting on surprise to do the trick for us. But 'neutralize' is coming to be the word I like best. Think about it."

"We'll know better after Monday, won't we?" Bumpy Stahlman suggested.

"We know right now," Gen. McCune said bluntly. "Once we let the initial advantage slip, we haven't really had any choice, have we? We aren't going to make any all-out assault. It would be suicidal. Let alone what it might mean in terms of open conflict with the enemy. We can't start World War III in the South Pacific."

"It's coming somewhere," Gen. Stokes said dourly. His colleagues looked at him with varying degrees of protest, halfhearted because basically they shared his foreboding.

"I'm not ready to accept that yet," Gen. Burford said.

"Nor I," Gen. Tock concurred, "even though sometimes it's awfully hard to see a way out."

"Awfully hard," Adm. Stahlman agreed somberly.

"Practically impossible," Gen. Stokes said.

There was silence.

"But not," Gen. McCune said finally with a sigh, *"completely* impossible. And to that we have to cling . . ."

"Well," Bumpy said in a businesslike tone to break the mood, "the immediate problem is Nanukuvu. What's the latest this afternoon from the island?"

"No particular change from what you already know," Zeecy said. "Everything proceeding on schedule, apparently—their schedule. The airfield work is progressing. Trees are being felled, the strips are being graded. No more troops have arrived, so for the moment, at least, approximately two thousand is apparently full complement. Subs continue to come in and out, a couple of the really big babies and half a dozen of the smaller ones, at latest report. No major naval vessels standing offshore—so far. Voice and code traffic continue at a busy pace. Moscow's keeping a very tight rein on this one, even more than normal. It seems likely it's being handled directly by the General Secretary: it seems to be his particular baby. Which makes it even more ticklish."

"What's the President doing?" Ham Stokes inquired. "Sitting around picking the lint out of his navel? When are we going to get some more guidance from him?"

"Are we going to get some more guidance from him?" Bumpy Stahlman wondered. "That's my worry."

"I think we will," Zeecy said, impelled by loyalty to his old classmate the

Commander-in-Chief for no reason he could quite analyze: he was feeling as impatient with him as they were. "He's making up his mind what to do, I think."

Ham snorted.

"Christ, if he doesn't know by this time we're all in the soup. Is every President this wishy-washy?"

"You know they're not," Zeecy said, "and I don't think he is either. He has an awful lot of things to consider, you know. It looks simple to us—at least, simpler—but there are all sorts of ramifications. At the moment, the order we have is what you know: keep on doing what we're doing. So—let's keep on doing what we're doing. O.K.?"

"O.K., yes," Ham agreed, "but I could wish the slippery soul would let it be known that he's with us. It would help."

"I'm sure he will," Zeecy said, not sure at all, "as soon as we get the hearing out of the way. A lot of things will be resolved then."

"I hope so," Bumpy said dryly. "They'd better be."

"Right," Brash agreed. "So we're all set then for Monday, right? You and Loy perform and we form a silent and impressive backdrop, ready to spring forward and perform when needed?"

"That's about it," Gen. McCune said with a smile as they stood and stretched and from behind a glass screen a colonel peeked out, saw the signs of departure and turned off the lights on Nanukuvu so that it subsided once again against the wall.

"Good," Gen. Burford said with a smile that still, to Zeecy, seemed to be concealing some inner tension.

"Brash," he said on a sudden impulse, "why don't you stop in my office for a minute? Something I'd like to talk to you about."

For just a second Brash's eyes looked wary. He hesitated for an obvious moment. Then he relaxed and Zeecy had the distinct feeling that some private Rubicon had been crossed.

"Sure," Brash said. "Of course, Zeecy."

"Now," Zeecy said when the others had gone and he and Brash were back in his office, "something's eating on you, friend. In fact, it's been eating for quite a long time. What is it?"

When Brash told him, at first haltingly but then with the more pragmatic flow of one who is gradually coming to terms with the worst, he expressed his fullest sympathy and support and asked if there was anything he could do. The conversation took a turn he had not expected. The day was full of surprises.

"You can give me some advice on whether I should retire now," Brash said. Zeecy gave him a startled look but it was obvious he was quite sincere. He explained his reasoning and the chairman sat back with a thoughtful frown.

"I don't know, Brash," he said slowly. "I'd hate to see you do that. You're not very far from retirement anyway, and it seems a shame to hurry it up for something that—well, that your retirement couldn't really be of much help to, to put it bluntly. I mean, what can you do for her that the people at Walter Reed can't? It's a great gesture, true—and I don't mean that invidiously," he added hurriedly, "it *is* a great thing to do, but—"

"She'd do as much for me," Brash said simply. "I want to show her how much I—well, I *care.*"

"For God's sake, man," Zeecy said, "she *knows.* Few women have ever been loved like Vi Burford. She knows it. You don't have to prove anything to her at this late date."

"I know," Brash said, "But I—I'd feel better, I think."

Zeecy studied him thoughtfully for a moment and came to the heart of it.

"What about the chairmanship?"

Brash smiled and gave him a candid look.

"What about it? You're going to push Ham into it, aren't you?"

Zeecy looked at him for a long moment.

"I'm not so sure—I'm not so sure . . . Anyway, I can't do any 'pushing.' It's up to the President."

"He'll certainly listen to you." Brash said, "No need to be disingenuous with me, Zeecy."

"I'm not being disingenuous," Gen. McCune said. "This President goes his own way, he always has as long as I've known him, and that's a long time. He'll consult around, of course, and I'll be asked, I'm sure, but no one individual's advice will be decisive."

Brash smiled.

"Yours more than most, I predict."

"Not at all," Zeecy said. "It may come down to something as simple as 'The Air Force has had it, now it's time to give the Army its turn.' You never know."

"I'd like to think it came down to a matter of ability and devotion to duty," Gen. Burford said somewhat stiffly. Gen. McCune smiled.

"Oh, it does, it does. But with an overlay . . . The question remains: do you want to quit when you're probably right on the verge of achieving what must be a lifetime ambition? At least it was for me."

"Oh, for me, too," Brash agreed. "And, of course, Ham." His eyes darkened. "No, of course I don't want to quit, damn it. But I think I should. I feel I—I owe it to her."

"Personally," Zeecy said, "I don't think you do. And I'm sure she wouldn't want you to. Have you discussed it?"

Brash shook his head.

"She's got too much else on her mind. I'm not going to bother her with my concerns."

"Which have always been hers, for Christ's sake," Zeecy said tartly. "Don't let yourself get too far away from home-base while being noble, Brash. She has a right to know what you're thinking."

"I know that!" Brash said angrily. Then the anger passed, he rubbed a hand that trembled slightly across tired eyes. "I'm sorry, Zeece, I'm under a lot of strain. You're probably right."

"Talk it over with her," Gen. McCune suggested. "I'll wager she won't be a bit surprised that you're thinking about it. And I'll wager I know what she's going to say."

"Yes," Brash conceded with a wry smile, "I expect you're right about that, too." The wryness deepened. "Maybe I just want to be coaxed."

Zeecy snorted.

"And don't give me any reverse-nobility, either. Stop castigating yourself and treat this like any other thing you two have faced together in your lives. It certainly isn't any bigger than her illness. In fact, to tell you the truth—" he too rubbed tired eyes—"this job is a crock. One has the glamor but one can't *do* anything. It's a very frustrating thing, basically. After I get out of it—" he looked grim and eager to do battle—"you're going to find me the biggest hell-raiser for reform you ever saw in your life. I'm going to blow the roof right off the building. I'll be making speeches and writing articles and testifying on the Hill until hell won't have it."

"Old soldiers never die," Gen. Burford said with a smile. "They just turn into reformers and try to fight the system that has put them where they are, is that it?" He smiled. "What makes you think you'll have any more impact than all the other reformers, Zeecy? They rise on the Hill—they make a fuss for a while—and they go . . . they rise in the building—they make a fuss for a while—and they go. The building goes on forever."

"May be," Gen. McCune conceded. "But one has to try from time to time, if only to keep the troops on their toes."

"I haven't noticed anybody getting them really alarmed," Gen. Burford said dryly. "A little agitated once in a while when somebody particularly powerful or popular raises hell with them, but basically not concerned very much. They know it will all die down in due course. Too many interlocking interests involved, in the building, in the White House, on the Hill. Too easy to raise the red flags of 'Prussianism' and 'military dictatorship.' Too easy to cash in all the I.O.U.'s on all sides. So on we go, stumbling toward destiny. I only hope destiny's waiting for us, otherwise we're all going to be in a hell of a fix."

"Exactly," Zeecy said, "just as we are with Nanukuvu, Exhibit A at the moment. . . . Anyway, Brash, to get back to you—nothing's decided on the chairmanship yet. Talk it over with Vi."

"But as far as you're concerned—"

"Stay with it," Gen. McCune advised. "It would be a wonderful, thoughtful thing to retire, but it really isn't necessary, in my opinion. You're very definitely in the running. Hang in there."

"I'll try," Gen. Burford said. "But—" he frowned and a deeply sad expression suddenly crossed his face—"it really wouldn't be worth it anyway, if she weren't around to share it with me."

"Well, on that," Zeecy said quietly, "I really can't advise you at all. Whatever you decide, Brash, I'll respect and support. Fair enough?"

"Fair enough," Brash said. "I appreciate your talking to me about it. Your kindness means more to me than I can possibly—" his voice grew husky and stopped. He stood up abruptly, turned and left.

Zeecy sighed heavily. A great preliminary to the evening with Luzanne to which he had devoted so much thought and anticipation. But maybe it didn't matter anyway. If it was meant to be, it would be. If not—if not, he told himself wryly, he and Luzanne would both survive.

He finished at the Pentagon shortly after 6, had his driver take him to Fort Myer. Renee had departed hours ago after her weekly struggle, amicable but intense, with Carleene over how to clean the house. With great relief and a final cheerful telephone call to him around 3 P.M., she had left for New York with the ambassador and his wife. The house was empty and somewhat cold.

He turned up the furnace, showered and shaved briskly, dressed in a conservative dark blue civilian suit with subdued tie, took the keys to the car which she had left in their usual place on the hall table and drove himself to the Washington Harbour.

Her apartment for dinner, Luzanne had said, would be the simplest, most obvious and therefore least likely to be observed of any place they might select in a city whose more prominent residents were almost always under someone's scrutiny, accidental or otherwise.

At the White House the man whose final decision they were all waiting for was preparing to host a state dinner for the prime minister of Singapore. The suave little gentleman was being given the full treatment. His tiny money-machine at the tip of the Malay Peninsula was as strategic as it had always been, its present-day importance increased by its humming commercialism and its steadily growing financial clout. The approaching return of Hong Kong to the erratic and uncertain mercies of mainland China, which was making the money-men of Taiwan increasingly nervous, was in turn making Singapore even more important to the economic well-being of Asia. In every way the city-state was worth keeping as an ally and encouraging as a bulwark against the increasing pressures of the enemy. The leader of Singapore was always welcome at the White House.

Leaving that aside, the President found himself tending to be quite bored by these never-ending visits which always demanded of him several hours of intense private bargaining and another three or four hours of pleasant but ritualized entertaining at a state dinner. Dining at the White House was the prize social event of Washington, and for those who did not live in it, it was always an exciting and thrilling occasion, given an extra gloss by the patina of history that overlay the Mansion. For him, too, it was always in some degree special and he always managed to rise to the occasion no matter how many after-dinner toasts and graceful compliments he had been required to deliver during his tenure. But inevitably after a time the occasion had become somewhat routine, and now he sometimes wished he could dispense with it altogether. But that would disappoint too many people, including his visitors and their wives to say nothing of members of the Cabinet, members of Congress, members of the diplomatic corps, members of the media and an occasional old personal friend or two.

A White House dinner was an elaborate gavotte of favors owed and conferred, egos stroked, politics, hard-headed business and the advancement of national interests. Its forms were as rigid, its rituals as unchanging as those of a Byzantine emperor's court. It was all very stirring and democratic, but its rules and procedures, scrupulously followed by each successive Administration, were by now virtually unbreakable.

Tonight would be no different from the rest. The guests would stream in at eight o'clock at the Southwest Portico in formal dresses and tuxedos; make their way up the staircase to the Great Hall; pass into the East Room where they would be formally announced. They would be served drinks, await with excited anticipation the playing of ruffles and flourishes by the Marine band in the foyer. The President and First Lady and their visitors would appear and the guests would form a line and be received. Each would be recorded by a White House photographer at the magic moment of shaking hands with the President, and in due course the White House social office would send them a signed copy with sometimes an intimate little personal note, depending upon how valuable they were, politically or socially, to the occupant. Then dinner would be announced, the many young military officers furnished by the Pentagon would see to it that each guest was ushered to the proper table. The meal would be served, after which the state visitor would toast the President with appropriate remarks, the President would respond. After dinner there would be some form of entertainment in the East Room, usually a singer or instrumentalist, followed by dancing. At 11 P.M. the visitor and his lady would depart for their embassy, the President and First Lady would go upstairs to the family quarters. The guests would be free to dance on for another hour. By midnight they would have departed and the Mansion would be quiet again.

So it went, sometimes as often as three times a month, as the unending stream of America's friends, partners, dependents and supplicants came to Washington. They always wanted something, the President reflected, and usually America wanted something from them, if only their assistance in keeping their particular corner of the world reasonably calm. So he supposed it all balanced out in the long run and he didn't really begrudge it, it was part of his job; but sometimes, as tonight, it was a little more burdensome than usual because he felt rather tired and hard-pressed.

Loy Buck had already entertained the prime minister at the Pentagon and soothed him with obliging responses to his modest requests for arms. Terry

Venner had spent a long and flattering hour with him at the State Department telling him just how important Singapore was to world stability. And the President himself had been closeted alone with him for two hours this afternoon for a wide-ranging discussion of Pacific problems.

It was during this final talk at the highest level that entertaining the visitor from Singapore had become a little wearing because he had raised the subject of damned Nanukuvu, as the Chief Executive thought of it, and had refused to be deflected by the President's well-known charm into some other less embarrassing and bothersome subject.

"You know of course, Mr. President," he had finally said, "that you must solve this problem very soon. What began as a minor irritation is now becoming a major threat. It cannot be evaded much longer."

"I'm not 'evading' it," the President had objected, with some mild asperity but not too much as there was no need to offend needlessly this astute little man. "It's a difficult thing to know what to do."

"The longer one waits," the prime minister observed with polite circumlocution, "the more difficult it becomes for one. I would venture to suggest, Mr. President, that if one has already delayed seven months, as one apparently has, it might behoove one to act now before the enemy gets even more entrenched. At least," he said politely, "that is how it appears to many of us in Asia."

"I'm afraid," the President said, "that my military advisers have been a little slow in deciding what to do. But that does not mean, prime minister, that we are not ready to take firm and effective action when the time comes."

"When is that?" the prime minister inquired, still politely though with a certain underlying impatience. "We understand work on the island is proceeding at a frightening rate. It is becoming a major threat to the whole region. How much longer can you afford to wait, Mr. President?"

"We must be prepared," the President said vaguely. "We must be sure all avenues have been explored . . ."

"Surely you have received some indication of attitude from Moscow by now," the prime minister said. "Is it necessary to explore further 'avenues'? Have there been any signs of cooperation at all, Mr. President?"

The President gave him a long look.

"None."

"Then why wait?" the prime minister inquired bluntly. "Why not move at once? It becomes harder by the day. Why make it more difficult for yourselves than it is already?"

"Would Singapore be willing to contribute a token force to a joint operation in the Pacific?" the President inquired, not quite sure why that idea had suddenly popped into his head but thinking that it wasn't such a bad one. Maybe an international force would be the best way out, at that.

The idea had obviously caught his visitor by surprise. The prime minister leaned back, eyes wide, expression startled.

"I had no idea," he said finally, "that you were contemplating such a thing, Mr. President. An international force! It is an amazing idea."

"Why?" the President asked, liking it more every second. "What's wrong with it? The South Pacific Forum is already in existence, Australia, New Zealand, the Marshalls and Marianas, the other island states. They've been on record for several years as wanting the region to be a nuclear-free zone. Perhaps we can persuade them to issue a new declaration based on what's going on in Nanukuvu. Then you could associate Singapore with them—we'll see if others will join—take it to the United Nations—"

"Mr. President," the prime minister said with delicate politeness, "the idea is admirable in concept but doubtful in execution if you wish, as you say, to form a so-called international force for military purposes. I have made it clear that Singapore is sympathetic to your desire to remove the threat of Nanukuvu, but . . . a military force?" He frowned. "I am not so sure, Mr. President, that we or anyone else would be willing to participate in such an adventure. Or, rather," he added hastily as the President's expression changed, "any such *military* adventure. The reason for that is very simple, Mr. President: we have no 'military force' to contribute. Even a token, as you suggest, would be beyond the limited capacities of my country and, I am certain, of all the rest. A *moral* offensive, however—a declaration—a protest—a united front against further introduction of nuclear arms in the region—that might be possible. Could it be done that way, do you think?"

"I think perhaps it could," the President said slowly, "though the preponderance of the advice I get is that we should go for the military option. However—"

"The military option is only good if one has the military strength," the prime minister observed.

"Exactly," the President agreed in a tone that sounded more down than he intended. His visitor looked alarmed.

"But if the United States does not have it," he inquired blankly, "then who does? What becomes of all of us?"

"Exactly," the President said again. "Not everyone remembers that as quickly as you, prime minister."

"We cannot afford to forget it," the prime minister said with a smile. "So you may depend on us to do whatever we can in this situation—short of the military."

"Good," the President said. "Perhaps you and Madame could remain after the dinner for a few minutes? We can go upstairs to the family quarters and talk this over with the Secretary of State." He smiled, a trifle dryly. "He will be pleased with this approach. Not a word to my Pentagon people, of course."

The prime minister agreed with a knowing smile and left for his embassy and a reception before returning to the White House for the evening. The President had remained alone for several minutes reflecting on the unexpected possibilities raised by his unexpected idea.

You never knew in this job, he thought, when something would occur to you as a solution for a problem you faced. For all his pushing for a diplomatic solution, Terry Venner had never come up with this suggestion. Yet it had been there all the time and none of the bright minds at work on the problem of Nanukuvu had thought of it, not Terry at State nor Al Brodovsky at NSC nor Joe Strang and the Doomsday Twins in the Pentagon. It had remained for him, the President, to get the inspiration, which was perhaps fitting and certainly welcome. He had really been up against it, he reflected wryly, not knowing until that moment quite how he was going to work his way out of the situation precipitated by the combination of Pentagon delay and public uproar.

He was not entirely sure now, but at least his conversation with Singapore's shrewd little leader had started things moving in a positive direction that he felt would be neither too aggressive nor too weak. He thought it would satisfy his peace constituency on the one hand and his more hard-line constituency on the other. He had to satisfy both if his political plans were to succeed on the scale that he felt would be fitting and appropriate to his position in history: a consideration to which, like all Presidents, he from time to time gave attention.

And now it was time to go downstairs and greet the glittering multitude. Two hundred had been invited tonight and all but three had been able to accept. He tied his tie, put in his studs, gave himself a last critical glance in the mirror, liked what he saw, and went along to the next room to collect his wife.

As usual she was not quite ready and he stood patiently waiting while she put the last touches on what she wanted the media to refer to as "another stunning ensemble for a radiant First Lady." She was sure they would, and he agreed. She looked smashing—his principal asset, as he often told her, which was not too far from the truth. She was among the principal ones, certainly, ranking not far behind his own highly attractive personality, excellent administrative abilities and profound political sophistication.

Under the North Portico they greeted the prime minister and Madame, a short, plump, brown lady of part-Chinese, part-Malaysian extraction who had an amiable smile, sparkling eyes, not much English but a charming disposition. The President murmured, "Don't forget after dinner," the prime minister beamed and nodded, the Marine band struck up ruffles and flourishes and they walked down the hall to the East Room, the prime minister's lady on the President's arm, the President's lady on the Prime Minister's arm. Just inside the East Room door they took up their stations and the long line began to pass before them, each announced by the briskly efficient young military aides. Twenty minutes of that and they were on their way along the Great Hall to the state dining room on the west side of the White House. An hour of eating passed to the pleasant accompaniment of the band's string section whose members wandered among the busily chattering guests playing tunes from light opera and musical comedy.

When it came time for toasts the prime minister was fulsome in his praise for the United States. The President responded in kind about Singapore. Both departed briefly from text, which caused some speculation among media guests and other perceptive diners.

"We want you to know, Mr. President," the prime minister said, "that in times such as these Singapore will cooperate wholeheartedly in any effort to preserve peace and security, particularly in our own part of the world where our modest efforts may hopefully be of some assistance."

"Now, as always," the President said, "we rely on our good friends in Singapore to take an enlightened and inspiring lead in those cooperative moves for peace which are nowhere more important than they are in the Pacific and Southeast Asia."

Later in the Red Room where the President and the wife of the prime minister mingled informally with the guests, while in the Green Room the First Lady and the prime minister did the same, the President saw Sen. Herron making his way determinedly over and braced himself for whatever blunt comment might be forthcoming. Cube, he recalled dryly, usually had some goody for him when he came to a state dinner.

"What was that all about?" he demanded now as he came alongside, bowed over the hand of the prime minister's lady and then turned to give the President's hand a firm, insistent shake.

"What?" the President inquired blandly as the ambassador of Denmark drew the prime minister's wife away in casual conversation.

"Joint efforts to preserve peace and security," Cube said. "Cooperative moves for peace in the Pacific and Southeast Asia. What are you two cooking up?"

"The usual boiler-plate," the President said airly. "Every state dinner toast has its quota, Cube. You know that."

"If it's some plan to salvage this Nanukuvu fiasco," Sen. Herron said, "you can forget it. Nanukuvu's finished."

"Oh, I wouldn't say that," the President said, thinking: well, there's another out if I have to use it. Let Congress kill it.

"Well, *I* would," Cube growled. "There won't be much left after Monday."

"I hope you won't be *too* rough on us, Cube," the President said. "We'd at least like a fair hearing. I'd like to think Cube Herron will give us one."

"I always try," Sen. Herron said. "I always try." He scowled across the room at the corner where Mario Escondido, who like himself had not been invited by happenstance, was exhorting the enormously tall ambassador of Ghana, looming above him. "Some people," he added dourly, "are not so forebearing."

"Yes, I know," the President said. "That's why we're counting on you. Keep that little weasel under control, O.K.?"

"I'll do my best," Sen. Herron promised with a wry smile, "but I can't guarantee it. Leaving him aside, though, you're still in trouble on the Hill with this one, boss. There's an awful lot of uneasiness. An awful lot of people want to know what comes next."

"And you really think," the President inquired, "that we can tell you what comes next without blowing the whole thing out of the water?"

"Maybe," Sen. Herron said, giving him a shrewd sideways glance, "you'd like to have it blown out of the water. It would solve a big headache for you."

The President returned a completely candid look, which he knew was the only kind that would be impressive to this old war-horse, and told him the exact truth.

"I don't know, Cube," he said as he turned away to greet the Speaker of the House. "At this point I honest to God don't know."

While the dancing continued in the East Room, the First Ladies went to the lounge in the Truman balcony to talk. The President took Terry Venner and the prime minister into the Lincoln study. He presented his idea, listened to Terry's delighted enthusiasm bolstered by the prime minister's cooperative friendliness.

"I tell you what," he said after they had sketched out a plan in fifteen enthusiastic minutes. "Why don't you sign my name, Terry, along with the prime minister's, and send out a confidential appeal for joint action to Australia, New Zealand, China, Japan, the Pacific islands and anyone else in the region you think might be receptive. Get at it right now and let's see if we can't get something we can release by Monday. All right?"

The Secretary of State beamed, the prime minister looked cordially obliging.

"Splendid!" Terry Venner said. "Just *splendid!*"

Ten minutes later they were on the way to the embassy to draft and send the message.

The President still didn't know what he would do, but at least there would be another option. It never hurt, he had learned early in the game, to have plenty of options.

Down a dark street in a dark section of Georgetown went that model young officer, Maj. Gary Stump, on his dark errand.

His mission came after another meeting, in the same place they had used before, with his newfound friend. It had been even better than the first time, he thought happily now as he walked rapidly toward his second, and far more dangerous, rendezvous of the evening.

Again they had been observed by the young sergeant from the Army's Criminal Investigation Command. This time he did not return to quarters but instead followed Gary with utmost discretion to an apartment building in Rosslyn, across the Potomac in Virginia, west of the Pentagon. There he sat in his car and waited, as ordered, prepared if necessary to spend what he thought would probably be a long, boring, exhausting and unproductive night.

Within an hour after Gary's arrival, however, things picked up. The major— or at least a short, compact figure which appeared from across the street to be the major—came back out. He was dressed, as he had been earlier, in civilian clothes. He wore a different overcoat than he had worn earlier and his face was concealed by a rainhat pulled low around his head, a scarf wound high around his neck—rather heavy gear, the sergeant thought, for a cool but relatively mild October night. He carried what appeared to be a small overnight bag. He went quickly along to his car, got in and drove off.

The sergeant called the information in and was told to stay with it and keep his superiors informed. Dutifully and discreetly he followed his quarry back into the District and, after a brief tour through teeming, garish, brightly-lighted, jiving central Georgetown, into what was evidently a very quiet, very wealthy neighborhood of beautifully restored old houses and heavy, overhanging trees.

There his quarry parked and the sergeant, after driving matter-of-factly on by, turned into a cross-street and, by some small miracle in that area, also found a place to park. He called in his location and asked for support. Then he left his car, doubled quickly back and began to follow, moving from tree to tree with all the effective skill he had been taught when he had entered two years ago upon his duty with the C.I.C.

For the better part of half an hour the quarry wandered, apparently aimlessly, through residential Georgetown. But, the sergeant noted, he moved in a gradually narrowing circuit. By the time another car passed the sergeant and discreetly parked some distance down the street, the circuit had narrowed further. It seemed to the sergeant and the two who now joined him that it was centering increasingly upon a shabby little Volkswagen with Bulgarian diplomatic plates, parked near the corner of R and 28th N.W. across from Oak Hill Cemetery.

On his third pass the quarry hesitated beside the car just long enough to toss something through its half-open window. Instantly the sergeant and his companions began to run, but not quite fast enough. Their movement alerted the quarry, he too started to run, pausing just long enough to toss a second object through the window. Then he fled through the dark streets, turned a corner, disappeared into a high-hedged garden and vanished.

In grim silence his pursuers coursed the area for another ten minutes or so but were unable to find him.

In the Volkswagen they found a manila envelope, encased in a plastic bag, containing perhaps twenty sheets of double-spaced typewritten matter. On the seat beside it they found an officer's cap. They went to what they presumed to be the major's car, called in the license number, were informed within five minutes that it was a rental checked out to another name. Disappointed by that but sure they had something of real import in the papers and the cap, they went to their respective cars and returned swiftly across the river to the Pentagon.

There it did not take long to convince the sergeant's superiors—if not completely the sergeant himself—that the quarry he had thought was Maj. Stump was someone else altogether.

On Nanukuvu, grading on the airstrips as of that hour was approximately one-fourth completed.

This was excellent progress, the commander thought, and a warm commendation from the most important office in Moscow agreed and made him happy. Everything was right on schedule on the island, he reported. Everything everywhere else, the strong, incisive voice from Moscow told him, was quiet, and that was good too.

He was advised, with a chuckle from the capital, that things would look even better on Monday when the unhappy American administration would have to undergo a grilling by Congress on its plans for Nanukuvu. Any attempt to really disturb the occupation of the island, the strong voice said, would certainly be impossible after that.

The commander was permitted to share the commendation and these good tidings with his men. Everyone was allowed to have an extra drink of vodka and everyone was very happy.

Above them through the placid Pacific skies went the message from the President of the United States and the prime minister of Singapore to Australia and New Zealand and the other nations of the South Pacific Forum, to China and Japan, to Indonesia and Malaysia and Thailand and all the other interested states in or near the Pacific basin.

Their response, it was hoped in Washington, would cancel by Monday any complacency that might be present on the island of Nanukuvu.

But of that, of course, no one at that point could be sure.

Five

1

The one thing everyone *was* sure of by Monday at 10 A.M. was that the Congressional hearing on Nanukuvu was going to be one of the biggest and best shows of the year on Capitol Hill; and, potentially, one of far-reaching consequences for the Pentagon.

Its chairman, in the numerous interviews he had given the media for Sunday's papers and news shows, had been careful to insist that it was just a "hearing," not an "investigation."

But he left no doubt that he was looking forward to it with some relish and with the expectation that it might well turn into a full-scale "investigation" before it was through.

Sens. Johnson and Castain and Rep. Aschenheim offered moderating voices, expressing the hope that it would be "a serious hearing with no unnecessary contentions, and with due regard for the best interests of the United States" (Luzanne) —"a hearing free from sensationalism in which we can determine whether the Nanukuvu mission is necessary, and if it is, why it has not proceeded faster in the Pentagon, and how we in Congress can help to speed the process" (Jerry) —"a short, informative, constructive and fair-minded hearing that will help the Pentagon and the President resolve what appears to be a serious situation" (Karl).

Mario Escondido left no doubt that his motives were pure as the driven snow, and that his only objective in participating at all was to assure a fair shake for all concerned:

"No patriotic American wants to interfere with the military in the pursuit of their duty to protect America's interests. At the same time we must make sure that this is not yet another typical example of Pentagon shilly-shallying and inability to function with the speed necessary in today's world. And we must, as always, make sure that American industry plays its full and fair part in producing whatever weapons may be necessary to assure the success of the mission."

"So much for Bridgeport, New Haven and New London," Jerry murmured dryly to Luzanne as they took their seats to Sen. Herron's right. The hearing was being held in the beautiful old high-ceilinged, marble-walled Senate Caucus Room, in the Russell Senate Office Building where all the major heroes and villains of the nation sooner or later appear. Mario and Karl were on Cube's left. A dozen other interested members of the Senate and House Armed Services Committees were in attendance.

Stretching out from the committee table along both sides of the room were the two press tables, jammed with major figures of the Washington media. The editor and correspondent of *Defense Eye* were squeezed in side by side with Red Roberts and a number of others from the Pentagon news room. Representatives of the wire services, the major metropolitan dailies and all the various special publications devoted to defense matters were present. Major foreign press were represented. The stars of the morning and evening news were also there. Against the wall on either side banks of television cameras stared down with impartial and all-seeing eyes. This was the media's chance to have what they had always demanded—and the Pentagon had always feared—the story of a major military operation before it happened. They were making the most of it.

Directly behind the witness stand were the Pentagon witnesses and their support team: the Secretary of Defense; Gen. Zoren Chace McCune and the Joint Chiefs of Staff; Secretary of the Army Clark, of the Navy Merriman, of the Air Force Ransome; Henry Milhaus, Assistant Secretary of Defense for Public Affairs, Brig. Gen. Harry Ahmanson, Harry Josephs and Assistant Secretary of Defense Helen Clark from Project Frio; Gen. Al Rider and his principal aide, Maj. Gary Stump, with Capt. Elizabeth Hogan and Lt. Broderick Tolliver of Operation Frio; Deputy Secretary of Defense Robert Cathcart; Secretary of State Terrail Venner; and assorted colonels, majors, commodores and captains from the four services, all bright, shining, scrubbed and polished, ready to spring into action the second one of their superiors indicated he needed a document, a cigarette or a glass of water.

These occupied the first two rows of the audience. Behind them assorted Pentagon wives, lobbyists and other hangers-on filled at least half the seats. Occupying the last half of the seats and standing three and four deep against the back wall, members of the general public lucky enough to get an assist from their Senators or Congressmen completed the audience.

The historic old room, Cube Herron noted with satisfaction as he banged the gavel and called the hearing to order, couldn't hold another body. Nor, he noted with considerable pleasure, was there a single major media personality missing. Cube didn't intend for his hearing to be a circus but he did want the country to pay attention. It was quite obvious that it was going to have the opportunity. His rosy cherubic face with its halo of white hair beamed out upon the room as he made his short introductory.

"This special joint committee of the Armed Services Committees of both houses, plus sundry other members who have expressed an interest, is convened this morning to hear witnesses concerning events on the island of Nanukuvu and subsequent activities of the appropriate arms of this government to respond to them. Mr. Secretary, will you open the proceedings, please. Do you have a prepared statement?"

"I have some notes, Mr. Chairman," Loy said in his quick, clipped, characteristic way. "I invite members of the committee to interrupt with questions or comments any time they please."

"In the interests of a coherent presentation," Sen. Herron said with a smile, "we'll try to restrain ourselves. At least for a few minutes." The audience laughed appreciatively and he looked at them with a fatherly twinkle. "The audience, incidentally, will restrain itself from any indications of approval or disapproval. This is serious business. Proceed, Mr. Secretary."

"Thank you, Mr. Chairman," Loy said. "Approximately seven months ago a landing was made by naval forces of the Soviet Union on an island called Nanukuvu, in the South Pacific in the general vicinity of the Marshall and Gilbert Islands—"

And he was off, relating the presumed slaughter of the island's innocent inhabitants, the sightings and death of Air Force Lt. Hague Smith—"which was the tragic but perhaps fortuitous incident which brought this matter to the attention of the United States"—the decision "by the Commander-in-Chief and the armed forces of the United States" to prepare an appropriate response —and in conclusion, in a firm and emphatic tone of voice that brooked little opposition, "The continuing determination, Mr. Chairman, to carry forward that response until this act of aggression by the Soviet Union, with its potential for disruption of the peace and security of the United States and her many allies in the South Pacific region, is corrected."

"Corrected?" Sen. Herron queried as Loy concluded. "An unusual word, Mr. Secretary. What do you mean by that?"

" 'Made right,' Mr. Chairman, as the dictionary has it: 'changed from wrong to right': 'removed as a threat to the right order of things': 'made to conform to the standard of what is right' in the dealings of peaceable nations with one another."

" 'Made right,' " Cube quoted again. " 'Made to conform.' How so, Mr. Secretary. How do you make the Soviet Union do something? With force? Isn't that what you're saying?"

"I'm not saying anything beyond the verb 'correct,' Mr. Chairman," Loy said crisply. "I do not think it in the best interests of the United States to inform the enemy of everything we are planning down to the last detail. I should be distressed indeed if I thought that was the purpose of your hearing here today, or if I thought any member of this committee entertained an intention so devastating to the well-being of his country and its allies and friends."

"Whew!" Delight whispered, not too inaudibly. "Listen to that arrogant bastard."

"He's not giving much, is he?" Red Roberts agreed with a smile. "Have to hand him that."

"I don't," snapped the editor of *Defense Eye,* "hand him *anything.*"

For the committee, too, the Secretary's tart rejoinder seemed to have come like the dash of cold water he evidently meant it to be. There was a little gasp along the table, a startled murmur from the audience. Loy Buck had come out fighting, there was no doubt of that. He did not go unanswered.

"Mr. Chairman," Mario Escondido said, "I resent that implication from the

Secretary! I think that's an awful way to address this committee, Mr. Chairman! Nobody here has the 'intention' to 'devastate' this country or its allies. I resent that, Mr. Chairman!"

"And the Congressman has no intention to try to make us reveal all our plans for Nanukuvu?" the Secretary inquired in an unimpressed voice. "Then we are indeed in luck, Mr. Chairman, and I must apologize for being mistaken."

"Well, you *are* mistaken!" Mario sputtered. "You're mistaken as hell!"

"All right, now!" Cube Herron said in an exasperated tone. "All right, now, Mario, cut it out! And you, Mr. Secretary, I'll thank you to remember that we don't take kindly on this Hill to implications that anybody up here deliberately wants to jeopardize the security of the country."

"No more, Mr. Chairman," Loy said in the same unyielding tone, "do we in the Pentagon take kindly to implications from up here that we are somehow betraying it or falling short in our duty to defend it."

"Mr. Chairman," Luzanne Johnson said pleasantly but firmly, "could we just concede that everybody here is patriotic, loyal, dedicated, concerned and determined to serve the country as best we can, and get on with it? It seems to me we're off on a tangent already. I thought you wanted to avoid that."

"Damn it!" Sen. Herron said, shaking his head as if to drive off a circling swarm of gnats and flushing all over his rosy face, "Damn it, I *do!*"

"Regular order, Mr. Chairman," Jerry Castain said in a calmly matter-of-fact tone. "I wish to ask the Secretary a few specific questions, if I may."

"You *may!*" Cube Herron said in such a tone of obvious relief that everybody, including Loy Buck and Mario Escondido, laughed. The tension was broken, at least for the moment.

"Good," Jerry said. "Mr. Secretary, how soon after the enemy action on Nanukuvu was the Pentagon apprised of it?"

"Almost immediately," Loy said. "I would say within an hour of Lt. Smith's death, isn't that right, general?"

And he turned to glance over his shoulder at Zeecy, who stood to give his answer.

"Yes, Senator," he said, "that is correct. The carrier *Dominant,* which was in the area—and, I might add, still is—to which Lt. Smith was attached, notified CINCPAC immediately, CINCPAC in turn notified me at once and I personally went immediately to the Secretary's office, which as you know is just upstairs above mine, and told him."

"And there was immediate action in the Pentagon?" Jerry asked.

"Meetings of all pertinent parties began almost at once," Zeecy said.

"And the President?"

"I called him immediately," Loy said.

"Thank you, general," Jerry said, and Zeecy sat down. "What did he say?"

The Secretary smiled.

"I am not privileged to reveal my private conversations with the President, but I think it's safe to say that it was very emphatically clear what he thought about it."

"He wanted to do something to counteract it?"

"It was very clear to me that he did."

"And you all, in the Pentagon, wanted to counteract it?"

"Most emphatically."

"Then why haven't you?" Sen. Castain inquired and there was a ripple of amusement through the committee and audience.

"Senator," Loy said, tone sharper but not too harsh, as this was, on the whole, a friend of the Pentagon, "as one who is familiar with the Defense Department and one of the great experts on the Hill in the whole area of defense, you are aware that things in the building sometimes take time. It is possible to move in a very short period of time to do something, but nowhere more than in defense is it true that haste makes waste."

"Time makes waste, too," Mario Escondido muttered just loudly enough to be heard. "Particularly in the Pentagon."

Loy Buck ignored him but obviously with difficulty.

"Mr. Chairman," he said, "if I may be permitted to continue my answer to the Senator from Indiana—it has been necessary to determine, first, what the strategic importance of Nanukuvu is, secondly, what its importance is to the security of ourselves and our friends and allies in the area, and thirdly, to decide what, how much, and when, should be applied to guarantee a proper and effective response. We could have mounted, I grant you, some half-baked, shoot-from-the-hip response, but that would not, in my judgment, have been the wise or effective thing to do. It has required very careful study and very careful planning—"

"But seven months, Mr. Secretary?" Jerry Castain interrupted. "Seven *months?*"

"It has taken that long, yes," Loy said, looking a little hard-pressed but maintaining his composure. "This does not necessarily mean that everyone in the planning areas of the Pentagon has been absolutely satisfied with that time period. Both Gen. McCune and myself have from time to time expressed a sense of urgency that has not always been reflected down the ranks. But there have been many factors and many people involved, and as with any human enterprise, it has not always moved as smoothly or as expeditiously as one might hope."

"But meanwhile the enemy's occupation of Nanukuvu has apparently moved as smoothly and expeditiously as *he* hoped?"

"He has achieved some success with his initial surprise, yes," the Secretary conceded, "but he still has a long way to go to achieve the complete success he apparently hopes for. Meanwhile, I would not want you to think, Senator, that everybody in the Pentagon has been standing still. *Nobody* has been standing still."

"But some have been standing stiller than others," Jerry Castain suggested with a smile. Again there was a ripple of amusement through the room.

"Some have had more problems getting things organized than we perhaps would have hoped," Loy said. "But, still, they *have* moved. To whatever degree has been possible."

"This is all very funny," Delight whispered to Red at the press table. "Except the delay could cost hundreds and *hundreds* of lives. If they ever get off their asses and get going."

"Why are *you* worried?" Red whispered back. "I thought you *wanted* this mission to fail."

"I do," she agreed, "but I hate to see such pathetic incompetence in anybody."

"By Christ, you're a generous girl," he remarked in mock awe, but with the amiable smile that always permitted him to say almost anything to anybody. "I didn't know you *cared.*"

"Honey," she said dryly, "I'm all heart."

"Mr. Chairman," Jerry said, "I should now like to submit to the Secretary, and ask him to respond to each one individually, the five questions I posed in the Senate a week ago when, together with my good friend Mr. Roberts of *The Wall Street Journal*"—he paused and smiled over to Red at the press table—*"Sweet,"* Delight hissed in Red's ear—"we first called public attention to what is known in the Pentagon as 'Frio.' In other words, the proposed mission to recapture Nanukuvu."

"I shall be happy to answer them, Senator," Loy Buck said, "but I think perhaps 'recapture' is something of a pejorative word."

"What would you suggest, Mr. Secretary?" Sen. Herron asked and they all looked at him with quickened interest.

"Whatever suits the methods with which we intend to persuade the enemy to abandon his plans," he said blandly. "It's a little too early to say, yet."

"Hmph," Cube Herron remarked. "Proceed, Senator."

"Thank you, Mr. Chairman," Jerry said. "The first question, Mr. Secretary, is: *Is it too late?*"

"According to the best intelligence reaching us," Loy said, "which is very good, since not only are our own intelligence-gathering methods quite adequate but the enemy in his arrogance is making very little attempt to hide what he is doing—the answer to that question is, No."

"Why is that?"

"Because developments on the island are still at a stage at which we estimate it will be at least another six months before he has completed what he apparently intends to do."

"What are those developments?" Karl Aschenheim inquired, leaning forward in the patiently intent way that made him a formidable inquisitor.

"That, Congressman, is something we regretfully cannot disclose in complete detail," the Secretary said, "because to do so would reveal some of our intelligence-gathering methods that must remain secret. Suffice it to say that the island can now accommodate submarines, that anti-aircraft defenses are in place, that a sizable complement of men has been established with barracks and supplies to house and feed them, and that work has begun on two air-strips—"

Karl Aschenheim looked amazed.

"Two?"

"Two. Of a planned size, apparently, to handle very large aircraft."

"That sounds like a really major installation," Karl observed with a frown.

"It accounts for our concern," Loy said dryly.

"But still does not account for your delays in acting upon it," Jerry Castain remarked. "So your answer to my first question is No. Very well, the second: *Has the Pentagon waited too long?*"

"That would imply that we have waited too long to be effective at all," Loy said, "and to that I would again answer, No. We believe we can still be effective. Providing," he could not resist adding with some tartness, "we are not harassed too much and are permitted to get on with it."

"No one harassed you for seven months," Cube Herron observed, "and you certainly didn't get on with it very far." And before Loy, flushing a little, could retort, he directed, "Proceed, Senator."

"The third question, as you will recall," Jerry said, "is closely related: *Can any counter-operation, however well-prepared and well-staged, successfully dislodge the Soviets from their bastion seven months after they started building it?*"

Loy nodded.

"This time, Senator, my answer must be Yes. Although again, 'dislodge' may not be quite the word. There are other options we can consider."

"What 'options'?" Mario Escondido demanded scornfully. "Seems to me the Pentagon is beginning to weasel, Mr. Chairman. Seems to me our brave boys with the flag wrapped around them are beginning to draw back from this precipice they're trying to take us to."

"Nobody is trying to take anyone to a 'precipice,'" Loy said sharply, as behind him the military and civilian heads of the Pentagon stirred uneasily. "We're doing our level best all the time to avoid a 'precipice.'" He appealed to Cube. "Can we damp down the rhetoric a bit, Mr. Chairman?"

"Don't forget I'm your chairman in the House!" Mario cried, rotund little body quivering with indignation. "I can use any kind of rhetoric I want!"

"Mr. Chairman," Jerry Castain said firmly before Loy, flushing even redder, could respond, "I believe *I* have the floor and *I* intend to use it." He leaned forward to peer across at Mario and snapped, "All *right*, Congressman?" Mario glared but subsided. After a moment Jerry resumed in a quieter tone.

"Now, Mr. Secretary, we come to question four: *Is it worth the time, the money, and most importantly the brave young men who would have to be sacrificed, to remove what may after all be a relatively minor threat to national security—*

since the island is so far away and the effort to recapture it—now, having waited so long—would inevitably be so great?"

Loy smiled, having had time to regain his normal composure.

"Again, Senator, semantics and assumptions. Who says 'brave young men' would have to be 'sacrificed'? Who says 'remove'? Those are strong words and it's a strong assumption they're based on. I repeat, there are other options."

"What *do* you mean?" Cube Herron demanded, not unfriendly but blunt. "Blockade them? Cut them off? Starve them out? What *is* the alternative?"

"Well, Senator," Loy Buck said calmly, "maybe that *is* what I mean—or maybe I mean an all-out assault—or maybe I mean something else. Since the Pentagon finds itself in a most unprecedented situation of having to testify in public about a military operation that hasn't happened yet, I'm just not going to *tell* you what I mean. It would be absolute insanity to tell the enemy in public session what we might or might not be planning, would it not? It would be utter asinine stupidity!"

"Well—" Cube Herron began indignantly. But the Secretary was having none of it.

"Would it not?" he repeated, and stared at the chairman with a deliberately stern and demanding gaze.

Cube Herron sputtered for a moment but common-sense and his own sense of responsibility brought the only answer possible.

"Yes," he conceded, ignoring Mario's fidgetings at his side, "of course you're entirely right. You can't do that. Perhaps you should proceed with your answer to Sen. Castain."

"Yes," Loy said, letting an obvious gratitude color his tone, "I think so. As to whether Nanukuvu is 'a relatively minor threat to national security,' that is a matter of judgment, and our virtually unanimous judgment—" out of the corner of his eye he was aware of a slight stirring from the Deputy Secretary but ignored it—"is that it is by no means relatively minor, but very major. You all have received copies of the map we sent you last week, which seems to me to speak for itself. The remainder of your question appears to be based on the assumptions I challenged earlier, so I don't think I need to repeat that."

"Very well," Jerry said, "Fifth and final question: *Do we, really, have the legal and moral right to conduct an operation, even if it did succeed, in an area where we have neither actual sovereignty nor a clearly-defined right to be there?* Both Mr. Roberts and myself, incidentally, checked quite closely into the assumptions underlying that one, Mr. Secretary."

"I know you did," Loy said, "and I don't question the sincerity or knowledge of those who advised you both on it. However, it seems to us that there is another assumption, based on history, self-interest, the interests of our allies, long and close association with island-states and many other nations in the area, and a general consensus accepted by both ourselves and by them, that we do in a general sense have both a right and an obligation to be directly concerned by the deliberate introduction of threatening force into the region."

"An assumptive right—not a legal right. Is that how you see it?"

Loy nodded.

"Basically, yes. But with the facts sufficiently persuasive so that we think we are doing the right thing, and will be doing the right thing when we in some manner remove, neutralize, thwart—" he smiled—"defeat, obviate, excise, eliminate or otherwise take care of, the threat posed by Soviet intrusion."

"Is it your contention that the South Pacific is an American lake?" Karl Aschenheim asked.

"Certainly not!" Loy said with indignant surprise. "But it *is* an area in which we have a primary and paramount interest, and one in which we intend to maintain that interest."

"Boy!" Delight whispered to Red Roberts. "Talk about American imperialism!"

"You talk about it," he whispered back. "I'm tired of it."

"I suppose you're all for it!" she retorted angrily.

"Sure," he agreed with an amicability he knew would annoy her. "I'm a real rootin', tootin', shootin' war-monger. You know me, kid."

She gave an indignant snort and turned her back on him, temporarily. He caught Jerry Castain's eye and winked. Jerry winked back and folded the notes he had been using in his interrogation.

"Thank you, Mr. Secretary," he said. "I think you've cleared up a few things for me."

"Not for me," Mario Escondido said. "The whole thing still looks pretty damned confused, to me."

"Maybe you'd like to interrogate next," Sen. Herron suggested. But Mario shook his head.

"No, I'll just listen and see what develops. I'll come in later, when it's important."

"Well, thank *you,*" Sen. Castain said with a laugh that was echoed by the audience. "I'm glad to know that's what you think of my questioning, Mario."

"Nothing personal," Rep. Escondido said airily. "Not at all."

"Good," Jerry said. "I was preparing to be crushed."

"Sen. Johnson?" Cube said. She nodded and leaned forward a little to her microphone. She looked this morning, Gen. McCune thought, absolutely lovely and absolutely self-possessed. She did not look at him, which showed him she was not quite as self-possessed as she appeared to be. Instead she gave the Secretary a pleasant smile and began by thanking him for his appearance. Then she bore in on what she considered the heart of the matter.

"Mr. Secretary, let me make the assumption that everything you say about the importance of Nanukuvu and the right of the United States to be concerned is correct. If so, how *do* you explain the Pentagon's delay in the matter? Hasn't it made your task extremely difficult by allowing time for the national and international uproar that now surrounds the subject to develop? Couldn't this very conceivably destroy your whole purpose?"

"The effects of the delay, Senator," Loy said, "you accurately assess. No one regrets them more deeply than I. *Why* there has been delay is a matter that has already been touched upon, and I don't know that I can offer much more enlightenment than I already have. In the Department of Defense, as you know, we have the second biggest portion of the annual budget, second only to the Department of Health and Human Services, to allocate, distribute and spend. It is an enormous task which requires a great many people and leads sometimes to inexcusable errors. Overall, however, considering the enormity of the job, I think we come off pretty well when all is said and done. We also have the armed forces to command, assign, post abroad or at home, keep in constant readiness, and deploy, when necessity unhappily forces us to do so, to further the best interests of the United States and to protect ourselves, our friends and allies. Here, too, errors and mistakes, sometimes tragic mistakes, inevitably enter in: the human equation perhaps too often controls, in both our major areas of responsibility. But here again, I believe that when all is said and done, our record is a good one.

"There is, I think—and I must apologize for taking so long to answer your question, but I think it's worth placing things in perspective—some necessity to do things in an orderly and organized way. And inevitably when you try to do that, you run into delays arising sometimes out of human nature, sometimes out of too much paperwork, sometimes out of inability to get everyone together at a given time on a given subject because the top people in the building just simply have so much to do—all these things play a part in what has been in this case, as you rightly suggest, an unfortunate and now handicapping delay. But given the size of the building and the size of its many, many responsibilities, I think it may have been almost inevitable.

"Which I know is probably not a satisfactory answer, but comes as close to the truth as I think you're going to find."

"You don't think inter-service rivalries have had anything to do with it?"

"Perhaps," the Secretary said with a rueful smile. "They always do, to some degree. But to the point of delaying things for seven months, no, I don't think they have been that important."

"Mr. Secretary," she said, "are you satisfied with the present JCS system and the way it functions?"

He considered his answer for a moment.

"I don't suppose there is anyone in the Pentagon from top to bottom who is satisfied with everything in it. And the JCS system is of course a very obvious target for complaint. There are changes I would like to see made, yes."

"No one ever seems to be able to make any," she observed. "I wonder why that is? We try to reform it from up here—the military lobby is so strong it survives us. Once in a while a Secretary of Defense will try to reform it down there—the deliberate inertia of the system defeats him. McNamara tried it: he's hated and despised in the Pentagon to this day. Short of cataclysm, it seems hopeless. And if cataclysm comes, it's hopeless anyway. The system

certainly hasn't done the Pentagon any good in this instance or in dozens—
probably hundreds—maybe thousands—of other instances."

"No, Senator," he agreed gravely, "it hasn't. It is something that deeply
worries and constantly concerns a great many of us in the building, including as
I said Gen. McCune and many other fine people in the military, as well as
civilians, and I know it has concerned a great many up here for many years. It
is a most serious matter. But the arguments against radical change are also
persuasive, and they also have their partisans. And a case can be made that
excessive centralization and excessive haste in our operations both military and
civil could be just as debilitating to the purposes of democracy as a more loosely
structured and time-consuming system."

She stared at him.

"So, as usual, there is really no one in the Pentagon who is responsible for
the situation we now face, is that right? It just happened, like some fact of
nature. Right?"

He smiled.

"Human nature."

She gave him a long and very thoughtful look.

"It isn't good enough, Mr. Secretary," she remarked soberly. "In this day and
age, it just isn't good enough. That's all, Mr. Chairman."

"Thank you, Senator," Cube said. "Congressman Aschenheim?"

Karl leaned forward.

"You said there were immediate meetings in the Pentagon when the news of
the Soviet occupation, I suppose we might call it, reached the building."

"Yes, sir."

"Without asking you for any details that might be confidential, have there
also been meetings at the White House with the President and his national
security advisers?"

"Oh, yes."

"How many?"

Loy smiled.

"May I say only—enough?"

"You may," Rep. Aschenheim remarked, not hostile but also not cracking a
smile, "if you think they *have* been enough. Have they?"

"Well, of course, Congressman," the Secretary said, permitting a slight impatience to surface, "there are many conversations that go back and forth between the Commander-in-Chief and his top people in the Pentagon. They
don't always have to be formal meetings. I'll say again—enough."

"All right," Karl Aschenheim said. "I won't press. If you're satisfied. And
would you say generally, again without revealing any confidential details, that
the Commander-in-Chief is wholeheartedly in favor of Mission Frio?"

Loy thought: damned if you do, damned if you don't, that kind of question;
not so dumb, old Karl. But he couldn't hesitate. He replied flatly: "I believe the

President to be wholly and enthusiastically behind this effort, whatever it takes."

"Oh," Karl Aschenheim said thoughtfully. "I see . . . He has conveyed this to you and to Gen. McCune and to all others involved, absolutely and unequivocally."

"We are fully satisfied that we have his complete support," the Secretary said in the same firm tone.

"Good," Rep. Aschenheim said. "Pity he hasn't conveyed that to the country."

He looked at Loy and Loy looked back, without expression and without response.

Karl Aschenheim let himself slump back in his chair, a big tousled bear of a man, gray-haired, bland-faced, looking like the plain honest country hick from rural Pennsylvania whom his constituents loved and had returned to Congress without a break for thirty years. But as they knew on the Hill and in the Pentagon he was plain and honest but he sure wasn't any hick. Not any hick at all.

"That's all, Mr. Chairman," he said. "Maybe I'll have a few for Gen. Mc-Cune when he gets on the stand. Thank you, Mr. Secretary."

"It's been fun," Loy Buck said with a smile, and for just a second Karl Aschenheim smiled back. Then he appeared to go into hibernation, until Zeecy came along.

"Congressman Escondido?" Cube Herron said. Loy braced himself and tension rose in the room. Mario was always a wild card. Loy knew the sheer weight of economic realities and comparative manufacturing capabilities had decided the recent Pentagon decision to give a prize contract to New Jersey instead of Connecticut, but he also knew most people in the country didn't know that. Many no doubt thought Mario's motives in criticizing the Pentagon were as pure as he pretended. He began, as usual, by draping that flag he had been talking about tightly and securely around his own chunky frame.

"Mr. Chairman," he said solemnly, "I want it clearly understood here—clearly understood—that if there is any real threat to the United States of America to be found 'way out there in the Pacific Ocean—" he made it sound as distant as Mars—"then I will be the first to give my own wholehearted and enthusiastic support to anything—*anything*—the Pentagon wishes to do to meet it. I give you my solemn pledge on that, Mr. Secretary."

"Thank you, Mr. Chairman," Loy said gravely. "We in the Pentagon, knowing how faithfully and diligently you work with us for the good of the country, are aware of the value of that pledge. And we appreciate it."

There were suppressed snorts at the press table, a ripple of tightly-suppressed amusement among the ranks of the Pentagon.

"Christ," Delight whispered. "I'm going to puke."

"I'll join you," Red agreed with a chuckle. "But not on Loy. He's not the one who deserves it."

"Mr. Secretary," Mario said in a tone suddenly businesslike and ferocious, "why do you think we in Congress should give our approval to a project that looks as though somebody is having a fit of hysteria over there? I'm prepared to give my support to something sound and sensible, but this thing! Who says there's a threat out there? How do we *know*? Has the media been permitted to go out and see? Does the world have anybody's word for it except the Pentagon's? How do we know what's really going on?"

Loy flushed angrily but did not speak until he had studied him thoughtfully for several seconds—to the point where Mario too began to flush. Finally the Secretary spoke in a cold and level voice.

"Are you accusing us of lying, Congressman?"

"I'm not accusing anybody of anything!" Mario said. "I'm just stating the flat truth of it, which is that all we have to go on regarding what may or may not be happening on some minor island in the South Pacific is what the Pentagon tells us. Is there confirmation from any other source?" He turned to Sen. Herron with an elaborate air of injury. "Is that so extreme, Mr. Chairman? Is that such an awful thing to ask? Am I so out of line to want confirmation from some other source in a matter as important as this?"

"Can't say you are," Cube Herron admitted. "That does seem perfectly reasonable to me. How about it, Mr. Secretary?"

Loy hesitated, collecting his thoughts, and as he did so Gen. McCune got up and came to the witness-stand. He glanced at Cube, who nodded and made a welcoming gesture. An aide moved a chair alongside the Secretary's. Zeecy sat down and leaned toward him. They conferred in whispers for a moment.

"Mr. Chairman," Loy said finally with a smile, "thank you for permitting Gen. McCune to join me a little ahead of his scheduled testimony. I apparently need his expert assistance."

"He'll be on the griddle soon anyway," Cube said. "Might as well get him started. What are you two going to answer to Congressman Escondido?"

"First of all," Loy said crisply, "we're going to answer that you have my personal word and that of the chairman of the Joint Chiefs of Staff that the situation on the island of Nanukuvu is exactly as it has been described to this committee and as it has been presented by Sen. Castain and Mr. Roberts, through the media, to the nation and the world. If the Congressman wishes to challenge that, he may do so." He turned to Mario and almost physically tossed him the dare. "Congressman?"

"I'm not accusing anyone of lying!" Mario said. "I'm not challenging your word! I'm just saying the fact is we don't have anything to back it up. The chairman agrees with me. So how about it?"

"If the Congressman wishes to come down to the Pentagon," Zeecy said calmly, "or if the entire committee—" he glanced at Loy, who nodded— "wishes to come down, we can show you intelligence and surveillance running back to day one on Nanukuvu and forward to the present hour which completely and entirely bears out what we say. But we are certainly not going to give this to you in open hearing, or under any but the most secure circumstances, because we do not intend to put our intelligence secrets on public display. Is *that* what you want, Congressman?"

"No, it isn't what I want!" Mario spluttered. "I just want something the country can *believe,* if we're going to accept this story! That's all! Just something we can *believe!"*

"Mr. Chairman," Luzanne said in a tone of what was, for her, rare impatience, "the Secretary and the general have told us how we can obtain whatever further proof we may want, what more can we honestly demand of them? Isn't it time for the Congressman to get on with his other points, if he has any?"

"Yes, I have some," Mario snapped, "and just because the Secretary and the general may have special friends on the committee doesn't mean I don't intend to pursue them!"

The audience exploded in excited murmurs, the media looked knowing, the Pentagon group tried with fair success to remain impassive. Cube Herron banged his gavel and turned upon the rotund little figure at his side.

"The Congressman will be in order and proceed, damn it!" he said in a tone that brooked no argument. "If you have something else, Mario, let's have it. They've made us a fair offer and called your bluff, now let's get on with it! The hearing will be in order!"

And he banged the gavel again as Mario teetered on the brink of some angry and defiant retort and then teetered back from it just in time.

"Well," he said grumpily. *"Well!* . . . I have no more questions of the Secretary, Mr. Chairman, but I do have some for Gen. McCune and the joint chiefs. Can the Secretary be excused?"

Loy gave him a wry look and laughed aloud.

"I'm sorry I'm such an unsatisfactory witness for the chairman of the House Armed Services Committee, Mr. Chairman. No doubt he'll make up for it next time I'm in front of *his* committee. Meanwhile, I'm perfectly willing to answer questions from other members of the Senate committee who may be present, if anyone wishes—?"

But after an exchange of glances up and down the table consensus emerged and Cube Herron stated it.

"Your cooperation is greatly appreciated, Mr. Secretary, but for the moment you may step down if you wish—or you may remain at the table with Gen. McCune, you wish. There are apparently no more questions for you at the moment, but we'd appreciate it if you could stand by."

"Surely, Mr. Chairman," Loy said amicably and rose from his seat. "I think I'll retreat from the line of fire for the time being and let the military have it."

And giving Zeecy's shoulder a friendly and encouraging squeeze which brought what Brash Burford called "the famous Zeecysmile" in response, he withdrew to resume his seat among his civilian subordinates in the front row of the audience. Aides again came forward, three more chairs were added. Zeecy sat directly in front of the microphone. Directly behind him, dressed like him-

self in full uniform complete with ribbons and medals, sat the chief of staff of
the Army, the chief of naval operations, the commandant of the Marine Corps
and the chief of staff of the Air Force.

Even the Pentagon's enemies, of whom there were sufficient both in the
room and in the nationwide television audience, had to admit they were an
imposing sight.

"General," Sen. Herron said, "and gentlemen of the JCS, thank you for
coming today to assist us in pursuing the truth of Nanukuvu and your Mission
Frio. We know how busy you are—"

"We're all busy," Delight whispered to Red. "What's special about that?"

"Nothing," he said, shaking his head in a tired way. "Nothing at all."

"—and we appreciate your cooperation." He paused and smiled, looking like
some cuddly but determined old kewpie-doll whom it wouldn't be wise to
underestimate.

"I let the Secretary get by scot-free in the last go-'round but I think this time
I'll exercise my prerogative and lead off the questioning. Gen. McCune, the
Secretary was very eloquent in rationalizing Pentagon delay. Let's have your
version."

Zeecy laughed, his very comfortable, at-ease, charm-the-socks-off-'em laugh.

"Mr. Chairman, you couldn't have hit on a subject closer to my own heart.
Let's face it, there have been delays in our approach to the problem of
Nanukuvu, nobody can deny it. And as the Secretary stated, he and I have
been on the side of the angels on that one, I guess: it's made both of us
impatient on occasion, and on occasion, downright frustrated and annoyed.

"But, Mr. Chairman—" he paused to take a casual sip from a glass of water
beside the microphone—"in defense of those who could perhaps legitimately
be charged with responsibility for delay, let me say, with the Secretary, that it
must be remembered what a huge and complex business we run over there
across the river. We spend more than $300 billion dollars a year, we manage an
armed force of more than 3 million, we have contracts out on some 50,000
industrial projects annually, and our mandate runs from the Pentagon to the
ends of the earth and into space. So it's a complicated machine and it's not
surprising if it doesn't always work with absolute efficiency. That it works at all
is perhaps more than we have a right to expect. That it works most of the time,
and most of the time well, is, I think, a tribute to the dedicated men and
women of both the civilian and military branches of the Department of Defense whom the Secretary, myself, and our colleagues here today have the
honor to represent.

"So: with the best will in the world, delays come, inefficiencies happen,
things that should be perfect are imperfect, things that should be inhumanly
brilliant are sometimes humanly dumb—it all gets involved with the human
factor. We try our damnedest and nine-tenths of the time—or maybe only
seven-tenths, but that isn't so bad—it all works out. Other times it moves more
slowly. Such, perhaps, has been the case with Nanukuvu. In the past seven

months we've possibly deserved criticism for delay. Now I think we're on track and moving out."

"Very eloquent," Sen. Herron remarked. "Toward what?"

"Toward whatever it takes to—" Zeecy hesitated for a split second over choice of words, selected the least inflammatory—"persuade the enemy that his adventure in the South Pacific is ill-advised and should be abandoned."

Karl Aschenheim stirred.

"How do you propose to do that?"

Zeecy smiled.

"As the Secretary said, we are not, of course, going to give you specifics as to what is planned. Our options include an all-out surprise attack on the island— some form of neutralization—various other methods and tactics that have occurred to us. We'd prefer to let the enemy worry about which one—or ones— we'll finally use—just let him realize that there are a lot of things we can do and that we're thinking about all of them. We're actually planning some of them. Which ones, let him guess." He smiled without humor. "That's his problem. Don't you all agree?"

And he looked blandly along the row of intent faces, skimming over Luzanne's as swiftly and impersonally as she had his.

"Of course we don't want to make you tip your hand in any way that would help the enemy," Sen. Herron said, "and that isn't really the point of my questions. You tell me, like the Secretary, that the only thing to blame for delay is human nature. But the delay has resulted directly in a situation of great public embarrassment for the United States that may really jeopardize the success of any attempt to, as you put it, 'persuade' the enemy to drop his plans for Nanukuvu. Not only has it done that, it has given the enemy seven months of unchallenged time in which to push those plans toward completion. So on all counts, delay in the Pentagon has been a very bad thing, in my judgment. And it can't very well be defended—at least with much real logic. Certainly its damaging results cannot be minimized."

"I'm sorry if that's the way you see it, Mr. Chairman," Gen. McCune said, while behind him the chiefs remained, as they had been so far, impassive. "We don't think it's too late to recoup."

"Good planners don't have to 'recoup,' " Karl Aschenheim remarked in a thoughtful voice. "They don't let themselves get into situations where 'recouping' is necessary."

Zeecy smiled, the smile a little tighter and not quite so confidently charming as before.

"We do the best we can with what we have, Congressman."

"I'm sorry, General," Karl Aschenheim said, "but I don't think you do."

A strained little silence fell, during which Delight had time to whisper, "Good! That's telling the arrogant incompetent bastards!" and Red Roberts had time to mutter, with increasing annoyance, "Oh, for Christ's sake!"

"I'm through," Cube said, "but I want you to know I don't think much of the

Pentagon's record on this one. I'm not saying at the moment whether I'm for or against this Nanukuvu idea, but I'm certainly against the way the Pentagon has handled it so far. It's been a sorry story, in my estimation, and I hate to say it, but I think it's been bad for the country. Maybe you can 'recoup,' general. I hope so. Senator Johnson?"

"Yes, Mr. Chairman," she said, voice steady, eyes impersonal, only a very faint flush indicating a very slight slippage in an otherwise excellent self-control, "I would like to find out a little bit about the way in which the final decision on what to do was reached in the Pentagon. First of all, though, has there *been* a final decision? Or is it still in limbo, as it were?"

"Senator," Zeecy said, solemnly but with a slight twinkle in his eye, "I can assure you Nanukuvu is not in limbo. We do have an Assistant Secretary of Defense for Limbo in the building, but he or she has not yet taken over Nanukuvu. There *has* been a decision, the details of which, as the Secretary and I have said, cannot be disclosed for obvious reasons. But it *has* been decided, that I can assure you."

"How?" she inquired and for a second he looked blank.

" 'How'? By the usual process."

"The JCS process."

"Yes."

She looked beyond him to the silent phalanx at his back.

"I wonder if I could ask the chiefs a question or two?"

"Certainly," he said. "We are all at your service."

"I'll bet," Delight whispered and this time Red didn't even try to reply.

When their chairs had been moved into a semi-circle at the table she turned first to Brash.

"General," she said, "are you satisfied with the decision?"

Brash gave a start and seemed to return from some private limbo of his own to answer her question, at first tentatively, then in a more positive tone.

"I'm satisfied that a decision has been made, Senator . . . Like any conclusion reached by five individuals, there were some differences of opinion on some points, but I think we've arrived at an agreement we can all live with. Yes, I'm satisfied."

"Would you say there was a deep division within the JCS on what to do?"

Brash looked at her thoughtfully, fully concentrated now.

"I wouldn't say a *deep* division, Senator," he said slowly, "but some division, yes. It's inevitable."

"But the final decision was a unanimous one."

"That is the JCS practice," he said somewhat stiffly.

"So that in essence it comes down to the lowest common denominator."

"Doesn't it always?" Karl Aschenheim murmured.

"No, ma'am," Brash said firmly. "No, sir, Congressman. There was a good discussion—a great deal of discussion—"

"You can say that again," Mario Escondido said. Gen. Burford ignored him.

"—and when it was over, we had reached a consensus on what should be done. I don't think you'll find any dissatisfaction with it."

"None that will be admitted, no," she said with a smile that softened her comment a little, but not much. "And would you say you were in the majority that finally forced—brought about—the consensus, general?"

"There was no majority," Brash said. "That isn't how we do things. There was discussion—a lot of ideas—kicking it back and forth—reaching an agreement. That's all. We reached one. We have one. Why does it matter, Senator, how we arrived at it?"

"It only matters," she said, "because it does go to the heart of the JCS process and it does result in a unanimity which does seem to some of us to be the lowest common denominator. This may not always be a good thing. How about you, Adm. Stahlman, are you satisfied with the result?"

"The Navy can live with it, Senator," Bumpy said in his most stately and dignified manner.

"You're not satisfied," she said flatly. He looked surprised and offended.

"I didn't say that, ma'am. I said we could live with it. We will—it is our duty to do so—that's it."

"Yes," she said. "And you, Gen. Tock?"

"Same thing, Senator," Tick said. "We can live with it. It may not meet all our objectives or all our objections, but it's been agreed upon after thorough study and it's the consensus. So what's the purpose in postmortem?"

"That's for me to judge, general," she said dryly and Tick promptly backed off.

"Yes, Senator," he said quickly. "Of course."

"So you're all agreed and it's one big happy JCS as usual," she said. "Does that include you, Gen. Stokes?"

Ham smiled.

"Not entirely." There was a stirring at the press tables but he disappointed them. "But as Gen. Tock says, it's the decision and we go from there."

"The Secretary said," she recalled, reading from her hastily scribbled notes, "that the intention is to 'in some manner remove, neutralize, thwart, defeat, obviate, excise, eliminate or otherwise take care of' the threat posed by the occupation of Nanukuvu. Which would the Air Force rather do, general, neutralize or eliminate?"

Ham chuckled. His colleagues looked at him with carefully suppressed concern, but of course he was not about to break ranks or inform the enemy.

"You know the Air Force, Senator," he said.

"That wasn't my question," she said with a smile.

He chuckled again.

"It's my answer."

"I take it 'neutralize' or 'eliminate' is still the main question confronting the Pentagon," she said.

"I can't say, Senator," he replied blandly. "There's no division in the JCS."

"None you'll admit to, anyway," she remarked, looking both amused and annoyed. He smiled back at her and said nothing. "That's all, Mr. Chairman."

"Let's have you two, Congressmen," Cube said, "and then we'll break for lunch. Congressman Escondido?"

"Gen. McCune," Mario said, "why was it felt necessary to conceal the situation in Nanukuvu from the Congress of the United States for seven months which would have been even longer if you could have gotten away with it?"

Zeecy hesitated. Then he smiled.

"Well, Congressman," he said dryly, "it wasn't a matter of 'getting away with it.' It was a matter of trying to decide what was best for the United States and its allies and friends in the South Pacific. It seemed advisable not to make a public fuss of it until we had reached that decision."

Mario Escondido looked belligerent.

"By a 'public fuss' you mean us—the Congress of the United States—I suppose."

"Well—" Gen. McCune said, and turned slowly and deliberately to let his eyes sweep across the press tables, the television cameras and then, turning almost completely around, the audience in back of him.

There was a wave of laughter as he turned back to face the committee.

"Very funny!" Mario said. "Very funny, I don't think! This is a perfectly legitimate inquiry by the people who vote the money. Don't forget that, general!"

"Never," Zeecy said calmly. "Nor do I forget that there are times when secrecy is necessary in government affairs, particularly military affairs. This seemed to be one of those times."

"Was that because you were really planning anything or just because you didn't want us to know how you were stumbling along over there in the Pentagon taking forever to make up all your minds about what to do?"

"I have told you our reason," Zeecy said coldly, "and I don't see any point in elaborating on it further. Or in engaging in a quibbling argument about it."

" 'Quibbling'?" Mario Escondido exploded. " 'Quibbling'? When it goes to the very heart of whether or not you were planning some sneak-in-the-night operation like Grenada, perhaps, behind our backs? We have a right to *know* these things before they happen!"

"Well, now you do," Gen. McCune observed tartly, "and God knows how much that's going to cost us in lives and money when it comes time to take action!"

"And when will that be?" Mario demanded sarcastically. "Ever?"

"Do you want us to or don't you, Congressman?" Zeecy inquired. "You seem to be in two minds about it."

"Of course I want you to do whatever is necessary for the security of the United States!" Mario snapped. "You just don't seem to know what it is, that's all!"

"Well, Congressman," Zeecy said, "I'm not going to get into that kind of shooting-match with you. Suffice it to say the problem of Nanukuvu *was* secret, now it's *not* secret, and we move on from there. With, we hope, your support and the support of your committee, and the Senate committee, and the whole Congress."

"Whatever deserves support will get support," Mario Escondido said. "Whatever doesn't, won't. It's as simple as that."

"Mmmhm," Zeecy said dryly. "Perhaps."

"Anything more, Mario?" Cube Herron asked, and collective breaths were held while the Congressman went through an obvious process of making up his mind, starting to ask something, then discarding it, then thinking of something else, then discarding it. Finally he shrugged in an annoyed way and sat back.

"Not of these witnesses, Mr. Chairman," he said. "What's the use?"

"Oh, Mr. Chairman," Zeecy said with a concern nicely balanced between sincerity and ridicule, "I hope we haven't frustrated the Congressman to that extent!"

"Be thankful," Senator Herron said; the audience tittered; and before Mario could gather himself together for what was clearly going to be an indignant retort, Cube said, "Congressman Aschenheim?"

"Just briefly, Mr. Chairman," Karl said, leaning forward, large and slow and to be reckoned with, "I'm a little curious, general, as to the support you're getting from the President of the United States."

"Yes, Congressman," Zeecy said with a smile much more cordial than any he ever gave Mario Escondido, "you've made that clear already. I can only endorse what the Secretary has said: he supports us wholeheartedly. We have no reason to believe he is not entirely committed to a solution of the problem of Nanukuvu."

"That will do what?" Karl Aschenheim asked.

"End the problem," Gen. McCune said, looking a little puzzled by the question. "Return peace and stability to the South Pacific. Cancel the threat to U.S. security and the security of our friends and allies posed by the creation of a major aggressive enemy base in the region."

"You're convinced it is aggressive," Karl said.

"What else can it be?" Zeecy inquired, again looking puzzled. "There's no other reason for them to have a base down there, particularly a base of that size and complexity."

"No, perhaps not," Karl said. "Aside from the basic purpose of terminating the threat, what else does the President support—if he supports that? Does he support any particular method of doing it? Any particular way to go about it?"

Zeecy smiled and repeated:

"He supports wholeheartedly, Congressman. That's really all I can say."

"Well," Karl said, sitting back. "If that's all you can say . . . I just wanted to be sure."

"Yes, sir," Zeecy said.

"Any further questions?" Sen. Herron asked, and without waiting for an answer, used the gavel and said, "We'll resume at 2 P.M. sharp. Everybody be here, please."

As they streamed out of the Caucus Room in a noisy babble of talk, gossip and laughter to seek the various cafeterias and restaurants of the Senate side a curious little incident occurred that was noted by almost no one because it was accomplished with great discretion and dispatch.

Two Army majors were waiting outside the huge oaken doors. As Gen. Rider, Maj. Stump, Capt. Hogan and Lt. Tolliver came out together one of the officers stepped forward quickly to intercept the general, flash an identification carefully shielded in one hand, and murmur in his ear.

For a second Al Rider looked completely astounded, and Gary Stump, though only Hogan noticed, turned white. Then the general's face became impassive, he turned to his staff with a quick nod that gestured them to follow him as he followed the two majors at a suitably casual distance around the corner, down the full length of the long adjacent corridor, around the next corner and into the stairwell leading to the floor below. There the officers halted. Gary by now had with great inner effort regained his composure. Hogan and Brod looked innocently puzzled and alarmed.

"I am Maj. Roseman, Army Criminal Investigation Command," the first officer said, "and this is Maj. Morrison. We must ask all of you to keep what is about to happen in strictest confidence at all times." He paused deliberately and let the tension grow. Then he focused a stern and solemn gaze upon his quarry. "Lt. Tolliver, I am afraid we must ask you to come with us for questioning. You may rest assured that all rights guaranteed you by the military code of justice will be scrupulously observed. We would appreciate it if you would comply with our orders immediately and without demur."

"But—" Brod said, turning absolutely white and actually swaying from the sheer shock of it, "but—but why? Why? *Why?*"

"We think you know," Maj. Roseman said, "and we think it would be better for you if you were honest and did not pretend ignorance. Come with us now, please. We have a car waiting at the side entrance, we can go right down these stairs. The less fuss, the better for all concerned. Come on, now. Sorry to trouble you, general—major—captain. You're free to go have lunch now. Have a good day."

The last thing they saw as they turned slowly away, close to shock themselves, was Brod's anguished face as he went obediently down the stairs between the two officers, looking back up at them as he cried incoherently, "General, I didn't—I don't know what—" And then in a tone of absolute desolution and abandonment, "Oh, Kathy! Kathy! *Kathy!*"

They walked slowly half the length of the corridor without speaking or looking at one another. Then Al Rider stopped.

"They think he's given the enemy copies of the plan for Op Frio and all the organizational and material requirements for the mission," he said. "I don't believe it myself but they claim to have proof. We'll have to support him in every way we can until it's proven beyond question. At least that's what I'm going to do."

"Oh, yes, sir," Hogan said, on the verge of tears. "I am too. He's *such* a nice kid."

"Yes," Gary agreed slowly. He sighed, a deep, unhappy sigh, so genuine that Hogan forgot all about the funny little moment when he had seemed to turn so pale, back there at the door when the majors first appeared. "But one never really knows, does one?"

At 2 P.M. exactly Cube Herron gaveled once again and the hearing resumed before the same crowded, attentive audience. During lunch Delight and Herb and a number of their more free-swinging colleagues had cornered Mario Escondido and been given a long, rambling, indignant and deliberately inflammatory statement about Pentagon inefficiency, the probably innocuous nature of Nanukuvu and the strong likelihood that infinite amounts of taxpayer money were about to be thrown down the drain in pursuit of "some harebrained hysterical overreaction on the part of the Secretary and the JCS." Many had filed this in full with their offices. It was a good antidote for "the snow-job the SecDef and Zeecy McCune are trying to put over."

Red Roberts and several of his more responsible colleagues from the Pentagon pressroom had managed to get a few moments with Sens. Castain and Johnson and Rep. Aschenheim and had emerged with a much more level-headed story carefully balancing obvious Pentagon delays with the inherent problems of the system and the apparently very real threat in the South Pacific. These reporters for the time being reserved judgment on whether the SecDef and Zeecy were trying to put over a "snow-job" or not. They were willing to give them the doubt and do what a dwindling number of conscientious reporters always did: wait and see. Perhaps the afternoon session would make clearer a situation whose full outlines and implications were still not entirely apparent.

The first witness of the afternoon took a lot of people by surprise, though not Mario Escondido, who announced with smug satisfaction and a triumphant amusement at the sensation he had caused, that the witness was being called at his specific request.

Senator Herron turned and examined him for a moment as though he were some unexpected form of insect life. Certainly Cube obviously thought his witness was.

"Very well," he said finally. "Mr. Framberg, take the stand, please."

"Yes, sir," Skip said, coming forward with a belligerent expression and a defiant air, red hair going in various directions as it always did, gray suit baggy and rumpled, a portion of hastily-stashed handkerchief hanging out of his right pocket—looking all in all, as Jerry murmured behind his hand to Luzanne, like the perfect popular picture of the absentminded scientist. He was obviously loaded for bear, however, and it was with a certain tensing among the ranks that his Pentagon colleagues watched his approach to the stand from his inconspicuous seat toward the back of the room.

"Your witness, Congressman," Cube suggested. "You start."

"You bet," Mario said with relish. "Mr. Framberg, I understand you have some involvement with this Frio thing. Can you tell us what it is?"

"Yes, sir," Skip said. "It's not Operation Frio, though. I'm involved with Project Frio."

"You mean there's something else?" Sen. Herron demanded, while Mario looked pleased at the stir this had brought among the audience.

"Yes, sir, there's two things," Skip said. "I thought you knew."

"No, we didn't," Cube said. "That's very interesting. Tell us about them."

"Yes," Mario Escondido echoed. "Everything."

"Well, sir," Skip said, "I don't really know very much about Operation Frio—"

"I think we pretty much have the picture on that," Cube Herron interrupted.

"Tell us about the project."

"As I understand it," Skip said, "Project Frio—or Proj Frio, as we call it in the building, Op Frio and Proj Frio—Proj Frio was established by Secretary Buck to handle what you might call the nuts and bolts of it—getting together the materiel and so forth for Op Frio. Particularly the ALCAC, and all that."

"We know what the ALCAC is," Cube said, "but for the benefit of the record, why don't you tell us?"

When Skip had, Cube asked blankly,

"Why does anybody want to modify that?"

"As near as I can figure," Skip Framberg said, "so all the services can get into the act." There was a murmur along the committee table, a restlessness among the Pentagonians. A small but satisfied smile touched the corner of Skip's mouth.

"Tell us about that," Rep. Escondido requested with relish. "That's what we want to hear about, how all the services have to get into the act. That's exactly the sort of thing we try to fight on this Hill all the time, all the services getting into the act. Tell us about it."

"Well, sir," Skip said, "I agree with the chairman, it's difficult to understand on the face of it why anybody would want to modify a perfectly good piece of equipment. I haven't been told all the reasoning behind it, but I do have some pretty good sources in the building—"

"Yes, Mr. Framberg," Cube remarked, "we've had the opportunity to notice that in the past. What did your sources tell you?"

"Not too much directly," Skip said. "I just pieced it together. When Op Frio was established to meet the threat posed by the enemy action in the South Pacific—"

"Do you believe that story, Mr. Framberg?" Mario asked. "Do you think there's a threat down there?"

The Pentagon ranks stiffened, but Skip, for all that many of them despised him as a troublemaker, was an honest young man.

"Yes, sir, I do," he said. "I think it definitely poses a threat and I think it has to be met somehow. My quarrel, like the committee's I guess, is with the way they're going about it. Or not going about it, rather."

"Yes," Mario said rather hurriedly. "Yes, well, that's your opinion, Mr. Framberg, and you may be quite right, some of us haven't decided yet. But go on about Proj Frio and the ALCAC. It's quite interesting."

"Yes, sir," Skip said. "It *is* interesting because it illustrates a side of the Pentagon that has always given *me* a lot of concern. As you may know," he added with a rather obvious show of modesty.

"We've had occasion to notice," Cube Herron said dryly. "What's your job at the moment, Mr. Framberg?"

"I'm a special assistant to the SecDef—Secretary Buck."

"For what?" Mario inquired.

"I don't know, sir," Skip Framberg said, and there was a ripple of amusement through the press tables and the non-Pentagon portion of the audience.

"You mean you're just there," Cube said and Skip nodded.

"Yes, sir. I study things."

"And did you study the ALCAC?" Jerry Castain inquired, trying to get things back on track.

"I presented a detailed plan for the modifications to the Secretary," Skip said with some pride. "He likes it, too. I believe."

He turned and looked suddenly and unexpectedly at Loy Buck, who did the only thing possible and nodded blandly.

"Very good," he agreed from his seat. "I do like it."

"Congratulations, Mr. Framberg," Mario Escondido said with elaborate sarcasm. "I'll bet that's the first thing you've done in the Pentagon that Loy Buck has liked in quite a long time."

"I wouldn't know, sir," Skip said with a sudden nervousness prompted by the realization that he was being led onto rather thin ice. "Anyway, I'm pleased about this."

"Great!" Mario said in the same tone. "I'm pleased for you . . . So the proposed modification of the ALCAC, even though you've apparently gone along with it and are contributing to it with rather notable success, illustrates, as you put it, 'a side of the Pentagon' that has always given you a lot of concern. What side is that?"

"A tendency sometimes to spend a lot of money on things that may not be really necessary, just so everybody can get a piece of the pie."

"And 'everybody' includes—?" Mario inquired.

"All the services," Skip said. "And the contractors."

"Who is in this case will be—?"

"Either Strategic Industries or General Growth Group," Skip said. "I understand they're both interested."

"Either S.I. or Three Gs," Mario said in a sour tone that indicated to the well-tuned political ear that neither had a major plant in Connecticut. "The same old tiresome, conniving, cost-busting, double-dealing, cheating—"

"Congressman," Cube Herron said sharply, "let's just hold down the colorful descriptives, shall we?"

"Just because they're big constituents of *yours,*" Mario commented, unabashed. "You know they've been in a lot of trouble sometimes."

"Not lately," Sen. Castain commented dryly, and there was general laughter, a little strained among the ranks of the Pentagon.

"They've paid their fines," Sen. Herron said with some annoyance and Mario nodded vigorously.

"Oh, sure and had their wrists slapped, and now and then their contracts have been suspended for a couple of months so the public would get the idea they've been disciplined before being allowed to go right back and do the same thing all over again. Oh, sure. Anyway, Skip—Mr. Framberg—you started to tell us about the ALCAC."

"Yes, sir," Skip said. "Apparently some one of the services suggested using it in whatever action might be planned against Nanukuvu by the Op Frio people, but with a little modification. And as soon as that was proposed, all the other services decided they wanted to put on some modifications too. *My* plan," he said proudly, "is designed to make it a better piece of equipment all around, not just bells and whistles to keep everybody in the JCS happy."

"You don't think much of the JCS, do you?" Mario inquired. Jerry Castain leaned forward impatiently.

"We've been all over that this morning, Mr. Chairman," he said sharply. "Let's get on with the rest of it now."

"Yes, sir," Skip agreed before Mario could make what was obviously going to be a noisy retort. "I have my criticisms, like everybody, but they're nothing unusual. The point here, and what really concerns me, is that here is a perfectly sound piece of equipment and there's this drive to change it, and the result has been a lot of delay."

"Which has not been good for either Proj Frio or Op Frio," Jerry remarked.

"No, sir."

"Whose idea was Project Frio, anyway?" Sen. Herron inquired. "Why couldn't everything have been handled by Operation Frio?"

"I'm not sure," Skip said, "but I have the impression the idea was Secretary Buck's."

"Why, Mr. Secretary?" Cube inquired. "Why the two-headed monster? Was that done to keep everybody happy, too?"

"It seemed to me at the time," Loy said, standing at his seat and again making the only response that made practical sense under the circumstances, "that it would be an efficient way to get things done, to have the strategic planning and the materiel planning going along simultaneously side by side. I am quite prepared to admit now, Mr. Chairman, that this was a mistake on my part for which I alone am responsible. I still think both things could have moved forward expeditiously side by side, but as we have already discussed at considerable length, this has not happened. *Mea culpa,* and there we are."

Which, he told himself with a wry inner amusement, was a lot better than saying, "I did it because as I told the chiefs, not really in jest, 'I'm not going to have you boys robbing the Treasury blind.'" Wouldn't *that* quote have given Congress and the media a field-day!

"Thank you, Mr. Secretary," Cube Herron said with an approving smile as Loy sat down again. "We appreciate your candor . . . So, Congressman, are we through with this witness?"

"With him, yes," Mario Escondido said, "but I'm still interested in Project Frio."

"So are we all," Sen. Herron agreed. "Any other questions for this witness?"

He leaned forward and glanced to his right and left along the committee table. Everyone passed. He turned again to Mario.

"Do you have any more witnesses on the subject, Congressman?"

"Indeed I do," Mario said with relish. Tension increased in the ranks of the Pentagon. "I'd like to call Mr. Harry Josephs, please."

"Mr. Harry Josephs it is," Cube Herron said. "Come right up, Mr. Josephs."

Small, gray, stooped, humble, innocuous-appearing, innocuous-acting, innocuous-sounding and about as innocuous, in Pentagon eyes, as a black widow spider, Harry Josephs came forward out of the audience blinking like some furtive night creature exposed suddenly to light. After he had been sworn, as they all were, to tell the truth, the whole truth and nothing but the truth so help him God, he settled himself uncomfortably on the edge of the witness-chair and leaned forward in a shy, strained, attentive attitude. No one, his posture seemed to say, could be more willing, more eager, more desperately anxious to do whatever the committee wanted. Mario Escondido obviously wanted him to blow Frio out of the water.

"Mr. Josephs," he said, "how long have you been an employee of the Department of Defense?"

"I've been in the Pentagon forty years," Harry Josephs said, "the last six of them as a principal assistant to Mr. William Murchison, Inspector General, OSD."

"So that you have a very substantial knowledge of government contract, spending and auditing procedures?"

"Oh, yes, sir," Harry Josephs said, blinking slowly and replying with an air of innocent candor. "I doubt if anyone except Mr. Murchison himself knows more."

"Good," Mario said. "Then you must have some definite ideas about Project Frio, of which, as I understand it, you are co-manager."

"Yes, sir," Harry Josephs said, "along with Gen. Harry Ahmanson. We were appointed by Secretary Buck."

"Why do you suppose he appointed two of you instead of one?" Mario inquired.

"Mr. Chairman," Loy said from his seat, "may I respond—?"

"No, sir!" Mario said firmly. "I'm questioning this witness, Mr. Chairman."

"Sorry, Mr. Secretary," Cube said. "If you want to rebut anything, there'll be time later. Proceed, Congressman."

"Mr. Josephs," Mario repeated, unable to keep a triumphant note out of his voice as Loy, shaking his head with an ironic smile, sat down again, "why do you think the Secretary appointed two of you?"

"I don't know," Harry Josephs said solemnly. "I have often wondered."

"Would it be because he distrusts the military and wanted you in there to keep an eye on them, and on Gen. Ahmanson?"

"Mr. Chairman!" Loy said angrily, again rising to his feet.

"Granted," Sen. Herron said as Loy sat slowly down again. "Suppose you stop fishing, Mario, and restrain your questioning to what this witness actually knows." His voice suddenly became hard and emphatic. "All *right,* Mario?"

"Well—" Mario said grumpily.

"Cool it down or knock it off," Cube directed flatly. "Maybe Senator Castain would like to take over questioning this witness—?"

"Not right now, thanks," Jerry said, "providing the Congressman proceeds in order."

"Mr. Josephs," Mario said sullenly to the witness, who had been sitting absolutely still while the high winds beat about his head, "what is your opinion of the whole Frio mission? Do you think it has any merit at all?"

Harry Josephs hesitated; blinked; hesitated; blinked again.

"Well," he said slowly, "you understand, Congressman, that we have not been told much about it, in Project Frio. It often happens in the Pentagon that various parts of a mission will not know all the details of the mission. Each component can have its own objective to achieve and then it's all put together by higher authority. It really wasn't until Mr. Roberts published his story and Sen. Castain made his speech that I really knew exactly what it was all about."

"And now that you do, do you think it's an ill-advised, exaggerated and probably futile idea?"

Again the Pentagon ranks were quietly agitated, but like Skip Framberg, Harry Josephs, now informed, was honest.

"I don't really know enough about it to say, Congressman," he said, "but from what I do know, I can understand why it's considered necessary to meet the threat out there."

"Oh, you can!" Rep. Escondido snapped while Loy and Zeecy exchanged a satisfied glance.

"Yes, sir," Harry Josephs said in a tone so earnest that it was obviously pointless to pursue him further on this point, "I can."

"Well!" Mario Escondido said. "All right! And what has been your experience in Project Frio, Mr. Josephs? Has everything gone along smoothly? Has Gen. Ahmanson performed his duties honestly and well? And what about Secretary Helen Clark? Has she been all right?"

"Secretary Clark and Gen. Ahmanson," Harry Josephs said slowly, as they glanced at one another not quite knowing what would come next, "are very *good* public servants. They have both been a little impatient with me, I believe, but—" he smiled shyly—"I never felt they actively disliked me for any reason."

"But they were 'impatient.' Why was that?"

"Well," Harry Josephs said, "I guess it's been because I've been one of those who disapproved of the plan to modify the ALCAC. I thought it was nonsense." A sudden uncharacteristic indignation came into his voice. "It's a perfectly good piece of equipment! It's perfectly adequate to do whatever they wanted it for! It doesn't need any modifications! That whole idea is just plain *waste!*"

"Your opinion carries a lot of weight with me," Mario remarked smugly, looking mightily pleased with his witness at last. "And why do you think it's being done, Mr. Josephs?"

"For exactly the same reason Mr. Framberg says. To make the services and the contractors happy."

"At a sizable cost in money and a very substantial cost in delay and loss of time for the overall mission," Mario suggested.

"Yes, sir," Harry Josephs agreed. "Such is my belief."

"Thank you, Mr. Josephs," Mario said. "No further questions of this witness, Mr. Chairman." He turned to his colleagues. "Does anybody want to defend monkeying with the ALCAC?"

He looked triumphantly along the committee table.

Cube Herron waited patiently.

There were no takers.

"Very well," Cube said, preparing to use the gavel. "If that's all, the committee will now conclude this—"

"Mr. Chairman," Luzanne Johnson interrupted firmly, "I think we should give both Gen. Ahmanson and Secretary Clark a chance to defend Project Frio."

"And I have another witness after that," Mario Escondido said.

"And I would like to call one more, myself," Jerry Castain said.

"It's a free country," Sen. Herron said wryly. "Come one, come all. All right, Gen. Ahmanson, if you will come forward, please."

Sworn and seated and looking very much in command of the situation, that very model brigadier general, Harry Ahmanson, USA, surveyed the committee with complete impassivity and composure as the chairman took over the questioning.

His testimony and that of Helen Clark, who was as calm, collected, unperturbed and forthright as he, was brief and to the point:

He had been appointed co-manager of Project Frio presumably because the Secretary felt that an essentially military project should have direct military input. No, he did not believe Harry Josephs had been appointed to "spy" on him (Mario's suggestion) and his relations with Mr. Josephs had always been perfectly pleasant. Like many in the Pentagon, he had been somewhat perturbed by the slowness with which the project got underway, and he had been "a little" impatient with Mr. Josephs because Mr. Josephs had made no secret of the fact that he was quite skeptical of the proposal to modify the ALCAC.

Nonetheless, he did not feel that Mr. Josephs had unduly dragged his feet, nor did he feel that what appeared to be some slowness on the part of the services in submitting their recommendations for the modifications had seriously hampered the project. Although interest and attention seemed to have been concentrated on the ALCAC in this hearing, there were other items of equipment and materiel that were being funneled through Project Frio and he felt that, overall, they were moving expeditiously and things were in good shape. He forebore, though hard-pressed by Mario, to criticize either the decision to modify the ALCAC or the Joint Chiefs, and responded with frigid and crushing dignity when the Congressman implied that this was because he was expecting to receive his second star at any moment. Members of the committee came to his defense indignantly and his appearance ended with Mario in glowering retreat and fulsome plaudits all around from the rest. Military Harry, as Red Roberts remarked to a savagely skeptical and continually whispering Delight, left an impression of integrity fully as effective as that of Civilian Harry.

Helen Clark was dressed with stunning simplicity in a plain black Halston dress that retailed at somewhere around $2,500 in the current market; the favorite strand of mixed pearls and rubies that always set off her long white neck so beautifully; and the single large rectangular pearl-and-ruby ring that did the same for her long white hands. Her coal-black hair was drawn back as always in a bun; her somewhat angular but beautiful features were as always striking; her large, intelligent eyes as always missed nothing.

She looked fit to kill and proceeded to do so, particularly Mario, whom she obviously considered a fool she did not intend to suffer gladly. She was fully as composed as Military Harry and, as a financially independent civilian who owed nobody on Hill or Pentagon anything, was considerably more acrid in her responses than either Military or Civilian Harry had dared to be.

Asked if she supported the modifications in the ALCAC she said flatly that she herself did not consider them necessary, "but, then, Congressman, I am as ignorant"—an exactly calculated pause—"as you are about the true needs and purposes of the Frio mission."

This brought a laugh from the room and a red-faced retort from Rep. Escondido demanding to know if she was charging members of Congress with being ignorant.

"Oh, no," she said quickly in her calm, level voice, "my answer only concerned you and myself, Congressman. I would not presume to judge other members of Congress."

"Then if you're against the ALCAC," Mario said loudly into the second wave of amusement, "why are you going along with it? Why aren't you opposing it like Harry Josephs? Why aren't you as honest about it as he is?"

"Firstly," she said, not at all perturbed, "Mr. Josephs in recent weeks has been as diligent as anyone in advancing the ALCAC program, whatever his private reservations may be. The same thing applies to myself. We have a duty to perform, given us by the Secretary of Defense. It would not occur to either of us to let blind personal prejudice or hope of political or other advantage stand in the way of our duty to the country. *We,"* she said with the gentlest and most unmistakable of stresses, "are not that sort."

"Are you saying—" Mario began indignantly and then stopped, probably because, as Red Roberts took occasion this time to whisper to Delight, he was afraid Helen would say yes. "So you don't like the ALCAC," he said rather lamely, "but you're still pushing it ahead as fast as you can."

"I certainly hope so, Congressman," she said. "In fact, it has gone through our hands and now is in the DSARC process, so it should be completed very shortly and ready to go."

"And contracts," he said, "will be let to either S.I. or Three Gs as Mr. Josephs says?"

"Mr. Josephs is correct."

"And which one do you and Gen. Ahmanson favor?"

There was a startled little movement in the Pentagon seats, but she was perfectly able to handle it.

"Whichever one can do the job best and fastest," she said coolly. "Which one would you like us to favor, Congressman?"

"Neither one!" Mario sputtered. "Neither one! I don't have any interest—"

"Yes, I'm aware neither is in Connecticut," she agreed with a pleasant smile, "so you really don't have the personal interest you have in some other contracts. It is quite clear to us in the Pentagon which ones are of most direct and profitable concern to you."

"I think," Sen. Castain murmured to Sen. Johnson as the room exploded for the third time in delighted amusement, "that our friend the Congressman would be well advised to leave Secretary Clark alone before she eats him up and leaves only a skeleton bleaching in the desert." Luzanne gurgled with delight. "Good for her, is all I can say," she replied. "Good for her! I don't think the little jerk has brains enough to stop."

But even Mario Escondido wasn't that dumb, and after two or three more feeble, and by now quite disheartened questions, he gave up.

"Mr. Chairman," he said sourly, "it is obvious that the Secretary is going to defend everything and everybody connected with Project Frio, and it doesn't matter to her one little bit whether the ALCAC is *ever* ready for this mission.

That could cause a lot of trouble Mr. Chairman. Just think of all the lives this delay could cost! Just *think* of them!"

"Mr. Chairman," Jerry Castain said sharply, "that is hardly a fair remark. It also illustrates the Congressman's own confusion, it seems to me. We thought you were against taking any action regarding Nanukuvu, Congressman. Are you or aren't you?"

"Well, I—" Mario began.

"Yes or no," Jerry demanded. "Yes or no!"

"I certainly don't want to do anything to jeopardize the security of the United States!" Mario said loudly. "On the other hand, I'm not going to stand for a lot of unnecessary frills and wasting of money, either! . . . So there," he concluded lamely, "you have it."

"I guess so," Jerry said, "though I'm not sure I know what it is. Shall we move on, Mr. Chairman?"

"I think we should," Cube Herron agreed. "Does anyone else wish to question the Secretary? . . . Very well, then."

Helen rose gracefully and returned, perfectly poised, to her seat. As she did so she gave Harry Ahmanson a wink that could not be seen by the committee but was observed with amused approval by her Pentagon colleagues.

"Mario," Sen. Herron said, "you said earlier you had somebody else. Do you still want to call him? Or her?"

"You bet I do," Congressman Escondido said, brightening visibly. "Mr. Deputy Secretary, will you take the stand, please."

There was a stir of excitement, a buzz of comment through the audience, a noticeable tensing of eyes, lips and jawlines along the ranks of the Pentagon. Big, burly and belligerent, Bob Cathcart got up from his seat at the very end of the row that held Loy Buck at its other end and lumbered forward to the witness stand, all 6 feet 4 inches and 233 pounds looking ready for battle.

"Do you swear to tell the truth, the whole truth and nothing but the truth, so help you God, Mr. Secretary?" Sen. Herron inquired.

"You bet!" the Deputy Secretary said roundly. "And nothing else but!"

"Very good," Cube said. "Better warn you, though, I expect Mario won't be the only one who wants to question you. If your testimony is what I suspect it may be."

"Come one, come all," Bob Cathcart said with cheerful zest. "I'm ready for you!"

"No doubt," Sen. Herron said dryly. "Mario?"

"Mr. Secretary," Rep. Escondido said, "when did you first hear about the Soviet landing on Nanukuvu?"

"When Secretary Buck decided to tell me," Bob Cathcart said. "Sometime the next day, I think it was."

"After he had met with Gen. McCune and the Joint Chiefs, after a White House meeting with the President had taken place, after it was known in half the building, is that right?"

"I wouldn't say half," Secretary Cathcart said with a rather grim smile, "but he sure didn't hurry about it."

"Wonder why that was, Mr. Secretary?" Mario inquired. Bob Cathcart snorted.

"Doesn't like me. Hardly a secret in Washington."

"Why?"

"Mr. Chairman," Luzanne asked, "are we here to explore an unfortunate and regrettable personal situation that exists in the Pentagon, which most of us know about, or are we here to investigate the progress of Mission Frio?"

"It's pertinent, Mr. Chairman," Mario said blandly. "Maybe if there was some cooperation up top over there, Secretary Cathcart could have been put on the job coordinating everything and this so-called 'mission' would be a lot farther along than it is."

"That's entirely speculative," Cube Herron said, "and I personally don't see any point in trying to stir up more trouble where enough exists already. Why don't you get on with it, Mario? And stick to the point, please."

Mario began a loud rejoinder and thought better of it.

"Mr. Secretary," he said abruptly, "what's your opinion of this Nanukuvu scam, anyway?"

"I object to that word, Mr. Chairman," Luzanne said. "It's pejorative and hostile and deliberately designed to arouse public opinion against the mission."

"Seems to me," Bob Cathcart observed bluntly, "it's aroused already. Are *you* getting a lot of mail *for* it, Senator?"

"None, for or against, that I'm going to let you drag into this record, Mr. Secretary," she said crisply and looked him squarely in the eye. "All right with you?"

He stared at her for a moment with an annoyed expression, but yielded.

"All right," he said impatiently. "All right. Let's get on with it."

"And let's stick to the subject," Karl Aschenheim spoke up unexpectedly. "If that's possible."

"He *is* the subject," Mario Escondido retorted, unabashed. "So, Mr. Secretary, for all practical purposes you've been sent to Siberia in the matter of Nanukuvu, is that right?"

"There hasn't been any great rush to include me," Secretary Cathcart said dryly. "Oh, I'll admit Loy's briefed me from time to time, there's been that courtesy, but as for any day-to-day involvement where I might have been able to contribute something—no, that hasn't happened."

"Very unfortunate," Mario said piously. "*Very* unfortunate. Could that be because you have disapproved of this whole peculiar business from the beginning?"

"Mr. *Chairman!*" Luzanne protested again. Cube Herron agreed.

"Just hold the adjectives, Mario, o.k.? Just get on with it."

"I repeat," Mario said belligerently, "you didn't like this peculiar business, did you, Mr. Secretary?"

"I couldn't see wasting the time on it, frankly," Bob Cathcart said. "I mean, they've been sneaking around out there for a long time and so have we, so what else is new? Why should we get all excited about it and make a big deal of it just because they're beginning to do what we've been doing in the Pacific for years?"

"Mr. Secretary," Karl Aschenheim inquired politely, "is that a fact, now? Have we been secretly seizing islands and slaughtering their inhabitants and building major sub and air bases down there in property that isn't ours? I've been on the House Appropriations subcommittee on defense for twenty years and *I* didn't know that." His polite amazement increased. "Are we *really!*"

Bob Cathcart flushed but didn't give ground.

"Sure we are! Everybody in the Pentagon knows it and I suspect anybody up here—of any stature—knows it too. I'm surprised *you* don't, Congressman."

"Not enough stature, I guess," Karl Aschenheim said with a wistful shake of his head. "Just goes to show. And where might some of those bases of ours be, Mr. Secretary? Can you name a few? I mean, I take it they aren't secret if everybody—of any stature—knows about 'em. Tell us." He looked very serious. "I think it's about time *I* found out."

For just a second Bob Cathcart looked as though he was going to let himself be provoked into a really angry retort by the needling he was getting from this usually calm and non-adversarial source. But with an obvious struggle he refused the temptation, at least for the moment.

"Well, Congressman," he said, "I'm not going to tell you if you don't know."

Karl Aschenheim studied him thoughtfully.

"Does that mean *you* don't know, Mr. Secretary?"

"No, it doesn't mean I don't know!" the Deputy Secretary snapped. "Everybody knows, I said!"

"Well," Karl said regretfully, "I guess if you won't, you won't. It puts a whole new light on it, though, to know we're a bunch of scalawags just like they are. Shoots our whole moral position, doesn't it? We're just as no damned good as they are. Well, well!"

"Mr. Chairman," Mario Escondido said indignantly, "if my distinguished friend from Pennsylvania is through harassing the Secretary—" there was a deliberately audible snort from someone in the Pentagon section—"maybe we can get on with this. I asked you 'way back there somewhere, Mr. Secretary, weren't you opposed to this Nanukuvu business from the beginning?"

"I didn't think much of it then," Bob Cathcart said, "and I don't think much of it now. I'm not making any brief for what they may be doing down there—which, as you said earlier, only comes to us through the OSD and the JCS, the media hasn't been allowed in to make any independent confirmation—but I do say we haven't any legal right to complain or interfere."

"And you don't think it's any real threat to our national security or to our friends?" Mario asked, expression openly pleased at this demolition, from within the Pentagon, of the Pentagon's case.

"No, sir, I do not," the Secretary said stoutly. "We've got plenty of stuff down there to stop 'em if they try anything funny. I don't believe it's a threat to us." He looked scornful. "I don't think the war party in the Pentagon has a leg to stand on."

"Oh, boy!" Delight whispered as a stir went through the audience, particularly the first two uniformed rows. " 'War party in the Pentagon!' There's a headline for you!"

"Not for me," Red whispered back. "But be my guest."

"Mr. Chairman," Jerry Castain said, "I find this quite extraordinary, the Deputy Secretary of Defense going on record publicly as opposing something that's been decided on as a matter of serious national policy by the Secretary and the Joint Chiefs of Staff. To say nothing of the President."

"Oh, has he decided on it?" Bob Cathcart inquired, sounding not at all impressed. "I didn't know that, Senator. When did he tell you that?"

"He hasn't told me that," Jerry said sharply, "but it seems to me implicit if the Secretary and the JCS are backing it. They wouldn't be otherwise, would they?"

Secretary Cathcart shrugged.

"Don't know," he said, shifting in his chair and looking thoughtfully at the committee. "They might. They're pretty independent over there."

For a good half-hour thereafter Sens. Castain, Johnson and Herron, aided by Rep. Aschenheim and several other members of the Senate Armed Services Committee, tried without success to break down the testimony of the Deputy Secretary of Defense and wipe out if possible the MAJOR NANUKUVU SPLIT IN PENTAGON headlines they could all see coming. But they weren't able to shake Bob Cathcart, who kept repeating firmly and with increasingly obvious satisfaction that he had been against Frio from the beginning, thought it was basically a lot of hysterical overreacting, thought the Soviet occupation was no threat and the U.S. reaction of no validity, and was convinced, and not afraid to say so, that a militaristic "war party in the Pentagon" had grabbed the issue from an unsuspecting President and was running with it.

The committee even recalled Loy and Zeecy to the stand in an attempt, led by Jerry and Luzanne, to refute the devastating skepticism and disparagement of Loy's nominal second in command. But Bob Catheter did not react or relent, and out to the world went, just as he and Mario had intended, the story of MAJOR NANUKUVU SPLIT IN PENTAGON.

Against that background the last witness at "The Special Hearing on the problem of Nanukuvu"—as it was entitled when the Senate Armed Services Committee finally had it printed up and released some weeks later, when the whole thing was over—came to the stand, at first, as something of an anticlimax. It was not long, however, before it became apparent that the headlines he might generate would be just as good, and perhaps much more significant, than the Deputy Secretary's.

His figure was tall and dignified. Every hair was in place. His face, as always, appeared calm, impassive and faintly supercilious, which was not really fair because he was quivering with excitement inside—was not at all impassive at heart—and had never really felt supercilious toward anyone in his life. But the Secretary of State—"Mr. Icicle" to his opponents in the Pentagon and his boss in the White House—was one of those people destined always to be misunderstood by almost everyone.

Fortunately for his current duties, he was usually misunderstood as being much more glacial, adamant and unyielding than he really was. This helped, in diplomacy. Actually, he often thought wryly, he was 100 per cent earnest, hopeful, idealistic pussycat. But he wasn't about to let on to anybody outside his immediate family.

Now he took the oath, squared his shoulders to their full unapproachable height, smiled and said gravely, "I am at your service, Mr. Chairman. Senator Castain, thank you for inviting me."

Jerry, who had received a call from him shortly after midnight requesting urgently that he be called to testify "on a matter of the very greatest importance which I can't disclose to you until I'm on the stand," bowed slightly, smiled in return and said smoothly, "Mr. Secretary, I'm delighted you could accept my invitation to appear. I thought the record wouldn't be complete without getting the diplomatic view of it. We're very pleased you could rearrange your busy schedule to be with us."

"Thank you, Senator," Terry Venner said, "it is my pleasure."

Of such are the stately minuets of Washington.

"Do you have any statement you wish to make, Mr. Secretary?" Cube Herron inquired.

"Mr. Chairman," Mario Escondido said, the usual sharp challenge in his voice, "I think we have a right to ask questions of this witness, don't we?"

"Certainly, Mr. Chairman," Terry said calmly. "I am perfectly willing."

He reached down to his briefcase, brought out a sheaf of papers in a brown leather folder that looked very official and placed it with conspicuous care very neatly at his elbow.

Then he leaned forward, hands clasped, a pleasantly attentive expression on his face and said, "Yes?"

"Mr. Chairman," Jerry Castain said in a voice that did not invite argument, "I think it is only fair that the Secretary be allowed to make any statement he wishes to make and *then* we can have questions. It's the only orderly way to proceed."

"I agree," Cube Herron said and looked once more at the small, chunky, self-important personage at his side. "All right, Mario?"

"Oh, all *right,*" Mario said. "I hope the Secretary will give us some idea of how he feels about Nanukuvu, though."

"Of course," Terry Venner said; took the papers carefully out of their folder; placed them carefully before him; and began to read in the clipped, aristocratic tone that was his hallmark.

When he had first learned of what he termed "the Soviet incursion" on Nanukuvu, he said, he had hoped a peaceable solution of the problem might be achieved through regular diplomatic channels. In pursuit of that he had advised the President to make direct contact with the General Secretary in Moscow. This had been done. The results were disappointing.

There was an excited stir at the media tables and through the audience. "Now maybe we're finally going to get the real inside story of Nanukuvu," Red Roberts muttered as he scribbled furiously. "What they *want* us to get," Delight retorted sourly.

Nonetheless, the Secretary said, he had persevered in his hope that a diplomatic solution might still, in time, be found. To that end he himself had held several meetings with the Soviet ambassador. Arrangements had now been made for further direct discussion between the President and the General Secretary. This time he was more optimistic that something constructive might emerge.

"With all respects," Karl Aschenheim interrupted, "why? It seems to me we're in a lot worse shape to argue about it now than we were seven months ago."

The Secretary smiled.

"It is my business, Congressman, to be optimistic. Suffice it to say I feel I have reason to be sanguine."

"Good," Karl said, sounding skeptical. "It would be nice to think so."

In any event, the Secretary went on, he *did* feel more hopeful, not only because of some new indications in Moscow of willingness to talk, but for another and potentially more important reason that he was now prepared to announce to the committee and the world.

He paused and looked thoughtfully at the faces across the table. For some reason no one could quite define, a sort of herd-instinct that began in the rows of the Pentagon and quickly spread back through the room, tension rose.

With deliberate care he set aside the pages from which he had been reading, took two more from his briefcase and placed them with exactitude directly in front of him. When all was ready and he had prolonged the suspense sufficiently to suit him, he looked up with a smile.

"You must permit me some small satisfaction in this, Mr. Chairman, because the discussions which resulted in what I am about to present to you began less than forty-eight hours ago on the direct order of the President of the United States. With his active participation and the efforts of myself and a most valued ally, this historic event has been accomplished in a remarkably short time.

"We have decided to call it 'The Declaration of the Pacific'—or, if one prefers a shorter form, 'The Pacific Declaration.' It is the belief of the President, myself and our most respected and helpful ally, the prime minister of Singapore, that it will provide a major, successful step, both in bringing the problem of Nanukuvu to a successful conclusion, and in furnishing a hopeful guideline to the future of the entire Pacific region."

He paused and looked up politely.

"Would you like me to read it, Mr. Chairman?"

"No, Mr. Secretary," Cube Herron said. "Mail it to us. Of course we want you to read it. You have us all on the edges of our seats."

"It better be good," Mario Escondido remarked dourly.

Terrail Venner shot him a dazzling smile.

"Oh, it is, Congressman," he said cheerfully. "It is . . .

" 'Whereas, it has come to the attention of the undersigned nations of the Pacific and South Pacific regions that an attempt is being made to establish a heavily armed and potentially aggressive base on the island of Nanukuvu; and

" 'Whereas, there is cause to believe that one of the major purposes of this installation is to serve as a command and refueling station for nuclear powered and nuclear armed submarines and aircraft; and,

" 'Whereas, in the policy statement of the South Pacific Forum in 1985, and in subsequent statements by that body and by other nations in the region, there was clearly expressed the abhorrence with which the nations and peoples of the region view the introduction of nuclear equipment of any kind into the region under any circumstances; and

" 'Whereas, their introduction for possible use in aggressive acts against any nation or combination of nations in the region is most particularly abhorrent;

" 'Now, therefore, be it

" 'Resolved:

" 'That the potential atomic base now being constructed on the island of Nanukuvu is, in and of itself, inimical to the best interests of the nations and peoples of the Pacific and South Pacific regions;

" 'That its construction can in no way be justified by any argument that it is necessary for the defense or security of the nation responsible for its construction;

" 'That it can only be regarded as a clear and present danger to the nations and peoples of the Pacific and South Pacific regions; and that therefore, its construction and its presence are unanimously condemned by the undersigned, who do now

" 'Demand:

" 'That said construction be stopped immediately, and that all forces of the nation responsible be withdrawn at once; and

" 'That the island of Nanukuvu be declared to be neutral territory within a Jointly Guaranteed Area of Peace maintained, and in due course extended, by all the nations and peoples of the Pacific and South Pacific regions, together with such other powers as may, for the sake of peace, wish to adhere to this Declaration and support such joint guarantees.'

"Signed, Mr. Chairman, by twenty-six nations, to wit:

"The People's Republic of China, Japan, Republic of Korea, Republic of

China, Federated States of Micronesia, Republic of the Marshall Islands, Palau, Thailand, Malaysia, Brunei, Indonesia, the Philippines, Papua-New Guinea, Tuvalu, Western Samoa, Australia, New Zealand, Vanuatu, Kiribati, the Solomons, Nauru, Fiji, Tonga, Canada, Singapore, the United States of America . . .

"We would hope, Mr. Chairman, that the Soviet Union will soon see fit to join in the guarantees. After, of course," he added firmly, "complying with the other requirements of the Declaration."

And he sat back, understandably and justifiably looked pleased.

There was a scramble at the media tables as many reporters hurried out to file stories. The television cameras swung across his triumphant face to pick up the generally impressed faces of the committee and then out to show the Secretary of Defense and the Joint Chiefs, who hoped their expressions were sufficiently agreeable, and so on to the excitedly buzzing audience.

Cube Herron let the agitation run on for a reasonable time, then used the gavel.

"The hearing will be in order," he said mildly. "Mr. Secretary, we must congratulate you on what is apparently a very real achievement—"

"As far as it goes," Mario Escondido interjected.

"Which is a damned sight farther than anything else we've heard here today," Cube retorted. "At least we've got some support, now, we're not out there alone. And at least we know where the President stands."

"We do?" Karl Aschenheim inquired blankly. "I'm not sure it's clear to me."

Cube looked surprised and a trifle annoyed.

"You heard the Secretary say this Pacific Declaration was instigated by the President and done at his orders. He wanted a diplomatic option, now he's got it. Seems clear enough to me. Whether the Pentagon is ready to back it up is another matter. How about it, Secretary Buck?"

"Mr. Chairman," Loy said, "do you mind if I come back to the table?"

"Not at all," Cube said. "Want you to." He chuckled suddenly, looking like a mischievous old pixie. "If the Secretary of State can stand it, that is."

"Oh, Mr. Chairman," Terry said as Loy came forward smiling, "we don't really fight, you know. We just disagree once in a while."

"That's right, Mr. Chairman," Loy said as a committee staffer placed a chair for him alongside Terry's. "It's usually an amicable warfare."

"Usually," Cube observed dryly. "Anyway, Mr. Secretary, what do *you* think of this Pacific Declaration?"

"I want to commend Secretary Venner," Loy said, "—and the President—and the prime minister of Singapore," he added smoothly, "for their diligent efforts on behalf of peace in the South Pacific. Every little bit helps."

"Mr. Chairman!" Terry objected, surprised and indignant. "I can't accept the description of this as a 'little bit.' I think it's a major step forward."

"So do I," Loy said quickly. "I don't mean that in any invidious way, just the way one uses that expression. I do think, however, that we'll have to wait a bit and see how Moscow responds before we can assess the impact accurately. *Has* Moscow responded?"

"It was only transmitted a couple of hours ago," Terry said. "You know they don't respond that fast, ever. The President and I have reasonable hopes that the response will be conciliatory."

"And if it isn't, Mr. Secretary?" Luzanne inquired.

"Then we'll have to take it to the U.N.," Terry said, ignoring another loud and skeptical snort. "But we're hopeful an appeal from twenty-six nations will be treated with some respect in Moscow."

"Even if some of them aren't much bigger than Nanukuvu?" Mario demanded.

"Their hopes and fears and human aspirations are just as valid as ours, Congressman," Terrail Venner replied in his starchiest tone. "Or Moscow's."

"Maybe," Mario said, "but they haven't got anything but sand and coconuts and a few seashells to back them up with. Which leaves it right up to us again, doesn't it? It still comes down to a confrontation between them and us, any way you slice it, isn't that true?"

The Secretary of State flushed. The Secretary of Defense came to the rescue.

"I'm sure we in the Administration hope, Congressman," he said firmly, "that this initiative will have the effect of persuading the Soviet Union that it is not advisable to proceed in the face of the massed opinion of the nations of the Pacific and South Pacific area."

"Massed opinion has never bothered them before," Mario pointed out. "How is this going to be different, Mr. Secretary? Particularly when there isn't going to be any penalty if they don't oblige? I mean, there really *isn't* anything anybody down there can do. Australia and New Zealand could float a few rowboats and loft a few butterflies, maybe, but for all the effective military force they could provide they aren't much better than Palau and Tuvalu. And apparently even we, thanks to you and *your* friends, Mr. Secretary—" he turned on Loy Buck—"aren't in a position to do much right now, either. So where's the powerful effect of this so-called 'Declaration of the Pacific' going to come from? Who's going to apply the pressure that will really do the job? I ask you!"

"Well, now, Mr. Chairman," Jerry Castain said in an exasperated tone as the two Secretaries glanced at one another with a harried, what-can-you-do-with-this-one expression. "There's such a thing as asking fair questions and such a thing as needlessly bullying witnesses—"

"That *is* a fair question!" Mario snapped. "Who *is* going to do the job if we don't, and who *can* do it if we can't? There's no answer."

"Mr. Secretary," Karl Aschenheim said calmly to Terry Venner, "I think this is an admirable achievement for you and the President, to get such widespread agreement on such a ticklish subject in such a short time, and I for one am prepared to wait a bit and see what the response is before engaging in a lot of inflammatory rhetoric about it."

Mario made a disgusted sound but didn't deign to comment. Terry responded gratefully.

"Thank you, Congressman. I appreciate your support. I am sure the President appreciates it too."

"It must have taken a lot of diplomacy, to get people to sign something so explicit and pointed," Karl remarked, "when they really aren't in much of a position to protect themselves if there's retaliation of some kind."

"I doubt very much that there'd be retaliation of a military nature," Terry said, "at least in the foreseeable future—and if we succeed in defusing the Nanukuvu situation. But in any event," he added simply, "sometimes principle *does* matter, even in such a world as we live in."

"It's got to matter," Karl Aschenheim agreed, "otherwise we're all lost . . ." He turned to Loy. "Does the diplomatic option suit you, Mr. Secretary?"

"Anything that attempts to solve a difficult situation by peaceable means," Loy said, "suits us. This myth that the Pentagon is always rarin' to go to resort to the military option is just that—myth. The last thing we want is conflict."

"Particularly when you aren't ready for it," Mario Escondido said spitefully.

Loy struck the table with the flat of his hand, so sharply and unexpectedly that everyone jumped. The tension shot up again.

"Mr. Congressman," he said icily, "we have had enough of that. We are far readier, all over the world, than self-interested critics who have some axe to grind with us are willing to admit or acknowledge. We are not perfect in every respect or every place, but we are sufficient for any foreseeable event. *Remember that.*"

"You have not been sufficient for Nanukuvu," Rep. Escondido retorted, dark, pugnacious face more pugnacious than ever, "and this record doesn't show anything to indicate that you will be anytime in the near future. 'Pacific Declarations' are nice but unless we can back them up they aren't going to impress anybody one little bit. We ought to cut our losses and get out of there. There's plenty of ways to take care of that base without going in there and without throwing our weight around. Let 'em sit there and rot, is my suggestion. What's wrong with that?"

The two Secretaries looked at one another and by tacit agreement kept still.

Senators Castain and Johnson and Rep. Aschenheim started to say something, and stopped. Sen. Herron did likewise, and stopped. In the audience Secretary Cathcart looked belligerent and approving. Gen. McCune and the chiefs sat impassive. Finally Cube Herron raised his gavel and brought it down decisively.

"Mr. Secretary Venner," he said, "Mr. Secretary Buck—we want to thank you, and all of you, for coming here to testify. This is a complex and dangerous issue but I think the country understands a little better now all the various considerations that have to be taken into account in solving it.

"Mr. Secretary of State, we wish you and the President well with your diplomatic efforts. Mr. Secretary of Defense, we hope things can be speeded up in the Pentagon. We want you both to know that most members of Congress want to help in any way we can. We may not have all the answers—sometimes think we do—but anyway, most of us *want* to do the right thing.

"If there are no further questions—" again he looked along the table left and right, again received negatives—"this special hearing into the problem of Nanukuvu is now adjourned sine die."

Again he brought down the gavel. One more chattering, gossiping, buzzing Caucus Room audience filed slowly out. One more major hearing of an ever-inquisitive Congress faded into history. The stately marbled room, emptied of its contentious contents, fell silent once again.

26 PACIFIC NATIONS PROTEST SOVIET BASE, the headlines said. VENNER HOPES MOSCOW WILL HEED PRESIDENT'S PLEA AS NANUKUVU SPLITS PENTAGON.

The evening news emphasized Bob Cathcart's scornful downplaying of the problem, Mario's "We ought to cut our losses and get out of there!" followed briefly by what appeared to be the feeble defenses of Loy Buck and Zeecy McCune. Lead editorials in major publications did the same. All expressed the hope that Moscow would heed "the statesmanly approach of the President, Secretary Venner and the twenty-five other concerned Pacific nations that have joined the United States in protesting the intrusion of a major nuclear base in the region."

Few had kind words for the Pentagon. Its delays, internal tensions and dedication to what was seen as "the alarming military option" brought sharp condemnation and, in many cases, more of the clarion calls for reform which, with predictable regularity, year after year rolled up like some great wave to the very steps of the impervious building and then, as regularly, drained slowly and inevitably away.

Six

six

1 "How they all takin' it?" Jim asked Carleene on Tuesday night while they watched the six o'clock news and saw one more brief replay of hearing highlights, plus new clips from across the nation and around the world showing vociferous, sometimes violent, disagreement with "any U.S. action that might upset the balance of peace in the South Pacific."

"None too happy," Carleene said, reflecting on her visits over the past two days to Mrs. Buck, Mrs. Burford, Mrs. Tock, Mrs. Stokes and Mrs. McCune. "Seems to me like one of those times when wives wish their husbands never set eyes on the military service at all." She gave him a sharp look as he sat, beer in hand, amicably smiling. "I know how *that* is!" she said, "so don't sit there grinnin' like a self-satisfied ole—ole *toad.*"

"I'm not self-satisfied," he said, grin broadening, "and I'm not no ole *toad,* neither. I'm just plain old Jim, who drives these guys."

"Who you been drivin' the last two days?"

"Gen. McCune—Gen. Burford—Gen. Stokes. None of *them* seemed very happy, either. Guess the hearin' really ticked 'em off." He looked sour. "Ev'body always givin' the military hell every chance they get. I don't like it, myself."

"Mrs. Buck says she *wishes* Mr. Buck would get out of it all," Carleene said as Bob Cathcart's face flashed on the tube for perhaps the thirtieth time in the past twenty-four hours telling the committee how innocuous the threat of Nanukuvu was, how worthless Mission Frio. "Course, she's wished that for a long time and it hasn't done any good. He keeps right at it."

"He enjoys it," Jim said with a lazy smile. "Just like I do. It's comfortable for me, but up there where he is, it's a real challenge. I can understand that. He's not the sort of man to sit around and do nothin'. He'd go crazy if he wasn't managin' somethin'. Although damned if I know why *any*body'd want to try to manage the Pentagon. Who needs it? . . . Can you get me another beer?"

"I didn't hear 'please,' " she observed, getting up and starting for the kitchen. "Some people wouldn't know how to handle a challenge if it came up and bit 'em."

"Now, Carly," he said with a chuckle, "no point in gettin' riled up. You wouldn't be happy if you didn't have me around to fuss at . . . Thanks. How's Mrs. Burford?"

"Poorly," she said, face somber in sympathy. "Poor thing. It's up and down. This mornin' was up. Tomorrow it may be down. Each time it's down it's a little more down. So—there it is. Rest of 'em pretty sassy, particularly that Zenia Stokes. I declare she's a pistol. Never saw the like of all that bustlin' around. He don't like it, neither."

"What's he goin' do about it?" Jim inquired with increased interest. "Get a divorce?"

"It's in the wind," Carleene said, "but I don't know whether they'll go through with it. Lots of gruntin' and growlin' when they both been home for lunch—which ain't often—and lots of stillness in between. Don't look good to me. I think he don't want to do anythin' right now, though, 'cause he might make chairman when Gen. McCune retires. He don't need no scandal."

"He's a smart man," Jim observed. "He won't have no scandal. I don't know whether he's goin' to make it or not, though. Gen. Burford's in there tryin' too. And of course they can always pick somebody nobody even thought about, that's happened. I expect the President thinks he can get our votes if he names Gen. Stokes, though. Might do that, just for that reason."

"Have to hand it to Gen. Stokes," she said as the news moved on in its standard formula to wars and killings, natural disasters, world and local tragedies, the downside of the day to the exclusion of all else—presented as always with an earnest smile and an up-beat intonation. "He's gone mighty far for a black man."

"Farther'n *I'll* ever get," Jim said with a chuckle. "Would you like to be married to a chief of staff, Carly? Would that give you a big ego jump?"

"Not me," she said with a sniff and a smile that softened it. "It's a heap o' headaches for any woman and I don't envy 'em *one bit.*" Her trained ear caught furtive sounds from one of the bedrooms. "J.F.K.!" she shouted. "Martin Luther! You stop fightin', now! You're gonna wake baby Zoren and if you do that Daddy's comin' right in there and tan your hides, hear?"

There was abrupt silence down the hall. They looked at one another and grinned.

"How about another beer?" she asked. He chuckled.

"You're goin' to have me all lickered up before the evenin's over, Carly, and you know how that makes me feel."

"Long way to go 'til then," she observed as the microwave bell sounded and she knew dinner was about complete. "You'll be calmed down by then."

"Want to bet?" he asked with a grin. " 'Bout time for little Zoren to have another brother or sister, don't you think? After all, it's better'n havin' some old chief of staff climbin' all over you, ain't it?"

"Stop bein' vulgar," she ordered, but with the little exciting smile he knew so well. "I *told* you I didn't want no chief of staff. You ain't much, but the headaches don't come with you."

"That's right," he said with satisfaction, grabbing her for one quick kiss before she pulled away and started for the kitchen. "I ain't got no headaches hangin' round my door."

"Good," she said, " 'cause from what I seen with my ladies, I sure don't want none."

And indeed in the past twenty-four hours she had seen plenty as she watched her ladies reacting to the hearing. She had happened to be with Mrs. Buck during the morning session, with Mrs. Burford and Mrs. Tock in the afternoon, with the other two today. Her presence had been welcome. She was virtually a member of all their families by now and her steadying calm and shrewd common-sense furnished a needed foil to Imogene's sputterings, Vi's dignified protests, Dorry's worried annoyance, Zenia's impatient complaints and Renee's icy and incisive comments.

Of the five, only Zenia expressed some agreement with the basic position set forth by Secretary Cathcart and Congressman Escondido. The rest were completely loyal to the Pentagon. Imogene, as Carleene had related to Jim, was provoked several times to repeat her often expressed wish that Loy would give up so thankless and pressure-filled a position and retire to the untroubled life she was more and more convinced was a necessity if he was not to drop dead on her hands one of these days.

Carleene's shocked expression told her that she shouldn't put it so strongly, but she couldn't help it, that was the way she felt.

"He's just so *tense* all the time," she said as they watched Loy, seemingly composed and in command of the situation, respond to the comments of the Deputy Secretary and the Congressman from Connecticut. "He puts up this good front but he's on edge inside, just the same. You know how men are."

"Yes, ma'am," Carlenne said, pausing in her dusting of Loy's memento-laden desk in the den to watch for a few minutes. "They feel they got to pretend a lot to each other. But they don't fool us."

"That's right, Carly," Imogene agreed. "They don't fool us."

She reflected, as Carleene resumed her work with one eye on the television, that Loy's discussions with the hostile elements in his dreams had become a little more pronounced in the past few days.

He was also more snappish than usual, his abrupt but usually kindly impatience with her had a sharper edge and his appetite was off, always a sure sign that something was bothering him profoundly. It took quite a serious worry to put Loy Buck off his food; "Iron Gut," as they used to call him at IBM, could eat his way through most crises without losing a calorie. It was only when he was really, deeply troubled that it began to show up at the table.

Vangie was worried too. She had telephoned yesterday. By now she was addressing her employer's wife by her first name, their shared concern for the Secretary forming more of a buffer for him than he perhaps would ever realize. It was a great comfort for Immy to know that she had an ally who could keep an eye on him during his hours away from home. Between the two of them, she

often thought with satisfaction and some amusement, they had Loy Buck
pretty well surrounded.

"Imogene," Vangie had said with characteristic directness, "I'm worried. Is
the Secretary eating much at home? He certainly isn't here."

"Not here, either," Immy had replied. "His appetite's fallen off badly just in
the last few days. I try to get him to eat a big dinner like he usually does, and a
relatively big breakfast, but he's been making excuses and leaving a lot. Do you
suppose it's just the general worry about Nanukuvu and this Frio business?"

"That's at the heart of it," Vangie said, "but what particular aspect, I haven't
been able to find out yet. He barely touches lunch, even when he has official
guests, and that isn't good. I've observed with all my Secretaries that you can't
do this job on nerves alone. You need to keep in shape."

"That's another thing," Imogene said. "How are his physical reports these
days? He dismisses them very casually when I ask about them, so I don't expect
I'll ever know. Does he mention them to you?"

"No," Vangie said. "He can be very close-mouthed, as I'm sure no one knows
better than you, and anyway, he wouldn't make more than a casual comment to
me, I'm sure. But—" she laughed, a small, prim, satisfied sound—"I have my
sources in the building after all these years. I hear his general condition is good,
heart in good shape, blood pressure under control, general tone good. So we
don't need to worry about him too much if we can just get his appetite back on
track. I keep changing his standard order, which is usually a ham or chicken
sandwich, salad and tea. I try to add more things, like soup and pie, but he
keeps leaving at least half of everything. I think, myself, that he's worried about
this hearing and he's also worried about the President. The President hasn't
called him in the last several days. It's unsettling."

"I am *so sick,*" Immy said in a sudden burst of candid irritation, "of politics in
this town! I'm even sicker of that than I am of the Pentagon, and you know—"
she uttered a small chuckle, half-wry, half-wistful—"how sick I am of the
Pentagon! *Why* won't the President call him? *Why* isn't the President supporting him in this business? *Why* aren't things simple, cut-and-dried and *honest?* I
never saw anything like it!"

"They are honest, Imogene," Vangie said dryly. "Washington honest. I suspect he'll hear from the President when the President is ready. Meanwhile he
isn't eating very well."

"All we can do," Imogene said, "is keep putting it in front of him. I'm doing
my best!"

"And I mine," Vangie said. "How are your plans for the party next month
coming along?"

"Fine," Imogene said more cheerfully, brought to a less worrisome subject,
her regular fall dinner for the top level of the Pentagon. "I think we'll plan on
around eighty. You can come over here sometime next week when it's convenient and we'll go over the list. You know who to invite better than I do, after
all your years there."

"At least," Vangie said with a chuckle, "I can keep out the less-desirables."

" 'Less-desirables?' " Immy echoed. "In the *Pentagon?* Vangie, how could you!"

"Watch me," Vangie said with a relish that was quite startling when taken in conjunction with her small, neat, sedately old-fashioned person.

And now a day later the hearing was being held and the President still hadn't called Loy or given any public indication of support, and here Loy was, forced to sit there at the witness-stand and lie about it to protect him. *Why* was politics like that! Because of course Loy was protecting himself too in protecting the President. He had to make everybody think he had the President's full support or his own position would be undermined, his own authority lessened. What an interlocking web it was and how easily everyone got caught up in it when they came to Washington!

She sat glumly through the rest of the hearing, not much cheered by Carleene's stoutly loyal, "I guess Mr. Buck, he really told 'em!" when the committee broke for lunch.

"He did, Carly," Imogene agreed. "But did anybody really listen?"

When Carly got back to Fort Myer and Quarters One, the committee was back in session and Mrs. Burford was just finishing lunch with Mrs. Tock, who often came over these days from Commandant's House, Marine Barracks.

It was sort of an in-between day, Carly could see at once: one of those days when Mrs. Burford moved a little more slowly, was from time to time a little vaguer, but was not really out of it, as she could be sometimes. She asked Carleene right away if she had been watching any of the hearing at Mrs. Buck's and Carly said yes, she had.

"And what is Mrs. Buck thinking of it?" Mrs. Burford asked.

"Not much," Carleene said as she began clearing away their dishes. "She's mad 'cause they's puttin' the pressure on Mr. Buck."

"And on our husbands, too," Mrs. Tock said. "Though I'll admit the chiefs aren't quite such direct targets as the Secretary and Gen. McCune."

"No, ma'am," Carleene agreed. "That Congressman, he's just hopin' to swamp 'em all in passin'."

"That's right," Mrs. Burford said as both ladies laughed. "That's his tactic exactly. He's not a very nice man, I'm afraid. At least not from the military's standpoint."

"Too bad he's chairman of House Armed Services," Doreen said. "He and Tick don't get along at *all.*"

"Nor he and Brash," Violet Burford said. "Or Loy—or Zeecy—or anybody." She frowned, her fine gray eyes troubled. "It's just a shame that people have to be subjected to that kind of thing from the Hill."

"The Pentagon hasn't bought him off enough," Dorry said with a cynicism that at first seemed to go oddly with her plump, pink, spun-sugar personality: but she was a shrewd and realistic little lady underneath it all.

"Can he be bought off 'enough'?" Vi Burford said, realistic herself. "It's always been our observation that that type is insatiable. Give them one favor or answer one demand, and they're back for more."

"We're fortunate to have Cube Herron on the Senate side," Dorry said, "or there wouldn't be any balance at all."

"Cube's a nice man," Vi agreed. "And he knows what he's talking about, too, after all his years on the job. Which is also nice."

"And there's Sen. Castain," Dorry said. "And Luzanne Johnson. And quite a few more. So it isn't all bad."

"Oh, no, not at all," Vi Burford said. "I just hope, though—" she said—paused—and frowned. "Now, what was I going to say?"

"*I* just hope," Dorry said smoothly with a glance at Carleene, who had stopped on her way to the kitchen but, at Dorry's nod, went on out—"*I* just hope that this doesn't damage the Pentagon or the mission too much."

"Yes," Vi said with perfect composure, "that's exactly what I was going to say. I hope it doesn't damage the Pentagon or the mission too much, because I know how much time and effort Brash and Tick and the rest have put into it. It would be a shame if all that were wasted."

"To say nothing of the encouragement it might be to the enemy," Doreen said as they took their coffee and went into the den. "I think if anything drastic happened to Frio, Tick might take early retirement. He's so convinced it's the right thing to do."

"Brash may too," Vi said. Dorry looked at her sharply.

" 'May'?"

"Strictly between us, he's thinking about it."

"Why?" Dorry demanded. Vi gave her a half-apologetic, half-defiant look.

"Because of me."

"You've been to the doctor, then," Dorry said quietly, "and discussed it with Brash. I'm glad, Vi. I'm really glad. It's better all around, fairer to you and fairer to him. But he shouldn't retire early. After all, he's got a good chance to be chairman—"

"That's what I've told him," Vi said, "but he says he's not going to listen. He says he's going to do what's best for me." Tears came momentarily into her eyes. She brushed them firmly away. "I *wish* I weren't such a burden to everybody!"

"You're not a burden to anyone!" Dorry said stoutly, though they both knew the time was coming. "And if you—" she hesitated for a second, then decided she could be candid now and went firmly on—"if you ever should be, then Brash will have plenty of help from Walter Reed and everything will be well taken care of. So don't you worry, and don't let him worry. And tell him *not* to retire early but just stay in there and keep fighting. He has as good a chance as anybody to succeed Zeecy; in fact, better, I think. Ham Stokes is so—so *abra-sive,* don't you think?"

"Brash says he's a very good general officer," Vi said, "and an excellent chief of staff. Not a very well-liked one, perhaps, but a very well-respected one. Which is no small recommendation."

"No," Dorry conceded. "I know he's good, Tick has often said so. I wonder how those two are getting along. Carleene tells me there's tension there."

Vi lowered her voice although Carleene had started the dishwasher and presumably was deafened by its gurglings and gushings—unless she was standing behind the door listening, which they thought she probably was.

"Carleene," Vi said, "links us all together like our own little private telegraph line, doesn't she? I wonder what she tells you all about me?"

"She's always very kind and respectful about you," Doreen said, "as I suspect she is about everybody. Carly's really a very nice person. I think she likes all of us, except maybe Zenia and Renee. I'm not sure she approves of Zenia too much—you know how they have these little antipathies toward one another sometimes that we just don't understand—and I have a feeling she's scared to death of Renee."

Vi Burford's kindly face crinkled into a smile.

"Who isn't? *I'm* scared to death of Renee!"

Doreen giggled.

"Me too. *What* a formidable character our dashing leader married!"

"He's run her a merry race, from what I hear," Vi said. "I'm not so sure I envy her that. In fact, in some ways—the ways that really count to a woman—I think Renee's actually a somewhat pathetic character." She chuckled. "She'd shoot me on the spot if she knew I thought so. But there it is."

"I know," Doreen agreed. "I often think about that too. At first glance Zeecy's the kind of man every girl dreams about. The only trouble is—" she giggled again—"every girl is *still* dreaming about him, at sixty-two. Nice for him but hell, I suspect, for Renee. Though of course she never bats an eyelash, at least in public. They must have some high old rows at home."

"At this late date?" Vi inquired. "I wonder. By now I expect it's settled into its final groove and they're just rocking along."

"Probably," Doreen said. She smiled a half-amused, half-wistful smile. "But, then, we all do, don't we, by this time? Maybe not about that particular subject, but just about things in general. The aftermath of the shave, in the washbasin every morning—"

"The insistence on reading the paper before you do, at breakfast—"

"The need to have rice pudding for dessert at least once a week, God knows why—"

"The insistence on getting everywhere *exactly* on the minute, you can't be *one second* late, no matter what—"

"The demand that you have the car washed at exactly the same place on exactly the same day at exactly the same time—"

"The demand that your closets be just as neat and uncluttered as his, which is easy to do after you've been military for thirty years but not so easy when you're just a mere woman—"

They started to laugh, helplessly but fondly.

"Anyway," Dorry said finally, "things in Quarters Six may not be quite so relaxed at the moment. Tick told me there's gossip going around in the Pentagon and among his friends on the Hill about Zeecy and Luzanne Johnson."

"I know," Vi said. "Brash has mentioned it to me too. I think it's been going on quite a long time—the gossip, I mean. Whether there's anything to it, I don't know. It's interesting, anyway."

"She seems to be a fine person," Dorry said, "the few times I've met her. And of course, leaving aside his wife's point of view, which we fortunately can, Zeecy's a fine man. I still hope for Renee's sake that it isn't true."

"She can handle it if she has to," Vi predicted, "but I don't wish it on her, either. Let's hope it *is* just gossip . . . More coffee?"

"No, thanks," Dorry said, "I really must run along—" she laughed again—"to get the car washed. Don't get up!" she ordered hastily as Vi, somewhat shakily, started to do so. Doreen came over and kissed her. "Dear Vi. We've had a good visit and a good gossip, haven't we? It's good to see you doing so well, and to know that you and Brash have worked it out between you."

"It was necessary," Vi admitted. "I was foolish to be stubborn about it." She hesitated, her face became shadowed but she obviously felt she must ask. "How is your son?"

"Oh," Dorry said, trying to sound relaxed but not succeeding very well. "No change, no change. But," she said with forced brightness, "we manage."

"So will we," Vi Burford said quietly.

When Carleene reached the quarters of the chief of staff, Air Force, at eight Tuesday morning she found the house as usual in something of a turmoil. The general was getting ready to depart for the Pentagon. The younger daughter was preparing to leave for high school. The youngest child, the ten-year-old boy with sickle-cell anemia, was playing with toy cars on the floor, his long, thin arms pushing them around his long, thin legs as he made a thin, crooning sound to them, his narrow, elongated head balancing precariously on his long, thin neck. Such a sad thing, Carleene always told Jim every time she visited the Stokes house; such a sad thing to happen to any child, any parents. Thank God for their healthy six, that's all she could say: thank God for *them*.

"Good morning, Carleene," Mrs. Stokes said briskly as she came in. "Did you sleep well?"

Mrs. Stokes asked this question so faithfully—it was her invariable opening gambit when Carleene arrived—that Carleene suspected, quite accurately, that

Mrs. Stokes herself did not sleep well. Mrs. Stokes, in fact, counted it a good night when she only woke once or twice and was able to sleep past five-thirty.

" 'Course," Carleene told Jim, "she's always runnin'. That woman's always *runnin'*. I don't think she *ever* stops. I can see why the general has a hard time with it. She's just like a little cricket, always jumpin' about, goin' places and doin' things. I'd get snappish, too, if I was him."

On this particular day the general seemed even more snappish than usual, Carly thought. His greeting to her was a terse, "Morning, Carleene!" as he came into the kitchen for a last hurried cup of coffee before taking off for the Pentagon and its endless gallons of the stuff. Other than that, he said nothing nor did he speak to his wife, who had followed Carleene into the kitchen and was standing, cup in hand, beside the sink. The general's expression looked bad, Carleene thought. They been havin' another of their quarrels, she told herself. Always quarrelin', quarrelin', quarrelin'. Not a happy house at all. Not happy.

"See you later," the general said, turning on his heel and leaving without kissing his wife goodbye or otherwise acknowledging her presence. The door slammed, the waiting car—driven by Jim, who had dropped Carleene off—zoomed up and faded out.

"Well," Mrs. Stokes said, "guess I'd better light a fire under my daughter. You can just do the usual today, Carleene. Don't disturb David, just let him play wherever he wants to."

"Yes, ma'am," Carleene said. "You'll be—?"

"I've got a meeting of the legal advisory board this morning," Mrs. Stokes said, "and an appointment with some people at the Department of Health and Human Services. After that I've got a luncheon with the committee to plan the Christmas fete here at the base, and then at one-thirty I'm going to be in the District visiting a law firm there. So maybe you could stay with David until I get back?"

"Yes, ma'am," Carleene said, though her heart sank: she felt sorry for the boy and liked him, but after all, she had five at home herself who would be needing attention along about then. She had brought little Zoren with her, as she always did these days, and none of her ladies minded. The other kids, though, would be raisin' hell by the time she got back. But she repeated, "Yes, ma'am," and got back to her cleaning of the kitchen. Under her breath she muttered, "Anythin' to please you plantation-owners," but her face remained impassive. She didn't care much for Zenia Stokes, who was even blacker than she was, though of course, Carleene admitted, a lot more stylish; but there was no point in rilin' her up. Carleene needed the money and, as with her other ladies, Zenia was part of the JCS and a passport to the big world.

Not, of course, that Mrs. Stokes ever took her much into her confidence, even on the days when she wasn't runnin' all over creation on her endless legal and charitable errands. Mrs. Stokes probably did a lot of good in the world, Carleene would admit that, but she was pretty close-mouthed about the general and what he did. Her white ladies *trusted* her, Carleene sometimes thought resentfully. Her black one never really did. On a sudden impulse she said,

"Saw the general at the hearing yesterday. Thought he handled himself mighty well."

"Fortunately he wasn't called on to say very much," Zenia remarked, "or he probably would have had Senator Herron and Representative Escondido crawling all over him. They don't like him much, I'm afraid." A distant expression came into her eyes. "I can see why."

"Why?" Carleene asked, feeling daring but deciding she couldn't just agree, maybe Zenia didn't want her opinion of her husband shared *that* much.

Zenia's eyes widened, and she spoke with an unexpected candor that quite startled Carleene.

"He isn't a very diplomatic man. He rubs them the wrong way up there on the Hill." She frowned. "He isn't very diplomatic about anything, actually. I imagine you've noticed that."

"He has his own way of doin' things," Carleene said cautiously. Zenia laughed without much humor.

"That he does," she agreed, "that he does. Anyway, it's probably just as well he didn't say more at the hearing. It was enough to have Secretary Buck and Gen. McCune parroting the official line without getting the chiefs into it. They're in deep enough already."

" 'Deep enough'?" Carleene inquired as David misplaced a toy, started to cry and Zenia found it for him. "They's just doin' their best, seems to me."

"Yes," Zenia said. "Well: I don't go along much with this Frio thing. I'm inclined to agree with Secretary Cathcart, that island isn't all that important to us and we shouldn't be wasting a lot of time and money on it. Also, I must say the Pentagon doesn't look very good, the way they've dillied and dallied about it."

"Seems to me it's important enough," Carleene observed as she got out the brooms and mops and prepared to really go to work. "Can't have them Russians down there threatenin' everybody."

"That's one view," Zenia Stokes said crisply. "Quite adequate for people who don't think. Be sure you give all the bathrooms a good scrubbing this time, Carleene. You didn't do such a good job last time."

"I didn't?" Carly responded, feeling vaguely that she had been insulted somehow but losing the thread of it in the necessity to defend herself against this unexpected attack. "I thought I did pretty well."

"Pretty well isn't good enough," Zenia Stokes said, sounding quite like her husband addressing some unhappily inadequate subordinate. "Those kids are little pigs at that age, as you know. So please be careful, o.k.?"

"Yes, ma'am," Carleene said sullenly.

Zenia didn't care, she had to have things done right since she didn't have time to go around cleaning up after the maid the way a lot of women did. She had to be able to rely on those around her if she was to accomplish successfully all the things she wanted to accomplish in this world.

The list, she told herself as she left a disgruntled but obedient Carleene to finish up the kitchen and get started on the rest of it, was lengthy but in no way beyond her abilities. She was perfectly capable of handling four meetings a day with all their attendant ramifications, though normally it was more like one or two. She prided herself that she had the brains, the breath and the energy, and she prided herself further that they were all good causes: helping distressed servicemen or their wives with legal problems, working on charities both in the Pentagon and outside, helping to organize worthwhile social events such as the Christmas fete, working on sickle-cell anemia, supporting various controversial social and economic causes, and finding time somewhere to do special legal work at home for the major Washington law firm she intended to join as soon as Ham's situation was decided one way or the other . . . and their personal situation, which was definitely in a state of tense and not very hopeful flux at the moment.

Ham's situation she regarded with mixed emotions, because of course if he should become chairman, she would probably be restricted as she was now, able to participate and contribute to many worthy things but not able to return to the full-time legal practice that her high intelligence, broad experience and encyclopedic knowledge equipped her for. Also for the two years of his term she would probably not be able to pursue, even in the rather muted way she had been required to do since he became chief of staff, those social and political causes in which she had invested a good deal of emotional capital.

Nanukuvu and Mission Frio, for instance. Protesters were massed at the River Entrance, in Lafayette Square across from the White House, on the lawn in front of the Capitol. Noted political activists, famous movie stars, famous academicians, top rock and roll singers, country-music stars, leading punk rockers and other prominent and well-informed citizens were holding vigil to protest any U.S. action that might in any way indicate criticism of, show opposition to, or otherwise upset the tender sensibilities of, the Soviet Union. The heroes of the hour were not Loy Buck and Zeecy McCune, who were trying to neutralize the threat, but those who asserted that no threat existed. It was much the more popular position, in late twentieth century America, and it was one to which Zenia Stokes found herself much attracted.

She would like to be out there carrying a banner or a sign of the sort that was appearing regularly now in the media: STOP FRIO, maybe. Or, KEEP THE PACIFIC PACIFIC. Or, NO U.S. IMPERIALISM IN PARADISE.

Unfortunately she did not have the time at the moment; and she was also under strict, loud and near-violent admonition from the chief of staff, USAF, that she was NOT repeat NOT to get involved in any of that God damned nonsense, this time. This time, Ham had said vehemently last night after they had watched one more demonstration march eagerly across the tube, was different. Not only because of the effect her inevitably publicized participation might have upon his career, but because this time it was a really serious matter on Nanukuvu, "and not one of your God damned liberal tea-party spasms about some God damned stupid thing."

"That's exactly why I ought to be doing my part," she had retorted with equal vehemence, "because it *is* important and it's not 'some God damned stupid thing.' What you people are proposing is a direct challenge to the Soviets, and that's entirely different."

"And why the hell would *we* be 'challenging' the Soviets?" he demanded. "Because, God damn it, they came crashing in there in the first place. *They're* the aggressors, *we're* not, but they've got the God damned world so turned upside down that a lot of half-assed, half-witted Americans actually think what's happening on Nanukuvu is *our* fault. *Jesus!*"

"Anyway," she said in the superior and condescending tone she knew would infuriate him further, "it doesn't matter really, does it, since the Pentagon has been so slow about it that nothing can be done now anyway."

"There are a lot of reasons for being slow!" he snapped. "We're in good enough shape to do whatever has to be done!"

"That isn't the way you came across at the hearing," she observed. His response was livid.

"That fucking Cathcart," he said, "and that fucking two-bit Escondido ought to be taken out and strung up by the balls. Of all the under-cutting, incompetent, self-interested, destructive, disloyal—"

"What's disloyal about trying to stop this crazy nonsense?" she demanded, her own voice rising. "Escondido's always got his own axe to grind, we all know that, but Secretary Cathcart's really sincere—"

"Secretary Cathcart," he said, "is working on a long-range agenda of his own. I know what it is but I couldn't prove it right now. Wait and see."

"He knows a bad idea when he sees one," she retorted, "and he's honest enough to say so. I agree with him!"

"Well, *you* would," he said in a disgusted tone. "Leave it to *you.*"

"Ham Stokes," she said, "I've taken just about as much as I'm going to take from you, always slamming my interests and my ideas and the things I believe in. I'm not going to do anything about Nanukuvu because I don't want to jeopardize your chances to be chairman—"

"Thanks."

"Yes," she said angrily, "thanks! You *should* thank me! This is one time when your precious 'reverse racism' you're always talking about wouldn't do you any good. I'll keep quiet this time and you *can* thank me for it, because I'm sure the President wouldn't want a chairman whose wife actually *thinks,* God forbid!"

He snorted.

"All the chiefs' wives I know *think.* That's what I like about them."

"Then why don't you like it about me?" she demanded, suddenly close to tears for some reason she couldn't quite analyze—mostly rage, she supposed.

"I've always liked it about you," he said more quietly. "I just don't like some of the things you think *about.*"

"Well," she said with an angry half-laugh, "I can't help *that.* And I can't help trying to do something about it. That's just my nature. It's the way I am."

"I'll be glad when you go to work for that law firm," he remarked. "Then you can channel all your energies into that and maybe I'll have a little peace and quiet around here."

"You mean," she said cautiously, "that you won't *mind* if I go to work for the law firm?"

"A lot better than having you sit around here sewing banners like Betsy Ross," he said, and chuckled suddenly at his mental picture of it.

She smiled with a happy relief.

"Then I can tell them I can start right away?"

But that was obviously the wrong thing to say. Ham's amused expression changed instantly to one of annoyed disapproval.

"Not yet! After we get the chairmanship settled. When I know where I stand. I don't want you messing it up for me until I have the President's commission right here in my hand. You do just what you said and stay out of all the crap until then, thank you very much!"

"But I thought you said—"

"*After* I know where I stand," he repeated. "Not before. And certainly not now, with all this stupid subversive uproar about Frio. I can't afford to have my wife mixed up in *that!*"

She managed to keep her voice quite steady, though it took an effort to conquer both her disappointment and her fear of Ham's reaction.

"If I can't go to work right away," she said, "then I'm certainly going to reserve the right to do *whatever* I please *about* whatever I please. And that's final!"

"Better not use the word 'final,' " he advised, staring at her with the expression that could make everyone from fellow generals on down the ranks wish they had taken up some other profession. " 'Final's a bad word to use. It could apply to a lot of things."

"Then let it!" she had said, picking up her book and storming out past the wide-eyed youngsters listening in the hall. "Just let it!"

And she had not spoken to him when he came to bed a few minutes later. Just turned off the light, turned on her side and, after a few more minutes of further furious (unspoken) argument, gone finally, fitfully, to sleep.

And now here was another day, one of the busiest she had lined up in several weeks, and fortunately she would be too busy for a few hours to think about it. Her days lately were often arranged with this kind of therapeutic oblivion in mind. But she knew something had to give. She had no intention of becoming involved in the protests against Frio, it really would hurt his career and she had always avoided going so far as to do that. And she really trembled at the thought of anything becoming "final" in their fragile situation, even though she knew she was more than capable of making her own way in the world.

The hard fact, and it was hard sometimes, had always been hard sometimes, was that she really did love her husband and she really did not want to lose him. But the minute he got his toy—the minute he became chairman—off she would go to the law firm. She promised herself that. In fact, she knew she would do it whatever the outcome on the chairmanship. If he didn't get it, he certainly couldn't object: if he did, no activities of hers could seriously hurt him then.

She just wondered why he had never seemed to worry much about hurting her. That was the thing that really hurt—being an adjunct of Gen. Stokes, not ever really a partner and a part.

Mrs. Gen. McCune had been the last of Carleene's ladies on the Tuesday after the hearing, and Mrs. McCune, as always, was pickin' away, partly because Carleene had come late from baby-sitting with David Stokes. Carleene admired, respected and feared Mrs. McCune, but she didn't really like her too much. She always felt that Mrs. McCune was lookin' down on her somehow, she told Jim. It wasn't a feeling she got from her other ladies, not even Mrs. Stokes who was a bit uppity and impatient with her sometimes but not in an unkind way. And Mrs. McCune wasn't unkind. She was just *superior,* somehow.

Carly, who knew no other French, had no way of knowing that this was an endemic Parisian condition that could only be handled by having sufficient self-possession to ignore it, genuinely and entirely. She let it bother her, just a little.

Mrs. McCune, who felt exactly as superior as Carleene sensed, never thought about it consciously at all. It certainly wasn't personal: she felt that way toward everybody.

She did, however, feel a certain impatience with Carleene that *was* personal, both toward her and toward her race. Now she was calling Carly's attention, for perhaps the thousandth time—*"Zut,* will they *never* learn!" she often exclaimed to Zeecy. "Not Africa, not France, not here, not *anywhere!"*—to the fact that she was not vacuuming under the two reclining rockers in the den. The chairs were where Renee and Zeecy sat for the evening news and whatever else (not much) they deemed worth watching. The chairs were on rollers, they were not all that heavy, it wasn't such a great exercise to move them sufficiently to keep the carpet clean. But week after week Carleene had to be reminded. And Renee had to remind herself, just as in former French Cameroon where her father had been in command, that there was no point in fussing too much: if you did you ran the risk of paralyzing them completely and getting only a blank and worried stare in response.

She made her point sufficiently this time so that Carleene did roll the rockers aside, did vacuum thoroughly, did roll them back again. That accomplished Renee felt as though she herself had accomplished quite a lot also. Her mildly exasperated mood was not improved when her husband's namesake, little Zoren, decided in his crib on the sofa that he was not pleased with the world and would give full voice to it.

"Sorry, ma'am," Carleene said, whipping open her blouse and preparing to go into action. "Best way I know to shut him up."

"Please do," Renee said. "I have a small headache this afternoon. It does not improve with the cries of babies."

"No, ma'am," Carleene said soothingly as little Zoren—already known in the family by both appellations, Little Zoren—went to work. "He'll be sound asleep soon's he gets his fill."

"It takes a lot, doesn't it?" Renee remarked as the baby pushed, pulled, sucked and gurgled with happy enthusiasm. "He will be a big boy."

"Oh, yes, ma'am," Carly said. "Doctor's already predictin' six feet and over. Tall as the general he's named for," she said proudly.

"Why *did* you name him for my husband?" Renee inquired. "It was very nice of you, he's very flattered, as you know—" Zeecy in fact, over her protests, had given the baby a one-hundred-dollar christening check, which she thought was a bit extreme—"but I know we've both wondered a bit."

"It's such a *nice* name," Carleene said as the baby finished and she buttoned her blouse and tucked him back in the crib. "It sounds so *military* somehow, like there ought to be a band playin'. General Zoren—Chace—McCune," she enunciated admiringly, rolling it on her tongue. "Maybe Little Zoren, here, will be a general himself, someday. It's a good name to live up to. The general's a fine man, Jim and I always say."

"Thank you," Renee said. She looked thoughtful for a moment. "He *is* a fine man, and who knows? The little one may indeed be a general himself, someday. Anything can happen." Particularly these days, she added to herself. Particularly in earnest, self-conscious, always-trying-too-hard America. Or was it too hard? In Africa as a young girl she would have said yes. Now, much older, she was not so sure. Who knew, with the world so different in so many ways, and in so relatively short a time, from the world in which she had grown up?

"I don't really care," Carleene said, staring down fondly at her son, "whether he's ever a general or not, 'long as he's a good child and a good man. That's all one wants in a son, right?"

She smiled up at Mrs. McCune and suddenly felt conscience-stricken, for of course she shouldn't have said that, Mrs. McCune looked so sad for just a minute. Fortunately Carly knew enough not to say anything more, and quick as a wink Mrs. McCune had regained her customary cool composure. Carleene couldn't help feeling a deep pity. Life wasn't so easy for these generals' wives sometimes even if they did live in fancy official quarters and stand at the head of the line. They paid their dues, she often told Jim. They paid their dues, and more.

Not long after that Mrs. McCune said she thought she would go lie down for a little while, her headache really was bothering her quite a bit.

"You be sure to do everything nicely for me, Carleene," she directed. "Come get me when you're ready to leave. I shall expect everything to be perfect then."

"Yes, ma'am," Carleene promised, hoping she could remember all the intricate directions Mrs. McCune had given her since she had started working for her. "I'll surely do my best, ma'am."

"Do better than that," Mrs. McCune said with a sudden smile that softened the rather severe planes of her classically pale and aristocratic face. "We want both Little Zoren and Big Zoren to be proud of what you do."

"Yes, ma'am," Carleene said with an answering smile. "I won't miss a thing."

That I doubt, Renee thought as she walked down the hall to her bedroom, which Carleene always made up first thing. But at least it will be sufferable until the next time.

Alone, she undressed slowly and thoughtfully; paused for a moment to turn this way and that before the full-length mirror, critically surveying a body that showed some slight signs of aging but was still remarkably svelte for sixty; put on the sheer silk cerise nightgown Zeecy had brought her from Brussels on his most recent NATO trip two weeks ago; and climbed into bed, pulling the covers snugly up to her chin.

She lay flat on her back, staring up at the ceiling. The headache throbbed busily along, just enough to keep her awake. But she would have stayed awake anyway, for a band in her head was playing for Gen. Zoren Chace McCune and now, as always, she could not send him back to barracks as easily as she wished.

She was not at all prepared for the phone call she received some ten minues later, or for the invitation it contained. But she accepted with alacrity, for something in her caller's voice told her that she was going to hear what she had foolishly convinced herself she was not going to hear.

She noted ironically as she hung up that her headache seemed to be gone, and Zeecy with it. In less than a minute she was asleep, beautiful body perfectly still, beautiful hair perfectly in place, beautiful mouth half-open, snoring gently; and so remained until Carleene knocked on the door almost two hours later and said the house was done and she and Little Zoren were ready to leave.

2 In his office off River Entrance, second floor, E Ring, Big Zoren at that moment was coming to the end of a day that had been largely concerned with various aftermaths, national and international, of the hearing. According to Clipper Corbus' *Early Bird* this morning, the flak had not abated much in the twenty-four hours since Cube Herron had used his gavel to terminate the contentious yammerings of Mario Escondido and the ill-concealed triumph of the Secretary of State.

News stories, editorials, commentators still kept up what Zeecy regarded as their cantankerous caterwaulings about the shortcomings of the Pentagon, the likelihood that Nanukuvu wasn't really of much importance to the United States and its allies and the noble statesmanship of the President and Secretary of State in so rapidly lining up twenty-five—count 'em, twenty-five—other nations (or "nations," depending on the point of view) to protest the introduction of a major nuclear base into the South Pacific.

And it *was* an achievement, Zeecy had to hand the President, and particularly Terry Venner, that. Despite Mario Escondido's scathing put-down at the hearing, the Secretary of State had managed to line up some real weight behind his "Declaration of the Pacific." Many of them might not have more than "sand and coconuts and seashells" to back up their protest, but Japan, both Chinas, the Republic of Korea and Singapore had substantial military clout, while Indonesia, the Philippines, Australia and New Zealand brought considerable moral, if not military, contributions to the effort. All in all it was an impressive list to which some contributed real power, some moral influence and a certain number, such as Nauru, Tuvalu and Vanuatu, contributed just by being there to swell the count.

Looked at from Moscow, however, it was still, as Mario had bluntly and accurately said, a contest between the only two capable of bringing to the issue real power. Most of the comments reprinted in the *Early Bird* were still overwhelmingly on the side of a diplomatic solution—which Zeecy and most in the Pentagon's operative levels felt was no solution. Few favored what was described by its critics as "the Pentagon's ever too ready willingness to resort to a trial of arms to decide this most delicate issue."

A trial of arms, it was pointed out, was on the face of it ridiculous. Nanukuvu was "a tiny island far away"; it was "a dot of earth which might conceivably be able to interdict certain sea and air routes, yet at the same time is itself vulnerable to blockade, isolation and eventual enforced desuetude." It should be "ignored . . . left to wither on the vine . . . cut off from any participation in any real threat to the Pacific and South Pacific regions . . . allowed to become, as boat-owners say of their expensive obsession 'a hole in the water' into which dollars (in this case rubles) are poured—to no purpose . . ."

LET NANUKUVU BE sternly admonished the lead editorial in the nation's most ubiquitous journal. ANOTHER SOUTH SEAS BUBBLE said its twin, turning history slightly askew to suit its own purposes. And over and over again, most uncomfortably for the chairman and chiefs, the SecDef and his assistants, the constantly recurring theme offered by another prominent gadfly in verse: "Latest Pentagon bumble brings U.S. stumble."

As near as he could figure it, Gen. McCune remarked to the Secretary in one of their numerous telephone conversations in the past few hours, the basic argument came down to: 1) Nanukuvu isn't worth bothering about—but 2) if the U.S. felt (wrongly) that it must bother about it—then 3) the Pentagon was to blame for the inability to bother about it in time to stop the kind of critical chorus that was now threatening its ability to bother about it.

"They're so messed up they don't know what they mean," Loy said. "So soldier on, general, soldier on. We'll get there yet, somehow."

"Still no word from the White House?" Zeecy inquired and Loy's tone abruptly sobered.

"No," he said with a sigh. *"You* know him. What's his game?"

"I know him," Zeecy replied grimly, "and at this point I don't want to even think about his game."

"Nor I."

"So—we'll soldier on."

"Yes," the SecDef said. "In the absence of anything more definitive."

But anything more definitive, Zeecy told himself now with a few colorful private thoughts about his old roommate, were obviously not going to be forthcoming until the President was ready. The White House spokesman had been asked this morning about the President's reaction to the hearing. His statement had been as bland and unrevealing as were his statements on most subjects these days:

"The President thought the hearing was most interesting and he is hopeful that the situation on Nanukuvu can be worked out without a major clash between this country and the Soviet Union. He feels the diplomatic approach he and the Secretary of State have initiated with the invaluable assistance of the prime minister of Singapore is a great step forward and will form the basis, along with other options, for a peaceable solution of this uncomfortable situation."

But as to the "other options," the spokesman refused to comment though bombarded with questions from Delight Jones, Herb Horowitz and many others. He also refused to respond one way or the other when Red Roberts asked point-blank, "Is the President in favor of some sort of military solution if the Pacific Declaration is ignored by the Soviet Union?"

So there they were, Zeecy thought, exactly where they had been for the past several weeks, with a little overlay of diplomatic nicety provided by the stubborn insistence and earnest idealism of the Secretary of State. Not that he was putting down Terry's idealism or his sincere belief in the diplomatic option: a lifetime's training and a lifetime's devotion to peaceful solutions was embodied there. But it *was* a distraction, coming just as the Pentagon was finally beginning to move in the tougher areas where, Zeecy and his colleagues were convinced, lay the only real hope of persuading the enemy to curtail his constant outward-pushing aggressions.

Personally, he gave the Declaration of the Pacific about ten minutes' life in the withering blast of Soviet disregard; but he supposed it was worth filing with the U.N. and referring to on every possible occasion if only as an embarrassment to Moscow. And it was heartening to know that twenty-five regional entities, even if some of them weren't much bigger than Nanukuvu itself, thought enough of the United States to follow its lead, go out on a limb and risk Soviet disapproval in order to protest establishment of a major atomic base in the South Pacific. It was a nice feeling to have support; and in the U.N. where he suspected there might yet be some formal interest in Nanukuvu now that it had become public, it would provide a nice bloc of votes the U.S. could call upon if necessary.

Basically, though, it was, and would remain, a military matter; and to that it was necessary to apply efforts and attention as though the hearing had never been. Mario Escondido and Bob Cathcart had deliberately done what they could to throw sand in the gears, and even such real friends as Cube Herron, Jerry Castain and—he hesitated on the name but then said it firmly aloud to himself, "Luzanne Johnson"—had been critical of the Pentagon. But that didn't change the basic fact as seen from the building. The Pentagon mission remained the neutralization and/or removal of the enemy installations now so well advanced on the island.

At the moment he was contemplating a brief review of the status of Project Frio. With one eye on the hearing, the members of the DSARC panel had approved the modifications of the ALCAC just before 5 P.M. on Monday and had released the invitations for bids, all in one amazing and uncharacteristic burst of speed. By eleven this morning both General Growth Group and Strategic Industries had responded with the bids they had obviously been holding in readiness for months while the Pentagon's acquisition process, Congressionally-mandated to be as slow and tortuous as most other Pentagon processes, had inched toward fruition. Helen Clark had sent around a memo to Loy, Zeecy, the two Harrys and Al Rider enclosing the two bids. Three Gs, Zeecy noted, was slightly under S.I.—a nice feather in the cap for young Walker Stayman, who had been Three Gs principal defense lobbyist for seven months, knew his way around Pentagon and Hill with self-congratulatory skill, and now lunched at Maison Blanche and dined at the Jockey Club with expense-account guests quite as a matter of course.

A feather in the cap for young Stayman. Tough times and big trouble for another youngster, for whom Zeecy had entertained high hopes and was still not convinced that they were invalid.

Al Rider had approached him when they all got back from the Hill yesterday afternoon. It was obvious he was upset about something and when Zeecy invited him to come along to the office for a talk, he accepted with alacrity. He told the tale he had to tell briefly and without adornment. When he had finished Gen. McCune shot him a sharp look.

"Do you believe it? Brod *Tolliver?*"

"Not for a minute," Gen. Rider said.

"Neither do I," Zeecy said flatly. "However . . ." He looked unhappy. "Many people have been fooled before by fine, 100 per cent, all-American boys. Maybe we have been too."

"I expect we'll be hearing more about it very soon," Al Rider said.

"Yes," Zeecy agreed as the phone rang. He picked it up, nodded at Al. His face became intent.

"Yes, general . . . Yes, I just got back. I appreciate your prompt call . . . I see . . . Yes, of course . . . Yes . . . Oh, really? . . . Well, if I might suggest—not having any real right to, of course, it's your bailiwick—why don't you examine the other staff members before you do anything drastic that would really destroy the lieutenant's career? Can't your fellows probe a little further before turning it over to the F.B.I.? I mean," he added as Al Rider looked puzzled, "we have been pursuing something else, haven't we? Why not go down that road a little further? Maybe it all ties in, somehow. Certainly I'd be very surprised if you found anything at all of a suspicious nature in Lt. Tolliver's life. You already have plenty in the other. Why not develop that angle? . . . No, of course I don't mean that the other individual you've uncovered is involved in anything treasonable. By God, that *would* be a scandal that would blow the top off the building! No, I mean that individual No. 1's private life may well make him subject to certain pressures that may well have led on directly to something like this. I'm sure Gen. Rider will give you every cooperation—"

"I'll testify for Brod myself," Al Rider said. Zeecy held up a silencing hand.

"Good, general, I think so too. Let's all just keep the lid on for a day or two longer and give your people time to go into it with absolute thoroughness before we turn to the F.B.I. or anybody else. I'll take full responsibility if there's ever any problem arising out of the delay, and you'll be pleased to know Gen. Rider's right here listening, so you'll have a witness if you ever need one . . . All right, general. Keep me advised at once if anything develops. Where is Lt. Tolliver, by the way?" He looked like a thundercloud. "Well, that's damned white of you," he said with a sudden biting sarcasm. "Let's hope she delivers all right, now that your people have terrified the poor girl out of her wits . . . All right, general," he said in response to sounds of earnest protest, "I'm sorry, I know your people didn't know, these things happen. I'll drop by to see them later . . . Hell, yes, I think that's all right! I'm not going to interfere with your boys, I'm just going to contribute a friendly word, that's all. I imagine the poor kids need one, right now . . . Very well, general," he concluded crisply, "thanks very much. Call me any time of day or night you think I'd like to be informed. I'm counting on you."

He hung up to find Gen. Rider studying him with a baffled expression.

"What was that all about? I got the gist of it but some of the details escaped me."

It was Zeecy's turn to relate recent history. Al Rider's expression changed from skepticism to shocked disbelief to increasingly appalled acceptance and finally to a palpable and quietly smoldering anger.

"Now there I was like you," he said with considerable self-disgust. "I prided myself I knew troops by this time. I thought Gary was a fine young officer, one of the best I've ever been privileged to have working for me."

"He still is, isn't he?" Zeecy inquired dryly. Al Rider nodded.

"Absolutely. But we can't have him handling sensitive matters with that kind of activity going on. Particularly with—" he stopped and again looked shocked. "My God, I can't believe it, but by God, you're right! *What* a scandal that would be!"

"Yes," Gen. McCune said crisply. "Exactly the sort some of our best friends in the media, such as *Defense Spy,* for instance—"

"And plenty more," Al Rider said grimly.

"And plenty more—would just love to hang us with, all over the world. Because of course it *would* go all over the world. So that's why—" he paused.

"That's why," Al Rider agreed, "a certain amount of necessary discretion is indicated here."

"Yes," Zeecy said with an exasperated sigh. "He'll have to be protected for the sake of the Pentagon, but why the hell that harebrained bastard—but charming," he added dryly, "oh, very charming—can't keep his equipment where it belongs, I'll never know!"

In spite of himself, Al Rider was unable to stop the tiniest gleam of amusement from coming into his eyes. Gen. McCune had the grace to blush slightly, but went on undaunted.

"I don't mean women, for Christ's sake!" he said sternly and Gen. Rider, again expressionless, agreed with a hearty, "No, *sir!*"

"But somebody like Gary Stump—!" Zeecy said. "My God!"

"I suppose as such things go," Al Rider said, "he is an attractive young man, extremely bright, extremely intelligent, extremely able and, in his tanned, self-assured California way, physically appealing. Not to me," he added with a wry smile, "but if one were so disposed."

"And apparently," Zeecy said, "as near as the Army Criminal Investigation Command can ascertain, this thing is quite a genuine emotion. Apparently it hit him out of nowhere and he doesn't seem to be able to shake it. Which is not the usual pattern, I'm told."

"And yet Brod Tolliver is the one who's supposed to be slipping war plans to the enemy," Al Rider mused.

"While Gary is really the one who has complete access to them through Op Frio—and maybe to other things as well through this new friend of his. It doesn't ring exactly true, does it."

"I hope you can keep your pal at C.I.C. under control until we can get this all sorted out," Al Rider said. "It *will* be hell if discretion *isn't* exercised."

"It will be," Zeecy promised grimly. "I'm going to see Loy about it immediately."

He picked up the phone, got Vangie, asked her if the Secretary was free, was told to come right up. "Now," he said as he shook hands with Al, "you go back there and make very sure that Stump and Hogan get a scrupulously correct but absolutely thorough grilling. Tell the C.I.C. I'd appreciate it very much if you could sit in on it, as commanding general of Op Frio. I don't think they'll object."

"Right," Al Rider said. "I look forward to it. Not with relish, but as a duty that must be done."

"In a situation where we just can't afford any fuck-ups," Gen. McCune remarked. Gen. Rider nodded.

"You can count on me," he said quietly. "Did I understand that Brod's wife has gone to the hospital?"

"Yes, poor girl," Zeecy said with recurring exasperation. "Those two boys who picked him up at the hearing apparently took him right home first thing— I guess they thought they'd surprise her burning secret documents or something. The result was to send her into screaming hysterics and premature labor, fortunately we'll hope not *too* premature as she was due in another week or so, anyway. But naturally it's not going to make it any easier. And as for its mental and emotional effects on her and that poor boy—" He frowned. "I *cannot* believe he's guilty and I *will* not until we know every last thing there is to know about little Mr. Perfect Maj. Stump."

"Is Brod at the hospital with her?"

"Under guard," Zeecy confirmed, "but I will say for them, once they saw the situation they decided to take him along there—well—accompanied, but at least he's there."

"And you're going to visit them later?"

Zeecy nodded.

"Count me in," Al said.

"Good man," Zeecy said, shaking hands again with an extra warmth. "The general told me they're going to let things ride with Gary until tomorrow morning, in the hopes that'll keep him confident and perhaps give them time to uncover a few more things."

"Then the general's got some suspicions, too."

"He's all right," Zeecy said. "He just has his own procedures to follow. See you at six, barring something unexpected . . . Vangie," he said two minutes later as she got up to show him into the Secretary's office, "you grow more endearing and beautiful every day."

"Zeecy McCune," she said, "it was lovely while it lasted, but surely you must know that we can't go on meeting like this. Our great days are over. They ended about fifty years ago."

"By God," he said with a grin, chucking her under the chin, a liberty she permitted no one else and no one else would have dared to take, "I think I was still in knee-pants at the time."

"And did that stop you?" she inquired, opening the door as Loy looked up with a smile tired but welcoming.

"Touché!" Zeecy exclaimed. "She outguns me every time, Mr. Secretary."

"Come in and sit down, Zeecy," Loy said. "You must have a lot on your mind, to come by this late in the day."

"Quite a lot, Loy," the chairman agreed as Vangie withdrew and closed the door and his temporary light-hearted mood turned as somber as the Secretary's. "Quite a lot, indeed."

Again they had stopped for a drink in one of Georgetown's many bars, eaten dinner in one of its more obscure but pleasant restaurants. A fierce impatience surged in his heart. They were wasting time—wasting time—wasting time. He had not felt like this in twenty years. His new friend was as calm, charming and casual as though they had all night. At the most it could only be three or four hours, as he did have to get home to his wife. Though apparently long-suffering, she apparently had a limit. "At midnight I turn into a pumpkin," he had told Gary the first time.

Prior to that hour there were a lot of things Gary wanted to do. With sure instinct, his friend was making him wait. For once, Gary recognized ruefully, he was on the receiving end of an ancient strategy. The certainty that the game would end as he wanted did not make it easier for him to take. He knew there was no point in expressing impatience but that did not make patience less difficult.

With great self-control he managed to smile and look animated and attentive while his friend chatted on innocuously and, it seemed to Gary, interminably about the news of the day as it affected the Pentagon. They discussed Op Frio, the hearing, the popular reaction, the latest enemy moves in other areas, various aspects of military life, what the Hill might be expected to do on several major civilian issues presently in the news and, finally, sports.

When his friend began speculating on how soon Washington might expect its first snowfall of the year, Gary held up a hand with a wry, protesting smile.

"Enough!" he said, but careful to keep it humorous. "Enough! Let's pay the check and get out of here."

"Oh," his friend said, seeming surprised. "All right."

"My treat this time," Gary said, reaching for it. His friend covered Gary's hand with his own and Gary attempted to pick it up. It made for a quick, unnoticed but pleasant little tussle which Gary won.

"Now," his friend said with a sudden thrilling seriousness as they left the restaurant. "The usual?"

"Why not?" Gary responded with a singing in his heart. "Why *not!*"

In the hotel Gary was moved by a sudden impulse to describe Brod Tolliver's "apprehension or detention or whatever you want to call it." He had cautiously avoided the subject during dinner but now everything was moving along so perfectly, he felt so happy and so relaxed and so uncharacteristically off-guard that he thought, what the hell. His friend had probably already heard about it through some top-level Pentagon grapevine, anyway.

His friend had not.

He paused half-undressed. His attention was riveted, he became very quiet. He asked Gary to go over the episode again, in detail.

Then he asked casually, "I assume *you're* in the clear, aren't you?"

"Certainly," Gary said indignantly, pausing too. "What makes you think I wouldn't be?"

"No reason," his friend said with a reassuring laugh. "No reason at all. I expect they'll question the whole staff, though, now they've got him. A bore for you."

"Oh, probably," Gary said in an offhand manner. He felt perfectly confident, perfectly calm: they had their man, they were convinced of it, he knew any questioning he might have to face could only be routine and corroborative of Brod's guilt.

He had long ago thought out the proper responses to nail *that* down conclusively and beyond challenge.

"It certainly won't be any problem for *you,"* his friend said with an admiring confidence that encouraged Gary's.

"Hell, no," he said, moving toward him in the darkened room.

His friend uttered a perfectly comfortable, perfectly natural laugh and backed away a little.

"Let's shower down," he suggested in a pleasantly humorous way. "I'm still sweaty from all those high-level meetings I had to go to today."

"O.K., let's," Gary said eagerly.

His friend smiled.

"Pretty cramped in there," he suggested. "You go first. I'll wait."

Gary hesitated but his friend urged in such a warmly encouraging voice, "Go on, man, go ahead!" that after a moment Gary shrugged and stepped into the bathroom.

"Don't go away," he ordered, a sudden huskiness in his voice. "I'll be right back."

"Sure thing," his friend said as he closed the door after him. "I'll be right here."

But of course, Gary realized with an awful cold fright when he stepped back into the room, he wasn't.

His clothes were gone, he was gone, everything about him was gone.

Gone, Gary realized as the fright deepened into terror, forever.

He dressed very slowly and carefully, the terror clamped around his heart. Very slowly and carefully he stepped out into the hall, went down the corridor, down the stairs, out into the dark night street and slowly and carefully, hardly seeing, to his car; got in, his small, sleek person feeling a hundred and fifty years old, and drove slowly and carefully home.

Over and over he kept thinking: I never should have said it. I never should have said it. Oh, God, you beautiful bastard, come back. I *know* I shouldn't have said it. You're right, *I know I shouldn't have said it.*

Across the street the sergeant from the C.I.C. yawned and took some more pictures. He already had some good ones of Quarry No. 2, whom he now knew by name. Quarry No. 1, he thought, appeared confused and distraught as he came later out the door, not at all the fleeting evil the sergeant was sure he had pursued to no avail through nighttime Georgetown.

Somebody got stood up tonight, the sergeant told himself with an ironic relish as he drove off to the Pentagon. Somebody didn't make it after all.

He wasn't into that sort of thing himself, he assured himself frequently, but, as with many a macho type, he certainly took a lively interest in it when it came his way.

Particularly when it was these two, one of them, he was now completely convinced despite the conclusions of his superiors, a traitor, and the other a fool.

Confused and distraught also on this troubled night for Frio and most connected with it was the earnest young figure, also small and sleek, who sat, wide-eyed and desolate, in a private room at Walter Reed Hospital trying to make some sense of a world that appeared to have gone completely mad.

One floor down and half a wing over, his wife was in labor and his child, if the Lord had any mercy left at all, was being born. Whole and healthy, he hoped, and with a good name with which to begin life. At least, he thought bitterly as he stared at the two faces that grew large, receded and grew large again while their steady drumbeat of questions fell upon him, the child's mother's name was a good one. God knew what the father's would be after these two merciless sons of bitches got through with it.

That he was now able to regard them as such after almost three hours of steady grilling was, though he was in no state to analyze it right now, an encouraging sign for Brod Tolliver.

For the first few hours of his ordeal—his sudden completely incomprehensible apprehension on the Hill, the grim ride back to his apartment during which his captors sat ostentatiously tight-lipped and refused all answers, the fantastic accusatory confrontation with Kathy that had sent her promptly into hysterics and into labor, the wild ride in the ambulance to Walter Reed, his two pals still wearing their iron masks, the hysterical goodbye to his wife as she disappeared into the delivery room, the silent march up to this deserted area of the hospital and this remote, isolated room, and the incessant verbal pounding he had received thereafter—he had walked through most of it like a zombie. He had appeared so shocked and disbelieving that his guards, or jailers, or whatever they were, finally concluded that he had to be shamming, nobody could be that paralyzed by events.

That was because they were used to confronting the guilty. They were not so often required to confront the innocent. And of course in fairness to them, as far as they knew, guilty he was.

Brod was in no state to be tolerant, however, and for quite a long time he was in no state to be anything but utterly terrified for himself, frantically worried for Kathy and totally unable to grasp what seemed a totally insane sequence of events. One moment he had been the trusted aide of one of the nicest general officers he ever hoped to meet, a man he liked, respected and admired, working with him and highly capable colleagues on a very important and very necessary project. The next he was consigned to the outer reaches of hell, accused of betraying the country he loved, giving secrets to an enemy he despised and deliberately seeking to destroy the very mission in which he believed with such wholehearted loyalty. It was absolutely crazy. It had no relation to the world in which he had grown up, joined the military, become a protégé of the chairman of the Joint Chiefs and done his excellent best to serve his country well. It was on some other planet, covered over with a gray haze and a sort of humming noise, through which at regular intervals protruded these choleric, demanding faces and harsh, demanding voices, increasingly angry and exasperated as he persisted in not giving them the answers they were sure he knew.

Along about now, however, Brod Tolliver was finally beginning to come out of it and get mad.

An hour ago, accompanied by his faithful companions, he had been permitted to go downstairs and see his wife. She was in a terrible state of tension and exhaustion and had barely known him, thus alarming him further. But he was assured by the colonel in charge that things were progressing reasonably well with no real cause for alarm even though it had now been some six hours since she had gone into premature labor. The colonel showed him that she was being monitored in every conceivable way known to medicine, and promised him that if it became apparent that a normal birth would not be possible without real danger to mother and child, they would take the baby by Caesarian if Brod agreed. He did so instantly and signed a paper to prove it. He was then allowed to sit alone with her for two minutes—one hundred and twenty seconds exactly, as timed by the younger of the two majors, after which he was told to kiss her and get on the stick, they had unfinished business upstairs. It was then that into Brod's hitherto dazed, dulled and traumatically docile mind there had come the phrase "merciless sons of bitches." After that, the world began slowly to right itself again.

It took a while, however, for this rising inner conflagration to transmit itself to the outside. For perhaps fifteen more minutes the younger major and the older, alternating, continued their unrelenting cross-examination. Brod suspected dimly that even in the military, this kind of solitary pummeling was quite irregular at this stage of the game, but hell, it was his word against theirs and how could he prove it? They weren't laying a hand on him physically— both, being at heart responsible officers, would have shunned that like the plague—and he had nothing with which to convince a court-martial or a civil trial for treason that he was being subjected to a mental pounding almost as bad. They were just taking advantage of his peculiar situation here at the hospital, trapped, as it were, by his wife's condition into a position where they could pretty much go after him psychologically as they pleased. But, he was able to reflect now as things slowly began to make sense again, they were losing ground.

No, he said, tone increasingly sharp, he had not taken the plan for Frio out of the office. No, he had not duplicated it with intent to give it to an enemy power. No, he had not been in Georgetown on the specified night. No, he had not rented a car and parked it at the specified place because, as he had already told them, he wasn't even in Georgetown at all that night. His wife could testify to that if they hadn't killed her and the baby with their damned nonsense. Very well, he was sorry if he had spoken disrespectfully, but that was how he felt and he couldn't help it. Well, he wasn't *going* to be able to help it, so he was sorry but there it was. No, he had not ever had any contacts with anyone from the Bulgarian embassy. No, he had not ever had any contacts with anyone from the Soviet embassy. He thought they were a pack of shits and he thought *this* was shitty too, if they wanted to know what *he* thought. Yes, he was aware he was an officer of the United States under military orders and in the presence of superior officers. Yes, he knew they were dedicated to the safety and security of the United States, what in the hell did they think he was? No, he had not hired a rental car on the specified evening and no, he had not driven it to Georgetown, and no, he did not there park it on said specified street and no, he did not traverse on foot sundry streets in Georgetown concluding at the corner of R and 28th N.W. opposite Oak Hill Cemetery and there toss into the window of a Volkswagen registered to the Bulgarian embassy a copy of the plan for Operation Frio.

And finally, no, he could not explain how his fingerprints *and only his finger-*

prints came to be on the copy of the plan found two minutes later by members of the C.I.C., and no, he did not also toss into the said Bulgarian-registered Volkswagen an officer's cap belonging to him, why should he? And no, he could not explain how his cap happened to be in that car.

But—

He stopped dead. It was perhaps the twentieth time these last two questions had been asked of him but he had been so dazed up to now that he had answered them almost mechanically—negatively, fortunately, but mechanically. All of a sudden they penetrated. Just as they did, the door opened and two stars of such dazzling magnitude appeared that the two majors were stunned into silence. For his part, Brod Tolliver almost burst out crying. But he didn't forget the two questions and he didn't forget the lightning that had struck like a cartoon lightbulb over his head. First, though, he had to greet his friends the chairman of the Joint Chiefs of Staff and the commanding general, Op Frio.

He did so with such fervent relief, looking so young and so forlorn and so vulnerable, that at that moment no one on earth could have convinced them of his guilt even if they had been presented with his signed statement admitting it.

"Gentlemen," Zeecy said in a tone that he did not often use but that could make much stronger men than the majors wish themselves somewhere else, "what in the *hell* is going on here?"

The older major gulped, wavered, but stood his ground.

"We are questioning Lt. Tolliver, sir."

"On whose authority?" Zeecy inquired, looking like a thundercloud with Al Rider not noticeably sunnier behind him.

"On the authority of the commanding general, C.I.C., sir."

"Yes," Zeecy said, "I know your general. We were talking on the phone just a short while ago about someone else who may possibly be pertinent to your inquiries. What are you questioning Lt. Tolliver about?"

"An episode that occurred several nights ago in Georgetown, sir."

"The attempted passing of the Op Frio papers to the Bulgarians," Zeecy said, and the majors looked first startled, then impressed.

"Yes, sir," they answered together.

"You see, I *do* know about it," Zeecy remarked. "Now, where does Lt. Tolliver fit in?"

"If we may, sir," the younger major said carefully, "we can tell you."

"Be quick about it!" Al Rider ordered and both majors said, "Yes, *sir!*" and launched hurriedly into their recitation.

The generals looked at one another without expression when they had finished.

"How does it happen," Zeecy asked without commenting on their response, "that you are questioning Lt. Tolliver, all alone, in these bizarre circumstances? This smacks of star-chamber proceedings to me. Don't you agree, Gen. Rider?"

"A fair description, Gen. McCune," Al Rider said solemnly.

"Well, sir," the older major said, "we didn't plan it this way, it just happened. You see, we took him in for questioning and then his wife—"

"Yes, I know that, too," Zeecy said impatiently. "You scared the poor girl out of her wits and she went into labor. So here he is and here you are. But that doesn't mean you could not be subject to very severe reprimand, gentlemen, about the way you've gone about this. It all seems most bizarre to me, most bizarre. And irregular, to boot. So what has Lt. Tolliver confessed to under these conditions, may I ask?"

"Not a thing, sir," the majors said simultaneously. The smallest trace of a twinkle came into the chairman's eyes and he carefully avoided looking at Gen. Rider, who was looking somewhere else himself.

"You mean you haven't broken him down in three hours of psychological brow-beating?" Gen. McCune inquired dryly. "You're slipping, majors. Slipping!"

"Perhaps, sir," the older said, again standing his ground. "But we have our duty to do and we expect to continue it."

"Under more suitable circumstances than these!" Zeecy snapped. He turned to Brod.

"Lt. Tolliver," he said severely, "Gen. Rider and I are asking you now on your honor as an officer and a gentleman, are you guilty of, or in any way involved in, the subject on which these officers have been questioning you? Think carefully before you speak and speak truly."

Brod gulped and looked, if possible, even more solemn than he had throughout the colloquy.

"Yes, sir," he said. "I mean," he said hastily, "no, sir. I mean, yes, sir, I *will* speak truly and no, sir, I am *not* guilty and I am *not* involved. But, sir," he said, back straightening, color rising, voice suddenly becoming excited, "sir—I think I have an inkling of who is."

"Very good," Zeecy said calmly. He gestured to the majors. "Gentlemen, sit down and put your feet up and relax for a while. Now, Brod, tell me and Gen. Rider and these two officers, who are probably—" the famous Zeecysmile burst forth—"not such bad guys when you get to know them—somewhere else. O.K., Brod, shoot."

And for the next fifteen minutes, quickly and excitedly and with a rising conviction in his voice, Brod did; and after that they all examined and cross-examined him exhaustively for another hour; and just about then there was a knock on the door, an orderly appeared, saluted and said to Brod, "Sir, with the compliments of the colonel, news from the maternity ward is that you have a fine son and he and Mrs. Tolliver are doing very well."

And then Brod really did cry.

Two phone calls came to the house in Georgetown shortly after midnight, one through the Pentagon switchboard, one on the direct red phone from the White House.

Loy was just beginning to drift into a light, uneasy sleep after returning with Immy from a dinner at the house of the publisher of the *Washington Post* when the Pentagon call came.

"God damn it!" he exclaimed, rousing uncomfortably on one elbow to take the phone off the hook. "Why can't they—"

It was the commanding general, C.I.C. He was extremely sorry to bother the Secretary, but there was now enough conclusive evidence to apprise him of an unhappy situation that could conceivably endanger the safety and security of the United States. He hated to be the one to bring the news, but he thought the Secretary should know that—

Loy listened for a moment, then broke in.

"Yes, general," he said sharply; then moderated his tone, the officer was only doing his duty. "Yes, general, I have already heard about that, unfortunately. It's one of the reasons I've been lying here tossing and turning, as a matter of fact. I'm trying to decide how best to handle it . . . No, I don't think you should do that just yet. I think you should put the lid on it absolutely in your shop until you hear back from me. Isn't that what Gen. McCune advises? . . . Yes, all right, then. Complete discretion is what is needed and *must* be maintained for the time being—perhaps forever. You and I will have to talk about that privately very soon. I'll get back to you tomorrow and we'll set a time. Meantime, I'll put things in motion at my end . . . Good, I appreciate your cooperation and I also appreciate your loyal efforts and those of your staff. I'll see you don't go unrewarded . . . No, my pleasure—if pleasure is the right word in such a sad situation . . . All right, then, general, thank you very much and goodnight."

"Wha' was that?" Immy demanded, swimming up from sleep.

"Just a routine headache in the life of a SecDef," he said, hanging up the phone and rolling over. "Go to sleep."

"I'm *trying* to," she said with drowsy annoyance. "Damned old Pentagon, anyway."

"Yes," he said, reasonable even under these circumstances, "I suppose you could say that. However—"

She was already snoring softly. And again the phone rang.

"Yes?" he inquired, trying not to sound too sharp because this time it was the red one.

"The President, Mr. Secretary," the White House operator said. Oh, *Christ,* he thought, mind flashing to two dozen potential trouble-spots around the hectic globe: what crazy bastard has done what crazy thing this time?

But it wasn't that kind of crisis, though instinct told him immediately that it was crisis enough for the building to handle.

"Loy?" the President said, sounding perfectly chipper at 12:47 A.M. "Sorry to bother you at this ungodly hour, Loy—"

"It is, rather," Loy said, managing quite a good chuckle, hoping to brighten the conversation: the President didn't sound upset, only determined.

"I *am* sorry," he repeated, "but you know, Loy, I've been lyin' here thinkin' about Frio—"

"Yes, Mr. President?" Loy said, abruptly wide awake and on guard.

"Yes, I have," the President said. "Haven't been able to sleep very well these past few nights, so I've been lyin' here thinkin'. And I've decided that the thing I've been thinkin' about most, the thing that's really got me goin', is Frio."

"Yes?" Loy said, holding his breath as the President paused.

"So I think," he concluded firmly, "that it's about time we all sat down again and reviewed the whole thing. What do you think?"

"If you feel that way, Mr. President," Loy said slowly and carefully, "although it seems to me that now that we have the hearing out of the way, and everything's moving forward in the Pentagon—"

"I was thinkin' about eleven tomorrow mornin'," the President interrupted. "You and Zeecy, and I'm sure ol' Icicle would feel mighty hurt if we left *him* out. And of course Al Brodovsky. How does that strike you?"

"Well—"

"That hour o.k. with you?"

Loy knew the mood and he also knew the Pentagon and Frio were in deep trouble.

"You're the boss, Mr. President," he said, voice deliberately impassive. "We'll be there."

"Good man," the President said. "Know I can always count on you, Loy. Thank you and go back to sleep now. Give my love to Immy."

"She'll appreciate that," Loy said. "Goodnight, Mr. President."

"He is the *most* inconsiderate man!" Imogene exclaimed, fully awake again. "Why does he *always* think it's so cute to call you in the middle of the night?"

"He does that to most of the Cabinet," Loy said. His voice became dry. "He likes to keep us slightly off balance. He thinks it keeps us on our toes."

"How can you stay on your toes if you're off balance?" she inquired with a sniff. He smiled ironically into the darkness.

"That's the point, I expect. I expect that's exactly the point."

She was back to sleep in five minutes but he was awake for much more than an hour. Around and around in his head went the call from C.I.C., the delicate human, political and public relations problems it posed, and the call from the Chief Executive with all the potential troubles and headaches it posed.

Maybe Immy was finally right, and he should chuck it all. But not, he told himself grimly, until I get Frio accomplished and the problem of Nanukuvu taken care of once and for all.

Somewhere toward three he went finally to sleep.

3 When Vangie came in with his coffee next morning he was standing at the window as he so often did, staring down across the river, now cold and gray, toward the massive government buildings and stately monuments of the white, imperial city. It seemed to her that he was especially troubled today, that he looked very tired and probably hadn't had too much sleep. A political instinct as sharp as his, and in some ways sharper after forty years in the building, made her pretty sure she knew what it was. The President had remained conspicuously absent in all the goings-on about Frio in the past few days. The Secretary and the rest of them were obviously out there on their own at the moment. It was no wonder he looked disturbed.

However, as always, he put a good face on it with nearly everybody. She flattered herself that he did not attempt much pretense with her.

"We've got trouble right here in River City, Vangie," he said with a smile as he took the coffee. "It's going to be a difficult day, I expect. Bear with me."

"Don't I always?" she inquired with a smile that seemed almost, in some quaint old-fashioned way, to be tucking him into bed and patting the covers. "We'll manage, you and I."

"That we will," he said, amused as she had intended by her proprietary air, which was always there and perfectly unabashed though usually hidden under her neat, impeccable discretion. "First of all, you can get me Helen Clark."

"Certainly," she said, starting out to her own desk. "Apparently, from the hearing, Project Frio is finally moving along very well."

"Yes, I think she's lighted a fire under them," he agreed. Vangie smiled.

"She's a very competent lady."

"And a very nice one," he said. He sighed suddenly and his expression turned bleak for a moment. "Which is why what I have to discuss with her is not going to be easy."

"I'll have her for you in a second," she promised. Cool and smooth as velvet in the snow, Helen's calm voice came over.

"Yes, Mr. Secretary. What can I do for you?"

"Can you come in for a minute, please? Something I want to talk to you about. Don't want to," he amended unhappily, "but must."

"Yes, certainly," she said, sounding alarmed. "I hope it's nothing to do with Frio."

"Not directly."

"I'll be right there."

Within five minutes she was.

"Sit down, Helen," he said, manner grave. "Have a cup of coffee."

"No, thank you," she said, expression frankly worried. "What is it, Mr. Secretary? Something I or my people have done?"

"No," he said, looking at her in a gravely concerned way that alarmed her even more; and proceeded to tell her, as considerately and gently as he could.

At first she turned very pale. Then came the protestations of disbelief. Then came acceptance and tears. And then came recovery and a shaky but determined promise to do whatever he wanted her to do to make the situation easier for everyone.

He told her what he thought was necessary and what he wanted from her; and after another brief moment of weeping she dried her eyes, straightened herself and stood up, lovely face even whiter than usual but calm again and ready for whatever might lie ahead.

"I'll talk to him," she said. "It will be worked out."

"Thank you," he said gratefully. "You're perhaps the only one who can do it. I have great confidence in you." He smiled with sudden warmth. "As always."

"Thank you, Mr. Secretary," she said with great dignity. "I appreciate your trust in me—as always. Do you want me to report back to you, or—?"

"Oh, no," he said hastily. "That won't be necessay. I know you'll do what has to be done."

"Yes," she said and for a moment her eyes welled up again. "But it won't be easy."

"No," he agreed, "dear Helen." He came forward on a sudden impulse and kissed her cheek. "Thank you so much."

For a moment, then, her control broke again and she uttered an anguished, "But *why?* Oh, *why?*"

"Who knows?" he asked gravely. His expression turned bitter. "There is no explanation. The whimsical humors of the Lord, perhaps. He seems to enjoy having a field-day with us humans sometimes."

"Yes," she agreed as Vangie appeared with great respectfulness, in response to his touch of foot upon the button beneath the rug, to show her out. "Life is such a roulette-wheel, isn't it?"

He made no response save a quick, unhappy nod, and turned again to the window to stare out at the powerful city, unseeing, almost unthinking, until Vangie returned.

"A very strong lady," was her only comment.

"The best," was his. He became quickly businesslike, returning to his desk, pushing aside the *Early Bird* and a mountain of dispatches on his desk. "I *do* have work to do here," he said with some irony, "but the Boss has sounded the tocsin and wants us over there at eleven. Can you notify Zeecy, please, and tell him to meet me here at quarter to? He can ride over with me."

"Right away," she said; started out; and turned back with the privilege of years and status. "I hope he gets off the dime and gives you a little support now!" she said, the abrupt colloquialism startling him into a welcome laughter.

"Why don't you call him and tell him that, Vangie?" he suggested. "It might surprise him so that it would just do the trick."

"I'd like to," she said with a ferocious little smile that suggested she just might, if the President didn't watch out. "He's such a—!" She didn't say it but her mouth twisted into frustrated annoyance.

"They all are, to some degree," he said, "but I will admit he is rather more so than most. I'll want that map of Nanukuvu and those latest reports that have come in overnight, please. Everything is going nicely from where *they* sit, anyway."

"It's a tough one," she said thoughtfully. "It's a tough one. Always has been and always will be. At least you're doing *your* best."

"Thank you, Vangie," he said, "you're a comfort in old age. *My* old age, that is," he added with a hasty chuckle.

"Nobody around here is as old as I am," she said, "but I haven't often seen one as frustrating as this. I'll go call the general."

"Please," he said and turned again to his papers. An hour passed in paperwork and calls from the Hill—Cube Herron, Jerry Castain and Luzanne Johnson all calling for brief, encouraging postmortems on the hearing; Mario Escondido, already moving on to the next project, calling to put on shameless pressure demanding that the Pentagon give him a pending prize contract for Bridgeport "or else."

"Or else what, Mario?" the Secretary retorted. "Suppose I just told you to take a running jump?"

"Better not," the Congressman said in an ominous voice. "I can make it plenty hot for the Pentagon, Loy, and don't you forget it."

"I don't forget it," Loy said, "and you shouldn't forget it works both ways. Suppose I call somebody like *Defense Eye* and tell Delight Jones the kind of pressure you try to put on us day in and day out. Suppose I tell her the chairman of the House Armed Services Committee is very peculiarly anxious to have certain contracts in his district, and that maybe she'd want to check into where all the money goes once the contracts have been awarded."

He expected an explosion, indeed rather welcomed it in his present restless and unhappy mood, but Mario, as often happened, responded with the unexpected.

"Hell, Loy," he said with a perfectly uninsulted chuckle, "I don't want their damned money, you know that. I just want their damned votes."

The Secretary had to laugh.

"You're incorrigible," he said.

"And in my own odd way," Rep. Escondido remarked with satisfaction, "incorruptible."

"Except with votes," Loy said.

"Oh, *those,*" Mario said cheerfully. "You can buy me with votes any time. Now how about that contract for Bridgeport?"

"In due course, Mario," Loy said. "In due course. It has to go through DSARC yet."

"DSARC!" Mario said with disgust. "DSARC! More damned alphabet soup! You run the most fucked-up place in town over there, you know that?"

"Thanks for all your help in making it easier," the Secretary said, but the irony was lost on Connecticut's finest.

"Not at all," he said grandly. "Call me any time."

"I'll do that," Loy said.

Just before he heard Zeecy giving Vangie his usual exuberant greeting in the outer office, he found an excuse to call another number in the building. The voice that answered was its usual pleasant, competent, agreeable self; nothing had disturbed it yet. Their conversation was businesslike and routine. He obviously hadn't heard from Helen—probably still too stunned, or planning her strategy, or both, Loy decided. He sighed: a hell of a business. He knew his gloomy thoughts were shared by Zeecy, because they had discussed it late yesterday afternoon when Zeecy dropped by. But Zeecy had apparently not lost any sleep. He seemed extra bouncy this morning, as though something he cared a lot about was developing as he wanted it to. Perhaps his mood was a good omen for this conference with his elusive former classmate in the White House. Loy did his best to join in the mood as they started across the river.

The Secretary of State was also feeling pretty bouncy today as he was driven the short distance from Foggy Bottom to the White House. The reasons were obvious in almost every editorial, column and television commentary. He was the spokesman of all who feared or abhorred a major argument with the Soviet Union, and that included a great many, not only in his own department where the let's-don't-be-beastly syndrome was everywhere predominant, but throughout the country, as well.

Terry Venner was the man of the hour, there was no doubt of that—he and the President, who of course was reaping the major benefit; and the prime minister of Singapore, who tended to be generally forgotten by the American public but had nonetheless been a real help. The President should be riding high today, Terry thought: and thus malleable to the only course of action that seemed to the Secretary of State to be consistent with the spirit and purposes of the Declaration of the Pacific.

That this really quite surprising achievement was a document before which the enemy would quail and go away, he was under no illusions whatsoever. It was composed of good intentions, earnest hopes, a lot of words and a piece of paper. Its "demand" for withdrawal from Nanukuvu, as Rep. Escondido had accurately if rudely said, rested in many cases on sand, coconuts and seashells.

Terry couldn't stand the obnoxious little man—thank God *his* department came under mild old Sen. Clawson of the Senate Foreign Relations Committee and very correct-thinking Rep. Harvey Starnmetz of the House Foreign Affairs Committee, smartest of the new isolationists. But Mario Escondido did have a way of putting his finger on it, uncomfortable though this generally was for all concerned. His realistic sarcasm concerning the underpinnings of Terry's much-cherished Declaration was nicely outweighed, in Terry's opinion, by all the nasty things Mario had said about the Pentagon in general and the idea of trying to stop the fortification of Nanukuvu in particular.

Now was the time, Terry felt—probably the very last time—to stop Mission Frio in its tracks and put the argument over Nanukuvu where he thought it rightfully belonged: in the hallowed halls of diplomacy in which he had been trained and employed all his working life.

Had the President's first direct approach to the General Secretary been fobbed off with minimal courtesy? Had his own contacts with the ambassador frittered out in their usual confrontation between earnest democratic hopes and brutally rigid totalitarian arrogance?

That did not mean that another try could not be surprisingly successful, if put forward now with sufficient authority and the knowledge that by now a fairly substantial military momentum was gathering behind the President. (Here the Secretary was forced to admit, but only for a moment, that the military did have *some* part to play in the equation—just, he devoutly hoped, not an active one.)

Anyway, this was the moment to drop the bluster, make a strong representation to Moscow, point to the overwhelming weight of opinion in the Pacific area and request—not demand, just request, firmly but politely—that the Kremlin abandon its obviously ominous plans in the area. Now that Nanukuvu had demonstrated the dangerously floundering nature of the JCS and the interminable nature of the Pentagon acquisition process, Terry felt that the time had come. He felt even more confident of this as he imagined himself, in buoyant thought, riding toward the White House in a gilded chariot, hailed by trumpets and wafted on billowing clouds labeled DISAPPROVAL OF THE PENTAGON and PEACEFUL MEANS IN THE SOUTH PACIFIC.

The trumpets became muted, the clouds parted gently, his chariot came softly down through them and bumped to a halt at the southwest entrance to the Mansion. As luck would have it his arrival coincided, as usual, with the long black limousine from across the river. His face put on its Be-Nice-to-the-Pentagon smile and he stepped forward, tall, erect, distinguished, impressive, to hold out his hand to his opposite number.

"Loy," he said, "sorry we didn't get a chance to chat more at the hearing—"

"Oh, that's all right," Loy said with that wry expression Terry found so disconcerting at times. "We each had our own agendas. Yours, I must say, is sweeping the nation two-to-one."

"I'm glad you realize that," the Secretary of State said, turning to shake hands cordially with Zeecy. "It may make *this*—" he nodded toward the beautiful white structure looming above them—"easier for both of us."

"Easier for you, maybe," the Secretary of Defense said, still looking wry but not, Terry noticed uneasily, at all daunted. "Not so easy for us. But I dare say," he added calmly as they started in, "I dare say we won't let you scuttle us without a fight."

"I'm not *here* to 'scuttle you'!" Terry exclaimed, lowering his voice to a near-hiss as attendants came forward to take the light top-coats they had worn against the early chill. "I'm just here to propose a sensible way out of this mess caused by Pentagon incompetence, and try to get us out of it with reasonable success and honor!"

"Oh, it's the Pentagon 'mess' that this is all about, is it?" Loy demanded, not bothering to lower his own voice much as Aleks Brodovsky appeared, smiling, hand outstretched. "I thought it was the mess caused by the enemy that was the problem here. That's what we're here to talk about."

"Both," Terry conceded hastily. "Both. But you can't deny that the Pentagon—"

"Gentlemen," the national security adviser said with firm pleasantry, voice riding over the start of Loy's indignant retort, "good to see everybody. I'm glad to see you all survived the hearing in good shape. Come right on up. He's waiting for us in the Oval Office."

Thus hurried along, they perforce had to drop their argument for the moment but both determined they would resume it upstairs. The President made it clear at once, however, that he was not going to permit any backward glances or recriminations this time. He started out by deliberately filibustering them into silence.

"Loy," he said, coming forward cordially to shake hands, "Zeecy—Mr. I—no, I don't think I'll call you that any more, Terry. How about shortenin' that nickname to one more heart-warmin'? How about 'Ike'? It did all right for somebody once, I remember."

"That would be fine with me, Mr. President," the Secretary of State said with a rather strained smile. "Whatever you like best."

"I like Ike," the President said, and chuckled. Then he sighed as he returned behind the desk and sat down to face them as they settled into their half-circle of chairs. "Lord, I wish he were here right now to tell me what to do! I'd give up this job in a minute if I could push it off on old Ike. *He was a pistol,* that man! Give 'em that big grin and that's all he had to do. 'Course in fairness I know he did a lot more than that, but that's what you saw on the surface. He made it all seem so *easy.* Well, gentlemen, I'll tell you somethin': it isn't." He sighed again, a touch Zeecy recognized and had always considered a trifle overdone, a bit more business than the stage could comfortably carry. "So, now! Here we all are again. And out there—yep, I knew it!" he exclaimed as Zeecy smiled and unrolled the map—"I *knew* you'd have it for us, Zeece, all full of your lines and symbols, it's about the best thing they teach over there in the

Pentagon, or at least the most prevalent, all that show-and-tell—anyway, out *there* we still have the island of Nanukuvu, which is not goin' to go away. Any more than the folks that's on it are goin' to go away unless we per*suade* 'em to go away. So what do I do about it? This is about the hundredth time I've asked y'all that question, I guess, and to tell you the truth—" his voice lengthened out dramatically, his eyes surveyed them with sleepy shrewdness—"to—tell—you —the truth, I still haven't got an answer. A really good, honest, practical, genuine *answer*. Loy?"

For a moment, thus confronted, the Secretary of Defense remained silent, obviously thinking out his response. Then he looked the President squarely in the eye.

"The question, it seems to me, Mr. President, is not what should *we* tell *you* to do about Nanukuvu but what *you* should tell *us*. That's where we in the Pentagon, I must confess to you, are somewhat lost at the moment. I don't know," he added with a glance at Terry, who looked sympathetic, "about my colleague from State."

"It *would* be of assistance, Mr. President," Terry said cautiously but not ducking the issue, "if we all might have some guidance at this point. It seems to me that we are now at one of the major turning points in what both Loy and I think of as the problem of Nanukuvu. We've had the build-up—a little slow, perhaps," he couldn't resist adding—"but beginning to move faster now. We've had the Congressional airing whose potentiality has been hanging over us for many months, and so presumably we won't have that interference to worry about again, for a while, anyway. We now have the Declaration of the Pacific, which it seems to me furnishes a clear, unequivocal and worthy path to follow —and so perhaps it is only fair that we *should* ask you. May we do so?"

"Old Terry!" the President said with a chuckle. "Old Ike—*my* Ike! I notice you got in a nice little plug for your own idea, there, Terry, and I have to confess, seein' as how it was a good part my idea too—"

"Largely," Terry said firmly, which prompted Zeecy to wink at him across the half-circle.

"Well, it *was* a good part, Zeecy, you old scoundrel," the President said, of course not missing it and more amused than annoyed. "Wasn't it, Terry? Didn't I get on the phone myself and call the chairman in Peking and the prime minister in Tokyo, and our friend in Australia and Mr. Self-Righteous in New Zealand, and a whole handful of those little rocks down there—"

"You called a great many of them personally, Mr. President," Terry said, "and it was enormously helpful in putting it all together."

"I stand corrected," Zeecy said. "Now what do we do with it? Is *it* the answer you want, Mr. President?"

"It helps," the President said thoughtfully. "It helps. But I'm not sure it's . . ." his voice trailed away. "It gives me a talkin' point and it gives us somethin' to take to the U.N., so maybe . . ." and again he trailed away.

"Mr. President," Loy said with more sharpness than he perhaps should have, but what he had often referred to privately as "the President's striptease act" was beginning to get on his nerves a little more than usual today. "Mr. President, what *do* you want on this issue? Do you want us to continue our build-up and proceed along military lines? Do you want us to cease our efforts and let the entire matter go into the hands of the Secretary of State? It's very confusing, frankly, for all of us. We would appreciate clarification. And *I* think," he concluded quietly but firmly, "that we deserve it."

There was a silence while the President appeared to be staring at some distant scene visible only to him, out there in the rose garden.

"I must agree, Mr. President," Terry Venner said.

"And I," said Zeecy.

"And I," said Al Brodovsky.

The President swung back, a twinkle in his eye.

"You're all against me!" he exclaimed with a chuckle. "I swear, I never saw anythin' like it, all against me! So what am I supposed to do?"

"Mr. President—" they began, but he held up a hand and, smiling still, forestalled it.

"All right," he said, "all right. You win. I've got to make a decision of *some* kind about somethin'! And I will! . . . But," he said, chuckling again at their eager forward-leaning faces, "not right this very minute." He chuckled yet again at their perturbed expressions. His face became quite severe. "I called you in here to give me some guidance and advice on what I ought to do, and all I get from you is a lot of complainin' that *I* ought to tell *you* what to do. So I guess it comes back to me, after all."

"Doesn't it always, Mr. President?" Zeecy inquired, the only one daring to say it, out of old friendship. And, using the old familiarity he never used except on the most extreme occasions, "Why the charade, Chuck? What are you trying to prove, pal?"

"I'm not tryin' to *prove* anythin'!" the President retorted, whether genuinely angry or not they were unable to tell. "I'm just tryin' to get my innermost circle, my top*most* advisers, to give me some guidance on what to do. That's all. But you won't, so there it is. I must say, Loy," he added suddenly, an apparent non sequitur but Loy knew in his bones that it wasn't, "I'm not very impressed with that Project Frio bit. Better tell 'em to step on it, over there. It's holdin' the whole thing up."

"Project Frio is now completely on track, I believe," Loy said evenly. "I'll pass along your admonition, however."

"Good," the President said, standing up. *"Somethin'* decisive has to happen *some*where. Got the whole wide world yappin' against Frio, got to give 'em somethin' to keep the wolves from climbin' on the sled, right?"

"Yes, Mr. President," Loy agreed, telling himself that what he thought was indicated was not indicated. "Project Frio, like all other parts of the mission, is now going full speed ahead."

"Good," the President said again as he moved them gently but firmly to the door. "And as for you, Terry, why don't you take that Declaration up to the U.N. this afternoon and file it with the Secretary-General?"

"It's already been done, Mr. President," Terry said. The President clapped him on the back.

"Good old Ike!" he exclaimed. "That gives me exactly what I need up there. Who said you were a stick-in-the-mud?"

"I'm sure I don't know, Mr. President," the Secretary of State said stiffly. "I certainly didn't say it of myself."

"That's right," the President said delightedly, giving him another playful buffet. "That's right, by God, you surely didn't! Take care now, y'all. You'll be hearing a lot from me in the next few days. We're goin' to get this Frio thing wrapped up successfully or die tryin'."

"Again," Loy said to Zeecy as their driver, Carleene's Jim, took them across the river. "Again, he baffles me."

"He loves to do that," Gen. McCune said. "He's always been like that, right back to the academy. But don't worry. He's made up his mind about something. Something's going to happen."

"I know," the Secretary of Defense said wryly. "That *is* what worries me."

At 6 P.M., from the White House spokesman in his last pressroom appearance of the day, they learned what it was.

"The President," he said to the attentive group of media regulars still on the job at that hour, "acting in his capacity of Commander-in-Chief, has decided to cancel a portion of the proposed Mission Frio, the mission designed to inhibit further Soviet development of the island of Nanukuvu.

"The activity known as 'Project Frio' is hereby terminated.

"The President believes it to be an unnecessary duplication of effort and a waste of time and money, both of which he is always desirous of saving in the Pentagon.

"That portion of Mission Frio known as 'Operation Frio' will continue until such time as it has served its purpose in resolving the problem posed by the situation on Nanukuvu."

In the SecDef's office he and Zeecy, watching this come over the evening news to the obviously pleased approval of the networks, made appropriate response.

"That's going to get him the praise he wants," Loy said bitterly. "Just listen to the vultures scream at us now!"

"One ball at a time," Gen. McCune remarked dryly. "They say that's the least painful way to do it."

In Foggy Bottom, the Secretary of State heard the news just as he was on his way out of the office and home to Marisa. He turned back and went to the window from which he could see, across the river, brightly lighted in the chilly dusk, the citadel of his competitors.

"Gotcha!" he said aloud. He hugged himself with a most shockingly uncharacteristic glee, unrecognizable for one wild, abandoned moment as "Mr. Icicle," or even "Ike."

"We're halfway home!" he told the arrogant damned bomb lovers exultantly. "Halfway home!"

In her beautiful apartment in Washington Harbour, Helen Clark sat staring dumbstruck at the little screen as its evening mentor turned to other subjects and continued to babble on in his pompous way about the worries of a troubled world.

She was in enough mental and emotional turmoil already, she thought with a bitter resentment toward the President, without adding this.

For the second time in a day, the second time in years, the composure that never cracked save on the rarest of occasions cracked again. It had deserted her once early today when Loy Buck had imparted his sad and deeply wrenching news and asked for her help in responding to it. Now it cracked again at what appeared to her to be a wanton and ruthless slap in the face for all her earnest and diligent work on behalf of Frio.

For the second time today Helen Clark broke down and cried. In some ways this latest news seemed almost worse than the first, or at least it added to it a burden that suddenly seemed almost unbearable.

She cried for quite a long time, deep, wracking sobs such as she had not uttered since the day her divorce became final.

Presently the storm passed. Helen the indomitable gradually regained control, or at least sufficient thereof to enable her to make the telephone call she had been desperately delaying—because she really didn't quite know how to go about it—ever since her talk with the Secretary.

She picked up the phone and dialed a number as familiar to her as her own. The voice of its owner responded promptly, at first seemingly as pleasant, competent, untroubled and calm as ever.

"Harry," she said, voice beginning to shake. "Harry, can you come right over? We've got to talk."

"All right," he said, sounding suddenly as deeply troubled and upset as she. "I'll be right along."

4

Hogan, she told herself to quiet an innocent but insistent apprehension, had always been a good girl. She had been a good girl as a baby, a good girl in kindergarten, a good girl in grammar school, a good girl in high school, a good girl at the University of Michigan, and certainly and beyond all doubt (save once) a good girl since she had joined the Navy twenty years ago. Her fitness report with unbroken consistency carried the word "excellent" in all categories; her rise to captain, no small rank for a woman, or indeed anybody, had been orderly and sure.

A whole string of commanding officers, reaching back down the years to her first overseas tour in Japan and coming right on up to Adm. Stahlman, in whose office she had been serving when detached for temporary duty with Gen. Rider at Op Frio, had paid glowing tribute to the intelligence, diligence and general all-around reliability of Capt. Elizabeth Hogan.

She knew she would probably rise no further in rank because she knew, and often told herself, that she just didn't have the little extra air of glamor and drive that characterized the few women who rose to flag rank. She knew she was intelligent, diligent, competent and absolutely dependable, but she wasn't bright, in the sense of sparkle. She knew that. She didn't have the edge of hardness and ambition that was really needed. She wasn't glamorous. She didn't glitter. She was, as she told herself humbly far too often, really a rather dull person.

Unfortunately, since that was the way she had very early in life begun to think of herself, that was the way her colleagues and superiors always thought of her. "Hogan's a wonderful, good-hearted gal and a great officer," they said, "but—dull, don't you think? A little dull . . ." And at various times and in various ways they tried to compensate for this with little extra kindnesses, invitations to Thanksgiving and Christmas dinners, inclusion in New Year's parties, the attempt, sometimes frustrating to them, to give Hogan a little more social life—and, indeed, just plain enjoyment of life itself—than she seemed to be able to manage on her own.

There had been a time, just once, long ago and now long deliberately buried beneath the accumulating sands of memory, when she had met someone who had seen through the Hogan-that-was to the Hogan-that-could-be. They had been stationed together at NATO headquarters in Brussels, and he had outwardly been much the same quiet, unassuming type, also destined to serve out an honorable Navy career but not rise to the dazzling heights that the more dashing and, yes, if need be ruthless, were slated to achieve.

All through one enchanted summer he had dated her three and four times a week, dinners, dances, picnics in the country, trips to nearby pleasant places that were golden and glowing because they were there together. For many weeks it went no further, but in September he had finally suggested, diffidently but with a dogged determination that endeared him to her even more, that they spend a weekend together in Paris. No one would know, he said, and it was about time. She blushed, hesitated, agonized overnight, and said yes. The world became even more enchanted, and when the weekend was over they were engaged to be married and were already planning toward the day when they would take early retirement and return to Michigan to take over the small but thriving hardware business her father had built up over the years.

The next day he and a fellow officer were driving to Ostend on official business when they were sideswiped by a drunken teenager who received a broken tooth, a bruised leg and the gift of continued life as a reward for his worth and responsibility. The fellow officer was permanently crippled, her fiancé was killed. The world stopped for Hogan and, for quite a while, did not resume again.

Eventually, however, it did because it had to; and, in a way providentially, though it was to tie her to the situation from which she knew now she would not escape in time for anything else, her father passed peacefully away of a heart attack in his sleep and her mother, shattered and beginning to enter upon what was to be a permanent state of "not feeling very well," was left alone.

Hogan had a younger, married sister and an older, married brother; and as is often the way, it fell naturally—at least her sister and brother thought it was natural—to her to assume the burden. Her siblings contributed regularly and cheerfully each month to their mother's support: on Hogan lay the heavy hand of daily care. Despite continued sinking spells, indefinable ailments and a general state of dependent desuetude, the doctors at Bethesda Naval Hospital told Hogan that her mother would probably live for many more years in just that dependent state. As long, in fact, one commander told her with a bluntness he hoped would prompt her to work out some other arrangement, "as you make it so easy for her to take advantage of you."

This firm comment had startled and upset Hogan but she knew it was true. That, however, did not make it any easier to find a solution; and presently, after being rebuffed gently but firmly by her brother and sister, and after a siege of wild hysteria from her mother when the three of them tried to suggest that she "might be happier someplace with people your own age," Hogan had, in effect, given up.

In the last couple of years, since her assignment to the office of the chief of naval operations, she had resigned herself to the thought that at forty, barring some extremely unlikely miracle, her years of having a chance for genuine happiness were over. She went to Kennedy Center from time to time with her friends from Tokyo days, attended most of the parties given by her friends in the CNO's office, in recent months had ventured out occasionally with Brod and Kathy Tolliver and had been invited several times to dine with the family of Big G, as they called Gen. Rider behind his back in the office. But it was not until Gary Stump had begun to be increasingly friendly in recent months that she had been able to achieve anything which in her mind could even remotely be described as Life.

And that, even though it had culminated a couple of weeks ago in the most intimacy she had known since that long ago weekend in Paris was curiously—unreal, somehow. She couldn't quite put her finger on it, any more than Brod could. They had not really compared notes, aside from Brod's occasional oblique comment, but her feeling was equally uneasy. This was not the happiness whose possibility, though consciously abandoned, still lingered somewhere in her heart. This was something a little different. And though for a little while she had been quite excited about it, and on their one occasion of intimacy had found him to be a skilled and imaginative lover, something still cautioned her to hold back.

This probably made it easier, she thought now as she sat in the office of the chairman of the Joint Chiefs of Staff facing Gen. McCune, Gen. Rider and a colonel from the Army C.I.C., to answer questions that she soon sensed were designed to lead back to Gary.

How long had she known him? (Only since the start of Op Frio.) Did she know him well? (The slightest hesitation, which was noted, and then: just as a good friend around the office.) What was her opinion of him as a fellow-worker? (Absolutely able, efficient—"a real brain," in full charge of himself, the office and every task he was asked to perform.) What did she think of Lt. Tolliver? (A thoroughly nice young man, also very intelligent, very capable—dedicated.) Had she ever had any cause to doubt in any way the loyalty or honor of Lt. Tolliver? (No, sirs, she had not.) Had she ever had any cause to doubt in any way the loyalty or honor of Maj. Stump? (Again the slightest hesitation, again noted, and: No, sirs, she had not. He, too, seemed absolutely loyal and dedicated.) If she were asked to imagine either of them betraying their country, which one would it be? (A long hesitation this time, so long that Gen. McCune himself took over the questioning.)

"I know that's a tough one, captain, but that's why we ask it, as I'm sure you understand—to try to get down to the essence of this."

"If I may ask, sir," she said, feeling timid but encouraged by Gen. McCune's kindly presence and his still-stunning good looks, which awed her as they did most, "could I be told what 'this' is? I mean, I have no idea what—"

"It isn't necessary for you to, Elizabeth," Gen. Rider said, but also in a kindly way. "At least not right this minute. I'll tell you myself when we've got a sufficient handle on it." He smiled his warmly pleasant smile. "Is that all right?"

"Oh, yes, sir," she said gratefully. "I didn't mean—I mean, I don't want you to think—"

"Just give us your best judgment, Elizabeth," Gen. McCune interrupted, but not harshly. "That's all we want. If you had to imagine a situation in which one of those two officers might betray his country, which would it be?"

"Well, sir," she said, emboldened by his encouraging air, "first of all, I couldn't imagine a situation in which either could do a thing like that—but," she added hurriedly as Gen. McCune stirred a trifle impatiently, "if I *were* to imagine such a situation, then I think I'd say . . ." she frowned and paused again, obviously upset.

"Just your best judgment, Elizabeth," Gen. Rider said quietly. "This isn't being recorded in any way, you know. This is entirely preliminary. We just want to find some guidelines on which to proceed further. Any help you can give us will be profoundly appreciated."

"Oh, yes, sir," she said earnestly. "I *do* realize and I do want to help. I don't mean to be difficult, but treason is such a—such a *terrible* thing, isn't it?"

"It used to be when Gen. Rider and I were growing up," Gen. McCune said, a sudden bitterness in his voice. "Nowadays I'm not so sure. So, captain: your opinion, please?"

"Well, sir," she said, "if I had to make a choice—"

"Make it, Elizabeth," Gen. Rider said.

"I think I'd—I'd have to choose . . . choose . . . Gary . . . I think."

"Why?" Gen. McCune inquired. "Give us your reasons, Elizabeth."

"I don't know," she said miserably. "That's what makes it so difficult. I don't want to say that about *anybody*, to begin with. And it's all hunch and supposition anyway. And—and—I just don't *know* why I say that about Gary, really. I can't put my finger on anything. I don't have proof of anything. I don't have any reason to be suspicious about—about anything." She paused as some vagrant memory or memories came to mind, memories she couldn't quite place, just then. The pause was noted but they said nothing. "But I just—" her honest eyes and guileless face were deeply troubled—"I just think if—such a thing were possible, then—then it might be Gary."

"Did Gary ever try to recruit you for anything?" Gen. McCune asked.

"Anything traitorous?"

He nodded.

"Oh, *no,* sir. Never!"

"Did he ever try to recruit you for anything else?" Gen. Rider asked gently. "Anything of a personal nature?"

"Oh, *no,* sir!" she exclaimed again; and promptly blushed a bright deep red and looked sad and utterly confused.

"Only in this room, Elizabeth," Gen. McCune reminded with equal gentleness. "It goes no further. In fact, colonel," he said, turning to the C.I.C. officer who had been listening silently so far, "would you mind stepping out of the room for a moment?"

"I'm not sure my duty permits it, sir," the colonel said earnestly. "I don't mean to be insubordinate, but—"

"I take full responsibility, colonel," Gen. McCune said with an air that brooked no denial. "Gen. Rider and I—and Capt. Hogan—will never tell anyone. You have our word. If you please."

"Yes, sir," the colonel said, doubtful and reluctant, but yielding. "With that pledge, sir."

After he had stepped out, Gen. McCune gave them an apologetic glance.

"I know I'm making that man violate his duty," he said, "but it's on my head and you're absolved of all responsibility."

"Who will ever know?" Gen. Rider inquired with a smile. "He won't ever tell anyone he retreated under fire—we won't ever tell anyone he did . . . Now, Elizabeth," he said with the almost feminine gentleness and intuitiveness that made him such an astute commander, "tell us about Gary. And again we remind you, only in this room. Our lips are sealed forever. Has he tried to be friendly with you—friendlier than just office-mates, I mean?"

For several moments she stared at him, eyes wide, unhappy and beginning to fill with tears. Finally she spoke in a near-whisper they had to lean forward to hear.

"Yes, sir, he—he has."

"A definite campaign to be friendly, you thought it was?" Gen. McCune asked in a manner equally gentle.

"Yes, sir," she said, looking completely miserable now. "I didn't think so at the time but I—I do now. And I suppose I fell for it." She gave them a woebegone look that made Gen. Rider lean forward and pat her on the shoulder. "I'm not—" she said, voice trembling, "I'm not a—a very happy person."

"Oh, dear," Gen. McCune said, not very happy himself at the areas of emotion this thing with Stump was pushing them into, but knowing it had to be pursued. He proceeded slowly but firmly to ask the inevitable question. "Did he ever persuade you to become intimate with him?"

"Yes, sir," she said finally in a whisper they could barely hear, weeping openly now. "Just—just once."

"Did he seem to you," Gen. McCune went on, hating himself for having to do it, but again knowing the query to be inevitable, "to conduct himself like a man on that occasion?"

The faintest smile, very wry, touched her lips for a moment.

"Oh, yes, sir. Fully."

"Score one for inscrutable Mother Nature," Gen. McCune said dryly to Gen. Rider.

"She's full of little tricks," Gen. Rider agreed. His voice, still gentle, became businesslike. "Now, Elizabeth, with all that in mind, looking back on it now, does it seem to you that his campaign of friendliness might have had some object in mind? That he might, indeed, have been trying to establish a foundation of trust that could in time lead to something that might be—well, traitorous?"

"I think now that it must have had some ulterior purpose," she said in the same bleak, utterly and pathetically honest manner as before. "No one could conceivably just want—*me.*"

"Oh, Elizabeth!" Gen. McCune said, deliberately impatient but also deliberately fatherly and encouraging. "That's a very foolish, stupid, untrue thing to say. It's also very unfair to yourself. You're an extremely intelligent, extremely nice and extremely wonderful girl, and someday before long some fellow with equal intelligence and equal character is going to come along and realize that."

"When?" she asked in a forlorn whisper. "It's too late."

"God *damn* it!" Zeecy exploded—something had to shake this girl out of her self-induced inferiority. "It is *not!* Stop defeating yourself! In the last analysis, you're the only one who can. . . . Now," he said, tone deliberately brisk, "if this *was* a deliberate campaign leading toward treason, why don't you think very, very hard for a moment about anything—*anything*—you can remember that might by the wildest stretch of the imagination indicate anything—*anything*—along that line. While you are," he said, getting up and going to the door, "I'll let the poor colonel return. He's probably dying of remorse and a stricken conscience out there. He let himself be intimidated into abandoning his post by the chairman of the JCS. He'll probably never get over it . . . The point here, colonel," he said when the C.I.C. officer, still looking disturbed and unhappy, had resumed his seat, "is that we have just asked Capt. Hogan to try to remember anything she possibly can about any conduct of Maj. Stump's that might appear to indicate in any way any disloyalty of thought or action toward the United States. Any words of his?" he asked, turning again to Hogan, who had had time to dry her eyes and become more composed. "Any actions of his? Any words or actions *about* him or *concerning* him from anyone else? Things that, in any area, didn't ring true?"

For several moments she obediently thought very hard while they sat back patiently and waited, watching her face intently. Again many thoughts marched their way transparently across it. Finally she spoke in a slow and deliberate fashion, obviously struggling to bring them together into some coherent whole.

"I'm trying to remember things in sequence as much as possible," she explained with an apologetic little smile, "so maybe they'll be of some help."

"Good girl," Gen. McCune said. "Take your time."

"Well," she said, "there was one funny episode quite a while ago that involved an officer's cap that belonged to Brod."

"Yes?" Gen. Rider said as he, Gen. McCune and the colonel all became abruptly very quiet. "Tell us about it."

"It was just that he lost it," she said. "In the office. And you don't lose things in the office, it's secured when we're not there, we even have our own special cleaning woman who comes in and she's thoroughly checked out and reliable. But Brod decided he was going to change his clothes in the office one night to go on to your quarters, sir, when you and Mrs. Rider gave that little cocktail party for us and the Proj Frio people. It was just for staff, you remember, and he was going to meet Mrs. Tolliver somewhere later, right after, with no time to go home and change into civvies. So he left his uniform hanging in the office. And next day he could find everything except his cap. It had disappeared."

"Did Gary come with the two of you to my house?" Gen. Rider asked.

"Yes," she said, "so I don't think it could have been—" She paused. "Wait a minute. We all started out of the door together and then Gary said—" her narration quickened—"Gary said he had forgotten something, and to go ahead, he'd be right along. He hit the code and went back in while Brod and I walked slowly along the corridor, waiting for him. In about three minutes, I'd say, he caught up with us and we all went along. But," she said, beginning to sound excited now, "he didn't start out originally with his briefcase but he had it when he came back out."

"Did either of you comment on that?" the colonel asked.

"No, sir, there was no reason. We all often take work home. But now that I think about it, it *does* seem odd that he would start out for a cocktail party without it and then go back and get it."

"Maybe he temporarily forgot that he wanted to do some work later, remembered as you went out the door and went back and got it," Gen. Rider suggested. "It happens."

"Yes, sir," she said. "Why don't you ask him?"

"We will, Elizabeth," Gen. Rider promised softly. "Oh, yes. You can be sure we will. Anything else?"

Again she frowned and looked thoughtful and delayed her answer for a few moments.

"One time," she said presently, "quite a bit later—in fact, only a few days ago, he was out of the office—I think you were all in the tank and had invited him to attend—"

"Right," Gen. McCune said. "The final paper for Op Frio."

"Yes, that was it," she said, again with a rising excitement. "That was it, because I remember now *two* things from that day."

"In order, please, Elizabeth," Gen. Rider said, and she smiled.

"Yes, sir . . . Well, first, while you were gone he got a call, which I took, from somebody—a man—who said he was from something called 'The Well-Favor'd Male' in Georgetown. Is there such a store, sir?"

"I don't know," the colonel said, "but we're sure going to find out."

"Good," she said, with a smile for him that transformed her plain and earnest face momentarily into something, Zeecy thought, quite a bit more human. "It sounds rather phony to me, now that I think about it. I mean, we all know Georgetown, but even for Georgetown 'The Well-Favor'd Male' sounds a bit too—too *much,* if you know what I mean."

"I think we do," Gen. McCune said with a smile. "And what was the message?"

"That Gary's suit was ready and he should pick it up at the usual time and place."

"We make progress," Gen. McCune observed, feeling a rising excitement himself. "And what did he say when you told him?"

"That he had purchased the suit there a while ago and they had been slow about it, so he was relieved to hear from them and he would pick it up and take me out to dinner in it sometime soon so he could show it to me."

"You may never see it, Elizabeth," Gen. McCune warned humorously and she responded in kind.

"I think I can survive without it, sir."

"Good. And what was the second thing that day?"

"Well, you recall, Gen. Rider, that the two of you brought your copy of the Op Frio plan back to the office and you told him to run off some copies for us?"

"That's right."

"So next day he gave them to us. But there was something funny about it—something that struck me for just a moment as a little odd, but I dismissed it and never even thought about it until just now when you asked me to try to remember things. I can see now what bothered me. It was the way he handed out the copies."

"Which was?" Gen. Rider asked.

"Well," she said, reconstructing the scene in her mind, "he got up from his desk and came over to Brod first, which was a little different, because while we're very informal in the office, as you know, sir, usually when it's something really important I get my copy first, as captain, and then Brod gets his, as lieutenant. Even when it isn't important enough for rank, Gary usually gives it to me first just because I'm a woman, I guess." She smiled for a second, then looked sad. "He's always so polite, Gary. He does everything so *right*."

"Yes," Gen. McCune said. "So he went to Brod first?"

"Yes, but he didn't *hand* him the copy, exactly. He held out the two copies, but I think now—yes," she said slowly as they became tensely quiet again—"I think when he handed Brod *his* copy, it was resting on top of mine and I don't believe—I *don't* believe—that Gary ever touched it. As I see it now—" her eyes narrowed and it was obvious she *was* seeing it—"his fingers were touching the edges of my copy underneath but they never touched the copy he gave to Brod. So," she said, looking at Gen. McCune, who slowly nodded, "the only finger-prints that ever appeared upon it would be Brod's, not Gary's. Is that a help to you, sir?"

"That, Elizabeth," Gen. McCune said with gratitude, "is an enormous help. I can't begin to tell you how much, though I think Gen. Rider, as he promised earlier, will tell you quite soon."

She looked pleased.

"And there's one more thing, sir, that I remember now. When Brod was—apprehended—at the hearing and the two officers from C.I.C. came up to us, for just a second Gary turned terribly pale and—I don't want to be overly dramatic about this, but this is how it seemed to me—it seemed to me he actually swayed a little. It was as though he had received a frightful shock for a second—as though he thought they were coming to get *him.*"

She paused and thought hard for a moment.

"That's about it, I guess. I'm sorry I can't remember more, sir."

Gen. McCune smiled.

"That's enough for our purposes, I think, captain. Quite enough. You have our heartfelt thanks, fervent gratitude and undying affection." He made a grand gesture, smile increasing. "Anything Capt. Elizabeth Hogan wants from now on in this building, she gets!"

"Better watch out, general!" she said with a sudden giddy relief and a lightness quite uncharacteristic. "I might want the moon!"

"The JCS," Zeecy told her jovially, "will approve it tomorrow morning. I think, gentlemen, unless you have further questions—"

They shook their heads.

"Thanks very much, Elizabeth," Gen. Rider said. "You can go back to the office now. I'm sure Gary will be curious about where you've been, but not a word of course, now or ever, to him or anyone. You may have to testify later, you know. I hope the thought doesn't bother you too much."

"Oh, no, sir," she said quietly. "If I can be of help, I really see no reason why I shouldn't be. In fact, I suppose in my heart—" for just a second she looked very sad again, but swiftly recovered—"in my heart, I always really knew there never *was* any reason why I shouldn't be."

"Thanks very much, captain," Gen. McCune said, deliberately breaking the mood. "You serve your country well." He suddenly beamed, very fatherly and encouraging as he could be with subordinates, who were invariably overwhelmed. "Be of good cheer! All is not lost!"

"No, sir," she said with a shaky little laugh, but sounding stronger as she saluted and went out. "I hope not!"

"Christ!" Zeecy said as the door closed behind her. *"Life* . . . Well, gentlemen, I guess the next step on the road before we turn it all over to the F.B.I. is a talk with our boy, right?"

"Yes," Al Rider said. "And I don't think I'd better call him on the phone. I'd better go get him and escort him down here in person."

"I'll go with you, sir," the colonel offered but Gen. Rider shook his head.

"No, I'll get him. He won't try anything funny with me. And perhaps he deserves to be escorted by a general." His expression, also, became sad for a moment. "After all, he *is* a good officer. And I'm the one who trusted him. So maybe the honors should be done by me."

In the "Cumulative Assessments Group" office on third floor, B Ring, Maj. Gary Stump, USA, fiddled nervously with the papers on his desk. He was alone in the executive section of the office. Brod was in custody, he didn't know where. Big G and Hogan were out, the general having departed casually an hour ago, Hogan having followed with equal casualness ten minutes after.

Some instinct had prompted Gary to get up and follow her at a discreet distance down the hall. She turned the corner. He paused and gave it a beat. Then he stepped swiftly forward and looked around the corner. Down the corridor, heading off together with a purposeful air, went Big G and Hogan, in the direction of E Ring.

He had returned to his desk feeling profoundly disturbed. His mood had to do with their stealthy, evidently prearranged departure together. And with the sad, all-pervasive melancholy that dulled the day and crippled all his thoughts, brought on by the abrupt defection of his newfound friend.

He was sure his friend would never betray him or do anything to harm him —or help him, either. He couldn't without implicating himself. He was not worried on that score. He was just sad—sad—sad, a dungeon-deep, thought-destroying devastation of heart and mind that he had not experienced (though he had occasionally given others the experience) for a good decade or more. Such things just didn't happen to Gary Stump. Gary Stump, who had thought himself long since invulnerable, just didn't put himself in a position where such things *could* happen to him.

But this time he had.

He had tried four times, very carefully but of course very foolishly, to telephone his friend in his office on the other side of the building. Each time the call had been refused. Each time he had tried again with diminishing hopes.

Now he had no more hope left. It was over and all he could do was grieve inside.

When Hogan returned alone he could sense that she was doing her best to appear matter-of-fact and everyday, but he knew she wasn't. There was an undercurrent of tension, and yet a curious satisfaction, which he sensed, with his great intuitive perception, at once.

He asked where she had been.

She said she had been on some final errand to now-defunct Proj Frio.

He managed to laugh and say quite naturally that he didn't believe her.

She managed to laugh quite naturally and respond that he'd better, because that was all she was going to tell him.

He was debating whether to keep prying for the rest of the day, confident he could break down her stupid and innocent heart if given sufficient time, when the door opened and Big G appeared.

"Gary," he said, in a tone that made Gary's heart jump, "can you come along with me for a few minutes? Gen. McCune wants to talk to you about the Tolliver situation."

"Certainly, sir," Gary said, standing up smartly, straightening his uniform, straightening his back, looking bright, willing and eager as always. "Anything I can do to help."

"Good," Al Rider said, standing back and gesturing him to go through the door first. "Please—"

Upright, able, efficient—highly intelligent, sleek and competent—Maj. Gary Stump accepted his unusual courtesy and stepped out smartly ahead.

After all, he *was* a good officer. Everybody knew, and respected, that.

At about the time Gary was entering the office of the chairman of the JCS, to be greeted with a casual informality that didn't fool him for one minute by Gen. McCune and some colonel he didn't know but whose insignia identified him immediately and brought a rising and barely controllable terror, the Assistant Secretary of Defense for Acquisition and Logistics and the former co-manager of the late Project Frio were arriving at Maison Blanche for lunch.

All about them they saw the same familiar faces and experienced the same sense of *déjà vu* that many of Washington's more prominent denizens feel whenever they enter those fabled and ubiquitous portals on a weekday noon.

Here at one table were Shorty Murchison, the inspector general, OSD, and Roger Venable, vice president (defense affairs) of General Growth Group. Here at another were Walker Stayman, vice president (defense affairs) of Strategic Industries and Tiny Wombaugh, Under Secretary of Defense for Research and Engineering. At still another were Hank Milhaus, Assistant Secretary of Defense for Information and Red Roberts of *The Wall Street Journal*. And at still another as luck and coincidence—which is not so coincidental in Washington in surroundings beloved of those either On the Make or In the Group—would have it, the editor of *Defense Eye* and her principal, and only, right-hand man, that demon reporter and exposer of all things evil in the Pentagon, Herb Horowitz.

It was just like old times, Delight remarked dryly to Herb, except that now that perfect bitch, Helen Clark, had apparently decided to go public with her little affair with Gen. Ahmanson. Delight had known about it for *weeks* and had taunted Herbie repeatedly for not being aware of it until she told him. He retorted once again that he did not consider sex gossip to be his principal interest in the Pentagon. She told him once again that it was the key to many things. He snorted and said, "Oh, for Christ's sake, Delight!" She told him he would know a lot more about the Pentagon and Washington, both, if he would just keep an eye on who was hopping into bed with whom. He retorted that it *wasn't* his main interest, his main interest was in exposing all the corrupt bastards, military and civilian, who were crawling through the building like roaches. She said it all went together. He retreated, as so often, into silence in the face of her positive and emphatic certainty.

As for Secretary Clark and Military Harry, they had decided to come here as some sort of psychological reassurance that their world was still a steady and stable thing, still in place despite Loy Buck's unhappy news for Helen and the

President's ruthless undercutting of their seven months of work on Project Frio.

When Harry had arrived at her apartment post-haste last night, he had already been much disturbed and upset. When he found her so uncharacteristically in tears, his own emotional turmoil had been greatly increased. She had almost literally flung herself into his arms, sobbing, "How could he? How *could* he?"

At first he had thought this referred to the President's action, as indeed it did, in part. When she had calmed down enough to talk coherently he found out that it also applied to something else. When she concluded her recital of what it was, he had given her a look of profound sadness and sympathy, taken her in his arms again quite simply and firmly, and held her tight. And presently she had quieted down again.

"Now the question is," he said finally, "what are *you* going to do . . . and what do you think *we* ought to do?"

"I'm going to do what the Secretary asked me to do," she said in a voice that shook a little but had regained some of its customary decisiveness. "I'm to call and pass on the order . . . and urge," she added with a lingering sob, "that it be accepted just as he wants it . . . and be acted upon . . . immediately."

"It won't be easy," he said, and for a moment she threatened to break down again. But steadied.

"No, it won't. It will be one of the hardest things—perhaps the hardest— that I have ever done. But the Secretary asked me to, and I owe it to him, and" —again her voice quavered but recovered—"to *him*. But, oh, Harry! It is *so* sad!"

"Yes," he said gravely. "But perhaps it can all be handled without too much scandal—"

"With none," she said firmly. "With none, if he will only listen to me and do what's best for him."

"Yes," he said again. A wry half-smile crossed his face. "He isn't noted for that."

"No, but this time—*this time,*" she said fiercely, "he had damned well better do it right or it will be the end of him."

"I expect he knows that," he said. "Are you ready to call him now?"

She took a long, quivering breath, steadied herself and picked up the phone. "Yes," she said. "I am."

After she had concluded a short conversation that consisted largely of firm orders from her, stunned protest—denial—admittance—silence—on the other end, she hung up the phone with a visible shudder and again broke into tears. His iron woman, Harry Ahmanson thought with an odd mixture of love, pity and gratitude, wasn't so iron, after all. She was a very strong lady in a very tough spot; but she had revealed to him beyond any denying later that she was very human underneath. For that he was profoundly thankful. It made the future much simpler for both of them.

"Now," he said briskly when it became obvious that the storm—the last storm of the evening—had cleared, "what about us? Our steed has been shot from under us. Shall we go on riding through thin air, or—?"

"It isn't thin air," she objected, giving him the cool, appraising glance that showed she was herself again, clicking on all cylinders. "I have plenty of other things to do besides Project Frio—you still have your career to think about— I'm sure Loy isn't going to abandon either one of us—"

"I'm not worried about that," he said. "I mean what should *we* do? How do we show *our* integrity?" He dropped the bantering tone, became thoughtful. "I think it *is* directly involved, you know."

"What do you want to do?" she asked with the calm directness that made her so effective a businesswoman and public servant. "Resign?"

"Early retirement for me," he said, "resignation for you . . . . We've in effect been dismissed, we've in effect been told that we're no damned good, that we've been wasting public time and money 'which the President,'" he mimicked in a suddenly savage voice, "'is always desirous of saving in the Pentagon.' So why hang around?"

"I can see it that way," she said slowly. "I could do that without regrets and go back to business. But you'd be sacrificing a lifetime career and a good chance of going on up the ladder. What would you do?"

He gave her a long, careful look of his own. Then he smiled.

"Marry you and become third vice president in charge of paper clips."

She laughed aloud, the first happy sound of the evening.

"If that's a proposal, it's the damnedest *I* ever heard."

"Well, it is," he said, laughing too. "So, Madame Secretary, make the most of it."

She gave him another long, appraising look, cool now, calm and alabaster-beautiful.

"Your desk may have to be out by the watercooler," she said with a sudden chuckle.

"And that," he said, taking her again into his arms, "is the damnedest acceptance."

So today they were at Maison Blanche, celebrating that and also "showing them," as she had said last night when he finally left around 2 A.M., "that we do things in style."

Few would have suspected, as they finished a light lunch and started out, that they were concealing both such happiness and such hurt over what they regarded as their public rejection—to which, they had finally determined after several hours of discussion, they were going to make such public and final response.

"Helen really is a stunner, isn't she?" Shorty Murchison said to Roger Venable, who nodded admiringly and agreed.

"They look happy together," Walker Stayman observed to Tiny Wombaugh, who also agreed. "I wonder if they're going to make it legal one of these days?"

"Have you talked to them since the President pulled the rug out from under Project Frio?" Hank Milhaus asked Red Roberts. "There ought to be quite a story there."

"There is," Red said, hastily throwing down his napkin and rising. "Pay the bill and I'll settle with you later. I can't let *those* two scoop me."

And he hurried out after Delight and Herb, who already had the secretary and the general cornered in the entryway.

"Secretary Clark," Delight said in a naggingly insistent tone, "are you going to take this crap from the President about Project Frio?"

Helen turned and looked her over at length from head to toe. Then she smiled the faintest of smiles, deliberately patronizing in a way she knew would infuriate.

"No," she said calmly as Red arrived and received a pleasant nod of recognition. "I'm going to resign."

For a moment there was stunned silence. Then Red turned to Harry Ahmanson.

"And you, general?"

"My request for early retirement," Harry said as calmly as Helen, "reached the chief of staff this morning."

"Wo*wee!*" Delight exclaimed. "You two don't fool around, do you?"

"Did you want us to?" Harry inquired.

"Hell!" Delight said with a grin. "Where would be the story in that?"

Her expression changed suddenly, became intent. She gave them a dramatically piercing look as Hank Milhaus joined them.

"Was there any other reason for the President to terminate your project? Was he dissatisfied with the way you were running it? Did he think there was anything funny going on? Were there any shady financial shenanigans involved? Was he upset about the influence of S.I. and Three Gs?"

Again there was silence as both Helen and Harry Ahmanson stared at her in disbelief. It was Red Roberts who replied.

"Delight," he said angrily, "for Christ's sake, what a hell of a line of questioning! How do you answer unfairness like that? Suppose they dignify you by answering, what happens? They deny, well, THEY DENY. And automatically nobody believes them. Why don't you ask the President those questions and stop this cheap-shot journalism for a change?"

"Oh, I will," Delight said calmly, "at his next press conference. Meanwhile, Hank, I think you ought to put *these two*—" Helen Clark for once lost her composure and looked furious—"on the podium in the press conference room and let everybody find out what their answers are. We aren't finding out right here."

"Well—" Hank Milhaus began, and hesitated.

"I will under no circumstances subject myself to this kind of guttersnipe journalism," Helen said. "Nor," she added calmly, "to this guttersnipe. Nor will the general."

"You'll be sorry!" Delight cried, voice rising angrily as other departing lunchers squeezed by trying not to be too obvious about their eavesdropping. "You always think you're so damned pure! You're always so pretty and perfect! You'll be sorry!"

"Come on, Harry," the secretary said, taking his arm and urging him out the door. "We've had enough of this, I think."

"Put them on!" Delight shouted at Hank Milhaus as the maître d', the manager and assorted waiters rushed up. "Put them on and let's *see* how perfect they are!"

"Delight," Hank said firmly, having done some fast thinking in the midst of the hullabaloo, "calm down. I won't put them on, you heard the lady, they won't come. But I think I can give you someone else."

"Better be damned good!" Delight growled as Herb grabbed her arm and pulled her away and Red Roberts stood staring after them with an expression of angry distaste. "That's all I can say!"

"Press conference in forty-five minutes," Hank said tersely. "Be there!"

Forty-five minutes to the second the room was filled to overflowing with Pentagon regulars and other correspondents who had hurried across the river from all over town. The television cameras were in place, the lights were on. The usual bank of microphones besieged the lectern. There was a sudden hush of excitement and craning, a few bewildered, "Who is its?" and a few knowing murmurs of recognition.

Into the glare of the lights, shuffling slowly along, blinking and peering and looking thoroughly confused by it all, came the last survivor of Project Frio.

"Thank you, ladies and gentlemen," Harry Josephs said in his mild, pokey little voice. "I don't know exactly why you want to see me, but Secretary Milhaus asked me and here I am. Oh," he added, an obvious afterthought just as Delight began a question, "I think I should tell you that now that Project Frio has been terminated, I am returning to my regular position in the inspector general's office, OSD."

"*You* aren't resigning, then," Delight said in a triumphant tone, and Harry Josephs looked quite bewildered.

"No," he said, blinking and shaking his head in puzzlement. "Why should I?"

"Secretary Clark and Gen. Ahmanson apparently are," she said. "Doesn't that suggest something to you?"

He blinked.

"Should it?"

"It doesn't suggest to you that they may have felt they should get out before anything suspicious came to light concerning their handling of Project Frio?"

For the third time Civilian Harry looked baffled, and blinked.

"Heavens, no!" he said. "Why on earth would anyone want to think that?"

"Because it looks very suspicious!" Delight snapped. "That's why!"

"Not to me," Harry Josephs said firmly. "Oh, dear, no, not to me. What do you mean, Miss—Miss—?"

"Jones," she said tartly. "Remember that, Mr. Josephs, Delight Jones. Of *Defense Eye,* a publication that doesn't believe in letting public servants in the Pentagon get away with *anything.*"

"Is it your contention," Harry Josephs inquired, seeming to focus upon her fully for the first time, "that Secretary Clark and Gen. Ahmanson have been trying to 'get away' with something? Because if it is," he said with sudden indignation, "I can tell you that I have rarely known such fine public servants in all my years in the Pentagon. And those began," he added with what was, for him, considerable sarcasm, "long before you were in the process of becoming a burden to your family, young woman."

There was a hoot of laughter from Red Roberts, echoed across the room. Delight glared.

"I am not here," she announced grandly, "to participate in any damned cover-up!"

"And I am not here," Harry Josephs said with surprising asperity, "to engage in any kind of character assassination. So I guess that makes us even. Now if somebody has a decent question to ask, I'll be glad to answer it. Otherwise I must get back to my duties in the I.G.'s office, where we spend our time finding more *real* wrongdoing in the Pentagon and among its contractors than people like you could ever dig up in a million years!"

Again Red Roberts led the laughter. When it had subsided with Delight still glaring furiously at Harry Josephs, who blinked calmly back quite unperturbed, he asked a polite concluding question.

"Mr. Josephs," he said, "as a representative of the I.G. and as former co-manager of Project Frio, have you ever discovered or heard of any wrongdoing, financial or otherwise, in the project? Or any malfeasance, maladministration or other wrongdoing on the part of either Secretary Clark or Gen. Ahmanson?"

"Never," Civilian Harry said calmly. "Never. . . . I can suggest a dozen other projects, Mr. Roberts," he added politely as laughter rose again, "into which you might look for things like that, and with some success. But not Project Frio."

"Give me a list," Red said. "I'll go after 'em."

"Come see me in my office," Harry Josephs responded with his first smile of the session. "I'll be happy to give you some ideas."

"It's a date," Delight said before Red could respond.

Harry Josephs gave her what was, for him, a positive glare.

"I wasn't inviting you, young woman," he said with a sniff. "I was inviting Mr. Roberts."

And with a last blink into the lights and cameras he turned and plodded off the podium and out of the room, to disappear once again into the labyrinths of the building from which he had come seven months ago to help with Project Frio.

"I assume that's all for today," Hank Milhaus said. "If so, I have a brief announcement to make. Secretary Clark and Gen. Ahmanson have asked me to announce that they are engaged and will be married in California some time in the next two weeks."

Delight snorted.

"How *sweet.*"

"Yes, isn't it!" Red retorted. "It's nice to have something happy happen around here once in a while in spite of you, friend."

"You're so damned sweetness and light about this place that I can't stand it!" she snapped as the conference broke up and they all straggled out.

"I try to keep a balance, Delight," he said, unmoved. "I recommend it to you and to some of our pals, here. It isn't easy but it has its rewards. The main ones being a sense of fairness and the boon of being able to live with oneself."

"Pollyanna!" she jeered. "Pollyanna!"

But though she had the last word she didn't look too happy about it.

Red smiled and went back to the pressroom.

He would let no grass grow under his feet with Harry Josephs. He would call him tomorrow and make an appointment.

And there was still Frio, of course. The Project might be gone but the Operation lingered on.

As an old Washington hand, he didn't think "lingered" was too pejorative a word to use.

In the office of the chairman of the JCS Gary was sitting on the edge of his chair, tense and white and shaking uncontrollably inside. They hadn't broken him down yet. But politely, patiently, inexorably and surely, they were getting there.

In his office, cluttered like all top Pentagon offices with many mementos of brave men and famous battles, Gary's friend sat aimlessly at his desk, staring out the window, eyes unseeing, thoughts whirling.

He knew what was happening to Gary. He did feel some genuine sorrow. But he was powerless to help.

He had no fears that Gary would implicate him when the questioning got to Gary's private life; he couldn't without implicating himself.

Gary's friend knew what he must do.

He had no choice.

Presently he called Loy Buck to tell him about it. The Secretary heard him out without interruption.

"I think you had better let me set the timing," was his only comment.

"Yes, sir," Gary's friend said.

"And in the meantime," the Secretary said in a voice level and without expression, "nothing, you understand me? *Nothing.*"

"Yes, *sir,*" Gary's friend said, chastened and humbled and really scared at last. "Not a thing."

After the Secretary hung up without further word, Gary's friend paused and considered this.

A small, reviving smile animated the carefree eyes and boyish face that had so smitten Maj. Gary Stump.

At least not in Washington.

5 "Now, Aleks," the President said, "I think it's about time I talked to that fellow, don't you?"

"Yes, sir," Al Brodovsky agreed. "I'll put it through."

While he was doing so, activating the "hot line," the small complex of computers, coders, teletypes and other electronic gear across the river in the Pentagon, the President thought about the opponent he must now address directly for—what was it, the twentieth, thirtieth, fortieth?—time.

The General Secretary was not a pleasant man and the President did not like him, in spite of his carefully cultivated public relations image for the bemusement and befuddlement of the great gullibles of the West. He smiled, he joked, he pressed the flesh and slapped the back, he campaigned for western public opinion with all the skill of the President himself. His wife tried to dress stylishly, smiled, smirked, laughed and liked fine clothes and fine jewelry—likings that were never photographed or shown on television back home to the 270 millions of barely subsisting socialist helots who would never know the rich and hypocritical privileges of the *Nomenklatura*.

They were a pair of pistols all right, the President often remarked. And they were clever enough so that some—too many—in America and the West managed to forget all about the pile of bloody corpses and bloody nations across which the General Secretary had clawed his way to power and over which he now presided.

But the President couldn't forget: he was elected not to forget, though many of his most famous and most vocal countrymen desperately wanted him to forget—as they themselves had either truly forgotten, or had deliberately forced themselves to forget.

The President was required to remember; and he also remembered that "that clown in the Kremlin" as he sometimes referred to him with a seeming amicability and a deep underlying revulsion—or, "that gangster from Georgia," in more heated moments—sat at the controls of a military machine so vast and overreaching that the President's own in many categories paled beside it.

It was not that he didn't possess sufficient power to blow the General Secretary's country to smithereens a thousand times over, the President often thought: but what the hell good would that do? The United States—the whole world—would also be destroyed in the process. War would profit nobody anything. But the threat of war . . . that was a different matter. That was blackmail on the greatest scale in history. And there, the President knew, the General Secretary had the advantages—of complete ruthlessness, complete amorality, complete treachery and bad faith . . . complete evil.

The word had been used by one of the President's predecessors and a great howling had arisen in America from those who had most to lose should the General Secretary's system ever triumph. In the face of it, his predecessor had backed down to some degree, in the necessities of appeasing his own most vocal countrymen and in the interests of getting along, with some degree of outward civility, with the General Secretary. The present President didn't use the word himself, but he believed it. And he knew it gave his adversary an edge that still might tip the balance of world history away from the erratic but noble light into which it was always striving to climb and falling back, and send it permanently into darkness and the final death of the human spirit and the human mind.

So: now he had to talk to the oily bastard once again—this individual to whom many of his gullible countrymen applied the soporific that soothed them so much—"just like us." He wasn't "just like us" and the President knew it. He was a vicious, deceitful, arrogant, ruthless—

But, what the hell.

The President had to talk to him again about Nanukuvu.

There was no way to avoid it now.

The national security adviser popped in the door, pointed to the special phone, dropped into an armchair across the desk and lifted his monitor phone. In the Pentagon machinery began to hum, tapes to turn, other official eavesdroppers to listen in.

"Mr. Secretary," the President said with a reasonable cordiality, "it is good to talk to you again."

"Also," the General Secretary said in the stilted but quite adequate English he had carefully learned; and, as always, with the lurking note of suppressed amusement the President knew he deliberately adopted to annoy. "It has been some time. Seven months, to be exact."

"Yes," the President said, more coldly. "Seven months. We do not like what has happened in seven months, Mr. Secretary."

"Many, many things have happened," the General Secretary noted blandly. "What is it that disturbs you, Mr. President?"

"The same," the President said. "It hasn't changed much, Mr. Secretary. Except as it's become worse."

"But *what?*" the General Secretary asked, professing a mild impatience. "That is what you must tell me, Mr. President. I am only an ignorant boy from Georgia—"

"Stop bein' so disingenuous!" the President said. "Talk honestly, if—" he almost said, "if you can," but thought better of it—"if we're to get anywhere with this talk today."

"And why must we 'get anywhere' with it?" the General Secretary inquired with innocent interest. "Everything seems good, to us."

"Nanukuvu is not good," the President said firmly, "and there's no use my pretendin' to you that it is. Nanukuvu is an increasingly disturbin', increasingly threatenin', increasingly inexcusable intrusion of Soviet power into the South Pacific. We want it stopped, Mr. Secretary."

"But why, Mr. President?" the General Secretary demanded with sudden indignation. "Why? Do you not have many military bases of your own in that area? We know there are several candidly displayed to the world, Guam, Palau, others; the base you managed to retain, the one *not* displayed, on that hidden island in the Philippines when the inevitable triumph of world socialism came to that country. And there are still more *not* displayed that we know about, Mr. President. Oh, yes, we have satellites and overflights and plain old-fashioned spies too, you know. We are aware of where you are. But we are not all the time demanding that *you* withdraw, Mr. President. Why, then, do you always complain at us?"

"This is the second call in seven months," the President said tartly. "Stop bein' dramatic, Mr. Secretary. We have let you proceed over there without much interference because we thought at first your intentions might be peaceable. But now—"

"You 'let' us proceed!" the General Secretary cried scornfully. "We *proceeded.* You could not stop us! You *let* us because your military were so slow in getting themselves organized that you could not possibly have done anything but *let* us, Mr. President! That is the straight of it!"

"We are generally a peaceful people," the President said, not letting his own indignation get out of hand just yet, "and we have hoped that we might be able to persuade you to either withdraw from the island or at least minimize its warlike aspects. We find now that this has not happened."

"You knew it from the first," the General Secretary said with a scathing bluntness. *"You knew it from the first!* Why did you call me seven months ago if you did not know it?" His voice became cold and emphatic. "This is a futile exercise, Mr. President. We are there: we will remain. Why should we not? You use harsh words to me. 'Increasingly disturbing. Increasingly theatening. Increasingly inexcusable. Warlike aspects.' Why do you use these words, Mr. President? Have we threatened anyone? Have we been warlike? Why are you disturbed? Why are we inexcusable? We have done nothing to anyone, Mr. President! And," he concluded triumphantly, "you can not prove that we have, because we have not. So, what is the purpose of this conversation? It distracts me from my duties. *That* is disturbing and inexcusable."

The President thought: *why, you son of a bitch.* But of course, though the General Secretary and Presidents had become increasingly blunt with one another in recent years, there were still some fragile limits. He allowed a long moment to pass before he replied. When he did it was in a firm and unyielding but civilized tone.

"Mr. Secretary," he said, "the United States regards your installations on the island of Nanukuvu as being a potential threat to the entire Pacific region today and very likely a *real* threat in the near future. We do not want to have an open confrontation with you about it—" the General Secretary snorted but the President ignored it—"but we must insist that those installations be held to their present level—"

"Ah!" the General Secretary said. "Ah, ha! Not 'withdrawn,' then. Not 're-moved,' then. Just 'held to their present level'! Quite a change, Mr. President. Quite a substantial change! The 'present level,' " he noted in a boastful tone, "is not a minimal level, Mr. President. It is quite sufficient!"

"For what?"

"To maintain peace in the Pacific and South Pacific region," the General Secretary said promptly, "against the growing threat of U.S. imperialist aggres-sion."

"How the hell do you get that one?" the President demanded with genuine anger. "Of all the twisted, vicious crap—"

"You have bases," the General Secretary interrupted. "Many bases. Some open. Some secret. You maintain major forces there. You seek all the time to use your influence there. You seek all the time to *expand* your influence there. You have designs. You make plans. You intend conquests."

"That is not true!" the President exclaimed.

"Perhaps not," the General Secretary said with supremely arrogant smug-ness, "but if we say so, everyone will believe it."

For several seconds the President was too angry to respond without saying something he might regret.

"So, Mr. President," the General Secretary inquired politely, "may I go now, and get back to matters which are really valid and important?"

"You may go now," the President told him, voice still charged with anger, "but I warn you, Mr. Secretary, if you continue to build up your installations on Nanukuvu there will be a most grave situation with the United States."

"If it has not happened by this time," the General Secretary remarked in the same smug, supremely confident way, "it will not happen. Goodbye, Mr. Presi-dent."

"Goodbye!" the President snapped. "And beware."

But the General Secretary made no reply, only uttering a loud and mocking chortle as he went off the line.

The President stared across the desk at Al Brodovsky, who was shaking his head with a worried air.

"That son of a bitch," the President said, *"That son of a bitch!* He isn't going to yield an inch on anything."

"And are we, Mr. President?" the national security adviser inquired soberly. "Are we?"

Again for several seconds the President was still, staring at him with a straight, unblinking gaze. Finally he pursed his lips in a determined line.

"Give me space, Al," he ordered. "I want to think."

"Yes, sir," Al Brodovsky said, "I'll tell the secretaries to hold all the calls. I'll be in my office."

After he left, the President sat for some time staring out into the rose garden, reviewing the conversation, reviewing his options, reviewing his situation.

None of the three was satisfactory, he told himself ruefully.

The conversation had apparently only heightened Soviet intransigence.

His options seemed even less than before.

And his situation, with an election coming next year and the tide of national and world protest rising against Nanukuvu, was not exactly conducive to a clear view of how best to go about being returned to office as triumphantly and decisively as his present still-high popularity would seem to guarantee.

Still high, he reflected, despite Nanukuvu. But that was because he had not been too closely identified with the Pentagon's campaign against it. Now he was being forced to, and he didn't like that. His jettisoning of Project Frio had brought him much applause from right-thinking folk and those major segments of the media that originated their ideas, controlled their thinking and verbalized their fears. But the basic problem still remained.

The General Secretary was in the process of doing what traditional American diplomacy had always said one must not do to the Soviets.

Don't be too harsh, the State Department had always cautioned. Don't be too intransigent. Don't force them into a corner without an avenue of escape. Give them an out.

Or—*boom!*

But that wasn't stopping the General Secretary from doing all of those things to the United States. He had power and no scruples about using it.

And no damned electorate, the President thought with an angry sigh, breathing down his neck while he did it.

So, what to do?

He sat for almost another hour brooding alone. He still had not reached a really firm conclusion when a call was put through from Al Brodovsky.

The national security adviser was quite upset.

What he told the President upset him, too.

But perhaps it wasn't all that bad, he told himself after a moment's reflection.

Perhaps the General Secretary had solved his dilemma for him, after all.

SOVIETS ASK SECURITY COUNCIL MEETING. CITE U.S. THREAT TO "PEACEFUL SOVIET IMPROVEMENT OF UNINHABITED ISLAND OF NANUKUVU." DEMAND U.N. "COMDEMN AND PUNISH U.S. IMPERIALIST AGGRESSION IN PACIFIC."

Those were the arguments, and when they were presented to the Security Council next day by the Soviet ambassador to the U.N., they were stated with great dramatic flair and much powerful righteous indignation.

Nobody, the President remarked dryly to Al Brodovsky, Terry Venner and Loy Buck as they watched the debate together on television in the Oval Office, could be more damned self-righteous than the Soviet Union when it was accusing someone else of intending to do exactly what it was intending to do.

"They've had a lot of practice," the Secretary of Defense remarked dryly. "They've been at it for seventy years."

"But sometimes," the Secretary of State began in a response that had also been much practiced in his department for most of those years, "don't you think they have some justifi—"

"No," the President interrupted flatly. "I do not. Do you?"

"Well," Terry Venner said, his enthusiasm for the diplomatic approach for once dampened a bit by the Chief Executive's uncompromising tone, "I think perhaps it could be argued that— . . ."

His voice trailed away at the President's expression.

"Not by me," the President said. "And not by the ambassador of the United States." His tone sharpened. "You haven't countermanded my orders that she fight this thing with everything she's got, have you?"

"Certainly not, Mr. President!" Terry said, shocked and offended. "Certainly not! You know I would never do such a thing! How could I?"

"I don't know, Ike," the President said, relaxing into one of his favorite poses, the sleepy-somnolent one. "But I just thought you might be tryin' to sneak somethin' through there, behind my back."

"I would never do such a thing!" the Secretary of State said stiffly. "You are the President and I am simply your servant. Certainly *not!*"

"O.K., Terry," the President said with a chuckle. "Relax. I know you wouldn't, I'm just havin' a little fun to brighten up this gloomy day." He turned back to the set. "Listen to that smarmy bastard carry on!"

And indeed the Soviet ambassador was carrying on, shifting from oozing righteousness to fierce denunciation to flamboyant indignation to pious nobility to stern demands for crushing retribution against the sinister, deceitful, imperialistic, aggressive United States—"the whole bag of tricks," as Al Brodovsky remarked with an exasperated laugh when the ambassador—one of the middle-aged bright young men with whom the General Secretary had packed the Politburo after his accession to power—concluded with a last ringing blast against "corrupt, evil, imperialistic circles in the United States that are using the pretext of protesting peaceful Soviet improvement of the uninhabited island of Nanukuvu as a screen for their own well-advanced aggressive intentions in the whole Pacific area. *This should be punished!"*

All lies, the ambassador of the United States retorted, patiently reviewing once again Hague Smith's unhappy sortie over the island, the undocumented but certainly clearly evident slaughter of its innocent inhabitants, the immediate steady development of Soviet installations: the atomic subs, the missile defenses, the two airstrips being hurried toward completion, the complement of two thousand men now stationed on the island.

"The Soviet resolution," she concluded—and of course there was one, encapsulating all the arguments the Soviet ambassador had shouted at such vehement length—"is a clear attempt to conceal the Soviet government's own intention to commit aggression in the area—perhaps not immediate armed aggression, Mr. President, but certainly its intention to attempt nuclear blackmail of many innocent nations just as soon as its unprovoked, unjustified and inexcusable militarization of the island of Nanukuvu is complete.

"We call upon our co-signers of the Declaration of the Pacific, and upon all members of the United Nations who rightly fear and greatly abhor the steadily encroaching aggressive imperialism of the Soviet Union, to join us in voting against this resolution both here and in the General Assembly. For our part, we shall of course veto it here as we assume some of our Security Council colleagues will also do."

Three more hours of debate were held, consisting principally of further angry Soviet denunciations—further acrid U.S. rebuttals—equally strong attacks on the Soviet Union by Britain, always supportive—China, always happy to fish in troubled U.S.-Soviet waters—and cautious but unwavering support for the U.S. position from the two signers of the Declaration of the Pacific who occupied temporary seats on the Council, the Marshalls and Vanuatu.

The Soviet resolution was then put to a vote and defeated 9–3, with permanent members Britain, China and the United States all casting their vetoes. France, equivocal as always, abstained.

"So much for that," the President said in a thoughtful tone that did not seem to his listeners to express quite the note of triumph and relief that might logically have been expected. "Now let's have lunch. I've instructed Mary Margaret to demand a General Assembly meetin' this afternoon. No point in wastin' time."

They relaxed a bit, had a mild drink, white wine in most cases, lunched in leisurely fashion on the light meal sent up from the kitchen, and at 3 P.M. returned to their chairs and their fascinated perusal of the workings of the world's most uniquely fantastic gathering of the large and the small, the good and the bad, the idealistic and the corrupt, the worthwhile and the worthless, the constructive and the destructive, the able and the inept, statesmen and mountebanks, geniuses and fools. To say nothing of quite a few clowns, most of them "underdeveloped" in more ways than one, Al Brodovsky remarked, who enjoyed nothing so much as kicking the United States around.

This they could safely do because the United States was a tolerant country that obligingly suffered, and at substantial financial sacrifice obligingly supported, the antics of what a majority of its citizens, according to frequent polls, regarded as the world's most pointless exercise in futility.

Still, as Terry Venner said with a conviction that made the old cliché ring true for one more time, "as long as they're talking they aren't fighting"—ignoring, of course, a dozen bitter wars that ranged from the tragic streets of the Middle East to the sinister jungles of Vietnam-threatened Southeast Asia.

But still, they *were* talking.

God, were they *talking.*

Nobody could deny that.

The upshot, at about twenty minutes after five in the afternoon, was that the General Assembly voted 87–84 to defeat the Soviet resolution, all signers of the Declaration standing firm. Partly this was due to the eloquence of Mary Margaret, who had one of her most effective and persuasive moments as U.S. ambassador to the U.N. as she argued brilliantly against U.N. condemnation of the United States and for U.N. condemnation of the Soviet Union. This latter was not accomplished because, on orders of the President which she could not quite understand, nor could his companions in the Oval Office who listened to his last-minute telephone conversation with her, she was restrained from introducing a U.S. counter-resolution to that effect.

Obediently she fell silent. Three votes and three votes only confirmed the U.S. victory.

"Just like I've always said," the President observed with a satisfaction that seemed a little overdone in view of the narrowness of the vote. "Give 'em enough rope and they'll hang themselves."

"But they almost hung us," Loy Buck pointed out. "Three votes isn't exactly an overwhelming margin, Mr. President. They've managed to whip up a great deal of sentiment against us, as usual."

"And as usual, on specious grounds," Aleks Brodovsky noted.

"Oh, well," the President said with a curiously unconcerned air that again puzzled them, but they finally put it down to his frequent unpredictability, which they had found usually had some reasonable final rationale in his own mind.

"Oh, Loy," he called as they started out. "Why don't you and Zeecy come by tomorrow morning at nine? I'd like to discuss this whole thing with you again, now that we've got this U.N. crap out of the way."

"Yes, Mr. President," the Secretary of Defense agreed, outwardly surprised, inwardly alarmed, thinking: *Now* what the hell?

The Secretary of State was inwardly alarmed too, and a little miffed at not being included. But perhaps, he thought as they all said goodbye at the Southeast Portico and were limousined away into the cold October night, this might be a good sign.

It could mean the President wanted to put the Defense Department on the carpet.

If it meant that, Terry Venner decided he would cooperate quite happily by staying out of it, thank you very much.

Promptly at 9 A.M. they were ushered in again to the Oval Office. It felt a little lonely without Terry and Al Brodovsky or anybody else around.

Both Loy and Zeecy had their forebodings, which they had shared on their ride over from the Pentagon. The President's greeting did little to allay them.

He was entirely too hearty and relaxed.

To Zeecy, who had known him so long, this indicated that he had made up his mind to do something that he knew other people wouldn't like and was therefore attempting with his often quite formidable charm to seduce them into agreement before he had even told them what it was.

Gen. McCune thought he knew what it was.

The Secretary of Defense, who had not known him so long but had studied his elusive personality with considerable thoroughness, had no doubts.

Operation Frio was in deep, deep trouble—probably terminal, he thought bleakly as they were gestured cordially to chairs overlooking the rose garden and were plied with coffee and doughnuts.

If this were the case it would explain the President's curiously placid reaction to the General Assembly vote yesterday.

He hadn't really been upset at all.

In fact, he had been pleased.

It had given him an out.

"Loy and Zeecy," he said expansively, seating himself opposite where he could face them both with an open and candid gaze, "I really appreciate you fellows comin' over here again so soon. You must be gettin' awfully tired of this place and of my own borin' and all-too-familiar features."

"Not at all, Mr. President," Loy said with an easy air and a friendly smile, deciding to play the President's game with him for a while. "I always enjoy both. They make my day."

"Chuck," Zeecy said bluntly, having decided it was time to cut the crap and come to cases, "what's this all about? Are you getting ready to scuttle us?"

For a moment the President's air of good cheer noticeably dimmed. An expression of open annoyance crossed his face. But it was quickly gone: this was to be one of his bloodless surgeries if he could possibly keep it that way.

"Zeece," he said with a chuckle, "you know me too well. Now first of all, I want you fellows to understand my thinkin'. It's very important you understand my thinkin'."

"I think we do, Chuck," Zeecy said, determined not to let him get away with any false humility or theatrics. "But go ahead."

"Thanks, Zeece," the President said dryly. "You really think I can? I'm allowed?"

"You're allowed, Mr. President," Gen. McCune said, dropping the familiarity as he decided his old friend was really going to talk candidly. "On with it."

"Well, sir," the President said, regaining his amicability but adopting a serious and thoughtful air which he no doubt did feel: it was, after all, a major decision and a major change of policy he had determined upon, sometime in the later reaches of a long and often restless night. "Well, sir, what I'm goin' to say may come as a surprise to you, but I want you to know I've given it a great deal of thought. Not only last night when I was tossin' and turnin' and decidin' what to do, but really for the past seven months. Your 'problem of Nanukuvu' has been a problem for me, too, Loy, even though you over there in the Pentagon may not think it has been, and even though you probably think I've just been futzin' around with it as though it were some old political football. It *is* political for me, I grant you that. But it's a matter of most serious strategic concern, too, and I've thought an awful lot about that aspect as well. I've been cogitatin'." He sighed, now quite sincere and without trickery. "I've been cogitatin' like hell."

"We are sure you have, Mr. President," Loy conceded, deciding to meet him halfway: maybe with a conciliatory approach something could yet be salvaged from what he now knew beyond all question was going to be an end to Frio and with it, unless he could persuade the President not to abandon Nanukuvu altogether, a de facto confirmation of the Soviet occupation of the island that had for seven months been central to their thoughts. "We're only sorry you haven't shared your doubts and worries with us much sooner. It would have made it much easier for all of us, particularly in the Pentagon."

"I know," the President agreed with an apparently genuine contrition. "I know. If I haven't it's because I *just haven't known,* Loy. I really just haven't known what to do."

"Certainly there has been no lack of advice from us, Mr. President," Gen. McCune remarked. The President gave him a tired, conceding glance.

"I know, Zeecy. I can't complain about that. You fellows have been pretty firm and united on it all the way through. You're supposed to advise me, and you've done so, I admit that. But there's one thing you can't help me do and that's *decide.* The final word has to come from right here. And it wasn't until sometime very early this mornin' that I finally made up my mind what it's goin' to be. And you know."

"Yes, Mr. President," the Secretary of Defense said. "I think we know. There wasn't any doubt in my mind after you seized the excuse to cancel Project Frio. I didn't really think Op Frio could be very far behind."

"I didn't 'seize the excuse,'" the President said sharply. "I'd been thinkin' about it for some time. It *was* a waste of time and money. There *was* no reason to change the ALCAC. It *was* made-work for the military and the contractors, with lots of jobs, promotions and taxpayers' money ridin' on it. It *was* goin' to be a boondoggle, pure and simple."

"Not quite fair, Mr. President," Gen. McCune said with a sharpness equal to his. "It may have been ill-advised and foolish, but it was not any deliberate attempt to give the services a field-day or waste the taxpayers' money. Gen Stokes proposed the idea of modifying the ALCAC because he sincerely wanted to perfect some aspects of it he thought hadn't been tended to the first two times around. Then the others came in because they saw the opportunity to get some of their pet ideas taken care of too. But it wasn't done in any flippant or unethical spirit, I can assure you. It was based on their best judgment of what was needed—their best judgment *at the time*. Which, after all, is what any judgment is."

The President gave him a thoughtful look and finally nodded.

"All right," he said, "I'll accept that. I didn't mean to slam your friends, Zeecy. I know the chiefs are a very responsible bunch, they wouldn't be where they are if they weren't. But I *am* questionin' the judgment itself. At that time or any other time. I don't think it was a wise one, no matter how sincere they might have been."

"Then why didn't you question it at once, Mr. President?" the Secretary inquired. "I established Project Frio because it was obvious the chiefs were going to balk and be uneasy with the whole mission if I didn't give them the ALCAC project. Maybe it was wrong to yield to them, but under our present system, that is unfortunately the way it has to be: you have to get them unanimously behind you if you're SecDef, or they indicate to you, in effect, that they aren't going to play ball. You have to keep them happy: it may be wrong, but that's how we have to operate under the present setup. So I established Proj Frio in what now appears in hindsight to be a futile and mistaken attempt to keep the services happy and at the same time keep them under some sort of control so that they wouldn't run completely wild with it."

"Bad as that," the President mused and Gen. McCune replied crisply, "Bad as that. Loy and I are among the Pentagon reformers, Mr. President. But I can tell you, it's heavy going."

"If you perceived some better way of doing this, Mr. President," Loy said earnestly, "or if you did not agree with the decision to modify the ALCAC, as you apparently did not, then you should have stepped in long ago, in my opinion. By the time you acted, Project Frio had become one of the symbols of our determination to take effective action concerning Nanukuvu. And your cancellation—not until this week, not until after the hearing, not until the national and international outcry had become too noisy to ignore—has become a symbol too . . . a symbol, I'm afraid, in the eyes of the enemy and of critics both domestic and international, of weakness and retreat."

He ignored the President's obvious signs of growing anger: the restless shifting, the rising flush. He found, suddenly, that he no longer cared. The President's mind was obviously made up; and so, suddenly, was his own. He knew now what he must do to satisfy his own honor and his own integrity. He ignored the President's reaction and went bluntly on. Zeecy, agreeing completely and admiring him enormously, watched silent and prepared to move in when the moment came.

"When you acted after so many months of delay, Mr. President," Loy said, "it looked to the world as though you were beginning to knuckle under to the Soviets and their domestic and international supporters. And once a President starts to do that it becomes a very hard thing to stop. The momentum grows. Perception becomes reality. When a President willingly puts himself on that downhill slope the ride gets out of control." He took a deep breath and concluded in a firm way he knew would burn the bridges. But now he wanted them burned and he did not care.

"Probably you *are* doing the right thing to surrender to the Soviets. But if that is your final decision, as it evidently is, it would have been a lot better for you and the country if you had done it a long time ago when a good face could be put upon it, rather than wait to this late date when it looks like a weak and politically motivated retreat forced upon you by the superior strength of the Soviet Union."

He stopped and for several minutes there was absolute silence in the historic office that had witnessed the hopes, despairs, weaknesses, strengths, nobility and shabbiness, achieved ambitions and failed hopes, of so many powerful men.

The President was furious as neither the Secretary nor his old roommate had ever seen him.

It did not matter to the Secretary: he was not going to be Secretary more than a few moments longer.

Finally the President spoke in a low, grating voice.

"You and your God damned Pentagon!" he spat out. "Your fucking, half-assed, promotion-seeking, service-loving, billions-wasting, jealous, competing, turf-hugging, tradition-bound, tradition-crippled, *system*-crippled Pentagon! I ought to get rid of the whole God damned lot of you! I ought to shut the whole God damned place down tomorrow morning and maybe the country would be better for it! Maybe the *world* would be better for it! . . . But of course," he said with a wryly bitter twist to his mouth, "that can't be done, can it? That's just not an option anybody has, is it? We're stuck with the Pentagon and somehow, by some God-forsaken miracle, we've got to muddle through with it. But God help us sometimes, is all I can say. God help us!"

Again there was silence. And finally Gen. McCune spoke.

"Mr. President," he said in a calmly level tone that belied the turmoil he felt at the thought that he was ending in this fashion and under these circumstances a lifetime of brilliant service to his country, "if Secretary Buck resigns, which it is clear he is going to do if you don't fire him first, I think it advisable and imperative that I leave with him. Since I, too, am a principal architect of Frio, and I, too, believe in it. Accordingly my request for early retirement as chairman of the Joint Chiefs of Staff, and from active duty with the Air Force, will be on his desk—or," he said dryly, "the desk of whoever is secretary by the time I get back to the building—within the hour."

And for the third time there was silence while they all sat, breathing heavily, terribly angry, terribly tense, staring at the rose garden, the pictures on the walls, anywhere except at each other . . .

It seemed to them that many minutes must have passed, though in actuality it may have been three or four. And at last, as Loy and Zeecy had known in their bones he would, when the last shout was shouted and the last unforgivable word said by everyone, the President cleared his throat, managed a fair facsimile of a smile and leaned back in his chair in the old, familiar, now-let's-just-talk-this-out-together way.

"Well," he said, voice sounding almost normal again, a humorous note struggling back into it—"now that we've gotten rid of all the bile that's in us—I've got to get the cleanin' crew in here first thing and get it off the rug, can't have the place messed up *this* way—maybe we should talk. Loy, I apologize for lettin' my temper get out of hand, I don't very often do that. But you got to me, I admit it—you got to me. You're not quittin', I'm not lettin' you. And you aren't either, Zeecy. Why, God damn!"—and he chuckled, sounding quite himself and perfectly at ease again—"You tell me I'm such a politician, now you just think how it would look!" He smiled at them, drawing them into the warm circle of self-disparagement with which he always thought he could charm subordinates—"My Secretary of Defense quits. My chairman of the Joint Chiefs quits. God damn, what a scandal! I just can't stand the kind of scandal you two fellows could blow up . . . On the other hand," he said, and now he sounded completely genuine again as he sighed a heavy sigh, "there's Nanukuvu. I can't afford to have *that* hangin' over me, either. It's not popular in Congress, it's not popular with the media, it's not popular with a whole lot of folks. My mail's runnin' heavy against it, and anyway, I don't need mail. I can sense this country, I always have, you know that." And finally they nodded, a cautious acceptance and understanding, if not friendship, beginning to creep back into their feelings toward him. "I can tell how the majority's reactin'. Nanukuvu is too far away, the threat is too problematical for most of 'em to grasp. *I* grasp it and don't you ever think I don't. But I can't go along with what the Pentagon's proposin', that's too much. On the other hand, what *is* the solution? Maybe there is none. It may be the enemy's found still another perfect spot to pinch us in, 'way out there in the South Pacific. Your 'problem of Nanukuvu,' Loy, may really be an insoluble problem for the United States. Unless you fellows can think of some way out that isn't war, that manages to keep the guise of 'peace' as we understand 'peace' in this Godawful century—" he paused and studied them and sighed again—"then that's it, near as I can see."

Another silence developed, not hostile this time but filled with racing thoughts and deep confusions, for he had posed it well, as he always did.

"Mr. President," Loy said finally, "first of all, my apologies too. I let myself get carried away a bit. But I do feel deeply about the threat posed by Nanukuvu, its vital importance to us and our allies in the whole region, the importance of our taking some stand that will preserve our influence and our ability to stop further Soviet encroachment in the area . . . and, I suppose," he added, with a wry look at Gen. McCune, who nodded, "that Zeecy and I have both been so frustrated with the general problems of moving the Pentagon forward at the pace we both think it ought to go for the sheer sake of national survival, that I let that frustration get to me too, in what I said to you. However . . ." He paused, became very thoughtful, spoke in a tone that indicated that at heart he wasn't yielding much. "If we are not to make a confrontational approach to the problem of Nanukuvu, then I do believe most sincerely, as I think Zeecy does too—" again Zeecy nodded—"that we must at least try to neutralize the island, either with blockade or with some sort of constant harassment that stops short of war but makes it uncomfortable and futile for them to remain there. My own feeling would be a *cordon sanitaire,* as it were, a declared perimeter through which they would be prohibited from passing—"

"In other words," the President said, "you do want a blockade, because that's really what you're talkin' about, 'harassment' is too vague and meaningless unless you put some teeth in it. And suppose they go through the blockade, then what? We're a long, long way from the Cuban missile crisis, you know. We've let them get far too strong for anything like that, now, particularly in a place that isn't too convenient for us even though we do have some big bases down there. So again I put it to you: what's a solution that can work, particularly after seven months? Is there one?"

"I'm not sure we have found it yet, Mr. President," Loy said, "but I am sure that abandoning all attempts to find it is a very, very bad and extremely risky course to follow."

"You want to continue Op Frio, then," the President said. "You want to keep the mission alive."

"I am afraid, Mr. President," Loy said levelly, though he knew he was risking a revival of argument that this time really could conclude in only one way, "that *not* to do so would double—triple—whatever—much, much worse—what I see as the bad effects of your cancellation of Project Frio. It would, in my estimation, be a terrible blow to our standing in the region and a final, implicit confirmation of the enemy's right to occupy as it suits him and do what he pleases without let or hindrance or even any very emphatic verbal protest from us."

"What about the Declaration of the Pacific?" the President inquired, not reacting just yet to this renewed challenge. "That's certainly verbal enough."

"Exactly," the Secretary of Defense said. "Exactly."

"Well," the President said, "I'm not goin' to equivocate with you, Loy. I *am* goin' to cancel Op Frio, because I don't think that's the way out. I don't think any of the Frio Mission is the way out. We've got to go some other route."

"Mr. President," Loy said, tense again, voice a little unsteady with the emotions he was feeling, *"why will you not take the strong action that is needed here?"*

"Because I haven't got the strength behind me in the Pentagon," the President said, "and because I don't have the strength behind me in the country. *That's why."*

"But you do, Mr. President," Loy protested desperately. "You *do* have it in the Pentagon—it's growing—and you *do* have it in the country, if you will just appeal to it. Don't walk away from it!"

"I'm not goin' to walk away from it," the President said in a voice growing angry again. "I'm goin' to pursue the diplomatic option available to me, which with the Declaration is now a good one."

"It's not enough," Loy said in a despairing voice. "It's not enough. It's got to be both options. One alone is *not enough."*

The final silence ensued. It did not last long.

"Then I take it you *are* goin' to quit," the President said. "You're goin' to put me in a hole."

"You'll extricate yourself, Mr. President," the Secretary said in a tone he strove to keep from sounding too savage—though he didn't really care much. "You're a survivor."

"And you, Zeecy?" the President inquired. "You abandonin' me too?"

"Just keeping the polish on my boots in good shape, Chuck," Gen. McCune said. "You know that's very important."

"Very well," the President said and it was obvious he was cutting his losses— or, it occurred to them in a split second's thought which they both rejected, was this what he had intended all along, to get rid of Frio's architects along with Frio? Surely he could not be that calculating!

"But, Loy," he added—"give me a little time to work out a replacement, O.K.? Don't make it seem too abrupt and as though you're leavin' in a huff."

"Mr. President," Loy said evenly, "any time I left in the next three months would be taken by the media to be 'in a huff,' you know that. Why don't we say twenty-four hours?"

The President sighed.

"If that's the best I'm goin' to get," he conceded finally, "that's the best I'm goin' to get." He stood up, held out his hand. The Secretary stood up and took it.

"No hard feelin's," the President said.

"No, sir," the Secretary said, "no hard feelings."

They meant it in equal degree.

"Zeecy," the President said, "stick around for a bit and talk to me, all right? I need an old friend's comfort and advice right now."

Gen. McCune hesitated.

"I *am* leaving, too, you know, Chuck," he said.

The President dismissed that with a shrug.

"I know, I know. But just stick around. I'll send you back in a White House car if Loy goes on ahead." He smiled, "You won't have to walk."

"Well—" Zeecy said doubtfully.

"Stay," Loy said. "I'll see you across the river."

"All right," Zeecy said with obvious reluctance. "I'll see you back there . . . Now, Mr. President," he said as the Oval Office door closed upon William Loyola Buck for the last time as Secretary of Defense, "what is it?"

"Don't talk to me in that tone, Zeece," the President said mildly. "Sit down again for a minute . . . Zeecy," he said earnestly, "countin' on our old friendship and all the great academy days and all, and our great association in the last couple of years here, I'm askin' you as a friend to please not join him in makin' a public row out of it. It *would* be bad for me, to have you both go at the same time. Of course I know—" he gave him a thoughtful look—"I know I can't dissuade you in the long run, you're goin' to do it. You're goin' and I can't stop you. But it *would* help me if you'd delay it a bit. Can I ask that?"

Zeecy thought for quite a long time. Chuck was persuasive, Chuck was seductive, Chuck could wear men down speaking in the tongues of birds and angels, he knew all that . . . but on the other hand, Chuck was an old and dear friend somewhere underneath all the Presidential trappings and the calculating sorcery created by the long, political years. He knew that too. There were the sentimental memories . . . and the possible effect a simultaneous dual resignation might have on the public attitude toward the Pentagon itself, over and beyond what it might do to the President and to Nanukuvu.

"I could serve out my term, I suppose," he said slowly. "It's only another three months."

"I *would* appreciate it," the President said with genuine relief. "Of course," he added thoughtfully, and Zeecy knew suddenly that their fleeting thought had been correct, the consummate politician had never been away for a minute in all their discussion—"of course, I *had* thought, maybe . . . I'll be needin' a more appealin' Vice President this time. I'd been thinkin' that maybe a military man with all your dash and pizazz, Zeece, and you've still got *plenty*, we all know that, might be— . . . *but,*" he said with a sudden candid air and a confiding smile, "of course if I'm goin' to separate myself from Nanukuvu, which I really must do, at least any aspects of it that can be attacked as warlike, I've got to separate myself from everybody who's been involved in trying to *make* it warlike . . . don't I?"

"It was never the intention of anyone in the Pentagon, Mr. President," Zeecy said with a sudden coldness in his voice, "to do anything *warlike*. It was always the thought, as it is always the thought with us, that if you are sufficiently strong and sufficiently firm—not belligerent, just firm, with the strength to back it up—that war will not be necessary. But I see your point, I follow your reasoning, I see your motives." He grinned suddenly and held out his hand. "I may not quite *despise* them, Chuck, but I do *see* them. Take care. I'll fill out my term. Thanks for even thinking of me remotely for V.P. It would have been quite a sensation, as the lumberjack said when he tried to make love to the buzz-saw, but it's not for me and never was. Good luck."

"Good luck to you too, Zeece," the President said, shaking hands with a fervent cordiality. "I knew I could count on you to understand everything. You always did."

"Not everything," Gen. McCune said. "But a lot."

Outside on the steps as he waited for the White House limousine to come for him, he shook his head and whistled. What a guy! What a President! In many ways, for all his wafflings on this issue, a good one. And wasn't that really how you had to judge a President—in many ways?

He felt as though a great weight had been removed from his shoulders. His abortive and never very serious thoughts about civilian politics were gone as though they had never been. Thank God he was out of that once and for all! Military politics, he thought wryly, were quite enough for him. He had done pretty well with *them,* over the years.

Loy had Vangie ring the house in Georgetown as soon as he got back to the building. Carleene answered and told him to wait a minute. Mrs. Buck was out in the garden.

"In this weather? That's surprising."

"Somethin' she had to prune," Carleene said. "You know how she is 'bout that garden."

"I know how she is," he agreed. "Can you get her for me, please? . . . "Immy," he said, "pack your bags. We're skipping town."

She sounded pleased and excited.

"A vacation?"

"Permanently."

"Loy!" she exclaimed. "You don't mean—you can't mean—Loy, you're *not* going to—"

"Oh, yes, I am," he said.

Immy began to cry, from sheer relief and happiness and the knowledge that now she need no longer worry, like the mother hen she rather resembled, about the physical and mental well-being of the man she had always adored.

At least not *quite* as much.

The first call Zeecy made when he returned to the building half an hour later was to the briskly bright colonel who was secretary of the JCS secretariat —the "purple suiters" as they were known in the building because of the mix of uniform colors on the staff. Staff members were apportioned with great exactitude among the services. They were supposed to forget their service loyalties and submerge their service interests in the sweet harmonies of the JCS. Of course the unceasing tug-of-war went on just the same. It was one of the more notable achievements of the system.

"Mike," Zeecy said, "I want the chiefs in the tank in fifteen minutes. I hope they're all in town."

Fortunately they were. Gen. Burford had just returned from a speech to a major civic group in Seattle. Adm. Stahlman had been deskbound for the past two weeks. Gen. Tock had just completed a tour of Marine installations in the Med. Gen. Stokes was due to leave that afternoon for a speech in Chicago but was free now.

In fifteen minutes as requested they were in the tank.

The pachyderms, the staff told one another, looked grave.

The head pachyderm looked gravest of all.

"Well, troops," he said as they settled back in their chairs and looked at him expectantly, "I'm going to give it to you straight. Loy and I have just been to the White House. He's canceling Op Frio as well—" there was an exclamation from Brash, a groan from Ham, a short, terse word from Tick, a sharp intake of breath on the part of Bumpy. "Loy is going to resign in protest—" consternation grew—"and I told Chuck I was going to too. There's an amendment to that which I'll tell you in a moment, but the bottom line is that Frio is no more and Nanukuvu is happily and securely in the hands of the Soviet Union. And many," he added somberly, "will be the consequences thereof."

"But how can he do that!" Brash protested. "We can't just walk away and let them have it!"

"He can," Ham Stokes said in a contemptuous tone. "He can do anything if he can sell it to the country. And this one, he can."

"You think so?" Tick asked. Ham snorted.

"Hell, yes. You've got those lily-livers on the Hill in an uproar, and those bastards in the major media caterwauling for it, and every dumb damn fool on a thousand Main Streets feeling confused and uncertain and uneasy about it, and here comes a clear, bell-like clarion call to get the hell out. Sure, he can sell it. He's *got* to sell it. It's his political bread and butter."

"Appeasement!" Bumpy Stahlman said with an anger rare for him. "Sheer, God damned, white-knuckle appeasement! What the hell's the matter with that coward, anyway?"

"He's not a coward," Ham said. "He's just a politician. There's a difference, if you can find it."

"In fairness to him," Zeecy said, and Ham asked, "Why?"—"in fairness to him, he does have public opinion to worry about and he does have, to be frank, the Pentagon to worry about. He doesn't think we've exactly done our job to perfection over here, and I must say—" he looked them calmly and squarely in the eye—"that I agree with him."

"You always were a damned radical," Tick growled. "I've never been able to understand how you got where you are, the way you've challenged the system all these years."

"My charmed life, Tick," Gen. McCune said with a smile. "Just put it down to my charmed life. Anyway, the President thinks we've been damned slow over here. He thinks that if we'd moved a lot faster on all aspects of Frio, he'd have been able to challenge the enemy much sooner and with much more effectiveness and the whole thing might have been contained. Now he doesn't feel it can be, short of the sort of confrontation I don't think even you, Tick, would welcome. So he's decided to scrap it altogether and go for the diplomatic option."

" 'The diplomatic option'!" Ham echoed in disgust. *"Christ!"*

"Foggy Bottom will be happy," Brash observed. "Terry Venner's going to jump with joy. I can just see the Soviets being frightfully impressed . . . You said you were going to quit too, Zeecy, but there was some amendment to it. What was that?"

"Well, as you know, the President and I go all the way back to academy days, so when he explained his political problem to me—" Ham made a face—"yes, he did, Ham, he's got one and it's quite valid from where he sits—he told me that if Loy and I resigned simultaneously with a blast at him, as I'm sure Loy will do—then it would create a difficult situation for him, with a re-election campaign coming up next year. So he asked me to stay on to the end of my term, which as you know is only about three months away. For old friendship's sake, I said I would. But he also made it very clear—" he looked thoughtfully at Ham and Brash, Ham looking annoyed and unappeased, Brash having that tired, drawn look he seemed to have almost constantly now that Vi's health was common knowledge and everyone was helping him worry about it—"that he could not afford to be associated politically with the Pentagon approach to Nanukuvu, or with anyone who had been notably active in organizing that approach . . . which means, I am very much afraid, that he will not select for next chairman of the JCS anyone now sitting in this room."

There was silence for a moment.

"Did he tell you that in so many words?" Ham demanded, but his tone showed he had already conceded: the fight was gone.

"Not in so many words," Zeecy said. "But he didn't have to. It's obvious, if you stop and think a minute."

This they did; and being men long experienced in the ways of politicians both military and civilian, and having long realized how dependent even the Pentagon's vast enterprises were upon the shifting sands of public opinion in a democratic society, they did not need the full minute.

Ham Stokes shook his head with a rueful air.

"Oh, well," he said, mocking his own bravado, "I didn't want it, anyway."

"Yes, Ham," Tick said dryly. "We all know that."

Brash Burford uttered a long, sad sigh.

"I can say that and mean it. I really haven't cared much lately, with Vi's health the way it is. I really feel relieved to be able to stop thinking about it. I really mean that."

"We know you do, Brash," Bumpy Stahlman said and they all nodded. "How is she?"

Gen. Burford smiled, a wan but gallant smile.

"We manage," he said. Tears came into his eyes and, quite unabashed, he dashed them away with a hand that noticeably trembled.

"Well," Zeecy said briskly, "so that's the situation and that's what we have to handle now. Just as a matter of interest, you might be interested to know that an attempt was made to give the plans for Frio to the enemy—"

"No!" Tick exclaimed, "Who was it?"

When he had told them, confining his account to Op Frio and no collateral issues, Ham said, "Son of a bitch! You just can't ever tell, can you? They're in there working, all the time."

"And all we can do is be vigilant—vigilant—and more vigilant," Bumpy said. "You can't prevent it all by any means—just keep a finger in the dike and hope for the best."

"But why a young fellow like that?" Brash asked in a baffled voice. "One of my own boys, a fine, fine officer, with everything to gain in the service—"

"I expect he had his reasons," Zeecy said, not considering it necessary to tell them what they were. "Anyway, he won't be in the service more than a day or two longer. After that he'll be in the hands of the F.B.I. and then Leavenworth for quite a long time, I think. It was all pretty ironic, when you think about it. The drop was intercepted—so the enemy didn't get the plans anyway. And now they've been canceled—so it wouldn't have mattered if he had."

"Maybe they'll still be revived," Gen. Stokes suggested, but in a tone that indicated he was not exactly optimistic.

The chairman shook his head emphatically.

"Oh, no, Ham. Come off it. Frio's dead. Another time we'll just have to do better." He smiled grimly. "There will be many such. We can count on that."

Back in his office he sat for a while going over routine papers and reports, thinking of the consequences of Frio's demise, already starting. Brash had announced that he was definitely going to go ahead and request early retirement: "There's nothing left for me here now, and Vi needs me." Ham said he was going to go home and talk it over with Zenia, "which will surprise hell out of her," he admitted with a candid grin, "because we haven't been exactly chummy of late. But maybe this is a good time to get started again." Tick and Bumpy had agreed that they would stay on, like Zeecy, to the end of their current terms and then leave also.

"In six months' time," Ham observed, "your friend Chuck will have himself both a new SecDef and a whole new JCS. Then he can do anything he damned well pleases, bless his little heart."

"Oh, he isn't that bad," Zeecy had protested, out of some lingering sense of fairness toward his old, charming, equivocal, calculating friend.

"He is in my book," Gen. Stokes said. "I despise the wishy-washy son of a bitch."

"He has his complaints about the Pentagon, too," Bumpy reminded, trying—obviously with difficulty—to be fair.

"That doesn't excuse him," Tick said dourly. "We deserve better support than that."

"And so does he, I suppose," Brash said with a tired smile as they left. "So there we are."

Now, moved by a sudden impulse to discuss all this with the shrewdest, most rational and most pragmatic mind he knew, Gen. McCune asked his secretary to put in a call to Quarters Six, Fort Myer.

"How about me coming home to lunch?" he inquired. "Got anything in the freezer?"

"I am astounded," Renee remarked. "However, come if you like. I shall endeavor to cope."

And by the time he reached home an hour later, she had coped indeed: a wonderfully warm and tasty spinach salad—the delicious seafood crepes from her own special recipe for which she was famous among Air Force wives around the world—a bottle of a California wine which he particularly liked, a great concession, knowing how loyal she was to her native products—and a soufflé that came light and airy and seductively aromatic from the oven at exactly the right moment.

"You're a hell of a good cook, you know that?" he inquired as she came in from the kitchen with a small coffee pot and two demitasse cups and led the way into the library.

"I know that," she said complacently, pouring the coffee and seating herself beside him on the sofa. "Why am I so honored, Zoren? You haven't been home for lunch in months."

"It's been an interesting couple of days," he said, and proceeded to tell her about them, starting with the sad conclusion of the bright career of Gary Stump and going on through the White House–U.N. visit yesterday, their conversation this morning with the President and concluding with the meeting with the chiefs.

She listened without comment save a sad shake of the head and a rueful "Zut!" for Gary, a wry, "He outthinks you all, that Chuck," for the President, a sympathetic murmur for Brash and Vi, an "Eh, bien, what can you expect in such a difficult situation?" for far-off Nanukuvu, abandoned to the enemy in the distant, sunny sea.

"And so you will stay on and complete your term," she said. "It is probably best. You will be gone soon in any event and it is pointless to be vindictive toward him." She smiled. "I imagine the Secretary will punish him quite enough."

"Loy is not in a mood to be kind," he said, "and I wouldn't be either, if we hadn't known each other for so long. But he's like all strong Presidents—they become a force of nature, after a while. And he does have a legitimate gripe about the Pentagon, difficult though it is for Ham and the rest to admit. They know it but they won't admit it."

"But Zeecy the objective always can," she commented with a wry little smile. "It is no wonder they have always considered you a radical."

"My virtues have apparently outweighed my faults," he remarked in a tone equally wry. "But I'll be glad to go, when the time comes. It's time to pass the torch and settle down."

"Oh?" she said, looking quite surprised. "Zoren Chace McCune, 'settle down'? I cannot believe it, Zoren. I will not be able to believe that, when *you* settle down."

"What's so astounding about it? It comes to all of us."

"But not you, Zeecy, Zeecy the eternal, chasing ladies forever down the halls of paradise. I had not thought to hear such resignation from you in *my* lifetime."

"Oh, come on, now," he protested. "Don't be like that."

"Well, it's true!" she said with a sudden brief but furious anger. "From the very first, it's been true. When we were dating it was true, when we were on our honeymoon it was true, all over the world it's been true! And *I* have been expected to be the perfect military wife and take it and say nothing!"

"And you have, haven't you?" he inquired, raising his arm just in time to fend off the slap she aimed somewhere in the general direction of his face. He caught her hand and held it firmly as she gave him an angry glare that he could tell, knowing her so well, was trembling on the verge of tears.

"I'm sorry," he said, rubbing her hand gently, genuinely contrite. "That really did sound horribly complacent, didn't it? I *am* sorry . . . You *have* been a very good wife to me, Renee, I couldn't have had a better. Always helpful, always supportive, always *there*. And beautiful, too," he added with the Zeecysmile that could charm even Renee, who knew *him* so well. "I've been the envy of the Air Force for almost thirty years. And not only the Air Force. Everybody in the military has heard of Renee McCune!"

"You are impossible," she said, hand relaxing in his, expression changing to its usually wryly knowledgeable acceptance. "You are unique, Zoren McCune, and I suppose I should thank God that I have been privileged to be your wife. It is a dream that has been held by thousands of ladies, I am sure. And only I, Renee, achieved it. That, I suppose, is worth something."

"Maybe a little," he said, smile increasing. "Not much in today's market, but maybe a little."

"Yes," she agreed. "I am informed that in today's market Zeecy McCune is no longer the prize he once was. I am informed that he is finally, at last, losing ground. I am informed that Zeecy McCune has even heard the word No. It is, indeed, time for you to pass on the torch and settle down."

"What do you mean by that?" he demanded, looking so surprised and chagrined that she uttered her characteristic short, sharp laugh.

"Suppose you give me your version," she suggested, studying his face with a quizzical expression. "I have already been privileged to hear the other."

"You mean—" he exploded. "You mean she actually—"

He knew he looked and sounded foolish, the protesting husband caught with the goods, but he was unable to keep himself from falling into that standard cliché, he was so completely surprised and taken aback. "What did she tell you?" he demanded angrily. "Some cock-and-bull story—"

"Your Senator," she said calmly, "does not tell such stories. She tells the truth. She is a genuine lady and she is my friend, which pleases me and I am proud to say it. She is also, though you may not be able to appreciate it for a while, your friend too, Zeecy. You see," she said in a kindly way she knew would sting, "we are both your friends, Zeecy. We want to take care of you. We want to protect you from yourself."

"Well, I'll be damned," he said, beginning to rally as the humor of it struck him. "Well, I'll be damned!"

And he began to laugh, quite genuinely and honestly amused; and after a moment she joined him and they sat there on the sofa side by side laughing like —well, like an old married couple sharing a joke. Which in this case, he was ruefully honest enough to admit to himself, was on him.

"What did she say?" he asked presently. "Did she give you all the gory details?"

Renee looked surprised.

"Why should she? She is not a supermarket gossip magazine. For which you may be very thankful. She simply said you had an idea she did not share, though she said she *had* shared it for some time. But she said she had decided some weeks ago that it was not possible or wise."

"Why didn't she tell me that!" he demanded in an aggrieved tone. "I gave her plenty of opportunity!"

"Because she said she did not think you would believe her unless she told you in person. And in a circumstance which you yourself had arranged. You see, she knows you, Zoren." She smiled, rather bleakly. "You are not the easiest person to convince, when you have set your heart on something."

"I suppose I *was* foolish to set my heart on it, wasn't I?" he said, remembering the perfectly tactful but perfectly firm fashion in which he had been gently diverted and sent on his way. "I suppose I *am* getting to be an old, senile lecher with no more brains than some—some sex-mad cadet at the academy!"

"Oh, Zeecy!" she said, mocking the hearts-and-flowers tone into which he had dramatically and automatically slipped. "My poor, helpless, senile old Zeecy! What a sad figure you have become! I can hardly recognize you any more! It is too pathetic, really it is!"

"All right," he said, starting to laugh in spite of himself. "You can make fun of me, but it was a great blow to my ego—"

"Nonsense! You expected it, in your heart of hearts."

"How do you know that?"

"Because you respect her. And if she had agreed, you would no longer have respected her. And it is necessary to your concept of her that you continue to respect her. So, you see, it was all inevitable from the first. Why did you even bother?"

He looked at her for a moment. Then he laughed again.

"Renee," he said, "you know me too well."

"I should hope so," she said tartly. "After all these years. That is why I was never worried."

"Never?" he said in mock protest. "Won't you allow my poor shattered ego that satisfaction? *Never?*"

"Never," she said firmly. "Not," she added with a sudden bleakness, "like some other times."

He said nothing because there was nothing to say. He sipped his coffee, not meeting the direct and hurting eyes that were turned upon him. The past was there, they both knew it: there was nothing more to say or do.

Presently he set down his cup with a businesslike air.

"Well!" he said. "I've got to get back."

He stood and she stood. He sought to kiss her lips, was presented with a cool and unyielding cheek, made do with that.

"That was, as usual, a marvelous meal. Do you suppose if I can get away from the office by six tonight that you could cook me another as good? Or would you rather eat out somewhere?"

She shrugged, outwardly her imperturbable self again.

"I will cook. It is good therapy, cooking. It takes one's mind off—other things."

"Good!" he said briskly. "Then you can expect me. In fact, Renee, I think you can probably expect me from now on. You're right, I'm getting to be a ridiculous old man. I'm going to retire in three months, after all!" He smiled the Zeecysmile, to which she responded this time with only a small, skeptical grimace. "I'm ready!"

"That is good," she said calmly. "I was ready some time ago, Zoren. I am glad our clocks are—how do you say it?—getting into sync."

"They are!" he assured her heartily as he put on his coat and hat, looking, as always, dazzling in his gold braid—so much so that her heart, as always, turned over in spite of everything. "I'll see you at six—from now on, if *I* have anything to say about it. And the chairman certainly should!"

He gave her a jaunty salute, turned and hurried out to Carleene's Jim, waiting patiently at the curb; hopped in, turned and gave her a last jaunty wave as they drove swiftly away.

She stood for a long time staring after him, not really seeing anything except, perhaps, the long parade of the past stretching back through happiness and pain, trust and disillusionment—held together by habit and love, which she knew she had for him, and he for her.

She didn't believe for a minute that he would "settle down" but she determined that she would cater to the mood while it lasted.

All she had to do, she reflected wryly, was live another twenty years, and Gen. Zoren Chace McCune might come dutifully home at night.

If it took that long, she told herself with a bitter and ironic patience, then that was what she was prepared to give it.

When the chairman got back to the Pentagon the news was all over the building: Loy Buck's resignation had been announced, and the President would speak to the nation that night on the subject of Nanukuvu "and the new opportunities for peaceful progress with the Soviet Union offered by the Declaration of the Pacific."

6

And so the problem of Nanukuvu moved inexorably on toward the end that had been implicit in its beginning.

Watching in the house in Georgetown, Loy Buck and Imogene thought the President looked a little drawn and tired. Watching with Renee in Quarters Six, Fort Myer, Zeecy thought the President looked in fine fettle. Watching in Delight's wildly decorated apartment in Adams Morgan, the editor and the chief and only correspondent of *Defense Eye* thought the President looked relaxed and pleased to be taking a step with which they jubilantly agreed. So, too, thought Skip Framberg and Deputy Secretary Cathcart in their respective residences.

Gen. Stokes and Zenia, Gen. Burford and Vi, Gen. Tock and Doreen and Adm. Stahlman, in their various quarters thought, as did Red Roberts and Gen. Al Rider, that the President looked under considerable tension and somewhat defiant, as though he could sense their massed disapproval. On Capitol Hill, taking advantage of a lull in one of the hectic night meetings that Congress always went into in the closing weeks of a session, Cube Herron had gathered his little group, "the Pentagon Regulars" as Jerry Castain had dubbed them, in his private office. *They* thought the President looked as though he had stuck in his thumb and pulled out a plum.

"And is about to say," Luzanne remarked, " 'Look what a smart little boy am I!' "

However he really felt—and actually he was probably closer to the perceptions of *Defense Eye* and the Hill contingent—he was able to command, by virtue of his office and his own intriguing personality, the eyes, ears and concentration of a great many millions in his own country and around the globe.

Nanukuvu was still a major preoccupation of national and world opinion-makers; still a major litmus-test, the world's leaders felt, of U.S.-Soviet relations; still an indicator of how determined the United States was to either (1) keep the peace by insisting on containment of further Soviet advances in the South Pacific or (2) keep the peace by seeking "the diplomatic solution" and, in effect, arriving at an accommodation with the obvious Soviet intention to extend Moscow's influence even further into an area where it had already made numerous tentative probings in recent years.

"My fellow countrymen," the President said gravely, giving the cameras the full impact of his most sincere and reasonable gaze, "I want to talk with you tonight about a problem you have heard and read much about in recent days—

the problem of Nanukuvu, a little island far away, about which we know nothing."

"There he goes!" Loy exclaimed to Immy. "God damn him!"

"Some Americans feel this island to be of major importance to the security of our country and the security of our allies in the South Pacific and Pacific regions. Many others disagree.

"The island, which hitherto had been considered uninhabited, and to which no one had paid any particular attention for many, many years, became a matter of concern to the military leaders of this country some seven months ago when it was occupied by forces of the Soviet Union.

"The leaders of the Soviet Union maintained at that time, and have maintained consistently since—"

" 'Consistently'?" Zeecy inquired. "Why not 'adamantly'—'arrogantly'— 'stubbornly'—'ruthlessly'? Why not some honest word like that?"

"—that the island was in an area over which no power exercised clear right and title, and that it was therefore open to occupation and development by any nation that wished to do so.

"This contention has been disputed by the United States on the ground that the island is in an area that is known to be, and is generally considered to be, within the general overall protection and friendly influence of this country.

"The Soviet occupation therefore became, in the eyes of some Americans—"

" 'Some Americans'!" Ham Stokes echoed disgustedly. "That's the second time. We're being carefully separated from the rest of the country. Watch this."

"—a major issue of concern. It was felt by the civilian and military heads of the Department of Defense that the United States should make a strong protest to the Soviet Union and, in effect, demand that Soviet forces and equipment be withdrawn and the island restored to its former isolated and independent condition.

"With this contention—"

"There's a friendly word for you!" Tick said scornfully. "Twice already, and no doubt more to come!"

"—I was, for a time, disposed to agree. However, I could only do so if those civilian and military leaders in the Pentagon who expressed such great concern were able to provide, in a very short time, the military strength with which to support such a protest to the Soviet Union. Every passing day, every moment of delay, made their position on the island stronger and our own position in trying to challenge it, weaker.

"Nonetheless," he said, and his expression became somber, "clear and obvious as this was, delay ensued. Not a week's delay—not a month's delay—but *seven* months' delay. Until as of today, our intelligence reports reveal a very strong Soviet presence on the island and indicate that it would take a very strong response, probably openly military in nature and entailing great risks of open conflict, to dislodge that presence now.

"Therefore the U.S. military strength which might in the beginning have been a weapon of non-belligerent and effective argument has now become, through these delays, a handicap in finding a peaceful solution. I now find myself, as your Commander-in-Chief, in a position where, if I attempt to bring strength to the argument, it will be too much.

"The strength which might have supported peaceful diplomacy seven months ago is the strength which now might precipitate the open clash that no sane individual desires and all abhor.

"I do not make any attempt to lay the blame for this situation at the door of the Pentagon."

"Not much!" Cube Herron snorted.

"It sure as hell isn't going to be laid at the door of the White House," Jerry Castain observed. "That's obvious."

"There are, as all Americans are gratefully aware," the President went on, "most able and patriotic men and women in charge of our Defense Department. Secretary William 'Loy' Buck has been a most diligent, able and effective administrator of that great department. My old friend and academy roommate, Gen. Zoren Chace McCune, chairman of the Joint Chiefs of Staff, and the Joint Chiefs have been equally able and diligent in the discharge of their duties. It is only with the greatest regret that even the slightest breath of criticism should be directed toward them. But somehow, even with the best will in the world on the part of top personnel in the Pentagon, the damaging delay did occur. And now we must move on from there.

"A week ago, as you are aware, I canceled a portion of the Pentagon operation which has been mounted against the Soviet presence on Nanukuvu—that operation which is known broadly as 'Mission Frio,' and which on a day-to-day basis has been separated in the Pentagon into two parallel activities known as 'Operation Frio,' the military side of it, and 'Project Frio,' the materiel and supplies side. It seemed to me that Project Frio was essentially a duplication of the planning and requisition going on in Operation Frio—an example of that duplicative and wasteful effort which has, in too many instances and on too many occasions, crippled the Pentagon in its attempts to pursue a strong, vigorous, clear-cut and effective policy on a given issue. Accordingly I canceled Project Frio.

"Tonight—"

"Do it, man!" Delight exhorted with a whoop. "Do it!"

"—I am also canceling Operation Frio, and am thus terminating in its entirety Mission Frio."

"Good for him!" Mario Escondido said. "Serves the bastards right!"

"All right, Mario," Karl Aschenheim said sharply. "You find a way out of this!"

"He'll do it," Mario said complacently. "That's his job."

"I do this," the President said, looking into the cameras with earnest sincerity, "because I believe it to be in the best interests of the United States, and of our allies in the Pacific and South Pacific regions, to remove from the consider-

ation of the problem of Nanukuvu even the slightest taint of a military operation. I do not believe that particular solution is possible now—"

"Here we go again," Brash said in a tired voice, but Vi, staring into some
place only she could see and picking aimlessly at the sleeve of her robe, made
no reply.

"—after seven months' delay in the Defense Department. I believe the only
solution to be the diplomatic one, and it is on that basis that your government
will proceed hereafter in dealing with the problem of Nanukuvu.

"I am confirmed in my decision by the recent vote in the General Assembly
of the United Nations. Although this vote of 87–84 against a Soviet resolution
charging this country with planning aggressive acts in the South Pacific was, on
its surface, a 'victory' for the United States, it was obvious that there is very
large international sentiment—very nearly a majority—in favor of a diplomatic
solution. This near-majority sentiment I must honor. I should be failing in my
duty to you, and to peace-loving peoples everywhere, if I did not do so. I shall
not fail that trust."

"Christ!" Red Roberts exclaimed. "What hypocritical crap!"

But nothing could have exceeded the air of utter sincerity with which it was
delivered.

"I regret," the President continued, and his expression became even more
earnest and sincere, if that were possible, "that in making this decision I have
taken a position which runs counter to that of some in the Pentagon. Principal
among these is the Secretary of Defense, my good friend Loy Buck—"

"As was, Mr. President," Loy said dryly. "As was."

"Horrid man!" Imogene exclaimed. *"Horrid* man!"

"—whose resignation was submitted to me earlier today. With great regret
and reluctance, I have accepted that resignation. I believe that after the passions of the moment have subsided, when he is able to reflect upon these
events in peace and quiet, the Secretary will perhaps regret the harshness of
the language which he used toward me in his letter of resignation."

And he picked it up and read from it with a put-upon and effective air.

"He says, 'I cannot in good conscience support a policy which amounts to
little more than appeasement in the South Pacific . . . From the first, you
have failed to give the Defense Department the clear-cut and effective backing
necessary to the completion of its mission . . . Despite the diligent and loyal
efforts of many fine men and women, both civilian and military, in the Pentagon, your own attitude has too often appeared to be one of unconcern bordering upon complete disinterest . . . The Pentagon cannot adequately perform
this or any other mission if it does not have the strong, determined and dedicated leadership of the Commander-in-Chief . . . As a citizen, I must express
my deep concern over the policy you apparently intend to follow in the only
region remaining on earth which is not already directly threatened by Soviet
encroachment . . . I most earnestly suggest to you, Mr. President, that only a
policy of strength *with* firmness can succeed in dealing with our opponents

. . . Do not, I beg of you, yield too easily that which it would take many millions of dollars and the blood of many fine servicemen to recover at a later time . . .'

"And he ends," the President said with a comical expression, "by assuring me that he has enjoyed working with me, and by telling me how grateful he is to me for giving him the opportunity to serve the country in my Administration." He gave a wry smile. "With such as that, who needs enemies?"

"He is clever, your Chuck," Renee said. "Oh, how he is clever!"

"Now, of course," the President said, and his tone became at one and the same time fatherly, indignant and warmly confidential, a marvelous combination if you can do it, Loy observed to Immy, "I am not following a policy of 'appeasement' in the South Pacific. And I have given 'clear-cut and effective backing' to the Defense Department. And I have held repeated White House meetings on this problem with Secretary Buck and my other advisers. And I have not shown an attitude of 'unconcern bordering on complete disinterest.' And I know the Pentagon must have 'strong, determined and dedicated leadership' from the Commander-in-Chief. And I *know* a policy of 'strength *with* firmness' is the only way to deal with our opponents.

"And I also know, fellow Americans, that I have twice conferred with the General Secretary in Moscow on this problem. And I also know that in the Declaration of the Pacific, supported by 26 nations with vital interests in the Pacific and South Pacific regions, including our own, I have strong diplomatic backing with which to go to him again and insist that we work out an amicable solution of the problem of Nanukuvu that will respect the interests of all concerned and provide a reasonable and responsible method for getting along together in that most important region."

"Doesn't he know," Al Rider demanded of his wife, "that the only method for 'getting along together' with the Soviet Union is to give in to it, and that if you don't do that, the only alternative is to stand up to it and tough it out?" He shook his head in bafflement. "Sometimes I don't understand this man."

In Moscow the General Secretary made no comment to the Politburo members who watched with him. But he smiled.

"In pursuit of this diplomatic option, which I am convinced is the one desired by the great majority of the American people—"

"Yeayyy!" Delight told him, "You can say that again!"

"—it becomes imperative that I have a Secretary of Defense who is compatible with myself and Secretary of State Venner—"

"Oh, oh!" Bumpy Stahlman said to his empty room and Clare, who was always with him somewhere, "here it comes!"

"—as we seek a peaceable arrangement in the South Pacific. I did not seek the resignation of Secretary Buck, but since I now have the duty to appoint a successor I find I can turn to one who is already high in the affairs of the Defense Department and thoroughly familiar with its workings."

Zeecy and Renee looked at one another.

"No," he said firmly, "it cannot be."

Across the river Loy Buck exclaimed sharply, *"No!"*

"It gives me great pleasure to announce the appointment of the present Deputy Secretary, Robert Cathcart—"

"Hot dog!" Skip Framberg shouted to his wife, yanked her out of her chair and waltzed her around the room. "Oh, *God,"* groaned Ham Stokes, as dismayed as Loy, Zeecy and all his fellow chiefs.

"—to the office of Secretary of Defense."

"And," the President went on as Jerry Castain asked blankly, "You mean there's more?"—"I should also like to announce at this time, because I believe it is necessary to maintain a continuity when dealing with so serious a matter as Nanukuvu, my choice to be the next chairman of the Joint Chiefs of Staff."

"Here is your hat," Renee said dryly. "What is your hurry?"

Zeecy was too startled and angry to make coherent response.

"The present chairman, as you know," the President continued smoothly, "is my old, dear friend and academy roommate, Gen. Zoren Chace McCune, a great officer who has served his country magnificently for forty years. His term expires in three months. He has expressed to me his desire to retire at that time, otherwise I should most certainly have asked him to continue in office for another two-year term."

"Liar!" Zeecy grated out. "Chuck, you God damned liar! You told me you couldn't have anybody associated with Frio. Oh, you *liar!"*

"But successful," Renee noted. "Oh, how successful."

"Being unable to dissuade Gen. McCune from his firm determination to retire," the President said, "I have decided to turn to one who has in no way been associated with the ill-advised and ill-starred Frio Mission."

"Well, at least *that's* honest," Zeecy said more calmly. "I'll hand him that."

"Therefore at the appropriate time I shall send to the Senate for confirmation the name of Adm. Richard Theodore Edgerton, presently CINCLANT, or commander-in-chief, Atlantic."

"Sniffles Edgerton!" Bumpy cried, shocked out of his usual dignity as his mind raced back forty years to Annapolis memories of the chronically rhinitic classmate whom nobody liked. *"That* little prick! Why, he's nothing but a God damned doormat anybody can walk over! Which of course," he added scornfully, "is exactly what he wants, isn't it?"

Clare agreed.

"My countrymen," the President concluded solemnly, "we have in the problem of Nanukuvu a difficult but not insoluble situation. Given sufficient determination, sufficient diplomatic skill and sufficient willingness on both sides to cooperate in finding a solution, I am confident that we and the Soviet Union can work out an agreement that will respect the rights of all concerned and make of the South Pacific region the truly nuclear-free zone which its peoples, we, and the Soviet Union, equally desire. In that hope and that confidence, I bid you goodnight and God bless."

PENTAGON 577

"Who says we and the Soviet Union 'equally' desire that," Luzanne demanded, "when they have already introduced overwhelming nuclear force to the island of Nanukuvu?"

"And who says they have 'rights' equal to ours or anybody else's in that region?" Jerry Castain agreed.

"*He* says," Cube Herron said, an unhappy scowl on his cherubic old face. "And he'll get away with it, too. See if he doesn't."

And of course he did. A nation whose people did not really want foreign adventures, even when their own self-interests and the interests of a stable world were directly involved, applauded from coast to coast. The media sang, academe was overjoyed, the statesmen and stateswomen of Hollywood were satisfied. Even the profoundly wise and intelligent gods of rock were moved to gibber their unintelligible blessing.

The statement of the Secretary of State, issued from Foggy Bottom immediately after the conclusion of the address he had helped to write, was dignified, non-gloating and fair.

"The President's speech," he said, "offers a clear and unequivocal path to the only solution of the problem of Nanukuvu that is possible in a civilized world—the diplomatic solution. In that effort he will have my full cooperation and that of my department in its entirety. I welcome and applaud his unfailing statesmanship, which has served, and will continue to serve, his country so well.

"On a personal note, I regret that indissoluble differences over policy have brought the resignation of my good friend William 'Loy' Buck, Secretary of Defense. I have enjoyed working with him in the Cabinet, and I wish him well in his future endeavors. He is a great and patriotic American. I am sorry he could not see his way clear to remaining with us while we work out the peaceable solution for the Pacific and South Pacific regions which the best interests of all concerned make imperative."

The statement from Moscow was briefer.

"The Government of the U.S.S.R.," it said, "welcomes the recognition by the President of the United States that the so-called Soviet 'occupation' of the island of Nanukuvu has been, and will continue to be, the peaceful development of a hitherto uninhabited island that belonged to nobody. The Government of the U.S.S.R. also welcomes his statement that the Government of the United States wishes to work with the Government of the U.S.S.R. to assure jointly and equally the peace and stability of the greater Pacific regions."

Which was not exactly what the President had said, but everybody was so pleased with the mild tone that nobody really wanted to upset harmony by pointing that out.

At the Cathcart home in Georgetown, not far from that of his predecessor to which he and his wife had rarely been invited, the new Secretary received telephone calls far into the night from all in the Pentagon who wished to climb aboard the new ship before it even left the dock.

On the Hill, Cube Herron may have growled, "I *don't like him.* We're going to give him a *hard time.* It's quite conceivable I can get enough votes to defeat the nomination." And Sens. Johnson and Castain may have immediately pledged all possible assistance.

Across the river in the massive building, few were taking chances.

Conspicuously missing from the calls, the new SecDef noted with angry frustration, were the chairman and members of the Joint Chiefs of Staff, and several of the top civilians. Bob Cathcart told himself he didn't care. Six months from now Zeecy and all the chiefs would be gone. Six months from now he'd have bounced all of Loy's boys who hadn't already left of their own accord.

He and the President, he promised them grimly as he went finally to bed, would have their *own* team then, and they'd handle Nanukuvu in their *own* way.

7

Once again he was staring out the window at the slow-moving river, now dull and gray under fast-scudding clouds, when Vangie entered with his morning coffee.

His resignation would take effect on Friday at close of business. All that remained was to tie up a few loose ends, wrap up a few lingering routine matters and get the hell out.

He knew the moment he saw Vangie that it would not be all that easy. Her eyes were red with tears, her prim little face alive with indignation beneath its bun of gray hair.

"Vangie," he said, hoping to forestall an emotional outburst from so contained and unlikely a source, "you are not to get yourself into a tizzy over this. That's an order."

"I'm not in any tizzy," she said, transferring the indignation momentarily to him for being so obtuse as to think such a thing. "I'm just going to resign, that's all."

"You mustn't do that—" he began but she gave him a scornful look.

"Work for *him?*" she demanded. "Work for that *great oaf?* Anyway, he wouldn't have me. He won't want anybody in here who knows what's really going on in the Pentagon. That would be too inhibiting for a fool like him!"

"Vangie, Vangie!" he said, beginning to laugh at her suddenly unleashed vehemence. "You mustn't say things like that about the SecDef."

" 'SecDef,' " she sniffed. "There's only one SecDef *I* know and that's Loy Buck. He's the best I've ever known and I've known four. As for that—that— *oaf*," she said again, "he's no more a SecDef than I'm George Washington."

"All right, George," he said, "calm down. He *is* SecDef, or going to be—"

"I'll bet the Senate won't confirm him," she predicted with angry relish.

"Don't bet on it. Anyway, I've made arrangements for you to stay on as a special consultant—"

"Don't you understand, Loy," she said, her concerned and most uncharacteristic informality somehow bringing home to him more than anything had so far the fact that he was actually leaving, "I don't *want* to stay around this building when you go. It won't be any—any *fun* anymore. I won't feel as though the country's being served as it ought to be anymore. I just won't feel *right.*"

He returned to his desk, sat down, took a sip of coffee and stared at her thoughtfully over the cup. Finally he nodded.

"All right, Vangie, if that's the way you feel, that's the way you feel. I don't want you to quit on my account but I'm flattered by your loyalty. I guess I've made a *few* friends in the building, anyway."

"Thousands," she said. "Thousands. What will you do now?"

"I don't know. I want to take Immy on a long vacation, first, and think about things. I suppose there'll be corporate board offers—maybe a chairmanship—I have a great many friends in industry still. A former SecDef usually doesn't want for something to do if he cares to be gainfully employed. Anyway, I have my pensions. I won't starve. But I certainly won't just sit around, either."

"Why don't you run against him for President next year?" she inquired with a sly little smile that showed how pleased she was with herself for having thought of it. "Maybe you could get Gen. McCune for your running-mate."

He looked at her in startled silence for a moment. Then he grinned.

"Vangie," he said, "that's the damnedest idea. I never even thought of that. But of course it isn't practical in any way. We're in the same party—I'd have to be a Bull Moose or something. And being a discharged SecDef isn't such an overwhelming selling-point with party leaders, you know. Or with the voters. And Zeecy, I'm sure, wouldn't be interested—"

"Ask him."

"No, Vangie," he said with another laugh. "Again, I'm flattered, but—no. It's just completely impractical."

"Wait and see what happens out there in the South Pacific," she suggested, the shrewdly calculating look of the old political hand coming into her eyes. "Maybe his decision won't look all that great when the Soviets are camping on New Zealand's doorstep, for instance. Or going after Australia. Or gobbling up all the little island states one by one. Maybe you'll have a real platform to run on, then."

"Maybe," he said. "I pray to God it won't happen that way, but—maybe. But, again—no. Don't ever tell anyone you had this wild idea, or I'll shoot you."

"Think about it," she said with serene conviction. "Think about it . . . Anyway, whatever you do, please keep me in mind. I really don't mind retiring at all, although I'll miss the Pentagon, of course. But if you find you need a secretary in your new job—" she gave him the sly little smile again—"say, in the White House—give me a call. I won't be leaving Washington. You know where to find me."

"Well, thank you, Vangie," he said, genuinely touched. "I give you my word I certainly will be in touch the minute I decide what I'm going to do."

"Are you very busy right now?" she asked. He looked surprised.

"What, this minute?"

"Yes. The staff wants to see you."

"I hadn't planned—" he began as she rose and went to the door.

"We did," she said, and in they all came, his usual weekly band of brothers: Joe Strang and the Doomsday Twins, Shorty Murchison, Tiny Wombaugh, Helen Clark, Hank Milhaus, Secretary Hugh Merriman of the Navy, Secretary Hill B. Ransome of the Air Force, Secretary of the Army Raymond C. Clark.

They took their accustomed seats and faced him for the last time.

"What do you do now?" he asked, trying to keep it light. "Sing 'For He's a Jolly Good Fellow'—or 'Blow the Man Down, Boys, Blow the Man Down'?"

"We've come here, Loy," Tiny Wombaugh said solemnly, "to tell you that some of us are going to quit along with you. And to let you know that those of us who aren't are only staying on because we won't be too involved with the jerk who's succeeding you, and we think maybe we can do some good for the country by sabotaging his more asinine ideas."

For a moment Loy stared at him, obviously moved. Then his expression became—not severe, because he was no longer in a position to be severe, but— serious.

"You mustn't say that, Tiny," he said, "and none of you must even think it. I appreciate your loyalty more than I can say—as I have valued your friendship and assistance more than I can say—but I can't countenance or be part of any disloyalty or 'sabotage' of the new SecDef. God knows I don't like him either, never have and that's no secret in the building—but you've got to help him as much as you can. He has some good qualities—"

"Name one," Joe Strang murmured and Loy smiled.

"All right, Joe, all right—and he will have the responsibility—"

"If the Senate confirms him," Hank Milhaus noted. Again Loy smiled.

"I think the chances are it probably will—of running this enormous, impossible, inconceivable, almost unmanageable machine that we have here in the Pentagon. He's going to need all the help he can get and I want those of you who stay on to give it to him. You, Tiny, I assume, and Shorty—" they nodded —"and who else?"

He paused and looked around the half-circle. The Secretary of the Navy spoke up with a smile.

"I may," Hugh Merriman said. "I haven't quite decided yet. After all, I'm Navy and the Navy has enough clout to survive even Bob Catheter as SecDef, I think. On the other hand, I'm with you on Nanukuvu. But maybe by staying here with the Navy's clout behind me I can do something about that, too."

"That's the way I feel," Hill Ransome said. "It won't be easy, obviously. But the Air Force has a bit of clout too, Hugh." He chuckled in his amiable down-home way. "I won't call it sabotage, Mr. Secretary, but I expect maybe we can do some good on Nanukuvu, too."

"I doubt that very much," Loy said. "The President has his mind made up. If you're going to stay I wouldn't advise rebellion. It's going to have to be all or nothing, I'm afraid."

"There are ways," Hugh Merriman observed with a smile. "I'd like to try them for a little while, anyway."

"I'm with you," Hill Ransome said. "If we find ourselves stymied we can always quit too."

"Good luck," Loy said. "I expect to see you both on the tiles within three months." His eyes flicked matter-of-factly across those of the Secretary of the Army. Ray Clark leaned forward.

"I'm with you, Loy," he said earnestly. "I think the President's decision on Nanukuvu is the absolute shits. That's my reason for resigning and I'm going to say so in no uncertain terms, just as you have. I can't in good conscience remain and see us adopt such a weak, sniveling, appeasement-minded policy in the Pacific. It's fatally mistaken, in my judgment. I'll make that very clear when I go."

"Thank you, Ray," Loy said in the same matter-of-fact way. "I appreciate your support and applaud your decision. I think you're doing the right thing."

"I'm sure of it," the Secretary of the Army said with heartfelt conviction. "I'm sure of it!"

"My resignation is already in," his sister said in her customary cool and level tone, looking her loveliest, "so there are no surprises from me. I haven't drafted my statement yet but it will follow the lines of yours and Ray's."

"Thank you, Helen," he said. A sudden smile, rather grim, lighted his face for a moment. "Are *we* ever cooking up a surprise for the man in the White House. It's going to be *quite* a sensation!"

"To which, of course," Joe Strang said, looking more roly-poly than ever—he's going to miss all that Pentagon ice cream when he joins the Beltway Bandits, Loy thought with amusement—"I am certainly going to contribute with *my* resignation. I could not spend one *day* in this building with that—that —*ignoramus*—sitting in this office. Let him get his own appeasers to do the job!"

"I likewise," said Jason Bard, Assistant Secretary (International Security Policy), a Doomsday Twin; and, "Likewise," said Jim Kraft, Deputy Assistant Secretary (Far East and Pacific Affairs), the other.

"I'm overwhelmed," Loy said. "And—" again he smiled—"the President will be too, I think. Of course Bob will be delighted to have you all clear out so he doesn't have to fire you. Though I don't think he'd mind doing so."

"I'm going to stick around just long enough to stage-manage all this for you," Hank Milhaus said with a grin. "Then I'm leaving too." He adopted an air of mock formality. "Gentlemen, the Secretary's resignation becomes effective at 1700 Friday, as you know. When may I have your resignation statements so that I may present them to Delight Jones and other good friends of the media?"

"The same," Ray Clark volunteered and they all nodded agreement.

They left with many expressions of friendship, confidence and regret that threatened to become quite emotional until he stood up and said sternly, "For two more days we have to run this monstrosity, so get back to your desks and get busy or I'll have you all court-martialed!"

The jest was mild but it broke the cumulative tension. With jokes and laughter and the ease of personal decisions finally made one way or the other, they filed out of his office for the last time.

When they had gone, Vangie came in, red-eyed again.

"For heaven's sake, Vangie," he said with mock severity, "stop leaking like the purple water fountain and get with it!"

Which made her laugh, shakily, dry her eyes and obey.

The chairman of the Joint Chiefs of Staff, she said, was on the phone wanting to know if he might drop by "just to chat."

"Of course," Loy said, feeling a sudden warmth of gratitude that even the massed loyalty of his staff had not quite aroused. For another two days he and Zeecy were still together at the pinnacle of this fantastic machine. They saw things from a vantage-point no one else in the building quite possessed. He knew this would be the last time the two of them would discuss it on a footing of shared responsibilities. He was very pleased that the chairman wished to do so.

"Zeecy," he said when the general came in after chucking Vangie comfortingly under the chin and offering her a handkerchief with a grand gesture that made her laugh some more, "how nice of you to come."

"I wanted to call you last night after the speech," Gen. McCune said, "but I decided you'd be too incoherent with rage to articulate clearly, so I didn't."

"Wasn't that the damnedest?" the Secretary said with a wondering shake of the head. "But shrewd—very shrewd. He turned it right around so that he'll have everything his way. It was a masterpiece."

"He can do it," Zeecy agreed. "He's always been able to do that, as long as I've known him. Even if it did require the rather unusual step of disassociating the Commander-in-Chief from the Department of Defense he's supposed to be the ultimate leader of. A very neat trick, if one can do it. And he did. Have you tried shaking your head yet, Loy? I haven't dared—our throats have been slit and our heads might fall off . . . Incidentally," he said, dropping the banter, "I thought that was a fine resignation letter you wrote. It said exactly what needed to be said and in a way that can't be ignored. He handled that very well, too, but the memory will linger. From now on everything about Nanukuvu is going to be measured against your statement and his. We'll see who wins out in the long run."

"I hope it was that good," Loy said with a smile. "I labored over it long enough . . . What *is* going to happen with Nanukuvu, in your estimation?"

"A continuation of what's happening now," Gen. McCune said. "But wrapped up in the sweet placebo of 'diplomacy' that will make it so much easier for the country to swallow. Are our friends of the Pacific Declaration ever going to be surprised!"

"They shouldn't be, God damn it to hell," Loy said with a sudden deep bitterness. "They've gone out on a limb for us. They deserve better than that."

"It's what happens when you get in the game with the big boys," Zeecy said. "You're apt to get trampled as they chase one another toward the goal-line. Not that *we're* doing any chasing, of course. We're barely in the game."

The Secretary sighed, a heavy, unhappy sound.

"We can't afford to think that, Zeece," he said. "We've got to think that there's a way out of this thing, and that he and Terry—"

"And Bob," Zeecy reminded dryly. "Don't forget Bob."

"—and Bob, will come up with a formula that will save face and achieve at least a little of the stability you and I have been hoping for down there . . . Of course we both know," he added with an unhappy honesty, "that he's entirely right in his strictures on the Pentagon. Things *have* moved too damned slowly. The system *has* triumphed again. The Kremlin has two enormous advantages on its side—history's greatest arsenal and the innate weaknesses of this building. They make a formidable combination."

"And yet," Zeecy said with a troubled thoughtfulness, "there are many brilliant people in this building. There are many fine, alert, intelligent, dedicated, hard-working, far-sighted men and women on both the civilian and the military sides. We have here in the Pentagon, in all probability, the greatest concentration of brains and ability in this country or anywhere. And yet—*and yet,* damn it! Too often when crisis comes the machinery slows down, the gears don't mesh, hare turns to tortoise, the system takes over and we crawl toward a solution when we ought to be racing . . . Not every time, of course," he added as if taken aback by his own vehemence. "On many occasions the system works brilliantly. But—"

"But on many others," the Secretary said gloomily, "it does not work at all. And it is on those unhappy and too-frequent occasions that the enemy finds his opportunities." He smiled, a sad and scornful smile. "And the media and the Hill make such a fuss about things that barely matter—about a $600 ashtray or a $640 toilet-seat—things that *we ourselves,* in the inspector general's office, OSD, discover and make available to them—some contractor dishonesty that *we ourselves* discover and make available to them. They do their best to convince the public that we try to hide the things that *we ourselves* uncover and make public and go after and successfully punish."

Gen. McCune snorted.

"All that is chickenshit. As chickenshit as the publicity-seeking motives and methods of the people who try to use it against us for their own purposes."

"There *is* a sickness in the building," the Secretary said slowly, "but it goes far, far deeper than that. It is a fundamental weakness, at the top, of interservice rivalry and inter-civilian rivalry and service-civilian rivalry . . . of everybody fighting for his own position or his service's position, and to hell with the national interest . . . of everybody having to agree on every detail before action can be taken . . . of endless obstructions and delays in order to gratify all sorts of conflicting aims and egos . . . of gossip and sabotage and deliberate undercutting for personal preferment or advantage that simply should not exist and rightfully should have no place at all in an enterprise as desperately vital to national survival as this . . . and on the lower levels, a weakness of fine people bogged down in too many bosses, too much detail, too much paperwork, too many restrictions on decision-making—"

"Many of them imposed by Congress," Zeecy remarked.

"Right, many of them imposed by Congress. But not all, Zeecy—not all. We have to be honest about that, too. A lot of it is Congress—and a lot of it is the system. And that's the final and perhaps most fatal weakness—that the interests of each have become so interlocking over the years that I sometimes really believe that the Defense Department is *never* going to work its way out of the mess and get back to being the alert and effective instrument of national policy and survival that a generally wishful and ill-informed citizenry thinks it is."

"It has to," Gen. McCune said bleakly. "It *has* to. Otherwise the game is lost . . . and with it," he added with a sigh as heavy as Loy's, "all that we have and hold dear."

For a minute or two they were silent, contemplating the deeply disturbing and inescapable conundrum faced by all who become familiar with the inner workings of the building.

And presently they left it, as sooner or later everyone does when confronted by the seemingly insoluble problems of the Pentagon.

"Well," Loy said, deliberately lightening the tone, deliberately breaking the mood. "Do you know what Vangie thinks you and I should do?"

"I can never anticipate what is going to come out of that clever little head," Zeecy said, smiling in response. "*What* does Vangie think we should do?"

"She thinks I should run for President and you should run with me for Vice President. Wouldn't that be a hell of a ticket?"

"The woman is mad," Gen. McCune said solemnly. "Stark, raving—so when do we announce?"

They laughed together, gloomy mood successfully broken, world restored again to the semblance of reasonableness and humor on which humankind has to proceed if it is not to dwell too fatally upon all the various abysses that lie beneath its feet.

"I'm tempted, I'll tell you that," Loy said, "but of course as I told her, it's sheer nonsense."

"Did you persuade her?"

"She said: think about it. I told her you wouldn't be interested, anyway."

"And what did she say to that?"

" 'Ask him.' "

"Better not, Loy," Zeecy said with a grin. "I might just. And then you'd have to, too. And then where would we be?"

"Leading a small parade on behalf of 'a little island far away,' to quote the President, which nobody really wants to think about."

"Yes," Zeecy agreed more soberly. "That would be about it . . . But—think about it, as Vangie says—think about it."

"Get along with you!" the Secretary said, rising and holding out his hand. "Thanks so much, general, for everything."

"Thank *you,*" Gen. McCune said, returning his handshake with a firm, congenial pressure. "It's been a real pleasure, Loy—a great privilege to be associated with so fine a Secretary."

"And so fine a chairman of the JCS," the Secretary said.

"I may bawl like Vangie if I don't get out of here," Gen. McCune said cheerfully. "Keep in touch."

"I will," Loy promised. "If Bob drives you up the wall too much and you want to let off steam, give me a call. I'll let you know where I am."

"Do that," Zeecy said. "I may well want to do exactly that. I keep telling myself that I only have to deal with the jerk for three more months. *Only three more months! God!*"

"And that's Pentagon time, too," the Secretary reminded him with a smile. "That's not real time."

He returned to his task of clearing up remaining odds and ends. Zeecy returned to his office. The phone rang. The voice he had not thought to hear again in any context except the official said hello.

"Hello!" he said. Then he remembered that he was supposed to be angry.

"I understand that you've been talking to my wife," he said sternly.

"Oh!" she said and uttered the clear silvery laugh he had come to value so highly in recent months. "So I have. I'd forgotten all about it."

"I'll bet," he said, trying to maintain his severity but finding it impossible as she giggled suddenly and said, "Oh, Zeecy! You know we both love you."

"I don't know that at all," he said, still trying to sound affronted but finding it increasingly hard to do. "I know Renee does. I don't know about *Senators.* They're a tricky damned bunch."

"She really does love you, you know. She really does. Why do you suppose she's put up with all your shenanigans all these years?"

"I suspect she's had a few of her own," he said darkly.

"Only because your conduct forced her to," she said. "Why have you been such a bastard, Zeecy?"

"I can't change my own nature," he said stiffly. She hooted.

"Oh, my, *that* old excuse. Well, it's time now that you did. Now that you've found out that I can't change mine, either."

"I have never been so humiliated in my life," he said, again trying to sound solemn but not succeeding very well in the face of her obvious determination to kid him out of it.

"It's good for you," she assured him lightheartedly. *"Good* for you. It's about time somebody took the great Gen. Zoren Chace McCune down a peg."

"Why?" he asked with a wistfulness he thought might inhibit her a little. But she was obviously shameless, and enjoying it.

" 'Why?' " she mimicked. "My poor Zeecy! Because it's *good* for you, I said. Especially as you sink into your twilight years with Renee there at your side to comfort you."

"I love my wife," he said stoutly. "Did you think I didn't?"

"Never," she said with a chuckle. "I just wondered how long it would take you to admit it to yourself and stop all this nonsense."

"I've *always* admitted it to myself," he said crossly. "And you certainly didn't appear to be averse to 'all this nonsense.'"

"No," she admitted more soberly, "for a while there, I wasn't. That was my mistake."

"But why?" he demanded, giving it a last game try. *"Why* was it a mistake?"

"Because," she said calmly, "I am a United States Senator with a lot of responsibilities and a lot of things to uphold, including my own common-sense. And fortunately, that was what saved me—oh, Lord, what a corny way to put it, 'saved me'—that was what kept me from making a fool of myself and letting you make a fool of yourself."

"You saved me from myself," he said with humorous irony—might as well be humorous, there was obviously nothing else to do. "You permitted me to let my better nature triumph. Boy, *there* are two fine clichés! What will you come up with next?"

"I don't know at the moment," she said with a gurgle of laughter, "but I'll try to think of something. Dear Zeecy: I *do* love you fondly, you know. And at your great age—"

"Sixty-two, damn it!"

"At your great age, it's nice to have a loving young adopted daughter of forty-seven—"

"My God," he said simply and she burst into full laughter this time. And so did he.

"All right," he said. "All right. I *did* make a fool of myself and you were right to show me I was one, and no doubt I should be gratefully faithful to Renee forever after."

"You should."

"Well," he said slowly. "Maybe I will."

"I think it would be nice. She'd appreciate it. And so would I. That way you could make both of us happy."

"And why should I make *you* happy?"

"Because I ask you to," she said sweetly. "How can you withstand an argument like that?"

"I don't think I can," he said with a chuckle. "At least for now. I'll have to think it over later."

"Don't do that," she said. "Just *do* it." Her voice became businesslike. "What are we going to do with this Godawful Catheter—Cathcart—nomination?"

He hesitated a second more—accepted—became equally matter-of-fact.

"Kill it, I hope. Any chance?"

"There's a lot of uneasiness up here about him."

"Nothing to what there is in the Pentagon," he said. "Increase it."

"Cube and Jerry and I and a few other people are doing our best. Want to come up and testify against him?"

"I *do* not! I have to get along with the big buffoon for three more months. I'll conspicuously *not* come up and testify *for* him, however. How would that be? Just tell Cube I don't want to be called, thanks very much. And the chiefs don't either. Leave us out of this one. All right?"

"All right," she said. "It can be arranged. Come up and have lunch someday soon, o.k.?"

"I can't stand to face you," he said with exaggerated solemnity. *"God,* the humiliation of it all!"

"Zeecy," she said, the silvery laugh ringing out again, "I really think you and I might become really good friends. Give me a call when you see your way clear."

"Probably next week sometime, after Loy goes."

"So sad," she said. "And so necessary. I'll look forward to seeing you then."

"And I you," he said wryly. "I suppose."

And he would, too, of course, he told himself as the hours passed and the thousand and one things in the day of a chairman of the JCS kept him occupied. She was a rare one, the senior Senator from Louisiana. And so, he had to admit to himself once more—he always *was* admitting it to himself, but sometimes he just forgot—was Renee McCune.

He was suddenly thankful that they were all friends. He did get home in plenty of time for dinner that night. Renee was surprised but he told her he had really meant it when he said he would. He said he really meant it this time, too. She smiled and said she could see that.

The Secretary of the Army methodically cleared the memorabilia from his office, left things neatly in order, turned finally to the last remaining piece of routine business.

It had been on his desk for two days.

He studied it for several minutes, face expressionless.

Then he scrawled the word "Approved" and signed "Raymond C. Clark, Secretary of the Army" in a large emphatic hand on the special memorandum from Gen. Burford detailing the national security aspects of the dishonorable discharge of Maj. Gary Stump, USA, and requesting permission to place his case in the hands of the F.B.I. for further investigation.

Then he stood up, straightened his shoulders, looked around the room one last time and walked out.

On Friday afternoon Hank Milhaus met with Delight Jones, Herb Horowitz, Red Roberts and a large and noisy group of media representatives.

No, he said, Secretary Buck would not repeat NOT hold a farewell press conference. His resignation letter spoke for itself and he had nothing further to say. He suggested that they direct any questions to Robert Cathcart, who, if confirmed, would soon be the new SecDef.

"Does that mean that Secretary Buck thinks he will *not* be confirmed?" Red demanded.

Hank Milhaus laughed.

"He's not predicting the Senate, Red, and you know better, too. But I do have a little news for you."

He was pleased to note that the multiple resignations hit them like a bombshell. Even Delight looked a little awed.

The media, whose members love to apply the word "massacre" to any wholesale administrative change that occurs on a given day, really had a picnic this time, even though Hank attempted to point out humorously that this was not a massacre but "more of a voluntary suicide pact."

The label was too good to resist and the conclusion that could be drawn from it too helpful to the favored side of the argument to be passed over.

Television made the most of it.

So did the newspapers:

FRIDAY NIGHT MASSACRE ROCKS PENTAGON
FIVE BUCK AIDES QUIT WITH SECRETARY
PRO-WAR FACTION BOWS TO NANUKUVU PEACE PLAN
NEW ERA DAWNS IN PACIFIC

The Building sits by the river.
The island sits in the sun.
They are many thousands of miles from one another.
But they have come together now and history
will not uncouple them.

Huge, squat, sprawling, seeming almost to breathe like some great antediluvian animal, awesome in its power and impact as it sits beside the river, The Building sends out its tentacles to the farthest reaches of the earth.

Its power is immense. Its influence is everywhere. What it decides or does not decide, what it does or does not do, affects not only the life of every American but the life of every human being on the planet. Its actions can decide the fate of nations, destroy or establish governments, turn whole peoples from one path of destiny to another, wither or preserve the earth. It can, and does, decide the fate of millions of its own and many, many millions more. Its reach extends to all the continents and all the seas and beyond them into space.

The mightiest nation, the tiniest dot of land upon the sea, may feel the touch of its hand. Before it the denizens of earth, as it suits them, may bow in awe, tremble in fear or jeer in hatred. It does not matter. The Building goes on, impervious, set upon a course at once so irresistible yet so glacial in pace that it takes years to start it moving, bring it to a halt or change its direction. In half a century it has become a force of nature, like the tides. Now in the closing years of the Anxious Eighties its influence upon America and the world has never been greater.

Now there will be changes in The Building. If Bob Cathcart's nomination is confirmed he will have around him his own selection of assistants. The JCS too will shortly change. Some familiar faces will disappear, some few faces, soon to be familiar, will take their places. There will be a shift in emphasis, a widely hailed—but essentially superficial—change in policy and direction.

Underneath, the machinery of The Building will go right on just as always.

It seems quite certain that the system will not be changed in any great essential, barring some miracle impossible to foresee—some internal reformation impossible to imagine.

(Not "barring another war," as some of The Building's top people complacently say when asked about the chances for real, fundamental change. Not even The Building will survive another war: and in the resultant wasteland, should it come, what wandering survivor will ever have heard of The Building and its system—or, in his tired mind, would care about them, if he had?)

No, the miracle will not come, in a system so closely interwoven and incestuously linked with its loudest critics, they of Capitol Hill. Things may shift a little on the surface, some window-dressing may be applied, games of musical chairs may be played. Official hyperbole may hail with loud self-approval some stately shadowplay of "reform."

Underneath, the game between the services, between the military and civilian sides, between The Building and the Hill. The Building and the contractors, the contractors and the Hill, will go on just the same.

Meanwhile on the island of Nanukuvu things will also go on.

The "diplomatic approach" will be attempted. Some sort of embarrassingly obvious face-saving will be worked out. Some sort of cynical sugarcoating will be offered by Moscow and accepted by Washington.

Here, too, nothing essential will be changed.

The airstrips will be completed. The sub pens will be enhanced. The missiles will be increased. The complement of troops will be raised to five thousand within a year. The store of atomic weapons will grow and grow and grow —and grow. And presently, as Vangie predicted to Loy, the pressure will begin: not very subtle, not very kind, not very tender toward unhappy American egos far away or the futile protests of helpless isolated governments closer by.

It won't be very long, now, before the enemy will be "camping on New Zealand's doorstep. Or going after Australia. Or gobbling up the little island states one by one."

And when they come crying, as they will, to Washington, Washington's words will be stout but its actions will be impotent. And there will be those in America, as there are always those in America, who will use their great means of communication to try to persuade their countrymen that impotence is strength and that retreat, in an age of awful consequences, is really victory after all.

The Building sits by the river.

The island sits in the sun.

No one would ever have associated the island with Death.

But Death has come—not only the physical death of A'afaloa and Nuku'ofa and their gentle families but death of another kind—the death of freedom, the death of the human spirit, the death of the human mind, the death of all the friendly things that make life for humankind worth living.

And The Building, having tried in all its ponderous and complicated ways to help the island and so stem in some small part the steady onflow of the New Ice Age, has failed.

It will have to try again, in some other crisis, in some other place, on some other day.

There will be, as Zeecy remarked, many such.

AFTERWORD

So sensitive is the Pentagon to any criticism, no matter how concerned or well-intentioned, that anyone in-house who can be associated with such criticism inevitably suffers in some degree.

Some of those who have assisted most freely and cooperatively with my research would be among the inevitable targets.

They would not be shot at sunrise: but certain uncomfortable disapprovals might ensue.

Therefore it is probably best that they not be named here. They know who they are and know, through often expressed gratitude, how much I have appreciated their help.

Suffice it to say that, after covering the Pentagon on an occasional fill-in basis when I was a reporter years ago, I returned before starting this novel to spend some weeks in the building and elsewhere in Washington, interviewing everyone from the SecDef to the manager of the motor pool, with way-stops at members of the JCS and many others both uniformed and civilian down the line. With a few notable exceptions—the SecDef himself being one—almost everyone I talked to, particularly in the military, was surrounded by a protective phalanx of aides.

Yet no number of aides, and no amount of bland official assurances that God's in his heaven, all's right with the Pentagon, can conceal the reality of intonations, expressions, the casual throwaway slur at a sister service, the indirect or brutally blunt in-jokes that reveal the tensions of a fiercely jealous, fiercely competitive environment.

A few spoke candidly.

Most did not.

They didn't have to.

Subtly but surely their attitudes toward their own responsibilities, and toward those (practically everyone) whom they regard as their competitors in the Pentagon, said it all.

There is, as Loy said, a sickness in the building.

God grant the building may heal itself in time, for in the final analysis no one else can.

A.D.

October 1984–December 1985